GRITS

Niall Griffiths was born in Liverpool in 1966 and now
lives in Wales.

Niall Griffiths

GRITS

V

VINTAGE

Published by Vintage 2001

4 6 8 10 9 7 5 3

Lyrics of 'Cowgirl' reproduced courtesy of Underworld and
Sherlock Holmes Music Ltd, written by Rick Smith, Karl Hyde
and Darren Emerson. Lyrics from the song 'Nancy Spain' reproduced courtesy of Barney Rushe and Tara Music Company Ltd,
written by Barney Rushe

First published in Great Britain in 2000 by
Jonathan Cape

Vintage
Random House, 20 Vauxhall Bridge Road,
London SW1V 2SA

Random House Australia (Pty) Limited
20 Alfred Street, Milsons Point, Sydney
New South Wales 2061, Australia

Random House New Zealand Limited
18 Poland Road, Glenfield, Auckland 10, New Zealand

Random House (Pty) Limited
Endulini, 5A Jubilee Road, Parktown 2193, South Africa

The Random House Group Limited Reg. No. 954009
www.randomhouse.co.uk

A CIP catalogue record for this book
is available from the British Library

ISBN 0 09 928517 7

Papers used by Random House are natural, recyclable
products made from wood grown in sustainable forests.
The manufacturing processes conform to the environmental regulations of the country of origin

Printed and bound in Great Britain by
Bookmarque Limited, Croydon, Surrey

TO MY GRANDPARENTS

ACKNOWLEDGEMENTS

Thanks to: Mum and Dad; Nickie, for loads of things; Linsey, Alex; Tony and Karen, especially for the loans; Ian Woodhurst and Richard Calvert; and David Snelson, for helping me get back to Wales in the first place.

For inspiration, money, support, company, etc., thanks, in no particular order, to: Matt Loader, Rich O'Regan and wee Ffion, Catrin Rhys, Deborah Jones, Jennie Wood, Harry and Claire and baby Ferdia, Griff, Gray Bass, Ken, Hilly and Jan, Clive Meachen, Paul Wain, Stevie Smythe, Chris Milton, and all the people I've ever drank with and laughed with and danced with. Further thanks to Catrin for help with the Cymraeg; Jennie for the money in particular; and Deborah, for far too many things to list.

Cheers to yis all. Nietzsche once said: 'And I should believe only in a God who understood how to dance.' To disagree would be daft.

GRIT: a wide, vague term for any sedimentary rock that looks or feels gritty ... [G]rits occur among the lower Palaeozoic 'greywackes' and are rocks that are on the whole fine-grained but contain larger, somewhat angular fragments (such as those in the Aberystwyth Grits formation) ... Sometimes the term is used for any hard sandstone bed to distinguish it, by a conveniently short word, from other kinds of beds in a sequence.

Wyatt, Antony, *Challinor's Dictionary of Geology*, Sixth Edition, University of Wales Press, Cardiff, 1986

GRIT: a rock composed of angular and poorly sorted quartz and other mineral grains; a rock more or less intermediate in grain-size between sandstone and a conglomerate. Many rocks are locally called 'grits' if coarse-grained and hard.

Nelson, A. and Nelson, K.D., *Dictonary of Applied Geology*, George Newnes Ltd, London, 1967

From *A Personal Guide to West Wales*, anonymous authorship, privately printed, p. 3

Fossiliferous, problematic, varied: geographically speaking, the Ystwyth valley area of west Wales is rich and diverse, so much so, indeed, that there are no better specimens in these islands than its Grits, its intrusive magma, its alternation of shaly agrillaceous mudstones and pale, hard sandstones. Aberystwyth town itself is sustained on such ancient, subterranean phenomena; mortared by ossified underground rivers of mud, it pays witness to the perennial battle of water and rock, the slashes of bright microgranite on the bared seacliffs the scabs and scars of this endless war. The planets' petrified dung, the cosmic patience of mudstone snaking its way into granite with a determination utterly ungraspable to any matter which operates within a humanly mappable time-scale. Yet within it, tattooed into its skin, can be discerned its very opposite: quick little flickers of life have left their marks here, here the segments of a trilobite, there the furrow of a snail. This is an area rich in fossils, tantalising glimpses into arcana long dead, but since these rocks date from the Silurian epoch, when all and only invertebrate phyla had evolved as far as they were going to, that diversity is necessarily and, some might say, disappointingly restricted.

Still: Here they are. They are here. Aros Mae.

THEY ARE MOVING

THEY ARE MOVING through these green and desolate hills, stumbling blearily through a landscape smeared in rain, trampling the sheep-shitted earth down above the bones of tatterdemalion armies who once stood here, determined, bekilted and still. The lip of a crag is not the only brink on which they teeter, as if afraid of the slow submission of scree; but now the only dragon which is pursued is smoked off a strip of silver paper cupped in trembling hands, protected from the wind, from the rain. It's merely drizzle, though, drizzle and wind; sometimes, and at night-time up here, these mountains shudder under thunder and the storm shrieks and the rain fumes like javelins swarming and the lightning leaps the lake on splintered stilts – but not today.

In the lee of a hillock tonsured by the razor wind, the boy called Roger, whose forefather's forefathers once stalked with bone bows boar on the cones of these volcanoes, snarls at the wind's whips and huddles further into himself and lights another match which like its five predecessors is instantly snuffed. He asks Colm for his Zippo and is handed it by badly bitten fingers, his sharply-focused mind narrowing his field of vision down to just this: the foil, the brown powder, the five-pound note rolled up into a tube, the weak fluttering flame. Colm's hand intrudes again and takes the lighter back then helpfully holds it steady beneath the silver paper, thereby allowing Roger to use both hands as a windbreak so that not one grain of the precious dust is lost. He hears a faint crackle and inhales the vapour deeply through his money snorkel, so deeply that his head presses back into the grass-muddy wall of the hill, hard enough to leave an indentation bowl-shaped, bowl-deep.

—What's it like, then, this stuff? Orright, is it?

Roger nods and exhales/sighs.

—Gettin a toot then, am I?

Roger nods again, smiling, and offers Colm his works. Lazily, languidly; his limbs already turning liquid.

—Good gear like? Not cut with too much shite, no?

—Pure bleedin brown boy. D'yew think Iain ud sell me anythin less, arfter last time, like? A fuckin told im, a did, a said enny more-a that fuckin . . . mm . . . fuckin *Nesquik* like an al fuckin . . .

Roger trails off and looks up blinking at his friends, scruffy apparitions in this land of ghosts, hair and clothes flapping in the wind. Pallid skin a-glow in the diluted sunlight.

Colm crouches down beside Roger, whose now tingling body he uses as a shelter from the weather, his limbs and head curled in tightly towards his navel like a woodlouse or a hedgehog or some other small creature in defensive attitude as he attempts to turn the heroin into inhalable smoke. Here, in these hard, huge mountains under the silvery wintry sun, there is no overlit realm but for that place which, shared and shining, throbs inside their skulls. They would be, if life were held under a magnifying glass, its focus; perhaps we can see and hear in them whole countries breaking apart.

Careful not to distract Colm from his delicate labours (he's not so stoned yet that he can feel entirely comfortable neglecting those considerations he'd expect others to grant to him), Roger raises slowly his heavy, humming head and stares with an almost wistful expression at Paul who has climbed a tall cairn and looks, hair flying in the wind, chest distended, for all the wide world like a dead tribal chieftain now in restless spirithood come back to judge the antics of these, his progeny. Roger squints, trying to make out the expression on Paul's face, but he doesn't even know where Paul is looking, whether at the ground, the sky, the ruffled and brackish lake, or the huddled and shuddering people; but nor, chest distended, hair flying in the wind, does Paul.

PAUL

NEEDS UH BIT more wine, this mixture does, so a tip uh load more red in, stir it about with uh mince an uh carrots an onions an garlic an tomatoes. When a taste it tho, a can still taste the fattiness an cheapness of thuh meat an, wirse, tha awful fuckin mildewy aftertaste yuh always get in this kitchen cos av the horrible mouldy walls, so a add still more wine an more herbs as well. There; that's not too bad. That black mould as now grown all thuh way up thuh wall behind the oven, an it infects evrythin cooked in ere with uh horrible, almost fishy, taste; cahn be fuckin good fuh ya. Still, a doan think anyone ul mind; ther all probly fuckin starvin by now. S'more red wine, a think, this time in me glass; an *that's* uh bloody turn-up fuh the books, that thiz any bloody wine left afteh the bottle's bin lyin around in thuh kitchen all aftuhnoon. A knock uh glass back an then pour meself anothuh, stirrin the stuff in thuh pan with me free hand.

—Look oo it is: Paul Pot. Wer's yer big white hat?

Colm comes boundin in an takes a full bottle uv cider out the fridge. Ee seems appy enough.

—Jesus! Wha the fuck's this?

Ee takes thuh ram's skull off thuh windehledge, sniffs it, an peers intuh its eye sockets.

—Malcolm found it tuhday, a tell im.—In a field in Cwm Rheidol somewhere a think it was. Parently it was full uv dead sheep, like the elephant's graveyard uh somethin. It shit Malcolm up; ee reckuns iz been cursed now.

Colm strokes the horns, rippled like coconut trees uh somethin.

—Yeh, ee's worried now that ee's brought evil intuh the house uh somethin just as fuckin daft.

Colm grins an goes: —Fuckin idyit.

7

—Yeh, a know, a say, smilin too.—But al tell yuh one thing; if anythin bad appens, a know oo's gettin the fuckin blame.

—Yeh. We can bern im at the stake.

Mairead comes in behind Colm. She's bin lookin a lot better than she normally does, thuh last couple uv days; still uh bit pale, like, an quiet, but a havunt for uh week uh two seener so drunk that she carn even fuckin move. Like at that party uv Iestyn's last month, down by thuh harbour; Mairead almost fuckin drowned inner own sick. No one ud giver thuh kiss uv life either cos er lips were all spewy; she didunt need it in thuh end tho, she just woke up an drank more.

Colm makes a ghostly noise, like: —WoooOOO, woooOOO!, an pushes the skull inter Mairead's face. Well, not *into*, like, just, yuh know, close to. She loves things like this – bones n stuff.

—Oh wow! Whuh did this come from?

She holds it an strokes it, er face rapt.

—Mal found it, Colm sehs.—Fuckin great ey. Lookit the horns on the bastard.

They fuss over it for a while an a make the cheese sauce. Thuh easy way; just open thuh packet, add milk an more cheese an heat through. Fuck all tha arsing about with flour an butter an milk, life's too short tuh stand thir stirrin fuh arf uh fuckin ower. Dull, dull, dull. A bring thuh sauce toer boil an leave it tuh stand an thicken while a drink more wine. A put uh dish over the pan tuh keep out thuh essence uv mildew flavuh. Am tellin ya, wir all gonta get fuckin bronchitis uh somethin; av told thuh estate agent's umpteen fuckin times about it but they do fuck all. As long's they get theh money, that's all they care about.

—Fuck me!

Mairead as noticed that thuh hedge tha used ta cover thuh window as now gone. Shiz starin out across thuh valley.

—A didunt realise t'view were sor nice. Oo chopped it down?

—Me, a teller, —earlier on tuhday. Hacked it away with uh machete. Took owers. A had a great time.

—Yuh can see alla way orver t'Comins Coch now. Incredible.

Colm replaces thuh skull an goes back intuh the front room, swiggin cider from thuh bottle.

—Malcolm! Wherjer get skully?

Mairead pours wine into uh glass an joins im, leavin the bottle in thuh kitchen, which is unusual, an good tuh see; she likes uh drink, does Mairead, an normally by now shid be too pissed tuh even stand or almost tha way, sittin in uh corner surrounded by bottles, chain-smoking an cacklin at nothin in puhticular. In fact, evrybody seems tuh be givin thuh drinkin an druggin a rest at the mo, even Colm, fuck, even Roger; that's thuh reason why am cookin this food fuh them all, only lasagne like, but some uv em as far as a know avunt eaten fuh probably weeks, definitely days. Last thing a saw Colm eat apart from speedbombs was a sweaty cheese roll in thuh Angel last Monday but, mind you, a havunt seen im between then an now so ee could uv eaten then, a suppose. But probly not. All uv em seem hungry; as well as bags uv booze thev all brought up crisps n stuff, an Roger's brought his idea uv a spacecake (uh Spar-bought Swiss roll sliced down thuh middle with resin sprinkled intuh it) an ther all wirkin up an appetite in thuh front room with spliff an videos – it was *Taxi Driver* before, it's fuckin *Beavis and Butthead* now. Roger's laugh sounds just thuh fuckin same: uh-huh, uh-huh. Me, I chopped thuh hedge down tuhday tuh wirk up a hunger an then went shopping, but a had tuh calm meself down aftuhwuds with a few cans uv Guinness an a couple uv pipes. Not bad goin, tho; a even bumped intuh Phil in town an ee offud me some acid cheap but a said no. Just say no, kids, just say no. Anyway, av cooked up uh fuckin shitload uv food fuh evrybody; a only hope theh bodies can take it. A know from past experience what disasters can occur when food suddenly replaces drugs; wirse than thuh other way round, al tell ya that. It can fuck yuh up badly, food can, in thuh wrong circumstances.

A hear Malcolm tellin em all about thuh field uv dead sheep, thuh Welsh equivalent uv thuh elephant's graveyard in Africa or India uh whirever it is. Roger's still goin: —Uh-huh, uh-huh, but at thuh telly or at Malcolm a dunno. A stir thuh cheese sauce an thuh mince again an try a glass uv tha poitín that Liam's brought back from Donegal; a knock it back in one an almost birn me fuckin throat off. Christ. When av finished coughing a pour a glass uv cold beer an down it tuh take thuh burnin away, an then a turn thuh ram's skull round thuh othuh way, so it's lookin out uv thuh window, across thuh valley. There yuh go, feller. See more now with all those hedges gone. See yuh brothers n sisters on thuh hillside there? Yuh could if yuh still had ya eyes.

A notice uh spider up in thuh corner in is web, one uv those ones with a tiny body an long spindly legs, those ones which Colm hates. Ee rirly does; a few times av seen im go white as uh fuckin sheet an be nirly sick when ee's bin suhprised by one, found imself sittin next tuh one on thuh wall or somethin. Thing is tho, ee's not bothered by thuh big, chunky, hairy ones; av even seen im pick them up. Strange. An look thir's a woodlouse as well, or a baby armadillo as Mairead calls em. Like uh diddy tank. Mr Spider ul av im if ee doesunt watch out.

Christ. Place's turnin into uh right fuckin bug hutch.

A drink more beer (Jesus that poitín) an arrange thuh lasagne in uh pan, put thuh oven on tuh preheat. The conversation in thuh front room as now gone ontuh porn films; for a moment me heart sinks uh little cos a think thev found me secret stash behind thuh dresser, but then a realise tha Malcolm's talkin about uh film ee saw ages ago. Phew.

—Yeh, rirly, no messin, ee shagged the sheep. Took is bleedein overawls dahn an rammed it strite up.

—Rammed!

—Nah, Mairead says.—It wern a ram, it were a ewe. Nowt queer about this bloke.

—What wus the sheep doin while ee wus shaftin it?

—Nothin, just eatin the grass. Wasn't arsed.

—Jesus. Did the feller leave the piecer straw in is gob?

A bend down tuh put thuh lasagne in thuh oven an someone tweaks me bum. A nirly bang me fuckin brains out on thuh hob.

—Hello, bach. How's it going, cariad?

It's Sioned, uv course, lookin fuckin gorgeous, er cheeks flushed a bit pink with thuh booze. Shiz wearin that ace old necklace she got offer granny, thuh one with thuh big chunky stones, makes er look sexy as fuck. Phwoar. A hugger an bend down tuh put me face inner hair, a havta bend down quite uh way cos am tall an shiz small. Er smell is fuckin lovely, even with thuh beer an smoke inner clothes an hair. A get anothuh pang uv guilt as am huggin er, probly cos uv thuh feel uv her, her body, her puhticular smell, an thuh sound uv her voice, all uv it so diffrunt tuh Banon an Colm's friend from Liverpool called Sarah oo came down tuh stay for uh bit when Sioned was away wirkin in Caernarvon or it might uv bin Camarthen, a get those two mixed up. Well, all thuh women uh diffrunt uv course but like, Sioned's thuh one oo am livin with, she's, yuh know, like me 'official' girlfriend . . . Shid fuckin kill me if she found out, shid go fuckin mad. It would breaker heart.

A carn deny tho that Banon n Sarah, both uv em, were good fun. Thev all been good fun. An fuck, anyway, ow do I know wha Sioned was up to in Caernarvon? Or Camarthen? A doan know, do I? She could uv shagged a diffrunt bloke evry fuckin night for all I know.

—Av ya seen what Malcolm found?

A show er thuh skull an take uh spliff from Liam as ee comes in for uh glass uv poitín.

—Yer had some uv this stuff, Paulie?

—Yeh. Blew me fuckin head off nearly.

—Aye, ut's potent stuff sure enough. Me uncle's best firewarter.

Ee leaves with uh arf-pint glass full uv thuh stuff, sediment settling an lookin like dandruff. Sioned puts thuh skull on thuh table an sits on me knee an we share the spliff. The feel uv er arse squashin on me legs is ace an starts me knob stirrin in me jeans.

A hear Colm's voice from thuh front room:

—The thing is, a mean wharrah alweys wonder about things like this right, is, a mean, ow would yer feel after doin summin like tha? Therd be two choices, it seems, two reactions, either summun like: I am the pits, the fuckin dregs uv humanity, the lowest ov the fuckin low cos I av let meself be filmed avin sex wither sheep; or summun like: I av done the werst thing I can possibly think ov, I av let meself be filmed shaggin a sheep, I cannot sink any ferther, therefore I am freed now from all moral conventions an I am liberated. I can now do wharrever the fuck a want. Yuh see? A mean, wouldjer be eaten up with self-loathing or wouldjer feel set free?

A wriggle me hips against Sioned's arse an she springs off.

—Oi! Am not avin yew servin up lasagne with a bloody arrd-on. Yew just calm yourself down, boy.

Me head hummin with thuh blow, a maker grab for eh tit an she bolts laughin intuh thuh front room an a follow er intuh uh cloud uv smoke.

—Phoah Christ! Yuh could cut this air withuh blunt fuckin knife!

—Ah if ut's not the chef. Sitchee down, now, wer just abou' ter put the film on.

A sit down on thuh floor against one uv the less mouldy walls with Sion, me fingers creepin down thuh back uv er jeans before shiz even sat down propuhly. A feel thuh smooth skin at thuh bottom uv er back with me finguhtips. God . . . a doan wanner cook, or even eat; a just wanner be in bed with Sion, strokin er, feelin er . . . Shiz laughin quietly an pushin me away, but it's no good; av got trousers like uh fuckin tent.

Roger, with uh spliff thuh size uv a fuckin pool cue hangin out uv is gob, puts uh film in thuh video. Thuh sleeves uv is grey T-shirt ride up a bit as ee does so an show is track marks, an a can see tha none uv em look fresh, which is good, unless uv course ee's jackin up somewhir else these days, which wouldunt fuckin suhprise me; Roger ud rip imself open an dig straight into is heart if all is veins collapsed. A tell ya, it fuckin scares me thuh way Roger hits thuh drugs, even moren Colm, or Malcolm, or Mairead with booze – but, then again, Roger scares me anyway; a right fuckin nutter sometimes ee is. It's not suh bad when ee's usin heroin, cos at least then ya can be sure that ee's not gunna flip out without warning like or anythin – ee'l just nod out quietly in some corner. When ee needs anothuh hit, tho, or thuh money fuh one, God, then no bastard's safe; yud av a better chance uv suhvival in Sarafuckinjevo.

—Ah no! Not *The Little Mermaid*! shouts Margaret from thuh corner. Ad fuhgotten she was here; maybe shud been asleep aftuh the hard day shiz had, wandrin round thuh town trine tuh seller electrical appliances cos shiz skint – irons, hairdryers, n stuff. Didunt get uh bad price fuh them in thuh end, or so she says.

Liam an Laura holler disapproval but Roger sits back with a big grin on is face an Colm beams happily. Malcolm fills up thuh bowl uv anothuh pipe an goes:

—*Taxi Driver, Beavis and Butthead* an now *The Little Mermaid* awl in wan arfternoon. God, wir twenniuth-century children . . . end av tha millenium culture-fuckers, oh yes . . .

A think the pot's gettin to im. Mairead starts singin 'Under the Sea', loudly an slightly drunkenly, an Colm snaps:

—Fer fuck's sake! Will yiz shut the fuck up so's we can watch the fuckin film! Wait at least til the fuckin song *starts*, Jesus.

A smile at Mairead an she snarls at thuh back uv Colm's head an then asks me ow long the food's gunna be.

—Not long now, a say. —Bout ten minutes uh so.

—Am starved, she sehs, an opens a bag uv pickled-onion flavour Monster Munch.

Good, a think, an take uh crisp off er.

Am pretty stoned now, and am puzzled by what people uh talkin about. Malcolm an Margaret are talkin about fuckin castles or somethin:

—. . .maybe wir bringin it awl dahn on arselves, Malcolm's sayin. —Ya know, like a self-fulfillin prophecy? If we say that wir playin witha ruins then we ar, even if wir not, or wirnt befaw . . . dja know what am sayin? A mean, it's *not* the end av tha wirld, but if we *fink* it is then it will be . . .

Liam looks at Colm an goes:

—Ah think ye'd feel free. Ah mean, all those fuckin shackles on ye, ye'd be rid uv em fe good, or ut least ferra while. Wooden rurly matter inny end ow ye gut rid uv em, ye'd just be glad tha ed gone. *Ah* reckun.

—Nah, nah . . .

Malcolm then starts gettin at Liam, but gently like, with no real malice, fuh bein idealistic, an Laura supports Liam, evrybody starts shoutin an blowin smoke intuh thuh air. On thuh telly, cartoon crabs an fishes dance an sing. A notice tha Margaret is ignorin evryone an concentratin on the telly screen, which could be bad cos sometimes she gets all upset when she watches kid's films, but that rirly depends uv course on what mood shiz in or what drug shiz on. A hear patterin on thuh window behind me; rain, Welsh rain, drivin rain, comin down like iron fuckin rods. A tirn tuh look an see water runnin down thuh window, see thuh few lights uv Comins Coch across thuh valley. Christ it gets dark quick now. Must be tha fuckin skull uv Malcolm's, bringin darkness down on us all. Or maybe it's just me, losin track uv time. Seems like av bin cookin fuh owers. Thuh spliff, too, yuh know.

A get up tuh go an check on thuh food. Mairead sehs:

—Djuh want a hand darlin?

—Nah, ts orright. Too many cooks, a say. —Too many wasters spoil thuh lasagne. Yuh can put stuff on thuh table tho if
yuh like.

Her an Sioned go to do that, an as a pass Mags a hear er say to
erself, quietly:

—A wish *I* lived under the sea. Ey av such fun down thair.

Shiz bin sayin stuff like that ever since er an Colm went snorkellin
last week, goin on about ow nice it'd be tuh live on thuh seabed
in a dome an stuff. Shiz goin off her head, I reckon. Maybe thuh
pollution's addled her brains; caused more damage, killed more
brain cells, than any amount uv drink or drugs evuh could.

In thuh kitchen a bolt back anothuh glass uv wine an wash me
phiz under thuh cold tap. Garlic an onion smell on me fingers.
Thuh lasagne's done a treat, thuh top all bubbly brown an crispy,
smells fuckin deelish, thuh garlic bread as well, fuckin loadser that
made by Malcolm. An Laura's brought a gigantic avocado salad –
typical Laura that, avobleedincado – an thiz Roger's cakes as well, so
thir should be enough fuh evryone, a hope, maybe even too much.
Am hopin that theh weakened stomachs ul be strong enough tuh
accept solids. Theh like little fuckin babies.

A sit down at thuh head uv thuh table, by thuh freezer, as Mairead
an Sioned bring in thuh food. Mairead's a little bit wobbly an am
hopin she doesunt drop anythin. Colm is sittin on me left, between
thuh end uv thuh freezer an thuh whitewashed wall (thuh mould
stays out uv this room fuh some reason); a imagine im cirld up in a
bank uv snow, fallin asleep. Ee's talkin tuh Margaret about proverbs
or somethin, a doan know why, ee's in one uv is tetchy moods:

—Yer can endow any fuckin phrase wither meanin that isn ther.
Oh, it's the wisdom ov the common man! Me arse. All slugs wear
hats on parsnips, ther y'go, ther's one. Keep sayin tha an sooner
or later irril come ter mean summun.

Evryone pounces on the food as if thev bin starved, which a
suppose they av, in a self-inflicted kind uv way. Colm rips garlic
bread apart with fingers so bitten that they must be rirly fuckin
sore, an passes some tuh Roger. A notice that thuh tip uv one
uv Colm's thumbs is almost fuckin angin off, thuh nail just a

thick black scab. A wonder what happened thir? A notice too
that Roger's got a new tattoo, a crude representation uv a magic
mushroom on is forearm, beneath thuh faded Celtic band, thuh
same design that a saw spray-painted ontuh thuh brewery wall in
town thuh othuh day. Looks as if it's done with a fuckin trowel
an tar, which knowin Roger it probly fuckin is. Roger's capacity
fuh destruction . . . imself as well as others . . . a dunno . . .

—Wearin a little woolly hat.

—Nah, irrud be a trilby, a trilby with holes cut out fer thee
eyepoles. Like a little slimy gangster, slidin towards the tufty grass
bit on the end uv the parsnip.

Malcolm, is cheeks all bulgy with food, tirns like a chipmunk
tuh Liam.

—Ya rirly reckon ya'd feel free then? God, ya mussun av a very
high opinion av yerself ta fink like that.

Colm joins in, cheese sauce dribblin down is chin:

—Juster fuckin opposite, man! Is self-opinion's so fuckin high
tharry dozen consider at all wha effects is actions could ever av
on others.

—Wha the fuck –

—Whar about the sheep? Ey? The poor fuckin sheep, innocent,
liker child –

—Now doan *you* fuckin start now!

Colm looks at Liam an goes:

—Oi! Doan you wrinkle at me tha limp shred uv salami yuv got
thuh fuckin gall ter caller top lip!

This makes me laugh. A do find it funny sometimes, thuh way
Colm uses wirds. Wha was it ee sed before . . . Yeh: earlier on
tuhday, when we wir all sittin round with thuh radio on, 'Word
Up' by Cameo came on an then anothuh song which contained
wirds like 'raise your hands in the air like you don't care' an
Colm looked up from the spliff ee was buildin an sed: —A fail
ter see how a simple elevation uv one's anterior forelimbs denotes
a devil-may-care an fun-loving attitude ter life.

Ee's always comin out with stuff like that. Fuckin loon.

Anyway, ther all still arguin an am concerned for uh moment
tha it's gunna get violent, cos it sounds it, but thuh expressions on
theh faces say othuhwise. Ther all havin a good time, a realise, a

know em all well enough tuh be able tuh see that. It's OK, it ul be awlright. Sioned, Laura, Maggie an Mairead ur all whisprin an laughin about somethin; occasionally Mairead looks up, chewing quietly, an stirs at thuh centre uv thuh table.

—Fuck me, Colm, mun! Roger shouts. —Ow much fuckin salt yer need, boy?

Colm grins an adds more. Fuckin snowdrifts on is plate, maybe ee likes tuh pretend it's amphetamine. A must say tho, evryone seems tuh be bearin up well, happy enough with thuh booze an thuh weed an thuh food, even if they are knockin back large quantities uv Liam's poitín. A think that maybe this is what they all need, rirly, thuh company uv each othuh as a, like, support kinder thing, a sort uv unaskt for help in assistin each othuh tuh knock thuh hard stuff on thuh head for a while. They wir all gettin pretty bad thir, for a time, Malcolm an Colm an Margaret speedin six days on thuh trot an then gulpin handfuls uv downers tuh knock em out for a couple uv days an then wakin up an startin all over again. None uv em ar twitchin or complainin, an a can tell that they avunt bin tooting or shooting secretly, in thuh bog or whirever, cos uv thuh way ther all attackin thuh food an beer. As fuh me, a had enough fuckin acid last month tuh last me a lifetime, an whenever a do speed n E now thuh comedown wipes me out fuh days an that's bad if yuv got tuh keep yuh wits about yer in order to successfully defraud the DSS. Ey can call yuh in fuh intuhview at any time, an if yuh too fucked tuh go, thel stop yuh fuckin dole. An me wages alone arn enough. An anyway, besides all that, a feel good enough without thuh drugs now; acid's legacy is tuh make thuh pot a bit more trippy, but nothin a carn handle. It's like, what it seems tuh me, it's like it's easier this way, wir all united through such things; united through thuh drug use and, when we stop it, united through that. An if a was a bit drunker ad say somethin about us all bein united through suffering or somethin like that, but am not thinkin about that at thuh mo. Without thuh drugs, it's easy tuh push such thoughts to thuh back uv me mind, an right now that's whir a want em tuh stay. An anyway, who is suffering, exactly? Look at them all . . . maybe some singeing uv the internal organs perhaps, a yellowish tinge tuh thuh skin, but that's all. Suffering: puh: fuck off.

The spacecake disappears in a couple uv minutes, washed down with thuh bottle uv brandy that Malcolm lifted out uv the Spar. An will wonders never cease, some people uh drinkin fuckin *coffee*. A shud take a photo. Well, coffee laced with spirits, but still. Altho Liam's lappin up the potch, Malcolm's knockin back pints uv beer, Margaret's chuckin vodka down er neck, an what's that in Colm's pint glass? Christ, it looks like blood.

—. . . drawn against Holland.

—Holland! Fuck. That's ut, then, wur ou'.

—Not necessarily. One–nil against Italy, remember, the fuckin faverits.

—Aye, but two–one against Mexico! Fuckin Mexico!

—An a nil–nil draw with Norway. Borin fuckin game that was, eh?

—No probleemo por May-hee-co.

Ireland's chances in thuh next round uv thuh wirld cup.

Rain on thuh window. Evryone's leanin back in ther chairs, smoking, hands on theh full bellies. A havunt seen em all so calm for as long as a can remember, none uv em shouting or scratchin like ev got fuckin fleas, none uv em cooking or choppin up powders on thuh table. Colm, even, puts his hand on Mairead's leg an gives her a big smile when she looks up at im. A think uv Banon an Sarah but then Sioned calls me cariad an touches me hair an I kiss her on thuh cheek. This is nice.

And then: mayhem.

Am just about tuh remark how evryone seems tuh be coping well with thuh food when fuckin chaos erupts. It starts with evryone's face turnin green; eyes begin tuh water an hands flap in thuh smoke an evrybody fuckin flips out. Liam suddenly launches into a monologue about rocks or somethin (ee did a bit uv geology in is year doin Earth Studies at thuh university before ee dropped out), fuckin disconnected babble; Colm lifts one arse cheek an lets out a loud fart which tirns into a gurgle an ee looks terrified for a moment before ee leaps up an sprints bow-legged to thuh bog yelling: —SHITE! Av follered fuckin through!; Roger suddenly lurches forwud an spews up in thuh salad bowl, splashes uv hot yellow bile an undigested gristle spatterin over Laura, oo screams an storms off, followed by Liam, ramblin now about granite; Margaret holds her head in er hands an starts tuh cry; Malcolm flies backwuds off is chair as if shoved by an invisible hand, smacks is head off thuh wall an crumples into a heap on thuh floor. Even thuh table seems tuh be rippling, wobbling like jelly, an phoar Christ, thuh stink – Roger's spew an Colm's guff. Jee-sus.

A carn help meself; a birst out laughin an a carn stop. Roger joins in, sick tricklin down is spotty chin. Some wirds come out uv me at Sioned an she chucks a glass uv wine at me but that just makes me laugh even more, a rirly carn stop, am findin the whole thing *so* fuckin funny, evryone's liker crap puppet, flappin about, jerking, all fucked up by food, an Colm's arse, then is gob, roar from thuh toilet behind thuh kitchen:

Bbbbbbbbbbbbbbrrrrrrrrrrrrrrraaaaaaapppp!

—Oh yer bastard! Dia-fuckin-rhea!

This cracks me up again an me lungs ache, but through me tears uv hysterics a can see a downside tuh all this: Mairead, with her head bowed, er face hidden in a curtain uv long dark hair which dangles in er plate. Bits uv onion an cheese an stuff are tryin tuh slither up the hair tuhwards er face, but that could just be thuh hashcake. A can hear her mumbling to herself but a carn make out any proper wirds an a can see er shoulders shaking. A hope shiz laughin too.

Roger gets up unsteadily an staggers out uv thuh room. A look at Mairead, an Mags, an Malcolm out uv it on thuh floor, an then at thuh table which is a fuckin bombsite. What a fuckin mess tuh clear up. Me laughter subsides as suddenly as it began.

Quick histry lesson: A was washed up here, on Aberystwyth beach, aftuh fallin off thuh Holyhead–Dún Laoghaire ferry about three years ago an a just decided tuh stay. Well, actually, a *jumped* off; a wanted tuh see if anyone rirly *would* shout; —Man overboard!, like they do in thuh films.

Nah, that's just uh joke. Thuh truth is, a carn rirly remembuh now why a came here; a just fancied a change from London, whir a was born to Irish Catholic parents from Limerick (am lapsed on both counts; am no longer Irish, or Catholic). Av bin livin in thuh house down Cwmpadarn Lane now for a couple uv years; Malcolm was already livin thir when a moved in, Mags moved in later, an a carn remembuh about thuh others. A met Sioned through one uv er ex-boyfriends, oo useter be me mate (in fact, ee invited me ere in thuh first fuckin place if a remembuh rightly), but oo av since found out is a complete twat. Av known Liam an Laura for a long time, a met Colm, Mairead, etc. through Malcolm. Geraint lived here, at Llys Wen, before ee got lucky enough tuh be able tuh fuck off tuh Florida. An Roger, it seems, as been around for as long as thuh mountains.

'Cwm' means valley, an Padarn was a saint (so Sioned tells me), so this is thuh valley of St Padarn or somethin a suppose. 'Llys Wen' means 'white court'. As if it rirly matters; it's just thuh place whir a live.

History, fuck, a was never any good at that. Hasunt it got somethin tuh do with William uv Orange?

Thuh town's full uv Hassidic Jews. They come here at a certun time uv thuh year, a doan know why: maybe it's somethin tuh do with one uv theh festivals uh summin. A nirly knock one uv em over as a tirn thuh corner at thuh bottom uv Penglais Hill; ee jumps back on to thuh pavement, lookin terrified, an a shout: —Sorry mate!, but a doan think ee hears me.

A pull in outside thuh job centre, whir av arranged tuh meet Roger (or, more specifically, whir ee told me tuh meet im). Thuh day's nice an sunny but with uh sharp hint uv coldness in thuh air; winter's not far off. Roger staggers out uv thuh Vale of Rheidol pub with someone else, spots me car when a flash thuh lights, an comes over. Thuh station clock says quarter tuh twelve. Oo's that ee's with . . .

Oh shit. It's Ikey Pritchard. Me heart sinks intuh me shoes.

A carn drive up intuh thuh mountains tuh see Bill with both Roger *and* Ikey . . . a wouldun be able tuh stand it. Roger's bad enough, but *Ikey*, God . . .

Thiz uh story about Ikey Pritchard. Ee's a psycho, a nutter, a first-fuckin-class hill-billy mad bastard; ee's from Tregaron way somewhir, but ee angs around thuh town a lot. Probly inbred. Anyway, thuh story is that Ikey was owed money, about five grand a think, by someone oo reneged on uh drug deal uh something, an this bloke just wouldunt pay up. Ikey torched is car, broke is fingers, shot is dog, but this bloke just simply wouldunt pay up. So Ikey an is mate came intuh town, found uh tramp, an made im an offer; they sed to im: —If yuh let us bury yer up to yuh neck in thuh woods for a few owers wull give yer a hundred quid. Thuh tramp agreed, so they took im out to thuh woods and buried im; just is head stickin out uv thuh ground, like, in thuh trees. Ikey stayed with im tuh keep im company while Ikey's mate went off tuh find this other feller, thuh defaulter, an bring im back to thuh woods. Ee found im, took im thir (Ikey was nowhere tuh be seen), pointed down at thuh protrudin head an sed: —Look, this feller owes Ikey money, an ee's bin buried ere like this fuh nirly two weeks now. Djer want this tuh happen tuh you? Thuh defaulter shrugged an sed: —A havunt got five grand. Yull havter bury me.

And at that, Ikey stepped out from behind a tree with a scythe an sliced thuh tramp's head off. Just one slice.

The feller paid up that aftuhnoon.

Roger gets in thuh car an Ikey sticks is head in through thuh window an goes: —Yoo hoo, Paulie poos!

A just grin at im an ee cackles. Ee fuckin reeks uv booze. Ts not even midday yet.

—Duntchoo fuckin ferget now a give Billy-boy a fuckin baccy, y'hir me like?

Ee sehs this tuh Roger, oo replies:

—Yeh, yeh, keep-a fuckin knickers on. Doan worry.

—Ah yeh but a fuckin know yew. Ee'l smoke it imfuckinself, in-a right then, Paul?

Ikey winks at me an then says, all serious:

—Vale. T'night. Six a'clock.

Roger nods. —Yeh. Rack em up an gerrum in.

Ikey slams thuh roof uv thuh car twice an sods off, walkin away pointin at me with a rolled-up *Daily Mirror*. Thank fuck ee's gone. A pull out intuh thuh traffic. Roger's smilin to imself an shakin is head.

—Fuckin Ikey, ee says. —Ikey fuckin Pritchard . . . hell uv a boy.

Ee points at a group uv Hassidics over by thuh twenty-four-ower garage.

—Ooer ese cunts? A seem evry fuckin yer round iss time. Why-a ee all wear ose darft fuckin clothes en?

A shrug. —Theh Hassidic Jews. A doan rirly know anything about em.

Roger looks at me, fuckin baffled. —Wha, eyr a fuckin *drugs* cult?

Now *I'm* baffled. —Ey?

—Well yew fuckin called em acidic Jews. Liker sixties wanky hippy thing?

—No, not acidic, *Hass*idic – Ha, Ha, *Hass*idic. Doan av a fuckin clue what it means like.

Roger looks out thuh window.

A drive out past Penparcau an ontuh thuh Devil's Bridge road an just keep goin up, up, up into thuh mountains. It gets colder n colder the higher we go; so cold in fact that thiz even bits uv fuckin snow at thuh sides uv thuh road. Am startin tuh feel depressed. Goin tuh see Bill always fuckin does this tuh me.

A park up when thuh road suddenly stops, arfway up a hill, an we get out an get thuh boxes an stuff from thuh boot. At thuh top uv thuh hill is Bill's house; well, hardly a house – four crumbling walls and arf a roof. Thuh other arf's just sheets uv corrugated iron which Roger nailed on ages ago. Bill couldunt do it cos ee's only got one arm; thuh other one got blown off in thuh Falklands war.

—BILLY! Roger yells. Am amazed ee managed tuh walk up this far. Ee must still be off the smack. —Billy boy!

Thuh view up here's fuckin incredible. Yuh can see fuh miles, mountains an valleys, Cader Idris in thuh distance with mist on its peak like a fluffy hat. It takes yuh fuckin breath away; so much fuckin *space*. A can see buzzards wheelin through thuh air in thuh valley below me, thuh size uv bloody wrens from ere. Never ceases tuh amaze me, lookin down on flying birds.

Billy pokes is ead out uv thuh shack door. Is beard angs down to is belly, or whir is belly would be if ee ad one, an is hair's a red, tangled halo standin up around is skull. Ee smiles, happily, an thiz absolutely no teeth tuh be seen.

—Ah, the boys, the boys, ee sehs. —Seventh bleedin cavalry. Christ a could kiss the both a yer.

We go into is shack. Av been ere before, several times, but it's always a shock; fungus – a mean real fuckin fungus, toadstools an stuff that looks like pasta shells, not just mildew like in Llys Wen – all up thuh walls, a fuckin *stream* runnin down one wall, loose planks for a floor, furniture made out uv crates an boxes, piles uv books an magazines all swollen n birst with thuh damp. It's dark an it stinks.

—What have yuh got for me then?

Bill sits down in a dead armchair. Behind im is an old Welsh dresser, covered in dusty white mould, with cloudy an faded photographs on it. Thuh people in thuh pictures look like ghosts. Whenever am up here, a always havter remind meself that Bill's only in is late thirties, ee's only ten years older n me; ee looks so fuckin decrepit.

A put thuh box am carryin down at is feet.

—Er yuh go, Bill. Bread, tea, sugar . . . all the stuff yuh asked for.

Ee nods an then looks at Roger.

—An ers somethin else is theh? Some powder?

Roger nods an rummages in is pockets.

—Yew wantin a shot now then?

Bill grins. —Do I shit in the woods?

Roger breaks thuh seal on a fresh disposable syringe, takes out lighter, spoon, cotton wool, wrap uv heroin. So ee must still be usin then, if ee carries is wirks around with im, unless uv course ee brought them along specially fuh Bill. Ee cooks up a shot while Bill drools an twitches in is seat, watchin Roger's movements with a massive need in is eyes.

A look around thuh shack. It's scary that anyone could live this way; no electricity, no toilet, thuh only heating is a fire uv gathered sticks built on a metal sheet in a corner, thiz no runnin water apart from that which streams down thuh fuckin walls . . . no people, no company, no telly, no radio, nothin. A void. Jesus.

—Ah Paul, Bill sehs, makin me jump a bit. —A can see yuh rendered speechless by the sparkle an salubriousness uv your surroundings.

Ee grins. Thir's a fuckin ocean uv sweat on is face, prompted probably by thuh imminence uv is fix. Roger ties is belt around Bill's one bicep, yanks it tight, an puts thuh end between Bill's teeth. Bill bites down on it and holds is head back, pullin it taut. Roger finishes cookin up an crouches over Bill tuh inject im. A carn see anythin cos Roger's got is back tuh me which is fine by me cos thuh only needles av ever ad in me life av been administered by doctors, an when a see people jackin up it makes me feel sick. A can tell, tho, when the drug's gone in cos Bill's stump stops jerking frantically an a hear im go:

—Aaaaaaaaaahhhhhhhhhh . . .

An ee leans back in is knackered seat. Thiz a huge fuckin smile in that mad beard somewhir. Is eyes are closed in ecstasy.

—Aaahhh . . . thir we go boys . . . thir we go . . . that's the stuff . . .

Ee's whisprin, mutterin to imself. Somethin about insects an birds.

Roger puts the works in a plastic bag, one uv those ziplock waterproof ones, an puts it on thuh dresser. Ee taps Bill's head, very gently, an Bill opens is eyes, which ar dreamy an far away.

—Yer gear's up yer, Roger sehs. —An listen to me now. Yer lissnin?

Bill nods an gurgles.

—Yer gunner put it in yer leg, or yer foot, *not* tha fuckin stump. Yew hear me, boy? Whir yer gunner put it?

—Me leg . . . me foot . . .

—Yeh. *Not* tha fuckin stump. Yew put it in *yur* an thass yew, brownfuckinbread. An if *tha* appens, al come an spread yer fuckin bones all over ese mountains, boy.

Bill grins an nods his head.

—OK now?

—Yeh.

—Right.

Roger nods tuh me an we get up tuh leave. Ee turns back tuh Bill.

—Al be back in another month uh so, so make it larst now.

Bill raises is one hand, slowly, an then lets it flop back down again on is leg. Ee looks happy, happy as fuck. When wir outside an walkin tuhwards thuh car, a hear im shout:

—Thanks, boys, an next time bring yer mates! Bring some pretty little fillies! Tell em not t'worry, ey'll be safe with me, am armless tell em! Tell em am armless!

An ee roars with laughter.

We get in thuh car. Roger is, unusually fuh him, subdued an quiet. Ee gets like this sometimes when we come out tuh see Bill.

Ee's known Bill a long time, apparently, thir's a bond thir cos Roger was in thuh army too for a time, although a doan know much about that. Ee never talks about it, or hardly ever.

Depresses thuh fuck out uv me, takin Roger out tuh see Bill. Am not gunna do it any more. Next time Roger asks me al make some excuse; al say the car's fucked, or am goin tuh see Sioned uh somethin. Am not comin up ere again.

A start thuh engine an Roger lights a fag.

—Will ee be awright thir, Rog, a mean with thuh needle and that? Ee won't get gangrene or anythin?

Roger splutters: —Course ee fuckin won't, boy, ee was a fuckin medic in-a fuckin army wanny? Ee knows wha ee's fuckin doin, Christ.

—Oh.

A drive down thuh hill. Roger's mumblin to imself, quietly:

—Fuckin ahl twat. Fuckin coward. Ad fuckin top meself if I ever fuckin end up like that boy. Put me n evry other twat else out-a fuckin misery.

We drive back intuh town, more or less in silence. A drop Roger off at a pub an then a drive back up tuh Llys Wen, willing summin tuh go wrong with me car so a can spend all aftuhnoon fixin it. A drive over a pothole down Cwmpadarn Lane an hear somethin start tuh grind in thuh engine: Nnnnnnnnnnnnnnnnnn. Ace.

It's a real pisser that thuh post comes early in thuh morning. A mean, if it's good, then that's awlright, but if it's bad (an it usually is), then that's yuh whole day ruined through worrying about it. Why carn they deliver it in thuh evening, or thuh fuckin aftuhnoon? Yud be able tuh sleep on thuh bad news then. Malcolm sed once that it's anothuh way uv undermining yuh defences, uv weakening yuh armour; an am gettin moren more inclined tuh agree with the cynical bastard.

Letter from the DSS: Dear Mr O'Riordain, it has come to our attention that you've been acting the cunt and working on the side whilst continuing to sign on. Please call in to see us at, on, in. Bollocks. Some fucker's grassed me up, an a think a know who – that fuckin mad bag Annie – so av got a story, an alibi. Thev got tuh fuckin *prove* it first.

24

In thuh dole office am kept waiting fuh arf uh fuckin ower nirly. This is done on purpose; they try tuh make yuh sweat an worry so yull botch up or fuhget yuh story uh summin like that. Am cool tho, am not rirly bothered; thuh only nuisance here is that av ad tuh take a day off wirk, an a need thuh money tuh goan see Sioned in Camarthen or Caernarvon or whirever she is. Still, a suppose a could use a rest day rirly, goan av a few pints or somethin.

—Mr O'Riordain? This way please.

Some sweaty specky tosser with a disgruntled gob like a cat's arsehole an kex too small fuh im. A follow im through a door marked 'PRIVATE ONLY', or 'PREIFAT YN UNIG', all thuh othuh punters lookin at me, wondrin what av done. As dole offices go, this one isunt too bad at all; compared to thuh ones in London, it's a fuckin palace, bettered only by thuh way-out-in-thuh sticks ones in thuh Scottish Highlands, that time a was up thir years ago cyclin round, little cosy sheds in thuh mountains with sleeping cats an gas fires. Most uv them ar probly gone now tho, like round ere; go out to thuh mountain villages now an yull be lucky tuh find a fuckin pub, let alone a shop or a post office. Just a few poky little houses.

—Have a seat, Mr O'Riordain, please.

—Ta. Call me Paul.

Fuck. Why did a say that? Ginger Specky looks at me as if tuh say: You takin thuh fuckin piss, mate? A tirn on me best chummy grin.

—We've asked you to come in on a very serious matter, Mr O'Riordain. Do you know what this is all about?

—Well, a read yuh letter.

—Mm. The situation is as follows: You have been an income support claimant for almost two years now, yet we received a telephone call yesterday morning informing us that, despite your status as a claimant, you are also working full-time as a manual labourer. If true, Mr O'Riordain, this offence can be punishable by a custodial sentence.

'Income Support': now thir's an intrestin phrase. It suggests that av *got* an income tuh support, so rirly, it's perfectly awright fuh me tuh be working cos then am gettin an income fuh the DSS tuh support.

—Mr O'Riordain?

Ee's raised is ginger eyebrows over thuh rims uv is glasses. A sigh n lean forwud (y'know, intimacy, trust); this ul be a piecer piss. Thir's no stone in this feller, a have enough experience uv this kinder thing tuh be able tuh tell that; ee's only about my age and, aftuh first impressions, doesunt rirly look too twatty; a mean, I wear glasses meself, and, like Colm, me fuckin beard grows ginger. A havter shave twicer fuckin day.

—Well, a say, clearin me throat. —This kind uv thing's been happenin tuh me quite a lot recently. Yuh see, a recently ended a relationship with a woman who's taken it extremely badly, and has decided tuh try an make my life as miserable as possible. I've had TV licence men round tuh thuh house, and a don't even have a TV; av had hate mail; policemen on a tip-off that am fencing stolen goods an dealin drugs; an order fuh twenty deep-pan pepperoni pizzas. And a hate pepperoni; wouldunt uv minded if they wir seafood, like, but . . .

Ee smiles.

—I even suspect her uv sabotaging me car.

The bloke begins tuh deflate a bit, his right-then-no-shite-from-you-sonny demeanour (which was farcical anyway) beginnin tuh slip away. Me story, by thuh way, is true; this fuckin Annie – she's a crazy bint, am tellin ya. She threatened tuh rip Sioned's face off in thuh wine bar thuh other night.

—If she gave her name, a say, —a can tell you as proof that er first name is Anne. Her second's Evans.

He nods, an a can tell ee believes me. Ee probly answered thuh phone imself, got shrieked at by some insane harridan. An anyway, if they rirly gave Annie's story any credence, then they wouldunt uv bothered tuh call me in, they woulduv just snooped on me straightaway an obtained proof. Thuh thought goes through me head that maybe a could tirn this situation to me advantage, get more money out uv it somehow; but nah, that might make'm suspicious. The DSS here tends tuh be quite lenient; ask a lot uv incomers why they moved to Aberystwyth an thell say somethin like: —Oh, tuh sign on. But it's startin tuh go thuh other way now. Theh becomin moren more strict.

—Well, in the absence of any evidence to the contrary, Mr

O'Riordain, I can only take your word for it. You understand, I trust, that any accusations of this kind –

Blah blah. A smile a little an nod as ee rambles on, wondrin what ee'd do if suddenly a stood up, dropped me kex, tirned me back on im, bent over an pulled me cheeks apart an let rip with a huge, wet, rumbling fart. Which a feel like doin; that fuckin chilli last night, oof. The bloke rambles on while a mentally map out thuh rest uv me day; post office tuh cash last week's giro, look for a cheap jumper fuh work cos it's startin tuh get cold again now, a bite tuh eat, a few pints, few games uv pool maybe . . . give Liam or someone a bell. Phone Sioned. Might as well enjoy me impromptu day off, ey; been fuckin ages since a last had money tuh blow. An thir's anothuh thought: Blow.

Blokey finishes speakin with an apologetic cough an a say somethin sorrowful-soundin about thuh inconvenience caused. As a get up tuh go ee takes off is spex, rubs is eyes tiredly an looks up at me with a sort-of grin:

—Between you n me . . . phew. A doan bloody envy yew, boy.

So a was right; ee *did* answer thuh phone.

—It's a downer awright, a say. —But what can yuh do?

A give im a shrug an a smile, y'know, men-uv-thuh-world-tuhgether kind uv stuff, an then am fuckin out uv thir, out into thuh fresh air again. That went OK, but a do fuckin hate those places; it's difficult tuh fuckin breathe inside em. Imagine havin tuh fuckin *work* thir, Christ. An it does bother me a little, when am in those places, that am doin somethin illegal, altho fuh me, that an soft drugs ar about as far as it goes rirly. Somer thuh others fuckin *live* by stealing, but I get too nervous, a start tuh sweat an stutter, ad get caught. This fuckin Annie, tho, man, a wish shid just fuckin fuck right off out uv me life an let me fuckin get on with it. Life's difficult enough. Sorry a ever fuckin met er now. Thir's always fuckin somethin, isunt thir? Always some shit yuv got tuh deal with, some fuckin hassle yuv got tuh somehow assimilate intuh yuh life. A know that some uv it's me own doing – Banon n Sarah, say, an this working on thuh side, but fuck oo can live on the dole alone, even in a backwater town like Aberystwyth? – an I accept the consequences uv doin such things; but shite always finds its way intuh yuh life, always fuckin manages tuh worm its way through thuh cracks an fucks up evrythin. Fuck. Annie. What can yuh do? In a town this size, things will always come back tuh get ya, yuh carn get away, thiz nowhere else tuh run, this is thuh end uv thuh fuckin line.

But things get better; at least for thuh moment. A cash me giro, buy a yellow jumper from Save the Children, meet stuttering Phil in thuh street an score some good soap off im. Nice one; didunt even avter go looking, just tirned thuh corner an thir ee was. A drive over thuh bridge to Trefechan, an go intuh thuh Fountain for a sarnie an a pint. No sooner am a through thuh door an a hear:

—Oi! Paul!

—Paulie, yer twat!

Colm n Malcolm n Margaret ar sittin by thuh fish tank, beaming, the table covered with empty glasses an bottles an overflowin ashtrays. Ther all grinding ther jaws an drummin on ther legs, speedin off ther fuckin faces by the looks uv things. 'Sympathy for the Devil' is on the jukebox, probly Malcolm's doin.

A wave over to em an get a round in at thuh bar. Thuh day might just tirn out awright after all.

Am workin on thuh roof uv an old chapel in Ystym Tuen. Thuh view up thuh valley is fuckin amazing, incredible, an a could stand n stare at it fuh owers; thir are times when a take thuh landscape fuh granted round here, but other times . . .

Yet what do a see all fuckin day? Slates an beams beneath me, my hand holdin thuh hammer; dull, dull, dull . . . But, in a way, a prefer it. If yuh stare at thuh lanscape too long, thuh mountains an stuff, it's like lookin at yuh face in a mirror, it becomes unfamiliar, odd, difficult tuh understand, even fuckin frightening. Whack thuh nails intuh thuh wood an lay thuh slates; much easier.

A tell ya what a do hate tho; those fuckin jets, thuh warplanes like, screamin over me fuckin head, low enough tuh almost knock me fuckin off. Fuckin dangerous. Fuckin cunts.

Life's never boring. Sometimes it's terrifying, sometimes it's nasty, but am very rirly bored. Much uv it a doan understand, an a hav uh suspicion that a don't want to, but it's always throwin surprises up in ya face when ya least expect it to. Yuh think that yuv got everythin mapped out, all ya plans fuh thuh day've bin made, an then . . . Life's never boring.

Sioned's off in Camarthen (or is it Caernarvon?), an anyway even if she was here a doan think ad wanter spend time just with her tuhday, but that doesunt necessarily mean that a wouldunt; shiz got a good knack uv makin me feel guilty, Sioned has, altho recently me emotions uv begun tuh play a steadily decreasin part uv ar relationship. Physically it's still thir − God, yes − but that's not rirly wirth much if yuv bin togethuh two fuckin years nirly an anyway physically am attracted tuh almost evry bird under fifty a see in thuh street even fuh fuck's sake Sharon, that bint from round Wigan way oo pisses evrybody off an who a think Colm shagged ages ago. Anyway, none uv this rirly matters cos Sioned's away an so, it seems, is everybody else; thuh only one oo answered thuh phone before was Mairead an she sed that she asunt got a clue whir Colm is, ee's fucked off out somewhir with her cash card, an altho a like Mairead an her company am not rirly in thuh mood tuh watch her get so drunk that she carn even speak. Shiz hittin thuh booze again, with a vengeance; at thuh party the other night she crashed out in thuh middle uv thuh floor an when she woke up a few owers later she couldunt find anythin tuh drink, so she went round thuh whole house pourin thuh dregs uv cans an bottles into a pint glass, fuckin flat, warm beer n cider an ashes n fag ends, bleuch. She drank it straight down fuh breakfast. Ug.

Poor Mairead. Somethin wrong thir, a think.

So a go for a walk tuh thuh castle. It's a nice sunny day, a bit nippy, but nice. On thuh way thir a bump into, speak uv thuh fuckin Devil, Sharon, oo more uh less ignores me cos shiz now found anothuh group uv people tuh tag along with and piss off, a couple uv gay blokes oo work in thuh Arts Centre an oo must be gettin fag-hagged out by er. She looks at me n goes: —Ulraaaaht, in er horrible fuckin whiny voice, an then kind uv sneers at me probably cos am on me own an she's with a group. Nasty fuckin piecer wirk, that one; a remember when Mairead got her inheritance, an Sharon was straight fuckin round thir on thuh scrounge, knowin full well that Mairead's too nice tuh refuse. She still owes er a fuckin grand nirly, an this was over a year ago. Mairead's fault, a suppose, fuh lendin it to er, but ow can yuh blame someone fuh bein kind? Thirl always be twats oo take advantage. Twats like Sharon.

One uv thuh gay blokes, Gwion, stops tuh speak tuh me but we only manage a couple uv sentences before Sharon drags im away, so a goan sit up against a wall in thuh castle an look out tuh sea. A light up a weak spliff. A jet screams over, makin me bow me head; a fuckin hate those things, thuh fuckin noise they make, quite awesome a suppose but they rirly fuckin put me on edge when they fly over like that; a havter grit me teeth an me hands curl up intuh claws an me heart starts tuh thud. They fly too fuckin low. Still, they are amazin things rirly; thuh fuckin *speed* uv thuh bastards. Ad love tuh av a look at thuh engine on one.

—Paulie.

A look up an see Roger, lookin fuckin awful; panda eyes an green skin an a canvas coat which a can fuckin smell. State uv thuh man. What a mess.

—Yew been to-a squat t'day, av yer?

His teeth ur yellow an look bloodstained. Thuh squat? Now why thuh fuck would a wantuh go thir? A descent intuh fuckin hell is what that is.

—No, a say, squintin up at im. Thuh sun's right behind is head so it's like is head's glowing, but thuh rest uv im is all blacked out. —Av, av just been ere.

—Sub us a ten-spot then, mun. A know a fuckin monkey oo needs feedin.

A shrug. —Am skint, mate. A would if a could. Al av some money tuhmorrow tho.

—T'morrer's no fuckin yewce, mun! A fuckin need it now duneye, see?

Ee moves off through thuh castle grounds in a kind uv jerky, spastic way, like ee's tryin tuh move fast but is bones an muscles av other ideas. A watch im go. Ee's gettin wirse. Ee's a shamblin advert fuh desperation. Colm's runnin thuh risk uv goin that way n all, an a feel wirse about that than a do about Roger. Roger's, well . . . a doan rirly like thinkin about Roger. A bad, bad geezer. Me head goes round in circles.

Thuh pressures friends put on yuh can be unbearable. An what's thuh definition uv a friend? People offun say that yuh can choose yuh friends but am not entirely sure about that; sometimes it's like yuh just find yuhselves next tuh each other, like stuff washed up on thuh beach. What is it that binds yuh together? Thuh local Nationalists like ul talk about nationhood, cultural unity, stuff like that; a doan rirly know what ther talkin about, but thuh plaque ere in this castle ul tell yuh that it was attacked an destroyed by an army partly made up uv Welsh mercenaries. Which means . . . a don't know. But a think that the stuff that binds yuh together as probly got more tuh do with, erm, a dunno, recognising somethin in others that either yuh want tuh see in yuhself or are too scared tuh see in yuhself; if anothuh person shows that quality, then yuh doan havter analyse it inside yuhself. Maybe. Ah, a dunno; it's all bollox anyway. Sometimes a think Roger has thuh right idea; numb yuh fuckin brain until it carn work any more. Easier that way.

Intrestin, tho, how wir all from diffrunt parts uv the country, apart from Sioned, oo was born ere; Roger's from South Wales somewhir, Merthyr a think, Colm's a Scouser, Malcolm's an Essex lad, Mairead's from somewhir in Yorkshire . . . tuh ask why wir all here, in this town like, is like askin why wir here on this planet. A doan av a fuckin clue about either.

A get bored an so a leave thuh castle an drive back up tuh Llys Wen, stoppin off at thuh Spar for a bottle uv vodka an some beer (it was a fib tuh Roger about not havin any money; a would av lent im some, tho, if a had more − it's four fuckin days til giro day, an a doan know when al be wirkin next). Thuh beers on ther own ul probly do me tho; am not very good at holdin me ale. Like thuh other day in thuh Fountain; Colm, Mal an Mags ad been in thir fuh owers before I got thir but a was still rat-arsed before them, even Maggie, oo's a girl an small. Snot such a bad thing, tho, a suppose; saves ya fuckin money.

A go intuh thuh house, intuh the mildew niff, an a can immediately tell that no one's in. Empty houses just have that feelin about them, that aura uv emptiness. Thir's a mound uv crusty dishes in thuh sink, an thuh livin room's full uv overflowin ashtrays an dirty plates an empty cans an bottles. Fuckin mess. Thuh room stinks uv Malcolm an Allen's feet; thev got thuh cheesiest feet in thuh whole fuckin world. Gorgonbastardzola, am tellin ya.

Thuh phone rings.

—Hello?

—Is that Paul O'Riordain?

—Yeh. Oo's this?

Thuh guy phonin me, it tirns out, is a vicar; apparently some mad feller that a know called Richard is in one uv thuh churches in town an is refusin tuh leave until I come an 'rescue' him (his word). Ee rirly is cracked, this bloke; not violently like, altho a wouldunt want tuh be alone with im if a was a woman – ee reckuns all women are in league with Satan. A gave im a bed one night, ages ago now, when a found im cryin an arf-dressed on thuh prom, an now evry other week uh so somethin like this happens. Ee's bestowed me with saviour status or summin. Poor fucker.

A drive back intuh town an go tuh thuh church, one uv those big, dark, Gothic lookin ones down thuh backstreets. It's a Catholic one; Our Lady of the Eternal Agony or somethin. Thuh vicar – a little old twitchy feller with a shiny bald head – looks at me like am the Second Coming an points over tuh Richard, oo's on is knees before thuh statue uv Jesus; a almost birst out laughin cos ee looks so much like Stan Laurel (Richard, a mean, not Jesus). A notice hymn books scattered around on thuh floor an pamphlets fuckin evrywhir, as if they'd rained from thuh roof; Richard must uv flipped out. A wanter get im out quickly cos churches shit me up a bit now, a always feel like am bein watched, as if am bein judged. A dunno, it feels like am under scrutiny cos a lapsed from Catholicism all those years ago. Maybe that's why a feel nervy an jittery in general like, cos Aberystwyth's so full uv bleedin churches.

—Richard. It's me, Paul.

Me voice echoes around thuh dark walls an Richard springs up an pelts over tuh me an curls up against me chest, cryin an ramblin on about somethin that a carn make out. Poor little bastard. Ee needs help; ee shouldunt be roamin thuh streets like this, ee needs someone tuh look after im, ee's a hurt person, one uv thuh many victims uv this life. Care in thuh community me fuckin arse. A take im out to thuh car an calm im down, stop im crying, then a goan buy im some fish an chips an take im ome tuh Llys Wen an give im enough vodka tuh knock im out. When ee's well away, a put im on thuh couch in thuh spare room. Thuh couch is fuckin crawlin with mould, but it's better than sleepin in the public shelter with the junkies an pissheads. An am glad Sioned's not here; shid kick Richard out an leave im tuh fend fuh imself. She hates im. Ee wakes for a moment an mumbles somethin about beams uv light an then falls asleep again. Poor little bastard. Still, at least ee gave me somethin tuh do tuhnight. Yuh carn just leave im thir now, can ya?

It starts tuh hit me, thuh E, as am gazin out uv thuh huge Arts Centre windows over thuh town. All thuh lights seem tuh suddenly run an flow tuhgether an become one huge birst uv brightness which explodes in me head an then surges through me whole body like electricity, spinnin me round, makin me move tuh thuh music. Malcolm had sed that this E wasunt much cop but, fuck, this initial rush is fuckin incredible. Am *flying*, am fuckin *soaring* over thuh sweaty crush uv people at thuh bar . . . Jesus . . . oh-hoooooooo! Look at me fuckin go!

A start tuh move through thuh crowd, movin sideways like a crab so a can slide in between people . . . place is fuckin heavin . . . Gorky's Zygotic Mynci ar on stage in thuh Great Hall, which is wir evryone ul be a guess . . . don't stop me now ya fucker! People's faces ar all sweaty an shiny an smiley, a see Black Jerry, oo sold us thuh E earlier, rubbin is girlfriend's bulgin, pregnant belly. Ah . . . how sweet . . . what a lovely sight . . . An thir's Mags, flyin as well, tryin tuh dance but Nigel No-Shoes keeps tryin tuh speak to er, is filthy feet caked in muck shufflin across thuh parquet floor . . .

CHRIST! An especially powerful rush knocks me back against thuh wall an a lean thir against it, smilin, laughin, feelin fuckin wonderful, feelin me hands shake. A doan take E offun but when a do a fuckin *love* it . . . Malcolm's right; thuh most appropriately named drug *ever* . . . foof, am off me fuckin face . . . this is just fuckin incredible . . .

Sioned's talkin tuh Catrin an Richard at thuh bar (not thuh mad Richard, another one); Richard's wearin a woolly hat an dancin with a stick an ee looks like that baboon off *The Lion King* . . . Sioned looks fuckin byooooooooooo-tiful, byoooooooooooooooooti-ful . . . what a lovely sound: byoooooooooooooooooooo . . . a see other faces a recognise, lots uv laughin faces: Irish Harry, Clare, Scouse

Neil an is bird Jennie, Deborah dancing, tall Matt twitching like a beanpole . . .

Colm sways out uv thuh crowd.

—Comin up, Paulie?

—Oh am *up*, am fuckin way, *way* up . . .

—Nice one.

Ee laughs an pats me stomach an goes off tuhwards thuh bar. A push meself away from thuh wall an let me legs jig me over tuh the entrance uv thuh Great Hall . . . a pass Sponge on thuh way.

—Awlright, Sponge? Ow's thuh window cleanin?

—Shite, ee says, an shows is teeth in a grin. Jesus, if ee ad one white one ee'd av a full snooker set.

A start laughin again, laughin at what Sponge sed, noise comin from a place in me chest which is open an clear an strong an OK . . . tinglin rushes through me body, fuckin waves uv loveliness just washin over me . . . walkin down the little corridor intuh thuh Great Hall proper an am like a rock star walkin out on stage or a famous footballer walkin down thuh Wembley tunnel . . . a can hear thuh people roaring . . .

—Paulieeeeeeeeeee!

Christ me ears! Squeaky Susie's dancin around me, wittering in her high-pitched voice. Am surprised people's beer glasses arn shattering in ther hands. Shiz so skinny that er skintight leggings ar like, a dunno, stockings filled with vegetables or summin . . . er bones all bulgy . . .

—How's the boy then, OK are we darlin?

A grab Susie's shoulders an we spin around tuhgether, havin a little dance. She weighs . . . well, hardly anythin; all she lives on is coffee, speed an vitamin pills. Er hormones ar a bit fucked up because of that diet, which is why er voice's so squeaky, apparently . . . but shiz a good'un. Fuck, *evryone's* a good'un . . . includin me . . . am high an am happy an am havin thuh time uv me fuckin life . . . oo-hoo, oo-hoo . . . feets do ya fuckin stuff . . . well if yuh like tuh swing on a star . . . doo-doo-doo, carry moonbeams home in a jar . . .

A love the way crap songs from me youth come back tuh me when am on E . . . out uv me memory . . . me da singin this song tuh me, swingin me round thuh garden in Kilburn . . .

Well yud be beh-tur off then you ar . . . or would you rather be a . . .

Arms clingin round me waist an Mairead swings in front uv me, er face split in a huge an gorgeous grin. Shiz wearin a gorgeous little dress all tight to er tits an she looks appy as fuck. She says somethin tuh me which a doan hear so a lean closer to er an a can smell er an she smells lovely.

—EY?!

—Ar! Yuh! Dan-cing! Wi me!

—Oh fuck yes, a say, an then wir off intuh thuh crowd rirly fuckin goin for it, am dancin me bleedin bollox off. Christ this is so much fuckin fun . . . this is what life is all about, innit, or at least it fuckin *should* be . . . yippie-ay-ey, yippie-ay-oooh-hooo . . .

Colm jerks past, kisses Mairead about thirty times on thuh cheek in quick succession an then slips me anothuh pill.

—Same again! ee yells. —Wiv all just done another so yis've got some catchin up ter do!

—An wharrabout me? Mairead yells, an Colm sucks is lip.

—Sher that one with Paul!

—Orright.

Colm goes off again somewher an a examine thuh pill in me hand. A carn see propuhly in thuh flashin lights but it's not thuh same as thuh one a did before; that one was big an pink, this one is small an white. A break it in arf, give arf tuh Mairead an we dry swallow em. She pulls a face as she gulps it down.

Oh isnt it rich . . . aren't we a pair . . . you with your feet on the ground . . . mine in mid air . . .

Later, after a few owers av passed in a fuckin amazin an joyous whirl, a start tuh come down as am leanin against thuh bar next tuh Colm. Well, not *come down* as such, just, y'know . . . the initial euphoria wears off, dunnit . . . am still fuckin hoverin tho, oh yes, still flappin me wings . . . yuh couldunt stop me if ya tried . . .

Mags n Mairead uh still goin for it on thuh dance floor, dancin opposite each other. Colm's watchin them. Mags is dancin rirly energetically, rirly, like, bouncin about, which she's sed tuh me she doesunt like doin much cos er breasts ar big an she feels embarrassed but now, well, no inhibitions here . . . which she shouldunt have; she looks like a queen, er short hair all stickin up with sweat, er silky top all clingin to er . . . Mairead's just off in er own wirld, a smile glued to er face. Colm's noddin his head tuh thuh music by me side an watchin em both, which ee has been doin for ages.

Ah . . . people ar alright. Ther themselves, yuh know what a mean? Ther just themselves, an all ther interactions an stuff make a certain kind uv sense an value. Thir ar always reasons why people do what they do. Always. No one lives in a vacuum.

. . . an solitaire's the only, game in town . . . daddah-dee-dum-dee, darroo-doo, duhduh-do . . .

A spring away from thuh bar, gettin some more dancin in before thuh DJ as is plug pulled. An before thuh Ecstasy completely wears off, uv course. Fuckin great night. A carn remember most uv it but a just *know* it was fuckin great.

—Who's she then?
—New family on thuh Close. She's the daughter.
—Shiz shaggin er brother. Im, ther.
—Er own *brother*?
—Well, fuck, fie ed a sista like that ad shag er n awl.
—That's disgustin. Prime-time TV as well.
—Oh yeh, irall goes on in Liverpool. Drugs, plagues, arson, bizarre deaths, an now incest.
—Look a that! Ther fuckin snoggin!
—Brother n sister. Awful.
—Actually, a think shiz a birruva pig.
—So's he.
—Prefer Sammy meself like.
—Her! Sour-faced bleedin cow.
Evrybody watching *Brookside*.

Sioned, Banon, Sarah.

SionedBanonSarah: three women in just over uh month. Not bad goin, ey?

Mm.

But sex is . . . well . . . sex is strange. Thiz diffrunt types uv sex; sometimes it's just friction, y'know. Attraction doesunt rirly enter intuh it – a mean, av offun rubbed meself on me pillow, an am not sexually attracted tuh that. Maybe me mattress; phwoar, look

36

at thuh ticking on *that* . . . An then thir's, like, *bodily* attraction, when ya fancy someone, ther face an body an stuff, an then thir's when ya fancy someone's personality, thuh way they speak an walk an laugh, thuh things they say, thuh jokes they make, what they like, don't like, all that stuff. An then uv course thir's the other thing, that which goes beyond all those things; love, a suppose yud call it, altho personally am not entirely sure that av ever felt such uh thing. But sex itself, thuh act, shagging, thuh movements, y'know, putting things in holes . . . a don't know. It's strange. Odd.

Sioned's sleeping with her head on me chest; a can feel thuh glue uv our sweat on me skin an smell my spunk an her cunt juice. Nice smells; meaty an raw. One good thing about Sioned, she doesunt smoke aftuhwuds; Sarah, tho, lies on her back with thuh ashtray on her belly, chain-smokin until a cahn even see thuh fuckin ceiling for thuh smoke, makin me eyes water an makin me cough. *Dead* fuckin romantic. A never wanter do it a second time with her cos after thuh first she always whiffs uv nicotine an ash an am wheezing like a fuckin sixty-a-day man. Banon, on the other hand, likes tuh talk an sing; sex gives er energy. Thuh last time (when was it? last week? week before?), she danced er fingers on me chest an sang 'The Raggle Taggle Gipsies O', an then a got a bit jealous cos she asked me if Colm is uh gipsy an a thought that she fancied im (she doesunt, by thuh way, an incidentally ee is, or partly; his dad, a think, is Romany. Or his grandad. Apparently Colm was born with uh caul on is head which makes im a lucky charm or immune from drowning uh somethin). Sioned, tho, just likes tuh sleep; sex tires er out. So does travelling all thuh way up from Caernarvon or Camarthen or whirever thuh fuck it is shiz been.

Sex, tho . . . a strange, strange thing. A mean, like, well, am not gay, right, but thir was this one time – an ad never tell any fucker this – thir was this one time when a went tuh bed with uh bloke. It was ages ago now, when a was workin in London; a left a job in a warehouse, crappy shelf-stackin thing, an we all went out that night tuh get pissed, an at closin time thir was only me an this other feller Andy left. A stayed over at is place in Islington somewhir cos ad missed thuh last tube, and, well, tuh cut a long story short, we were drunk an ee got intuh bed with me. Well, on thuh couch this was; a was sleepin on thuh couch. A didunt push im away or anythin, a just remember, like, lookin up at im as ee straddled me hips with is knees an kind uv grabbed both our pricks tuhgether in is hand an like wanked us both off at thuh same time (one thing a do remember clearly – mine was a full bell-end bigger). A cahn deny that a enjoyed it; in fact a came a bucketload (no way a could stop meself rirly). But that's thuh thing, ya see; am not gay, this was just, like, in thuh spirit uv experimentation, a was *seduced*, an even if a *was* gay, which am not, then this Andy's not thuh type ad go for. Ya see what a mean? A doan fancy men, an a certainly didunt fancy Andy, an yet . . .

Or like when a shagged Derwen Browntree's missus. A didunt fancy er eetha – fuck no, scraggy old boot, witchy, sour-face – this was more, like, revenge on Browntree cos ee's an arse. Ee owns a few pubs in Aber, thinks ee's Al Capone . . . Dai Capone . . . A wirked in one uv is pubs once behind thuh bar an ee was *such* a fuckin tosser . . . complete arsehole. So a shagged is wife an ee found out an sacked me, tho rirly a was lucky a didunt get beaten in. But a was *able* tuh shag is wife, that's thuh point; thuh desire for revenge, an not sex, made me hard an able tuh do thuh biz. A mean . . . how?

Mm.

Evrything's confusing. It all puzzles me.

Apart, maybe, from this; Sioned sleeping on me chest, snoring softly, thuh clock ticking, thuh sheep bleating outside. Nice.

Thir's one thing botherin me tho; av bin tryin tuh remember fuh ages . . . what was thuh name uv that rabbit in *Watership Down*, thuh kind uv Aryanish one, thuh second-in-command tuh the nasty bastard, General Woundwort? A cahn fuh thuh life uv me remember. It's rirly gettin on me wick.

Uuuuuuuuuuuuuuuurrrrrrrrrrrrrrrrrrrrrrrkkkkkkkkkkkkk *fuck*.

Some fuckin hangover this is goin tuh be . . . ooh . . . what a fuckin mess . . . me eyes open with uh ripping sound an a see that am on thuh couch in Colm's an Mairead's pad. Sioned's not ere. Thuh low table by thuh couch's covered in bottles an cans (which isunt unusual) an overflowin ashtrays which stink an make me gag. Thiz uh whiteish crusty splash on thuh TV screen, which could be milk, thuh cassette player's still switched on an is humming in me ears an av still got me boots on an thir's a patch uv cold, caked puke on me shirt. Fuck; it was me best white one n all. Me head feels full uv diarrhoea. Av got sevrul long n horrible owers uv discomfort ahead. Fuck.

A get up painfully an limp into thuh kitchen, dimly remembrin somethin bad happening. Tuh get to thuh kitchen av got tuh go through thuh bedroom, an a notice that thuh bed's empty, but thuh sheets're rumpled an thiz uh faint smell uv spew, altho that could be, an probully is, me. A get meself a glass uv water an go out intuh thuh yard; thuh sun an thuh green grass uv Constitution Hill, over thuh yard wall, ar too fuckin bright an hurt me eyes.

—Paul.

Mairead's sittin in a patch uv sunlight on thuh floor, her back against thuh whitewashed wall, a can uv lager at her feet. Evrythin's too bright, far too fuckin bright . . . thuh brightness seems tuh make a sound, like a fuckin *roar* or somethin. Mairead doesunt look too good; er hair is long an greasy, shining in thuh sunlight, and er lips're all cracked an swollen. She holds er hand out unsteadily an shows me somethin wrapped around er finger; a baby lizard.

—Say hello to the tiny dinosaur.

It's fuckin amazing, rirly wee, perfect in evry detail. Even its tiny little tongue flickerin out tuh taste thuh air.

She puts it gently un thuh floor an it scurries away into a crack in thuh wall. She takes a long swig out uv thuh can an offers it tuh me, but a shake me head an just sit down by er. Oh me fuckin skull. Bang bang bang.

—Ower yuh feelin then?

—Like shit. Whir's Col?

She shrugs. —Dunno. Ee never come back last night. Duh yuh not remember losin im on the prom?

That seems strange; not that we lost im, ee's always fuckin off on is own, but that ee was in thuh prom pubs in thuh first place. Ee normully never goes in them, sayin that ther too full uv fuckin students n rich kids. Which is true, like, but in thuh nice weather it's nice tuh sit outside at thuh tables an watch thuh sea. An a havunt got thuh faintest recollection uv bein on thuh prom at all. A doan remember a fuckin thing.

—Why did yuh smack Sioned?

Ah shit. Me heart plummets.

—Is that what a did?

Mairead nods an gulps at er can.

—Hard?

—Well, a dunno that. A could ear yuh borth fuckin screamin at each othuh from thuh end uv t'rord when a were comin back. Ad given yuh the keys, remember? An a knocked ont door an Sioned orpened it an then legged it down the rord. Said yud it er.

It begins tuh trickle back now, through thuh haze. It wasunt a closed fist, a remember that clearly, just like a slap tuh get er away from me an tuh stopper goin on, gettin on me fuckin nerves. Ad asked er tuh do somethin an she refused an then started tuh av a go at me like she does, goin on an on, no one else goes on like Sioned especially when shiz drunk; nag nag fuckin nag. Still . . . a don't suppose a shoulduv belted er. A can be an arse too when am pissed up.

—Yuh should stop doin it, Paul, Mairead says. God; fuckin lecture alert. Why do all women always fuckin go on? —Get eh grip. A knor that Sion can be uh pain at times like but it's right fuckin out uv order tuh it er like that. Yur a bloke, yuh can never understand what it's like, the fear an pain an real fuckin anger. That's worsen t'pain, the fuckin rerge inside an knowin yer powerless t'do owt about it. Av met sor many wankers oo uh free wi the fists, yull never be able tuh understand what it's like. That's one thing al say fuh Colm; ee asn actually hit me yet. Threatened to, like, an ee's grabbed me an stuff, but ee's never rurly, y'knor, punch to the ferce . . . dornt meant that ee wornt in future, a course. Ee probly will. Blokes're all t'fuckin serm.

Am beginnin tuh feel like a real shit now, thuh more Mairead goes on. A mean Sioned, Christ, she's two feet smaller than me, shiz tiny, Christ me hand's the size uv er whole fuckin head. Oh fuck . . . even if she *is* a fuckin black belt at karate. Am a shit an a shouldunt uv fuckin done that.

Mairead finishes er can, burps.

—Want one?

—Yeh, awlright.

—Well, fetch one fuh me too while yuh thur. Ther in fridge.

A goan get two cans uv cheapo Spar lager from thuh fridge, which is empty except for arf a bottle uv Martini, a shrivelled lemon an a carton uv milk. A give a can tuh Mairead n sit back down by er. Thuh sun's rirly fuckin hot; gunner be another nice day.

—So. Wotcher goin tuh do tuhday? Yuh gunner goan find Colm?

—Nah. Ee'l come crawlin back later on, when ee's run out uv money. Ee allus does. What about you? Yuh gunner see Sioned?

—Ah, shiz probully back up at Llys Wen. Al go back later, give er time tuh calm down like. Taker some flowers uh summin.

—That would be nice.

A swig at me can, an then wait for a bit tuh see if it's goin tuh come back up. It doesunt, so a drink it all an then rinse thuh sick out uv me shirt an we polish off thuh Martini while it dries on thuh line an then we both go intuh town to thuh offy. Thuh prom is packed with tourists an those Hassidic Jews uh still around n all. A buy us both burgers at thuh kiosk an we go for a couple uv pints outside thuh Glengower, then Mairead goes off ome with er carry-out tuh get drunk an a sit thir on me own with a paper an another pint. Gladys Trevithick, off er fuckin face on somethin, tries tuh join me but a tell er tuh fuck off an she does. It would be nice tuh av some company but not *her*, Christ . . . evil old witch. Those poor fuckin children. It is fuckin awful, tho, drinkin away a hangover on yuh own, specially if yuv got summin tuh be ashamed of. A remember Colm sayin once that a bloke oo hits a girl is thuh lowest uv thuh low, the scum uv thuh earth, an at this moment in time a reckon ee's probly right. A feel like fuckin shit.

A down me pint an then another. Am a bit too pissed tuh drive after that, but it's only, like, threeish an a cahn face goin ome yet. What a rirly feel like doin is drivin out to thuh mountains with a bottle or two; a feel thuh urge tuh stand in a place whir a can see somethin with me naked eye which would take me sevrul days walking tuh reach. A doan know why, like, a just do.

This is difficult tuh believe. No, this is fuckin im*poss*ible tuh believe. A feel sick inside, like am about tuh heave, thiz a horrible taste in thuh back uv me throat . . . thir's images runnin about in me head that a don't, *can't*, look at.

Fuck. How could she? How could *he*? Fuck. My friend.

This life is full uv shocks. Big, dirty, nasty shocks, things that come round thuh corner tuh boot yuh in thuh face before yuv even had time tuh *think* about defences. Ya helpless, ya useless against these things . . . thir's nothin ya can do. Apart from fill yuhself with enough fuckin chemicals tuh neutralise these shocks. Christ, what a life. What a fuckin life.

Shock one is findin out al never see Roger again. A never liked the lad that much like, but, God . . . a wouldunt wish what happened tuh him on me wirst enemy. No, praps a would. Ad wish it on fuckin Malcolm.

Shock two is Sioned tellin me that shiz shagged Malcolm. *Malcolm*! A mean . . . why? She was dead quiet in thuh car from thuh station tuh here, quiet when we ate thuh pasta ad cooked, quiet when we wir makin love, quiet when we wir in the shower . . . an now ere she is tellin me that she got off with Malcolm. Malcolm. Fuckin Jesus Christin twattin cuntin fuckin *hell*!

A just sit thir on thuh edge uv thuh bed, shakin me head, starin out thuh window. A can see sheep, white blobs on thuh hill goin up tuh Comins Coch, a can see rooves uv houses, a few clouds, a big bird wheelin in thuh sky, probully a buzzard . . . a can hear me heartbeat, drownin out Sioned's whines:

—Sometimes yew need *com*fort, Paul, can yew not under*stand*? A was drrrunk, Chrrist, *hurrrtin*, a felt all alone after what yude done . . . a mean, *rrrirly*, what did yew bloody ex*pect*? Yew carn go on doon it for ever, a mean sooner or later –

A can hear er wirds but a carn see er sayin them; er head's bowed an all er hair's hangin down over er face. Am reminded for a moment uv Cousin It out uv thuh *Addams Family* an then a quickly seem tuh leave meself, me mind, a seem tuh drift outside uv meself an become like an observer, not a participant in what's goin on, an part uv me picks out a spot behind that hair curtain whir a imagine er cheekbone tuh be an then me right fist slams into it hard an a feel hard bone crunch against me knuckles an she flies back across thuh bed, screaming, er legs kickin an er head in er hands. Then am up an puttin thuh boot in again an again, a don't aim a just kick, an then am in thuh hallway flingin open thuh door tuh Malcolm's room not knowin what am goin tuh do, fuckin clueless. Me body's like an engine that am operatin by remote control; am in fuckin pieces, am in fuckin bits. Am not really here.

An then: Shock three. Malcolm's room; it's empty. None uv is stuff's in here, ee's gone, fwsst, fucked off; no books, no tapes, no clothes, no posters on thuh walls, just a bare mattress on thuh bed an a polka-dotted wall whir ee used tuh bounce a baseball against it, thuh prick. Ee's gone. This room is not lived in anymore. It is empty.

Fuck.

A stand an stare for a bit an then back out onto thuh landing, closin thuh door quietly behind me as if someone's in thuh room asleep. A doan know why a do that. Thuh door goes 'snick' as it closes. An a stand thir, completely fuckin baffled, rirly fuckin shaken up like, an a can hear three things; one, Sioned crying an gurgling in thuh bedroom, screamin somethin about bleedin beneath, a dunno, a carn rirly make it out; two, Mags spewing up in thuh bathroom; an three, Allen roarin with laughter downstairs at somethin on thuh telly. An then thir's a fourth sound as a jet screams over thuh house, low enough tuh rattle thuh fuckin window-panes.

Fuck. A just stand thir lissnin, rubbin me knuckles. What thuh fuck do a do now?

A use thuh Abergynolwyn Castle infuhmation board display thing as a buffer an chug gently against it to uh stop, thuh wooden ridge at thuh bottom uv it pressin intuh me belly. Over it, far away in thuh mist, a can see Bird Rock, risin out uv thuh landscape like a giant, warty thumb. Drizzle comes down as a tirn tuh watch um all shamblin out uv thuh castle entrance; Laura an Mairead, smilin as they come up on thuh mushrooms; Malcolm an Colm hackin at each other with invisible axes, or they could be swords, a carn tell; Liam brushin moss an stuff off is leather jacket an goin on about ow nobody bothered tuh elp im down off thuh wall.

—Whur the fuck wur you fuckers? Fuckin leavin us stuck fuckin up thur . . .

—Well, yer shouldn av climbed it inner ferst fuckin place yer idyit, should yer?

We stand thir in thuh rain. Colm, beginnin tuh twitch as thuh speed ee bombed earlier takes effect, olds is and out tuh test if it rirly is raining, as if all thuh water fallin on is head isunt proof enough.

—Fuck. Rain.

—Oh, yuh dornt say, Mairead says, all sarcastic like. Colm just ignores er.

Shafts uv bright sunlight break through thuh shiftin cloud cover an one uv em falls directly ontuh Bird Rock, lightin it up. It stands out like uh beacon burning, evrywhir else around it dark, as if thir's no rain on it, as if it's uh tiny piece uv the Caribbean, weather an all, uprooted an replanted here in Wales. It looks fucking amazing.

—Lookit that, says Mairead, an as if that's a signal we're all off, whoopin an boundin tuhwards it, runnin an roaring over thuh muddy ground an gettin all covered in shite, tryin tuh reach thuh sunlight an thuh shelter before thuh clouds're blown over tuh cover it again.

Yuh see, thuh thing is with Sioned, right, is that shiz so at ease with erself. A mean, she knows oo she is, whir she's from, an whir shiz goin to, or at least she *seems* to. I, on thuh other hand (an most uv thuh other people a know), avunt rirly got thuh first fuckin clue about any uv those things, an a think that's what frustrates er about me and pisses er off. A can understand why, a suppose; shiz solid, an am watery, as she never fuckin tires uv tellin me, an that's why a guess she nags me all thuh fuckin time. But, fuh fuck's sake, shiz got fuckin solidity tuh spare; why carn she use some tuh support me, or at least offer me some sort uv foundation? Doan get me wrong like, a can look after meself; but . . . well, by way uv an example, Sioned isunt even bothered by thuh closed-inness, crampness, uv livin in a place's small as Aberystwyth, whereas it sometimes drives me fuckin barmy; yet, instead uv talkin tuh me about it, an tryin tuh, y'know, point out thuh good things, shill sneer an call me wishy-washy an treat me like a fuckin kid. What fuckin good does that do, ey? Steader makin me feel important an wanted she sometimes just makes me feel even more unnoticed an insignificant than a normally fuckin do. Shill even use thuh language barrier as a defence; if a ask er tuh explain erself more clearly like, in an argument or somethin, shill say that thir's no point in tryin cos she can only explain erself clearly in Welsh. She

44

speaks English better than fuckin I do, an besides, did she fuck give me any credit fuh spendin all that fuckin money an time (two nights a fuckin week!) tryin tuh learn Welsh at nightclasses. Jesus. An she's so fuckin touchy; if a call her a name, even just messin about like yuh do with mates, like, y'know: —Yuv birnt thuh toast yuh daft cow! or somethin, shill sit an sulk until a apologise an not just apologise but apologise profusely an licker fuckin boots clean. She even taints me relationship with Banon, makin me ill at ease an broody when am with her (av given Sarah thuh Spanish Archer, the old El Bow); a know that's a terrible fuckin thing tuh say . . . a mean, am two-timing Sioned with Banon, not thuh other way round . . . but thir yuh are. Banon's more fuckin fun anyway. *And* better in bed. Not that Sioned ud ever make any effort tuh understand *that* . . . that's er fuckin problem; she never tries tuh empathise with other people, an shill never, an a mean *never*, change er opinions. About anything. Ever. Shiz got no fuhgiveness in her at all, and a vindictive streak that runs a mile deep. Like a seam uv coal.

So anyway, am fucked if am stayin sober tuhnight. Wuv driven – or, no, *I've* fuckin driven – out to thuh pub in Pontrhydygroes for uh meal, thuh arrangement (made by Sioned only, a might add) bein that I stay sober, bored, an pissed off in order tuh drive us ome while she chucks thuh fuckin vodka down er throat an as a great time. Loads uv fuckin fun. An tuh make matters worse, thuh drive out thir goes through a landscape which reminds me uv both thuh Scottish Highlands and Snowdonia, an a start thinkin about thuh times a spent in those places, when a was younger, freer, happier. A understand ow Colm feels now when ee's always goin on about Brittany. Or Mairead with Spain.

—What's wrong bach? Sioned asks. In a voice like shid use to a fuckin cat or summin. —Yuh look sad.

A shake me head. —No, am awlright. Ad just like a drink, that's all.

—Well, have one then.

—Yeh; pint un a fuckin arf. Great.

She understands *that* reasoning, awlright. If a tried tuh teller about thuh Highlands an Snowdonia an this fuckin loss inside uv me, shid look at me as if a was talkin Swafuckinhili. Am tryin, tho, am rirly fuckin tryin tuh keep it tuhgether, if only she could fuckin see it. Am goin tuh be twenty-fuckin-nine next month. Sioned's twenty-two.

Inside thuh pub, which is heaving, a make straight for thuh bar. A group uv local fuckin inbred-lookin farmers start speakin tuh Sioned in Welsh; she blushes an answers em back, says summin which makes em laugh an point at one uv ther number, a fuckin barrel-chested no-neck arsehole like a bulldog on its hind legs. Jesus, someone wipe thuh fuckin drool off is chin, will ya?

A give Sioned er double vodders an coke. Pint uv Guinness fuh me; thuh first uv fuckin many, al tell ya that.

—What did those cunts want? a asker as we walk away from thuh bar.

—No, she says, —they wurr oo-kay. Just bein boys. She taps me glass an a nirly fuckin spill it. —Remember, now: pinten a half's the limit, cariad.

My hairy fuckin arse it is. Am gettin fuckin shit-faced even if it means wir fuckin walkin ome.

We find a table in thuh corner by thuh fireplace, choose food from thuh menu an a go up to thuh bar tuh order it. While am thir a knock back a double whisky an order up another stout, an another vodka fuh Sioned. Thuh booze is goin straight tuh me head an thuh effect, as it always is when am in this mood, is part mellow, part anger. Intrestin, like, but a doan rirly know ow tuh cope with it, which tends tuh accentuate thuh anger. A think uv Colm tellin me about the effects uv takin crystal meth with Colombian brown heroin – doan fight it, ee says, just enjoy thuh rollercoaster ride – an knock back another double whisky.

—Yuv gone n got another *pint*! Sioned says as a sit back down. —Yurr oonly all*owed* another half!

A shrug. Little do you fuckin know.

She goes on: —A know yew, yull be *pissed* ahfter that one, an *then* whurr will we be? Ey? Ower *fuck* will we get back hoom then?

A shrug again. —Fuck knows. Get a fuckin taxi. Walk. *I* doan fuckin know.

She gets all fuckin indignant at this. —So what's brurrt this on, then? What have a done now?

A gulp ahf thuh pint an try tuh tell er, but it's rirly fuckin difficult cos a carn rirly impress upon er thuh way a feel unless a tell her about

Banon, an Sarah n all a suppose, an that would rirly fuck er up, an no matter ow much she pisses me off a doan wantuh do that to er. A mean, thuh fuckin bruises on er face avunt completely gone yet; a doan wantuh hurt er like that inside as well.

—Look, bach, if yew *rurrly* wanter get pissed then do, but *please* dunt be a pain in the arrse. Av oonly ad two drrinks, *I* can drive us back if yew want or, Duw, let's us *both* get pissed an go arvs on a taxi aye?

—Wha, a say, —an leave thuh fuckin car here? An ool it be oo ass tuh come out n get it in thuh fuckin mornin, ey? Me, that's oo.

—Well, we can arsk Mairead if urs is workin or Liam or even get anothurr taxi. Wuv got the money, ant we? Dim problem.

Thuh food arrives an a order a bottle uv white wine; fuck thuh cost, a cashed a giro tuhday, *and* got fuckin paid. A bang back what's left uv thuh Guinness an start shovellin in thuh food, somethin pasta, a carn remember now what thuh fuck it was a ordered. Thiz prawns in it, a think. Sioned's got hare which shiz eatin with er fingers, bits uv flesh in er teeth. Evry so often she spits out lead shot; it goes *spang* on er plate. She looks like some kind uv Celtic queen, thuh brass torque round er wrist, thuh long blonde hair, thuh old leather waistcoat. A notice those fuckin yokels nudgin each other at thuh bar, starin at er like, as she sucks on a bone; am about tuh say somethin to thuh fuckers, tell em whir tuh fuckin go like, but without lookin up Sioned says:

—Please dunt, bach.

—Don't wha?

—Dunt say anythin. Dunt cause trrouble. Ther armless, ther just bein *boys*, like yew do when yuh with Malcolm an Liam an people.

This pisses me off. —Not like fuckin *that* a don't! Fat fuckin cunts with the tongues angin out like fuckin dogs! Ey probly only fancy yer cos yuh look like the fuckin sister!

A realise that am speakin loud; people at thuh other tables uh lookin an whisperin. At last th'er fuckin noticin me now, am thinkin, but me anger is subsiding with thuh booze an a doan wantuh upset Sioned any more, an am afraid that er coolness an reasonableness might drive me into a right fuckin rage if a stay so a concoct a plan. A plan. A pour us both some wine an wait for

47

er tuh go to thuh bog, which is a long an tortuous wait cos a doan trust meself tuh speak to er an stay calm, but thuh silence feels so fuckin awkward . . .

—What's yuh food like then?

—Awlright, a say. —Nice.

—What is it, then?

—Pasta an prawns. .

At last she gets up tuh go to thuh bog, an luckily fuh me shiz on er period so a know shill be in thir a while, so a go up to thuh bar (those yokels av fucked off now, probly tuh meet some sheep somewhir), get three triple gins, takem back to thuh table an pour em intuh me empty Guinness glass, fill the rest up with wine, take a deep breath an knock it back in one. A havta cover me mouth tuh suppress thuh gag reflex like an a can see through me tears some dog's-arse-gobbed biddy and er hubby cluckin disapprovingly at me. A grin at them an burp, down thuh rest uv thuh wine. Then a leave a load uv money – well, enough tuh pay thuh bill – under Sioned's plate an then, after a few more doubles banged back up at thuh bar, a go out intuh thuh night. Outside, in thuh car park, a think am goin tuh be sick, but a fight it back an start walkin, back tuhwards Aberystwyth with me thumb out, an a dunno whether it's cause thuh roads uh fairly empty or cos it happens rirly quickly but only about three cars go past me before a collapse an black out in a hedge at thuh side uv thuh road, a squashed fuckin hedgehog or summin, some unlucky splattered thing, pickings for thuh red kites which ar rumoured to av returned tuh nest around ere.

From *A Personal Guide to West Wales*, anonymous authorship, privately printed, p. 18

Here, there is a fault of colossal proportions, a fault which gapes along the twenty miles of the Ystwyth valley down to the edge of the sea, a fault disguised by the surface attractions of the slaty cleavage which always, always, insists on distance: once adjacent points here are now separated by metres measurable in their thousands. The foldings and contortions of the strata testify to the slow writhing of rock, a restlessness which will allow no permanence; these patterns, here, will never be static, nor complete, nor perfected, they will for ever be in a process of formation for as long as loosened rock obeys the pull of its parent planet, which is for ever. The land shifts, its signature mutability, the impossible timescale of its stamp concomitant with the utter inscrutability of its hard and granite heart.

Here, there are questions, questions concerning temperature, reaction, diachronicity, questions doomed to be always unanswered. Vast retreats before the presence and consequent recognition of a force infinitely greater, stronger, crueller. Torture.

THEY ARE LOCKED IN

THEY ARE LOCKED in a pub in which they have been drinking for several hours and they are enjoying themselves in their usual manner, ravaging, savage, and lost. Look at the dragon rampant; he howls above the hubbub, walks as if led by his pelvis, has the bulbous and bloodshot eyes of one fraught with amphetamine and alcohol, lust and roar. Some intense sort of energy crackles in his speech and rises like nicotine to scorch the yellowed ceiling. A familiar face floats up in front of his and his vision clouds red as flame.

Malcolm nudges Paul. —Av ya seen Roger? Fuckin off is *face*.

—A know. What's ee on?

—Christ, ee bombed abaht a gram av crystal meth yestaday, ee'l be aht av it fa days. Colm n awl, whireva the fuck *he* is.

—Wasunt ee with us before, back at thuh house?

—Well, in body, yeh. Neva even offad me one fuckin dab, tha cunts. An ennyway, whair did they get crystal fuckin meth from? Larst birra whizz *I* ed was fuckin icing sugar.

—Ther not goin ta be able ta find ther dicks fuh weeks.

—Roger ul be pleased, then, cos ee's neva fahnd his befaw.

Malcolm resigns himself to alcohol alone and finishes his pint in a gulp. He knocks back his vodka chaser and struggles up to the bar.

Roger misses this conversation, being otherwise engaged in stamping on the hands of a moustachioed and beer-bellied someone in a narrow alleyway behind the pub, someone with whom he has had a long-running and brutal feud for reasons now long lost. The hands continue to twitch, fumbling brokenly on the bloodied and spittled cobbles, so Roger stamps on them again, harder this time, one palm against the mossy brick wall for support, stamping with the heels of his boots until the hands cease moving and he can re-enter the pub, surreptitiously, through a side door.

—Liam! yells a voice in the crowd. —Give us a song, yer twat!

Liam declines, half-heartedly but nevertheless uncharacteristic-ally; usually, he does not need to be asked to sing. He hides his face behind a gulp of Guinness.

—Ah naw, naw . . . landlord wouldun like ut.

—Shite, man, that's wha ee as these fuckin lock-ins for!

Smiling sloppily, swaying slightly in his seat, Liam begins to sing 'Mary McCree', and the crowd around him fall quiet. At the bar with a fresh pint of Wrexham's, Roger feels rage begin to drop away and squints at Liam through sore eyes, jaws working, teeth grinding. A softness now starts to work with the sulphate to hum and buzz inside his head, his beating breast, and he begins to think that he loves Liam for his gentle Irish voice and the words of his chosen song which seem to sum up perfectly all loss and all pain and all subsequent anger. Purple thoughts flash through his reeling brain, flash and vanish and are immediately replaced by others of their kind; Liam's alcoholic mother and his exilic life, his childhood spent next door to a war zone, Roger's own memories of a tour of duty in Ulster before being discharged extremely dishonourably, blood, impact, theft, things crumbling away, crumbling away. Another chemical rush through his body is prompted by the general cheer which accompanies the end of Liam's song and he turns to a girl standing at his right elbow whom he had silently appraised earlier and tries, unsuccessfully, to refrain from babbling in her ear.

A cry from Paul:

—Sioned! It's your turn now!

> Hen fenyw fach Cydweli
> Yn Gwerthu losin du

Roger's hopes rise at not being rebuffed and he stops talking with difficulty to listen to Sioned sing, his mind now offering personalised pictures of crags, valleys, hills, stone. Sioned is beauti-ful, he thinks, and his hips twitch involuntarily and his fingers curl into claws at the feel of phantom flesh and when Sioned's song ends and they all launch into a bellowing version of 'Dicey Riley' he roars along vigorously, the girl at his side matching him in pitch and enthusiasm:

Poor-or old Dicey Ri-hi-ley
Has taken to the sup!
And poor-or old Dicey Ri-hi-ley
Will never give it up!
It's off each morning to the pub
And then she's in for another little drop
And the heart of the road is Dicey Riiiiiiiiley!

She walks along Fitzgibbon Street
With an independent air!
And then she's down by Summerhill
Where all the people stare!
And now it's nearly half past one
IIIIIIIIIII'll just drop in for another little one
And the heart of the road is Dicey Riiiiiiiiley!

As they all repeat the first verse the girl joins in with huge zest and
Roger steals a glance at her and sees flushed cheeks and clean teeth,
mousy hair tied back in a ponytail. Little make-up. He will leave
with her tonight, he thinks; he will go back to her room or take her
back to his and he will fuck the arse off her tonight, he thinks, he will
shag her senseless, screw her daft, and as Colm, who has reappeared,
begins to sing about being a man you don't meet every day (and
'thank fuck fer *that*', whispers Mairead), and as blood congeals on
slimy cobbles and rats watch a man pull himself brokenly into
a mossy wall on shattered hands, Roger clasps the girl's hand,
sweating, hoping that she will not notice the faint trembling in
his fingers which anyway is not due to nervousness but to scalding
anticipation and the uncommon strength of the amphetamine he
has ingested and especially to the last residues of rage leaving him,
crumbling away, crumbling away, to be replaced by fires other, yet
still of their kind.

ROGER

GRAFFITI ON-A WALL in-a New Gurnos like, biggest fuckin estate in-a ole uv Ewrop, fucked fuckin place like am fuckin tellin yew, Merthyr fuckin Titfeel, a fuckin *real* Wales fyer boy, none uv-a fuckin mountains or lakes yer jes fuckin sewage an dumps n boxes t'fuckin live in like, a *real* Wales, a place whir am fuckin *from*, Indyin fuckin reservation in-a middle-a Great fuckin Britain like (an Geraint the twat now standin on-a *real* fuckin reservation over in-a steyts like with feathers an spears an fuckin peyote) a pleyce-a gwehilion o boblach boy, too fuckin right, ewman fuckin weyst like, waste-a ewmans, gahbidge like, rubbish, shite, yer's fuckin graffiti on-a wall in-a New Gurnos:

Croeso i uffern.

Yew fuckin twat.

MONDAY

Stayn streyt this week, boy. Streyt's a fuckin ruler like. A woz gettin bloody bard ferra bit like, t'smack woz like avin a fuckin pee, jes, like, summin a did, so av got t'stey streyt, least ferra bit like, no smack, no speed, stayn off-a fuckin bevvy an all – a know wha appens when a don't, fuckin chaos, mun, fuckin nightmare like, blank out an weyk up all fuckin bloody in-a fuckin cell or ozzy. A can teyk booze with-a skag, most carnt . . . fuckin *I* can tho. Too fuckin right. Fuckin survivor me, boy. But a dunno what's werse like, tha or this, this's fuckin *borin*, mun, dull; ow long's it teyk like t'recover from-a binge? Might uz well sayer rest-a me fuckin life, coz thass wha tslike, y'know, a want fuckin drugs like *yew* want air. Know what a mean en?

Bu' iss fuckin boredum, mun . . . doin me fuckin ead·in, aye. A mean, lessee like, wha av a done t'day? Al tell yer: gorrup twelveish like, et some toast an en sicked it streyt back up agen like, ad about twenty shits (summin wrong with me insides a reckun like), smoked a big spliff, watched a bit-a telly. Ad seven wanks, knob red-raw now like, randy as fuck like, picked me nose (nowhere neer as nice as it is on-a smack), farted, pulled-a matted irr out-a fuckin plug-hole (all fuckin wiry an jet black from at fuckin Goth cunt downstirrs), cleaned me room up an *fuck* a shite in yer mun, fuckin mounds-a mould an socks yer could fuckin snap like, yewsed johnnies from larst fuckin *yeer* (carn shag on-a smack, see?), a went-a corner shop fer milk an baccy, watched telly, watched telly, watched a bit more telly . . . ardly rockin fuckin roll now, is it, ey? S jes fuckin dull, mun, dull dull dull, an-a werst-a it is all-a fuckin stuff yer *don't* do, or see, a fuckin insides-a yer like-a fuckin brick, evrythin teysts like fuckin muck like, s'prised not t'see orange fuckin dust on-a paper when a wipe me bleedin arse like. Avn phoned Colm, or Malcolm, or enny fucker else – Colm ul be probelly fuckin manic on some mard fuckin cocktail ee's invented like, at twat Paul as bin-a bit fuckin snotty recently, moody fuckin cunt at ee is . . . A carn even eat like; av got t'weyt fer me fuckin guts t'settle down a bit b'fore a can even fuckin *think* bout eatin agen. So whirr's all-a shite comin from en? Fuckin streynge tha, like . . . Ope a can fuckin sleep t'night. Might see meself off with another toss like, tha new porno with tha Chinky tart in . . . oo yeh. A member-a Chinky fanny when a wuz in Ong Kong with-a army like, some fuckin tricks ey knew aye, am fuckin tellin yer, mun, foo. Meyk yer fuckin irr cerl aye.

Fuck. Never felt so fuckin orny as when a come off-a smack. Never. Might jes fuckin go out like an—

A phone's ringin. Not fuckin arnsrin it. Be some fucker probelly with a big fuckin bag-a powder an-a fuckin big grin on's feyce. Fuck, mun, if fuckin Colm wants-a kill is fuckin self en ats is fuckin bisness. An al tell yer fuckin wha, if tha fuckin Margaret doan fuckin watch out shill do-a seym fuckin thing an all. Fuckin –

—Roooooogeeer!

One-a em stewdent cunts from down-a stirrs. A keep shtum.

—Griff's on the telephone!

A stey quiet an ee fucks off. A can eer-a cunt on-a phone like:

—No, am sorry, he's not in, I'm afraid. Can I take a message?

At meyks me larf, a fuckin message from Griff. Probely summin like: —Ram-a fuckin receiver up yer fuckin arsehole until yer fuckin bleed yer tarty fuckin stewdent cunt. Griff, mun, Jesus . . . some fuckin crew round yer, mun, ey? Fuckin Aberystwyth, mun, mouth uv-a fuckin river like, seaside town by-a sea, come an visit an see a biggest fuckin concentreytion-a junkies an baddies an nutters at yew've ever fuckin seen, mun. A ceym yer t'fuckin get awey from all em fuckin . . . well at's fuckin it fer me, mun, am fuckin tellin yer, a least ferra fuckin bit; does me fuckin ead in like . . . av got more t'fuckin live for an fuckin gettin off it like, fuck, a wuz ternin inter fuckin zombie-man. Could go see Liam a spose, ee's a bit more streyter an ee others like but ee still gets beyond, still likes a fuckin larf like . . . Liam knows-a score. Even if ee is a fuckin grumpy Mick cunt at times like.

More t'fuckin live for an fuckin drugs. Too fuckin right mun.

Sfunny like ow missed sleep from-a ole fuckin month ago catches up with yer. Am fucked, mun, knackered, all-a fuckin sudden am apserfuckinlutely fucked like. Weysted. Only, a avn slept proper, without knockin me self out like, for's long as a can fuckin remember nerly; fuckin months like. Ope a can fuckin manage it, mun, a rerly fuckin do.

TUESDAY

A bit better. Terrible fuckin night tho like, ardly enny fuckin kip, tossin an ternin an, yeh, fuckin tossin agen, but t'day like av even dug me fuckin weyts out agen, found em in-a back-a me wardrobe underneath a pile-a nicked coats tha av never bin able ter flog off. Not fuckin s'prised, tell yer-a trewth like, orrible lookin things ey are; corderfuckinroy. Wha yer dad ud wirr like. Ennyway, a did a few reps each fer me chest, tris, bis, some sits, chins, push-ups . . . muscles're stiff's fuck now like but a feel all light-eaded like an me dick feels ten feet fuckin long (exercise alweys meyks it feel arf its actual length, ha ha). Wirked up a good fuckin appetite an all, so a went to-a Chinkie's on-a prom, best fuckin chips in-a town, mun, got meself chips, mixed veg, chicken, portion-a curry sauce, took it all back yer an washed it down with guess fuckin wha? Milk, ass fuckin wha, yer twat yer! Good fuckin scran an-a cold pint-a full cream an a feel fuckin *ace*, mun, jes fuckin ace, even if I am on a fuckin bog evry five fuckin minutes like. Curry sauce streyt fuckin threw, oof. Pissin out me arse like. Larst month, fuck, larst fuckin *week* even, a thought-a eatin ennythin apart from speedbombs would-a bin fuckin orrible, enough t'put me off me fuckin drugs. Iss uz meyd me reelise like tha, rerly, am a eater, a do rerly like me food . . . Am startin to, without-a drugs, startin t'reelise like oo a rerly am. Am Roger fuckin Price, mun . . . A member food alweys bein yer when a was a kid back on-a Gurnos; Sundays, mun, foo, ole fuckin family round-a fuckin teyble, twenty-fuckin-three uv uz like, ewge fuckin pots-a stew an cawl an loaves-a size-a fuckin cars, a cheaper that wey, see? Evry twat chips in like, no fucker goes ungry. An me man n aunties could cook up well n all, pervidin a course ey could leave-a fuckin bottle alone f'long enough like an me cunt've an ole mam ud leave *em* alone. Al tell yer wha sbard, tho, or wha can be bard if yer lerrit be like, an ass gettin inter food too fuckin much; yew've got t'be cirful's fuck with-a food when yer comin off-a drugs, av seen people get fuckin obsessed like, Christ mun, fat fuckers in a fortnight ey ar, fuckin sick, mun, yew've got t'fuckin watch out like, got t'steyn fuckin control. An thass fuckin bard, tha is, thuz ulweys things on yer fuckin back, mun, ulweys things yuv got t'fuckin fight . . . tsall a greyt big fuckin war, innit?

Telly agen t'night, smoke some weed, lie back. Werk up some munchies an ger inter that multipack a crisps a nicked from out-a fuckin Somerfield. Not bard, ey, fuckin bag-a crisps a size-a me fuckin pillow like an a fuckin nicked em. Ow? Fuck off; treyd fuckin secrets boy. A stealin buzz elps t'meyk iss bein streyt a bit more bearable like but agen a need t'watch out a don't get fuckin gripped. Fuckin awful tha would be aye, trine t'stey on-a streyt like an a get fuckin gripped with a multi-pack a fuckin Hula Hoops up me fuckin jumper. Mind, ad *avter* get streyt in-a fuckin cell, woulden I, ey? Nick's sound fer hash like, but enny'in else, ferget it, boy.

Rest me veins . . . ey fuckin need it n all. Not jes a ones av bin stickin a needle in like but the ones on me fuckin legs n all, a big berst ones from yompin in full fuckin pack when a wuz in-a fuckin army. A need me fuckin blood, mun, a need-a stuff t'keep on fuckin flowin like . . . A member tha time, few months ago now like, a tried injectin inter me knob, reasonin tha a didn yewse it for ennythin but pissin out uv ennyway . . . it wuz a fuckin nightmare, mun; when a stuck a needle in tha ewge fuckin blue vein, y'know a big bastard on-a underside like, it meyd a kind uv small explosion-a blood; it jes seemed t'berst out like, all around-a needle point, jes sudden like, a quick red splutch . . . a fuckin shit meself, a did. Thought me ole fuckin feller wuz gunner drop off er an en. Congealed quick tho, like, but it wuz rerly fuckin orrible . . . never tried it agen. Scar's still there. Knob's orright, tho. Bir itchy. Gets a bit inflamed when a wank like.

All-a horrors av gone now like, a brown horrors. Ey only ang around ferra little bit like, an en ey go awey. The horrors . . . a bones ternin t'jelly, splintered like, split, a horrendous fuckin aches an a . . . Nah; horrors be fucked. *Ey* wern horrible. A can survive fuckin enny'in boy. Ulster now, at wuz-a fuckin horrors; a smack withdrawals ar jes a pain in-a fuckin arse comperd ter fuckin Ulster like.

Larst night, in bed like, a ad a toss an imagined Sioned doin loads-a derty things with Colm. Dunno why, like, ferst time ever. Maybe am a bit lonely. Fuck it ennyway. An Sioned wuz a right derty bitch, some uv-a things she did, mun, oof.

WEDNESDAY

Signin-on dey. An look; a carn normully fuckin feyce signin on without a shot or a dab or at least a smoke or a few pints, but t'dey like a jes walked in yer, signed on-a dotted, an fucked off. Easy. Nah, well, thass not entiley wha it wuz like; a stood in-a fuckin queūe an sweated like, got all fuckin panicky, nerly wen off me fuckin trolley mun. Fuckin ate those pleyces, I do. Orrible fuckin things.

—Have yew done any work, paid or unpaid, in the previous fortnight since yew last signed on, Mr Price?

Stuck-up fuckin cow. Can see right up yewer fuckin nostrils when yew tilt yer ead back like tha, yew smug fuckin bitch. An yeh, fuckin course av done some fuckin werk yew darft ole bag, think a could survive on me fuckin dole? Larst fuckin month a sold off two ounces-a uncut billy, streyt off-a fuckin boat down

Fishguard like, runnin round Aber trine t'get rid like a blue-arsed fuckin fly, an so far iss month av tried t'kick a fuckin drugs inter touch an thass a ardest fuckin graft av ever fuckin done, mun, werst fuckin job av ever ad, an avin t'deal with-a likes-a yew yer smelly ole fuckin cow dun meyk it enny fuckin easier. See?

A wen on a bit uv a spree arfter a signed on. A bought some loose baccy from a t'bacconists – sweepins, like, two quid un ounce, quite good iss week; ts a bit uv a lucky fuckin dip bine sweepins like, cos sometimes eyv swept up-a load-a fuckin menthol or fuckin pipe baccy, shit like tha, but t'dey ey wir orright like – en a wen in to-a Spar fer me bread an milk an a nicked a big block-a cheese, some pepper, soap, an-a packet uv smoked salmon. Yew might as well go for-a fuckin luxuries if yewer not fuckin payin fer um aye? At's ow a get Bill's supplies fer im, a nick em, seyvs fuckin spendin money on at ole twat, dunnit, ey? A seyved meself a good few quid like, an got-a bonus buzz. Saw Malcolm outside, on-a street like, an ee wozn lookin too bard, puttin some weyt back on like but ee's alweys bin a skinny cunt ennywey; a told im t'watch ee dun get fat. Ee wanted me t'go fer a pint-a two like, dinnertime an tha, y'know, but a sed no, which wuz dead fuckin ard t'do, am tellin yew; two pints terns inter three, four, twenty-fuckin-five, an en ts a fuckin speed-run t'carry on more fuckin drinkin . . . no such fuckin thing's a couple-a pints, mun, yer fuckin kiddin yerself if yer think-a is. So a said no. Colm, tho, if a ad-a met fuckin im, a probelly would-a gone; ee's one persuasive twat, that fucker is. Ee says things like, a coupla pints ud be a good test a will-power, see if yew can deny yerself, only in a Scouse accent like, it's a test-a fuckin strength, so yer go fer a fuckin pint with im an nex thing yer know ee's orderin up is fuckin twelfth an meykin fuckin speedbombs under-a fuckin teyble. A wuz glad a didn run inter *im*. Ts funny ow Colm meyks is speedbombs; ee meyks em out-a Rizlas an tears a glue strip off fore ee swallers it. Can yer fuckin believe tha like? Ee eats andfuls-a armful drugs an ee woan eat-a fuckin gum off-a fuckin Rizla. Ee's a fuckin odd one, tha cunt, good fuckin larf tho; av yer in fuckin stitches when yev both ad a few like, some uv-a fuckin things ee says, mun, Jesus.

An speak-a the fuckin devil, oo phones up at teatime? Am cookin meself up some leek soup, tippin some flour in t'thicken it like cos it looks like me bleedin piss an a fuckin phone goes an one-a ose pricks from down-a sters shouts up t'me so a goan answer it like. A carn ardly ear Colm cos yer's loud music in-a background like, but a can easy tell it's im cos-a is fuckin accent an-a wey ee's talkin ten fuckin werds to-a second:

—Roger, thiz fuckin loads uv us, man, me, Liam, Mags, getcher fuckin arse down ere, la, wuv got some fuckin crystal, Jesus, one fuckin dab an Christ alfuckinmighty am speedin me fuckin tits off man!

A tell im al meet im in about un ower an put-a phone down like. An am tempted mun, Christ am rerly fuckin tempted like, but a stey in instead an watch-a fuckin telly. Me sweat still smells-a fuckin sulphate an it's been, wha, four fuckin deys since me larst hit-a whizz? Fer fuck's sake. Smokin about fifteen fuckin roll-ups evry fuckin ower. Probelly werse fer me an-a fuckin smack like.

It's-a fuckin boredom, mun, at's-a fuckin werst thing. A pain an-a horrors, ey go awey arfter a while like; but iss fuckin boredom mun, it just fuckin angs on. Bored t'fuckin fuck. Got t'keep it goin, tho, iss streytness, jes fer a few more deys; ole things fucked if a don't.

Terrible night's fuckin sleep.

Nothin's ever fuckin easy. Nothin is ever fuckin easy, mun, an tha rerly fuckin gets on me fuckin nerves, rerly fuckin pisses me off.

Bored. Fed up with-a telly watchin, fed up with wankin. Fuckin bored I am.

THURSDAY

Knew it fuckin knew it. Knew fuckin Jed ud phone t'dey. Fuckin tempteytion's too fuckin much mun.

Jed leys us on-a ounce-a whizz nerly evry week, if ee can ger it like, an a cut it n wrap it, meykin about thirty grammes fer a tenner each like, a flog em off, give undred an sixty back t'Jed fer ee initial ley-on an pocket-a fuckin diff. Tidy. All profit like, plus a get me own whizz free, or treyd it in fer a smack. So, two choices: either let Jed ley us on an meyk over a undred quid fer a night's werk or wait till t'morrer an get ninety fuckin quid income support t'larst us two fuckin weeks. Wha would yew fuckin do? Ey? Tell me tha, yer fuckin twat.

A pick-a gear up from Jed's like an teyk it ome an step on it with flour in me room. An er's no arm in avin jes a few dabs meself like, fer-a energy like, av got t'run round-a fuckin pubs an pleyces unloadin it all like, so a av a few dabs like an fuck me stiff it's good fuckin stuff. Pure fuckin sulphate from Jed iss time, am fuckin tellin yer. Kicks in quick, art thuddin, chewin me fuckin cheeks off, feel just fuckin fine. Boredom jes drops afuckinwey like, oh yeh, yer's fuckin good times ahead boy too fuckin right mun. Al see Colm first like, get rid-a a quart or so thir like streytafuckinwey like, plus ee's a mate an mates alweys get sorted ferst. Er yer go Col, teyk a fuckin quart at-a fuckin discount boy. Sort yer right out, mun, bam. Will do a few lines like an go out an get fuckin lashed; time t'fuckin meyk up, I yav.

Av got me coat on an am out-a fuckin ouse in a second. Thirty wraps-a whizz in me fuckin pocket.

. . . MONDAY AGEN?

Whir-a fuck am I like? . . . Ey? . . . Oo me fuckin head.
   Like. Fucked is wha a am, mun, fucked.
   Fucked.
   Yer fuckin twat.

Ts fuckin lovely, mun, iss pleyce whir a go . . . fuckin lovely. Leaves on-a pond, sun threw-a branches uv-a trees like, singin-a birds, lovely fuckin buzz in me ead . . . doan ever wannit t'wir off. No fuckin wey. Yew carn get this feelin from enny'in else, a mean it, mun, nothin, nothin fuckin ever comes close ter this . . . jes the buzz . . . the brown buzz . . . no twats round yer t'bother yer, no fuckin dole offices like, no fuckin coppers, nothin, no aches or angovers or comedowns . . . am free yer, I yam. Free. Free's a fuckin bird like.
   Am fuckin tellin yew mun . . . ts fuckin lovely, fuckin gorgeous, iss pleyce whir a go.

. . . av got t'wirk things out yer, mun . . . got t'fuckin wirk things out . . . a bard fuckin idea, this, a think iss's gunner tirn out t'be a bard fuckin idea . . . snot fuckin easy, iss, snot fuckin easy like . . . so much fuckin stuff t'wirk out av got like, so much fuckin . . .

Arm comin up strong on-a fuckin acid an-a mushies; two fuckin Purple Ohms an two andfuls a mushies, big ones n all . . . an *strong*, ese ones, am fuckin tellin yew, fuck am on *fire* an me fuckin ead's about t'fuckin explode . . . terrible fuckin pressure inside me fuckin ead mun . . . terrible . . . bard fuckin idea like . . . too fuckin right . . . iss's gunner be too fuckin much, mun, a can tell it's gunner be too fuckin much . . . fuckin skag's better fer yer . . . too right . . .

Ese fuckin mountains yer ar so fuckin *big*, an am on me fuckin own among em, tiny a am, am-a size-a a fuckin fly like . . . Seemed like a good fuckin idea yesterday like; drop some acid, gerrout into-a ills, go travlin inside like, wirk things out . . . Now, tho; fuck. Av got a fuckin shitload-a stuff t'wirk out mun, am fuckin fucked-up inside like . . . Llŷr thinks ee can elp me like, lend me is fuckin cottage while ee's down in London, an is cottage's fuckin miles awey from fuckin ennywhir like, iss ain't-a New Gurnos, iss ain't even Aberfuckinystwyth, iss is a surface uv-a fuckin moon . . . avn got a fuckin *clew* whir a am . . . Wales somewhir like . . . land-a fuckin song . . . land-a screams more like . . . Llŷr brought me out ere at night-time like, a mean a axed im to like, an en ee fucked off an left me, on me tod, ere, whirever-a fuck it is . . . oh Jesus mun, oh me poor fuckin ead . . .

Am sittin on-a rock lookin out over-a valley, an a can see fer fuckin miles. A grass an-a trees ar like, *movin*, wavin an hummin, an-a can almost see em shootin out sparks-a energy like, fuckin flickerin purple lightnin bolts shootin out an cracklin . . . an all-a plants grow well by yer, if yer lissen ard yer can ear a roots slurpin up blood out-a a soil, thousands-a fuckin skeletons in-a fuckin ground yer, mun, all-a em murdered, massacred, a can imadgin a slaughter ere, fellers in kilts with swords an axes oldin up severed eads, hackin at twitchin bleedin bodies on-a ground, a ole fuckin valley a swamp-a fuckin blood, a fuckin waterfall over thir runnin red . . . ear-a squelchy noises ey meyk as ey walk threw-a guts, fuckin necklaces-a intestines mun, shit an pain an screams an blood an agony an beggin, pleadin fer fuckin mercy off some cunt ool show yer fuckin none, some fuckin mad demon ool teyk is time killin yer can yer see-a fuckin look on is feyce an in is eyes . . .

. . . like I must-a looked. When I –

Av got bard fuckin things ter wirk out yer, now fuckin lissen t'me, mun . . . Dead fuckin bard ey ar . . . dead . . .

A sun goes behind-a clouds as a watch an a shadow pours up-a ole fuckin valley. Like a fuckin tidal wave-a tar or summin.

Am a fuckin killer. A fuckin *murderer* I yam mun, a fuckin psycho killer oo walks round free mung yer all, jes imadgin one night me brushin parst yer in-a pub an yell av touched-a fuckin killer, some-a my nasty evil might jes rub off on yer like an yell become a fuckin killer yewer self, oooooooooo . . . av killed a feller, mun, am tellin yer a took-a twat's life like, an not quickly or nicely either, oh fuck no, not with a gun, oh no . . .

Fuck me, mun, iss is gettin too fuckin bard . . .

. . . too fuckin bard . . .

It wuz when a wuz in-a army, a fuckin fusiliers like, an a wuz tourin in-a province, asslin-a Micks like, bashin-a Paddies . . . ass why a wen off fuckin AWOL, mun, am not bein a buffalo soljer fer no cunt, Taffy v. Paddy like, fuck that . . . A never fucked off cos uv-a murder like, fuck no, tha wuz jes like, a fuckin symptom an not a fuckin cause, a mean, fuck, Liam's a Paddy, an Colm's arf Mick as well, fuckin gippo too, so yer see a doan fuckin mind-a Irish, some-a em ar greyt blokes, ass not why a murdered one-a em, tha wuz jes a scrap tha gorrout-a and like . . . Jes pissed up an scrappin in-a carpark outside iss pub in Down . . . a mean, fuck, if yer losin en yell do fuckin enny'in t'win, woan yer, ey? Yew or fuckin em, pal, yew or fuckin em . . . so ennywey a bottled-a cunt. Well, a fuckin moren fuckin bottled im, didn I, a smashed-a fuckin bottle over is fuckin ead an a stuck a fuckin spikey end in is fuckin feyce, stuck it in an stuck it in agen an agen an agen . . . a jes like blacked out like a do sometimes like an jes carried on stickin til is ole feyce wuz fuckin mush . . . a remember im, even without-a acid a still fuckin remember im, pleadin an cryin, a remember im screamin as is eyes popped, a remember im pissin isself agenst me fuckin leg . . . well, in tha wha a wuz fuckin bred for, mun, in tha wha a wuz taught t'fuckin do like? Oh aye, fuckin taxpayer's money spent t'teach me t'kill like, t'kill without fuckin mercy an ter use wha ever a could get me fuckin ands on t'do so, a mean kill, kill, fuckin *kill*, not jes, like, damage or injure, but get rid of, kill, makem not fuckin yer enny more like, away fer good, never fuckin assle yer agen . . . Sliker fuckin IRA boy, eyd yewse enny fuckin thing ey could get-a fuckin ands on, make bombs outer nails an put em in fuckin prams, bits-a steel, fuckin garotte yer with barbed fuckin wire, explosives rigged up to-a car cigarette lighter like . . . Sa right fuckin idea mun; Free Wales Army bernin down oliday cottages, sprey-peyntin a English off-a fuckin road signs? Useless. Does fuck all. Yer might as well piss in-a fuckin ocean boy. Can yer imadgin-a cunts up yer in fuckin Westminster? Oh dear, I rather think Wales should be granted autonomy, old bean, the natives have begun attacking road signs again. I think they're really rather peeved . . . Fuckin bollax. Showem some fuckin strength, boy.

Christ, me ead's fuckin bangin . . .

An ese mountains yer look jes like fuckin Ireland, ey do, em pleyces a went to when a wuz AWOL. A got as far as fuckin Wicklow on me own two fuckin feet; a fuckin ad ter, no fuckin way a could itch like, any twat oo picked me up could-a bin either IR fuckin A or British fuckin Army. A eyt berries an stuff a could nick from-a fuckin farms an a caught fish in-a rivers, right fuckin Rambo a wuz, an al tell yer one fuckin thing it wuz-a best fuckin time-a me fuckin life like, oh Christ aye, even tha fuckin blood on me ands began t'feel good, yed berrer fuckin believe it, mun, fuckin outlaw a wuz, a wanted fuckin man, best time-a me fuckin life, oh yeh yed berrer fuckin believe yer's still fuckin wolves in Wales yer fuckin twat . . .

N a did, didn I, a rely fuckin *did* enjoy it . . . ard as a fuckin rock a wuz; kneelin above im like a God, broken bottle in me and like-a fuckin sword-a justice. Christ, a wish a could-a seen meself.

Spent a long fuckin time in em fuckin ills, em mountains . . . yeh, a did-a decent fuckin thing an fucked off out-a eyr fuckin feyces an wha fuckin appens? Ow wuz a fuckin rewarded? Fuckin prison, lock-up, dishonourable fuckin discharge, an think ow much fuckin werse it would-a bin if ey could-a fuckin *proved* tha a wuz-a fuckin murderer. Doan bir fuckin thinkin about, boy. A member Bill's story about tha fuckin officer on-a Giant's Causeway, some fuckin poncey English cunt, an ee wuz jes fuckin standin yer like an lookin out t'sea an some fuckin local fanny axed im fer-a light, so ee goes back to-a Land-Rover, like, t'yewse a fag lighter an when ee presses it in – BOOM!, an is fuckin legs're gone. Blown off. The fuckin bitch ad wired up-a fuckin bomb to-a fuckin electric circuit like in-a car while ee'd bin standin yer lookin at-a waves, soft cunt, a prick should-a bin fuckin watchin is fuckin back like, a bomb wuz jes big enough t'blow im away up ter is waist, no legs, no dick, no balls . . . Bam. Meybe's one day like erl be-a technology t'gather up all-a molecules-a is dick n balls an rebuild em an stitch em back on like, but fer now all he've got's fuckin memories. Poor cunt. Is own stupid fuckin fault tho; should-a bin fuckin lookin. Ulways watch yer fuckin back.

. . . Yer's a fuckin bomb in me fuckin ead mun, a fuckin fewse yer fizzin awey . . . a think it's a dud, tho, a doan think it ul explode like, it'll jes sizzle awey in yer . . . But then another immense fuckin shadow pours down-a fuckin valley below me like an teyks me fuckin breath awey an a start t'get all cold an shivery like an am sheykin an me fuckin ead's spinnin an a fuckin acid's *rushin* right threw me fuckin bloodstream . . .

Ts orright, tho; am used t'this, fuckin acid's easy boy, an when-a rush subsides like a teyk-a andful-a downers out-a me cammy jacket (come prepird, like, *ulweys* come fuckin prepird) an knock em back with-a quarter bottle-a brandy. En a jes sit n wait like while-a acid effects start t'slip awey an arfter av spewed up a goan fall asleep in a little cave in-a valley wall, a tree idin it like, an when a weyk up owever much leyter it is meybe nex fuckin dey like fer all a fuckin know a muss still be fuckin trippin cos am lookin right at-a fuckin dragon, a real fuckin dragon fuckin croppin-a grass about ten fuckin yards awey on-a top uv a valley wall . . . silhouetted, like, agenst a evenin sky . . . a real fuckin dragon . . .

Nah, a know it's not *rirly* a dragon like, but av yer ever noticed ow weird fuckin things ulweys fuckin appen to yer when yewer trippin? A mean, not jes, inside yer ead, like, a mean rirly fuckin *thir* like, in-a real fuckin wirld . . . A mean, lissen, av only ever seen two deer in Wales in me ole fuckin life like an now yer's a fuckin stag eatin a fuckin grass right in front-a me fuckin eyes mun. Jes standin yer, eatin awey. Fuckin mad, iss is, am tellin yer, iss is too fuckin creyzy . . .

A red-sky sunset behind-a stag looks like fuckin fleyms comin out-a its gob an pourin across-a sky an down-a fuckin valley birnin

68

fuckin evrythin an en a stag looks up like as a fuckin jet screams over, fuckin low an screamin mun *screamin*, fuckin orrible noise ose cunts meyk like but's like-a fuckin stag's screamin yer, screamin an breathin red fire . . .

Am on a fuckin mountainside, freezin, windy, full-a fuckin drugs an still trippin me fuckin box off an yer's a fuckin dragon standin ten fuckin yards awey screamin an breathin fire.

Fuck. Wha would *yew* do? A carn fuckin move.

It jes carries on eatin-a grass. Even tha fuckin jet didn bother its arse like . . . probelly used to-a fuckin things like, eyr ulweys fuckin flyin over ere . . . Look a the fuckin horns on it, mun . . . Av ulweys known yer's deer in ese mountains like, eyr some fuckin posho English cunt's private erd, parently ee breeds em so's im an is fuckin posho meyts can fuckin come up yer an shoot em. Fuckin English cunt. Some English cunts're orright like, a mean fuckin Malcolm comes from fuckin Essex, as English as yer can fuckin be without avin fuckin Windsor as a second neym, an ee's a sound twat (most-a a time; a fuckin shite-arse twat, iffa trewth be fuckin telt, but thir y'fuckin go, boy), but a cunt oo owns ese yer deer must be a *right* fuckin cunt . . . a mean, ow-a fuck can yer fuckin buy wild fuckin animals? Am glad one-a em's fuckin escaped . . . no am fuckin not. Look-a a fuckin thing; it's fuckin *ewge*, mun, fuckin ewge, a can imadgin its fuckin orns plowin threw me fuckin belly like, a can see it reysin its fuckin ead to-a sky an me fuckin impaled on its fuckin antlers like screamin an twitchin, a can imadgin-a fucker tramplin over me fuckin feyce . . .

Soon's a can move a chuck a stone at-a bastard an it fucks off farst over-a top uv-a mountain but am fuckin rattled t'fuck now, mun, am scird fuckin shitless t'tell a fuckin trewth, so a fuck off back t'Llŷr's cottage an drink meself fuckin unconscious by-a fire. Fire's ee only light, no fuckin leccy yer, fuck no, iss is wild fuckin Wales boy . . . a keep imadginin at fuckin stag prowlin round ee ouse, starin in at-a window with glowin red eyes . . . snortin . . . tossin its ead . . .

Arfwey threw me second bottle-a brandy an a crash out, but am woken up by-a voice in me ead tellin me wha a havter do, so a meyk a speedbomb with-a full fuckin gram in it an clean an en load Llŷr's old untin rifle. (Grantin a gun licence ter Llŷr wuz fuckin sick; ee'l shoot fuckin ennythin. A mean it; foxes, cats, sheep, horses, dogs . . . One day soon ee'l find a nice cosy spot on-a ill overlookin-a town an jes start pickin people off. I know ee will. Yer can see it in is fuckin eyes, boy.) Am still feelin a bit trippy like an a need t'be alert like so a wash-a speed down with-a load-a fuckin orange juice an go back out into-a mountains agen, wirrin a big fuckin coat iss time, partly ter ide me rifle under like an partly t'keep out-a fuckin cold; a nirly froze me fuckin bollax off yesterdey.

Fuckin amazin ese mountains ar, yer should fuckin see em . . . ey give off a weird energy, like, an it's stronger in some pleyces than in others, it kind uv fuckin throbs an hums, an when a reach-a spot whir a saw-a stag (quickly, like, am speedin me fuckin feyce off by now like) it's like a can feel iss energy flowin threw me body, growin inside me like, sliker can feel me body bulgin an distortin with iss force an power . . . a look down an a-see me legs cheynge, see em an me arms go all thick an warped an bulgy . . . a feel me feyce an it feels like-a fuckin lion's ead or summin . . . it's not scary, iss, in fact a trewth is it feels fuckin greyt . . . streynge tho; me mind pleys some odd fuckin geyms, it does, specially on-a acid, yer's so much fuckin shit bin threw it over-a yeers like . . . Fuck, tho, av never felt so fuckin *alive* like, so fuckin powerful mun, so fuckin *wild* . . . Some fuckin hikers pass by, rambler tossers like with eyr fuckin rucksacks an stewpid fuckin boots on, an a look on eyr fuckin feyces when ey fuckin clock me like, me with me muscles all warped like an a fuckin ead uv a lion on me fuckin shoulders, ewge fuckin gun in me ands which now look like bunches-a fuckin bananas . . . A stick me tongue out at em an meyk a growly noise as ey pass by an ey nir fuckin shit emselves like, ey fucking leg it over-a hill an a piss me kex larfin at eyr fuckin feyces, Christ, yew should-a fuckin seen em, mun . . . Ey probelly fuckin loved it. Madgin-a fuckers back ome over-a fuckin border, tellin eyr poncey meyts over-a fuckin cheese an wine about eyr fuckin hikin olidey in Wales:

'Oh yarse, rilly rahther hex-hiting. Hauthentic Welsh hill-billeh, ite hanting his suppah . . . Rilly rahther quaint. Toby was all fawer hinviting him back to thar hotel, bat Hi poo-poohed thet hi-dear; hay mean, cen you imargine what he wad hev dan with the san-dried toe-mahtoes?'

Fuckin arseholes.

A sit down in-a shelter uv a rock, by-a remains-a somethin's dinner; feathers an clumps-a dried blood an gnawed bones. Shreds-a flesh. Probely the dinner uv a fox or a badger, most probely fox . . . a like foxes, I do. Cool little fuckers. Eyr a ardest fuckin animals t'kill, foxes ar. Ard little bastards, aye.

Am a hunter as well. Am like a fox; I can hunt. A know ow t'sit dead fuckin still, ow t'weyt . . . even with a fuckin whizz inside me an iss fuckin mad energy off-a fuckin mountains am a good enough fuckin unter t'sit still an jes weyt . . . weyt . . . yer run songs threw yer head, yer think, y'sit dead fuckin still, y'let yerself remember things . . . jes let stuff run threw yer head, think fuckin control, mun, control . . . become a fuckin lion.

An see? It might uv teyken fuckin owers, like, but all good things come to ose cunts ooer strong enough jes t'sit an weyt.

The stag comes over-a hill an starts t'eat-a grass agen. Same fuckin spot n all; stewpid twat. A weyt a few more minutes so it starts t'think tha, like, evrythin's orright, y'know, so it starts t'feel seyf an relaxes, an en in one movement a jump t'me feet an aim an pull-a fuckin trigger. Its ead snaps back as if yanked on a rope an a shot rumbles down a valley. It's strugglin ter get back up on its feet (or ooves a suppose a should sey) but am on top uv-a fucker in a second with me fuckin knife in me and, it screams like one-a ose fuckin jets but a whinin noise in me own throat's louder an it kicks its ooves an tries t'toss its ead t'stick me with its fuckin orns but a bullet went right threw its fuckin neck so its ead jes flops about like a fuckin limp dick. It smells like shit an sweat an mud an a stand on its feyce t'keep it still while a slice its fuckin throat; a hack once an blood sperts out like-a fuckin geyser all over me fuckin legs . . . a imadgin more trees growin on iss spot, in-a future like, a branches uv-a trees lookin like-a antlers uv a stag . . .

A blood jes pours out, so much fuckin blood, mun, rivers uv-a fuckin stuff, an its breath tirns inter a wheeze an its feet flop about on-a grass. A squat down by its feyce an watch it die, strokin its shoulder with me and. Coarse fur, like a fuckin Brillo pad or summin; a thought it would be softer. A light goes out, a bulb switched off inside its skull. It's dead still but-a fuckin blood still gushes out; am standin yer in a red fuckin bog. Dead things ar fuckin weird, mun; ey seem ter av a fuckin life uv eyr own, ey do. Like tha fuckin ram's skull uv Malcolm's; it fuckin looks at yer, mun, it knows yer fuckin business. It knows yer fuckin thoughts.

An a stag's skull ud be much more fuckin impressive than tha twatty ram's skull, but a carn get-a fucker's ead off; me knife's not fuckin sharp enough t'cut threw a sinew, never mind-a fuckin bone. All a do's meyk a big ragged ole beneath a fucker's chin so en a try un skin it but a fuck tha up as well, me ands ar tremblin fer some fuckin reason probelly coz-a a speed but ennywey am a fuckin unter not a fuckin tanner, me job's t'kill, not meyk fuckin weystcoats. Fuckin fur n leather clothes t'sell at Mach market ter twats oo like t'think eyr in touch with Celtic culture, like ose fuckin hikers before . . . Wankers; *iss* is fuckin Celtic culture, mun, iss fuckin slaughterhouse yer; a stag's a fuckin mess, doan even look like a fuckin stag enny more, doan look like enny'in much sept-a fuckin abattoir . . . blood, guts evrywhir . . . a exposed muscle whir a tried t'get a fuckin hide off, all shiny an glissnin . . . dozen look fuckin real even. A fuckin ravens an kites an foxes ul av a right tidy feed t'night, aye. Yer's one-a yer stags fer yer, yer fuckin English cunt. Didn fuckin know yer's still fuckin wolves in Wales, did yer? Avn got a fuckin clew.

A rinse meself off in-a pool by a waterfall an go back ter Llŷr's cottage. A stey thir fer another night, boilin up loads a fuckin pans-a water on-a fire so's a can av a hot bath an clean all-a fuckin blood an shite off meself. Me clothes're fucked like, fuckin caked, but eyr-a only fuckin ones a brought with me an Llŷr's teyken all is with im so a avter fuckin wir em. A sit up threw-a night, feelin a acid an billy an other stuff leave me system; t'wards dawn a fall asleep fer a couple-a owers, an when a weyk up a feel . . . ow do a fuckin feel? Like evrythin's fuckin left me an a can start all over agen. Which, a suppose . . . is orright.

Hitchin back ter Aber's a fuckin pain in-a arse like, but a ventchly get a ride off-a army truck. A umpity, bumpity army truck. An ow's tha fer fuckin irony, ey? Carn elp but fuckin larf, mun, carn elp but fuckin larf.

Yer I am, back yer agen, in iss gorgeous pleyce . . . jes lyin yer an watchin-a leaves fallin off-a trees, twistin, twistin threw-a air an landin so softly on-a still, dark water . . . jes floatin yer ey ar

. . . ah yeh . . . nothin ter bother me yer, mun, er's jes me an-a leaves an-a water. Nowt else. Feels like home it is I've come to, like, feels like fuckin home, mun, see.

Aahh . . . look-at a little junkies; ey should all be wirrin L-pleyts, or LS-pleyts: Lerner Smack'ead. Eyv got wha looks like some orright brown but eyr choppin it up on CD ceyses an snortin it, fuckin *snortin* it – a weyst-a good fuckin eroin, al tell yer. Fuckin soft. Little fuckin pricks.

FuhfuhPhil's sittin back on-a couch, watchin em an smilin, lookin like-a proud fuckin uncle a summin. Ese little twats yer ar is meyts, jes come up like from fuckin Southampton or somewhir, an ee's showin em round-a town, a galleries an squats an stuff, opin tha ayl see im as some sort-a fuckin ard man if ee interduces em t'other, *real* ard men. Know what-a mean? Like, y'know: —This is Roger, one-a me best meyts. Fuckin wanker. Colm's findin all-a iss very fuckin amusin like, but am gettin fuckin pissed off; it's fuckin stewpid, an embarrassin. A doan like Phil, a never fuckin av; ee's a fuckin tosser t'tell yer a trewth.

One-a-a amateurs – a right fuckin arse wirrin a nice new overcoat an a stewpid fuckin floppy woolly at – snorts a line-a skag an en sits back on-a couch.

—Oh maaaan, ee goes. —That's a nice toot . . . good gear this . . . whoof . . . betcher don't get gear like this out ere, ey?

Colm larfs an gives me a look like: Jesus Christ, oo-a fuck-a *these* fuckin no-marks? A jes sheyk me ead. Av bin off-a brown ferra while now like, couple-a months meybe since a ad me last hit, but ese twats yer need a bit uv fuckin guidance. Ey need someone t'show em ow it's done.

A look over at Phil. —Iss is Gail's room, innit?

Ee nods.

—An shiz a diabetic, int she?

—Erm . . . yeh.

A sigh. See wha av got t'put up with yer? Am surrounded by clewless twats. Jesus.

—So av got t'spell it fuckin out f'yer then, do I? Whir. Does Gail. Keep. Her. Needles?

An en ee starts t'fuckin um an ah but ee's stuttrin so fuckin bard

73

tha by-a time ee's on is third fuckin wird Colm's back from-a fuckin bathroom with two new syringes in-a plastic wrappers. Good one that man.

—Ah duhduhduhdon't rih-rih-rrrrr −

—Oh fer fuck's sake, Phil, just shut the fuck up ey, Colm says as ee teyks off is belt. —Gail gets dese fuckin things free. An ar yer gunner tell us tha she never fuckin uses em ter jag smack erself, as well as fuckin insulin?

Phil sits back with a beamer, all fuckin sulky like, an folds is twiggy fuckin arms over is weedy fuckin chest. Colm jes sheyks is ead an goes: —Prick, an en taps up a veyn on is arm.

The girl baby junky, one-a em fuckin Goths like, z meykin a spliff an watchin Colm's evry move, fuckin fascineyted by wha ee's doin. A mean, iss is a real thing like; iss is a fuckin PhD in eroin use iss is, snortin it's fuckin GCSE. A bet shiz never seen iss in er fuckin life. She looks fuckin gobsmacked. Not bard tits on er tho, a muss sey . . . ad be rippin fuckin inter that if er wirnt more fuckin important things t'do.

—Oi, a sey t'Floppyat. —We pass ar drugs round yer in Wales.

A give im a look like: Gerrit fuckin out, cunt, an ee does streyt afuckinwey. A teyk spoon an cottons out-a me jacket pocket; even when am off-a smack a carry-a wirks round with me, it's arder t'stop doin that en it is t'stop fuckin usin. A mean, yer never know, do yer? A get some water from-a sink in-a corner uv-a room an cook up. Gothtart's gob's angin fuckin open.

—Shut it, bach, yill catch flies.

Er meyt, another tosser wirrin jeans four fuckin sizes too big fer im, goes over to-a stereo like an wha does a fuckin cunt put on? 'Mr Fuckin Brownstone' by Guns n fuckin Roses. A tell yer, ese twats need some fuckin lessons, boy . . . ey avn got a fuckin clew.

—Get this fuckin shite off!

Bigjeans looks round. —Well, wha' jer want on then? A mean −

—Enny'un, shrugs Colm. —Juss doan pley tha fuckin wank.

A record gets cheynged an, oh yeh, a might-a fuckin guessed; 'Heroin' by-a Velvets. A better choice like, but still fuckin corny as fuck . . . Ese kids − real fuckin amateurs, ey ar. Ey still think evrythin should av a fuckin soundtrack. Well, av got somethin t'tell yew, children, life's not fuckin like that . . . Ah, eyl lirn. All ey need's a good fuckin tutor.

Still, tho, a Velvets ar orright; when other bands wir fuckin witterin on about fuckin flowers an stuff, a Velvets wir talkin about-a fuckin *real* things in life, drugs an death an shaggin . . . y'know, fuckin *real* stuff. John Cale, ey; a fuckin proper Welsh prince, mun. Too fuckin right.

Floppyat's fuckin mutterin t'imself like on-a couch, slaggin off-a music. Ee's goin:

—Ow old's Reed now, fifty? Over fifty? Fuckin past it anyway . . . he should uv got out when ee was still cool, he should've fuckin walked it like he talked it, man. Would've been better all round if ee ad've fuckin died . . . kept is, y'know . . .

—In-integrity, Phil says, noddin all fuckin solemn an serious like.

Colm looks up from-a big bulgin vein ee's tapped up an goes:

—Oh a see. So wha yer sayin is, right, is tha a life lived completely an to the full can only be perfected by the necessary brevity ov its duration? Wharrer loader fuckin shite.

Iss cracks me up. Floppyat jes looks down at is knees, not knowin what t'fuckin sey like, an en ee objects when Colm pours-a rest uv is gear into-a spoon but ee's completely fuckin ignored; ee might uz well be a part uv-a fuckin furniture. A Goth gasps when Col sucks-a blood back inter-a needle barrel, t'boot it like, an ee grins an en pushes a plunger in an growls as a brown shoots up t'wards is brain.

—Ow is it then?

Ee wrinkles is top lip, but a can see that ee's flushed an sweatin, is fingers tremblin a bit like. —Not bad, ee says. —. . .Ts orright . . .

A look a the underside uv is cotton; ts all spotty with wha ever a skag wuz cut with like, so a yewse a same one fer me own shot. A stir right at Gothgirl an sing along ter 'Afterhours' as a cook up a spike meself, an en oh fuckin yeh yer it is agen – fuckin waves, mun, ese lovely fuckin waves yer flowin threw me ole fuckin body like, fuck ow could a ov *ever* fuckin let iss fuckin feelin go . . . Christ . . . iss gear int too bard, av ad a lot better like but fuck av ad a lot wirse . . . oh yeh.

A think am gunner spew up but a feelin passes. Thank fuck;

pewkin me fuckin ring up yer ud look fuckin darft, mun. Dead fuckin uncool . . .

. . . back on-a smack, downin-a brown . . . am appy as fuck. Colm's sittin cross-legged an rockin back an forth, larfin quietly t'isself an singin along t' 'Pale Blue Eyes'. Goth, Floppyat an Bigjeans ar sittin like-a three darft monkeys on-a couch, stirrin at me like as if am some sort uv fuckin god. Which is exactly ow a fuckin feel. FuhfuhPhil's jes . . . well, oo-a fuck cares wha ee's fuckin doin?

Yeh, iss as fuckin shown em. A first fuckin lesson in-a proper use-a eroin. A should be fuckin wirrin a mortar-board an cloak yer with a fuckin scroll under me fuckin arm like . . . Sound as a fuckin pound, mun, am fuckin tellin yer. It carn get enny better an iss.

Colm woan fuckin move. Ee woan move, an am in need-a summin pretty fuckin bard.

A rap-a back-a is ead agen with me knuckles.

—Colm . . . weyk fuckin up, mun, yer cunt . . .

Ee dozen budge.

—A need some-a tha fuckin whizz off yer, mun, bring me fuckin back up agen . . . am crashin yer . . .

A feel like fuckin death yer, a do. A feel like fuckin shit.

Colm's hand's in a circle uv light, a big fuckin scab on-a end-a is thumb, all crusty, like, an black. A wuz gunner axe im bout tha before like but summin appened an a fergot, like, a carn fuckin remember wha now. A techno from-a party down-a stirs's so fuckin loud tha it vibreyts-a fuckin floor, meykin Colm's and do quick little jumps. If ee dozen fuckin answer soon a tell yer, mun, al fuckin boot the twat aweyk. Ee dropped another fuckin E not-a fuckin ower ago, whass wrong with-a cunt like? Ee should be fuckin dancin about by now . . .

A feel like fuckin death, mun, am tellin yer.

—Colm, mun, teyk-a fuckin edge off us, mun . . . am fuckin crashin yer . . . less both av-a snort an go back down to-a party ey, come on mun . . . Colm, mun, c'maaaaaahhn . . . Colm . . . Colm! . . . Colm! COLM!

A squeeze is and's ard as a fuckin can but ee's avin fuckin none-a it an am gettin rirly fuckin pissed off. A cut on is thumb's opened up agen with me squeezin an's bleedin, but if ee wants t'lie yer like a fuckin zombie an miss-a fuckin party en ee fuckin well can like, al goan get me own fuckin whizz off some fucker else. Cunt. Tight-arsed cunt ee is.

A drag meself out-a room an down-a stirs back to-a party. A noise-a iss fuckin taffy techno like its me like-a fuckin rugby tackle, does me fuckin ead in. A see Mags over-a other side uv-a room, bouncin around like fuckin mad like, er tits goin creyzy, an a wave er over, knowin shill av stacks-a fuckin billy on er. Tidy. Am crashin. A feel like fuckin shit. But tha fuckin Colm, mun, Christ, at's-a larst fuckin time a ever give tha twat enny-a me fuckin drugs, al tell yer fuckin that. Cunt.

Gareth – ginger-eaded cunt a met in Swansea nick – is one cheeky cunt, ee is; ee even teyks-a selection uv is own teyps out with im when ee goes screwin cars. Wooden be so bard like if ee wozn inter such crap fuckin sounds; Iron fuckin Maiden or some fuckin shit blarstin out as ee tirns-a corner by-a Central ter pick us up.

—Whass iss then? A sey. —A fuckin *Mini*? Gone down in-a fuckin wirld, yew av.

Ee gets all fuckin insulted like.

—Wha, yer think iss is fer fuckin *fun*, boy? Iss is fuckin *work*, mun, *work*; coppers ul pick us up, wir in-a fuckin Merc or summin. Inconspicuous, iss wey, see?

Yeh, an ee screws screechin off an does sixty before ee end-a Portland fuckin Road. Inconspicuous me arse. Darft cunt.

Ee tells me about Llangollen as we ead up into-a ills on-a coast road, parst-a Penparcau estate an out t'wards Aberaeron. Gareth's jes come back from Llangollen. That's wha ee does, iss cunt, ee goes around to-a towns in Wales, kicks up some shit, gets awey with wha ee can an en legs it back ter fuckin Aber an leys low fer-a while before fuckin off an doin a seym thing agen somewhir else. Eel run out-a towns, sometime. Ee's bin doin it fer fuckin yeers ee yaz.

—We'd all bin up it, ee's seyin. —Aller us, even tha fat cunt, Tomos, yer know im? Fuckin sumo wrestler, im, boy, thought ee wuz gunner fuckin crush er. Only sixteen, she wuz, but fuck shid av yer doon things tha even *I* didn know about, fuckin beggin fer it she wuz, ennythin fer a few downers or a bag-a brown, an I mean fuckin *ennythin*.

Ee sheyks is ead with-a memory an does a little smile. Ulweys full-a stories ee is when ee comes back from is travels like. Probelly bullshit, most-a em; a mean, Gareth, ee's a fuckin mess; guess wha ee wuz inside fer? Fuckin poaching. Stealin fuckin trout. Never fuckin tells ennybody tha, tho, it's ulweys jes: —Oh yeh, av done me time, eight fuckin months in Swansea gaol boy, meyks-a fuckin man-a yer aye. Bit uv an arsehole, like, all in all, but yer's no one better t'go screwin ouses with, al tell yer that.

—. . . an yer she is, ee's seyin, —on-a fuckin couch like, ternin fuckin blue, an Hywel, ee wuz a one oo gave er er hit in-a first fuckin pleyce, like, guess wha ee goes an does? T'bring er round, like, a mean yer she is like, naked, on-a couch, ternin fuckin *blue*, ee only goes an jacks er up with base fuckin speed, dunnee? Seen *Pulp Fiction* too menny fuckin times, tha boy. Ennywey, soon's she starts spewin an thrashin about like-a fuckin eppy, am fuckin out-a thir boy, fuckin sharpish like, streyt in-a car an back fuckin ere, no messin. Frothin at the mouth she wuz. Fucked off n left im to it like. Hywel's fuckin problem.

Ee tirns inland jes before we hit Aberaeron, up into-a mountains.

—Wuz in-a *Cambrian News* ee other dey. Dead like. Fuckin sheym, boy; best fuckin ump av ever ad in me fuckin life, an at's no messin. Even ose slags in Milford, a ever tell yer about them? Ey wir –

Fuck this.

—Yid bess be fuckin right about iss fuckin pleyce, a sey in-a loud voice ter shut-a twat up. At's is problem, Gareth; never knows when t'keep is fuckin gob shut. —Cos if yer fuckin not an somethin appens –

—Av *told* yer, ee says. —Stop fuckin wurryin. Wan ole cunt, on is own, no dogs, ouse's full-a fuckin silver an swords an fuckin elmets an stuff from-a war like. Vet'run ee is. Piece-a fuckin piss, boy.

—Aye, well, it fuckin bess be, at's all am fuckin seyin.

But a know it probelly will be. Av told yew; no better person t'go screwin ouses with an Gareth, borin twat that ee is. One thing al sey fer im; if ee tells yer ee's caysed a joint, then yer know it's bin fuckin caysed. Least it ad fuckin better be, fer is seyks. If

Gareth didn av iss skill, a would-a knocked is fuckin teeth in yeers ago, mun.

Ee pulls-a car over into-a dirt track, idden by trees. Yer wooden know it wuz thir if yer wirnt lookin fer it like. Yer's a single light shinin threw-a trees. Pitch black otherwise.

—A can see a fuckin light, a sey, softly like.

—Ts orright. Ass jes an outside light ee leaves on. Am tellin yer, ee's ulweys in bed by iss time; arf ten on-a dot.

We get out-a car with ar bags an ead t'wards-a light, threw-a trees, steppin high like so we doan get caught by-a fuckin branches an brambles. Gareth's got a little torch, one-a ose fuckin pencil jobs like, which ee shines on-a ground so we doan trip over. Am thinkin ter meself: Pey off Jed. Give Liam back-a thirty a owe im. Up ter Camarthen fer a greyt big fuckin binge. Pey off-a landlord; ha, a fuckin retired vicar gettin is rent from profits uv-a fuckin burglary. Get some new boots –

—Yer.

Gareth goes round-a side uv-a ouse an a follow im, out-a wey uv-a light. A ouse is fuckin tiny, one-a ose diddy little whitewashed cottages like, two-up two-down with a coal shed out-a back. A window freyms-a rotten an soft an a push one in dead fuckin easy, with only a bit uv noise. Ts only a small window like, but a can squeeze in easy cos uv all-a fuckin weyt av lost recently an Gareth, bein a scrawny cunt, can fit threw ennywey.

Me art booms like it ulweys does wance am inside, an a need ter slash. Gareth shines is torch-beam across-a walls an fuck me, a pleyce's like a fuckin museum; swords, medals, big silver pleyts on-a dresser. Me art beats faster. A can jes meyk out Gareth's grin in-a dark, is fuckin teeth shinin like, an en wir fillin ar bags, slowly like an cirfelly, tryin not t'meyk enny noise. A go streyt fer-a glass ceyse full-a medals an stick it in me bag, side-on like, so-a glass woan get smashed by stuff on top uv it. A can ear me breath roarin in me fuckin eers. Yer's fuckin sneyks in me fuckin belly. A reach up on-a wall fer-a funny-lookin elmet; all curved an stuff. Looks Japanese or somethin like. A look a the pitchers on-a walls; a group-a soldiers, one soldier on is own, a woman like in ose ole films with-a bonnet on an stuff. Am tryin ter meyk out-a regiment on-a soldier's uniforms when summin sharp sticks in me side.

—FUCK!

A spin around but's only Gareth, stewpid cunt, messin about with-a samurai sword, pretendin ter be fuckin Bruce Lee or summin, posin with it an meykin Chinese noises:

—Hroooooooorrrrrwaah! Yew Taffy sorjer, sey bly-bly to fliggin head!

Ee lunges. Is top teeth-a stickin out over is lower lip an is eyes-a all slitty. A start t'laugh, a don't want oo but a carn elp it.

—How yew rike sam-uh-lye steel in berry?

A teyk another sword off-a wall as well an we start ter mess about, dancin around like, goin: —Aaaaaaaahwah!, an fightin each other. It's dead fuckin funny like, an a get rirly fuckin into it but then a become awir that wir bein fuckin watched cos a reelise tha a can see Gareth's feyce more cleerly cos thir's more fuckin light from somewhir an me ead starts ter pound.

Gareth spins round an a see-a ole cunt is standin yer in is nightdress like in-a fuckin *Carry On* film in-a doorwey. Ee looks like a fuckin scarecrow, all thin n spindly like, like-a ole fuckin spider. A carn meyk out enny uv is features cos a light's behind im in-a hall but then a feel sick when a see tha Gareth's reysed a sword over is ead an is grinnin like a fuckin maniac.

Oh fuck. A teyk it all in dead quickly: The light off the sword. A ole twat in-a doorwey. Gareth grinnin like-a fuckin lunatic.

Yer's a patterin on-a floor an at's a ole boy pissin isself. Yer's a whinin sound an at's im screamin, ee's on is knees with is arms wrapped round is ead. Is gown's ridden up is legs like an a can see is dick an balls, all shrivelled an useless-lookin.

—Na, na, plis, dwi'n erfyn arnoch chi, na! *Na!*

Is voice is like . . . a dunno, a screypin sound . . . it's orrible . . . it's fuckin orrible an a wan im ter stop . . .

—Duw, Duw, plis!

An en me n Gareth-a both out uv-a fuckin window an leggin it threw-a trees, fuckin larfin like in issterics, fallin over, wild men uv-a fuckin woods. Am goin fuckin mad I yam, a feel like fuckin pissin meself as well an spewin up at-a seym time an en wir in-a car an fuckin arsin it awey, evvy bags an-a sharp swords on me knees.

Gareth is fuckin manic as ee drives.

—Jer see-a fuckin feyce on im, boy? Jer see it? Ee thought a wuz gunner fuckin stick im!

—So did fuckin I, a sey.

—Yeh, an me! Ee's larfin like-a mad fucker, whippin through-a leyns, breyks screechin. Me art is fuckin boomin.

Jesus . . . what-a fuckin night, mun, ey? Arm still fuckin tremblin as we drive down on to-a coast road an ead back inter Aber, an a start ter tremble even fuckin more when a notice-a weyt uv-a bags on me knees. Hevvy, ey ar. Dead fuckin hevvy. Jesus. What-a fuckin night.

Fat Charlie's dead. A ird Griff n Jerry an all em talkin in-a boozer iss mornin like: Fat Charlie's dead. An en, iss arvo, a saw it in-a *Cambrian News*, agen: Fat Charlie's dead. Well, didn rerly sey tha, like, y'know, ey yewsed is proper neym like . . . Davies, a think, Charles Davies . . . but a knew wha ey meant. Fat Charlie: dead. A didn know-a bloke tha well, person'ly like, jes a few bevvies once-a twice like, an one time-a both uv us knocked shit out-a some fuckin Shoni boys on-a South Beach, but's still a bit uv a fuckin blow like . . . Fat Charlie's dead. A yewse t'seem round yer all-a time, ulweys round-a town ee wuz like; an ow could yer fuckin miss im, ey, size-a a fuckin bus ee wuz aye. Am tellin yew, bloke tha size, mun, Christ, must-a dropped enough fuckin drugs t'fell-a fuckin ox like. I yerd it wuz a combineytion like tha killed im, a mixture-a smack an downers an booze an curry, an that it wuz-a fuckin curry tha did fer im inny end like, chokin on it like when ee wuz crashed. Some fuckin life, iss, innit ey? Yer do in enough fuckin chemicals t'put bleedin Boots out-a fuckin business like an wha is it tha fuckin finishes yer? Fuckin curry, mun, *food*, a tell yer, food's-a werse fuckin addiction uv all, an Paki food-a werst uv-a werse. Fuckin bard news iss is, mun . . . Fat Charlie dead.

Al tell yer summin now; stey off-a fuckin food. Fucks yer right up, food does. Stey off-a fuckin food.

Colm's bin fuckin dabbin an snortin at-a whizz since fuckin Tuesday an is, like, apserlutely fuckin wired. Look-a is eyes, mun; bright fuckin red, big as fuckin pleyts, is jaw's wirkin awey ten to-a fuckin dozen. Ee's about t'fuckin explode, ee is, an if ese cunts yer doan stop windin im up soonish eyr on ferra fuckin feyce-ful-a fuckin fist, al tell yer that.

—Ey, Roger! Ee weyves us over. —Comen meet these wankers ere. Ee sneers at-a arseholes sittin opposite im. —Fuckin Princer fuckin Dyfed me arse.

A fuckin wine bar's packed, mun, an-a can see all-a twats around Colm tryin not t'look at im or even, like, acknowledge tha ee's thir, some-a em with tha expression yer see on-a feyces-a people around pissheads or speedfreaks or nutters, y'know, like eyr scird-a a fuckin explosion or summin. Opin ee'l go awey. An eyr fuckin right t'be scird, an all; av told yer, Colm's off is fuckin box, mun, an al tell yer another fuckin thing, enny cunt gives me enny fuckin assle ternight like an ey'll wind up in fuckin Bronglais. Am teykin no fuckin shit from no cunt t'night.

A elbow me wey over ter Col, spillin fuckin pints left, right an fuckin centre. G'warn, jes sey somethin, yer twat yer . . . A see some-a a others over in-a far corner; Liam's singin (agen), Mairead's crashed out agenst-a wall (agen). Liam must be pissed cos, from wha ee's singin, ee's obviously feelin breyve:

> They come wi tanks an trucks an guns
> Come ter take uwey ar sons
> Ellycopters in the sky
> But they'll get ther own by-an-by.

Malcolm gives us a concerned look, like t'call if a need enny elp like, but-a larst fuckin twat ad call on in-a scrap ud be tha shitein twat. Ee'd sooner fuckin suck up than fight, ee would, a fuckin tosser. If yer doan want-a fight, en at's fine; but doan meyk a cunt-a yerself in order t'fuckin avoid it like. Cunt's trick, tha is.

> When ee gets off the boat back home
> Ee'l uv left is legs out in Athlone
> O ee will never ferget the day
> When ee ran into thee Aye! Ar! Ae!

Oh yeh. Somethin's about ter kick off orright. Fine by fuckin me. Am jes in-a right fuckin mood fer it, I yam.

—Oh yer knees, Rog, Colm says, weyvin is and at-a Twat Twins feycin im. —Presencer fuckin royalty ere, uh so this fuckin gobshite sez.

A know ese twats. Eyl call emselves Nationalists, like, whine on about fuckin revolution an kickin out-a English like, an en eyl piss-a fuckin kex at-a first sign-a assle. Tossers, arseholes; no fuckin threat ter no fucker, but fuck ow ey love t'think ey fuckin ar. Wankers. Eyr idea-a freein Wales is ter sing 'Y Gafr Goch' in-a English pubs. Pricks. Sieffri Lewis once sed tha ey suffered from 'delusions-a Glyndŵr'; a fuckin love that, a do. 'Delusions-a Glyndŵr'. Fuckin right n all.

A sit down next-a Colm an knock back me Bushmills in one.

—Iss right, then, is it, boys? Yew gunner seyve us from-a narsty English, then, ar yer? Prince fuckin Llywellyn is it.

A one in-a Ponty shirt looks at us.

—Dun ay know yew? Ee says. —An we met before?

We yav, yer, but-a jes stir the twat out. A met im a few weeks ago, at iss very fuckin teyble in fact, im an is skinny fuckin meyt; ey wir tryin-a seym trick on Mairead an Sioned, tellin em ey wir descended from some fuckin Welsh prince or some fuckin shit. An soon's a remember tha, now, a know fer sure tha ese two ar gunner get a kickin. It wuz only on-a cards before, like, but's a fuckin reycin certainty now, mun.

A seym fuckin bullshit twice. Christ . . . doan ese two ever get fuckin *bored*?

—An whir is it yer from? One-a em's seyin. —Yer not Welsh, ar yer?

An as if iss int bard efuckinnough, a other cunt says somethin to us in Welsh, fuckin smirk on's feyce like-a Bob fuckin Spunkhouse off-a telly.

—Doan yew talk yer fuckin shit, boy, a sey. —Am New fuckin Gurnos I yam, me family's bin in fuckin Wales fer fuckin centuries, yer stewpid fuckin cunt!

Iss, by-a wey, is trew. Me ancestors – or some uv em, ennywey – wir fuckin Puritans, can yer fuckin believe it, me fuckin family's older fuckin Welsh than Cader fuckin Idris, an cunts like ese think eyv got a fuckin right ter be smug about comin from-a hills an speakin-a old tongue. A tell yer, ey think eyv ad it bard like, with-a pressure from-a English, but ey wooden larst two fuckin minutes on-a Gurnos like. No fuckin wey. Now *yer's* fuckin pressure for yer, livin on-a Gurnos; yer wunner see oppression? In action, like? Look-a a New fuckin Gurnos, boy, down in Merthyr Tydfil. At's-a real fuckin Wales fer yer, yer twat.

Colm's larfin in-a feyce-a ese arseholes, an it looks fuckin greyt; ese two twats tryin t'act all heroic an noble like an-a wrecked, scruffy little gyppo like Colm is larfin in-a fuckin feyces. An at's a fuckin situation, boy, teyk it or fuckin leave it; no fuckin eeroes enny more, mun, an al strangle-a fuckin life out-a yer with yer fuckin dragon scarf, yer wirthless little prick. An a will, n all; a know ow fuckin easy it is ter kill someone. It's jes like givin up smokin, or smack; yev jes got t'rerly want-a do it.

—Oh is tha right, is it? Colm's seyin. —Oooo, am shitein me fuckin kex ere. An al tell yis summun else, yer ugly little prick –

Yer's a light in Colm's eyes which isn drink or drugs as ee chucks a pint in Ponty Top's feyce, an en as ee lunges over-a teyble at im Colm's quick with-a whizz an ee grabs iss twat's hair an smashes is feyce down smack into-a ashtrey. Fag ends an people scatter, an Colm smashes-a ead down agen, oldin im by-a eers, an a tell yer, ese cunts're slow, far too fuckin slow t'be causin assle like iss; av even got time t'watch Colm smash-a ead down a third fuckin time before a tirn to-a other cunt an drive me fist streyt into is fuckin feyce, smack on is fuckin nose, crunch, broken a reckon, a hope. Felt it squash, I did. Bam. Tidy.

Colm's oldin a ead up by-a hair all caked in blood an ash an's gunner give it another go like but iss wine bar's a regular boozer like so a grab im by-a arm an drag im awey, people scattrin out uv ar road an starin. Twats, all uv em. Malcolm an Paulie ar gawpin at us over-a eads uv-a crowd as we scarper awey, across-a front uv-a band in-a meyn bar (more fuckin Blues Brothers songs like), evry cunt starin, an outside into-a cool air. Me fist feels jes fuckin ace; full-a fuckin power.

—Fuck me tha was fun.

Wir leanin agenst a wall, outside like, larfin like an pantin, an am opin tha ose two twats'll follow us outside whir a can give em a proper fuckin kickin. Am watchin-a fuckin door. A landlord might

uv seen us, as well; a ope ee asunt, like, but . . . well; so fuckin wha
if ee as.

—Come ed, Col says. —Less goan av another dab by the river.
Av got stacks left. Tha fuckin prick'll be coughin up fuckin teeth
an ash by now.

—Old on a mo then. No rush like.

—Nah, come on! Fuckin leave it, man, thell be cryin to the
fuckin landlord by now, Jesus.

Am wantin ter ang around ferra bit like, see wha appens, but
Colm teyks us down to-a riverside an we dab into is bag-a pink
whizz. A beer garden's empty, like, cos it's winter an it's fuckin
freezin. A can see lights on-a river, an bits-a broken glass in-a
gravel, an a babby's shoe left in-a mud.

—A rerly fuckin hate gobshites like tha, a rerly fuckin do. Colm's
grindin is teeth cos-a the speed_like but it sounds like ee's growlin
like a dog. Oh no, a think; a can sense a fuckin rant comin on. —A
mean, Tryweryn! Thee fuckin accused me uv Tryweryn! Me! Tha
wasn fuckin me, tha was fuckin Liverpool City Council, before a
was even fuckin born ennyway. Twats. An, fuck, didn the same
fuckin council take me granny's fuckin caravan away frommer
in the sixties an sticker inner fuckin council ouse on ee edge
uvver fuckin dump outside fuckin Aintree? Jesus fuckin Christ,
nowan's gorrer fuckin monopoly on sufferin, fer fuck's sake . . .
dick'eds . . .

Ee treyls off, an en as-a speed rushes threw im ee laughs an nudges
me in-a ribs with is elbow. A laugh as well, but am beginnin t'not
feel so fuckin good, a doan know why like . . . a avn slept ferra
couple-a nights like, an am like, aweyk but dreamin, y'know wha
a mean? Am dreamin about tha boy in Down (glass spikes in is
eyes, a gushin blood as red as-a Man Yewnited top ee ad on –
which in itself wuz-a good enough reason ter bottle-a fucker), an-a
stag with its skin an ead angin off (its ooves kickin in-a swamp-a
blood), an evrythin fuckin else . . . tha ole feller pissin isself with
fear, Gareth standin over im with-a sword . . . doan fuckin get me
wrong, mun, am not seyin sorry fer fuckin ennythin, am meykin no
fuckin skewces or apologies ter no cunt fer nowt. But it seems like,
sometimes . . . oh a doan fuckin know. Am like-a fuckin animal, av
bin tirned into-a fuckin animal by them cunts high up in iss fuckin

wirld . . . a mean, ferget-a fuckin English, like, eyr not wirth fuckin worryin about mun. Ther jes pricks, fergettable fuckin pricks; yer ar wirse fuckin . . . oh yeh, a mean, al sey a hate-a fuckin English so's ter wind-a cunts up like, but it's sometimes-a fuckin Welsh emselves, a fuckin Wales v. Wales fixtures, a small fuckin neytion-a fuckin fuck-ups . . . Carn even pley fuckin rugby enny more. Carn even sey eyv got that, now. An when wuz-a larst fuckin time ey beat England? Ey? Iss int-a fuckin seventies enny more, boy . . . ose deys're well fuckin over. A member-a istry lessons at-a school, only fuckin lessons a ever wen into; a yewseter mwch off-a rest uv-a dey but go inter tha one, istry. A fuckin know about istry, mun, I do, a know tha ee Irish ad-a go at-a Welsh, an-a English betreyed whass tha cunt's neym, tha bloke oo me ole cunt uv-a grandad wuz called after, Caradoc, yeh, ee wuz betreyed to-a fuckin Romans like but, fuck, at-a treaty-a fuckin Aberconwy oo wuz it oo birnt down-a fuckin castle? The Welsh, aye, a Welsh fuckin army, we betrey arselves wirse an enny other twat could ever fuckin do. Don't put the fuckin bleym on . . . fuck . . . an ennywey, ow fuckin long ago wuz all iss? Ey? Gerrout uv-a fuckin past, mun, ass why ey ulweys fuckin arp on about istry, cos eyr scird fuckin shitless uv-a present. Tossers.

Aye, a fuckin well know about istry, I do.

—Oi, Roger. What's up, man? What's the face for?

Iss whizz, as it starts-a kick in, meyks me want t'do streynge things, like meybe tell Colm bout Northern Ireland an wha a did over thir, but a fight it down an smoke a couple-a fags instead an jes enjoy-a rush. Fuckin good one n all.

—Cut with crushed up dexies, Col says. —Blow yer fuckin mind, or what's lefter the bastard!

A look at im ter see if ee's bein snotty like, but ee's larfin, which is lucky fer fuckin im. Meyt or no, am not in-a fuckin mood ternight, am jes not in-a fuckin mood . . . Colm's orright, tho, ee's not rerly-a snotty type, not like tha fuckin Malcolm can be sometimes; a suppose am jes bein a bit para with all-a speed an stuff like.

Colm's all up fer goin back inside t'find-a others an by now am rushin ter fuck like so a sey yeh an we climb back up-a riverbank an go back inside-a pub, whir-a crappy fuckin band's still pleyin more fuckin Blues Brothers songs. Fuck, Christ almighty, mun, cheynge-a fuckin record, will yer, do somethin new.

Fuckin hate mornins like iss, I do. No fuckin money, ee only fuckin letter a court summons fer non-peyment-a council tax. Me feyce's all fuckin swollen from at kickin a took larst night outside-a fuckin rugby club. Wankers; took fuckin six-a the cunts t'bring me down, a fuckin tossers. Av membered-a feyces, like, oh yeh; al go fuckin after em with-a fuckin hammer. Pricks. Juskers a got a bit stroppy with one-a eyr tarts, oo wuz fuckin arskin fer it ennywey, a slag. Stuck-up fuckin bitch . . .

A go back ter bed.

A fuckin ate mornins like iss, a rerly fuckin do.

Ikey goes:

—Ah, does yer good, a birruv what yer fancy, an opens another bottle. Gin iss time. Ee swigs it from-a neck an wipes is lips. —Ahhhhh . . . ah yeh, evrythin in moderation, a sey, includin fuckin moderation!

Ee looks over at Griff an laughs is fuckin machine-gun larf. Woody fuckin Woodpecker. Griff's pissed off is fuckin feyce, dribblin down is chin, is eyes arf-shut. Yer's-a pool-a spew on-a carpet between is feet, an it's *is* bleedin room, as well.

Tha last shot a took's ardly fuckin done ennythin apart from meyk me feel jes about fuckin normal so a teyk out me wirks an cook up another one, iss time yewsin more-a tha fuckin chalkdust tha Scottish Iain's got-a fuckin cheek t'call eroin. Al avter av a fuckin wird with tha cunt, al tell yer that fer nowt. Yer's a bluish lump jes under the skin on ee inside-a me elbow whir all-a chalkdust's beginnin ter gather. All kind uv crunchy to-a touch.

Ikey's watchin me like an sheykin is ead.

—Hell uv a boy, yew, Roger, aye . . . wha yer pumpin yer veins full-a tha shit for? Ey? What's wrong with jes gettin pissed?

A jes wrinkle me nose at im an concentreyt on wha am doin. A know, from experience, like, ow fuckin yewseless it is t'try an expleyn a attraction-a brown ter those oo've never teyken it an av got no intrest in teykin it; pure impossibility, boy.

A get me bubbles an-a stuff dissolves, too fuckin slowly a reckon.

It's near a whole fuckin wrap av cooked up yer an fer extra strength a yewse one-a me old cottons. A fill me syringe an tap up a veyn. Tha few months off-a skag wuz good fer one thing, at least; it geyv me poor fuckin veyns a rest. Now eyl tap up in no time.

Griff gurgles as a stick-a spike in.

A blood in-a barrel looks . . . jes fuckin gorgeous . . . a wey it spreads an fans. Me gob goes all dry as a weyt fer the hit . . . a calmness . . . a lovely fuckin . . . mm . . .

Slowly, like, a push it in.

An fuck me, look-a this a carn fuckin breathe, mun, what's fuckin −

Am meltin yer meltin, me ole fuckin body's tirnin fuckin liquid yer an now am breathin too fuckin much yer's too much fuckin breath comin in like am slidin down like oil like blood goin down down in-a smooth an flowin cage to −

Blackness.

Black as fuckin coal.

BLACK

. . . whir-a fuck am I, like? Wha-a fuck's this? . . . A first thing's a feelin uv bein *so, fuckin, wrecked* tha a jes carn fuckin expleyn . . . An *never* bin this wrecked before . . . Jesus . . .

Whass tha rumblin noise? Am a movin?

A fuckin am, yeh, am fuckin movin yer . . . an yer's voices, as well; wha-a fuck's appenin? What's goin on?

—Yew don't. Tell. Ennyone. Nowan, yew got that? If I fuckin find out a yewv bin fuckin blabbin al −

—Jesus, Ikey, give it a fockin rest yew cont! Me lips're fockin sealed, mun, Christ.

Ikey, an Griff. Wir in-a car, a reelise tha now; fuck knows oo's, tho. A can see branches-a trees above me, goin past-a window. Must be nirly dawn. It's a struggle ter sit up. Snice yer, lyin back, movin, warm . . . smacked off me fuckin feyce . . . fuckin lovely . . .

—Whass appenin yer then, boys?

Griff an Ikey scream an look around at me fuckin terrified like it seems an Ikey yanks-a car over to-a side uv-a road, smashes it into-a fence. A see sheep run awey an see a old shack by-a side uv-a road an a know, then, whir we ar; by-a reservoir, a Nant y

88

Moch reservoir. Yer's a sign by-a shed which sez jes fuckin that: NANT Y MOCH, an a arrow pointin left.

—Jesus, Pricey, yew fuckin twat!

—We thought yew wir fuckin dead, mun!

—Yew ever do tha agen an al kill yer me fuckin self!

Iss is all a dream . . . it's appenin like, a know it's appenin, but am not a part uv it, mun . . . av never bin so wrecked in me life . . .

—Yew fuckin wanker.

What's Ikey so pissed off about? Ikey . . .

—Nerly geyv me fuckin art attack, mun, Christ. Tew fuckin owers we wir kickin yer for! Tew fuckin owers! Thought yew wuz a fuckin goner, boy . . .

Am movin in slow motion as a search me pockets fer me fags. Ad rirly fuckin enjoy a smoke now . . . yer's bulges all over me body; a can feel them, evvy bulges like . . . An what the fuck? Yer's nothin in me pockets 'cept bricks, big fuckin bricks an rocks. Ow-a fuck did they get thir?

A teyk em out one by one an dump em on-a floor. Thud, ey go, thud, thud. Evvy fuckers.

—Wha yer lookin for then?

—Me fags. Whirv me fags gone?

Griff ands us a lit B an H. Tha ul do. A pull on it deep an . . . fuck . . . am so wrecked . . .

A think am gunner spew so a get out-a car, ose two twats watchin evrythin a do. Whass up with ose cunts? never seen a bloke stoned before?

After av spewed (only a bit, like, yer's nothin in me stomach but bile), a sit down by-a side uv-a road an look out an down over-a leyk an-a mountain behind it. Sun's comin up over it all, meykin a leyk go all orange like . . . ts like-a water uv-a leyk's goin over me, fillin me veins, all warm an ace . . . fuckin lovely, mun . . . Christ . . . yer's nothin inside me but peace.

Griff sits down.

—Yew orright then?

A jes nod. At's all a can fuckin do, like; nod an smile.

—Look-a all this, ee says, sweepin is arm over the view. —Fockin amazin, innit, ey? Oo needs bleedin skag when yev got-a real thing ere?

A jes look-a im an smile an sey yeh.
Smile.
—Yeh.

Hen wlad fy nhadau; an if so, en wha *is* this fuckin land? *My* father wuz a ole fat cunt oo ad me mam like a whipped fuckin dog, ulweys pissed up an smackin us about like, fuckin laughin at me when a ceym ome from-a school speakin-a Welsh ad lirned. Oo once took us all on-a dey out t'Porthcawl an fuckin drove off an left us yer, left us t'find ar own wey back ome, nine fuckin yeers-a age a wuz. Teach yer t'survive, bollacks; fuckin teach yer ter lie an cheat an steal an ate yer own ole fuckin man. An is dad before im wuz-a seym, an probelly is an all like, so if iss *is* a land-a me fuckin fathers en it's a land uv old, fat, evil cunts oo carn keep eyr fuckin ands off-a fuckin bottle an-a scabby little dicks inside eyr fuckin kex. A fuckin *Mabinogion*'s summin at we annoyed-a teachers by not readin for ar omewirk; fuckin Dic Penderyn's a subject fer evry wanky fuckin amateur folk singer around. Shite on it fuckin all, mun, it means fuck all t'me. Apserlutely fuck all.

Cachar ar dy ffycin 'steddfodau.

Whir ar-a cunts? Ahf eight, Colm sed, ants now fuckin nine . . . A wuz with tha Rhodri ferra bit, like, y'know tha twat out-a tha band Dom like, but ee's fucked off an now am on me tod . . . Ahf eight at-a pub on-a prom, at's wha ee fuckin sed. An a doan even like-a fuckin pleyce; run by tha twat Browntree, it is like, ee's around yer somewhir, im an is fuckin meyts . . . Fuckin Colm. Ee'l be leyt fer is own fuckin funeral, that twat, which ul come sooner an ee fuckin thinks if ee dozen get is fuckin Scouse gyppo arse in geer.

Pub's fuckin packed, mun. End-a summer an all tha, all-a fuckin stewdents come back like. Fuckin arse'oles, most-a em, think ey know it fuckin all like, stewpid fuckin clothes an ircuts, fuckin cars bought fer em by-a rich fuckin daddies . . . Twats. Al tell yew one thing about studyin, my friend; yer can lirn far more on sites an in fact'ries an lock-ups an yer can ever fuckin lirn at unifuckinversity, an at's a fuckin trewth. A mean, lissen, boy, lissen yer ter ese twats at-a next fuckin teyble:

—No because what Lynch does, y'see, is to reveal the American

Dream as the warped and surreal nightmare that it actually is for those whom it excludes. For example, take that scene in *Fire*, or even let's say *Velvet*, where the Leland stroke Hopper character –

—Ah but Simon –

—No no, hear me out, hear me out . . .

A mean, wha kind-a fuckin bollacks is tha? Them an eyr fuckin hats an pointy little beerds . . . Do ey know fuckin ennythin about-a real wirld, ey? Do they? Course not, mun, ey avn got-a ferst fuckin *clew* about ow people reely live . . . Fuckin wankers, ey ar; money in-a bank an-a seyf pleyce ter live an ey know fuckin fuck all . . . English cunts, ey ar, yer can tell by-a posh accents. Fuckers. Look-a em – yer see oo wir rewld by? Oo wir fuckin under-a power uv? Ey? Queer little tossers oo'd shit emselves if yer looked at em a wrong wey, wankers oo'd birst inter fuckin teers if yer spilt yer Guinness on eyr fuckin dungarees. Arse'oles, boy, at's all ey fuckin ar. Ow-a *fuck* did iss all come about? Ey? Ese pricks with-a power an us with fuck all? Ow the fuck did tha appen?

Meyks me fuckin mard, mun, it does, mard as fuck . . .

One-a em, tho, it must be sed, is a shag an a fuckin ahf, am tellin yer, long dark air, wirrin a top all tight on-a tits, showin-a belly like all flat an brown . . . Jes a wey a like em. Rip inter *tha* in no fuckin time, boy, am fuckin tellin yer . . . Sort tha slag right out, too fuckin right, boy. A begin ter feel some stirrin in me kex so a cross me legs under-a teyble an look out-a sea, but me eyes-a drawn back an a thank fuck am wirrin sheyds. An ennywey, why-a fuck shoulden a fuckin stare, like? She obviously fuckin wants me to, wooden wir tha fuckin top if she didn't like . . . Fuckin tits on it, mun, Christ, wha a could do ter tha. Avn ad a shag in fuckin weeks – months, even – not since tha slag a pulled in-a Ship, an she wuz a fuckin boot if-a trewth be teld, nowt like iss fuckin piece yer . . . Not tha shid be fuckin intrested in a fuckin junky like me, oh no . . . fuckin snob . . . Shiz like ose tarts on-a telly; lookin down eyr fuckin noses at yer like, fuckin sneer at yer ey do, larfin like cos ey know yer gettin tirnd on by em . . . Bunch-a fuckin slags. Yer can look but yer carn fuckin touch; well fuck that – fie wanter touch al fuckin touch, a will, no fuckin messin around. No cunt fuckin sneers at me like, an at's-a fuckin trewth.

Jesus Christ . . . nirly an ower fuckin leyt. Eyr gettin a fuckin gobful when ey tirn up, a bunch-a fuckin twats ey ar. Keepin me fuckin weytin.

Al tell yer oo iss bird looks a bit like: Mairead, Colm's tart, or Laura if she ad dark air . . . Laura's a snooty cow as well. Ad shag it, like, but . . . Tho Mairead, now, shiz a right fuckin slapper she is; fit, like, but a right fuckin goer. A know newmerous twats oo've been up er, like, she drinks like a fuckin fish an lets enny fucker av er. Tha twat oo's in-a TA, tha bald-eaded twat, sheyven like, Twmi's is neym, well, ee ad er, an ee told me tha shid get so fuckin wrecked like tha shid fall asleep when ee wuz givin er one. Iss pissed im off like, as it would, so one night, ee sed, ter pay er back like, ee weyted fer er ter nod off an en tirned er over an stuck it upper arse'ole, geyv it to er in-a shitter like, an she wuz so fuckin out uv it tha she didn even stir, jes compleyned about bein sore in-a mornin. Fuckin ace, ey? Still, ee's a bit uv a tosser tha Twmi; a liar, like. A gobshite, Colm'd call im; an a wonder if *ee* knows tha story? Summin ter think about thir, innit, ey?

Yeh, a like-a brunettes, a do, dark eyes, tits jest-a right size like, not too big, not too small, jes a nice gobful . . . altho ter tell yer-a trewth ad shag ennythin if a wuz fuckin randy enough, stick it in-a fuckin knothole if it ad airs round it like . . . Like now; orny as fuck, mun, I yam, been on-a fuckin billy all dey like an tha ulweys gives me-a orn. Bin snortin an dabbin since larst fuckin arvo, yesterdey, like . . . glad a dropped ose moggies before, like, calm me down a bit like . . . iss is wha appens when yer come off-a skag; orny an ungry, ungry fer ennythin but food, at's fuckin me, boy.

A eer a load-a noise comin from further down-a prom like, Liam's Irish voice callin ter someone on-a beach. A can see um all a few undred yards awey, runnin all over-a pleyce, all over-a fuckin road like, climbin on-a railins, balancin on-a walls . . . bout fuckin time n all. A cunts. Am nirly out-a bevvy, but one-a those fuckers can get um in now.

Desp'rit times, mun, desp'rit fuckin times . . . Av bin cookin up me old cottons fer three fuckin deys, eatin-a fuckin carpets mun, goin off me fuckin trolley . . . So: desp'rit fuckin measures.

Am idin in-a garden underneath-a window ter Scottish Iain's pleyce. Ee lives above a shop, which is good like cos at means tha yer's no fucker downstirs oo might spot me like an arsk me wha am doin, or even fuckin run upstirs an tell Iain. Even phone-a fuckin coppers like. Now tha ud be bard . . . Voices an ard techno ar comin out uv-a upstirs window, so a ley me old towel out on-a grass beneath it like an light a fag an weyt. Shoulden be too fuckin long now, like, not if fuckin Dyfed an Powys constabulary get eyr fuckin skeyts on like . . . New Chief-a Police in-a *Cambrian News* ee other dey wuz goin on about ow ee's goin ter stamp out-a drugs menace once an fer all in west Wales an all at fuckin shite. Fuckin bollacks, mun. He've offered a reward ee as fer infermeytion leadin to-a arrest-a known dealers. Cunt. As if a need eyr fuckin rewards; a can meyk me fuckin own, I can. Too fuckin right, boy.

Iss garden's a right fuckin pit. Cans an bottles, even fuckin babby's nappies, ewsed like, all over-a fuckin pleyce. Fuckin Iain should –

BANG! BANG! SMASSSHHH!

Ah, that ul be the door. Fuckin chaos from-a room above:

—Fuck! Get rid!

—Oo is it, Iain, tell me oo it fuckin is!

—Gerrout me fuckin way!

—*GET FUCKIN RID!*

An oh yer yer it comes now, a lovely fuckin reyn, out uv the window come wraps-a whizz an geer, little plastic parcels-a pot an pills . . . Ey all float down, dead fuckin butterflies like, comin ter rest on me leyd-out towel. Desp'rit measures, av told yew. A fuckin syringe whooshes parst jes a fuckin inch from me fuckin nose an sticks in-a ground like-a miniature version-a tha sword at ee end-a tha tossy film *Braveheart* with tha cunt Gibson in. Could-a fuckin skewered me thir, tha fucker could . . . could-a been fuckin bard, that.

—Whir's ya warrant! Show us yer fuckin warrant then, cunt!

—What's goin on, will someone please tell me what the fuck's goin on!

—Gerroff! No fuckin rights, pal!

A bundle me towel up seyfely like an stick it inside me jacket which a zip right up t'me throat. A yank me hood up over me ead as a leg it across a garden an over a fuckin wall in-a single fuckin bound, fuckin Superman, at's me. All me aches slippin awey, fuckin lucky bag in me jacket. Fuckin ace. A leg it ome in record fuckin time. Tidy.

Yew ever noticed like ow, when yer trippin, weird fuckin things ulweys start ter appen? A mean *rerly* appen, like, not jes in yer ead, a mean *rerly*, in-a wirld . . . Streynge things. Ulweys.

Paulie comes inter the pub whir me n Malcolm n Colm uv bin drinkin all mornin an arvternoon. Malcolm's jes done some dodgy deal like with knocked-off videos or somethin so ee's flush like, which is fine by me cos am fuckin brassic an so's Colm, but thass not unusual fer tha scroungin gyppo twat.

Paul stands thir an goes: —What uv yuh all got planned fuh tuhday? Anything? Whadjer say to us all droppin uh trip an fuckin off somewhir?

Iss sounds good like, but am a bit weary-a trippin since-a larst time which nirly blew me fuckin ead off like, but Paul's got old-a some Penguins like which ee assures us-a nice n mellow, as if a doan fuckin know like, as if a need enny fuckin drug advice off tha fuckin amateur, so we all drop one each like an ead out-a town in is knackered ole car, a Manics on-a stereo, roses in-a hospital an all tha fuckin stuff like, mun. We teyk off into-a mountains, out parst Bill's pleyce an inter Strata Florida like, whir we jes lie on ar backs in-a grounds uv-a ole abbey an weyt fer the acid ter kick in an do its stuff like. Am jes lyin yer . . . A fuckin sky, mun, an-a grass; iss is wha av ulweys fuckin loved about trips, iss is fuckin acid at its fuckin best like, boy, buzzin in me ead like-a fuckin bees, all four uv us laughin like an talkin an chewin on-a grass stalks like fuckin farmers. Or fuckin sheep. Thiz nowt bard about this hit, mun, iss is pure fuckin fun, boy, even Colm agrees an ee's not normelly one ferra acid, an Malcolm carn stop fuckin larfin ter imself. Paulie's darncin about like yer's music ee's lissnin to but yer's nothin cept-a birds an-a insects . . .

Ace.

We goan look at Dafydd's greyve, Dafydd ap Gwilym like, yer know, tha poet cunt, an as arm standin yer lookin a start ter feel-a energy-a iss pleyce, a start ter madgin monks bald an in brown gowns like walkin round yer an chantin to-a gods . . . a gang-a blokes with birnin torches an pitchforks outside-a geyts . . . but slike am not madginin iss at all, slike am rerly fuckin *remembrin* it, yer know wha a mean like? Like a can rerly fuckin smell-a fleyms an ear-a fuckin voices like, n almost as if a can feel people walkin parst me, fuckin breathin on me . . .

Fuckin ameyzin iss is, mun. Bess fuckin buzz iss is, am tellin yer.

—Not a lot lefta this plice, is thair? Malcolm says, lookin round. – Funny fuckin feelin abaht it tho . . . kinda plice samwan like fuckin Phil'd gow on abaht, ya know, ger all fuckin hippy . . .

En ee does an impression-a FuhfuhPhil, only without-a stutter like, an it's so fuckin spot-on tha we all piss arselves larfin like:

—Oi went aht ter Stratter Florider terdie, dropped a trip an cime ap boi Dafydd's grive. Quoit freaked me et the toime.

Ee sounds jes fuckin like im, with is shaky, wimpy voice. A larf me fuckin ead off, mun.

We ang about ferra bit, jes fuckin about like, enjoyin-a hit, an en we go to-a pub in Ponty whassit, fuckin long neym like, whir we stey til it's dark an en Paul drives us out ter the pub in Goginan, the Druid like. Good boozer, a Druid; in-a deytime yer can see right out across-a valley, see-a little white ouses on-a illsides like, see-a smoke comin out uv-a woods jes like tha fuckin programme *Twin Peaks* . . . fuckin smart . . . dead calm, like, an nice . . . Fuckin buzzin yer, boy, a acid's jes floatin me along, like, hummin, dead fuckin lovely, mun, an am jes about ter go up-a bar an get another round in with Malcolm's dosh when the streynge thing appens, as it wuz fuckin bound to, sooner-a leyter, like, as it ulweys without fail fuckin does: the door birsts open an some ole twat comes runnin in nerly fuckin in tears mun all fuckin beamin red-feyced like an sweaty an jes about ter shite is fuckin kex:

—Quick, *quick*! Outside! Oh my God it's outside! Yuv *got* ter comen see it, quick before it goes! Quick! In the bloody sky by Christ!

Evryone's jes fuckin stirrin at im like, yer know, like: Oo the fuck's this?, an en ee legs it back outside an we all leap up an follow im, Colm n Paulie n Mal fuckin gobsmacked, mun, like me n all. We go outside an-a ole bastard's standin yer in-a middle uv-a fuckin road like, pointin across-a valley like an jabberin on to isself but's pitch fuckin black mun, yer carn see-a fuckin thing cept-a nighttime like. Jes darkness. A mountains on-a other side uv-a valley-a jes big blobs uv deeper blackness. Yer's fuck all ter see. An ee ole feller's stampin is foot like an pointin an yellin an yer's people tryin ter calm im down like but ee's not fuckin avin enny uv it:

—Am bloody tellin yew! It was *there*, a say! Saw it with me own bare eyes I did, a bloody spaceship it was, in the sky, big as a bloody church, boy! Lights goin on an off, makin bloody bleepin noises it was! There! Clear as bloody day!

Iss meyks me larf like cos yer's no bloody dey yer, mun, black as fuckin tar it is see, in fact's not much-a fuckin ennythin part from-a moon an a night an a stars. A shout over ter the ole fucker:

—Ey, it wozn Richey James Edwards pilotin iss spaceship, was ee? Only he've fallen off-a fuckin planet, mun.

—Think it's bloody funny, aye? Think it's all a big bloody joke, son? Well let me tell yew av bin farmin ese hills fer near thirty yeer an a never in all my born deys –

Ee rambles on. Muss be a mad cunt. Either tha or ee's jes ad a midnight fuckin snack-a mushies, aye. A barman teyks im back inside ferra drink like an me n Col n Paul n Mal all jes stand yer lookin at each other an larfin like, but en a get another acid rush like an a start ter think about spy satellites in-a sky watchin us like, we think eyr fuckin stars like or spaceships but eyr fuckin satellites mun, with cameras an telescopes so fuckin powerful ey can see-a fuckin fillins in yer back fuckin teeth. Watchin evry fuckin thing yer do. Teykin photographs uv yer. Recordin yer voice.

—Jesus Christ, Malcolm sez. —What appened then? A mean what the fuck was *that*?

A shrug. —A jes got a bit para like, a sez, an ee looks at us all fuckin puzzled like an en we all birst out larfin agen an go back into-a pub. Colm's streyt up to-a bar, gettin more drinks in with Mal's money. A ole feller's in a corner with-a crowd-a people, knockin back-a whisky, nirly fuckin cryin.

—It's the trewth! Am tellin yew, it's the bloody *trewth*!

Poor ole twat, a suppose, like. Spaceships in-a sky. Liked me crack about Richey Manic, tho, a did. Wozn flyin iss fuckin rocket wuz ee? Ha.

An am flyin me fuckin self, or the acid's flyin me like, another rush liftin me over to-a bar, next ter Colm, oo's fuckin hoverin an all. Yeh, unidentified flyin objects, thass fuckin us alright, boy. Am tellin yer, tho; streynge things, when yer trippin. Ulweys. Am right, arn I? Yeh. Course a fuckin am.

Some good fuckin fun lass night, boy, aye; all-a us wir thir, good fuckin boys all, me, Griff, Sieff Lewis wirrin a big woolly at an lookin like a fuckin Celtic Snoop Doggy Dogg, Ikey, Llŷr, fuckin loads-a us thir wuz. In-a Angel this wuz, like. Oh aye, an that fat cunt with-a fuckin tash oo a taught a fuckin lesson to in-a alley behind-a Ship the other week thir, that night a shagged that tart when a ad the crystal meth like. Fuckin arse'ole im, aye; couple-a yeers ago now, that cunt went threw me fuckin pockits like when a wuz crashed out over at Iestyn's house. Took all me fuckin money, drugs . . . wanker. Thought ad fuckin fergot about it, ee did (an so did evry cunt else al bet) but av got a fuckin long memory I yav, boy, too fuckin right. Ennywey, a wuz in-a mood ferra fuckin scrap like but iss cunt clocked me lookin at im an fucked off shiters. A wuz appy ter see is fuckin ands wir still in fuckin bandages like, oh yeh. Arse'ole. A wuz jes about fuckin ready ter teyk off after im an give im another fuckin lesson in respect when Gareth pulled me over to-a fruit machine.

—Roger. As the bin enny busts round yer recently? Drugs like?

—Yeh, a sey. —Jed, fer one. Some fuckin grass . . . an if a find out fuckin oo . . .

—Well, yew av, mun, ee sed. —See tha twat over yer, a one in a blew jumper like?

A looked over at the bar like an saw iss fuckin short-arsed twat in a blew jumper standin yer with-a arf, lookin round at evryone like. A remember, ee'd bin yer all fuckin night, jes standin yer, eyein evry fucker up. Wondered oo ee wuz, a did; yer doan come ter the fuckin Angel an spend two owers over one fuckin arf unless yer up ter somethin like.

—Well, ee's yer grass, Gareth sed. —Member when a wuz up in Pwllheli? That cunt wuz thir an all. Soon's ee left, people wir gettin busted left right an fuckin centre. Seym thing in Swansea like. An in Brecon. Am tellin yer, boy, that fucker's yer grass, ee's yer snitch. Fuckin pig spy, that cunt is like.

97

So we go round, like, whisp'rin in evryone's eer, tellin em about iss fuckin spy. An evryone's fuckin well werked up like cos-a pleyce's bin fuckin dry fer months, Jed on remand, Iain awey somewhir, all-a dealers leyin low like, wiv all bin fuckin *nnnnng* fer fuckin ages like, so we all gather round-a corner by-a pool teyble, out-a public view like, an rack up-a balls an start pleyin. Pretty soon an Ikey brings iss fuckin blew jumper cunt round a corner, and on is fuckin skinny shoulder like.

—Some uv my good friends would like t'meet yew, sir. Ah . . .

An we wir on im like wolves. Ikey wuz oldin is arms back like, screamin ee wuz, wir all reachin over each other's fuckin eads ter get a good fuckin shot in like, gettin in each other's wey, a coulden reach cos a wuz stuck be'ind fuckin Griffiths like an yer know ow big ee is, fuckin man mountain boy, so a got me cue an reached it over Griff's shoulder an fuckin jabbed it like dead ard in blue jumper fucker's eye. Should-a seen-a cunt swell, mun, fuck; five seconds an ee coulden even see out. All blue it wuz, matchin is fuckin jumper like. Tidy.

—Iss is wha appens ter grasses round yer, boy! Ikey wuz yellin in is eer. Ee wuz fuckin beggin like, goin:

—No, please! I don't know what you're talkin about! Let me go, please, I –

Ikey twisted is arm back an ee screamed as summun snapped like an en we stuck im in a corner be'ind the pool teyble, Ikey standin guard over im. Sittin yer ee wuz in-a puddle uv is own shit n piss, beggin, pleadin, cryin like-a fuckin babby. Disgustin as fuck ter see, it wuz.

We carried on pleyin pool like, evry now n agen teykin ar frustreytion at a missed shot out on is fuckin grassin cunt. Not tha a missed menny shots like, fuckin hustler that a am, but a still got a good few fuckin digs in like. Sieffri, yer know ow shit ee is at pool, ee wuz on-a cunt all-a fuckin time like, fuckin cue on is bollacks, fuckin black ball bounced off is fuckin ead (ee passed out ferra bit after tha one, but we brought im round with-a pint in is feyce like), chairleg on is fuckin kneecaps . . . An all-a time unless ee wuz out uv it like iss grassin bastard never stopped beggin; even when Ikey smashed all is front teeth in with-a cue ball, oldin is ead back like, ee still carried on, pleadin, cryin, not tha yer could unnerstand a fuckin wird ee sed arfter that like . . . jes fuckin gurgles it wuz, mun.

Kept im thir ferra good two owers we did, a reckon. Coulden fuckin reckernise-a cunt arfter a while like, is ole ead like a fuckin black ball's big brother. Deserved evry last fuckin bit uv it, ee did, the fuckin snitch. Ee finally managed ter esceyp like when Ikey broke a glass an started walkin toward im, all slowly like. Doan rerly know ow ee managed it like; jes pure fuckin terror, a suppose. Didn even know ee wuz gone like til a saw the treyl-a blood an piss an shit goin out-a fuckin pub door. Ikey wanted ter follow im with is bleyd like, but Griff eld im back; too menny potential witnesses out thir, see. Bad boy, Ikey is. Ee'd uv cut the cunt ter shreds like an a fuckin mean tha, mun.

Ennywey, a pigs caught up with us when we wir all eatin fuckin kebabs outside D'Okays, leyter on like. Fuckin greyt it wuz: —Never seen the boy in me life, officer. Couldn do fuck all, like, cos we all ad an alibi; Angel barman sorted it, sed ee adn seen us in is fuckin pub all night. So we get ar fuckin drugs back, y'know, all-a dealers come back out uv idin, an a fuckin grass fucks off. Tidy. Wharrer fuckin night tho, boy, yer should-a fuckin been thir, God, yew would-a fuckin loved it.

—AH YER FUCKIN CUNTIN BASTARD FUCKIN . . .

Me fuckin ands-a sheykin so fuckin bard tha a drop me fuckin wirks fer the second fuckin time, can yer fuckin believe tha, boy, me nice clean fuckin wirks all over iss fuckin slimy fuckin kitchen floor. Iss fuckin squat, mun, some fuckin people aye . . . ey live like fuckin pigs, mun. Some-a em a crowdin in-a doorwey like, fuckin gawpin; ese fuckin gyppo cunts oo live yer, if yer can fuckin call it livin.

—An wha the fuck a *yew* fuckin lookin at? EY?

Ey back off.

—FUCK OFF NOW AFORE A FUCKIN SMACK YER!

Ey leg it.

—CUNTS!

Young kids like . . . a older squatters ar all browned-out up-a stirs like. Wish I fuckin wuz.

A pick me wirks up, too fuckin wired ter clean em like, an cook up another hit. Av got ter grit me fuckin teeth yer; nirly a ole fuckin wrap all over-a fuckin kitchen floor. Fuck. Jes when a fuckin needed it most like n all . . . A gerrit right iss time, too fuckin right a do, pump me veyn up in two fuckin seconds an jack it streyt fuckin in, not even both'rin ter boot the fucker. Me veyns ar fuckin sinkin, av bin ferra while, but eyr not fuckin yewseless yet, boy . . . oh no . . . some fuckin survivor I yam aye. Didn even check fer blood . . . might av missed-a fuckin veyn . . .

Mmmmmmmmmmmmmmmmmmmmmmmmmmmmmmm.

A slide down on ter-a floor, among-a rubbish an-a mould an-a crusty spew an-a spilled fuckin fixes. Ese cunts'll av a stonedest fuckin silverfish in fuckin Wales, mun. Am tellin yer . . . Mm.

Rrrrrrrright! Av got ter fuckin move, boy, carn stand yer fuckin about. A old a bin-bag open with one hand an chuck all me old clothes in with-a other. Teyps an stuff in a sports bag, weyts n things streyt into-a fuckin shoppin trolley on-a doorstep. No fuckin messin about yer, mun.

Am lookin up an down-a road like, opin a don't see me ole twat uv a landlord out on-a fuckin scrounge fer is fuckin rent. Nirly three fuckin ton a owe im, a do; took iss long afore ee sirved is eviction notice, a stewpid cunt. At's men uv-a cloth for yer, aye. If it wuz me, now, ad av yer out on yewer fuckin arse arfter a week, no, a fuckin *dey*; at's ow yev got t'be in business, boy, fuckin rewthless like. Show no fuckin mercy.

—Oh . . . are you leaving us?

One-a ose fuckin stewdent English cunts from downstirs like, the specky one. Lived jes below me, ee did; a yewse ter eer im wankin sometimes at night like. A ignore-a twat an leg it back up-a stirs fer the rest-a me geer, jes a larst bits like, y'know, me bong, me sceyls, me one book (*The Chronicle of Welsh Events*, at's all yer fuckin need that is, boy, oh yeh, it's all in fuckin yer). Back down-a stirs agen.

—Where are you going, then?

—S none-a yewer fuckin business, boy, yer doan need ter know. Orright?

—But what about a forward address for mail and stuff? Where should I –

Jesus. Some cunts avn got-a first fuckin clew. A slam a door on im, the larst time al close that door . . . al never be in at ouse agen like. Unless, uv course, a find meself runnin short; some fuckin geer ose stewdents av got aye – CDs, videos, tellies, the fuckin lot, mun. Woulden fuckin believe it aye.

A teyk one last look up at what wuz me room window en a scarper down-a road with me trolley full-a stuff.

Ts only the self-deluded cunts or the amateurs oo talk about feelins-a immortality. Skag, all drugs, ey doan meyk yer believe tha yew can live fer ever, no fuckin wey, mun; wha ey do is, ey show yew yer own death, an show tha it's not wirth fuckin worryin about. That's all. It's when yuv seen death like, when yuv fuckin *caused* it, tha yer know it's fuck all ter be scerd uv. It's easy. Smack sorts it all out fer yer, boy.

See, a know al die young. A know av not got tha long left yer, on iss fuckin planet like, an a eroin tells me tha that's orright, an not t'fuckin worry . . . No fuckin bother. Av ulweys known like, since a wuz a babby like, tha am gunner die young. An at's fuckin easy, that is. Wha a won't fuckin do ever is die like-a boy in Down, pissin me fuckin kex with-a bottle in me feyce. Stickin out like. No fuckin wey boy. Al die like-a fuckin eero a will, teykin loads-a yew fuckin bastards with me. Oh fuck yeh.

From *A Personal Guide to West Wales*, anonymous authorship, privately printed, p. 24

Albeit in a different state, the ice remains here, as, too, does its moraine: watch the mountains seeking to shove the small town into the sea, which burns and returns like a memory. The glacial diversion, the obvious incised meander suggest randomness or a mutation from plan and purpose, as if the timeless tryst at Aberarth between the Irish Sea ice and the ice of more local origin was mere chance, happenstance. Perhaps it was; but the graded bedding effect of the beach here is due to a sudden ongoing influx of rock particles of all shapes and sizes, some stubbornly retaining their original dimensions and others crumbling to powder under the terrible pressures of constant contact. The larger screes and arrested avalanches, the crashed masses of rock debris, ensure that never will be forgotten the periglacial conditions of this area, those conditions which characterise slow centuries of rage and ransack, conditions which prevail after the ice itself has departed for another state and all that remains is frost, crystalline, curious fronds of coldness.

THEY ARE CELEBRATING

THEY ARE CELEBRATING St Patrick's Night, sustained by colcannon and sausages which Colm, in a rare and surprising instance of food hunger, cooked for them earlier and which they washed down with large quantities of stout, Bushmills, Jameson's, poitín. A flask of the latter has been smuggled into the pub in Liam's side pocket and is being used to top up pints beneath the table with a surreptitiousness which is, in fact, unwarranted; the barman has already gleefully accepted several measures of the illegal liquor and is now yelling for Liam to sing 'Mary McCree', although Liam cannot hear him over the combined noise of the fiddle player, the roared requests for drinks, and the plangent ruckus inside his head. The usual pub hubbub.

—Ey, Liam, what's up with you? Colm asks, distressed at his friend's sour expression. He is determined to make everybody have as good a time as he is. —C'mon, cheer up, yer bastard! Sona Lá Fhéile Pádraig, fuck's sakes, c'mon.

—Aye, same te you n all.

—Oh yer grumpy fuckin cunt.

Colm looks around for a happier face and finds Paul's.

This night is, for Liam, as are nearly all these occasions, an unfortunate concourse of sensation: the scattered Gaelic phrases, the accents, the fiddle and bodhran playing, the headlong rush towards drunkenness in the stifling pub heat, the taste of the poitín and whiskey, all these things threaten to drag him back to memories of strained and awkward family gatherings in Donegal hill inns, nearby rumbles of war, his mother's breath rising and reeking on a screech. He is remembering, reluctantly, news reports and whispered bulletins in the cracked mouths of strangers, the slap and crack of a palm on his face, his sister's either all-seeing or un-seeing eyes above her slack and drooling mouth. Even the froth on his Guinness recalls the crusts of sea salt in the cuffs of his father's trousers and on the frayed peak of his hat, so he gulps it down and holds the empty glass aloft so that Laura, who is struggling for purchase at the bar, will see it. She smiles and nods and is then lost in the crush. Liam feels a hand gently squeeze his ribs.

—Give us a smile then, doll. Tha looks raht misrubble.

He turns to Mairead, whose uncommonly happy expression cheers him; she rarely appears this content, and Liam is pleased to see her this way. He smiles and sees, over her shoulder, Colm loudly and slurringly and with extravagant hand movements telling Paul his grandmother's recipe for colcannon.

—It wuz special, y'see, the wey she made it, av never *ever* tasted colcannon ennywher neer as good as me mamo's, fuck it wuz ace, she'd *fry* the scallions, yer see, an the kale n all sumtimes, in butter, an then put the cream in . . . only a little bit, like, not too much cream . . . a yuce ter love goan round ter me granny's when a wuz a kid . . . an sumtimes it yuced ter make me fart so me granny ud call it Colm's cannon insteader colcannon.

Paul laughs at this and Liam grins. He notices a scabrous slice, deep and dark, on the end of Colm's thumb and wonders briefly how it got there before turning back to Mairead who is smiling at the overflowing ashtray in the centre of the table.

—Ts nice te see yis smilin, Mair, so ut is. Ah doan think av seen ye this happy since . . . fuckin ages. Things uh goan bettur fe ye now, eh?

She shrugs and finishes off her Jack Daniel's and Coke. —Nah. Am just pissed off mi ferce.

—Ah well, ad bettur getchy anothur then eh?

—Ta, yir a love.

He stands and then immediately falls back again, on to Mairead, who laughs and catches him. He has forgotten the potency of his uncle's poitín and has, in the course of the evening, drunk a sizeable amount of it along with numerous pints of heavy stout and many shots of whiskey. Drunkenness has now come upon him not in steady increments of inebriation but in one sudden muddling rush.

—Jayz . . . ah'm pissed so ah am. Pissed's a fuckin fahrt.

Mairead holds and rocks him, laughing. His elbow is digging sharply into her breast but she doesn't mind.

—Oi! You! You triner tap up my berd?

—Too fuckin right ah am. Shiz too fuckin good fe ye, Col, so she is. In tha right thur, Mair?

—Av bin tellin im that since the der a met im.

—Whur's Laura gone fe tha fuckin pint now? Dublin? Ah . . .

Laura, looking sweaty and flustered, hands Liam a fresh stout. Blacker than black, heavy and rich, a raised shamrock patterned in the foamy head. He takes a big, deep gulp and flops sideways against Laura, who encircles him with her arm.

—Christ, Liam, how drunk are you . . . completely trousered . . .

She kisses the top of his hot head and plays with his ponytail. He springs upright again, slaps the top of the table, roars, tries to roll a cigarette. Tobacco falls to the floor.

—'Mary McCree'! 'Mary fuckin McCree'!

—Oh God, Liam, sing it fer im will yer an shut the fucker up. At's all ee's been seyin all night, 'Mary bleedin McCree'. Gettin on me wick.

With guitar accompaniment from the band Liam sings the barman's request, and a large section of the pub falls quiet to hear him. It is mournful and moving, sung stumblingly and with little hope. In the relative silence which follows Liam nods to Colm who clears his throat, sits upright, and begins:

Gooood saaaave ar graaacious –

Then before the uproar can properly take hold a grin splits his face and he flaps his hands laughing, says: —Nah nah am only messin, and croaks into 'Liverpool Lou'.

Across the table, Malcolm leans over to Sioned.

—Ain't like this on March tha first, Sion, is it? Why down tha Welsh go craizy on St David's day like tha Irish do on St Patrick's?

Sioned shrugs and curls her top lip. Her cheeks have flushed pink and her bright blonde hair in the dim pub light looks lustrous and lithe and alive.

—Well, some do, some do . . . a dunno . . . fuckin chapel, innit. Yull never appreciate the influence of eh chapel hir if yur not Welsh. Strew. Think uv it, rrright; the 'Wearin uv the Grreen' compird to 'Siospan bloody Fach'.

—Well, yeh, agrees Malcolm. —It does seem somewha odd that a song abaht a diminutive kitchen implement was chowsen ta celebraite a national day.

—Bloody shit. But it could be a Welsh celebration too tho cos St Patrick, he was Welsh. Born ere ee was.

Malcolm looks over at Liam. —Nor, Liam, do I see wha wearin mustard n cress in ya button'owl as got ter do wiv St Patrick.

—Ts fuckin shamrock, ye soft get!

—Could maker nice little salad ahter that.

An exuberant roar is heard from the other side of the bar.

—Wharrer they so fuckin appy about?

—Fuck knows. Go an fuckin ask em.

The bodhran player starts off a strong, rolling rhythm. Paul drums along with it on the table top, spattering people nearby with warm splashes of flat beer.

—Oi! For fuck's sakes!

Malcolm produces a wrap of amphetamine from his cigarette packet, tips half of it into his lager and passes it on to Colm.

—Nice one. Good on yer.

—You've still got yours, yeh?

Colm nods.

—Well, saive tha fer laiter, when we start ta flag. Keep us gowin.

—Orright. Probly sooner un yer fuckin think tho with this bleedin stuff. Sulphate me arse; ts nerly pure fuckin self-raisin if yer ask me.

The bodhran rolls on. Liam kisses Laura wetly and then turns to Mairead, who is swaying in her seat dreamily, languidly. She hasn't expressed any disapproval at Colm dabbing speed behind the shield of Paul and Liam thinks that maybe this is a good sign; Mairead frowns on Colm's amphetamine habits simply because the drug makes him unbearable to her, exponentially exaggerating as it does his natural enthusiasms and energies. Colm must be a terrible person to live with, Liam thinks, and silently admires Mairead's endurance – and remains puzzled at her commitment.

—Keep with ut now, Mair, stay up now. Sno fuckin good this nonsense, this broodin all a day. Fucket. Gets ye fuckin nowhurr.

Mairead leans forward in her seat.

—Oh am happy, am happy, she says. —An am dry; look out, av
got t'get ter bar.

Liam pulls his knees in so Mairead can squeeze past him. The
bodhran rolls on.

LIAM

Ah . . .

The breeze an the seagulls an the waves.

Ah do like warkin on this beach, Tan y Bwlch, berrah thun
the wan at the othur end, by Consti like, at the bohttom uv
Cliff Terrace. Thass juster bit borin, tha wan – pebbles. Ah like
the rocks n stuff hur, all jagged an black an volcanic, ey remind
me o' tha Ingmar Bergman fillum, the wan whur the feller plays
chess with Mr Death, carn remembur wha ut's called now, yurs
since ah'v seen ut. Bu' yeh, ah like rocks ennyway, *all* rocks, all
life comes out uv the rocks, ah lurned tha if fuck all else when ah
did tha bit uv geology in me yur up at the uni. Diddun fuckin last
long tho, shur enough; money an all tha shite, yeh know. Ye carn
be a student now, juss carn survive, less ye're fuckin rich, o' course
. . . An ennyway, te tell ye the truth, ah doan think ye can rurly lurn
ennythin in lecture theatres an classrooms tha ye carn lurn bein out,
like, in the wurld, if ye know wha ah mean. All ye need's a right
fuckin outlook an attitude an a bit uv imagination an knowledge is
hur fe the takin. Shur it fuckin is. Wance thur wur no universities,
wuz the now?

Ah offun do this, cum walkin on the beach on me own. S
fuckin lovely, so ut is; a flask o' Jameson's an a spliff or two an
am afuckinwey. Grand. Those fuckin jets which scream oveh yeh
ead ur a pain in the fuckin ahrse butchy can get used te evrythin,
av alweys sed tha, an am fuckin right, ah am; ye can get used te
evrythin if yer around ut fe long enough. A mean, look wha ah
lurnt te put up with, back in Ireland; fuckin next-door neighbour
te a war zone, on yer toes all a fuckin time, next step could be yer
last, n me mam bein a fuckin demon with a drink, no money, me
da not fishin, eatin spuds seven nights a week an only one meal a
dey . . . ye can lurn te cope with fuckin annythin. Ah tell fuckin

Colm tha when ee starts goin on an gettin all depressed like ee does sumtimes, an tha fuckin Malcolm too; the doan agree wuth me like, bu' fuck, shuren theh still around, arn they? See.

Ah finder big rock te sit behind, out uv the wind, take ou' me flask an spark up a spliff. Nice grass this . . . sey wha ye like about Stutterin Phil – ee deals a good bit uv gear. A rotten clump uv seaweed in front o' me smells like fuckin shite so ah move away over te another rock an pull the collar uv me overcoat up around me face. Cosy an snug. The whiskey's fuckin great goin down, warmin me up, an am all mellow an calm with the weed. Griff used to deal sum good soap as well afore a fuckin peelers got old uv im wuth several undred fuckin Es in the glovebox uv is cahr. Stupit ahrse. Is own fault n all; ee ires a cahr in Ponterwyd, drives oveh te Birmingham te score, gets wrecked testin the merchandise like, leavin is own cahr in Ponterwyd fe three deys longer'n ee sed ee would. So yer man gets suspicious like an phones the coppers oo watch is cahr an grab im when ee cums te pick ut up, an im now with a glovebox full uv fuckin white doves (ah bet Paul Daniels couldunt do *that*). Fuckin eejit, rurly; grand bloke, but Christ, whur wuz ee keepin is fuckin brain tha dey? Shur, yeh, we all fuck up oncer twice, bu' sumtimes just once's enough te ruin yer ole fuckin life so ut is. Purr bastard. Fuckin twiddlin is thumbs an wond'rin wha appund now down in Swansea nick, callin imself all the stupit curless bastards under the fuckin sun.

The big rock keeps the wind off. Ah lissun to ut whinin, an the gulls screechin, an the waves breakin hiss on the beach . . . ts fuckin grand. An al tell ye sumthun else; ts not in the church whur ye can find God, ut's in places like this, the wild places, beaches an forests an mountains an lakes . . . That's whur ut all began te go wrong ah reckun, when they startud te build places whur we could supposedly meet God an ignore all the places whur ee actually is. That's one uv the reasons why ah stopped bein Catholic, like, cos none uv em could ever fuckin understand tha kind uv thinkin. Ts like, fuckin, deviate from wha they call the propur course uv things an ye get fuckin outcast. D'ye know wha ah mean? An fuck, oo's got the fuckin right te sey wha the propur course uv things *is*, ey? . . . Well, that's not fe fuckin me. Oh no. Never was, never will be. Ye know ah'm fuckin right.

Ah can see a ridge uv lahnd on the horizun, ur wha *looks* like a ridge uv lahnd . . . Probly just a cloud ur a fogbank ur sumthun. Ye cahn see Ireland from hur. Ut's sixty miles awey, an the horizun's, wha, twenty, ur thurabouts, so ut definitely cahn be lahnd. Wishful thinkin, aye, ah suppose, bu' fuck knows wha ut is ah'm fuckin wishin for . . .

Ah walk furthur down the beach, lissnun te the stones crunchin under me boots. Reminds me uv tha bit in tha fuckin buke *Ulysses* tha a tried te read only cos we wurnt allowed te do ut at the skule, a thought ut ud be durty ur sumthun like, the only bit uv tha fuckin buke tha a could ever bring meself te read te tell ye the truth . . . Ah mean, great fuckin wurk ur no, ut's a load uv fuckin shite in places, like a diffrunt shaggin language . . . What's tha phrase now tha ah can never propurly remembur: 'Ineluctable sumthun uv the visible' ur sum such shite an then sumthun about light bein in is eyes. Now wha the fuck's tha supposed te fuckin mean, now, ey? Well, about as much ah suppose as tha nonsense me mam kept cummun ou' wuth the last time ah sawrer, an hur throwin hur best fuckin crockery at the press. Smashed ut all te fuck so ut did, the press *and* the fuckin crockery. Bits. Splintered all te shite. An all ah could make out was stuff like 'fuck off' an 'cunt' an shite about me desertun me own fuckin mothur, leavin er te look after me sistur on hur own, an me sister bein all broken up like ahftur bein caught up in tha explosion in Derry . . . purr gurl, purr Roísín . . . twinty-three yurs old . . . in a wheelchur now she is, cahn walk ur talk, cahn rurly do much uv ennythin, God love hur . . . purr Rosh, my sistur . . . Ut wuz a fuckin Proddy bomb n all. The UVF publicly took responsibility un the fuckin news. Cunts. Ah wuz *this* close te fuckin enlistin ahfter tha, so ah fuckin was. But, fuck, ut's war; wha can ennywan expect? An wha did me mam fuckin expect n all, fe me te stey an av no fuckin life te speak uv just so's she can av sumwan te drag around be the ponytail like she does when she's pissed? Ah mean, Jaze, ye can be pushed only so fuckin fahr an then yuv got te do sumthun about ut. Shur ye fuckin huv. Wuv all got ar breakin points an ah fuckin reached mine tha dey so ah fuckin did. Shull be over thur now, waitin fe me da te be off with the tide te catch fish so's ee can put fuckin food on the table, an soon as ee's out tha fuckin door shull be straight te the fuckin cistern fe the bottle uv Powers. Lyin in er own puke on the front fuckin doorstep when ee cums ome, like she was tha time ah came home wuth me leavin results, fuckin failure in Irish ah got, ow's tha fe fuckin heritage, ey? Aye, well, not tha ah hud much fuckin oppertunity fe me homewurk like; ah mean, *you* try fuckin studyin the declension uv Gaelic vurbs when ye mam's smashin evrythun te fuck in the fuckin kitchen an ye sistur's wahntin er colostomy bag changin, makin tha orruble fuckin whining sound like she does when she needs sumthun . . . Ah Christ. Ah hud te fuckin leave. Erin go bragh, aye, but not with a sistur oo's little mur thun a cabbage God love hur an not wuth a fuckin mothur like mine . . .

Ah fuck ut. Ut's all over wuth now.

The spliff an the whiskey's buoyin me up, makin me feel light an enurgetic, so ah climb to the top uv Pen Dinas, tha oul hill fort with tha monument on top te the Napoleonic wars ur sumthun. Built by a one-legged veteran it wuz, apparently; fuckin amazin, rurly, one feller cartin all those fuckin stones up hur, all a fuckin scaffoldin, mortar, an him wuth only one leg . . . either amazin ur stupit, ah cahn make up me mind. Ah can almost eer Roger splutt'run with laughter an callin im a soft twat, ooever ee wuz, an meybe ee's right in a wey; ah mean, why go te all tha trouble enshurin tha a war is rememburd? All tha fuckin murder . . . Shur, an meybe all those fuckin murals on a Falls an Shankhill Roads'll be painted over wan dey. An meybe me mam'll stop drinkin. An meybe ah'll win the lottery. Ah bollox. An annywey, ah doubt very much tha Roger wuz thinkin o' tha kind o'thing when ee sed tha. God alone knows wha ee *was* thinkin of tho.

Tha thought about the lottery, evil fuckin thing that ut is, starts me off thinkin abou' money, an how ah'm goin te get more wance av spent this last tennur in me pockut which ah'll no doubt do this ahfternun, an wha ah'm goin te do then, Laura's fuckin peanut n button wages not goin very fuckin fahr wha wuth rent arrears an all tha shite, but thinkun on tha kind o' thing alweys gets me depressed so ah turn me back to the sea an look out inland instead, over the hills . . . the shapes an formations; grits, spurs, mudstone, granite, truncations, scree . . . takes me mind awey from all tha fuckin money shite. So tha fuckin uni wuz good fe wan thing, at least; not much fuckin else tho, but ut did seem like a good idea at the time. Least ut offud me a tickut out uv Ireland. Ah, what's the fuckin point, ey? That's why ah like stones, an rocks, an landscapes, cos the stones ur responsible fe evrythin, thur the furst cause, thur like God – evry time a see sum granite ah think 'daddy'. An the sparkly bits in granite remind me uv the fish-scales stuck te the skin on me da's hands an on is boots, an is hat . . . Fuckin incredible the wey evrythin's linked. Fuckin amazin wurld so ut is.

Ah did get wan more thing out uv uni tho. Thur wuz a feller in me class oo went a bit mad. Well, a lot mad, a *fuck* uv a lot mad if the truth be telt . . . Ee became fuckin obsessed with rocks an geology, landscape, natural histurry an stuff, ee used te rant on about how human lives were mapped by the rocks an all kinds uv crazy shite like tha, an ee wrote some strange guide te this area, Aberystwyth like, which ee tried te get published but ut wuz turned down by a load uv places an tha made im wurse. Ee flipped out in the end, in an out uv North Road ee was, usin all kinds uv drugs both prescribed an illicit, rantin away at evryone an pissin imself in the street in full view uv evry fucker . . . dead fuckin sad so ut was. Av got a photocopy uv is guide which ah keep in me flat, an ut's bizarre fuckin stuff. A still read ut evry now an agen bu' . . . well, te tell ye the truth, a find ut a bit dull. Bit borin. This feller, tho, ah think ee drowned imself in the end; well, ee *did* drown, ah know tha, but whether ut wuz suicide ur an accident, no wan knows. Purr fucker. Ah cahn even remembur is name now . . . Just anothur nutter attracted te this small town be the sea. An ut seems te attract an awful fuckin lot.

So: that's wha else ah got from me time at universuty – proof tha ah'm not the only wan oo thinks some fuckin bullshit, thank Christ.

Ah stand an look out over the town, the castle an the harbur and, behind thum, the long, curvin promenade. The hills surroundin ut remind me uv Donegal, the times ah'd go out campin with me pals when ah wuz a kid. So green, these hills ar. Like Donegal, only without the shadows cast fuckin constuntly by a pissed-up mothur.

Anothur good swig from the flask an anothur spliff. All a people movin abou' in the town below me, so wee an insecty. Ah could just nod off hur so ah could, just drift off te sleep . . . an ah do fuckin well deserve a rest. Uf anny fucker deserves a fuckin rest, ut's me. Diddun ah long ago get off me fuckin ahrse an do summun fuckin positive wuth me life? Too fuckin right ah did. Left the place which was bad fe me (both Donegal *and* uni), wurked on a site, found a flat, a good wommun . . . When ah furst came hur ah had thurty fuckin quid in me pockut. Ah slept on flurs, in the fuckin public sheltur with the winos, ah ate fuckin dulse an crabs off the beach . . . Like Marc, tha feller out by Llanilar; when ee lost is rights te dole ee rigged up a light powered by a cahr batt'ry in a rucksack an went poachin fe trout an salmon in the rivers at night-time. Ah went out wuth im wance, amazin fuckin sight, so; the light beam movin through the dahk rivur, yer man stabbin at the fish with is spear made out uv a cahr aerial . . . Ee made a fuckin good livin out uv it ferra bit so ee did, afore ee began te like is smack too much. Ah havunt seen im ferra while now, ah told im te fuck off ahftur ee lifted sum money from Laura's purse. Bout a tenner ah think ut was. Ah seem te remembur Laura givin im a fiver as well, tho tha wuz prob'ly just te make im go . . . Shiz a good wommun, Laura is, no fuckin doubt about tha, even if she does fuckin yell like me mam sumtimes when she gets angry. Does me in tha does, but shur ah can live wuth ut. Ye can get used te fuckin evrythun. Shuren ye fuckin can.

Yeh, that's wha ah'll do; smoke me spliff, huv a wee sit, go back down into town for a couple uv scoops, go ome around teatime an cook Laura sumthun nice fe when she gets ome from wurk. At least wuv got food in the fridge now; menny times, fah too menny times, ut's been empty. An then when wuv eaten wull go te bed an ah'll shag hur senseless, if she wants te, like. An, fuck, ah'll tell ye, ah do love shaggin tha wommun; if ye could see hur, Jaze, shuz gorgeous, yuv nevur seen such breasts, Christ . . . Wurds like 'tits' doan do um justice – thur breasts, *breasts* . . . Shuz a lovely lookin wommun my Laura. God, she is. Ah'd eat me chips out uv er knickers so ah would.

Ah start te get a wee bit hard, thinkin like, an ah become awurr agen uv the monument behind me, pointin up to the sky like an immense mickey. Ah laugh te meself. Now that's sumthun wurth celebratun, ah reckun. Too fuckin right.

*   *   *

Ut's quite a long drive out te Abergynolwyn, but's alrigh'; Laura drives while ah take chahge uv the cassette deck an the four-pack o' stout in the seatwell. The purr cahr's fucked now – an ut's only a Citroën CV, so ah suppose ut wuz fucked te begin wuth – but ut gets ye from A te B, yer know, an wha the fuck elser cahrs for? We used te live out hur in Abergynolwyn, Laura an me, in fact ut's whur we met; ah wuz livun in the oul police station hur when ah furst came over te Wales, livun in wan uv the cells that ud been convurted inte bedsits like. Odd experience so ut was; av been locked up loads uv fuckin times but ah nevur thought ah'd end up livun in a fuckin cell. An the gahdun uv the place wuz, like, the prisoner's exuhcise yahd; wee little walled-off patch uv gravel an beneath the gravel wuz a worn-down groove all a wey round ut, close te the wall, worn down from all a pacin feet over the yurs. Mickah, the feller who ah shurd the place wuth, still lives ou' hur but in a diffrunt house now. An that's whur wur off te tenight, te see Mickah. Scenery round hur's fuckin stunnun so ut is but's pitch black now so ah cahn see anny uv ut.

Ah'm feelun a little bit strange, cummun back hur. Ah doan do ut very offun . . . Ah'm remembrun summun Colm said wance, when ee wuz talkin abou', ah dunno, love ur sumthun ah think ut was, about how it ul inevitably be lost ur sum such maudlin shite. Talks a load uv shite that mahn sumtimes. But ah remembur im sayun how we alweys go back te those places which ur loaded wuth significance fer us, y'know, whur ye kissed, screwed, wha'evur . . . returnun like criminals te the scene uv a crime, Colm sed, ur a fox back to a shed full uv slaughtered chickuns. An ah'm beginnin te feel a bit like tha now so ah am, but ah don't rurly know why, ah mean, Laura's wuth me, shuz hur, be me side, in the cahr, so ut cahn be as if ah'm visitun a site uv lost love ur enny bollox like tha now can ut? Nah, just Colm an is bullshit. We pass sum roadwurks with a 'REDUCE SPEED NOW' sign an a remember the lahst time we came hur, Colm wuz in the cahr with us as well, an ee saw tha sign an sed:

—Oh look – 'REDUCE SPEED NOW'. Well, who uh we ter disregard Dyfed County Council imperatives?

An then ee startud te dab agen at is ever-present bag uv

amphetamine. Fuckin stuff ee cums ou' wuth sumtimes . . . ah tell yis, tha boy hasunt just kissed the Blarney stone, he's fuckin *shagged* ut.

We drive down t'rew the village, pahst all the oul places – the police station flats, the wee shop, the pub . . . The hillside whur ah used te wurk, collectun moss; the hedge whur ah saw a weasel cummun ou' uv a dead sheep's stomach; the skule pleyground whur ah had a fight with tha oul fucker an dislocated is kneecap; the town clock under which Batty nurly choked on is own vom; the field whur ah furst shagged Laura, oh yeh, just pahst midnight in amung the daisies an the sheepshit . . . All the oul places. Still hur.

Mickah opuns is door when we knock an is dog, Trapper, cums boundin out te jump up at us an lick us. Fuckin great dog, Trapper is, like all dogs ar – the unconditional adulation. Shur, doan we all need a bit uv that from time te time?

—Ahts youse two! Cum in, Jesus, cum in.

We follow im inte a cloud uv pot smoke like grey fuckin candy floss.

—Still smokin like a fuckin chimney ah see then, Mickah, eh?

Ee waves is ahms un grins, like: Wha didjer expect? Big fuckin grin on's face . . . Sound feller, Mickah. He fetches sum could cans uv Guinness from the fridge an builds a spliff as we sit by the fire an talk abou' all kinds uv shite. Laura gets quickly stoned an stahts talkin te Trapper; ee's sittun thur, so ee is, eeurs cocked, lissnun, understahndun evry fuckin wurd she says, ah'm fuckin shur uv ut. Thuz a log fire goin on behind Laura an she looks beautiful in uts light. *Evrythun* looks beautiful in uts light.

—So annyways, Mickah, ye still got yer bahn?

Ee nods. —Why?

—Well, ah sey, gettin to the real point uv this visut likes, —wur thinkun uv gettin a crowd tegethur an meybes stoppin in ut ferra weekend like, uf that's alrigh' wuth yis.

—Sound. No problem. Only yer carn stey inner old one, y'know the big one? Cos av got somethin growin in thir now. Yis can rent the newer one tho.

—Ta. An what uv ye got in the oul wan then, as uf ah doan fuckin know?

Ee grins. —Show yer.

We all, Trapper included, follow Mickah out the back to his bahn which, just as ah thought, as been convurted into a fuckin cannabis greenhouse, a miniature fuckin herby jungle. Jaze, what a sight.

—An not just enny old weed folks, oh no, Mickah says. —This stuff ere is yer surefire strong-as-fuck blow-yer-fuckin-brains-out superskunk. Super-fuckin-*duper* skunk a should sey. Yull have never smoked ennythin remotely like this stuff. A got me hands on some cuttings an seeds last time a was over on the Isle of Man.

—Jesus.

Ah stroke the leaves an sniff up. Ut's strange, ut's as if thur's a hum in the air hur, a throb sort uv, ah feel as if ah'm standun in the lair uv sum wild animal, ur a missile silo, ur sumthun like tha. Scury, but kind uv excitun at the same time, in a wey.

—Av got sum already dried inner house. Al give yis a blast.

So back in the house an Mickah skins up. Ee's been smokin since, likes, the late fuckin seventies ur summun an is nur fuckin immune to the stuff so ee puts abou' a teenth in each spliff. Ah should uv reelised, rurly, an refused; bu' like Colm an Mags wuth speed an Mairead wuth the bevvy, ah can nevur resist a toke.

Burns me fuckin t'roat off when ah inhale. Laura declines, cos shuz drivin, so Mickah an I smoke it urselves. Ut smells an tastes like, ah dunno, grass syrup ur summun, sickly, sugary, an ah'm in no bleedin time at all stoned as a fuckin bastard. This reelisation cums on me suddenly, as ah'm closely studyin the ghost uv a bahcode on the Rizla packut which wuz used ferra roach an which is just visible beneath the moist cigarette paper . . . Bahcode. Ah'm stoned. Ah'm so fuckin stoned, ah mean, rurly rurly rurly stoned; fright'ninly stoned, acid-trip stoned, evilly stoned (no no not evilly) nurly fuckin flippin ou' screamin stoned . . . Ut stahts off wuth me needin te shite, urgently like, ah mean ah need te consciously hould me hole tegethur, an then ah becum awurr uv Trapper breathun an slobberin an snufflin like sum dog-demon, too loud, fah too fuckin loud, *unnaturally* loud . . . then the heat from the fire's too fuckin hot, scorchin me, blist'rin me skin, so ah shift awey, wrigglin on me ahrse like, but the movement feels daft an crippled an sumhow false an Mickah's talkin at me an ah try te concentrate on wha he's sayin but ah carn understahnd a fuckin wurd, he's talkin in a series of whoops an grunts an gurgles which shurly cahn be fuckin right

121

what's fuckin wrong with the mahn . . . ah make ou' sumthun like 'fifty fuckin times in the face' but in wha context is tha? What's the fucker on abou'? It sounds twisted an undeniably fuckin sinisturr an maybe this is wha goin insane feels like, losin yer fuckin mind *ah'm* losin me fuckin mind hur so ah am . . . Ah'm needin out uv hur, fahst, but ah doan know how te go about ut. Ut ul look rude; Mickah might think ah'm a prick. An besides, ah'm not even shur that ah'll be able te fuckin move. As soon as ah move me muscles ul unclench an ah might shite meself. Oh Jesus. A dunno. Wha. Ah fuck. Ah fuck. What do I –

—Liam. Are you OK?

Ah look up an Laura's leanin t'wards me like an hur face's too big an too red. Jesus I –

Be normul be normul just do just sey sumthun fuckin normul –

—Whur's Mickah gone?

Christ was tha my voice? Ah sound liker fuckin toad so ah do. Warty. Waaaaaaaaaaaaaarrrrrrrrrtttttttttttttyyy.

—He's gone to the toilet. Do you want to go? You're as white as a sheet.

An then before av even reelised that ah'm movin ah'm up an out the front door, Laura's shoutin sumthun te Mickah an ah'm inside the cahr, me head tucked down inside me jackut, the leather cool an clingy on me face which is at a temperature too high fe human life. How can I how can I –

What the fuckin –

My mothur.

Ah feel the cahr move an kind uv get lower as sumwan gets in ut; ah know ut's Laura, but the pressure feels too big, like a buffalo ur sumthun. A buffalo in the cahr. Ah imagine lookin up an seein it thur, a bison in the driver's seat, an ah hav te fight back hysterical giggles. Ur meybe just hysteria. Jesus Jesus Jesus.

—Are you OK? What's wrong?

Me sistur.

Her legs.

Ah manage te summon a shred uv sanity from sumfuckinwhur in me fizzin, sizzlin brain. That's what's inside me skull right now, lahd in a fryin pahn: SSSSSSSSSSSSSSSSSSSS.

—Too fuckin stoned, ah manage te mumble. —Please doan talk te me, just drive now, will yis.

She does. Superskunk. Fuck tha.

The sound uv the cahr's soothin at furst, a cahm rumble like, cept when ut goes up a hill an whines like a tortured animal, an ah think ah'll be able te hould it tegethur just about, just the skunk just the skunk, Christ, so ah pull me face out uv me jackut an see in front uv me a huge fuckin lake, the moon glowin off ut, the warter like molten lead. Fie could just sit down by the warter . . . fer five minutes just . . .

—Laura, Jesus, stop the cahr will yis. Ah'v got te gerrou'.

—What, I –

—Lemme fuckin OU'!

She pulls over quick an then ah'm down thur by the lake, squattin in the reeds, me hands in the clear warter, so fuckin cold but so *clean* ut feels, pure . . . ah feel an probly look fuckin stupit but ah cuddun give a shite.

—For God's sake, Liam, what's wrong? What's up with you?

—Tha fuckin cunt Mickah. Spiked me fuckin drink with a trip ah'm shur ee fuckin did.

Cahn believe ah just sed tha. Jesus. Fuckin eejit, fuckin gobshite ah am.

—Don't be silly now. You're just a bit too stoned is all it is.

Me hahnds ur tremblin in the warter which tinkles t'rew me fingers like glass. Paht uv me wants te imagine sumthun wuth great big teeth an eyes surgin out uv the lake at me, but ah fight it back. Eyes all bulgy lifeless the size uv footballs surgin t'rew –

– teeth like fuckin –

Ah'm OK ah'm OK. Just the weed, the superskunk. Too strong. This will go away soon.

—It will pass, Liam. Laura puts her hahnd on me shouldur an ut feels awlrigh. —Sh now. Be calm. You'll be OK in a bit.

Me hahnds in the lake. Ah hope so. God ah fuckin hope so.

Ah remembur this wan time, few yurs back now (Christ the time just runnun awey like ut does), when me mate wuz up at the college in Belfast an ah went te stop up thur wuth um ferra weekend – lots n lots uv drink an drugs an ah shagged an American student who looked a little bit like yer wan from tha crap fillum *Far and Away*, wha wuz it er name wuz now . . . Kidman, aye, Nicole Kidman. Ah remembur this mot blabbin on abou' fuckin Noraid an shite an ow ur uncles donated munny to um, sed she wuz Irish cos er great granda knew sumwan oo'd wance seen a pitcher uv Cork cuntryside in a buke ur summun arsey an tenuous like tha. Fuckin Americans eh, what's wrong with um? Ah, ah suppose we all wahnt sum history, doan we? Sum kind uv legitimation . . . Annywey, this mot wuz just like: —Oh, ah jest luuurrv your awk-cent, yer know? She just wahntud te see blokes in balaclavas carryun Armalites so she did. So, uv course, ah took advantage – who fuckin wuddunt? – an gaver wan back at ur halls uv residence. The tricolour an céad míle fáilte up on er walls thur. Annywey, a remembur Ciaran, me mate, gettun stopped an surched be squaddies on the wey back te is digs wan night; they wurnt too bahd, like, Brummies ah think they wur, an they let um keep ould uv is stash. Sum fuckers wudduv confiscated it an then smoked it thur fuckin selves. An ah saw blokes in camouflage wuth big guns, a saw tanks in the streets, armoured fuckin cahrs, hellycopturs. A saw a blastud out shopfrunt with jam on the pavement outside uv ut; a saw a tattered group uv crippled Proddies on a march ('march'! Fuckin hobble more like). One uv the best fuckin weekends uv me life so ut wuz. Wha' ah duddunt see, tho, wuz men with pistols wearun ski masks; ah diddunt see um, an yet ut seems like ah remembur seein um. Ah'm shur tha av not ever seen um wuth me own eyes; but, te be shur, thur a big fuckin paht uv me life, me memmury. In tha strange?

Fuckin wine bahr's packed ou', an the noise is dead loud – shitey blues cover bahnd n all – but ah can still heer um talkin, an what's this thur goan on about now, crisps is ut? Mairead's singun the praises uv Monster Munch an Malcolm's goin:

—Well, yeh, I used ta pitch me tent firmly in tha Monster Munch camp, but I'm driftin more an more ovah ta tha Discos site now. Jast a bivouac at tha mowment like, a pup tent if ya will, but a can see that am ganner afta fink abaht rentin a marquee pretty soon.

—Oh no no no, Sioned says. —Discos? Can't *stand* the bloody things. Look like bloody blistered *skin* they do.

—Twiglets!

—Nor them either. Sioned shakes hur head an she looks rurly, genuinely disgusted. —They look like clubs for tiny cavemen.

—Thuz allus yer Bombay Mix n all, uv course, Mairead goes on. —Coupler bottles wine an uh grert big bag o' that stuff an am a happy happy lass.

An ah must sey, she does look happy. Probly the booze but. At least, she looks happiur than she did when ah sawrer urlier on tedey, cummun out uv the travel agent's shop. She diddun see me tho; a wuz behind er like, she came ou' wuth ur hood up ovurr er head an ut wasunt even raining, as if she wuz in disguise ur sumthun. Ah was goin te call out to er but ut looked like she diddun want te see annywan; goin fahst she was, dahtin inte the neerust pub. A wonder wha she was up te?

Ah drift awey, over te the bahr. Packed, so ut is; am elbowin me wey t'rew, people's sweaty fuckin breath on me face. Has ut's advantages, tho, this place, when ut's heevun like this; brushun yer arms across tits, rubbin yer mickey across ahrses. Laura's awey at er mammy's, so me eyes ur roevun, not tha ah'd ever do annythun abou' ut; ah'm stayin faithful so ah am. Thur ah sum oo'd shag annythun, but not me; ah'm not like tha so. An ah love Laura.

Colm's at the bahr havvun a bit uv a blether wuth sum wee fresh-faced student gurly. Ee's leanun over ur like a predatory burd:

—No, believe me, shuz sayin, —a know cos am a marine biologist.

Colm's grin widens. —Oh, yer ar, ar yer? Ar yer sure yer not just doin a marine biology option in the second year uv yer environmental science course then?

The gurly gets embarrassed an ah laugh te meself, but's rurly up te the mot, innit? She wahnts te call erself a marine biologist, then let ur. So wha? Not doon anny hahm te annywan, shur ut's not.

Unlike tha annoyun fuckin gobshite Mags is talkun te. The Cackler, Malcolm calls um, is reel name's Ian ah think. Ut's a good name tho, tha, the Cackler, cos ee *is* – like a fuckin donkey so, an ee does it all a fuckin time so ut's becum, like, is definin characteristic. An ut's so obviously fuckin fake, rurly fuckin annoyun, grates on me fuckin bones. Prick tha he is. Ah know tha we all need a badge, yer know, sum kind uv noticeable pursonality trait peculiar te ahselves in order te, like, convince ahselves uv ar own individuality, but ut doesunt make ut anny less annoyun. Ee cackles in Mags's eer an she gives us a look, like: rescue me, yer fucker, but ah just grin an shake me ed. Yer on yer own hur, Maggie; ah wuddun speak te that fucker if ye paid me.

Thur's Roger, wuth two uv is psycho mates, Llŷr an Ikey. Thur all slouched over in the cornur, scowlin at evrywan, aggression cummun off um in waves. Roger gives us a lazy, knackered-toothed grin. Is teeth ur fuckin awful, an ee's got a big white scar on is lip ah doan know what from which makes im stur ev'ry now an agen an say: —What-a fuck uh *yew* fuckin lookin at? He's been gettun back inte the skag recently, more fuckin fool im; he'd knocked it on the head ferra bit thur but ah know Roger – ee's the kind uv eejit oo'l always go back te the stuff. *Needs* ut so ee does. Least ut keeps um quiet, unless ee's ahftur a fix. Ah hope, ah do rurly, tha wan dey ee'l jack ut in fer ever, but ah doubt he evurr will. Addiction's a fuckin terruble thing. Rurly; ut's a cliché, ah know, but ah reckun most people doan reelise how truly fuckin terruble ut is.

Ah get me pint an sip ut, lookin round. A seer face ah reckunise.

—Howyeh, Dewi, Cerys ad the babby yet?

Dewi grins. —Yesterday, mate. Near didn fuckin make it; ad it in the car she did, on the way ter Bronglais.

—Oh Jaysus. Evrythun OK now tho?

—Ah yeh, theh both doin great guns. Little girl. Fiesta.

Ee's glowun wuth happiness, knockun back the vodka.

—Fiesta? Cos uv the cahr she wuz born in?

—Nah, mate, cos uv the fuckin wank mag tha inspired er conception.

He slaps me on the back an squeezes pahst te the bahr.

Ah see Phil, the skinny dealer oo looks consumptive go up te Roger an Llŷr an Ikey, probly tryun te flog um sum geer ur summun. Ee'd best fuckin watch umself unless ut's a beatun ee's ahftur. If Roger's not smacked up (and, bein in hur, ee's probly not), then Phil's in danger; if ee's got geer an Roger's got no munny, then . . .

Ah take me pint back t'rew the bah, see Paulie laughun like a mad fucker wuth Roy an Mark an Iestyn. Thur all out tenight, eh? Giro dey fe sum o' thum. Evrywan laughun, drinkun . . . even Margaret thur, oo's now got rid uv tha cacklin cunt (no easy thing te do, im being such a fuckin clingy limpet fucker); even she seems happiurr tenight. Fuckin long face on ur normully unless shuz speedin ur sumthun which ah reckun she probly is now, lookit, rantin sum nonsense te Allen. Laura reckuns thur's sumthun goin on between Margaret an Colm, but ah'm not so shur. Thur may be, ah mean ah cahn sey fe certun like, but . . .

So fuckin wha, annywey?

Ah pass Colm agen. Ee's now whisp'run sumthun in the gurl's eer, which is makin hur laugh. Definitely flurtin. Bu', agen, so wha? Is ut not up te him wha ee does? Liven let fuckin live ah sey. If ah'm in a good mood. Ah feel sorry fe Mairead tho, too fuckin right ah do; shuz gentle, kind, she doesunt desurve the shite she gets. Which is the wey in this fuckin wurld, ah suppose. Kindness is seen as weakness an people will prey on that. Christ, what a fuckin life.

When ah go back inte the lowurr room, ah hurr Mairead sey:
—Nor, nor, t' Jacob's Club.
—A crap biscuit! Sioned yells, drunk now an animated. Shuz tiny, Sioned, but she can drink like a fuckin fish; she puts ut awey be the gallon. Hollow legs, must be. —Booooooorring! If thir was awards for dull biscuits, the Jacob's Club ud win. Hands bloody down. Al go for me faverrit a reckon, the Penguin.
—Ick, Malcolm goes. —Only twatheads eat Penguins.
Oh fe fuck's sake. This is gettin borrun so ut is.

Ah lean back agenst the wall an drink me pint an that's when ah see ut, the ghost, the ghost uv tha kid ah went te skule wuth who was blown te bits in Armagh. Pádraig Bíog we used te call um cos is name was Patrick an ee was fat as fuck, yer know, sarcastic like, 'bíog' meanun 'tiny' in the Gaelic. Ee lost loads uv weight ahftur leavin the skule an the lahst ah hurd uv im ee'd been blown up, purr bastard. Anothur innocent dead – just a civilian, ee wuz. But ee's hur, now, in this fuckin wine bahr, lookin healthy and, ut must be said, a bit fat agen, hur in the wine bahr, drinkun Guinness an havvun a crack wuth is mates. Ah wonder if thur all dead as well? They look pale enough . . . Meybes ah should go ovurr thur an av a few wurds; ey, Paddy, what's ut like then, the othurr wurld? What wuz ut like te be blown apart? An ar yis glad te be back at all?

Little Paddy says sumthun te is ghost mates, ah cahn heer wha, an they all crack up laughun. Ah, djer see tha now? Even ghosts can av a good time. Ah. Thur's a fuckin lesson te be lurnt thur so thur fuckin is.

. . . ah wish Laura was hur. Ah'm so fuckin bored.

The pahty took a turn fe the wurse when tha crowd uv cunty fuckin students came in ahl wurrin togas, so wis all came up hur te this attic room, but not afore Roger gave wan uv um a dig in the jaw an Colm purred red wine ahl over wan when ee tried te chat up Mairead. Thur probly phonun the fuckin peelers right now, bunch uv fuckin tossers tha thee ar. Tha fuckin Sharon's around sumwhur as well, tryun te tap Mairead fe murr munny no fuckin doubt; ye can alweys tell when Sharon's hangun around leeching cos ye can hur Colm fuckin grindun is teeth tegethur. Cahnt sey as ah blame um, eithur, rurly; shuz a twat n a hahf tha Sharon wan. Ow Mairead hasunt gobbed er wan yet ah doan know. Too fuckin nice so she is. Too daycent.

But, well, shur ut's nice up hur. Ut looks sort uv set up, like, fur a fillum ur sumthun; Mairead an Sioned singun 'Bunch of Thyme', the rest uv us sittun around um, lissnun, lookun. Malcolm's concentratun hahd on choppun up powdurr on a CD case (Meatloaf, ah notuce; best fuckin use fer ut so); Colm's sittun cross-legged, head bowed, chain-smokun, noddun on diazepam ahfturr a four-day speed binge; Paul's strummun alohng on tha guitah ee nicked from the bedroom down the sturrs. Ut's nice hur, it is; wur all cut off, isolated; safe.

Margaret opens up a new bottle uv stolun wine; Colm n Malcolm filled a bin-bag full uv booze from the kitchen te bring up hur wuth us. Good plannun tha.

> All yooooooooo whoor blooo-ming in yur prime
> Hall-waaays be-ware-hare, to keep yur gar-din fair-air,
> Let nooooo-one steal uh-way yur thyme.

Thur fuckin beautiful, the pair uv um, fuckin gorgeous so thee ar. Thur voices ur soarun like burds t'rew the smoky room.

The whizz kicks in quickly an me scalp starts te tingle.

Laura sets abou' openun sum murr wine.

TWANG! A string breaks an evrywan laughs. Thul survive, ah'm thinkun, ahl uv um, evry lahst wan, thur ahl fuckin survivors, yis can see ut in thur eyes, even yur mahn Roger thur, noddin out in the cornurr wuth is jeans caked in boak; even im, yeh, too fuckin right, even he has 'survivor' written ahl fuckin ovurr im.

What was tha ah wis lookun fur the othurr dey now, ah think ut was flunkies; annyway, wha evurr the fuck it wuz, while ah wuz lookun ah found me rosary beads, in the drawer, beneath me rolled-up socks. Thur they wur. Haddun even thought abou' thum fur . . . too fuckin long. An, God fegive me, ah saw thum an ahl ah could think uv fur a moment wuz those lovebeads tha the fat gurl pushed up the Chinese gurl's arse in tha porn film o' Paulie's which we found an watched lahst week. Hiddun behind the wardrobe ut was; Malcolm found ut. Doan ask me wha ee wuz doon behind the press in the furst fuckin place, cos ah doan fuckin know likes.

But, God . . . me rosary beads.

Ah sit on the edge uv me bed with a hahd-on an thread me beads t'rew the fingurs uv me right hand.

Fuck. May God fegive me. Me rosary beads.

Ach, ah'm fuckin well sick uv this, these fuckers ulweys fuckin cahllun me naive an idealistic, ah've hud just abou' fuckin enough uv ut so. People sey ut offun enough an ut becomes like a bahdge, a definun characteristic, like ye know: Oh Liam? The idealistic Irishman? Pisses me off so ut does. Specially tha fuckin Malcolm wahn; if ah evurr refuse to agree wuth is fuckin end-uv-the-wurld apocalypse shite then, accordun te tha twat, ah'm naive. An not only tha but judgementul, as well; ee tilts is fuckin ed back all snooty likes an passes judgemunt on me fe bein judgementul. Whuz the fuckin sense in tha, ey? An, annywey, ah'm fuckin none o' those things; all ut is is tha ah'm more hopeful than most fuckers. Ah doan bulieve, as most do, tha things ur irredeemably bleak.

Annywey. Fuck ut. Ut's VE dey, an the papurrs an the telly ur full uv ut, full uv oul black-n-white, grainy footage uv explosions an aeroplanes an shots uv othurr, oldurr remembrance Dey parades, oul codgers wurrin berets an medulls an gettin ouldurr an ouldurr wuth each wan. This is ohn the telly in Colm's an Mairead's gaff, tho thuv got the sound turrned down an ur playun some mad techno stuff, which is, rurly, a fittun soundtrack, ahl booms an electronic fury. Colm looks up a' me un Laura as we go in, is eyes red an hevvy; ulready ahf pissed be the looks.

—Yis awlrigh'?

—Yeh, ee says, soundun annythun but. —Been onner bevvy fer weeks, man.

Mairead mutturs: —Too fuckin right tha has, an Colm snaps at hur te shut the fuck up. Oh shite, ah think; ut's gunner be wahn uv those fuckin nights.

Ah goan put me beer in the fridge, which is empty apaht frum a bottle uv Martini an a pint o' milk an some mouldy stuff on a plate. Ah pour a Martini fe Laura an take ut back inte the front room, which is full uv bukes, an smells uv pot smoke an a whiff from the cage uv Colm's rat, Plague. Nevurr gets cleaned, tha purr wee fucker; livun in uts own shite so.

Colm's sayun: —It muster seemed like thee ender the fuckin werld. A mean, imagine i', God, the blitz, the atom bombs, the Holocaust . . . fuck, it *was* the end uv the werld; it was a catastrophe from which will never fully recuvver. Thee end uv fuckin histery, thee end uv fuckin evrythin.

—Yer fuck, ah sey, sittun down on the flurr. Tha kind o' talk pisses me off; ah mean, look a' me purr sisturr: even she's recovurrd, in a wey – shur an shiz still alive, in she now? Ur even tha mate uv Roger's, oul Bill . . . Ah doan sey this te Colm, tho; in the mood ee's in, tha would just lead inte a debate on the meruts uv euthanasia urr sumthun. Instead ah sey: —Shur, diddun me oul granda recovurr, ey, an ee was in the thick uv ut. In the desert, in Africurr.

Colm goes: —Yeh, so did mine. Both uv um; one was caught twice byer Nazis in Crete an escaped both times, anee other was oner the ferst tuh liberate one uv the concentration camps. Doan know which one tho. Never yuced ter talk abahr it unless ee was drunk. Anna doan fuckin mean tha, ennyway, am not talkin on a personul level, a mean as a species, as a race. The Nazis an wha they did effectively ended fer ever any fuckin faith at all in the perfectability of humanity. Yer just too naive ter realise tha.

—Ah now Jaysis, doan *you* fuckin staht off!

—Christ am only fuckin messin, Jesus, keep yer fuckin wig on. An ah know ah shouldun sey this, likes, shouldun get personul if ye mean ut, but ah cahn help ut. Ut was tha fuckin crack agen abou' beun naive. Colm can take a raggin, annywey.

—*Me* wuth a wig! Ah say. —*Me!* Shur, that's wha *yur* gunner fuckin need uf anny fuckin murr falls out yer head.

Ee just says: —Roar, all deadpan like.

—Yull be a fuckin egg-ed afurr yur thurty so ye wull. Gleamun cue ball. Avtur stey uwey from the tables in the pubs case sum wahn tries te pot yur head.

—Bellow.

Ee looks pissed off. Is eyes all hooded ovurr.

Mairead rolls a spliff on the scabby coffee table. Thur's some cans an a nurly empty bottle uv Bushmills on ut; they probubly arsed the whole fuckin lot between um in the pahst owurr ur so. Ah tell Colm, just te make conversation like, abou' the lahst time ah was ovurr in Donegal, when ah tolt me da abou' Colm beun born with a caul on is ed.

—An ee says te go ovurr wuth me next time so yis can bring um luck on is fishin trips. All the fishurrmen try an av sumwahn like yeself wurrkun wuth um on the boats.

Colm just nods. —Yeh, am sepposed ter be safe from drownin or some such shite. Accordin ter me nan, ennyway. Ee takes a big gulp uv is drink. —Av never drowned yet, tho, so a seppose ther must be some fuckin truth in it.

Then ee downs the rest uv is drink in wahn, as if te make some sort uv point, but ah'm fucked if ah know wha. Ee probubly doesunt know imself. Oo knows wha goes t'rew tha fucker's head, ur annybody's, fe tha mattur; shur, ahn we ahl fuckin mysteries?

Colm knocks back a glass o' whiskey an Mairead mumbles sumthun which ah doan heeurr to im an then springs up off the couch an walks quickly out uv the room. Colm yells at hur back an then pulls a pot uv milk from undurr the table, wahn o' those placcy two-pint jobs likes, an hurrls ut across the room, in Mairead's direction. Ut burrsts on the wall an milk sprays evrywhurr; the books, cahput, the rat. Some uv ut dribbles down the wrinkled face uv un oul soljurr on the TV screen, an some uv ut splashes inte Laura's hurr.

—Oh for God's sake!

—Sorry, mutturs Colm. —A didn mean ter splash yer. A was aimin fer that fuckin arsehole ther.

Mairead comes back inte the room with a glass uv Martini, big spliff in hur gob. Colm looks at hur like ee's abou' te fuckin put is glass in hur face ur sumthun.

Ah wave me ahms an stahnd up. —Look, Jaysis, fuck all this nonsense, all this shite. Ah thought we wur goun ou' somewhurr.

We do. Laura whispurrs te me tha ut might be a bettur ideurr just te go home, but ah shake me head. Colm just needs te cahm down a bit, that's ahl; ee's got tha look ee gets sometimes, the rurly wired look like ee's been off is face fe days an Mairead's probubly gottun a bit wound up wuth ut ahl an ut ul ahl cahm down soon, afturr a few murr bevvies in the pub. Ut'll ahl sort utself out.

Outside the flat, on the road, me n Laura fahl behind, an let Colm an Mair walk ahead uv us. Evry now an agen ah see im give hur a shove, in the shouldurr like, but she just ignores him an carries on walkun, ahms folded across hur chest totully unruffled. Ah, she can be a cool wan, tha Mairead. They keep this up ahl the wey across town te the wine bahr, an not fe the furst time ah have te admire Mairead's endurance, an have te wondurr agen at why she puts up wuth so much shite from Colm. She must see sumthun in im that *ah* certunly don't. Oh yeh, ee can be great crack so ee can, but te live wuth um? Fuckin nightmurr that would be. Ach, ah suppose ut's a recipe fe disasturr, the whole fuckin thing – two pisshead fuck-ups togethurr.

When we reach the wine bahr, Colm's ulready sittun in the yahd wuth Iestyn, both uv um watchun a wee kitty lap spilt beer up off the table.

—Look at this yer, Iestyn says. —Little babby alky cat. Hellish cute, innay?

Ah bend down an go: —PSSSSSSSTT! in the cat's eeurr an it runs uway. Laura cahn stahnd cats, an nor can I; bloodthursy little fuckers so. Ut's thur nature, ah know, but thur so fuckin indiscriminate in wha they torture an kill.

—Oh yer fuckin twat, Colm goes. Ee loves cats; now *thur's* a big surprise, ey?—What the fuck jer goan do that for?

Ah ignore im. —Whuz Mairead?

Ee shrugs. —Fuck knows. Doan giver shit either.

—Shiz gone t'a bar Liam, Iestyn says, an ah ask im if ee's plannun on havun anothurr pahty soon.

—*Christ*, no, ee says. —Am still scrubbin the blood an puke outer the walls from-a *last* one.

Ah go inside, get drinks, an bring um back out te the table. Ah'm feelun cahm tonight; cahm, an quiet, an awlrigh'. An maybe that's what's needud hurr, te prevent Colm from flyun off the handle like which ee's threatenun at anny fuckin minute te do, the fuckin eyes on the basturd, sumthun fuckin wrong with tha boy so, ah'm tellun ye. Ee just ignores Mairead an she does the same te him as they both get murr n murr pissed, rat-ahsed, ah can hahdly understahnd a wurd eithurr uv um ur sayun, but later on, when wurr headun back te mine ah see tha thur holdun hands.

Ah nudge Laura. —Lookit.

She just nods.

—Wha the fuck's up wuth *yur* gob, then?

She scowls an shakes hur head. —Nothing, Liam. Just leave it, OK?

Christ. If ut's not wahn thing ut's anothurr. Angurr rises up in me chest but ah bite ut back. No fuckin point. Still an ahl tho, why the fuck cahn she just let ut go? So Colm an Mairead have a row; thuv made ut up now, havunt they? Jesus . . . Ah let go uv Laura's hand. She says nothun.

Up ahead, Colm's stopped te speak te a beggar, ye know, tatty blond mohican an a skinny dog on a rope. Ee's a new wahn, ah havunt seen is face afore; but thur's murr n murr uv um evry fuckin day. Colm gives im a coin.

—Twenny pee fer the lad, Liam?, ee slurs.

Ah shake me head. —Ah'm skint so.

We walk off an furthurr on Colm turns round te speak te me, a snarl on is lips. Oh yeh, ah think, hur we fuckin go; ah can see wha ee's gunner say from a fuckin mile off.

—Yer tight-arsed fuckin twat. Why unt yer give the poor bastard a coin? Poor fucker's got no owce.

133

—Shur, ah say, —ee'l only go an spend it on the drink.

—Yeh, so? Why's tha so fuckin bad? That's wharree wants, Christ, ennythin ter make is miserable existence a little bit berrer. Ee's go' nowher ter fuckin sleep ternight. In *this* weather.

—Ah'm shur ee'l find space in wahn uv the squats.

Colm just shakes is ed an turns uwey. Ah doan say annythun murr. Colm's got is Mr Righteous hat ohn, an ah refuse te get inte an argument wuth um over this. Bottom line is: ah will not help te accelerate annywahn's premature death. Shur, if ah knew tha beggar was goin te spend the munny on food, shur ah'd slip im a fuckin fivurr; but ee won't, ee'l spend ut ohn cans uv Special Brew te drink in the fuckin street. Ah won't force annywahn te do what ah won't do meself. Shur ah fuckin won't.

Back at the flat, an Laura slinks off wurdlessly te bed. No surprises thur like, so ah crack opun tha bottle uv Irish Cream ah've had stashed in the press fe ages.

—Enny potch left, Liam?

—Nah, Colm, ut's ahl gohn. Shur, diddun we finish the lahst drop uv ut at Iestyn's pahty?

—Aye burrah fuckin know you, tho, yuv probly gor another four fuckin bottles idden away somewher.

—Ah, shut ye gob an get this down ye fuckin t'roat.

We drink an Mairead builds a spliff. Colm doesunt smoke weed, so ah end up just talkun an smokun wuth Mair, mainly abou' VE day an ahl tha. Shuz ravin ohn abou' ahl the signal fires that av been lit on the surroundun mountain peaks; if ye stahnd in the middle uv Aberystwyth, ye can see ahl the peaks around the town ahl lit up. At this time they look like flames in the sky, cos uv the dahkness likes. Mairead thinks this is ace, fe some reasun, but ut seems te me tha the intention's the same as the buildun uv tha column on the top uv Pen Dinas – te make us ahl rememburr war. So then war becomes a constunt paht uv owurr lives, which results in ut beun unstoppable. An whur's the fuckin sense in tha?

Ah lissun te Mairead talk an she lissuns te me an then ah'm as stoned as a basturd.

—Ey. Whur's Colm gone tuh?

We get up te goan find im an fuck me ut's difficult te stahnd, me legs ur fuckin jelly. We find Colm in the kitchen, just stahndun thur lookun out the window at the bonfire on top uv Constitution Hill. Size uv a matchflame from this distance, among the stahs. Flickering orange flames in the black night sky.

—Looker tha.

We stand thur, the three uv us, ahl slightly swayun, squintin ou' at the wee red flicker in the big, black night. A phrase comes inte me head, ah doan know why likes, just ahl uv a suddun ut's thur: War Wounds.

Ah'm fucked. Drunk an stoned as a cunt so ah am. Sleep well tonight ah will.

—Yeh, me n all, Colm says, an ah reelise with a jolt that ah'd spoken out loud. Christ. —I yavvun slept since fuckin . . . wha, Wednesday? Colm turns te Mairead fe confirmation but she just shrugs. —Al sleep liker fuckin babby ternight; wake up evry two owers ter cry an shit meself.

Colm smiles at is own joke an flops agenst Mairead.

—Am fuckin blitzed.

—Aye, meen all, says Mairead, dead quiet.

Ah don't rememburr them leavun, nor do ah rememburr goun te bed, but ah meet Mairead in the boozurr the next morn an shuz got bruises all up hur ahms and, she says, down hur legs. Apparently, on the way home, Colm kept collapsun agenst hur an forcin hur, accidentully like, inte walls an cahrs. Hurr ahms ur ahl spotted black, like a leopard's. An hur legs, she says. See? War Wounds. Ah told yis.

—AH YIS FUCKEN STUPIT GET!

Afore ah can stop meself, ah've chucked the peppurpot at Laura, ahd as ah fuckin can; ut smacks inte the back uv hur leg – PLAK! – an she scahpurrs out inte the bathroom. Ah can heeurr hur cryun.

Stupit fuckin cow tho. Fucken asked fe tha', so she fuckin did. Ah've told hur befurr; annybody its me an ah'l fucken well dig um back, mahn, wummun, young, oul, annyfuckinbody. Took enough o' that fuckin shite off me mam. No murr.

Ah retrieve the peppurpot an replace ut on the table. Table's ahl set; cutlery, bowl uv good grass, bottles uv wine. Ah sit thur ferrah bit an drink a glass uv red an then ah goan knock on the bog durr.

—Laura, ah sey, softly likes. —C'mohn, now, come back ou'. Ye cahn sit in thur ahl night. Geraint ul be hurr soon annywey. Ee's come all the wey from Florida te see us.

—Go away.

—Ah, come ohn, now. Ye shouldunt uv hit me furst. Ye know tha'. Come on ou', now, let's av a glass uv wine.

She flushes the chain an carries on cryun.

—Ah ye cummun out?

No answer.

—Laura?

Silence.

—Ah, well, fuck yis then.

Ah punch the durr an walk uwey. Bollox to hur, me an Geraint ul get wrecked on owurr own; she can stey in thur ahl fuckin night if she wahnts te. Fuck hur. Ah'l boot the fuckin durr down if ah need a piss, so ah will.

Ah look in the oven te see how the food's doin. Ut's grand.

From the top uv the mountain ye can see fe miles an miles, see othurr peaks fahr, fahr uwey in the distunce, breakun t'rew the mist. See the wee town below, wee clusturr uv white cottages an churches, the hillsides runnun down te ut ahl covurrd in the wet sphagnum moss stuff tha ah used te gathurr when ah lived heeurr, in bags te sell. Made fair munny doin tha so ah did; people buy ut fe thur gahduns, thur hangun baskuts an ahl tha kind uv shite. This wis ages ago like, but still now, as ah look at ut, ah find meself estimatun ow manny bags wurth thur ah in each patch, an ow much theed fetch. Assessun these hillsides in monetary turms. Which is fuckin stupit, so ah stop ut.

—Is that thuh roof uv thuh barn wir stayin in?

Paul points down inte the valley, the village. Ah squint along his fingurr.

—Ah think so . . . yeh, cos thur's the othurr bahn next to ut, see?

Ah ulways rememburr tha, the two bahn rooves next to each othurr, the landmahk ah used te look fe whenevurr ah climbed these hills. All the green mountains, the whitewashed houses, the smoke currlun up from the chimneys . . . could be a Donegal Gaeltacht.

But's not quaint, tho, ur attractive in an idyllic-rural-settin kind uv sense, al tell ye tha'; live hur ferrah while, an yull soon see wha' goes ohn. Things yud nevurr fucken believe.

—What does Mickah keep in thuh othuh barn? Djer know?

Ah shrug. —Load uv oul junk. Fucked ou' fahm implements an stuff. Not much.

Ah mean, as if ah'm gunner tell this bunch uv wasturrs tha the bahn's full uv homegrown hybrid superskunk; d'ye think it ud still be thurr at temorrow's sunrise? Tha fib te Paul, tho, abou' the junk, was a big mistake; ah should uv minded is fucken jackdaw habits, his fuckin tendencies te hoard – the garage up at Llys Wen's fuckin overflowun wuth junk so ut is, axles, sideboards, presses, mattresses, rabbut hutches, axes, spades, all kinds uv shite an useless stuff. Burrstun at the fuckin seams like.

Is eyes av lit up.

—D'yuh think a could just –

—No way, ah sey. —Feget ut. Ut's locked ulways annyway, an uf Mickah's not takun the keys wuth him, then ee's hiddun um somewhur, ah doan know whurr. Somewhurr inside is house, so just fuckin feget ut now.

—Maybe just a peek through thuh windahs then? Just a little –

—Blacked out.

—Blacked out? Why, if ee only keeps bits uv junk in thir?

Oh fer fuck's sakes. —Ah doan av the furst fuckin clue wha ee keeps in thur. Ut's just a fuckin storeroom, but ut's Mickah's fuckin bahn, not yurrs, so just leave the fucker alone an keep ye nose out.

The fuckin grin on im.

—Ah mean ut, Paul. Uf that's interfered wuth in anny way –

Then somewahn – Malcolm, ah think – yells from furthurr down the path:

—Ow my good fuckin God! The horrah, the horrah! I fink am goin ta be sick!

Ahl the othurrs – Mal, Colm, Mairead, Laura, Sioned – ur all gawpun at sumthun down in the ditch which bordurrs the field, an ah can see this big flock o' flappun black burds wheelun abou', screechin. Ah light up a spliff an go down te see wha ahl the fuss's about, thinkun uv Mickah's superskunk an the reasuns why ah doan want the othurrs te find out about ut. Te tell the truth, ah doan think ut's so much wurryun abou' thum raidun the bahn as ut is wurry abou' meself beun tempted te smoke some wuth um, an wha might happun if ah do. Ut's evil fuckin stuff so ut is, feget fuckin acid ur 'shrooms; tha fuckin weed's the fuckin elevaturr te hell.

Malcolm's face is ahl kind uv animated; equal measures uv intrigue an disgust. —Brice yaself, Liam, ee goes. —This is fuckin hideous.

Ah look inte the ditch. Thur's a sheep in thur, uts front legs rotted uway te ragged, black stumps, draggun utself t'rew the mud an shite. Wan uv uts eyes, as well, as gohn, leavun a leaky an mushy sockut, an uts fleece's caked an matted wuth ahl kinds uv crap an muck. Purr wee basturd.

—Footrot.

—Yeh, an oner those fuckin berds as ad it away with one uv its eyes. A sawrit peck irrout. Colm's face is ashen, is eyes ahl wide.

—. . . fink am goin ta fuckin vom . . .

—It's the Captain Ahab uv sheep.

Sioned's gohn greenish, Colm n Malcolm ur coverun thur gobs wuth thur hahnds, eyes like fucken tennis bahls. They look like thur in awe. The main thing ah notuce, tho, abou' the sheep, is tha', despite evrythun, ut's still gettun on wuth uts life; stumpun alohng, chewun dock leaves an wartercress in the muddy ditch. Uts front legs av mostly gohn an ut's ohnly got wahn eye, but ut's still just doin uts sheepy things, ye know, chewun the cud, doun wha' sheep do. Ut even baas up at us in a slightly pissed off way. Ah cahn elp but admirre the wee fucker. Malcolm, tho, wuth is end-uv-the-fuckin-wurld shite, doesunt see ut in tha way:

—Ya know wha this is, down't ya? It's tha angel of death. We ah lookin et the first fuckin herald ov tha cammin apoca-lypse.

—Yeh, fer you, Colm says. —It's come ere specificly fer *you*, cos of its mate's skull yuv gorron yer bedroom windersill. Ad fuckin leg it if I was you.

Malcolm goes ohn, as ee fuckin usually does: —We will be ashered inta the next world by a rotten, one-oid, shit-ciked sheep. Jast fuckin reward fa a useless, wasted, drug-addled life.

This gets a laugh, but ut's a thing wurth thinkun abou' seriously, rurly. Ye know, ahl tha stuff abou' punishmunt an reward. Not now, tho.

—Well, if that's fe me, wha will come fe yer mahn Roger?

—Me mind's not capable.

—Nowt as horrific as wha ee can cornjure up f'isself, Mairead says.

Sioned: —Or what he's *made* of himself.

Roger, uv course, isunt heeurr, othurrwise they wouldunt be talkin about im like this. Ah did try te find him te invite him wuth us like, but ee's nowhurr te be found, ee's fucken disappeared. Ah hurd vague rumours about im beeun spotted in Aberystwyth somewhurr, but ah could nevurr find im fe meself. Ah'm awurr that ee's gettun bad on the smack agen, but ah've an awful feelun that ee's rurly fuckin flipped ou' this time, rurly lost the fuckin head. Last time ah saw im was about a month ago ah think, at some pahty likes, is face black an blue, eyes like fuckin piss'oles in durty snow. Ah offurrd im some acid, as ah recahl, just mild stuff like, Purple Ohms, an he refused, which ah thought was a wee bit odd. Ah'd ulweys ad Roger down as a ten-tabs-a-day mahn. Annyway.

Colm, up on some stupit fuckin concoction, goes off inte wahn uv is rants, stahndun on an outcrop uv rock, is ahms flung wide.

—A mean just fuckin look a' all dis! Look arrih! Look ow far yer can see, an wha' does it fuckin tell yer, ey? Wha does it fuckin scream in yer eer like a bad fuckin dream, like the fuckin roar in yer ed when someone's just twatted yer?

Ee points te the sheep. Like some demented preachermahn ee is, which is probubly intentionul.

—Look arrih, just fuckin look arrih. Oo made tha? Tha unfor-tunate an vile scrap uv life? Wha kind uv twisted fuckin brain, wha fuckin demons' dreaming, wha fuckin fevered nightmer . . . wha warped an mental . . .

Mairead goes: —Colm? If yer dorn't mahnd an even if yer do, shut up.

Fuckin Colm an Malcolm an thur endtime nonsense. The wurld ul go ohn, like ut ulweys fuckin has; if they havunt lurnt tha yet then they nevurr fuckin will.

We start walkun off up the track, furthurr inte the hills. Colm is behind me somewhurr, ramblun ohn te anny wahn who'll lissun:

—A wen out with this gerl once oo ad a vibrator. She never cleaned it or any'in, an then wen she was changin the batteries an ad ter take the screwy bottom bi' off like, ther was all these little white werms wrigglin round inside . . .

T'rew ponds an trees an mist we go, ahl uv us lookun like mad basturds, mud on owurr faces an clothes an twigs an grass an stuff in owurr hur. Like wild men uv the mountains.

—. . . an a thought ter meself: wha' kind uv God makes a werld in which ther ar such things as both tigers an wermy dildos? Wha kind uv werld is i' which can contain eagles soarin across the sky an vibraters fuller maggots? A mean . . .

Sioned makes a disgusted sound. —Yew've *rrruined* dildos for me, yew av, Colm, *rrruined*.

Spliffs get passed round, dabs uv whizz, mild trips, bags uv dried 'shrooms. Mairead swigs constuntly at a hipflahsk full uv, ah dunno, vodka probubly. Loves vodka, Mairead does. Loves annythun slong as ut's alcoholic. Ah panic ferra momunt, thinkun wuv lohst wan, but then ah rememburr tha' Margaret didunt come wuth us; shiz gohn off te Sheffield ur somewhurr. At the top uv the mountain we 'ooh' an 'ah' ovurr the view ferra bit then tern an walk back down, me lookun down at the oul peeler station whurr ah used te live. From this height an angle ah can see right down inte the yahd, the prisonurr's exurcise yahd likes, an ah recahl the strange sensation uv goun inte a cell an beun able te go out uv ut whenevurr ah wantud te. Just wahkun in an beun free te leave whenevurr ah felt like ut . . . openun an closun the big steel durr meself . . . puttun posturrs up on the wahls. Drinkun in thurr, smokun spliffs, playun loud music . . . Jaysis, strange things in this life, this wurrld, shur enough.

Wahkun back inte the village an wurr ahl bellowun:

> And on that wing thir was a feather
> A rerr feather, a rattlin feather
> An a feather on a wing
> An a wing on a bird
> An a bird in a nest
> An a nest on a leaf
> An a leaf on a twig

An a twig on a branch
An a branch on a limb
An a limb on a tree
An a tree in a hole
An a hole in the bog
An the bog down in the valley O!

Big breath an then, dead fuckin loud, owurr voices ringun in the mist an the mountains:

Roll, roll! The rattlin bog,
The bog down in the valley O!
Roll, roll! The rattlin bog,
The bog down in the valley O!

Then silence ferra bit an Mairead's littul voice goes:

On that feather there were a louse –

An evrybody else protests:
—Oh fer fuck's sake!
—Nor agen, nor afuckingen!
—Av had enough!
—No more!
—Me throat, me throat!

An just at tha' momunt wan uv those fuckin jets screams ovurr owurr heads, ah duck instinctively, all ye can heeurr is the rurr uv ut's engines, a horruble sound which fills the whole fuckin wurld. Ah hate those basturd machines; ye can nevurr get uway from thum, ye think yer miles uway like, beautiful fuckin scenery, lakes, forests, an then wan uv those cunts screams ovurr an makes ye fuckin shite yer kex. Does ye fuckin head in like. Course, if ah could *fly* wan, then it'd be differunt – ah'd love thum then, appreciate thum fe the remarkubble pieces uv engineerin which they undoubtedly ar. But ah carnt, so ah hate thum. Basturds.
—Fuckin hate those things.
—Yeh. Imagine bein *attacked* by one.
—Yew get used ter them livin yer, boy, Sioned goes, ahl

wurldly-wise likes. —At's all this country is ter this fuckin Government aye, one big fuckin firin range. Show off theh new toys.

Wurr ahl a bit tired an subdued when we go inte the pub in Abergynolwyn. Ahl the punturrs turn round an sturr at us, an ah reelise how we must ahl look te thum, unfamiliar faces like, like fuckin troglodytes just down from the mountain, durty skin an clothes on us, ahl uv us up ur down on some fuckin drug ur combination uv drugs. The bahmun rememburrs me, tho, so that's alrigh', an Sioned ordurrs fe evrybody in Welsh, loud enough fe the locals te heeurr.

We take owurr drinks ovurr te the fireplace, steam risin from us as if wur ahl fuckin evaporatun. Wur still attractun some funny looks tho, an even Colm sits thurr quiet an wuthdrawn. Malcolm looks fuckin shell-shocked, Sioned an Laura exude exhaustion, an Mairead's pissed as a faht. Some fuckin bunch us, eh? Ut's nice, tho, sittin heeurr, the fire cracklun, pint uv well-pulled Guinness in me fist. Tha' is, ut's nice until wan uv the local fuckin fahmer boys, halo uv white hurr an a face uv strawberry jam, comes ovurr te us an stahts givin it the gob.

—Druggies, he says, standun thurr hands on is hips. —The lot uv yer. We do not want druggies round yer. An whir is it that yer all from then?

Ah fuck. Is mates up at the bahr urr like, givin us daggers, an Sioned, tired an irritable but still bold like she ulways is, says somethun Welsh in a raised voice te this red-faced cunt. Ee looks a bit taken aback like an goes te say somethun else but Sioned talks ovurr him:

—Oh bollacks, boy, a wunt do yew the faver uv talkin to yew in yer own language cos whatever a say in any bloody language yew won't bloody lissen to anyway. And dunt yew worry, we're fuckin going; as if wid want ter stay in the same pub as un *arrrrse* hole like yerself.

Ah fuckin love this ah do, this big fuckin fahmurr lookin like a twat in front uv wee, female Sioned. But ut's certunly time te leave, cos ah can tell tha this fucker's goin te give wan uv us a dig soon; ee'l av te, rurly, te regain is self-respect. That's ow these things wurk. If Roger was heeurr, now, the pub ud be rubble awready; but the only wans oo'd be up ferra bahney would be Paul an Colm, an thurr both fucked. Ah'd fight, as well, if ah had te; Malcolm ud probubly run. Which isunt, given the circumstances, such a bahd fuckin idea.

Ah knock back me bevvy.

—C'mahn. Let's go.

—Yeh, says Colm, grinnun in this feller's beetroot face as ee walks pahst im, talkun loud so the othurr fuckers can heeurr as well. —Let's all goan get completely fuckin wrecked on loads n loads uv highly illegal an dangerous drugs. Malcolm, al swap yis some E ferrah blast uv yer smack if Paul ul give us a go on is coke. An a bagsy ferst shot on the syringe!

We to the bahn. Wurr ahl a bit down agen now like, an wance back at the bahn Laura goes up te bed, sour fuckin face on hurr agen an Mairead mixes up an enormous vodka an tonic in a casserole dish. Malcolm chops up some speed on the table top, an Colm just twitches abou', pickin things up an sniffun thum, restless an wrecked. Wur ahl quiet, not talkun much likes. Fuck ut ahl. The full moon beams in t'rew the window. Ah sit thurr sippin a whiskey an lookun at ut. Ut looks like an acne'd face.

—Av just adder fuckin orrible thought, Colm says. —That ther's a face peerin in the window, but the body's over ther on the topper the mountain so is neck's about three miles long.

Sioned heats knives on the stove fe hotties. Surprising, rurly; she doesunt usually go much fe weed.

Paul. Whur the fuck's Paul?

—Ey, Mairead, wher d'ya find the casserole dish?

—As annywan seen Paul?

—Yeh, stumblin across the yard about ten minutes agow.

—Oh no! Maybe Necky's gorrim!

—Oi! Aller yer, come un see this!

Paul's stahndun in the doorway, flush-faced an pantun. —Yul never fuckin buhlieve this! ee shouts, an me purr heart sinks. —Tha othuh barn, it's not full uv junk at all, it's full uv fuckin marijuana! Loadser thuh fuckin stuff! It's ace, it's a fuckin *fielder* the stuff!

An ee olds is hahnds out, a huge fuckin bundle uv skunk in thum.

—Look at this! Some uv it's already dried!

Uproar. Oh well.

★   ★   ★

—Bless me, Fathurr, fer ah've sinned an ut's been a lohng time since me lahst confession.

An ut has, as well; so long, in fahct, that ah cahnt even rememburr the lahst wan. Ten yurrs ago? Twelve? Ah must uv been abou' fifteen, ah suppose, back ovurr in Donegal likes . . . shur, ut was probubly somethun like drinkun urr playun wuth me mickey that ah needud te confess te. The wurrds, tho, the oul wurrds, they still come out in a rush, an this place, the atmosphurr, the gloom in the box an the priest's face t'rew the mesh an the silence . . . ut ahl feels so familiurr still. Ye cahn nevurr get uway from this. An the feurr hasunt gohn, eithurr, oh no; that's still hurr as wehl. Tha' nevurr goes uway.

—May God help you to confess your sins with true sorrow.

Strong southern Irish accent; Cork, ah think. Shur, meet an Irishmahn outside Ireland an he'll be wan uv three things; a priest, a gangsturr urr a navvy. Urr a wasturr like meself.

—And, ah, can you tell me how long ut's been, approximately, since yurr last confession?

. . . wha' can ah answurr te tha'? 'Fifteen yurrs, Fathurr'? Nah . . . Ach, wha' am ah doun hurr? Why did ah come hurr?

Without sayun anothurr wurrd ah get up an leave, out t'rew the church pahst all the hopeful an repentunt faces an out o' the big woodun durrs inte the mornun sunlight whurr ah can breathe agen: aaaaaaaaahhhhh. Fuck. The relief, as wehl; thur's anothurr thing which nevurr goes uway.

> Oh ah'm awful shift-eeeeeeee
> Ferrah mahn uv fift-eeeeeeee
> Catch me if yer cahn
> Me name is Stan
> Shur aym yurr mahn!

Grahnd. The less said abou' tha fuckin episode the betturr.

Ah go inte wan uv the prom pubs ferrah few scoops; good drop o' stout an a mornun papurr. Tha fat fucker Browntree's hurr, holdun court wuth a load uv beer bellies, ahl uv em fuckin puffed up an ohn thurr way te beun righteously rat-arsed cos thuv ahl just been te church; cleansed now, they can embahk with impunity on anothurr week uv bullyin the defenceless an beatun thurr wives. Wankers. Teday's the furst day uv all-day Sunday openun; not tha ut was evurr difficult gettun a drink on a Sunday before likes, but ut is slightly upliftun te see the archaic an restrictive licensun laws beun loosened anothurr notch. Twinty-furr-owurr drinkun just round the cornurr, eh? Tis already if ye know whurr te look. Always has been.

Thur's a bunch uv boys in the cornurr, eviduntly drinkun uway lahst night's speed n E, cummun down hevvy. Thurr faces urr bone white, thurr eyes tiny sunk in grey-black rings. Wan uv em – wee fucker in specs an woolly hat – looks like he's abou' te burrst inte teurrs at anny momunt. They look like ghosts, sittun thurr. Dead things. Wan uv em ah recognise – Llŷr ah think is name is, good mate uv Roger's like – an ee gives me a small, fucked nod an goes back te is lahgurr.

Ah feel like gettun smashed now, locked, wrecked, out uv ut, shite-faced, so ah finish me pint an walk round te Cliff Terrace te cahl at Colm's. Mairead's uway ferrah few days; hurr mamo an granda own a wee cottage in the mountains above Aberdyfi somewhurr, so shuz gohn te stop thurr ferrah bit on hurr own. A rest from Colm an stuff, ye know. Just wahnts te be on hurr own wuth a keg uv fuckin vodka probubly. Colm's a wahn so ee is. Sound bloke te get wrecked wuth, tho, if yer feelun up te ut.

Music hits me when ah'm hahf way up the road. Ah cahnt make ou' what ut is at furrst cos ut's ahl distortud likes wuth ut beun so fuckin loud, but then ah recognise the tune: 'Thirsty Dog' by yer mahn, what's is fuckin face now. Nick Cave. Apt. Ah bang fuck out uv Colm's durr. Ow can ee stahnd ut so fuckin loud?

—Ah ut's yerself, William! Ee yells when ee opuns the durr, ahl mock Oirish like. —Top o' the bloody marnin te yer, Mr Herlihy, ahnd is ut not a foine marnin! Will ye not come in ferrah drap o' the holy warter!

Ah follow im in an ee turrns the music down, thank Christ. Me fuckin eeurrs wurr beginnun te bleed thurr. Ah see empty bottles scatturrd around his bed, a bra hung ovurr the lamp (probubly deliberately placed thurr, for effect, like), fag butts wuth lipstick stains in the ashtray. Colm's flat is a mixture uv chaos an tha strict, rigid tidiness tha amphetamine obsession generates. Ah mean, lookit; the durrty t-shirt draped ovurr the purrfectly-aligned towurr uv books in the cornurr by the telly. 'S full uv stuff like tha.

—Mairead uway, is she? ah ask, knowun full well she is likes.

—Yeh, why?

—So yis urr fuckin abou'?

Ee just looks at me. —Er name's Carol, shiz fuckin ace in bed an ter get wrecked with, an shiz gone back ome ter Birming'am now, if it's enny fuckin bisness of yours. Which it isint.

Ah can tell ee's pissed off so ah try te lightun things up a wee bit.

—Did yis find hurr taint?

—Er taint? What's tha?

—Ut's the piece uv skin between hurr cunt an urr arsehole.

—That's a perineum.

—Nah, ut's hurr taint.

—Why?

—Cos ut ain't hurr cunt an ut ain't hurr arsehole.

—Oh Jesus.

Ee sits down on the couch an continues choppun speed up inte lines ohn the coffee table. Thur's a glass full uv thick, red stuff which ah take a swig uv an nurrly fuckin spew straight out agen.

—Jaysis Christ! What the fuck's tha?

—Bloody Mary.

—That's nevurr a fuckin Bloody Mary. Tastes like mouldy fuckin sturr-fry so ut fuckin does.

—That's cos uv the soy. A had no Worcester sauce so a used soy instead.

—Yer fuckin thick.

Fuckin disgustun so. Ah go an drink some warter te get rid uv the taste, an when ah go back inte the front room Colm snorts a long line uv pinkish powdurr up is nostril, gags ferrah bit an then sits back sniffun an sighun.

—Ennywey, ee says, —av been takin it easy fer the last few days so av gorrer tiger in me tank an am rairin ter fuckin go. Yer up fer it? Djer fancy a birruv drug abuse?

Ee leans close te is speedlines an calls em useless basturds.

The phone rings.

—Hello?

Ee lissuns ferrah minute, smilun, an then replaces the receivurr, shakun is head.

—Tha was Roger.

—What did ee want?

—A red-hatted emu fer is tracter or summin. A don't know, a couldun make out a blind fuckin werd ee sed.

—Av ye seen him raysuntly?

—Nah, not ferra while. Ee's usin quite hevvily agen at the mo a think. A herd ee spenter night in the cells last week, on Thursday a think it was.

—Why? Wha' did ee do?

Ee shrugs an rolls a fivurr up inte a tube. —GBH or assault or summin. So a don't suppose ee can be usin *tha* hevvily if ee ad the energy ter fill somebody in.

Ee snorts anothurr line.

—Jaysis, ah say, —wha is ut wuth Roger? Why's the mahn so fuckin violent? Fuckin psycho so ee is.

—Nah, Colm says, sniffun wetly. —All ee needs is a little birrer love.

—Ur ye usin yerself, now?

—Wha, skag? Nah. Avvun touched a toot fer, what, fuckin months now.

—Good on yis. Does yer no fuckin good tha stuff.

—A can feel lazy an fucked without the use uv drugs, djer know wharra mean?

The phone rings agen.

—Popular teday, Colm, eh?

—Yeh. A pay people ter ring me up so i' looks like evryone thinks am ace.

Ee answurrs ut, an then is face drops an is voice goes a wee bit poshurr, slowurr. Ah heeurr him arrange te pay some munny across ur somethun an then ee uts the phone down.

—Landlord.

—Wha did he want?

—Is fuckin rent is wharree wants. Oh yeh, yer can av yer fuckin rent, burrits in the form uv ahf un ouncer fuckin amphetamine now, mate.

—Ah, ye should ulways pay yer rent, ah say, but tha reminds

147

me: ah hope Laura's paid owurrs up te date. Am not urrnin at the mo likes, so she pays wha the housing benefit won't, ahfturr thurr fuckin rationed compassion. She still gets behind tho, bu' God . . . ah hate gettun behind like, ah hate beun in debt, bu' one uv the dullest fuckin things in the wurrld, rent, utility bills, poll tax, tha kind uv shite. Ah hate ut. Got ter fuckin do ut, tho; no fuckin choice. Colm, tho, ee'l be alrigh': ee'l do wha ee ulways does – ask Mairead te pay the arrears. Which she will.

We do a big line uv whizz each an crack opun some cahns uv lahgur. This is good speed, so; straight inte me bloodstream, boom boom boom, the tinglun in me face, me scalp, the detergent taste which makes me gag . . . cool, expansive, happy as fuck.

—Yis goun ter see The Selecter next week?

—Up at thee Arts Centre? Too fuckin right! 'Too Much Pressure', djer remember i'?

We spring up an do a little bouncun jig goun: —Hirrup! Hirrup! Hirrup! Hirrup!, but ah have te stop cos ah can feel me tits jigglun abou' undurr me shurrt an ah doan like ut. Ah need te lose some weight. Ah'l have te get back inte the whizz, an ah must say, the way tha lahst line's made me feel, that's not an unattractive ideeur.

Colm's eyes ur fillin is face. —Ey, Liam, wharrer we doin in the fuckin house? It's the ferst day of all-day Sunday openin, we should be in the fuckin pub ter celebrate. *Calls* ferra celebration, this does. Am thinkin lots n lots uv whizz an an all day sesh, wharrabout yerself?

Ah'm thinkin: Laura me mammy confession rent wipin the drool off me sisturr's chin blessed art thou among women long pointless days ahead this burning this burning a little house in Eglwys Fach an a pet dog but ah say te him: —The very same me mahn, an we leave the house tegethurr.

BARMAN

A GOOD NIGHT that, aye. Not bard at all.

Third lock-in this week. Cunts t'get out at arf bastard four in-a morn like when ther all pissed up an settled in, but a good night nonethefuckinless. This's the best time uv-a night, this is; standin yer in ee empty pub, all nice n clean now arfter ee bar staff uv gone, smell uv-a beer an-a fag smoke . . . The ringing in me ears. Took a fair whack n all, tidy it looks in-a till; carn f'get *that*, now, can we, boy, eh?

Ey wir all in yer t'night, that crew, ur most uv em anyway. Nirly alweys ar, like; oh aye, yer's seats in iss pub perfectly moulded to-a shapes uv eyr arses. Not that I know much about eyr arses, like, altho yer's some on-a girlies I'd like t'get t'know better, oh yes . . . ardly know anythin about em at all, in fact, despite eyr regular custom; a mean, it's just, like, ey give me money, an I give em drinks. Simple as tha; pure consumerism, like. Just another source uv income, ey ar, that's all. Oh a *like* em, aye, or some-a em, a carn deny tha; a mean, Duw, ey pey me fuckin rent, dunney? Not tha a *like* the money so much as *need* it like; am on me own now, see, missus carn work six feet under out ther in Llanbadarn, now, can she eh? The big C it was that took er; aye, gets us all in-a end like, that Cirrhosis. Fuckin killer. By-a time she was gettin treatment for it it was too bloody late – too bastard busy ter notice anythin was wrong, see? Kept seyin yer was nowt wrong with er, but a should-a known somethin was up, the blood should uv told us that. No time tho, see. No time ter notice anythin but work work fuckin work. Five years ago now, that was, or six; somethin like that anywey. The time just goes by.

That Irish feller with-a ponytail an-a hooch; oof, fuckin firewater that, boy, aye. A like a tipple-a that, I do. The mountain dew like. Is tart reminds me uv ow me missus used t'be, all ose years ago like, when she was young; fuckin gorgeous fer one thing like – ad look at er an ferget ow t'breathe – an quietly spoken, like, never seems t'swear. Bit fuckin snooty an all tho like, shiz oner them modern wimmin, y'know; a mean, yer's ow times av changed, boy, a called er 'girl' t'night when a gaver er change, y'know, like 'diolch girl', an she looked at me all cold like an tutted an sed sideways to er boyfriend: 'Am a *woman*.' A doan rirly understand em ese days – a mean, yer think shid be fuckin pleased t'be called a girl. An anyway, woman, girl, what's a fuckin diff? An it's not as if a carn tell that shiz a fuckin woman, er wither tits pressin out that tight top an er fuckin legs up toer ears! Fuckin arse on er n all, foo, Christ, am tellin yer.

Ah well.

An tha Scouse lad (like sparrows, Scousers ar; fuckin evrywhir, boy), scruffy little bastard with-a ratty hair. Always larkin, ee is, always loud, drinks like a fuckin fish (an at's not fuckin *all* ee does; av seen-a fuckin oles in is left arm, oh aye. See, eyes like-a fuckin buzzard, me – a never miss a trick). Goes out with that girlie with the grin; er ole face, no, the whole fuckin pub, lights up when she smiles, not that she does a lot uv that. Looks depressed most uv-a time like. Doan see why she feels-a need t'put all ose fuckin rings through er face, either; puts yer off, that does. An she drinks far too fuckin much – av seen er over ther, like, in-a corner by-a fruity, on er own, all dressed up like on er own, whisky after whisky after whisky. Ferra woman, like, she carn arf put the fuckin stuff away; reminds me uv me missus. Sad, like, innit? An tha other binty as well, er with the short hair an the boots, looks like a fuckin soldier like, she likes er fuckin vodka, she does. Knocks back bottles uv the stuff, am tellin yer. A think the Scouser's knockin *her* off n all; at's what ther all like now, boy, believe me, bein a barman all iss time yer see what goes on – like fuckin rabbits ey ar. Daft, rirly, a mean what with iss fuckin AIDS thing like . . . still, ad probly be doin-a same thing if I was ther age. A wish a was. Used t'stick it in anythin, me, anythin in-a skirt. Ey never wore trousers in em days, see.

Well, t'tell-a truth, a doan rirly know any more if I rirly want that age back agen. I ad fun, like, but it was a fuckin struggle . . . but a know one thing, an that's a doan fuckin like the age I yam, no fuckin way, boy, carn walk up-a bleedin stairs without puffin an blowin like the fuckin Devil's Bridge train, an not one uv the fuckin diets a go on ever seems t'make any fuckin difference to-a size-a me fuckin belly. Avunt seen me feet fer years, never mind me fuckin nudger. Someone told me once that-a most effective diet was-a no stout one, but fucks ter that bi Christ – couldn't live without me Beamish, me. An yuv got t'keep one pleasure, at least, avunt yer, eh?

Generally speakin, like, a prefer em to-a stewdents, that much must be sed. Oh yeh, ey can sometimes be as loud as the stewdents, like, but in a different way; the loud cos the enjoyin emselves, that's all, whereas the stewdents tend t'be loud cos ey think it makes em stand out in-a crowd, ey want evryone t'look at em. Which a suppose ey do, but in-a different way; a mean, yer's not many-a my fuckin customers uh pissed an singin after two pints uv fuckin Caffrey's. Butty other bunch, now, well, on occasion eyv bin in at eleven soon's av opened up an steyd in til av closed thirteen, fourteen owers later like. Ey like-a drink an-a company, that's all; a stewdents like showin off.

Not all uv em, uv course, some uv em ar perfectly alright people. An Christ, ey feed the cat an put fuckin margarine on me toast, dunney, eh? Too fuckin right ey do. Carn complain rirly. The stewdents ar fuckin good fer this town when all's sed an done, with eyr spendin. An besides, yer's not one uv em as scary as that other lad, im with-a cropped ed an-a homemade tattoos all over is fuckin hands. A bleedin eyes on im as well, am tellin yer, fuckin *mad* ey ar . . . ee scares-a fuck out uv me, a doan mind admittin it; ee's never give me any trouble, like, or not inside-a pub anyway, ee normly goes outside like t'sort things out, but yer can see it in is face tha' ee's not all there. A nutter. Ee reminds me uv those pictures yer see uv that Charles Manson twat, y'know im with-a swastika between is fuckin eyes? An ee's got fuckin arms like pincushions n all, all bruised an holey, an a remember iss one night ee just fuckin stood an stared at that stag's head up on-a wall there, at's all ee fuckin did fer owers on end like, just stood there, starin. Snot fuckin normal behaviour that, ey? Is neck must-a ached all t'fuck arfter like. Just standin there, in evry twat's way, the people all millin around im like, too bleedin scared uv im t'complain, not that a fuckin blame um. What the fuck was ee seein ther, eh? It's not even a real stag. Drugs, yer see. Oo fuckin needs um? An a mangy ole fuckin thing n all, that fuckin head is; it's only still up there cos me missus loved it. Al bin it soon like, before it falls off-a wall an brains some poor bastard.

Oo else is the now . . . ah yeh, that small girlie wither blonde hair, speaks an sings-a most beautiful Welsh yuv ever fuckin heard, boy . . . One time a taped it, secretly like, but with all-a racket in-a bar yer couldn't hear a thing. A know er name, n all – Sioned it is, Sioned Elfyn. Er ole man used t'drink in yer, an is father before im. A remember im comin in, years ago now, all pleased that is daughter (not Sioned, her older sister) was goan off t'university. Nice one, we all sed, good on yer like. An en ee comes in-a next day like, fuckin *purple* with anger, goin: 'Rrrrrrright! That's it! She's disowned! Shame on the fuckin family! No bloody daughter of mine goes off to a foreign university!'

Took me ages an several bleedin on-a-house whiskies t'calm im down. Tirned out she was leavin fer Nottingham the next morn.

Sioned goes with that tall feller with-a glasses. A loony; not like ee other feller, a mean a *nice* loony, y'know . . . fuckin Irish jigs in-a middle uv-a packed pub.

An ey all like a drink – so what? Maybe a smoke an all, but am partial to-a blow meself, boy. No arm in it, it's not proper drugs like, not ee ard stuff, it's just like, relaxing, y'know . . . Why some-a em seem t'want t'kill emselves with that other shit . . . a doan fuckin know. Baffles me, it does. What uv ey got t'be depressed about, ey? Smore fuckin opportunities fer the young ones t'day than er ever was when I was eyr age. An a bet none uv um's ever lost a wife. Eyv got, what, forty, fifty fuckin years ahead uv um? A wish I fuckin did; the things I'd do . . . Fifty fuckin years t'chuck away, down-a drain. At's just fuckin cowardice, that, if yer ask me, like; weakness it is.

Ah well. Fuck it. It's up ter them, int it? It's eyr lives, like, ey can do whatever ey fuckin want with um. An anyway, a wouldn't exactly say that eyr depressed, like, not rirly; eyr fuckin larfin most uv-a time, singin, larkin about, even tha other feller, the tall, skinny one with the cockney accent an the blond hair. Grumpy bleedin twat, ee is, sometimes; rollin is fuckin eyes like when a tell im av got t'go change-a Guinness barrel. Needs t'get isself some fuckin patience ee does, that lad.

Yer should've seen um ee other week ther, when Ireland beat Italy in-a World Cup on-a telly; av never seen so much fuckin joy. Ey were so happy ey were smashin glasses.

Av bin yer, doin iss, fer thirty bleedin years nirly, an av seen em all come an go. People drift through Aberystwyth like nowhere else on irth, believe me, an a saw a good few places when-a was in-a navy. Oh yeh. It's ee end uv-a train line, see; yer carn go any further west like. People come an people go. An ese ones ul go n all, an ther'll be others ter take eyr place, others just like um . . . An wher do ey get eyr money from, ey, at's wha I'd like t'know; ey spend a fuckin fortune in yer, an ey carn be workin . . . Best not t'arsk, rirly. An anyway, all money spends-a fuckin same dunnit, no matter where it's fuckin come from. Just got t'think uv it like that, a suppose. A doan care where ey fuckin get it from as long's ey give some uv it t'me.

Meself, a need a little bit uv somethin ter help me sleep now, usually a blow an a few whiskies. Bought some new smoke before off that Irish feller an is mate with the dog, a new type called superskunk or somethin stewpid like tha'. Darft bloody names ey come up with, eh? Ey sed it was strong stuff like, but it just looks like Chinese green tea t'me. Ope it's not too strong; makes me a bit para sometimes if it is. Get the bloody heebee-jeebies, a do. Does funny fuckin things ter me mind like aye.

Well, iss is me off t'bed. Eyl be yer inner morn, waitin on-a pavement outside fer me t'open up like. Only I doan open up t'morrer, one uv-a day staff does; am down ter Glanyrafon like t'stock up at-a cash n carry. A need some bleedin cockles, amongst other things; the Scouser an that tall bloke with-a glasses reminded me uv that t'night when ey were puttin cockles up eyr noses an snortin em back out agen. Ey picked em all up off-a floor like, an-a ones ey didn't the cat et, so er was no mess, but's still a bit fuckin disgustin like, innit. Still, it made *them* laugh. Big fuckin kids that ey ar.

Kids a never ad? Christ, mun, doan make me fuckin laugh! Oo'd want them fer children, eh?

Al just tirn-a lights off. Bed an-a smoke-a iss new gear. Tidy. New day t'morrer.

From *A Personal Guide to West Wales*, anonymous authorship, privately printed, p. 30

Freefall, in thrall, all returns to water's call: the town is sliding, subsiding into the sea. Slowly, imperceptibly slowly, but occasionally a full reclaim is achieved with catastrophic rapidity, such as the congregation which gathered in a now-gone chapel below the castle ruins sometime in the last century and which crumbled, quickly, into the waves below. Steady erosion, insidious elemental dissolution, or the combined weight of flesh and wish and worship, there could really only ever be one result – reclamation, irrevocable and total, as witnessed in those porous striations of rock which can do nothing but absorb to the point of saturation then split, and become other. Twinned with skin, the rock can be said to suffer; skin's kin, the rock can be said to suffer.

Sometimes, countries cannot choose the manner of their deaths.

Sometimes, human bones and jewellery are still found buried in the sand.

The mouth of the river will become the river; if nothing else, the wind has chiselled that into the rock.

THEY ARE SLEEPING

THEY ARE SLEEPING, or, rather, indulging in those torpid twitchings and intermittent restless writhings which, for them, pass for sleep. Dawn, and the weak sunlight which creeps through the cracks in the curtains reveals floor and furniture peppered with empty bottles and cans, crisp packets, ashtrays overflowing, smeared glasses and mugs. Here a mirror with a patina of powder and a razor blade rimmed with fine white dust, there a demolished packet of Rizlas and a ziplock bag of dried grass, scattered twists and flakes of tawny tobacco. Somewhere, a syringe, greasy fingerprints on the barrel, a tear of blood on the spike now dried to rust. A charred spoon. A ball of cotton wool, stained. The prints on these not Roger's; he, this morning, sleeps in hospital, prostrate under temazepam.

Never really meant to be what they are or where they are, they nonetheless can sometimes snatch or sometimes tease from the air a thing which will fit them and which they will wear like a crown, a thing which will allow them to possess their hours both light and dark with the confidence which lines well-rehearsed will give to a costumed actor. Some of them may sometimes think that they have donned a shadow; others may believe, however temporarily, that they both speak and hear in sunlight bounced off a breaking wave in a silver fan of scalpels. So however shallow their sleep, however short and spiky and shredded by dreamy termites, it still allows the assimilation of a controlling compulsion, a necessary mulling retirement neither long nor short enough, perfectly balanced in fact in its insufficiency since it means they will wake in hunger.

And the sunlight slides. Gently over Malcolm's head atop a flung overcoat, the skin on his face the colour and texture of raw sausage. What dreams bubble his eyelids can only be wildly guessed at; with each bleat of a sheep from the field outside, the crusted corners of his mouth twitch and a tiny groan escapes. In the shaft of sunlight which illuminates his wasted face, minute motes and pinheads of dust drift and then, silently and madly, swirl in the turbulence of his exhalations. His nostrils are fungal runnels, slightly bloodied.

Move with the sun, over the slumbering hump that is Laura, Liamless as he sleeps under a boat on a beach in Cornwall, and down the disrupted hallway where vomit dehydrates by the telephone and into the main bedroom where Paul and Sioned lie, back-to-back and entwined. The topography of the duvet mirrors in miniature the landscape outlying the house; the spurs of elbows and knees and shoulders, softly sloping uneven valley walls, the narrowing, joined point at the apex where the lower limbs are entangled. The silvery sheen of sweat on ankles touching suggests a stillness several hours long. On the ceiling above them, mould continues to spread and grow.

Drift again, out of the bedroom and down the hallway, disturbing a breakfasting bluebottle, over the coconut-hair doormat which bears the faint impression of Margaret's boots and into the satellite bedroom, where Mairead rests. Her bare arms curl out on to the pillow, her hair is a spread black fan. Her lips are slightly ajar and the morning sunlight glints off her teeth and the metal rings in her face. The rumpled duvet rises and falls gently, gently, her breathing steady and soft. Last night's alcohol has blotched her face and cracked her lips but, sleeping now and freed from those waking pressures which furrow her forehead and darken her eyes and drag her face downwards, her beauty can be discerned. Her long lashes flicker in the lingering sun.

Behind the north wall of this bedroom, in the kitchen, Colm sits at the table, staring. At irregular intervals he gulps from a glass of red wine or sucks at a cigarette but mostly he just stares. Every now and again he sings the first few words of a song and then stops abruptly, looking furtively around the empty room as if embarrassed. His hair is wire, his eyes are laced red, his skin looks suicidal. Ask him why he is there and he would have no answer; probably he would continue, simply, to stare. He squints into the sunlight as if looking for a certain something and waits for one of the sleeping others to move, as Mairead rests peacefully behind the wall and a well-fed fly orbits his head.

MAIREAD

FUCK IT. THA hear mih? A said *fuck*, it.

A do fuckin hert this, a hert it a hert it a hert it – bein workin up ba Colm bellowin in kitchen. He's bin all quiet an sulky lahk fer past few days, flahyin int' rerge at drop uv a hat, an a knor fuckin why, n all; er's got nor munneh an ee warnts t'get trashed. Av given drinkin a rest lahk as an attempt t', lahk, mek im feel better, y'knor, solidariteh an support an sor on, an let mih tell you 'tasunt bin fuckin easer, but ee never nortices such things. It's juss me, me, me wi im . . . a mean, lissen t'bastard, now, in kitchen:

—Oh Jesus fuckin cuntin Christ! Fer fuck's sakes! Useless fuckin wankin cuntin bastard fuckin arse'ole . . .

Bangin pots an plerts an pans around lahk a spoilt little kid. A fuckin hert this, a do. Sometahm soon a knor al werk up an Colm worn't be in t'bed, ee'l be in pub somewhere wi mih cash card. Why cahn't things ever be fuckin easer, eh? Why cahn't theh?

One uv t'grert things bout castles is that, cos thee wuh built on, lahk, vantage points, tha can ser fer mahls an mahls around when tha stands in um – which, uv course, was thee intention, t'be erble t'spot attackin ahmies when thee wuh still far off. Ah mean, from ere, ah can ser Bird Rock which is fuckin mahls awer, t'cormorants flappin around it size uv gnats from this distance. It's incredible. Ah can imagine the surroundin hills swarmin wi cavalry, blorks on beautiful horses armed wi shields an spears an swords, other fellers in kilts creepin through trees. God, wha must it uv bin lahk in those ders? Ah can picture it, clerlih, hear t'horse's hooves, smell t' horsecrap . . . Those mushies must ber tekkin effect. Ah strork t'moss on castle wall; soft an smooth an damp, lahk t'fur uv some kahnd animal.

—Look at them all, Laura sers, givin me a nudge. —Mad.

Ah turn round an look down int' castle grounds. Such children; Liam's spread-eagled lahk a starfish, halfwer up a crumblin wall, shoutin:

—Ah'm fuckin stuck! Ah'm stuck! Ah cahn get fuckin down so!

Malcolm, standin on top uv t'wall, shoots Colm wi an invisible bow an arrow, an Colm gors: —Oof!, an flings is arms out, collapsin backwuds, int' grass.

—Yuv done fer me! Yuv skewered me through an through!

—Oi! Ye carn fuckin leave me hur as it's a fuckin *limpet* that ah am!

Such children. Fuckin daft, all uv em. Me n Laura laughin on t'battlement, me head beginnin t'spin.

—Look at Paul! What the hell's *he* playing at?

A follow Laura's pointin finger, up up up, an ser Paul runnin lahk a trern across top uv one uv t'high walls, dead dead high, dangerouslih high.

—Jesus. Fee falls off an il brek is bloody back uh summat.

—Kill himself.

—Paul! Get down! Yil fall off!

Er looks up, squints, wervs an then carries on chuggin along. Ow orld is he? Twenty ert or summat? Yih can hear im mekkin trern noises:

—Chuffchuffchuffchuff . . . chuffchuffchuffchuff . . .

An ee others:

—Ah cannat fuckin move! Geez a hahnd down now one o'yez!

—Oi! They didn fuckin *av* machine-guns in them days!

—It was a bleedin crossbow!

—Oh yeh, a crossbow goin budda budda budda?

—Chuffchuffchuff . . .

—Boilin oil then: fsssssst!

—Fe Christ's sake ah'm slippun fuckin off!

—Aaagh! Yuv melted me alive, yer twat!

—Whoooo, whoooo! Chuffchuffchuffchuff . . .

Mad. Comin up summat chronic on them mushies. So like little children. Thee all need lookin afteh.

★   ★   ★

Uh prorgram comes on telleh, summat about drug abuse in rural areas lahk, an evrihone stops what theh doin an looks up t'watch. Frorzen, lahk statues; Roger with ee electric flex tied round is bicep an clamped tight in is teeth, vern on is arm poppin out lahk a blue rorp; Colm hunched orver in chair, about t'chase heroin off a foil wrapper from a KitKat; Malcolm wi chopped up cocaine on mih merk-up mirror, uh rorled-up tenner on t'wer to is nose. Normly, lahk, ad problih object tuh this – Roger jackin up er in mih flat (a carn stand t'saht uv it; needles, ugh), Colm usin heroin – but am too fuckin stoned n drunk, too fuckin *trashed*, t'care. Colm's orn fuckin choice anywer. Sup tuh him.

A voice on telleh reels off some statistics, sers: *Soon, it will be rare for a young person under thirty in Wales to have not tried marijuana*, at which wih all laugh. This blork's fuckin BBC accent lahk.

—A was *bored* with marifuckinjuana fore a wus *ten*, yer darft twat, Roger sers with t'flex snerkin out uv is mouth.

—Ah yud berrer watch it then, Colm sers. —Yer might be addicted to the stuff. Yul be injectin it next.

In some rural areas, heroin is as cheap and as easily available as a bag of sugar.

—Yer fuck! Oh yeh, see this bagger brown yer, mun? Bought it from the corner shop, I did. Sixty pence a pound it wuz. Fuckin wanker.

—A go' confused thee other day an sprinkled me Weetabix with skag. Fuck's sakes.

Children as young as twelve are now reported to be drinking heavily . . . Users attest to the lack of opportunities in the countryside, resulting in boredom, as the main reason for their continuing abuse of drugs.

—Oh, puh-leeeeaaase!, ah ser.

—Yeh. An all-night sesh by the side uvver lake inner mountains, sittin byer big fire, comin down an watchin the sun rise over the water. Borin as fuck, tharriz.

—Member tha rave on Ynyslas sands larst week like? Or the one in Dol-y-bont? Member ow we all fell asleep like cos we wir so bored?

Malcolm sniffs an sers: —Awl these prowgrems are miles wide of the mark. A mean, neva ev I hird one stite that a long-term effect av prowlonged drug abuse is a tendency ta incessant fuckin sarcasm.

A laugh at this, but Roger just sters at Malcolm an is ferce clouds orver lahk an then ee starts spittin fuckin sparks:

—An wha the fuck's *that* supposed ter mean like? Eh? Fuckin incessant sarcasm, whatjer fuckin mean by that then?

—Roger, ee's just messin, man, Colm sers, an a put mih hand on is arm (which feels thin as a fuckin reed lahk) an that seems t'calm im down a little.

—Yeh, well, ee'd fuckin bess be like's all *I* can fuckin say. Cunt.

—Now offence meant, mate, Malcolm sers, lookin terrified. Roger's starin at im, still chewin the flex in is clenched teeth. Ah can see glints uv copper where he's, lahk, gnawed awer the rubber. —A was bein, sawt uv, ironic, ya know, self-deprecating. A mean, wha a said was itself sarcastic . . . so I was like . . . tikein tha piss aht uv meself n awl . . .

Ee shoots me a worried look an Roger sers summat else which a carn't mek out cos er's bitin down hard on t'flex again now, slappin up a vern on is weedy arm, slappin t'skin rully hard, almost vilently lahk. T'vern rises reluctantly an ee grunts an reaches fer is syringe on t'terble.

T'prorgram gorze int' some blinkered an narror-mahnded discussion about E an rerves an drug-culture in general lahk, an prettih soon evihone loses intrest an just does theh drugs. Roger nods out on couch, to a general sigh uv relief, Colm snorts some coke wi is heroin t'keep im up lahk an jabbers shite wi Malcolm, an I just get drunker n drunker n drunker. Some good techno on t'stereo, a spliff or two, an am awer. Smashin. Oh look anotheh naht uv drug dependency despair an desorlation, oh look how sad wih all are. Me arse. Yuh can all go screw.

Malcolm tells us that er hurd from . . . wuh it Robbie? Tha blork oo's gorn off t'Paris soon? Yeh, ah think it wuh him – that parts uv t'woods b'hahnd Goginan uh haunted, well, not suh much haunted lahk as odd, strernge; sehs people ee knors wunt tek theh kids thur, sehs t'ground's tund sour uh summat (tha wuh the wud ee used, 'sour'). Soon's wih hear that, well, uv course, wih want t'go, ur at least Malcolm an ah do; wuh fuckin *rerrin* t'gor, but Margaret an Colm ur a bit wirreh:

—A dunno, a dunno about stuff like this, Colm sehs. —Seems liker laugh before yer atchly get ther, like, bu' . . . a remember this one time like –

—Ow fuck awl thet. Let's just gown see what it's like eh? Malcolm sehs. —Maker change if fuck awl else. A mean, Mags, what wer you plannin on doin taday?

Shih shrugs. —Dunno. Anythin. Pub, pool, pissed, a s'pose.

—Exactly. Ya do thet *avry* fuckin day.

—When av got the money, yeh. An anyway, a fuckin *like* doin that. Carn think of anythin ad rather do, t'tell yer the truth. 'Part from go swimmin maybe.

—Yeh, well, it's fuckin freezin taday, innit? An this al et least be differant, ey, a change at least, wown't it? Jast gow dahn inta tha woods, av a sniff abaht, then gow n awl get wrecked in the Druid. Sahnd.

—Oh well. S'pose.

So that's decided then. Ah can understand Colm's rerluctance, tho; er's got Romany blood, from is nana on is dad's side ah think, an as clichéd as it sounds lahk ee seems, well, kahnd uv tuned in t'certun things, y'know, t'spirits an so on. Slike, one tahm bout uh yur ago now when ah started t'fell strernge in t'flat, a feelin uv a presence ur summat . . . it's hard t'explern; it wuh lahk bein watched alla time, an assessed, an spied on lahk. . . . Raht fuckin weird it wuh. An an remember ah wuh lyin in t'bath smorkin a spliff an wishin that this weird feelin would go awer when Colm cerm in with a peculiar grin on is ferce an sat on edge uv t'bath an said in a low, strernge voice:

—He's here. Can yer feel im around yer? Ee's been inner flat with us fer the past few days . . . Av yer felt im watchin over you?

Ee explerned that this presence wuh t'ghorst uv a dead ancestor, an that ee wuh benign, an good, an wuh ere t'see that wih curm t'no harm, but ah just couldn't get rid uv t'feelin that ah wuh bein judged. Ah just couldn't sherk it. So ah asked this ghorst ur spirit ur phantom ur whatever it wuh t'gor awer, niceleh lahk, an ee did. An ee ant bin back since, ur at least, if ee as, then *I* avunt felt owt.

Things lahk that offun happen to im, ur so ee sers, anywer. When ee wuh in France, in t'Camargue, Colm wuh sittin wi some people watchin t'gypsies rerce an trerd theh horses, an some uv these gyppos kept pointin orver at im an talkin about im an callin im orver. Colm couldn't understand what thee wuh sayin lahk, cos they wuh talkin in French lahk, so ee asked one uv t'people ee wuh with t'translert an it wuh summat lahk:

—They're asking you to go over and join them. They're saying that you're one of them and you should return to the fold.

Odd, eh? It must be summat uv a burden, tho, ah suppose . . . in a wer . . . carryin such stuff around wi yuh . . . Me, tho, ah find it nice. A find it attractive. It's intrestin.

Any rord, we ead off in mih car, which is still just about workin, mekkin noises under t' bonnet summat chronic. MOT's nully run out on it, an ah reckun it ul cost fuckin lords t'fix; it's an ex-police car lahk so ee engine's had uh real fuckin hammerin, it's still got belts int back seat lahk that t'prisoners wuh handcuffed to an stuff. It gets us out t'Goginan, just about, an down int valleh, whur ah park up undeh a big old friendly-lookin tree at t'sahd uv t'path. Smells fuckin gorgeous here, it does, trees afteh a rern, t'soil, t'earth . . . An quiet, too, raht quiet; not even any birds singin.

—Av got a few dried 'shrooms on me, Malcolm sehs, —if anywan's intrested like. Not very many. Probly abaht ten, fifteen each.

—None fer me, Colm sehs. —Carn stand the fuckers.

—Maw fa us then.

Wih compress t'mushies int small, swallowable bundles, start t'eat em, an then uv course Colm wants some too.

—A fuckin ate takin em like this, ee sers. —Look arrum. Ee orlds a bundle out on is palm. —Aller fuckin stalks stickin out, looks liker baller those orrible little fuckin creepy long-leggedy spider bastards. Ick.

But ee swallers um down anywer, wih all do, washin um down wi some old an tepid vodka that's bin in t'car fer fuck alone knors ow long, months probleh, mebbe even years. Tersts fuckin awful.

Wih set off, int woods.

—This is, lahk, a real adventure. Am all excited, ah ser.

—Yeh. Look at that.

Margaret points to a free-standin wall, slahtly blackened wi old an charred beams stickin out from it lahk spokes uh summat. Sall that remerns uv some house, a holiday cottage ur summat probleh. Thus a faded, bareleh legible Rhyddid Cymru porsteh stuck to it, peelin awer at edges. Wih walk on, deeper int trees.

Sfuckin amerzin, this, out int forest, all green, trees sor thick an high . . . Trees aren't in regular, clorned rows out here, or nor, theh mad, haphazard, an wild, followin nor pattern but theh orn, which is just ow it should be, ah reckun. Ar feet crunch an squelch through t'leaves an bracken an mulch. Ah feel free here, rulleh free, a feel freer than ah hav done fur a long, long time, not since ah went up t'mih nana's cottage in Aberdovey on mih own hav ah felt lahk this. Totully free. Fuckin loveleh feelin this is. Rent arrears, fuel bills, council fuckin tax, theh can all go screw. This is t'plerce fer mih, oh yeh. If thuh wuh vodka flowin from uh spring, then, God, t'garden uv fuckin Eden this would be.

—Erm . . . what exactly are we lookin for?

Ah shrug. —Nowt in p'ticular lahk. Just, ah dunno, some kind uv feelin ur summat a suppose.

—Innit ace, anywye, tho?

It is, an it sters erce until wih get out uv t'woods an find arsens in an old, disused quarreh. Not a very big one lahk; wee, in fact, just a few jagged horls in ground, each one about as deep's as, ser, a house. All grey an jagged in t'smooth green. A mist has started t'come down here n all an evrihthin's startin t'look kind uv ghostleh an unreal.

Malcolm just sehs: —Ow shit.

Mags's eyes ar fuckin huge: —Now a *don't* like this. Oh no. A don't like this one tiny bit.

—You orright, Mags?

It maht just be t'mist but sher's pale, pale as milk, er eyes t'size uv hubcaps on mih car. She looks lahk sher's about t'be sick.

—Am alright. Juster mushrooms, a think . . . made me belly feel a bit funny . . .

—Ah haven't got owt off um yet, ah ser, but am not rully sure that's t'truth . . . a mean, ah carn't rully tell . . .

—Nor av I, thank fuck, sehs Colm. —Doan know why a fuckin ate um now. Hate the fuckin things.

—Jast say no, Colm, jast say no. Diddan ya eva heed tha *Grange Hill* wawnings?

169

Ar voices uh dampened here, thuz hardleh any noise at all. When ah speak, mih voice just serms t'stop dead about an inch in front uv mih ferce. An it's lahk t'air is pressin on mih, weighin on mih, ah feel lahk av bin tightly wrapped in a grey blanket ur summat. It's raht fuckin odd.

In a kind uv tacit agreement wuh all start t'follow t'quarreh path back around t'woods t'wards mih car.

—This is a bit . . . weird, Malcolm goes. —A can feel . . . things . . . ghosts, around us.

Colm sherks is head, raht serious. —Am tellin yer, ther's bad things here. Rerly bad things. Things that rerly fuckin don't want us here.

—Oh fer fuck's sakes, don't fuckin say that.

A rub Mags's arm an whispeh: —You OK?, an shih nods. But then shih mutters, softly lahk:

—Am not fuckin likin this. Onestly. A rirly don't feel right.

—Probleh just t'mushies.

—Yeh.

Colm's gone raht quiet, er's not sayin a wud. When wih get back t'mih car ih gors off fer a piss an comes back a couple uh minutes lerteh lookin all wurrid.

—Comen look a' this, ee sehs. —Strangest fuckin thing.

—Wha' is it?

—Fuck knows, a carn rerly explain. Yul avter comen av a look.

Wih look at each otheh then follow im through t'trees an int clearing, whuh thuz lahk, summat, a dunno, some fuckin bizarre kind uv sculpture, ah havunt a fuckin clue what it is: a door, just a normul house door lahk, standin upraht in t'ground, a length uv red rorp flung orver top uv it wi an empty clear plastic barrel tahd t'each end wi sawdust sprinkled b'neath um, on either side uv t'door. Am baffled. An some kind uv squiggles screrped int pernt on t'door . . . odd symbols an sherps . . . lahk fuckin hieroglyphs ur summat . . .

—What . . . the . . . fuck?

Colm sherks his head. —A mean, *why*? Ey? Why? In the middle of the fuckin forest, why the fuck would anyone want ter fuckin . . .

—Coulda been kids messin abaht a suppowse, Malcolm sehs.

—Yeh, but still . . . Colm reaches out t'touch it an Margaret shouts: —NO!, or at least, a *think* shih shouts; thuz hardly anneh sound to her voice at all. T'mist an stuff just sort uv swallers it up.

—Why not?

—A dunno, just, just don't. Er voice's tremblin. —It looks liker fuckin portal or somethin . . . it might try n pull yuh through if yuh touch it. Shih wraps er arms around erself an shivers. Shih looks rilleh upset, rilleh unsettled.

—Ah fuck it. Malcolm spits on t'floor. —I reckon it wuz jast kids muckin abaht anywye. Little cunts.

Colm agrees: —Yeh, ey probly purrit ther ter scer shite out uv a few dick'eds come out ere ter take some mushies.

—Yeh. Let's gown get shit-faced inna Druid.

That perks us all up again an wih leg it back tuh car, a start it up an fuckin miracle it wuks fust time, even in this mist, which is sor wet it's lahk some kind uv floating pond. A can feel me hair stickin t'mih ferce in sorked strands. A drive back up t'valleh to t'mern rord an pub.

—Well, we didn find any standin stowns, but we did find samthin, didn we?

—Yeh. Fuck knows wharrit was tho.

—Al tell ya what, Malcolm sehs. —A jast wish ad neva fuckin fahnd that sheep skull. Am tellin ya, eva since ah fahnd it av ad eeva bad luck or things appen ta me which're jast, like, fuckin bizarre. A mean it. Am gonna chuck the fuckin thing away.

Wuh drive in silence fer a bit, t'car labourin up t'steep valleh wall. Then:

—One thing, tho, Colm sehs from t'back seat. —Tha clearing tha tha fuckin statue thing was in, it was pretty big, wasn it?

—What clearing?

—Av just sed, the one with tha fuckin door thing in.

—Yeh, suppowse so. Baht tennis cawt size. Why?

—Well, that's the way we walked when we ferst gorrout uv the car, through tha part uv the woods. A remember the bernt house. Ow come we didn notice it then?

An all uv a sudden am hit wi t'notion tha if we went back t'look fer the clearing raht now wud never be erble t'find it an it's lahk summat drops in car, lahk some big, invisible wert falls from t'roof. Malcolm blors air out through is teeth an Maggie gors:

—Christ, let's urry up an get to this fuckin pub. A need lots n lots n lots n lots uv beer.

A put mih foot down, but a carn help smiling. Am feelin fuckin exhilarated, if t'truth be telt, an it's not ornly from t'mushies, it's lahk thuz some kind uv electrical charge in mih blood. Ah feel fuckin grert, ace, spot on, on raht form; this is one uv t'reasons why a curm t'Wales in fust plerce.

A park up opposite t'Druid pub an wih get out an stand thuh lookin out oveh t'valleh. A big cloud uv steam ur mist ur summat rahses up out uv t'woods. So much sperce; vast, huge, it is. Diddy white cottages on t'valleh floor an sides, about a mile b'neath mih feet.

—Looks like *Twin Peaks*, dunnit?

—Ey, Mally, member tha time me, you n Paulie n Roger came out ere when we wer on acid an tha old feller came leggin it inter the pub screamin tha ther was a UFO outside? Djer remember?

They both laugh at t'memory an ah smile even more. Am feelin, fer some reason, very very happeh. Am gun get rat-arsed t'night, an bollox t'drahvin horm; wih can sleep int car, ur al drahv horm pissed. Whatever; that's not important. Just wert n see wha happens.

Ah can see t'orange glow uv a real fire int windors uv t'pub orver rord. Ah carn't wert t'be in there.

—Al get um in, a ser. —What wih all havin?

T'otheh naht, lahk, when a wuh up at tha rerve in t'barn nir Dol-y-bont, a remembeh sterrin at one uv them fractal things projected ont barn roof, norticin t'sherps within sherps within sherps, alla them mirrorin each otheh, an a remembeh thinkin how life wi Colm is lahk that, how an hour wi him mirrors a whorl der, which mirrors a week, which mirrors a month, which ur all mirrored in t'whorl length uv tahm av knorn him. A typical der starts off nice (morst uv the tahm), then becomes tense, then upsetting, then bitter, an then, finally, dull. And, nor doubt, when am on mih deathbed, mih whorl life ul be mirrored in time a spent wi Colm, cycles wi'in cycles, worlds wi'in worlds. Never-endin spirals. On an on an on.

Still, at least teder, lahk, thuz a chernge; ee maht be on another one uv is moanin jags but at least a can understand wha ee's talkin about – ee ant bin erble t'string a fuckin sentence t'gether fer t'last few ders, out uv is brerns on downers, lahk, so a supporse 'am fuckin bored' merks a nice chernge from incoherent grunting, even if it is windin me up summat chronic. Wuh borth just sittin round t'flat lahk, drinkin red wine an lissnin t'that new Black Grape album. Just relaxin, lahk, y'knor, just tekkin it easeh, but ee starts gorn on about ow wuh shoulden be werstin such a nice sunny aftehnoon indoors an ow a should drive us out somewhuh nice before am oveh t'limit on t'alcohol.

Well, a think, orright. It *is* a nice der, an it's nice t'be erble t'talk t'Colm wi'out im fallin asleep evrih few minutes, so wuh get in car an a drive us borth out t'Ystrad Fflur, y'know Strata Florida, t'abbey an t'flowers an Dafydd ap Gwilym's grerve an so on. Dead nice out thur it is. Colm terks theh wine wi him an necks t'lot before wuh even out uv Aberystwyth.

—Mebbe ad lahk a drink mesen when wuh got thur, did yuh eveh think about that?

Ee just shrugs. —Shoulda brought two bottles then, shouldunt yer?

Fuck's serk. Selfish fuckin bastard . . . Am t'one doin t'drivin, while ee just sits thur an gets ferried about drinkin all t'wine. Prick. Thinks am is fuckin chauffeur. Arse'ole.

But it is peaceful in t'abbey, raht calm, t'sun on hills an t'birds singin awer. Amerzin, n all, alla orld carved tiles on t'floors uv t'little recesses whuh t'monks used t'gor an pray, sor orld, wi carvins uv animals an Mary cradlin t'berbeh Jesus an sor on, amerzin it is, but alla bleedin time from Colm it's:

—Thiz a nice little pub in Pontrhydfendigaid, yer know, dead nice irriz, av been in ther before. Will nip in ther onner way bakh, yeh?

A mean, evrih five fuckin minutes ee sers this or summat similar lahk, an ee's fuhgettin that it's up tuh mih t'drive us fuckin horm so al not be erble t'drink much anywer. An am tryin here, am rully fuckin tryin t'keep t'urges at bay, t'fuckin clamouring insahd

173

mih fuh booze, t'terst uv it, t'buzzing in mih head, but that dorn't fuckin bother him, tho:

—Oh, so why the fuck djer say inner car tha yer'd like a drinker wine when we gorrout ere, then, ey? Yer diddin want any wine at all, did yer, tha was just another fuckin thing ter av a go at me for, wannit?

A just sigh. Not wuth gettin wukd up wi im when er's in this mood. —Let's just go un sit ba Daffyd's grerve an smork a spliff, eh? Wunt that be nice?

—Doan even fuckin like pot. Yer know tha.

—Oh well, suit yuh fuckin self then. Mornin twat.

—Yeh a fuckin will. Al be in the fuckin pub.

Ee skulks off down t'rord an a gorn sit in t'sherd uv t'tree whuh t'poet's buried. Lovely an cool. A lean back an light up t'spliff that's bin dryin out in mih glovebox fer fuck alorn knors ow long. So relaxing hir it is, an a have t'ser, it's merd even more so by t'absence uv Colm scowlin an moanin an gettin all restless an snappy. Ee'l bih back soon, tho, a knor that; ee's ornleh got enough munneh fer a pint uh two, unless he's bin hidin some, which ee probleh has cos we got a cut-off nortice for t'gas this week. Me, tho, av got a twenty stashed in mih purse which a fulleh intend t'spend on t'wer horm on a grert big bottle uv Martini, a giant fuckin bottle uv dry Martini an a lemon an some Silk Cut an some tonic ur lemonade ur summat an a couple uv bags uv thorse Spar cheesy balls. Ace. Altho mebbe al give t'cheesy balls a miss . . . ur mebbe get one bag ornleh; a feel as if av bin puttin a bit uv wert on recentleh lahk . . . a horp not. A fuckin hert bein fat, a do, an am cursed wi a slor metabolism; ornleh av t'look at chocolate an that's it, am a porkeh. A run mih hand orveh mih tummeh, but it dorn't feel too bulgy, which is good; when a wuh a kid, a wuh raht chubbeh . . . well, a wuh a fat fuck t'tell truth . . . an, Jesus, did a get some stick: yuh knor t'kind uv thing – fat slag, pig, oink oink called afteh mih int plerground, all tha fuckin cruel an heartless stuff that children ser. Rilly fuckin nasty stuff (a dorn't tell many people about this now; theh react t'yuh differentleh, as if in t'past yuv committed some vile an hideous crime. It's lahk: —What, you wuh once *fat*? Oh Christ, get the fuck away from me! Yuh might fuckin *relapse*!). Kids will try theh hardest t'merk otheh kids' lives a sheer misereh for whateveh tiny an negligible reason; sometimes theh dorn't even need a fuckin reason, lahk, thel just merk one up, lahk, if theh decide that yur a slag then yuh ar: a slag if yuh wir merk-up, a slag bicause yih tits grow earlier than morst ur if yer periods start earleh, a slag if yur pretteh, a slag if yur not . . . Fuh me, lahk, it wuh bicause a wuh blackmailed int sleepin wi someone when a wuh dead young – twelve, a wuh, ur thurteen, mebbe; raht young anywer, wi a blork oo wuh in is middle twenties (now, uv course, a realise that thuz summat deeply wrong wi blorks lahk that), an it wuh a fuckin mental rape – y'knor, al chuck yuh if yuh dorn't give us it an tell evrihone yir a slag, that kind uv thing . . . So a did, an uv course by t'end uv t'week evrih one in t'whorl fuckin school knew. An then it wuh: 'I laid Mairead' on t'bikeshed wall, 'Mairead Morgan is a fuckin slut' an sor on all oveh t'bog walls. Awful, it wuh. Horrible. Even some uv t'fuckin *teachers*, Christ . . . a remembeh on one report card it said that a lacked imaginertion fuh English an mortivertion fuh PE, thuh inference bein uv course that a wuh fat, fat an thick, fat, thick an lazeh. Fuckin bastards. An mih form teacheh readin mih report card an lookin mih up n down an sayin: —Yes, a lack of motivation for physical education, yes, I can see that quite clearly, yes . . . then grinnin all pleased wi imself while t'whorl class cracked up. Fuckin cunt. Nor teacher's insult is *ever* fuckin fuhgotten. A horp a bump int im some time in t'future, preferably when am all dressed up t'go out, laugh at im droolin, leerin . . . fuckin old bastard. An a wuh neither fat ur lazy; well, a bit plump, mebbe, but . . . truth is that a wuh just sor fuckin consumed wi self-lorthin an hertred . . . thuh wuh a hurricane in mih head.

It wuh around that time tha a tried t'top mesen. About fifteen fuckin year orld a wuh . . . Fifty paracetemol lahk, hospital, stomach pump . . . nightmare it wuh. Still, tho, a supporse it got better afteh that, that wuh, lahk, t'turnin point, an then a started tekkin singin lessons an t'music teacher said a had a grert voice an a talent which a should merk t'morst uv, which a still try t'do now. Specialleh when av had a few bevvies; booze helps mih tuh sing, an it keeps mih slim by suppressin mih appetite lahk, an plus it merks mih feel fuckin grert. A think it wuh just before t'orverdose tha a discovered booze. Yeh, it wuh. Arf bottle uh whiskeh out uv a friend's dad's

cabinet lahk, necked t'fuckin lot in t'garden. An it merd me feel
. . . an it merd mih think that –

Oh fuck it. Am startin t'get a bit depressed, now, thinkin back
orver all this stuff. It's all in t'past, fuck it, it's just anotheh chain
yuv got t'try n get rid of. Livin in t'present is a skill wuth cultivertin,
as Malcolm allus sers, an t'present's not too bad raht now: av got
munneh that a dorn't av t'wuk for, thanks t'me granny lahk, altho
how long it's lahkly t'last wi Colm dippin int it alla fuckin time
a dorn't fuckin knor, fuckin Sharon n all – nine hundred fuckin
quid a lent tha fuckin cow an not a penny uv it back. God, yuh
shouldn't be nice in this wuld, yih should neveh be fuckin kind;
people see that as a sign uv weakness an then theh fuckin strert in
thuh, can yuh lend us this, can yuh lend us that, al pay yuh back
next week, promise . . . Fuck em all. Wankers.

An a must ser, ad sooneh av nor munneh at all an mih grandparents still alive than lots uv munneh an borth uv em dead.
Which is –

Which is raht fuckin depressin again. Pot does this tuh mih,
sometimes, merks mih dwell on sad things; thuh annoyin thing is
that yuh can neveh tell when it's gorn t'hit yuh that wer. A need
booze t'counteract it lahk, but then t'buzz is sor fuckin nice that yih
dorn't stop until yuh too pissed t'even rerse yuh glass. Or rorl orveh
out uv yuh orn sick. Lahk at Iestyn's parteh that time; a turned blue
apparentleh – a dorn't remembeh, lahk, a wuh unconscious. But a
can neveh wur mih nice red dress again.

What can yuh do?

Ah fucket, as Liam would ser; it's easy. Am here, in Wales, am
slim, av got some munneh t'quench mih thirst an am slightleh
storned an t'sun's shinin down. Colm's in t'pub, wertin fuh mih,
an Colm *can* be nice, carn't he? Sometimes, yeh, ee can . . . So fuck
em all. An if am a slag, so fuckin what? Yur a ignorant, brernless
fuckin dickless arse'ole in that case.

Dim probs.

A bury t'roach under t'grass, ser tara t'Dafydd an drive down
t'rord int Pontrhydfendigaid. A find Colm in t'little pub thur, in
dark an dingeh corneh, arf a pint left an a mound uv ripped-up beer
mats ont terble in front uv im. T'smell, that loveleh pub smell; rich
an yeasty an dead fuckin ace.

—Drink up then love, a ser. —Al buy us a big bag full uv booze on t'wer horm an wuh can get trashed. Ow does that sound?

Ee grins an knocks back is drink an we bellow out folk songs all t'wer horm, mernly 'Three Score and Ten' cos that's t'one a knor all t'wuds to.

Up at Oxygen which this week is in t'union bar at universiteh an a tell yuh, Christ, am absoluteleh fuckin *flyin* on this E, well out uv it, soarin soarin wer wer up thur. T'nerm Ecstasy is right, thur uh nor fuckin wuds fer this joy, rapture, a can ser mih hur flyin in t'strobes an mih body's pumpin pumpin all mih limbs, mih skin one grert big tinglin sheet an mih ferce lit up in a permanent grin. Out t'corneh uv mih eye a see Colm at bar standin thur watchin mih dance, am free, am free, am free an buzzin all t'fuck flyin through these flashin lights t'music like some life-givin force ur summat an when it stops then I will too but ah knor it will never stop, never ever ever. T'whoops on this track keep pushin mih left leg forrud; ey sound lahk Liam did when ee wuh attemptin t'yodel in car on t'wer up here an Malcolm said ee sounded lahk a UFO in some crap fifties sci-fi film, woo-OOOO, wooo-OOOOOOH . . . Mags is dancin opposite mih, bouncin about, t'sweat glissnin shinin in er cropped hur she looks sor fuckin happeh an beautiful, er hipster trousers below er flat belly er legs pumpin pistons, shuz raht gorgeous, eckfuckinstatic lahk, t'naht a do not care if muh suspicions that shiz shaggin Colm ont sly uh true ur not am just gonter enjoy, enjoy . . . Paul's orveh thur wi Colm, lookin lahk er's just eaten t'dawn . . . Men keep slidin in t'dance by us but wuh dismiss em wi smiles (theh beer monsters, unaware uv t'etiquette; rule three – yuh dorn't chat owt up when theh dancin at plerces lahk this; wuh here for t'dancin an t'drugs, nowt else), t'thought creeps unwanted in a fight it but it still creeps in that any one uv these blorks could be t'campus rapist (wuds in mih head wantin t'be hurd: tortureterrorabusehumiliationpain) but then it creeps out again of its orn accord lahk an oh God am happy am sor happy a dorn't knor if one person can handle sor much happiness am soaring am fuckin soaring, dancin happeh happy as fuck.

Sometimes, in t'night lahk, when Colm's still out somewhur ur is crashed out snorin on t'bed, a go into mih secret drawer. In thur, a keep alla letters an mementoes from time a spent in Spain, all kinds uv stuff; maps, matchbooks, napkins, swizzle-sticks, letters off an phortos from ex-boyfriends, stuff lahk that. A just dip int shoeboxes which contern all this stuff an touch it an look at it an sometimes when a look up again, it's dawn. T'sunlight shinin through t'curtains. Sometimes t'nights arn long enough.

Shoulda remembered, rerleh, shouldn't ah; it's Wednesday aftehnoon, ahf der up at uni lahk, sor town's fuckin heavin wi students. Thuz a group uv them standin round t'cashpoint machine, an one uv them nudges is mert an looks mih up n down as am tekkin some munneh out an gors:
—Ad give *that* one.
Ah look him up an down in turn, from is unlerced armeh boots to the ridiculous yellow hat, an ser in mih best scornful voice:
—Nor yih fuckin wouldn't.
Ee gors red an is merts laugh an whoop too loudleh an merk raht arses uv themsen. Fuckin students. Thuz anotheh group uv them in t'travel ergents as well when a gor in thuh an do what a have t'do; ah nortice that thur all buyin der returns t'Dún Laoghaire. Outside, ah think ah catch a glimpse uv Liam in street so a dive int nearest pub on mih orn, down a few vodkas on mih orn . . . Feel immediately better. Thuz students in ere n all, in a few diffrunt groups; one group's bein loud n obnoxious an arsy, anotheh's just drinkin an talkin an laughin. Ah dorn't think that all students ar wankers; some uv them ar perfectly OK people lahk, just tryin t'improve theh lives, y'knor, just tryin t'mek summat better fuh thesen . . . It's t'otheh type tho, t'middle-class type, t'loud, toothy, braying ones, students with a capital S, self-consciousleh wacky, abusive, ignorunt, *Pulp Fiction* porsters on t'walls, inflerted wi a far too large sense uv t'scrap uv intelligence thev got; *them* ar t'fuckers I hert. Yuh knor t'ones ah mean, yuh seem fuckin evrehwhuh.
Ah finish mih drinks an gorn av a look in t'windor uv that shop down Pier Street; t'dress is still thuh, t'brown stripy dress av ad mih eye on fer erges. A try t'picture mihsen in it, what al look lahk, which uv course's nowt what a rully look lahk when am standin wi it on in front uv t'dressin room mirruh . . . but still . . . it looks

178

quite good on mih, it does, an anywer ah *feel* good in it, which is t'mern thing, innit?

Ah put mih orld clorthes back on – torn leggings, washed-out jumpeh an sor on – an tek t'brown dress up t'counteh. Sixty fuckin quid. Well . . .

Thur uh two prime examples uv t'genus Student Arsehole at counter. These two ar t'kahnd uv people am talkin about, loud enough so that t'whorl bleedin shop can hear that thuh tryin t'buy uh mannequin's leg, horldin it up, strorkin it, just gen'rulleh bein complete twats:

—Gwooooah look . . . if only *real* bloody women had legs like this . . .

—You don't need one of them real things now, my son!

Not that eitheh uv yuh uh eveh fuckin likeleh t'get one, a think t'mihsen. T'lass behind t'counter's on t'phorn, tryin t'find a price fer t'leg:

—No, no, not the whole mannequin . . . just the leg, aye . . . two boys . . . Ten pound? The one leg?

Student Grant an is mert whoop an holler an hand orveh uh tenner. T'lass's kind uv laughin, lahk, shakin huh head:

—Oh, you two . . . mad you are . . . d'you want it wrapped?

—No thank you. I want to admire it in all its svelte beauty.

Ee horlds it up above is head lahk a tropheh an roars. Fuckin dickhead. Ee nortices mih then an grins but a tun mih back on em an as am payin fer mih new dress a hear thum leavin t'shop:

—Why did we buy it? *Why* did we buy it?

—Simple. We saw it, we wanted it, and lo, it was ours.

Then theh cheer again as theh goin down t'rord. Mih intestines uh cringin fuh thum, mih cheeks uh burnin red; do thah not knor what utter pricks theh mekkin uv thumselves? Ah well. Bollocks to em. Idyits.

Ah tek mih new dress on mih orn t'public bogs int castle an put it on in one uv t'cubicles. Mih orld stuff gors back int bag; am not gunna throw it awer, lahk, thuz important stuff in pockets an anywer chuckin orld clorthes awer is a waste, no matteh how knackered theh ar; yih can alwers chop em up t'merk summat else, ur use um t'patch horls an sor on. Ah carn't stand needless werst.

An, ah mean, one uv mih faverit short skirts used t'be uh jacket; merd it mesen, ah did.

A feel raht good in mih new dress, an a walk int Ship an Castle all proud. Orld feller at bar gors:

—Now there's lovely, an a give im a grin.

Ah sit in corneh in mih new dress an a start drinkin. A drift around t'pubs on mih orn, meetin people a knor an people a dorn't knor. In t'wine bar, after t'sun gors down lahk, thuz a group uv dickheads torstin a mannequin's leg which is propped upright in centre uv terble whuh evrihone can see it, so ah leave afteh ornleh one drink.

Evrihthink seen through a haze.

An through a haze a gorgeous lad, funny, lerdback, strong Manchester accent; ee admires mih new dress. Ee's doin Celtic studies up at universiteh, but it tuns out ee knors Colm. Whureveh t'fuck *he* is.

In mih new dress, in mih haze, a get as drunk as a possibleh fuckin can an werk up at horm, on t'bed, on mih orn, no Colm, still in mih new dress ornleh now it's covered in sick. A tek it off an look at lerble: HANDWASH ONLY. Bugger.

> Come back to me my Nancy
> And linger here for just a little while
> Since you left these shores
> I've known no peace or joy.

Lassies' night in. Well, lassies' couple uv owers in before wuh gor out t'pub, me, Sioned, Margaret, two bottles uv vodka an a Christy Moore terp on player. Ace. Summat t'sing, t'yell, t'shout at top of mih voice:

> No matter where I wander
> I'm still haunted by your name
> The portrait of your beauty stays the same
> Standing by the ocean, wond'ring where you've gone
> If you'll return again . . .
> Oh where's the ring I gave

To Nancyfuckin Spain.

Wuh fall about wi laughin, an then laugh more lahk cos wuh laughin at arsen bein childish; slippin a swearwud int song, which is childish in fust plerce, which merks us laugh even more. God, what uh wuh lahk. Trio uv stupid bints us, arn't wuh?

Sioned tops up t'glasses.

—Anyone gooin to the Cnapan festival this yur, then?

—Dunnor, a ser. —When is it lahk?

—Didn't yew go last yur?

—Yeh, a ser. —Oo else went now? Colm uv course, Malcolm . . . you wuh thuh, wunt yuh?

—Yeh, with Paul, Sioned sers. —But a was ever so sick as a parrot. *Siiccckkkk*. Spent the whole bastard weekend feverish in Paul's bleedin car.

—Oh yeh, ah remembuh that. Dint Sharon gor as well?

—Oh Christ! *That* bint!

Margaret merks a cross out uv er fingers an Sioned merks a spittin sound.

—Ah still remembuh Colm wuh speedin is ferce off and –

—Now *thir's* a surprise.

—Oh! Says *yew*!

Mags smiles, all sheepish lahk.

—. . . an it wuh rully earleh in t'mornin around sixish lahk, an ee ad such a fuckin gor at Sharon, Christ . . . rully nasteh, ee wuh; gorn get a fuckin personaliteh, ee said, gorn fuck off an die, get out uv is life an sor on . . . yuh should uv hud him. Ripped er apart, ee did. Made er cry lahk.

—Good on him, Sioned sers. —A dunt blame him, *purse*-unally; never liked that one, I yavunt. Nasty bloody piece uv work aye.

Mags gors: —She never fuckin liked *me*! Said about three fuckin words t'me in all the time av known her.

—Ah, she hates all women, Sioned says. —Most bloody blokes, too, it seems.

—Ah, shuz not all bad, a ser. Even after all shuz done, ah supporse ah still feel a little bit sorreh fer Sharon.

Sioned snarls. —Christ, Mairead, yur too bloody nice for yur own good, yew are. Now if it was *me* she still owed nine hundred bleedin pounds to after all this time . . .

—Ah think shull per it back, ah ser, but am not entirely shur ah believe that. It alwers helps t'think positive, tho, even if yuh ar bloody kiddin yersen. Ah mean, it's lahk wi drugs; it rully dunt help t'think, just afteh yuv tekkin it lahk, oh this E's just fuckin aspirin, or this speed's just fuckin baby laxative, does it now? Yuv got t'think positive. Even whuh twats lahk Sharon uh concerned.

Sioned sherks her head. —A wouldn't fuckin count on that.

—Yeh, but what about Colm? He –

—Different thing, tho, innit? Yew *live* with Colm. He's yur boyfriend.

—Dunt that merk it wuss?

Sioned just sherks her head. No arguin wi huh sumtahms. Raht stubborn she is.

Mags chernges the subject:

—Who played last year, at Cnapan? Anyone good?

—Lords uv people, ah ser, —a can't rully remembeh . . . ah wuh wrecked. Dom, they plerd, a remembeh that, an some drummy salsa type band, bout fuckin fifty uv thum thuh wuh all runnin round t'marquee hammerin awer on drums. Fuckin ace, it wuh. Colm'd bought some whizz off Jerry before wuh set off – fffffffffff. Out uv it fuh three fuckin ders.

—Didunt someone let yer tyres down? Mags sers. —A seem t'remember somethin about that.

She dint come t'Cnapan wi us; a dorn't think ad even met her then. —Yeh, some little fuckin arseholes, a ser. —Ah saw thum, pleryin fuckin frisbee, an it must uv bin them an ah thought if one uv you little wankers sers one, fuckin, thing . . . A wuh rully fuckin angreh. Fuming. Good job Paul had that compressor wi him.

Sioned nods. —Yeh. It's handy, sometimes, him bein such a bloody jackdaw.

Wuh drink more vodka. Christ, wuv merd one big bastard uv a dent in it; an fuck me, this is t'second bottle. Just then ah remember summat.

—That wuh the fust time wuh met you, Mags, remember? At Llys Wen in t'mornin before yuh went t'wuk at t'students' union? Dyuh remeber that?

—Oh, was that then? Ad only moved in a couple of days before. A already thought it was a fuckin madhouse n stuff, an then one mornin the kitchen's fuller these wasters all fuckin wired on speed an stuff. A was fuckin scared; a thought, who *are* these nutters? She laughs.

—Yup, that wuh us.

—Didunt we all get stoned that mornin? ·

—As bastards, yeh.

—Yeh, an then I adter go to fuckin work! Split fuckin shifts in the union bar! Horrible. Fuck knows how a managed it. A was wrecked. Mind you, it was nothin unusual; a did the whole fuckin summer stoned. Evry fuckin day.

Wuh laugh. An then just witter on about all kinds uv shit. T'night gors by ant vodka disappers.

> Give the Wicklow boy his freedom
> We must give him back his liberty
> Or are we going to keep him in chains
> While those who framed him up, hold the key.

—Wuv arranged t'gorn meet t'men, a ser, cos a supporse someone as t'ser it. Alla thum – Colm, Paul, Malcolm, Liam, Iestyn, fuckin evrihbodeh – ar wertin fer us int prom pub. —Wuh already ahf ower lert.

Mags shrugs. —Bollocks to em. Am avin a good time.

—Yeh, ah ser. —Me too. Let's gorn get anotheh bottle. Al per by cheque.

An this wuh do, tumblin out uv t'flat yellin an mekkin a fuss, already ah fwer t'bein rat-arsed. Two blorks ont otheh sahd uv t'rord nortice us an stop an stare. One uv um gors: —Yeeeeeeeeess, lay-deeeeeeez!, an wuh just stand thuh, lahk, lookin at im.

Sioned gors: —Av yew *rerly* just said what I think yew av?

—Whir yer all off to, all dressed up sexy?

—Dunno yet, Sion sers. —Not sure. Whur ever yew pair uv tossers arnt going.

We leg it down rord, laughin lahk three kids, t'blorks standin thuh behind us lookin lahk twats, not knorwin what t'ser. One uv em calls afteh us: —Well, that's a relief, yer buncher fuckin slags!

Right. War.

—Oooooh, there's clever!

—Get back tuh tha bedsits an wank over yer porn mags cos that's t'clorsest yull ever get to a propeh shag!

—Yer dickless little pricks!

—Wankers!

An more uv t'serm. Thee shout summat else afteh us but wuh laugh an ignore thum, theh behind us, gone, pathetic, insignificant specks. Wuh gor int town t'Spar, off ar fuckin heads, blorks whistlin at us, callin wuh orver:

—Wheee-ooooo! An where ar you three goin?

—Lookin good ternight then!

Which, a havter admit, wuh ar; am wurrin this small, multi-coloured dress a got last month in Machynlleth market, Sioned's wurrin a big billowy dress orver a pair uv Caterpillar boots an Mags as got on ripped an ferded orld jeans wi t'hugest boots av eveh seen an a little taht black top which shors off er tits an er flat tummeh. The cow, she neveh as any probs stayin slim. An a feel that a look good sor consequently a *feel* good, jer knor what a mean lahk?

Outside t'Spar, Margaret meets someone she knors, a rully fuckin irritatin blork wi bad teeth oo's got t'kind uv laugh that meks yuh wanter smack im one. Ee seems t'lerbour under t'misapprehension that is laugh is actually amusing, so ee exaggerates it furtheh, which merks it grate even wuss. A dorn knor is propeh nerm lahk, nor do a rully want to; Malcolm calls im the Cackler, which is good enough. A can hir is stupid fuckin false cackle from inside t'Spar as a buy two big bottles uv vodders an some tonic.

—Let's get completely rat-arsed, Sioned, eh?

She grins. —Too rright. Let's drink til wir *sick*.

Wuh orpen a bottle ont wer horm an swig it strert from neck.

> Six long months a spent in Dubberlin
> Six long months doin nothing at all
> Six long months a spent in Dubberlin
> Learnin ter dance for Lanigan's ball!

The Cackler follors us ferra bit an tries t'tell us that wuv got t'wuds wrong an tries t'cadge some vodka from us an all but Mags tells im, quite nicely lahk, t'sod off, an thank fuck ee does. Wuh do a little celebrertary jig int middle uv t'rord outside t'cinema an a police car pulls up. Bearded ferce out uv t'windor, lookin us up an down. Is pink tongue comes out an licks is lips bitween t'gingery bristles. Fuckin letch.

—Noswaith dda, ferched. Shwd i' chi?

—Oh, wir great, thanks, Sioned sers. —Just goin home for a few drinks, yer know.

Ee sniffs. Christ ee can't keep is beady eyes off Mags' knockers.

—Ydych chi'n feddw?

—Not yet, noo. Soon bloody will be, tho, aye! She horlds up one uv t'bottles an smiles.

Ee sniffs agen, an is eyes slide all slimily orver us agen. Ah reckun ee's thinkin uv summat else t'ser so's ee can gawp at us some more lahk so wuh dismiss im fust:

—Well, thanks fer yuh concern, officer, wull be off horm now.

—Nos da! Take care driving now, there's some right dangerous people about!

—Diolch y fawr, constable!

An wuh leave um sittin thur all sweaty in is car, wagglin ar arses exaggeratedly. Ee's probleh strorkin is ard-on now, sittin thur starin, lickin is lips. Christ, t'wer ee wuh fuckin lookin at us, as if we wuh thur ferrim t'pick, as if wuh could just be selected an bought . . . Puh; men an the libidos, frantic an indiscriminate. The all t'fuckin serm. Oh yeh, thur ar some exceptions, mebbe; Malcolm, frinstance, t'other naht when ee wuh askin mih about mih ornleh gay experience, that wuh just, lahk, curiositeh, talkin about things when drunk, yer know . . . Harmless. Morst uv um tho; morst uv um ar like that fuckin copper.

—Didjer see the fuckin face on im! Is eyes were nearly fuckin bulging out!

—A thought ee was gunner go off thir an fuckin *then*! Sex-starved, probably, poor feller. Imagine what's going thrrough his head right now; us three, handcuffs, trrruncheons!

—Oh Jesus! Oh good God!

—Still, oo can bloody blame him ey? Arn we all just fuckin gorgeous?

Wuh shout an yell an leg it back t'flat an am horpin t'fuck that Colm worn't be thur wi a lord uv drugged-up nutters in tow. A dorn't want fuckin owt t'spoil this, am avin a fuckin grert time. T'flat's still empty tho when wuh get thur, empty except fer Ratty (Plague: stupid name) an Christy ont stereo:

> I went down to the hazel wood
> Because a fire was in my head

Wuh flop down int' seats an pour drinks.
—Women an vodka, ey, a raht potent combination.
—Too fuckin right, girl!
—Hundred per cent bloody proof, innit?

An a wek up ont carpet, stereo hissing, gob lahk a dirteh oven, t'smell uv spew an a smile on mih ferce. Sioned an Mags ar all bundled up ont couch t'getheh, under one duvet. Ther smilin too.

A big, boomin voice werks mih out uv muh drunken slumber an a lie thur, hungorver t'hell, lissnin to it; Colm int kitchen merkin tea an singin 'Oró Sé do Bheatha 'Bhaile', that Gerlic song that ee sang endlessly fuckin endlessly wi Liam last night int pub. The tried t'teach it t'mih but Colm sings it t'the tune uv 'What Shall We Do With the Drunken Sailor' which am sure is wrong. But, anywer, it's morning, ee's singing, an mih heart lifts; not cos ee's got a grert voice ur owt like that, sjuster gruff Scouse bellow rully, but cos it means that ee's happy, so it ul be easier fer me t'be happier too. A worn't havter put up wi is fuckin moods. Ts not offun that a werk up an feel lahk this. It rarely happens this wer.

An awurr uv t'risks alraht; not just AIDS lahk but t'rerpist as well, yih dorn't avter be on t'campus t'meet the Campus Rerpist, it could bih fuckin anybody – but am doin it all t'serm. Colm does it, sor can ah. An besides, it's not as if am not experienced in this, it's not as if ah dorn't knor what to expect, av done this fuckin hundreds uv times, it's sor pitifully easeh – yuh just give a certain look int bar, yuh pretend yuh find em intrestin an pretend t'be impressed an that's it, yur away. Easeh. Yuv just got t'utilise yuh natural talents.

His room is like morst; messy, a bit sweat-smelly, clorthes ont floor, dirteh dishes, porsters ont walls. Am somewhat dismayed t'see that Pamela Anderson's on one uv em, poutin above er ridiculous tits, but . . . well, did ah rully expect owt else? The all sor similar, morst uv em, t'slight softness around t'middle, the need, t'rough fumblin fer mih clit. Ardleh any uv em touch mih breasts, or strork thum; t'best yih can horp for is a cursory grab. And, as usual, this one gives mih an irriterted look when ee carn't get t'condom on, as if it's *my* fuckin fault.

—Here. Yuh want me t'do it?

—No. I can manage.

Ee flicks mih hand awer, snarls an grunts as ee rorls t'rubber down orver is veiny, stubby knob. A look at it an a carn't elp thinkin uv Colm's in relation; his is definitely bigger (it's a source uv endless borsting fer Colm, is bein well-hung), an darker in colour – t'end uv it, ah mean. Funny how the all so different. A think uv Colm's narrow hips an his soft, hairy tummy, his tiny pink nipples an wide shoulders, wondrin what ee's doin wi um right at this very morment. The all so similar, an yet so different; this one pushes mih gently back ont bed, is tongue prorbin in mih mouth, is big hand strorkin mih thigh. A clutch his sides an orpen mih legs, strorkin is balls as ee rorls bitween em, scratchin softleh wi mih nails t'merk im gasp. A guide im in, an it stings a bit cos a wunt rully wet enough, but a soon moisten up an follor is thrusting. Just like riding a bike, this is; yuh never forget. Grunts in mih ear, slobber on mih shorlder; too fast.

—Slow down, will yuh . . . tek it easeh now . . . bit slower . . . ah yeh . . .

A like it when is pubic bone presses int mih clitoris but ee's goin too fast fer that so a lock mih legs bihind is back, just above is arse, an force im t'slor down. Ee decelerates an starts t'grind, is hips an is teeth, a gorgeous sensertion which ah can feel even through mih drink-numbed senses . . .

—Yeh, like that . . . that's good . . . keep on doin that . . .

Ah can see is teeth above mih int dark, a dull creamy glint. Mih hips go up t'rub mesen agenst im an mih toes curl up an mih thighs shudder an mih belly ripples in an out, unstoppable an uncontrollable like falling or flying mih breath comes faster louder an it builds an builds an –

—Ooooooooooohhhhhaaaaaaagh am comin am commmmmmmm . . .

And ah release it all, evrihthing, in a long, lovely groan, all weak an warm an lovely jelly . . . but as soon as it starts t'subside ee's awer agen, ten t'fuckin dozen, a dorn't av time t'wind down cos ee's a fuckin blur agen, thrashin full speed afuckinhead, ah mean fuckin gabba techno style BPM am talkin here. Av ad my come lahk sor ah just let im get on wi it like an a find mesen fer some reason thinkin uv Colm agen an is perpetual air uv bewilderment an t'thought comes t'me that ee'l allus be separate, even to himsen (an what fuckin 'splendid secret'? *Who?*). An a dorn't knor why but a start t'cry, but ornleh a little; a nearleh allus feel sad after av come lahk, an t'booze dorn't help. Ornleh a few tears, not so much that it merks it difficult t'conceal from this groaning blur above mih oo jerks an thrashes madly fer a few seconds an then abruptly stops, sighs, an rorls off. Plop as t'condom hits t'floor at side uv t'bed.

—Uuuuuurrwaaagh . . . fuckin . . . fuckin lovely . . . smashin . . .

—Mm.

—Didjer come then?

—Yes, a ser, an kiss his shorlder, or whur ah imagine is shorlder t'be, int dark. This seems t'please him an ee starts t'breathe deeply, asleep within a few seconds. God, ee reeks uv beer; but then, probly, sor do I. A raht long session this has bin . . . can ardleh remember owt . . . a carn't even remember what is ferce looks lahk. Stubble, ah remember stubble, an a gap in is teeth which merd im look boyish an nice. Green eyes. Nice green eyes.

Ah wert until am sure ee's fast asleep an then a delicately extricate mih arm from bineath his heavy head. Ah remember Roger an Malcolm, yestider a think it wuh, talkin about t'Coyote Arm Syndrome; when yuh werk up hungorver next to an ugly lass int mornin an yer arm's trapped bineath er sor t'avoid wekkin er up an avin t'talk to her or, God ferbid, shag er agen now yuh sorber, yuh chew yer orn arm off in order t'escape like a coyote caught in a trap. T'loss uv a limb is preferable t'loss uv a bit uv self-respect a supporse is t'idea. One thing puzzles mih tho; why a coyote? Why not a fox? The do t'serm thing an all, the mutilate thesen if the trapped, like a coyote, or a wolf, or a jackal or whatever. So why not a fox?

Anywer, fuck it, that's what a do now – a escape. Softly, an as quietly as a can, a feel around ont floor fuh mih clorthes: boots, socks, jeans, shirt, bra, knickers. A pick summat up, some garment lahk, an mih fingernails brerk through a thin crust uv summat an a realise that it's is boxershorts. Ick. Ee must uv bin leakin int pub when ah wuh chattin im up, or when we wuh neckin in that shop doorwer. Ick.

When am fulleh dressed, a stand there lookin down on this sleepin sherp int dark. You wunt one uv t'wust, ah think t'mesen; you – whatever yuh nerm is – wuh just like morst uv em – so, so average. An ah can picture it int morn, you wi yuh merts down pub, boastin awer, t'words yull use, 'picked up', 'slag', 'gave it one', 'loved it'. A right goer, yull ser, gaggin fer it, yull ser, but yuh worn't tell em that this slag wuh gone when yuh work up, will yuh? No. But she will be, this tart, shill be long fuckin gone when yuh werk up, an if she ever bumps int' yer around town which in a plerce this size is bound t'happen yull look at er an yuh worn't av a fuckin clue why she did it, will yer? Yull wonder why she went, wonder why there wuh nor number or phone call, an it ul never even cross yuh mind that a just couldn't bring mihsen t'sleep by you, in fact t'ster clorse t'you fer any length uv time longer than wuh necessary t'get what I wanted from you. Oh yeh, yuh weren't too bad like, but . . . a ornly wanted, needed, yuh for one thing. An a got it.

A leave t'room silently an creep downstairs, grorpin mih wer through this unfamiliar house int darkness. Down t'hall an through t'kitchen, where ah nortice moonlight gleamin blue off glass; a bottle uv gin by cooker. That ul do me. A tek it wi me out front door where a find mihsen in one uv thorse narrow, hilly streets down by t'harbour. A can hear seagulls, an t'night is cold an windy an almorst entirely wi'out stars. A wonder if Colm'll be at horm, an what al ser to him if ee asks me where av bin. But ee probly worn't ask that anywer. Ee probly worn't even be horm. A start walkin in that direction.

Too lert; mih knickers uh full uv blood. A raht fuckin mess.

Ah terk um off an insert a tampon quickly sor a dorn't leak ont floor, fetch t'bowl from bineath t'sink, fill it wi watter, an put mih undies in it t'sork. The watter immediately turns red an cloudy, like red fog rollin in orver t'sea . . . a heavy one this month . . . it reminds me uv t'miscarriages, thorse years ago, before a met Colm . . . it must've bin all thorse pills which brought t'last one on, at least that wuh what t'doctor sed . . . but ah remember the –

Nah, dorn't think about that. It's in t'past now.

Am drunker than ah realise, as a sit down ont bog a stagger an havter support mesen wi one hand ont windorsill. Runny shit rushes intuh t'pan, almorst completely liquid. Ah havunt eaten for . . . how long? That packet uv dry rorsted peanuts yesterder . . . ham roll t'der before that . . . erm . . .

Colm torld mih once that he read that t'Nazi doctors would tie Jewish women's legs t'gether when they wuh giving birth. Ah havunt stopped thinkin about that . . . imagine it . . . t'berby suffocatin, t'mother bein torn apart . . . what evil fuckin bastards . . . imagine it . . .

All t'dead berbies, all t'aborted children. Sometimes ah think uv um all, the tiny people burned in hospital incinerators, flushed down toilets . . . ah remember that wanker Leon, Leon Leatherbarrow, when ah wuh livin in Leeds lahk, punchin mih int stomach t'bring miscarriage on when ah torld im ah wuh pregnant. Arsehole. Still, ah perd im back; when ah curm out uv hospital ah werted until ee wuh pissed an then ah poured lighter fuel down is trousers an set fire to it. Left im runnin about t'room, screamin, all doubled orver, slappin at t'flerms wi a pillow. Ope it burnt is fuckin dick off. Never father a child now.

The blood in t'bowl wi mih knickers in reminds me uv t'sterned river by t'dye-wuks back in Huddersfield. Similar, t'wer t'colour spreads an billows . . . dye-wuks clorsed down long ago now, but t'river bed is still bright red. Amerzin, it looks. But fuckin horrible at serm time.

Thuz a bottle uv red wine ont windorsill. Ah terk a big gulp from it as sour crap trickles out.

Liam an Colm ur int kitchen. A can hear thum talkin, one uv Liam's stories:

—The landlord uv the Mill. Ye know the mahn? Ieuan? Beard, blondish hur?

—Erm . . . no, a don't think . . .

—Ah well, fuck ut, ut's not importunt. Annywey, even he couldunt hahndle ut, an ee's been puffin like uh fuckin chimney since the fuckin seventies like, done the fuckin lot: trips, mushies, *loadser* fuckin mushies, t'ree fuckin hundred in wan go's is record. But this superskunk now; ee couldunt fuckin hahndle ut. Freaked im right fuckin ou'. Ee kept goan ohn about how he needud te shite desp'rutly, ee wuz ahlmost fuckin *crine*, ee wuz goan: Jesus, Liam, what huv ye fuckin done te me? Wha' huv ye fuckin *done*? Thought ee wuz goan mad, the two uv us fuckin did. Fuckin ahful so ut wuz. Ee got threatenin, ee did. Mad. Ah wuz feart fer me fuckin life.

—Fuck. Wha' did yer do?

Evrih time ah terk a swig uv t'wine more shit runs out a couple uv seconds lerter. It's as if it's pourin strert through mih, runnin like a watterfall strert through mih whole body, all mih bags an tubes . . . Quite intrestin, rully. Ah think ah'l just ster here.

Liam shouts from t'kitchen: —Oi, Mairead, wha' the fuck yis doin in thur? Touch uv the oul dia-ree?

—Yeh! Colm roars. —Come out an avva fuckin bevvy with us!

Ah drink more wine an sherk mih head. Ah think ah'l just ster here.

Granma?

. . .

Granma? Granny?

. . . I'm here. Can you not sleep?

It's OK, ah will soon. Ad just like t'talk wi yuh fer a while . . .

That's fine. It's not as if I've got a great deal t'do, now, is it?

No, ah suppose not . . . tell mih agen; what's it rully like, bein dead?

Worry. All it is mainly is worry. And boredom. Much the same as being alive, really.

Why t'worry?

Well . . . *you* should know.

Why's that?

For instance; that one sleeping next to you. Colm. Is he really good for you, do you think?

A dorn't know, Granny, really . . . sometimes ah think sor. Ah can never rully tell. Sometimes ah think yes, sometimes ah think nor . . . He meks mih happy, he meks mih sad. He's intrestin t'be wi, he's dull t'be wi. Ah dorn't rully know.

Ah, that was always your burden, wern't it? Uncertainty.

Yeh, ah supporse . . . am sure about one thing, tho; ah'm sorry ah spent t'money this wer.

Well, it's up to you. It's yours, you can do whatever you want with it. All I ask is that you don't let Sharon get away with stealing nine hundred pounds from you.

Oh a worn't, a worn't.

Yes, you probably will. You're too kind, in some respects. And kindness is a very heavy weight to carry, Mairead: people will take it from you, twist it, and give it back to you as something completely different. Something uglier.

Ah knor that now . . .

. . . are you sleeping?

Nurly.

You were always my favourite. I saw myself in you. I gave you your name, I named you after my own grandmother.

I know.

Born not twenty miles from where you're lying now.

I know.

Yes, of course you do . . .

. . . Granny?

What?

I wish you wuh still alive.

I know you do. Go to sleep now.

OK.

Fuckin mmmmm drunk as fuckin fuck . . . can ardly fuckin see even . . . where . . . Colm? Z that you?

Fuck knorsssszzzzzzzz . . .

. . . police phorned bifore an sed thee wuh horldin im but a dorn't knor where ur what for . . . dorn't fuckin care either . . . drunk as shite . . .

Geraint? Is that fuckin Geraint?

—Thought you wuh in fuckin Florida still . . .

—A saw yuh yesterday, Mairead. Do yuh not remember then?

Am movin . . . am bein fuckin carrid . . . a voice out uv t'dark tells mih summat about Roger bein dead but ah think ah'm just dreaming . . . ah ornleh saw Roger t'otheh der . . . ee wuh wurrin bandages on is wrist . . . who's falling? Where t'fuck am ah?

—What?

Wings an rumble and white fluff height. Nnnn, rrnnnn. At's what al see. Am fuckin *wrecked*. Thuz a voice mumbling in mih ear as ah fall down int whiteness but ah can't understand one fuckin word.

A rully fuckin hate that phrerse 'drug uv choice'. It's shite, it's meaningless. *You* dorn't choose t'drug, *it* chooses *you*, whatever effect it has that irons out yuh creases, counteracts yuh black energies, merks yuh horny, not horny, happy, whatever . . .

Sor am a what, am a fuckin drinker. A *heavy* drinker. Sor fuckin what, lahk? Why uh people sor fuckin afrerd uv that? It's not as if ah'm a fuckin bank manager, ur a bailiff . . . am not part uv thorse invisible forces that shatter an then trample on other people's lives. A just like a drink. Lots uv um.

A knor what t'liberals would ser, thed ser that a dorn't have a choice but a have, ah fuckin insist on that, it's my fuckin choice t'nullify all this, t'drink it down an down int a pulpy, harmless paste. It's all too jagged, too bright wi'out t'booze . . . too many scalpel edges.

Ah merd this choice a long, long time ago. Other drugs, ah mean, E is good; oh yeh, E is fuckin grert, but it's what it sers, tha knors, ECSTASY, rimoved from this wuld lahk, tortally divorced from what a knor as reality. Least wi t'drink t'wuld still tends t'be thur somehow, some wer, just whitewashed a bit, yuh knor, foggy an opaque . . . like tha woolly white when yuh flortin orver t'clouds . . .

That whiteness is nice. A like that whiteness. A dorn't think ah could live wi'out it, t'tell the truth, a rully rully dorn't.

From *A Personal Guide to West Wales*, anonymous authorship, privately printed, p. 33

Positions precarious and points perilous; frozen rockfalls and avalanche, scree . . . A colossal consumption; the Ystwyth valley is the ever-widening maw of a vast and greedy fault stretching to slurp at the sea, bestubbled along its length with the stumps and debris of shattered boulders, each piece microcosmically mirrored, each dimension – the large, the small – caught in the commonality of slow disintegration. Shared is the susceptibility to erosion, a collapse from which there can be no escape, ever. The fault is the furrow of an immense land-lamprey, its offspring the tiny tunnels in the rock surface; winding ridges, writhing runnels, stunning patterns made by the unknowable activities of organisms now anciently gone, ineradicable traces of shy and tiny lives, made ungraspable aeons ago. Each track weakening the rock still further, even now, even now. From twitchings, continental collapse can come.

THEY MOVE ALONG

THEY MOVE ALONG the valley wall, dimly processional through the driving snow which, falling relentlessly, dampens their yelps and insulates their shouting which is becoming steadily weaker now since they have walked far and still have far to go. The house lights on the valley floor a thousand feet below, are, when visible through the swirling snow, mere matches about to be doused. The destination is Mairead's grandparents' cottage, clutched in these mountains and in this blizzard through which they wetly, whitely, stumble. Some of them stride purposefully, heads bowed, arms wrapped around themselves; others leap and caper manically like scarecrows animated by some fantastic force. Through the mad lace of the snowstorm, though, they are all phantoms, shadowy and insubstantial. It is New Year's Eve.

—What a fuckin wey te spend the first few owers uv ninety-five, lost in a fuckin blizzard so. Jaysis.

—Captain fuckin Oates, ey.

—Where?

Apparitions in the snow they are, this one silently gliding, that one leaping from drift to drift, driven by the hot chemical energies which sear through blood. Mickah's dog, Trapper, pelts back and forth between the moving shapes.

—Go gerrum, Trapper! Where's Sioned? Go on, go finder!

—This's the best fuckin advertisement fa class-A drugs ya could eva hope ta have! Malcolm's voice is barely discernible through the falling snow. —A mean, am *warm*! This is unbefuckinlievable! It's *lovely*!

—Flyin on tha last E, man, am fuckin *fline*.

—Look at awl this! So fuckin beautiful! Jesus, it's *so* fuckin beautiful! If a hadta die here then a wouldn't fuckin mind, onest, a wouldn't mind fuckin *dyin* here, if a hadta.

—Ah, don't tempt it. It might very well come ter tha yet.

—Yeh, Colm says. —Thel find us inner mornin, frozen in mid-walk. A mean, a carn feel it, like, burram sure it must be nerly fuckin cold enough ter freeze the blood in yer veins, it fuckin must be. Let's all gerrin daft positions so when de find us they can av a laugh, yer know, on all fours with ar arses stuck up in thee air an stuff.

—Fuck's sake, Colm! Sioned is heard to yell. —Just shut yur bleedin gob!

Colm, grinning, moves through the white towards a Sioned-shaped shadow only to find that it is one of the previously unknown people whom they had drawn to them earlier, back in the pub in Aberdyfi. He squints at the unfamiliar girl's screwed-up face, and tastes snow on his tongue.

—Oh. Ooer you?

—How far is this house?

—Miles, fuckin miles, he says, flatly. —Didjer not do enny E?

She shudders and shakes her head, then her whole body, her face like a clenched fist.

—Ah yer should've done, Colm goes on. —It's fuckin amazin, and then he vanishes back into the blizzard calling for Liam, who can be heard somewhere nearby saying:

—Ut's not at all warm. Christ, no, ut's not at all warm so ut's not.

The snow falls. It flumps to the floor and the world is white.

—Jesus, av just thought; the sheep. The poor fuckin sheep.

—Yeh, what do the sheep do in weather like this?

—God knows. Die, probly.

—Sheep, Trapper! Go get the sheep!

A small dark shape darts off into the white murk. Mickah watches his dog for a moment and then resumes the slurred and disjointed conversation with whoever it is he has been talking at for the last mile or so. Mickah is dangerously drunk.

—. . . oh yeh, av seen it, I yav. Just a row uv cottages, nice like, butcher av a closer look like an eev all got the same door knocker, a devil's head door knocker. Cos ther all Satanists, see? It's like a kind uv code, so they can all reckernise each other like. Up Llanegryn way. Strue, av seen it. Seen it with me own bare eyes. Yuh doan b'lieve me? Eh? Yuh doan b'lieve me then?

The shape in the snow drifts off, woolly hat pulled up into two peaks, and Mickah continues the conversation with himself. He is beginning to lose his footing on the slippery ground; his eyes, more closed than open, are sprouting little caps of ice.

Other voices drifting, swirling with the snow:

—Christ, tha fuckin taxi driver. After drop yis off at the cattle grid me arse. Could freeze ter fuckin death out here.

—Ah, no, fair play te him now, ye can hardly blame the mahn. Would *you* want te drive a bunch uv drugged up nutters t'rew *this*? God, could slide off the road an end up in the bottum uv the Happy Valley thur.

—An talkin uv which – wher *is* the fuckin road?

—Yeh, an whir's this fuckin house? Wiv bin walkin fer fuckin miles.

—Ah left a light on, Mairead says. —Will see it soon enough.

She tugs at the hem of her skirt, a tiny velvet tube which reaches maybe mid-thigh. She congratulates herself for deciding to wear her thickest tights underneath it, although they of course do nothing for the metal rings in her face which now feel like chips of pure ice, burning with cold. She thinks how her tampon string must be like a tiny icicle between her legs and looks around for Margaret.

—Mags! Is that you?

—Yeh. A think so, at least. Can ardly fuckin *think* am so cold.

—Come ere then so ah can . . . fuck me! Look at tha hat! It's completely fuckin iced orver!

—Am not wearin a hat. This is me fuckin *head*.

Malcolm gallops past them, a gangling shadow, chased by a bounding Trapper.

—Cahhhm on! Lines a whizz an glasses uv whiskey back at the house!

He vanishes.

—Fuckin loon. Ee'l freeze t'bleedin death.

Margaret shivers. —Christ, av never bin so bleedin cold.

A deep voice begins to sing 'I'm a Man You Don't Meet Every Day' and gradually, out of the falling, sprawling snow, other voices join in. An uneven string of singing shapes along the valley wall, drifting singing shadows in the weightless white.

—Nah! Colm yells. —Yer singin the fuckin Pogues version! Sing the proper one!

> I'm a piper by trade
> I'm a raaaambling young blade
> And there's many a tune
> I can play-aaaaaaayyyyy

Liam almost trips over a lump in the snow and recognises, with horror, Mickah's jacket. He hauls him up into a sitting position and slaps hard his slack, bluish face.

—Mickah! Get fuckin up, mahn! Ye cahn fuckin sleep hur now!

Mickah slowly shakes his head. —Just ferra bit . . . just need to lie down ferra bit like . . .

—No fuckin wey mahn! Yull be dead within fuckin minutes ye soft get! Yer gettin up an walkin so ye ar ye useless fuckin . . .

—. . . just ferra bit an al be alright then . . . al . . .

Liam opens a wrap of speed up under Mickah's nose.

—Lick this.

—Naw . . . al be sick . . .

—Bettur than bein fuckin brown bread. Eat the fuckin thing now.

Mickah obediently licks a mixture of snow and sulphate crystals off the small square of paper and Liam yanks him up onto his rubbery feet.

—Now walk. Walk wuth me n Laura.

They prop him up between them and march him onwards.

Ahead, in the billowing clouds, Llŷr floats over to Colm.

—Roger's not around, is ee? Only a could use a toot when we get back, somethin-a take-a chill out, like, know what a mean?

Colm shakes his head and water flies out of his hair.

—Nah, ee's back in Merthyr, a think. S wher ee sed ee was goin, ennyway, although if ee as then fuck knows why cos ee never sez any'in but bad about the place.

—Um.

—Al tell yer what, tho; if it's skag yer after, al do yer a ahf bagger brown fer another E.

—Ah, now, well . . .

And they haggle there, on the side of the mountain, in the snow which continues to fall, softly falling now that they have crossed Windy Gap and are sheltered by a mountain peak from the lashing wind. A signpost for Llyn Barfog protrudes from a deep drift like a finger raised in warning.

—Look! There's the sign! Not far now!

—This is fuckin incredible. It's like the head of a vast pinter Guinness.

—Gunter die we arr, Sioned mutters. —Not gunter make it, boy. Fuckin dead yer we arr.

—Don't be daft, Paul says. —Not far tuh go now. Will be OK.

Margaret's voice, trembling slightly as the MDMA (or whatever toxic concoction was sold to her under that name) begins another rip and rush through her tired body, cuts through the curtain of snow:

—A can see a light! Look! There's a light ahead!

A candle in the darkness, reachable warmth and shelter. Those who are able to – those who are drug-driven – yell in triumph and break into a run; the others somehow find another shred of energy and determination to put behind their staggering.

—Ah torld yer wud mek it, didn't ah! Mairead puts her arm around Sioned's shoulders. —Wuh thur, look! Wuh serf!

—Duw, Sioned whispers, her voice gulped by the snow. —Diolch, Duw.

Bounding, shouting figures in the descending ice, flailing limbs and grinning faces scything through the snow clouds, sudden, shadowy propulsion towards the solitary light. Were it not for the soundproofing effects of the snow these mountains would ring to their joy.

Malcolm crouches in the cottage doorway, teeth chattering, hugging himself.

—Christ, what kept ya? Bin ere fuckin owers it seems like, Jesus, urry up an let me in am ahf bleedin dead with tha cowld. Fuck.

Mairead opens the door while Paul fetches buckets of coal and logs from the ramshackle outhouse and soon there is a roaring fire with boots and Trapper roasting and steaming on the grate, socks like the shed skins of snakes. Powders and pills are strewn across every available surface and the air is soon thick with smoke. Glasses of whiskey gleam amber in the firelight. Those who had been snagged earlier in the pub sit quietly by the flames, watching and listening, warming themselves. Malcolm makes moves towards one, but she can only tremble and clack her teeth. Nice teeth, Malcolm thinks. White and strong.

—Sussussorry, she manages to say. —Fuhfuhfuckin frfrfrozen.

—Ere, wawm yaself up.

He takes a knitted blanket from the sofa and drapes it across her shoulders. She nods and wipes a dewdrop from her nose. Nice nose n all. Snub, sort of. Retroussé? Is that what it's called?

—Well, ere it is, lads an lasses! Mickah, who has made a remarkable recovery, raises a half pint of brandy. —Happy New fuckin Year!

—Y Flwyddyn Newydd hapus!

—Aye, Nua bliain sona ter yis all!

Drinks are gulped, powders snorted, pills popped. Llŷr, pleased with his heroin for Ecstasy transaction, chases off Bacofoil in the corner. Laura falls asleep on a glowing Liam. And Colm breaks up the half-finished jigsaw on the coffee table, a lake scene in Switzerland or somewhere, to consternation from Mairead:

—Oi! Tha twat! Took mih fuckin owers that did!

—Ah well, yer shouldun be so anal, then, should yer? He busies himself with the pieces, thumbing and snapping them together, forcing them to fit. —Jigsaws ar fer anally retentive people oo always want evrythin in its proper place. People ooer ruled by routine.

—Bollocks. Tha's just a pern int fuckin arse Colm is what yuh ar.

—Fuck off.

—Ah now, here! Liam yells. —Ut's New Year's fuckin Eve!

—There. That's berrer.

Colm sits back, beaming and sniffing, pleased with his handiwork.

And Margaret, the initial euphoria of the rush subsiding, stares fixedly at what has become of the jigsaw; now tree has been joined to roof, lake to sky, bush to wall, cloud to boat. A window looks out of water and a branch pokes from a chimney. She stares at the puzzle, now jagged and uneven, a depiction of a nightmare place full of snares and sharp edges and she goes on staring as steam begins to rise from her clothes and beyond the walls the snow continues to fall and cover the cottage, the surrounding mountains, all of Wales.

MARGARET

A SAW IT advertised in, where was it now, the Bon Bon a think: ROOM TO LET IN SHARED HOUSE, that kinder thing y'know, an a telephone number an stuff. A already knew the house like cos a used to live up by it, on the Waun; a used to pass it when a walked down into Llanbadarn to go to the pubs thair, the Gog an the Black like, an a remember thinkin then what a lovely house it looked, what an ace place to live it seemed an stuff. So a rang the number an a was ever so s'prised like that the voice on the other end was cockney:

—Well, it's a bahstard uv a plice ta foind, sow ya moight be better off gerrin a tahxi . . .

But, liker say, a knew whairabouts it was, so a caught a bus up to save some money an walked down Cwmpadarn Lane. Comin up to winter it was, as a remember like, an the little stream down thair was pretty full, almost overflowin an stuff, an a remember aller hedges so green an frosty an stuff like an a could hear the sheep in the fields an stuff an a saw a little frog. An when a got to the house, to Llys Wen like, the steep driveway was all iced up an stuff an a nairly went smack flat on me arse walkin down it, tryin to avoid the car thair which was tryin futilely t'get up the drive like; it'd get halfway up an then the wheels'd spin like an it'd slide back down to the bottom again. A leant down an smiled in through the side window an saw some sour-faced lookin girl who refused to even look at me; Christ, a thought, a hope *she* doesn't live ere. She didn't, as it tairned out; it was that Sharon one, y'know the one from Wigan is it or somewhair like that? Don't see much uv her now, thank God – she never *did* like me, she didn't.

So, anyway like, a knocked on the door an stuff an this tall, skinny bloke answered lookin utterly pissed off. He looked over my head an went:

—Oh fa fuck's sakes. She still fuckin ere is she? Shiz bin ere on tha couch fa fuckin days an now shiz finely got tha fuckin hint an got er fuckin arse in geah ta gow she cahn get up tha fuckin drive. Well, al tell ya; she thinks shiz stain ere anotha fuckin night shiz got anotha fuckin think comin. She can fuckin wawk owm. Bag.

Then ee looked down at me as if, like, only just realisin a was thair.

—Ow shit am sorry. Arm Malcolm. You're Margaret, yeh? Margaret Jones? Fuck yud betta come in.

A started t'laugh, an he joined in. He looked wasted, as a remember; is skin all sallow an stuff an is eyes all red. A couldn't av looked too hot meself, tho, not havin slept for two bloody nights nairly; ad bin whizzin away over at a party in Dol-y-Bont.

A followed him into a house which whiffed uv dampness, mildew an stuff like, but a liked it straightaway; y'know when somethin just gives off a good feelin, a good welcomin feelin? Well, it was like that. An it was a fuckin madhouse as well; thair was the noise uv the car strainin outside, hard techno blastin out from up the stairs, some crappy game show loud on the telly, nobody watchin it. We wair standin out in the hall an the phone rang, an when Malcolm picked it up a haird a Scouse voice boomin out uv the receiver, all tinny an insecty like but still bloody loud, ee must've bin roaring:

—Malcolm, yer ole twat! Wer scorin supplies fer Cnapan, whatjer want? Urry up an give us yer order cos the money's about ter go!

—Col, arm just in tha middle uv showin somebody arahnd tha house, yull afta –

—Boy or gerl?

—Girl, she –

—What's she look like? Is she fit?

—Shiz ere now, right ere, listen, I –

—Wer off right now like so whadder yis want, quick cos the money's goin! It's about ter go enny minute! Quick!

—Two bags. Just get us two bags.

—Is that all? Christ that's nor enough!

—An a pill then. Yeh, get us a pill as well, two bags an a –

The line went dead – brrrrrr. Malcolm replaced the receiver an shook is head an took me round the house like. It was fuckin brilliant. The front room was a mess uv bottles an plates an clothes an stuff, with a deep voice behind the couch goin:

—Hello? . . . Hello? . . . Hello? . . . over an over again. A could see trainers an the bottoms uv a pair uv dead mucky jeans stickin out. An then a remember some lanky bloke with glasses an a grin – Paul, this was – draggin a mattress down the stairs behind us an another voice, an Irish one, shoutin at him:

—Yis're not takin tha fuckin mattress up Cader Idris. No fuckin wey. Wha the fuck a ye playin at mahn? An wha, yeer goin in fuckin *sandals*?

—Hello? . . . Hello? . . .

Someone came out uv the kitchen drinkin melted ice cream out uv the tub. Allen this was, before ee ad that row with Malcolm an left.

—Want some Neapolitan milk?

—No ta.

—Al sift out a choc'lit piece if yuh like. There's still a few solids left.

—No, it's alright.

Malcolm was shakin is head, grindin is jaw. Laughtrack from the telly, the techno from upstairs, an now Perry Farrell screamin from the kitchen as well. Mad it was.

—Hello? . . . Who's thir? Who's that?

Malcolm jerked his head at the couch. —That's Geraint. Ee's off ta fuckin Florida soon, lucky cunt, so ee's celebratin by tryin ta drink imself ta death as quickly as possible.

—Paul! Am not climbin the fuckin mountain wuth ye draggin tha fuckin mattress so am not. Ah Jaysis, oo let the fucker at the mushroom tay? Ah told ye te keep im awey from the mushroom fuckin tay!

—Prefer the raspberry ripple meself, but they wir outer that in the Spar.

—Hello?

The doorbell rang, an someone shouted:

—Malcolm! It's Sharon! She can't get up the drive!

Malcolm held his head in his hands.

—Oh fa fuck's sakes! Ow, fuckin, *long* . . .

—Mint choc chip's not bad, like, but goes all claggy when yuh melt it. What yuv got tuh do is – ·

Malcolm said t'me then:

—Look, the room's at the topa the stairs, straight in front a ya as ya gow up. If ya want it, it's yours, ya can av it. Will sawt aht deposits an shit later, yeh? An down't mention that ya sub-lettin eeva. That fuckin Sharon's not stain ere one maw fuckin minute . . .

A decided t'get out uv thair an hole meself up in the room, so a squeezed past Paul an is mattress on the stairs.

—Watch y'self thair then.

—Put the fuckin thing back ey, Paul, stop bein so fuckin daft. Jaysis Christ.

It was *mental*. An a loved the room immediately; big, slopin ceilings, a bit uv mildew like but fuck that, the window lookin out over huge green fields t'Comins Coch. Bedlam from downstairs. One drawback, a remember thinkin, would be that ad have t'walk back up here from town through the college, an this was when the campus rapist was at is most active like, but even that didn't put me off. A mean, the place was so kind uv welcomin an stuff . . . a just felt at home thair, an bollocks to the mildew and the fuckin rapist. Amazin how quickly yuh get used t'facin dangers, isn't it? An a remember findin a big spliff on the windowsill; movin-in present or not, a smoked the bastard lyin on the bed.

Chaos from downstairs:

—Yuv bin ere since fuckin *Tuesday*!

—Well, ah carn fuckin elp it, can ah?

—Right, that's ut. Ahm not fuckin goin so am not.

—Well, just uh cushion then. Wuh gunner need summin tuh sit on when we reach thuh top aren't we, a mean will be fuckin knackered.

—Hell fuckin O! Will some fucker tell me oo's thir!

—Phone a fuckin taxi then! Look, ere's tha fuckin phone, right? An ere's tha fuckin numba! The fuck're ya waitin for!

—Ey, Paul, ya know tha legend abou' Cader, tha if ye sleep on ut yull wake up eithur insane ur a poet? Well, guess. G'wahn, just take a wild guess.

—Geraint! Yew just leave that fuckin ice cream alone!

—Shall we av just one more cup uv that tea before we go? Ey! Let's take uh flask uv it with us!

Mental it was. Yeh, a could definitely live ere, a remember thinkin t'meself; a clearly remember thinkin that, as a lay back on the musty bed an listened an smoked the spliff. It just felt like home. Ages ago this was, now. About two years, a think.

Speed's ace, a love it I do, but the comedowns are fuckin terrible. So fuckin *down* . . . An like anythin else, the nicer it feels when yur up, the worse it'll be comin back down. That's a rule. A mean, me an Colm scored a half-ounce off Phil two days ago, an it was ace like, but now . . . a feel like fuckin shit. Absolute fuckin shit. Physically, mentally fucked. An a feel as if av done somethin so vile, so hideous . . . a don't know what, like, specifically, just somethin unforgivably bad. The best way t'cope with this, av always found, is to just drink through it, an that's what wiv both bin doin for the past few hours, just drinkin pint after pint an starin at the fish in the fish tank an chain-smokin an stuff in this dark an dingy pub with the rain beatin on the windows. Colm looks fuckin wasted. Is skin's like a raw sausage an yuh can ardly see is eyes, all shrunken they ar an stuff. It's Sunday afternoon. A feel like fuckin shit. An sittin opposite us is the Fat Family; fat mum, fat dad, fat boy, fat girl. Thev all got huge plates uv food in front uv them an stuff, an every so often one uv them looks up and says through a mouthful:

—Nice chips.

An that's it; that's all they say to each other. Nice chips. On a rainy Sunday afternoon in a small Welsh town by the sea. Nice chips. Lifelessness personified. If a had t'draw a picture illustrating how a feel, ad draw a fat, vapid-faced man saying: 'Nice chips'.

—Jesus.

Colm looks up at me all helpless an stuff. He looks like a small, frightened child on is first day at big school.

—Am so fuckin bewildered, Mags. A feel so fuckin . . .

Strung out strung out strung out. Struuuuuuuuuung ooooouuuuut. When a finally get t'fuckin sleep . . .

—They *are* nice chips, yes. Nice chips, you two?

Me eyes're beginnin t'sting. A think am gunner cry. Hopeless. Everything's so fuckin hopeless.

—Let's gerrout uv ere. A carn fuckin stand it, Colm says.

—Alright. Whair juh want t'go?

Ee shrugs. —Let's gerrer bottle an go sit in the castle.

—OK.

We sip ar drinks.

—Nice chips?

—Mmmmmm.

Colm lights a cigarette. A can hear him wheezing as ee inhales. My God. Is it rairly wairth it? Ey? Is anything rairly wairth it?

Ey, look at this – am about t'be chatted up. It doesn't happen t'me very often – most blokes're put off by the cropped hair an stuff a suppose – but now here's someone swayin across the courtyard an sittin down opposite me. Little ratty beard, spiky hair, drunken brown eyes. Not bad at all. No Jason McAteer, like, but he'll do. (Me, Sioned an Trish decided the other day that Liverpool are the best-looking football team; Trish went for Jamie Redknapp and Sion for the goalie. But the number 4's the man for me.)

—That's a nice top, this feller says.

—Thanks.

An ee's right, it is – a rairly like this top. Bought it in Shrewsbury like. Short, with black straps across me back, showin off me little snake tattoo. A feel dead good in it I do.

—It looks good on yew, that top does.

—A know.

—But it'd look better over the back of the chair in me bed-room.

A bairst out laughin, a can't help meself. The bloke grins, all embarrassed an stuff.

—Am not very good at this, am I?

A smile at him. —Not rairly, no. But at least yur tryin.

Ee laughs. —Oo is it yewer waitin for then? A mean, I assume yewer waitin on someone, sittin yer on yer own like.

An just then Phil comes into the courtyard with Pinkbits, the sixteen-year-old dealer (an one uv the best in town, it must be said – specially for E). The bloke leaves an Phil gives is back such a nasty fuckin look . . . oh God, a hope ee's not goin t'start off on all that shit again . . . a thought ee was over all that crap . . .

—Thuh that wuhwuhwas Sh sh sh sh Sieffri Luh, Luh, *Lew*is. Whuh what ddddid huh huh huh huh huh *he* want then?

—A dunno. Just talking. Christ.

Ee looks me up an down, all pissed off an stuff. A want t'fuckin smack im. Pinkbits sods off somewhair, probably sensin obsession rearin up in Phil. Christ, a don't see why a should have t'justify meself t'this arsehole, but what's fuckin infuriating is that a find meself doin exactly that:

—Ee just came up t'me an started talkin, a didn't even know who ee was! Fuck's sake! Can a not even speak t'whoever a want t'speak to now? Jesus, what's up with you?

Ee sits down opposite. A can smell the stale sulphate comin out uv is leather jacket, all detergent an sickly. Ee always smells like this when ee gets wairked up an starts t'sweat.

—Av av av av av av av guh got yuh you a ppppp *puh* resent. Ee smiles, or tries to, an slips me a tab of acid which a eat straightaway.

—OK.

—Am suh sorry, it's juh juh juh juh just th that –

—No, no, it's alright, a say, tryin t'smile as well. It feels uncomfortable on me face, like a growth or somethin. —Don't worry about it.

No, that'll be right, don't worry about it an let *me* do the fuckin worryin an stuff, worryin over what could have happened thair with Sieffri, worryin about how fuckin long it's goin t'be before a good-lookin bloke chats me up again. Jesus . . . a thought fuckin Phil was well over is stupid bloody obsession an stuff. A told im straight, a said yur a nice bloke, but friends only, nothing more than that, an ee seemed to accept it, like, but . . . ah Christ, a don't need that shit, specially not now when av just dropped acid an stuff, the thought uv which immediately starts t'make me feel a bit self-conscious, y'know, awair uv me tits pushin out against me top an stuff, which makes me go a bit red, which makes me go even redder, but thank God Phil's not lookin (ee'd probably mistake my redness for the blush uv lust or somethin), ee's handin out tabs of acid t'whoever comes along. Ee's still leanin over the table t'wards me tho, still all kind uv proprietorial an stuff.

Dewi comes over an sits down, lookin awful. He's a nice

bloke, around forty-ish like, a recoverin alcoholic with a complete kleptomaniac for a wife.

—Anyone seen my Cerys? ee asks, lookin like ee's about t'bairst into tears. —Shiz gone off shoppin like an was supposed ter meet me here over n ower ago . . . avunt got a clew where she is . . .

He looks dead, dead worried, as if ee's about t'go fuckin mental.

—Shiz got the kids with er an all. Christ, if anythin happens . . . a told er, a fuckin told er I did . . .

Phil slips im a tab.

—Ere. Thuh this ul ul ul s s s s s sort yer out.

Personally, a fail t'see how acid, in his state, will help Dewi out at all, but ee eats it and of course it's up to him. He's an adult, isn't he? He can do whatever the fuck ee wants to. A feel me toes begin t'tingle an stuff an am already startin t'regret droppin that tab, moreso when Griff takes Dewi's place across the table from me. He's a monster, Griff is, from Anglesey a think; ee frightens me like, even if ee as always been nice t'me, y'know, friendly an stuff. Ee's just so fuckin huge an mad-lookin. An thair's a rumour goin around that ee's wanted for murder, which wouldn't surprise me if it was true, oh no. He looks immense, like a fuckin buffalo or somethin, an his tattoos are too brightly coloured. Lurid an raw. They look sort uv painful an stuff.

—Fockin other night, boy, ee says, starin into me face. —Up in-a mountains out at Llŷr's pleyce like, with that twat Roger, yew know im aye?

A nod.

—Aye, smack, booze, fockin sound weekend aye. Ennywey, the Sunday like, me fockin hound comes back in-a middle uv-a fockin night like, only fockin draggin a sheep in, wannee? Fockin sheep's focked, mun, like iss it was –

An ee pulls a face, is eyes all kind uv wonky, head back, tongue out, an a nairly bairst out laughin cos ee looks so much like Phil when ee gets angry.

—Fockin blood evrywhir mun, up-a fockin *walls*, Roger's fockin freakin out not knowin whorra *fock's* goin on like, ee's woken up by-a fockin guts slappin im in is feyce like, so's a knock at-a fockin door like inner an Roger's goin farmer! farmer! tryin t'ide iss fockin chewed-up sheep like but's too fockin big see, an me fockin rotty's goin fuckin nuts at-a fockin door like so a opens a door, dunneye, an a fockin dog jumps out: BANG!

A jump an evrybody in the courtyard looks around then quickly away again when they see that the noise was made by Griff. He's fuckin mental, he's hyper, Christ knows what ee's on. Am startin t'feel . . . a dunno. Uncomfortable.

—An a fockin dog flies back in, no fockin ead on im. One gunshot like. Llŷr's cottage, boy, oof . . . a fockin abbatoir aye. Whorra fockin night like. An tha cont Roger's still fockin up thir, killin off-a farmer's sheep, gerrin is revenge. Fockin crazy boy. Woulden fockin mind like burrit wuz *my* fockin Rottweiler. Am not arsed. Got-a cont fer free anyway – when ee wuz a pup like, a nicked im from-a seym fockin farmer oo shot im!

Ee roars laughin, as if this was the punchline. A don't rairly know what t'do so a laugh as well, but am thinkin uv Rōger out thair in the mountains, stalkin sheep with a knife . . . rippin them apart . . . grinning as ee washes is face in a cupped handful uv hot blood . . . ew, God, steaming . . .

Griff slams is palm into Phil's shoulder, hard enough t'knock im sideways.

—Ey, Phil, yew yewseless stutterin cont. Lay me on-a tab.

A can see he doesn't want to but he's so freaked he's trembling, an ee gives Griff two with a shaking hand.

—Th th th th th three quid each, buh buh buh buh buh buh but yuh yuh yuh you can a a a a a a a a –

Griff leans in t'wards Phil, is hand cupped around his ear. —What yew sayin thir, Phil? Speak up, boy, a carn fockin eer yew!

—A a a a a a a a a a *av* um f f f f f f f f –

—Av um fer nowt? Is that what yewer tryin ter sey? Well, thank yew very fockin much! Ee claps im on the back. —A teyk back evrythin av ever said about yew, boy, a rirly fockin do. Apart from the smell! Yew fockin stink!

He eats the acid an ruffles Phil's hair an goes away, wipin is hand on the arse uv is jeans. Phil sighs with relief. A feel sorry for him, a mean yuv *got* to rairly, he's so pathetic, but the truth is that he's the wairst dealer ever, and he should find another line uv wairk. A mean, the other day like, ee was baggin up speed and hash in his house like an thair was a knock at the door, so ee peeked out of is window, saw two big men in dark suits on is doorstep, panicked and flushed all is gear down the bog. Then ee composed imself, opened the door, and spent the rest uv the afternoon rummaging through is drains: they wair Mormons.

Phil's face is white. White with a delicate tinge uv green. Am comin up strong now.

—Bah bah bah bas bas bas bas bast, bast, bast –

—Oi, Phil, come over yer now, yer cont!

A can almost hear the clunk as Phil's heart hits the floor. Griff, standin in the bar doorway with Black Jerry, beckons im across an ee scoots over t'them. God, he's so nervous that it'll take im about ten minutes t'say one waird. A feel another pang uv pity for him again; like that mad bloke Richard oo Paul knows, Phil's one uv life's victims. An invisible sandwich board with 'LOSER' on one side an 'EXPLOIT ME' on the other is permanently hung over is shoulders.

So am just sittin here on me own, comin up quickly on acid. Fuck, no, the whole fuckin *courtyard's* comin up on acid, Phil an Pinkbits av supplied evrybody it looks like, the whole place's startin t'flip out; people're crying, dancing on the tables, havin beer-fights, laughin manically . . . am not sure if it's just me or if the whole place's suddenly gone insane. A hear a deep an demonic voice in me ear:

—So . . . ee's gone n left yew on yer own, then, azzy?

A look up an see Jed, James Jedburgh, the Jedi Knight, the size uv a fuckin truck. Ee's alright, tho, covered in tattoos (a notice a new fire-breathing dragon on is neck) an built like a brick shithouse an stuff but he's a big fuckin softie rairly. Wouldn't harm a fly. But now, tho, at the moment like, thair's a leer in is eye an is teeth are lookin far too yellow:

—Left all alone then ar yer?

A nod an try t'smile.

—Yew two made a date then?

—What for?

—What for? The weddin, uv course. When's it gunner be? Yew decided yet?

This throws me. Am fuckin baffled an stuff here. Absolutely.

—*Ey?*

—Yer know, you an Phil. When're yewse tyin the knot?

Then it hits me, like a fuckin club or somethin, an a stand up an put me jacket on. Jed looks sick as ee realises an ee tries to apologise:

—Oh fuck am sorry, a rirly fuckin am, it was FuhfuhPhil yer see, ee sed yud got engaged like an –

—S'alright, don't worry. Not your fault like.

—A was wond'rin why a couldn't see any ring like. An a was wond'rin as well why the fuck yud wanter goan get hitched ter that twat, ter tell yew the trewth like. Ee seemed so sure uv imself, when ee told me, like, a mean a had no fuckin idea, I –

—It's OK, it's OK, don't worry. Just tell that tosser t'fuck off from me when ee comes back.

Am nairly in fuckin tears now an a leave as fast as a can, away, away, away from that deluded dickhead an is absurd obsessions, an halfway down Eastgate Street ee catches up with me, panting, red in the face, is glasses all steamed up an stuff. Rage tastes like iron in me throat an am gritting me teeth so hard am surprised they don't break.

—Suhsuh suh sorry a about that, it it it it it wuh was Griff, ee ee ee ee ee ee wuh wuh wuh wouldn't lih lih lih let mmmmmme a a a away, huh he –

A tairn on him then an somethin snaps. A can feel it, hear it, break inside: SNAP, like a stick. Thair's people lookin but a don't fuckin cair. Am pokin him in is pigeon chest an a can see spittle flyin out uv me mouth an onto is leather jacket:

—How many fuckin times have a told you? EY? Am not fuckin interested, d'you hear me, djer want it FUCKIN WRITTEN DOWN? AM NOT! FUCKING! INTERESTED! *AT ALL! EVER!* D'you understand me now? Ey, you stupid little prick?

Ee's fuckin gobsmacked like, both figuratively *and* literally cos av just twatted him in the face.

—Yull do as a friend, altho if you want t'remain that then yud best not fuckin tell anybody else any stupid shitty little fuckin lies like wair engaged, djer understand that? Is that fuckin simple enough for you?

A bloke walks past smirking an a can see what he sees; another hysterical woman, red-faced an sweaty and shrieking like a harpy, making a spectacle uv herself in the middle uv the street. Am about t'tell im t'fuck off but a start t'cry instead, a don't want to like but the acid's enhancing evrything, all of this shit, an a feel me face collapse. Phil reaches out for me so a run away from him, away to the train station an taxi rank whair a catch a taxi back up t'Llys Wen an totally ignore the driver an shut meself away in me room. All fuckin afternoon an evening a have t'endure the fucking acid an stuff; luckily it was fairly mild, an a was able t'take the edge off it with a Valium, otherwise fuck knows what a would've done. Probably somethin a fuck uv a lot wairse than lie on me bed an cry an listen to the radio. Some people might say that a overreacted back thair like, that Phil's sad an lonely an in need uv pity an understandin an tolerance an stuff, but they don't understand about me an how absolutely fuckin sick I am uv that tosser doin stuff like that, ee's always fuckin at it. Ee just won't let me be my own person. It's fuckin difficult enough t'know yursel as it is without some sad bastard insisting that yur somethin which yuh most definitely ar *not*. An what makes it even fuckin wairse's that a haven't had a boyfriend for so fuckin long; a few shags like, but nothin special, an Phil spreadin those stupid fuckin rumours jeopardises me chances uv meetin someone who a like. And I'd like t'meet someone like that, oh yes, am so fuckin lonely . . .

A find another Vally in me bottom drawer so a eat it an then soon thair's sleep, or at least a kind uv vague swooning. At around sixish thair's a knock on me room door an guess who it fuckin is, comin in all sheepish an apologetic an stuff an standin thair lookin weedy an ignorant. Then he stops bein apologetic an starts bein somethin much, much twattier:

—Yuhyuhyuhyuhyuhyuh you luh left mihmihmihmihmihmih-mihme ul ul ul ul alone! Av buh buh buh bin wuhwuhwuh wwwwwwandrin the stuhstuh stu*reets* luhluh –

—OH FOR FUCK'S FUCKIN *SAKE*!

A bury me face in the pillow an scream.

—WILL YOU FUCKIN LISTEN TO ME YOU IGNORANT LITTLE FUCKIN PRICK! WHY WON'T YOU FUCKIN LISTEN TO ME!

A rairly fuckin screech this, so loud that it hairts me throat. The blood drains from Phil's face. The drugs're still in me system an the room is kind uv blurry an stuff, dreamy like, an Phil's just like an unpleasant apparition standin at the end uv me bed. I wish that rairly *was* all ee was. A take deep breaths, tryin t'compose meself. A see an empty Smirnoff bottle on the windowsill an a think about smashin it over is thick fuckin skull. Oh a know, a know he's lonely too, but Christ, why can't he fuckin just *listen* t'what a say? Why can't he understand that am simply not interested in him, an that a want him t'leave me alone? I don't want him, a never have, a never will. It can't be *that* fuckin difficult t'understand, Christ.

—It's juh juh juh just that . . . M Margaret, uh uh uh uh I thuh thuh thuh thuh think a a a a a a a a –

—Oh Jesus, don't be a wanker! Shut the fuck up!

—Buh buh buh buh but a a a a a a do, a fuh fuh fuh fffffuckin luh luh luh *love you*!

A shove him violently off the bed an stand above him. His eyes shine with, with, a dunno . . . God, is he fuckin *liking* this?

—A can't fuckin handle this, am only twenty-two years old for fuck's sake!

A run into the bathroom. An thair I am, sittin on the toilet with the lid down, head in me hands, goin fuckin mad. After a while a hear me bedroom door close an then a hear the house door close downstairs, so a sneak back into me room, which offers little solace now that it pongs uv stale speed an BO. That sounds cruel, a know, but it's fuckin true, man; thair's many things Phil needs, an foremost among them is a good wash. Thair's a note on me pillow:

SO SORRY
PLEASE UNDERSTAND HOW
I FEEL ABOUT YOU
HERE'S A LITTLE PRESENT
'SWEETS 4 THE SWEET'

The 'present' is another tab uv acid. A think about taking it an then a think about throwing it away, but in the end a just stash it in me bottom drawer; you never know when such things might come in handy. Laughter, both real and on the telly, drifts up through the floorboards from downstairs so a dry me eyes, wash me face an go down into the mouldy living room. Sioned an Paul ar cairled up t'gether on the sofa. Mairead an Colm ar asleep in the corner, both uv um utterly wrecked by the looks uv things. Colm, a notice, is wairin a washed-out old tartan shirt.

Malcolm's openin a bottle uv vodka.

—Mags, quick, comen sit dahn an ahl pour ya a drink. Bill Hicks's ownly just stahted.

—Ta.

A sit down on the floor and he hands me a glass uv straight vodka.

—Where's the Gibberer? Gone, as he?

He always calls Phil that – 'The Gibberer'. A smile an nod yes an sip me vodka.

—We ird ya shoutin befaw, Malcolm says. —A was gonna go up an see if ya wir orright. Ya wir, yeah?

A nod. —Oh yeh. Just Phil bein a tosser.

—Ah well. He points at me glass. —Knock it back, darlin. Plenty maw where that came from.

A do just that, an pretty soon am happy, or as happy as a *can* be, under the circumstances like. But that's good enough, a suppose. At least, it'll have t'do.

God, what a day. What a fuckin day. Lookin forward all week t'me giro cheque an this mornin whair is it? No fuckin housing benefit cheque either an me rent's *well* overdue. Ad had it all planned out as well; get dressed up nice an stuff, go inter town, cash me giro, buy an eighth uv hash and a quarter whizz, chop the speed up at Roger's or somewhair an flog a few grams off, thereby gettin me own two grams free an makin some money t'get wrecked on.

Now tho? Fuck it.

A go inter town to the job centre, wait ages in the queue. Angry faces an screaming babies. When it's eventually my tairn am told t'go round the corner to the social security office, which a do, take me little paper tag (number 73) from the machine an wait. They av a similar machine at the deli counter in Somerfield. Quarter-pound uv mature Cheddar an a couple uv onion bhajis please. Them an three or four bottles uv strong red wine. Gwor. An that's another thing a was goin t'do with me money t'day, buy some fuckin food; av bin on rice an peas for the last six days.

Fuckin boring, depressing places these are. Always full uv scowling people. An thair's a couple uv young kids, about sixteen or seventeen, a suppose, talkin t'Sponge the window cleaner, over by the plastic plant, boastin about their court appearances yesterday:

—Yeh, an possession uv a teenth, one uv em says, too loudly. —A teenth! An yer's me with a bleedin ninebar in me pockit while am standin in a fuckin dock, boy!

A must say, a don't see gettin caught as anything t'boast about; gettin away with it is surely more reason t'show off. But a suppose that becomes so ordinary, rairly, a mean y'do it all the time, like havin a bath or a cup uv tea or somethin. It's just part uv yur life.

Boring boring boring. A can feel meself deflating, shrinking . . . this place saps all me energies. It was in ere that a saw Fat Charlie for the last time, y'know before ee choked an stuff. Maybe it was this that killed im – just bein in here. Poison in the air-conditioning, another way uv keeping the unemployment figures down. Christ, Hell can't be any wairse than this; a social security waitin room for all eternity.

Fat Charlie's funeral soon. Is sister invited us all. Av t'get meself something decent t'wear, *if* a go – a didn't rairly know im that well. None uv us did. A liked im, tho, what a knew of im. He seemed alright. Poor bastard.

Bzz! '73' flashes up on the board so a go up t'the counter, speak t'the man through the smashproof glass.

—Erm hello, am wondering why me giro didn't arrive t'day.

A give im all me details and ee sods off for twenty minutes. Christ, this is hard fuckin wairk. An poorly paid as well. Sponge gets a counter payment an leaves all smiley an stuff an the kids start writin on the walls in blue felt tip. The feller comes back an tells me that am under investigation for having undeclaired airnings: What fuckin undeclaired airnings?

—Your work at the students' union.

—Yeh, a declaired that on the form! A didn't hide anythin!

—Well, according to you, your employment was terminated

there on the twenty-third of the fourth, but your ex-employer states that your employment was *actually* terminated on the twenty-eighth. Now, what we need to do here is –

Oh for God's sake. Five days. Five lousy fuckin days, an now av got no way uv quenchin me thirst or even, fuck's sakes, eating. How the fuck're you supposed t'survive an stuff, ey?

Ee goes on for a bit an when ee's finished a go round to the housing benefit and go through the same tortuous, dull shit again. Apparently, housing benefit is stopped automatically as soon as income support is. So what do a do? Me rent's in arrears.

—Well, hopefully, Miss Jones, it will be sorted out within a week . . .

Christ. An in the meantime, what do a tell me fuckin landlord? A mean, he doesn't even know that am signing on, an no DSS tenants was one uv the stipulations, not that that mattered at the time a moved in – evryone in the house is claiming in some form or another. But av only just gone legit an stopped sub-letting and a think ee suspected a was so what do a tell im now? He only needs a reason t'chuck me out. He thinks av got a regular income. A can't exactly tell im that me benefit's bin stopped so ee'l av t'wait for is rent now, can I? It ul be OK if a can avoid im for a week, if me claim's reassessed within that time. *If.*

Shit.

This day is fuckin awful. Terrible, horrible. Torture. At the end uv this day al be less than a was when a woke up this morning. All this shit, all this stuff, it takes things away from you, it rips and snatches pieces off you. Yur diminished, shrunken . . . incomplete.

An all a need is twenty pounds for merciful oblivion, twenty quid t'take me away from all this. Use drink as a glue – put the bits back t'gether again. Or if not that, then get so fuckin pissed that you don't fuckin cair.

So a trudge all the way back up t'Llys Wen (which is a fuckin hike, believe me), get some stuff, walk all the way back down again. Am utterly fuckin knackered, walkin around with a heavy sack over me shoulders. No fuckin money and in need uv a drink, that's one uv the wairst things in this world uv wairse things. Av got t'bacco in me pockit and enough money t'buy a *Big Issue*, which a do, an am wanderin around imagining what it would be like in the Ship an Castle right now; dark and safe, the gas fire on making that little sputtering sound, old men drinkin quietly at the bar, me with me cold lager an feedin crisps to Murphy the dog. Rain on the windows. It'd be fuckin lovely.

Ah Jesus. No. Fucking. Money. An this bag on me back's gettin dead fuckin heavy. A go into the Trading Post.

—Av got some stuff t'sell, a say.

—Aye, well, let's see it then.

The old duffer who runs the place watches as a take the stuff out the sack; an iron (never wear smart clothes anyway), a sandwich toaster which took me fuckin ages t'clean an stuff (al just use the grill from now on), a calculator (?), and a hairdryer-and-cairling-tongs set (never used em since a had me hair cropped). He's fingering them, tuttin an goin: —Mmm, an am wairking out what al accept for them in me head; maybe two, two fifty for the iron; fiver perhaps for the toaster, altho al accept three (bollocks, Maggie, yud accept fifty fuckin pee girl), another fiver for the hairdryer-an-tongs; say two, two fifty for the calculator. Call it twenty quid. No, be realistic – fifteen. Can get drunk on that. Shit-faced if a go the offy.

The old bloke clears his throat and launches into a coughing fit, stuff that sounds like molluscs gurgling up into his throat. Christ, he's old. Either that or very, very ill, maybe both. When he's finished, he wipes his eyes with the cuffs of his jumper and says in a strained voice:

—Eighteen quid. Can't go any higher. Take it or –

An before ee can say 'leave it' av got me hand out for the money and a can almost taste the beer. Eighteen quid, not bad, nice one smashin cheers ta good on yer. That'll do.

It's fuckin beautiful here, it is, under the water. So fuckin beautiful . . . A don't cair about the pollution an stuff cos it's just so beautiful here. An besides, a haven't seen any real evidence of pollution as yet; certainly no turds or condoms, just the odd crisp bag or Coke can, bleached white by the salt an sun. They say that the wairst pollution is the stuff you can't see, but a dunno about that, an anyway if it *is* true why fuckin worry? What you can't see can't hurt you,

223

or, rather, what you can't see you don't give a toss about. And, God, far be it from me t'concern meself with sea pollution when a pump me body full uv drugs an drink, poisons, at evry available opportunity. Not that a feel the need for any uv that down here . . . it's just so beautiful, here under the water . . . Liam an Mickah an all them drop acid an go swimming at night-time, but just this is exciting enough for me, a don't need anythin more . . . safe an lovely, weightless, am flying, drifting over the rocks an through the waving seaweed, me breath in me snorkel sounding like Darth Vader. A can see Colm ahead uv me, the sunlight ripplin zebra stripes across is back. Ee's pulling imself languidly over the rocks an stuff, slowly kicking is legs. Thair's a hole in the crotch uv is shorts an sometimes when ee kicks like a frog a catch a glimpse uv is grollies, all shrivelled like walnuts. A want t'laugh. A smile and bubbles escape.

God, it's lovely here. Am so happy here.

Colm waves me forwud so a go up t'swim alongside him. Ee's pointing down at the sandy bed a few feet below, at a huge crawling crab, rairly fuckin big, its shell about the size uv a saucer. Its claws are stretched out t'wards us to scare us off an a can see is eyes. He looks pissed off. Colm dives down to it an it scuttles away under a rock. A spit me snorkel out an sairface for some air (catchin a split-second glimpse uv Malcolm an Mairead drinkin beer on the shore), one deep breath before a dive back down again. A wedge me fingers under the rock so a won't float away an peek under at the crab; thair ee is, claws stretched an open in warning, is eyes on their stalks stairin right at me. Jesus. A look up at Colm. Bubbles trickle upwards from his smile and is eyes behind the glass uv is mask're very blue. Is hair waves like seaweed.

Me lungs start t'ache an stuff so a swim back up to the surface, me head immediately hot from the bright sun. Colm appears in front uv me. Wair facin each other an treadin water, thair's wind drivin grains uv sand into me face an a can hear children playin somewhair.

—God. That was fuckin *ace*.

A want t'go back down again. Straightaway.

—Shall we go back down then?

—Yeh. It's berrer down ther, innit?

A replug me snorkel and submerge. And instantly, evrythin's OK; am in an underwater garden, the seaweed swaying like tiny trees, rocks gleaming pinkly in the sun. A little grey fish with black stripes sees me and sods off, so fuckin fast – one second it's there, the next it's gone, a tiny puff uv sand in its place. A just float thair, spread-eagled like a starfish. Colm swims underneath me. A just float thair, me eyes closed, not wanting this to ever, ever end. A want to swallow water til me lungs're full. A want t'sprout gills. A want t'manacle meself to a rock so al never float back up to the surface.

This is all thair is – floatin in several feet uv polluted water off the coast uv west Wales on one uv the very few hot days uv the year an a rairly don't want it to ever, *ever* end.

Fuckin money.

Havin no money prevents you from doin so many things, but it's not rairly the big things that bother me, a mean am not arsed about good food and clothes an havin a CD player an stuff; no, it's the little things, *they're* the ones that get t'yer, things like havin t'eat dry toast an black coffee for breakfast, rollin up dog ends from the ashtray t'smoke, havin t'wash yur clothes in the bath cos you can't afford the fuckin machines in the laundrette, foldin the bog roll over the shitty part after yuv wiped once so you can av another clean surface t'wipe again. Avin t'bundle kitchen roll between yur legs cos yuv run out uv tampons an can't afford any more, it rubbing all sore an stainin yur knickers. Some uv these things are bairable, like, just about, cos livin in a shaired house like a do thair's normally someone with some spair milk or marge or a Tampax or somethin, but evrybody else here is poor as well most uv the time so a can't get a sub for drink or drugs. And fuck a could do with both.

The day stretching ahead uv me, empty, yawning, boring. Nothingness, emptiness. Utter fuckin boredom. Nothing t'do. Nothing a *can* do.

Fuck it. Four fuckin days til giro day. Am expectin a tax rebate (a little one, thirty pound or so), at least av applied for one, but what comes through the letter box this morning? Bills: gas, electricity, council-tax arrears, owed rent. It just never fuckin ends. Poverty would be tolerable, like, a mean goin without things an stuff, y'know, if there wasn't faceless fuckin wankers in offices demandin that a give money t'them when a haven't got enough for mefuckinself. Shit, what a wairld.

It's pathetic: shakin the fuckin furniture, hopin t'hear the jingle uv coins. Evryone else's out as well so am alone an bored, bored bored fuckin bored. Not even thirty fuckin pee for a bastard *TV Times*. Jesus.

evrih*thing*evrih*thing*evrih*thing*evrih*thing*evrih*thing*evrih*thing*

The song comes on again.

—*Again?*, a say, an Robbie twists around from the front seat.

—It's mah faverit, ee says. —It's mah farewell song. Ee breaks into a big grin. —You up on the E yet?

A shake me head.

—Ah, yuh will be soon, yuh will be soon. *I* am. One uv the best av had in fuckin ages, al tell yer that. Aven't ad one this good for ages.

A watch the mountains speed past the window, just vague dark humps in the dusk. Wair off to a big rave in the hills, a kind uv fairwell party for Robbie cos ee's off t'Paris in the morning. He's in the front seat with Dai, who's driving, an am in the back with Phil, oo's stairin out the window an grindin is teeth on whatever complex combination uv drugs ee's up or down or both on t'night. Am just waitin, waitin for the E t'kick in an stuff. The anticipation's part uv the pleasure, providin you aven't been given a dud, uv course, in which case the anticipation only ends when it becomes disappointment, which is *not* my idea uv a good time like. Robbie got these pills for us, tho, so they should be alright; knows is E, does Robbie.

whydon'tyoucallme, afeellikefly-in*too*, whydon'tyoucallme, affeellikefly-in*too*, whydon'tyoucallme, afeellikefly-in*too*

It's that Underworld song, the one off the fairst album; 'Cowgirl' a think it's called. A fuckin love it, it's brilliant, but this is the fifth or sixth time it's bin played, since we got in the car it's been this non-stop, an am gettin a bit sick . . . an then, as it explodes, a realise that a wasn't listenin to it properly before like an that it's absolutely fuckin perfect, flawless, incredible fuckin energy an drive . . . God . . . It sounds monumental, like, massive; it equates, in me mind, with Robbie leaving, and forms an image in me head uv a giant statue toppling. Av always liked Robbie. An this is, just, this is perfect; the song, the car, fuckin evrythin . . . sometimes things wairk, don't they? Sometimes they just come t'gether, oh yes.

Christ, am up on that E.

Oh yes.

—Louder!, a shout. —Tairn it up some more!

Dai does, an instantly the car is filled with mad, intense, amazing noise; am twitching like mad in the seat, me arms churning at me sides as if am like running on the spot, Robbie's yellin somethin over is shoulder about standing stones in this area – what area? – an the song's going right, fuckin, through me, movin me limbs, shakin me head, the bass rumbling and roaring way down deep in me bones my God a feel fuckin *great*. An it's goin t'get even better.

A want t'make sure evryone else feels the same way, so a nudge Phil an ask im if ee's alright, an instantly is expression changes from what looked like worry t'what could be called joy.

A tap Dai on the shoulder. —*You* alright, Dai?

Ee makes a circle with is thumb an forefinger and nods.

—Ow about you then, Robbie?

He twists his body around so that he's looking over the back of is seat at me an goes, slowly an thoughtfully:

—I'm leaping . . . over tall buildings . . .

Ace! Fuckin ace! A laugh an just go with the music as we drive through the mountains. A wish a could see out, see the landscape, but it's pitch fuckin black n stuff an a can't see a thing but that in no way weakens the way I'm feeling, full of hope an happiness, God, E is a great fuckin drug it is one uv the fuckin best. Oh, a know it can backfire – didn't it put Colm in the hospital that time? – an that poor girl in the paper who died after taking er fairst one at her eighteenth birthday party – but a can already tell that this one's sound, clean, powerful . . . a feel fuckin invincible.

A dance in me seat until Dai tairns down a farmtrack an in between rows uv trees an suddenly the car's filled with light, multicoloured light. Thair's a big barn thing in the woods ahead uv us, music blasting from it, lights bairsting from its windows an stuff, an it looks like a giant spaceship as landed in the trees, something from that old *Close Encounters* film. People ar darting around outside it, drinkin out uv bottles silhouetted in front uv a bonfire, dogs leaping for sticks, people running, jumping, climbing on each other's backs, it looks fuckin great an mad an fun. A leap out uv the car an leg it fast over to the lights.

—Mags! Ey, Maggie!

It's Colm, drinking from a can by the fire, an Mairead an Malcolm an Paul an Sioned an loads uv other people. A run over an hug them all, talkin ten to a fuckin dozen, thir all happy and off their faces an havin a great time. God this is ace. Malcolm's doin a kind uv swirly dance, is feet skimming the orange flames. Thir's someone out uv it, comatose like, on the floor.

—Oo's that? Is ee alright?

—Gareth, Paul says. —Ee got let out uv prison tuhday an took too much, erm, methadone a think. With uh shitload uv booze as well. Carn move im now.

Phil says that thair's a van they can put im in so im an Paul carry Gareth off (ee just flops in thir arms like a rag doll) an the rest uv us go into the barn. Instantly through the door an the music smacks me in the face, deaf'ninly loud like, an the *heat*, God, hundreds uv people dancing, moving, wispy clouds uv steam risin up in the strobes t'wards the barn roof t'float around the nutters dancing on an hangin off the beams, about thirty feet off the ground. Fuck knows ow they got up thair like. A see a little bird, a sparrow or somethin, fly in through one door an flit over the heads uv the dancers an then fly out the other door back into the night an this seems gorgeous to me, an amazin, beautiful little event, an me heart swells like an a leap into the crowd an start goin mad, dancin me tits off t'the music, good fast trance, not too hard, like, just banging, dancing music. It's all fuckin great.

A dance for ages. That's all a do, a just dance. A get covered in sweat, me own an other people's; the E roars through me an keeps me goin for fuckin owers. Some dark, sexy bloke in a Wales away football shirt keeps supplyin me with water an grinnin at me all the time. An a keep seein this funny little bloke wairin a green baseball hat an square green shades, movin around all hunched over like, makin slow choppin motions with is hands, a serious expression on is face. Looks fuckin hilarious. Thair's loads uv people here, evry few minutes a see someone a know, I always do at these kind uv raves. A feel ace. So ace that am even glad t'see Phil makin is jerky way over t'yell into me ear:

—Just puhpuhput Guh Guh Gareth in a v v v v v an! Rim rim remind me tttttttttttttttt*oo* chuh check on im l, l, l, l, l, later!

A nod an carry on dancing, bouncin about madly, glad a wore me sports bra — if a hadn't've then me buzzies'd be in agony by now. And ad have two black eyes. Droplets uv sweat fly off me face, shining in the lights; it looks like am sweatin pure colour.

Liam drifts past me, is face bright red, a bottle uv amyl held up to is nose. Ee takes a huge sniff then throws is head back, is eyes popping out, roaring with enthusiasm.

Malcolm dances by me side for a while, is eyes bulging, is jaws working away. Jed trundles by fat and beaming an Malcolm follows im, fumblin in is back pocket for money. Sioned floats over the crowd, hoisted up on Paul's shoulders. Colm stands swaying in front uv the DJ box, bent backwards at the waist, eyes closed, the picture uv fuckin ecstasy. Iestyn, Dewi, Llŷr, Laura, Roy, Squeaky Sue, Sam n Antonella . . . a procession uv friendly, lovely faces an a dance an a dance an a dance.

A don't know how many owers later it is but the DJ starts playin some jungle, which a don't like t'dance to, an am thinkin that maybe a should av a rest anyway so a stagger over to the door an go outside an instantly a can't breathe; it's daylight an the view just, like, stands up and roars. In the foreground, collapsed bodies lie around the ashes uv a fire and, behind them, green hills stretch for miles and miles t'rise up into a valley again, immense mountains wairin scarves uv cloud beneath a giant, silvery sky . . . Absolutely fuckin gorgeous. Beautiful. A sit down by a tree t'smoke a fag an look at the landscape. The sweat dries all cool on me skin. Me ears ring.

Thair's some Brummie blokes a few feet away, complainin cos thev run out uv drugs. A see Pinkbits, sittin in a crowd by the dead fire, prick is ears up at this an come over t'offer them some whizz. The Brummy guys look up at him, an you can almost *hear* the relief on their faces.

—Ow much yer got, like?

Pinkbits shrugs. —Much as yew need. Loads.

One bloke pulls some cash out uv is pocket an goes:

—Cahnt yerself luck-aye am heterow-sexual.

A laugh an then stair some more at the view. The funny bloke in the hat an the square shades jerks through the vista, doin exactly the same movements as ee was doin several hours ago – the choppy hands, the fixed grin. Like some kind uv woodland sprite or somethin. A can feel the E b'ginnin t'leave me now, slowly like, an now for the fairst time in many hours a start t'feel the unpleasant onset uv a real, unadulterated emotion: fear, fear uv the shattering, horrible comedown that lies ahead. Not nice. No fuckin way. Altho whether the fear is of feelin a real emotion rather than what that emotion actually *is* . . . a can't say.

—Mags. Ow ya feelin?

A look up an see Malcolm.

—Christ ya wir fuckin gowin for it last night, wirnt ya?

—Yeh, a say. —A think am goin t'be payin for it shortly tho.

—Well, ya down't afta, just yet. Ee sits down by me. —Wuv awl just chipped in an bawt a load maw billy an E. Plan is ta drive over ta Ynyslas, get some bevvy on tha way, ya know, kick back, chill out . . . av a bit av a party in tha dunes. Keep tha buzz gowin. What jer reckon? Ya up for it?

Christ. *Course* a fuckin am. A spring up an follow im over t'Paul's car. A load uv faces ar pressed against the windows, from the inside like n stuff.

—Robbie comin with us?

—Nah, Malcolm says, grindin is jaws. —Ee fucked off a few owas ago. Ad ta catch is plane. Ee'l be arfway ta Gay Paree by now.

A wave over at the car an Paul revs the engine in response. As if the car is a big, friendly dog growling in greeting. Tingling starts in me legs again, me teeth begin t'feel strange . . . Djer know, a think am b'ginnin t'come up again on that pill. Yeh, am almost certain that a am.

—So yew never tried it then like?

A shake me head.

—What, not even once?

—No. A shrug. —Av ad stuff similar, y'know, DFs, Mogadon an stuff, downers. Am more uv an uppers pairson rairly, speed, dexies, E, y'know. The other stuff doesn't rairly do it for me like.

Roger blows out air an shakes his head. —Ey can be just as fuckin bard f'yer, if not fuckin werse like. Av seen too menny fuck-ups on-a speed like, I yav . . . A mean, look at fuckin Colm, mun!

A smile. A wouldn't quite call Roger a smackhead, not at the moment like (he goes through phases), but ee's certainly startin t'talk like one – stupid junkie contempt for anythin except heroin. A mean, take that bloke Methadone Mickey as an example; ee sits in the corner shivering, smellin uv shit an sweat an puke, skin like a week old pizza n stuff, dribblin into is patchy beard, an ee tries t'warn me off amphetamines because, t'quote im: 'They'll fuck yer pretty head right up.' That's actually what ee said t'me the other day, round at Phil's house like: 'Amphets'll fuck yer pretty little head right up.' Arsehole. An am like, oh an smack won't, is that what yur sayin then? A mean, Jesus. If a wasn't speedin me face off a wouldn't be fuckin sittin ere talkin t'you anyway, you borin bastard. An the thing is, right, all the fuckin junkies an wasters think they can give me advice cos am the youngest; it's only Roger, in fact, surprisingly, oo often treats me like an equal. A don't cair what people say about im, people're always slaggin im off (behind is back, like, never to is face), sayin ee's a psycho n stuff, but ee's always been sound t'me. A know ee can be a bit uv a nutter, like, an ee's bigoted n stuff, but . . . well, thair's reasons for evrythin, isn't there? A mean, ee was in the army for a while like, so a b'lieve, an ee spent some time in Northern Ireland, before the ceasefire like . . . that must be enough t'send anybody fuckin mental. God.

—If enny twat asks yew, y'dint fuckin get this from me. OK?

A nod yeh an take the wrap out uv is hand.

—Ow much?

Ee waves is hand, dismissively like.

—On-a house, tha one. Gerruz a wrap-a whizz ur summin when yer can like. But don't yew chase moren arf in-a go, like, an doan tell enny cunt oo gave yer it. An keep away from-a fuckin needles n all.

—Alright. Ta very much.

A want t'dash straight ome an do it, like, see what all the fuss is about, but that gay lad, Gwion, the one oo Sharon always fag-hags around, comes over an sits down at the table. Ee's not, like, the flamboyant type n stuff, not rairly, but evryone knows he's gay, not that ee tries t'hide it or anything. Roger's face immediately tairns nasty; is top lip cairls back from is yellow teeth an is eyes cloud over. Givin off waves uv coldness n stuff. It's like sittin across from an open fridge.

—Oh, Maggie! And how are you then, my love?

Me n Gwion talk about trivial stuff for a bit an then a think ee gets the message off Roger an ee leaves, with promises to get together for a gin an Abba night or something. God, a deaf n blind pairson could get the message off Roger. Ee seems, like, pairsonally insulted an offended an stuff.

—Tell me why-a *fuck* yew give-a time-a fuckin day t'that queer little fucker, ey? Sittin yer by im, yill get fuckin con*tami*neyted, mun, ee's more uv a fuckin tart en *yew* ar. Why-a fuck yer bother, then, ey?

A sigh an shrug. —Ee's a nice bloke. Does no harm t'no one.

Ee laughs, a real scornful, vicious laugh. —Nice bloke be fucked! Yew woan be fuckin sayin at when yewer weystin awey in-a fuckin AIDS clinic, will yer? Ar, yewer too fuckin young, mun, yull see sense in a couple-a yeers, aye.

That's it. A fuckin hate that, all that patronising bullshit. Av changed me mind – Roger *is* a tosser. Ikey Pritchard comes over, swayin, pissed off is face, steadyin imself with a hand on people's heads, a bottle uv Newky Brown like a weapon in is hand.

—Ey, Ikey mun, tell Mags yer about em fuckin queers. Teller-a fuckin germs, mun, g'wahn, clew er in. She woan fuckin lissen t'me like.

A pretend t'see someone a know an leave, quick as a can without causin offence. Am not takin any more uv that shit. An besides, the heroin is humming in me pocket so a leave the pub an catch a bus up to the Waun, go back t'Llys Wen an shut meself in me room. Bottle uv Spar cider, Sonic Youth on the stereo, matches, tinfoil . . . av never done heroin before but av watched others doin it enough times t'give me a fairly good idea uv what t'do, an anyway it was free so what does it matter if a fuck it up an it doesn't wairk? I aven't lost anythin, av I?

A open the wrap (as usual, a square from a porn mag), exposin a small amount uv chocolate-brown powder (only a taster, I imagine; Roger wouldn't part with a full wrap for nothing, now, would he?).

A delicately tip about half uv it on to the tinfoil. Me hands're shakin a bit n stuff. A roll a fiver up into a tube, put it in me mouth an hold a match under the foil. The powder begins t'crackle and smoke so a run the flame along the underside uv the foil, back an forth like, followin it with the money tube, suckin up an inhaling the coarse, claggy smoke. It's gone. The powder now just thin black ash.

A sit back.

Nothing. Sod all. Did a do it right n stuff? Just a horrible fuckin taste in the back uv me throat like, that's all. Did I –

– did i –

– oh fuck –

It *rushes* in in a split second an then me head's in the bin an am chuckin me lungs up into the fag ends an ash an banana skins an used tissues n stuff, so much vom that a think it's never goin t'stop. Yurk. Oh Christ, yeh this is fuckin great this is; oh, yuv got a drug that ul make me spew up for ever? Oh yeh, sounds fuckin great, al av some uv that. Jesus.

Then, tho . . . when av finished a sit back on the bed. Which has never felt so comfortable. *No* bed has ever felt this perfectly comfortable. Sonic Youth av never sounded so cool, clever, accomplished. Me clothes . . . me skin . . . evry fuckin cell in me body is humming and buzzing thair is no badness thair is no badness. Anywhere. Ever.

Ah, thair's no use tryin to explain. No one could ever understand . . . Here is something . . . A dunno, a don't feel lonely any more. A just feel ace. I am truly myself.

One thing, tho, a think t'meself – al never ever inject it, no fuckin way. Fuck, al never even chase it again; nice t'try it once, yeh, but that's it now. Yuv got t'try these things once, at least, haven't you? New experiences an stuff, sensations . . . it's what life's all about, or *should* be, anyway. A mean, what brought me to this town in the fairst fuckin place? Got t'explore, got t'seek. Got t'try these things. An yeh, am glad av tried it once. Pointless tryin to explain rairly like. Am buzzin t'fuck an that'll do me.

A lie back on me bed, arms over me head, just, like, laughin softly to myself . . . waves uv pleasure . . . oh God . . . it kicks in an it kicks in, an when yer think it can't kick in any more, it kicks in.

Fuck. Wow. God.

Colm nudges me in the ribs an nods over to the bar, whair the pub's owners – a Manchester couple called Ron n Babs – ar havin another row. Always fuckin rowin, they ar, like, sometimes rairly bad; Ron threw the whole fuckin till at Babs once, the bloody customers ad t'call the police an stuff. Ron's an ex-boxer; mashed nose, bright pink face, white hair. Ee's also, like is wife, an alky.

—Ah yih fuckin ignorunt *pig*!, Babs screams an chucks a full pint at Ron oo ducks down b'hind the bar. She storms off out uv the pub. Ron appears again, a big grin on is face, wipes up the spilt beer an broken glass an resumes the conversation ee was avin with one uv the old blokes at the bar. A don't know what ther talkin about; graves or somethin, a think:

—Oo's eh thuh deeds?

—Well, a checked the records like.

—Yeh, an what did theh say? Oo's name uh thuh deeds in?

—Mine.

—Ah, well, thir yer fuckin go then, the fuckin grave's yurs. Yer can dig the ole cunt's bones up if yer like, give em t'yuh fuckin dogs. No fuckin rights t'be buried ther.

Colm rubs is face and smiles. —Nice to av a floor show when yer comin down, innit?

—Yeh.

An am comin down fuckin fast, too, so fast a can hear the fuckin air whistlin through me earrings. Wair both drinkin heavily in order t'maintain, or regain, am not sure, the high we wair on all fuckin day yesterday an nairly all uv the night. Good speed, we ad, but it was cut with laxative powder; a managed an ower's sleep just b'fore dawn like an woke up with a streak uv runny crap in me bed. God, sometimes it's sick t'be human n stuff. All those fuckin fluids . . . a tell yer one thing; you can say a big tara t'dignity when you're involved with drink an drugs. Yuv just got t'let yur self-respect go like n stuff.

Colm looks at me. —You've gorra funny face.

A laugh. —Oh thair's nice, it was lovely two pints ago!

Ee grins an raises is arse cheek.

—A think am gonna fart.

Am about t'tell im that that might not be a wise move when thair's a wet rumble in is pants an is face tairns ashen an ee dashes off t'the toilet. Am sittin thair laughin on me own, me head in me hands.

—Funny over ther, is it?

A look up at Ron, oo's grinning pinkly. —Yeh, yeh, a say. —It's hilarious.

—Good. Nice ter see the young 'uns avin a good time, eh? Ee, yer so full of fuckin life . . . Ee winks. —'Nother two lagers, is it?

—Yeh, alright. These ar almost out like.

Ee brings the pints over an a wave uv comedown sadness breaks over me. A start t'think about Colm, the way he is, the things he does . . . a know one thing; a could never fuckin live with im. A just wouldn't be able t'put up with im . . . like the time we wair all round at is house one afternoon like an we ran out uv booze so Mairead gave im thairty quid t'go out an get some more, an ee comes back two owers later pissed off is face with a baby rat in is pockit. That kind uv thing would drive me fuckin mad it would. Sometimes a think ee's mad imself, or gettin ther; some uv the things ee says, they can only be the product uv an addled brain. Like the other night when a was in bed, sober n stuff like, just readin an avin a spliff, y'know, up at Llys Wen like, an Colm came in absolutely off is fuckin face an sat on the edge uv me bed an started . . . well, it was fuckin scairy, it freaked me out n stuff; is eyes rolled back in is head an ee started ranting on about the San Andreas trench or somethin an fish with eyes on stalks with bodies that ar just a great big gulping fanged gob an disembodied claws twitching on the sea bed an all this crazy fuckin stuff . . . a pushed im rairly hard an ee fell off the bed, looked up at me an said:

—*Fuck* knows wher a was then, an left the room.

Fuckin odd. Quite frightenin, rairly. Sometimes it's like a can sense things comin adrift inside Colm, breakin loose of ther moorings an floatin about inside his body, his head . . . Still, tho . . . a do like im. A can't help it, a just do.

—Guten abend, Margaret, wie gehts?

Oh no. A know that fuckin voice. A look up an oh shit it's Oxford John, with Paul. John's a Nazi obsessive, ee ardly ever talks about anythin else, specially when ee's pissed, which is when ee becomes the biggest pain in the wairld. Ther's a mutual dislike b'tween im an Colm, an Paul's not too keen on im either, but Paul'll put up with anybody. They sit down at the table an Paul opens is mouth t'speak t'me but John launches into a rant about war crimes or somethin, some fuckin Nazi crap. A spy Colm retairnin from the bog. The *look* on is face when ee spots John.

—. . .a mean, y'know, what actually *is* a war crime? Would *you* like t'define what a crime uv war actually is? An then uv course there is the question of actual *proof* . . .

Paul says: —Orright, Col?, an Colm sits down b'tween us an announces that ee's just followed through. Paul laughs an John looks at im with disgust, which Colm notices an is eyes light up. What follows here should be intrestin:

—Ah, Christ, it wuz disgustin, a disgusted me fuckin self. Yer know the bogs ere, the layout like, ther's like a cubicle, an then a piss-pan wither sink in a different bit? Yeh? Well, a hadter go into the cubicle ferst, like, ter clean, yer know, wipe all the cack away like, not ser much solid cack as just thick juice, like, yer know, poo juice like fuckin mulligatawny soup, an it ad all run down me legs so a hadter wipe irall up with bog roll which broke like so a gorrit all over me fuckin ands as well . . .

Me n Paul ar laughin ar fuckin eads off. John's lookin at Colm with the utmost contempt, which uv course provokes Colm t'new heights, or depths, dependin on how you look at it:

—. . . so *then*, right, *then*, a hadter waddle out uv the cubicle inter the bit with the sink in, me kex around me knees cos a cuddun pull em up cos then ad get runny shite all over me fuckin jeans again, wuddun I, an am standin ther like with me kex around me ankles washin smears uv cack off me legs hopin, no, fuckin *prayin* that nobody comes in ferra piss a mean can yer fuckin imagine it, ey, Ron strollin in ferra wee an me ther with me kex down washin me fuckin arse . . .

Paul's almost in fuckin tears. John is now affecting detachment, whistlin quietly to imself, stairin around the bar.

—. . . so then, when a wuz finally clean, a hadter fuckin waddle back inter the cubicle bit wher the bog roll is like so a could trine dry meself off, an then back ter the sink ter wash me ands. Fuckin orrible it was. That fuckin speed was cut with fuckin laxative, am never scorin off Derty Derek again. But ennywey a did it, a cleaned the cack off an now ere I am, cleanest fuckin tiger in the jungle. Rarin ter fuckin go. No shite on me, oh fuck no. You orright ther, John?

John looks at Colm, nods, an then tairns back t'Paul:

—Anyway as a was saying, these things have got to be proved. And why, tell me this cos it's something I've always wondered about, why *isn't* 'I was only following orders' a legitimate excuse?

Colm shakes is head an murmurs: —Jesus Christ, looks at me, an shrugs helplessly. Thair's real despair in is face, in is eyes, a mean real, dark, huge despair. It makes me feel a bit sad.

—Did yer get any sleep at all last night, Mags?

—A bit, a say. —Bout an ower ur so.

Ee nods. —A diddun ger a fuckin wink. I avn slept fer about three fuckin nights. A tried, like, bu' . . . a just ended up makin a film in me ed. Ther's this kind uv fantasy a go through in me ed ter elp me get ter sleep . . . Am stuck inner blizzard, inner forest, an av got ter make some kind uv shelter quickly before a freeze ter death, so a burrow a hole in a snowbank, a big, deep hole, an a know av got ter dig it quickly before me energy runs out. A go through irall in me head, evry step in the procedure. An normally, by the time av crawled inside the hole like an unrolled me sleepin bag, gorall warm an snug, am asleep.

John's still blabbin in Paul's ear but Paul's lissenin t' Colm, stairin intently at the side uv is face. Is eyes behind is glasses ar all kind uv glazed n stuff. Another one oo spends most uv is days with a fuckin bottle in is hand.

—Diddin fuckin werk last night, tho, *or* the night before tha, Colm says. —God, when a finally *do* get ter sleep . . . it'll be fer fuckin *ever.*

After a while, Paul an Colm leave fer another pub but John wants t'stay here. Ad sooner go off with the other two but a feel obliged t'stay with John cos . . . well, am slightly ashamed t'admit it, like, but a used t'go out with Oxford John. A know, a know, fuckin embarrassin n stuff . . . a was young, still a fuckin teenager, ad only just arrived in Aberystwyth after runnin away from home like, a was lonely an vulnerable an felt like a needed some protection. God, we all make mistakes. Just got t'fuckin lairn from them, innit?

—A know eesh yur friend, Mags, but . . . John's drunk as fuck. Slurrin is words, wobblin in is seat. —That fuckin gyppo bastard . . . carn fuckin stand im. Dirty fuckin thievin gyppo *cunt*.

Ee flops against me an a shove im off.

—Don't you fuckin slag my mates. Orright? Just keep yur gob shut. A don't cair whether you like em or not, just don't fuckin slag em t'me.

Ee falls against me again.

—Ah, we adsum fuckin good times, dinwe? Me n you, ey . . .

Oh yeh, a think; some fuckin great times I ad, me sittin there on the bed in yur grotty little bedsit drinkin White Lightning cider an lissenin to yur theories uv how Adolf Hitler was this wairld's saviour. Fuckin wonderful they wair.

—Ey, lissen; Nicola's away, she's gone back to er mother's for the weekend. Me room's all empty . . . whatjer reckon?

A look at is face. A remember how a used t'be with im, kind uv like: Yeh John, I agree with anythin you say n stuff. Now, tho . . . am older, more experienced. He can't control me any more, no matter ow much ee thinks ee can. Am a different pairson now.

—C'maaaaaahhhnn . . . just like old times an all that . . . c'mon, they were good, you fuckin loved it, you *know* you did!

—Alright, then, a say. —Got t'go the offy on the way, tho, yeh?

We leave the pub, passin Babs tryin t'strangle Ron by the fruit machine, an go to the off-licence. John can hardly walk, bouncin off cars, shoutin in German, bellowing 'Tomorrow Belongs To Me'. It's dead fuckin embarrassin. Ee buys a bottle uv brandy in the Spar an we go back to is room, which is nothing like a remember it, the difference bein that now it's got a woman's influence, y'know, the perfume bottles on the dresser, the ornaments an stuff. Which isn't me, I'm a messy cow I am, an lookin round this room now, this room in which a once drank, laughed, cried, slept, waked, fucked, fought, et cetera, a feel a pang uv somethin in me belly, a don't quite know what it is. Just a slight twinge. Just a tiny, tiny pain.

John makes a grab for me tits.

—No, not yet, Christ, calm down . . . sav a drink fairst.

Ee flops on the bed and a open the brandy. A was younger, av bin younger in this room . . . Christ, am only twenty-two now, but, y'know . . . a was nineteen in this room. So unbelievably young. There was an extra two, three years uv possibilities ahead uv me, stretchin ahead . . . anythin could've happened. Evrythin did.

Ah fuck it. John and his twisted obsessions.

—Any glasses?

Ee flaps is arm at the sideboard an a take two tumblers out uv it an fill em both up with brandy. John knocks is back in one, makes a grab for me, an a fend im off until ee falls into a coma, ur somethin very like it. Snoring, heaving lump on the bed. When am certain that ee's not goin t'wake up a retrieve is jacket from whair ee dumped it on the floor an go through is pockits. A take twenty uv the thairty quid in is wallet. A go to the door. Then a go back to the wallet an take the other ten. Then a leave the house, wonderin which pub Colm n Paul'll be in now . . . well, al just av t'try em all, won't I? The White Horse is the closest. That's as good a place t'start as any.

A get picked up outside the university. A young couple, crustyish lookin, in a van. A red van.

—Where y'goin?

—As close t'Sheffield as you can get.

—Ah, not bad, then, wir for Manchester. That do yer?

—Sound.

Am asleep before wair even out uv Wales. Rude, a know, but . . . am completely fuckin exhausted n stuff. A got the phone call on Thursday, just when a was packin me stuff t'go t'Abergynolwyn with all the others. Me friend, Reuben . . . hung himself in his halls of residence in Sheffield. Reuben who a knew in Shrewsbury. Reuben who a went out with when a was about seventeen. Reuben who a used t'get drunk with, on Scotsmac an Concorde wine. Reuben who a shaired me very fairst wrap uv speed with. Reuben.

Reuben dead in Sheffield, hanging from the window frame in a tiny, anonymous room.

Am nudged gently awake in Manchester, outside the bus station. Fairst thing a see when me eyes open ar buildings, tall buildings, noise n buses n smoke n people. So long since av been in a city. Rain evrywhair n stuff. A thank the couple profusely an buy a ticket for Sheffield at the booking office. Tramps, permanent fixtures uv any bus station anywhair in the country, ask me for money but a can only spair coppers. Half an ower wait for the Sheffield bus. A can't goan av a pint cos av hardly got any money.

Reuben who used t'torture frogs. Reuben oo was good on the guitar. Reuben oo smashed up is father's car.

A go an sit outside t'watch the city. It seems so fuckin immense after Aberystwyth, but in the kind uv way that seems t'deny any sense uv space, or freedom. Which isn't t'say that those things can be found in a small Welsh town by the sea, like, or in the countryside surrounding it. Oh no. Common misconception, that.

Reuben who always wanted t'go to Peru. Reuben who was, if the God's honest truth be told, a bit uv a dickhead. Reuben now who is dead.

A smoke a fag an listen to the roar of the city an feel the clammy, dairty rain on my arms, on my face, an wait for the Sheffield bus.

Here it is; one uv those large, bay-windowed new development flats overlooking the harbour. A thought as much. A double-check the address, hoist me bag over me shoulder an ring the doorbell. Gradually, a stooped figure takes shape b'hind the frosted glass, and a voice, slightly frail but deep too an with a surprising power, comes out uv the intercom speaker:

—Yes? Who is it, please?

A lean down to the microphone-thingy an say in me best polite tones: —Am from the home-help agency. Am the stand-in for this week?

The door is slowly opened by a wizened, Barbara Cartland type, leaning on a Zimmer frame an so heavily made up that she looks kind uv creepy and clown-like an stuff. Still, tho, there's a kind uv superiority in her bairing an stuff, a kind uv self-confidence in her eyes set in panda rings uv blue shadow as she scans the ID card I hold up to her an then looks me up n down.

—Oh. I was, ah, expecting a young lady.

—I am, a say, smiling. —It's the short hair. A feel like pullin me jumper up an sayin 'What jer think these are, then?' Young fuckin lady, Jesus Christ. Is she fuckin blind?

—Oh. Yes, well.

She still looks unsure, but she opens the door and ushers me in t'one uv the best bastard flats av ever seen in me life; thiz a big open fireplace, expensive-lookin paintings on the wall, all kinds uv valuable ornaments an stuff propped up about the place, on shelves an tables an stuff. A wall-sized window offers a stunning view over the harbour to Pen-yr-Angor an Pen Dinas, which is a great green shape in the mist. The place smells uv perfume an fresh flowers, which don't quite succeed in masking that smell you always get around old people, that slightly disturbing whiff uv off milk and wee. Still, tho, what a fuckin flat; what an ace fuckin place t'live.

—You're a new one, aren't you, the old lady says. —I've never seen your face before.

—No, a say. —Am just a stand-in y'see. If any uv the regular home helps call in sick or whatever, then I'm called in t'do the rounds for them. Am just temporary, like.

—And what's happened to Sally, my regular? Nothing serious, I hope?

—No, a say, —just a bit uv a cold, but rairly I haven't got a fuckin clue what's up with her; could be fuckin leprosy for all I know.

—Well, the biddy sniffs, sittin down in a vast armchair by the fire. —I suppose it *is* a reputable agency . . .

The displayed wealth uv this place is, like, too much t'take in all at once. One uv those jade ornaments alone probably cost more money than al see in a whole fuckin year. An ad bet that that's a *real* Turner above the mantelpiece thair . . . Christ. Bein a non-Welsh speaker in this job is a positive boon; you get sent out to all the houses that belong to the rich English incomers, those oo can afford t'spend ther last years in comfort an luxury by the sea n stuff while the natives, or most uv them, ar left to die in the council houses in Penparcau or Llanbadarn, surrounded by insects and damp. An hasn't it always been that way?

The woman keeps glairing at me short hair. Er eyes keep flickerin from me head t'me breasts b'neath me jumper, as if shiz baffled by some incongruity or somethin. A try t'smile and ignore her assessing gaze.

—Now. A think we have evrything here. One pastie, Cornish . . . A reach into me bag an she tuts and goes:

—Oh, for heaven's sakes *no*, dear, in the kitchen if you don't mind. I can't abide crumbs, particularly in my living space. They bring all the insects in.

—Am sorry.

A take me bag through into the back kitchen an unload the stuff on the spotless ceramic wairktop. It's like a show kitchen, it is, all glitter an gleam; am terrified t'even bloody breathe in it, it's so fuckin *clean* an disinfected an stuff. God, she must av a whole fuckin army uv helpers runnin round after her, makin what life shiz got left not just bairable or comfortable but positively fuckin luxurious. A mean, that blazing fire in the front room, she's not agile enough t'light it of a morning, she must av er own personal fuckin firelighter. Christ. A wonder how she made her money. A wonder how she manages t'live like this.

—Crockery below the sink, cutlery in the drawer, trays in the corner unit, a hear her say in the other room. —Cornish pasty, tinned peas. You have those?

—Oh yes, a say. —Evrythin you asked for.

—And the fancy? The cream fancy?

'Fancy': puh. It's a fuckin *cake*, yer daft old bat.

—Yes.

—Good. Slice of white bread, thinly buttered, pot of Earl Grey, no milk, no sugar. And bring the cruets *to* me, please, do *not* attempt to season my food yourself. My regular help is well aware what a stickler I am for seasoning.

—OK.

Jesus, I'm thinking, old habits die hard, don't they? They wair right in the agency; this one *is* a fussy old bag. Evrythin she just told me a had written down anyway, includin instructions not t'use the salt an pepper. Still, tho, at least shiz not hangin round me peerin over me shoulder like some uv em do, altho er pins can't be that good, what with the Zimmer frame an stuff. Wonder ow old she is.

A put the peas an pie in the microwave, prepair the tray an tea, an take it through to her when it's all ready. She wrinkles her top lip – a small kink in that thin lipstick gash – at the presentation as a place it on the little table over her knee an starts taking tiny bites. She talks to me as she eats an a lissen to her stories, ow many grandchildren shiz got an what ther all doin, all that kind uv stuff. One uv em, called Christine, is a doctor in London and has apparently got:

—The most *beautiful* long hair, *such* a shine to it, completely breathtaking. All the way down her back. Stunning, it is, like silk, *silk* . . . she turns heads, she does, wherever she goes. All the male doctors in her hospital, oh, such characters they are, all of them, you see, they –

She talks on and a nod an say: —Mmmm, at regular intervals, but am rairly miles away here; am tryin t'see myself at her age, what al look like, the place where al be living . . . it's difficult t'do. A can't imagine meself ever bein that close t'death, danglin on the end uv such a long rope uv time n days n years n stuff. Sittin alone in some home al probably be, stairin at the walls an the telly . . . a big fuckin black void ahead uv me. And, wairse, p'raps a big black void b'hind me as well, me existence cancelled out by dementia or just plain boredom, me youth only a dim an bairly recollected confusion. Christ. What a fuckin life. A shouldn't be thinkin like this; am only twenty-two years old.

—. . . a think you'll agree? Hmm?

A look up an shiz smilin at me through a curdled mustache uv cream.

—Oh yes, a say. —Entirely. May a use yur bathroom please?

Her face puckers up a bit in distaste but she says: —If you must. Beyond the kitchen.

A take her tray through to the kitchen with me, fill the sink with hot water an put the dishes in it. Then a go into the bathroom, lock the door, an open the cabinet above the sparkling clam-shell-shaped sink. This is it, this is me bonus: drugs are like insects – there's a million different types an yull find some uv them lurking in the most clean an well-lit places. The most well-scrubbed, hygienic areas always have thin little cracks uv darkness for them t'hide in. Yuv just got t'know where t'look like.

Row upon row uv lovely little brown bottles . . . the equipment to temporarily annul pain is evrywhair. All types uv pain necessitate all types uv possible cure, and here we have Valium, codeine, diazepam, Xanax, Stelazine, Dramamine, all types uv inviting stuff. A take a few from each bottle an put em in me pockit an then, thair, b'hind the incontinence pads yes! she shoots! she scores! a bottle uv

DF fuckin 118s. Great stuff. Yer can't beat that morphia hit, the cocoon, the capsule, that lovely warm safe bubble . . . oh yes.

A flush the loo, then wash n dry the dishes in the kitchen an stuff an then go back into the front room with me bag.

—Well, that's it, a say. —Your usual help will be back with you t'morrow a should imagine. Is thair anything else you need before I go?

An am kind uv shocked t'see that in her eyes as she looks up at me is somethin like, well, a dunno, fear. Some kind uv unreachable depths . . . all confidence, all snobbishness, completely fuckin gone.

—Oh, stay for a little while, she says. Pleads, almost. —Have some tea and tell me about yourself. Shall we make a fresh pot?

A smile. Oh well, a think, a might as well; shiz not that bad an old biddy after all like, an a might never come here, to her flat, again. The pills ar bairnin a big hole in me pockit but, t'tell you the truth, a rairly could do with a nice cup uv tea.

Erm . . . Mairead's a sound girl. A like her a great deal; many a good time av ad with her, out drinkin n dancing n stuff . . . a don't want t'ever upset her, like, but Colm: Colm's sittin across the kitchen table from me in is an Mairead's house an everybody's crashed out in the front room apart from Mairead who's lying wasted an unconscious in the bed an Colm's sayin things t'me . . . things a never thought ad hear im say . . .

—. . . an a alweys av. A think yer fuckin gorgeous. A tell yer, if ad never met Mairead like ad . . .

Me head's humming. The speed's wairin off. It's about five o'clock in the mornin an thair's a glass uv beer goin flat on the table.

—. . . a mean, oo's ever gonna find out ey? Fuck, would *you* tell ennyone? A know *I* fuckin wuddunt. A mean, yer know, no one ul ever find out's wharram sayin cos all we after do's keep ar fuckin gobs shut like, an . . .

Birds're twittering outside. The kitchen smells faintly uv fried onions, an thair ar dusty, webby loops hangin from the ceiling. Hundreds uv books in the old, disused fireplace. An Colm's eyes ar blue an ee's smiling and is hair is all greasy an messy an stuff, an av always thought the name Colm is cool and his fingers ar all bitten an thair's a deep cut on the end uv is thumb. An then he's over me an is tongue's deep, deep in me throat an a can taste t'bacco and alcohol. Is tongue's tickling, caressing the inside uv me mouth all around, evrywhair, over me teeth, tongue, gums . . . a want to bite it, hard, a want to bite it off . . .

Ee opens a bottle uv red wine an we sit on the kitchen floor drinkin it an kissing. God, such strange things happen . . . this is mad. But a carry on doing it.

Round about eightish Paulie comes through t'use the toilet an me n Colm fly apart, it must look so fuckin obvious n stuff, but ee doesn't say anything, ee just smiles wastedly on his way back through. Mairead's asleep, drunk in her bed, an I'm in her kitchen with me hand down her boyfriend's jeans, fumbling, tugging, pullin the skin back softly t'hear him gasp, I like hearing him gasp . . . caressing Colm's column. The column uv Colm; a almost start t'laugh but a control meself, not knowin how he'd react. Ee'd probably laugh as well but y'never can tell, rairly. Men and their dicks.

Ah God. What am I fuckin doing? The answers come: Enjoying meself. Tryin t'stop feelin lonely. Getting off with someone a fancy, av *always* fancied. An that's it. It's that fuckin simple.

We go to the nearest pub on the prom when it opens an drink all day, talking, touching, playing pool, stairin out the windows through the rain at the sea. Round about teatime we go to the public toilets b'hind the pub an lock arselves in one uv the cubicles, the smell uv piss an disinfectant an stuff. A flyer for Oxygen is pinned up on the door. An the things we do then . . . Colm sucks my nipples an gently fingers my cunt, me clitoris. Ee sits on the bog an gets me t'bend down in front uv im an worms is tongue up my arsehole, which no one's ever done t'me b'fore an it makes me squirm an groan. I kneel on the cold tile floor b'tween his legs an lick an suck his cock, balls, thighs. A notice a crusted ring uv talcum powder around is foreskin an am reminded for a moment uv a Polo mint. He smells clean, washed, meaty an fresh. A put a finger up his bum an he pants so much a think ee's goin t'pass out, an ee yelps as a take it out which a like t'hear so a put it back in again. The stubble uv me hair tickles his skin. The sleaziness uv the location, this scummy public bog an stuff, somehow adds t'the excitement of it all an a come so fuckin hard when ee's fuckin me up against the cold wall, a come an cry out, an then ee's got is hand over me mouth an is face pressed up t'mine cos thair's people in the toilet, drunken blokes singin some song about Swansea an am standin thair still an silent an me cunt's twitching, tryin t'draw more uv Colm's knob into it an me fingers're diggin into is back, me legs up around is waist . . . splot, splot as fluid hits the tiled floor . . .

The blokes leave an a urge Colm t'fuck me harder, harder, this is Colm my friend Mairead's live-in boyfriend fuckin me oh yes fuckin me an a fuckin love it a rairly fucking love it, tryin t'fuck some calmness into myself tryin t'produce that gorgeous blotting white-out in my head . . . Colm comes and yells and my head is on his chest an a can hear the boom uv his heart. Lovely, lovely . . . such tinglin fuckin loveliness as we wind down t'gether an stuff, is dick shrinking an softly sliding out uv me. Thair's a light dimming in my head and I don't want it to dim.

An the better you feel the wairse it'll be in the future, when the pleasure wairs off cos it can't last for ever. Y'see? Thair it fuckin is again. The better you feel now, the wairse yur *going* t'feel. I know that now.

We return t'Colm's house and get drunk, or drunker, with Malcolm an Mairead. Mairead's manic on a bottle uv tequila, happy an ranting. And what is thair f'me t'say? What the fuck can a say? We all get shit-faced an watch the telly, Liam an Laura come around with some weed, a wake up wrecked in the morning on the couch with a woolly blanket thrown over me, me eyes stingin t'fuck cos a was too drunk t'take me contact lenses out. What can a say? A don't know what t'say.

I shouldn't've done it.

It was fuckin ace and a rairly hope we do it again. Soon.

Ah fuck it. Thair's *nothin* t'fuckin say. Nothing.

The other night it was, me n Sioned ad been out t'Trish an Rhun's house t'watch that film *Communion*, y'know the one about the aliens an stuff? An we wair a bit freaked out n stuff drivin back in Paul's car, ee was off climbin some fuckin mountain somewhair with Harvey n Allen an a flask uv mushroom tea, an wair drivin down one uv the tiny lanes in the mountains outside Devil's Bridge like, couldn't see anythin apart from the stars an the patch uv illuminated road in the headlights, an suddenly thair was a clunk an the whole car instantly filled with light as if someone ad shone a powerful searchlight through the back window. Me heart leapt down into me boots an a could feel me face goin hot with horror. Sioned swairved over the road and stopped an a could hear her breathing.

—What . . . is . . . that?

—Oh Christ, was all a could whisper back, an we wair just sittin thair bathed in this bright light n stuff an a was rairly fuckin scaired n stuff, a mean fuckin terrified, me heart thumpin like mad an a sick feelin in me stomach an a was expectin little skinny grey men with huge black insect eyes t'come peerin in the windows. A was trembling. Sioned pulled a crowbar out from under the seat an went out into the night an bairst out laughing; that relieved laughter with the slightly hysterical edge to it. A got out too then, into the windy darkness.

—What is it?

She said through her laughter: —That stupid bloody *lighttt* thing that Paul rigged up in the back uv the car on bonfire night. Look. It fell over.

She pointed with the crowbar at the fallen light. A remembered then; Paul, in one uv is ridiculous fuckin handyman moments, ad strung a light across the roof in the back uv the car, the station wagon like. A don't know why; it was somethin t'do with firewairks or somethin daft like that. He's mad; if thair was nothin t'fix, ee'd break somethin just so he could fix it.

—That's all it bloody was.

—Fuck, a said. —A nairly ad a fuckin heart attack then.

—Bollax to yur hearrrt, girl, Sioned said. —Djuh know what av gone an done? Only pissed in me knickers, avunt I?

An then we started t'laugh, t'laugh cos the whole thing was so stupid n stuff, an if any aliens had've come down then an saw us like that − standin in the mountains among the sheep an wind n stars, laughin uncontrollably at a glowin car an smellin uv pee − they would've thought us defective specimens an gone lookin for better examples to take with them back to Zob or whairever the fuck it is they come from.

★   ★   ★

Christ. A terrible shock, that was.

Am just driftin around the town aimlessly, just wandering n stuff, me last fiver from the cash machine bairnin away in me pocket like, just walkin along the promenade. It's that time uv the year when all those Hassidic Jews come t'visit Aberystwyth, a don't know why like, they do it every summer; the town's fairly quiet with all the students gone n stuff an before the main influx uv tourists comes in an then all uv a sudden the place's full uv these fellers wairin long black coats an bowler hats an funny plaits in ther hair. Y'see them in the Spar, lookin bewildered at the Mini Chicken Kievs an the Hungryman oven meals for one. Anyway, thair's a bunch uv em millin about on the pier by the amusement arcade an am wonderin how t'get maximum enjoyment from this last, solitary fiver when fairstly a fuckin Tornado jet roars over, low enough t'touch with a long stick n stuff an makin a noise louder than the tyrannosaur in *Jurassic Park* like, an then secondly thair's an ear-splittin BANG! which shocks the shit out uv me; a mean, a fuckin ducked at fairst cos a thought the jet ad dropped a bomb or somethin or maybe broken the sound barrier an then a realised that it was a flare. Such a fuckin shock, tho, those two things t'gether like, the jet an the flare, horrible. Like somethin out uv Hell. An the Jews get thrown into a panic; the elder ones're goin mad, reelin about like pissed penguins, probly thinkin about the wrath uv God n stuff an some uv the younger ones're just rigid an stairin out t'sea like, as if ther amazed that it's not parted all the way to Ireland or somethin. Mental. A watch them for a bit cos it's quite funny in a way but then a start t'feel a bit sad; they look sorrowful and pitiful n stuff, as if they don't belong here, gentle, strange aliens not suited t'this wairld uv screaming war machinery an noise an steel an people drowning out at sea.

Poor bastards. An those fuckin planes, a tell yer . . . a fuckin hate them. A still remember the time several uv them buzzed that open-air rave at Kerry a couple uv years ago, dead fuckin low . . . thousands uv dancers, all on one an havin a great time an then suddenly the fuckin skies wair ripped open an all these planes came howlin through. Rairly fuckin freaked some people out n stuff, a mean thair wair breakdowns, collapsings . . . am

248

sure the pilots wair under government orders. Am fuckin *sure* uv it.

Anyway.

A carry on drifting. Well, t'tell the God's honest, a know exactly whair am drifting to; the offy for a cheap bottle uv red an a bag uv crisps an ten fags an then t'the castle t'drink an smoke an eat an watch the waves. 'Drifting' me arse; yuv even brought a fuckin corkscrew, Maggie, who're you tryin t'kid?

At the castle, a sit in the sun with me back against one uv the ancient, mossy walls. Me n Colm came ere once t'drink away a speed comedown. Actually, wiv done that here a few times. Several. Fuckin loads uv times in fact, altho we normally go to a pub. God, ad fuckin love some speed now. That's my drug, amphetamine; sod heroin – that was an experiment, a momentary aberration in me drug career. Never again. Ace t'try once, tho.

Just a fuckin experiment. Me whole fuckin *life* is just an experiment, an one which a sometimes dread isunt controlled by me. Always sairchin for new sensations, experiences . . . that's why a came here, to Aberystwyth. A just drifted here; ran away from home an ended up here, y'know, a small place, by the sea, mountains n stuff . . . it's odd; this is a place that people just seem t'drift to. End uv the train line. A mean, take Squeaky Susie as an example; I asked her once what brought her to Aberystwyth an er answer was the kind uv thing that a lot uv people say around here:

—Oh, y'know, oi just ferncied a day away, y'know, aht uv London. Came ere, got pissed, fergot ta get back onna bus. End av story.

Wair all from somewhair else, or most uv us. Sioned's not, she was born here, her family's been ere since, erm, ever. I come from Shrewsbury, or Amwythig a suppose a should call it round here, a border place, a no-place rairly, a buffer zone b'tween England an Wales. A mean, a don't even have much uv an accent, do I? A could've gone anywhair, but Wales seemed a better option. So am here; am just here. As ar Colm n Malcolm n Mairead n Liam an evryone . . . wair all just here. A don't think it's cos uv drugs. Ther just stations on the journey, overnight stops in Drugdom . . . it's as if we wair all just dropped here without any background or history. We hardly ever seem t'see ar families, ar mums n dads; a carn speak for any uv the others but personally I don't see mine because . . . well, a just don't. Av made up with them again now, an a phone em evry month or so t'let em know am still alive n stuff, an a do love them, but . . . a dunno. It's just my life. One day al get the urge t'move on an when that day comes al do exactly that; pack me stuff, get on the train, and sod off, providin av got the money uv course so a hope the urge comes on a giro day . . . just bugger off somewhair else like. Maybe somewhair like this, altho a can't imagine thair ever bein such a large concentration uv druggies an psychos an wasters anywhair else as thair is here. This town's odd for that; thair's so fuckin many uv em in such a small place. The drug and personality problems here are so noticeable, so conspicuous, cos ther so concentrated. It's a town that evry drifter seems t'get to sooner or later. The homeland uv the drifting class, if that's not a contradiction an even if it is so fuckin what? Christ, *wair* contradictions, us drifting people, aren't we? Rootless, anchorless shadows in a world of forced fixed values and steady consumption. We'll always be around. Thair'll be a drifting class in 100, 1,000 years' time, only instead uv driftin from town t'town they'll be driftin from planet to planet. Maybe Mars'll become the Aberystwyth uv the twenty-second century: Ah, a just came ere for the day, got pissed and forgot t'get back on the rocket.

A finish the wine and head home. A see Liz on the way; small, pretty Liz who a always feel big n gawky around. We talk for a bit, an she tells me that thair's a party happenin at the weekend at Rolf's house out in Pontrhydygroes, a tell her al see her thair an we go ar separate ways. A like Liz. Colm knew her when he lived in Cambridge, then lost touch with her when he left. Didn't see her for years. Had no idea she was here until he bumped into her in Boots the chemist.

On the way home me eyes're scannin the ground for money an me brain's whairlin with ideas uv how t'get some cos one bottle uv wine does nothin rairly except give you a taste an a craving for more. Shouldn't uv fuckin drunk it rairly; one bottle's more frustrating than none. It's a long fuckin walk home an stuff an when a eventually get thair thair's a note pinned t'me bedroom door:

CALLED ROUND
HELP! – NO MONEY NO FOOD NO RENT
NO GAS NO DRUGS
WILL CALL AGAIN LATER
PHIL XXX

A tear it down, crumple it up and chuck it away. A mean, for fuck's sake. The selfish prick. If yuv got no money then go out n fuckin get some; *I've* got no fuckin money either but you don't see me emotionally blackmailing people into giving me some, do yer? Christ.

Am pissed off now, but in a way that's good cos now the day ul go faster. Anger's something. See? Halfway thair already.

A lie back on me bed an smoke me last fag an listen to the sheep outside. Thair's a mildew patch on the ceiling directly above me shaped like a crude drawing uv a knob an balls. Which makes me think uv Colm, an a wonder how al react the next time a see him. Hopefully we'll both be off ar faces an then it won't be so difficult, not difficult at all in fact, altho it'd probly never feel awkward for Colm, only for me. And Mairead's blitzed most uv the time as well. Not that that makes me feel any less guilty . . . but . . . a did enjoy it, didn't I? Yes, Maggie, yer did. Tell the fuckin truth. You loved it.

Me hands move down over me breasts, tummy, hips . . . a haven't eaten for a couple uv days an me ribs're prominent but me belly still feels big – why the fuck is that? An me tits feel far too large an me legs far too thin. A have a sudden, nightmarish image uv meself naked with all me physical shortcomings gro-tesquely exaggerated, matchstick fuckin legs wobbling under the weight uv an enormous pot-belly an saggy veiny tits, it's horrible, an before a can stop meself av walloped meself closed-fist in the tit, far too fuckin hard, far harder than a meant to. Ow . . . a massage it softly, feeling stupid. Sometimes a feel as if me dead grandad – the one who was born in Ponterwyd – is watchin over me, an a hope he had is head tairned then. A feel fuckin daft.

A drift off . . . the afternoon goes. Goes in a doze. In a doze an a daze, the day's daze, dozy hazy dazy lazy. . . . Noises from downstairs wake me up around teatime, loud voices n laughter n people messin about. Male voices.

—Ah yis must huv some fuckin ice now! Carn drink wahm fuckin gin, makes me fuckin boak.

—I'll have yours then.

—Yer will in me ahrse!

—Yer never fuckin paid for it, did yer?

—No, an nor did fuckin *you* fe yis whiskey. Fuckin close, tho, wasn it ey?

—Christ yeh. A thought fer fuckin sure that checkout gerl ad seen us.

—The lemonade. Oo's got the lemmerfuckinade?

Clatter uv bottles and cutlery, the bam! bam! uv an ice tray bein whacked on the wairktop.

—Annywan else in, Malcolm?

—Danno. Paul's not, ee's taken Roger aht ta see that one-ahmed cunt, what's is fuckin face now, Bill. Samwan else might be tho. Avva shout n see.

—Mags! Allen! Harvey! Uh yis in at all? Thir's a bag uv booze waitin te be drunk down hur so thur is!

An then am boundin down the stairs, liking now the feel uv me large, firm breasts beneath me loose top, already almost happy:

> Cardigan Bay, a wish you wair vodka
> Cardigan Bay, och aye!
> Cardigan Bay, a wish you wair vodka
> I would drink you dry!

Oxygen this month is fuckin ace, up at the union in the uni, ace fuckin music, amazin fuckin E an stuff . . . this E; it whooshes through me an a feel like a rag doll picked up and shaken by a dog, a big, friendly, bouncy, bounding, slobbery smiley dog . . . Mairead's dancing opposite me an she looks fuckin ace. The strobes . . . Christ, a feel so fuckin cool an happy, me limbs won't stop moving . . . this is fuckin incredible . . . thair's a slight self-conscious streak to this E hit, it always affects me that way, but at the same time a feel gorgeous an exciting an evrybody's ace, cool, sexy . . . this is fuckin incredible . . . out the corner uv me eye a notice Colm leanin against the bar, watchin me, so a put more energy into me dancing, sway me hips, try t'look sexy which a *know* a fuckin do . . . Mairead does as well . . . a lean t'wards er:

—You look fuckin gorgeous! a yell over the music. She smiles an goes:

—*What?*

A say it again: —You! Look! *Gorgeous!*

—*WHAT?*

A flap me hands an smile and continue t'dance. Then a smile an continue t'dance. Then a just continue t'dance. It's fuckin ace.

—Another pint, Mags? Lager?

—Orright, a say, an knock back the last few inches in me glass. —An a chaser? They do cheap shorts ere.

—OK then. Vodka?

—Cheers.

—Two pints of lager and a vodka then. Comin up.

—An get some more change for the pool.

Martin goes off to the bar an a rack the balls up on the table. Three games t'one in my favour it is; am playin fuckin ace t'day n stuff. If a had the choice, tho, a wouldn't be ere with Martin, but am skint an ee's buying, so, y'know, I am. Ee tried it on with me at a party last week but a knocked im back; ee was quite persistent an stuff, but I was avin fuckin none of it. Ee's one uv those blokes who find it difficult t'understand why girls don't want t'go out with them; ee thinks it's cos a don't want a relationship at the moment, or cos am afraid uv bein hairt n stuff, an ee just can't grasp the real reason, which is that ee's a ginger, overweight, patronising tosser oo a fancy about as much as a fancy psoriasis. Anyway, t'day ee's bein extremely generous, either t'buy me affection or as a way uv apologising for bein so overbearing an insistent last week. A don't cair what his reasons are; am just gonna exploit the situation for all it's wairth.

—Here y'are.

—Ah cheers.

A knock the vodders straight back an sip the lager.

—Oo's tairn is it t'break?

Ee points at me with is cue. —Yours.

A smash the balls apart an a red goes spinnin off into the corner pockit. A knock in another couple an then bring the cue ball t'rest against the side cushion; nice one. When am in the mood for pool a can play rairly well n stuff; av even beaten Malcolm once or twice, even Allen as well, an ther fuckin professional standard almost. It's all down to a lonely childhood, Malcolm says; ee didn't av any friends when he was younger like so ee used t'spend all day in the pool hall is dad wairked at in Colchester.

—Ah shit.

Martin's shot goes well wide an the white ball trundles into the pockit.

—Oh nice one, a say. —Not so much a in-off as a in-instead.

—Another vodka?

—Wouldn't say no.

Ee goes t'the bar again. Ah, he's alright, rairly; ee's just like most blokes, y'know, with an ego inflated beyond all reasoning. It's funny compairing how people see themselves with how you see em y'self; the difference is always vast. Still, a suppose it all comes from a deficiency; a lack of self-confidence or something which demands compensation. Sad rairly.

Me pool playing gets wairse as a get drunker, which is perhaps what Martin wants; a mean, y'should see the way is eyes light up when ee wins a game. Of course, bein beaten by a woman is just not fuckin on, is it; such a thing compromises Martin's sense uv is own masculinity an superiority. Still, ee's not all bad, rairly; thiz nothin rairly dangerous about im, like, ee's just a bit risible. Pathetic almost. But ee's OK.

We get staggeringly pissed an Martin invites me back to is place for a whisky an a smoke. Am unsure n stuff, but ee's all apologetic like an persuasive and anyway what the fuck else would a do? It's only about four o'clock. Thiz many drinkin owers ahead. So a go with im over to is house up Cliff Terrace, next door but one t'Colm's like, an knock meself out with draw an Jameson's. Am swaying in the seat. A can hardly fuckin see.

—If you want to crash, please use the bed, Martin's saying. —Honestly, it's OK; please trust me. You don't want that kind of relationship with me, I know, and I accept that and respect your wishes. Please trust me. If you want to sleep, sleep. You look wasted. Al crash out in the armchair if I have to.

An I *am* sleepy, rairly fuckin sleepy, so a stagger over to is bed an flop down on it. The sheets smell kind uv oily but they feel so fuckin comfortable, a couldn't stay awake if a tried like, am completely fuckin wasted. A feel me eyelids closing like steel doors swingin shut.

Am asleep. Am fuckin miles away like.

When a was goin out with Oxford John, ee'd sometimes feel me up when a was asleep. It was nice, sometimes; ad be woken up by warm tinglings, gorgeous rubbings . . . but a haven't slept with John for years an a don't even want to any more but this is odd cos ee's here now kissing me, is tongue's right down me throat n stuff, one uv is hands is tweaking me nipple an the other one's rubbing me fanny an it feels ace, maybe it's Colm, am responding and writhing but the dimensions uv this tongue are unfamiliar an thair's a knob pressing into me thigh an Jesus, Martin, get off me you dirty fuckin −

—Away! Get fuckin off me! NO!

A try t'push im away but ee's holdin me rairly tight an a can't fuckin move, ee's panting and sweaty an is whispering frantically in my ear:

—Nearly there oh God yes nearly there don't move this feels so nice I love you I love you oh I fuckin love you . . .

—Fuck off! Fuckin get off me!

Is thrusts get faster an then ee spurts over me dress, groans, an staggers away t'sit in the chair. A just stair at im. A feel fuckin sick. A don't know what t'do. What the fuck do I what the fuck −

—I can't fuckin *believe* . . . what you've just done . . . I . . .

Me heart is thudding. A feel sick. Me teeth are grinding t'gether.

He can't look at me. His eyes are all over the room. —I thought you were into it . . . am sorry . . .

Ee starts trembling, huddled up in the chair, is arms wrapped around himself. Tears roll down is red, flushed cheeks. Am s'prised, lookin at im thair, ow quickly me anger subsides, to be replaced by contempt and derision. Drunken fat fuck crying an shaking, is limp dick flopping out uv is fly like a slug with flu. Jesus Christ.

—Am really really sorry . . . I thought you . . . A couldn't stop
. . . God, I'm so cold . . . so cold . . .

Is favourite black silk shairt – the one he wore t'try an woo me
last week like – is hanging over the back of is desk chair. A pick it
up, wipe the spunk off me dress with it an chuck it into the corner.
Martin's just stairing at the floor, quaking an sniffing an stuff.

Am not angry. A don't rairly feel anything. A just don't fucking cair.

Thiz nothin a can find t'say to im. A put-down would be
superfluous, an anyway a can't think uv one. A just say: —Wanker,
and leave is house.

Colm and Mairead aren't in so a head home, up the big hill t'Llys
Wen. Arfway up Penglais a start t'cry. Tears uv anger, nothin else;
anger at myself for trusting that piece uv shit, anger at myself for
getting so wrecked. Fuck.

Anyway, that was *my* Sunday. That's what a did t'day.

Lying in me bed. Night-time. Straight and a wish a wasn't, altho
sleep'll probly drag me under soon . . . Stairin into the darkness an
stuff. The whole house is quiet except for the squeak uv bedsprings
from Paul n Sioned's room.

Fuck.

An am thinking only one thing:

That a never fuckin asked for this life. A never expected all this.
Get restless, leave home, nothing nowhair's any fuckin better. Thiz
always stuff y'never asked for or wanted, stuff forced into your life
by uncontrollable powers, not that yuv been invested with much
control t'begin with anyway. Like puttin a soft-bodied animal into
a box uv iron spikes an shaking it vigorously. Wuv got none uv the
resources and qualities needed t'get us safely through this fuckin
wairld, this fuckin life. Colm says stuff like:

—So what's wrong? Yer inner pub with me, yuv got booze,
drugs, fuck what more d'yer want, gerra grip, fuckin cheer up.

As if that's enough like. And Colm, God, ow many times av a
seen im depressed, ow many times av a comforted im when ee's
crying and stuff on a bad comedown? Ee needs more than this.
I need more than this. A don't know what, precisely, but a need
much more than this fuckin life can give me. Not that a think am

more important or anythin, God no, am not better than anyone else, evrybody's got reasons for what they do . . . no, fuck, wait, I fuckin well *am* better than some people − selfish people, killers, rapists . . . am better than them. Yes a fuckin am.

In whose eyes? Me own? . . .

It's all about context n stuff, isn't it? A mean, when Colm's shagging me like an ee whispers in me ear that am a dirty slut n stuff, ad much sooner hear that than fuckin Martin saying that he loves me. D'you know what a mean? It's all about context.

Nobody will ever appear t'me unexpectedly in the middle uv the night and tell me not t'be afraid. No one will ever appear in singing and in light. Fuck it all.

A hear Sioned groan, very faintly. The squeaking stops.

Life promised so fucking much. The most unfaithful thing uv all, the biggest fuckin betrayal . . .

What am I do −

What am I −

This will never satisfy me. It's been more difficult than I ever thought possible.

Christ, listen t'me. On an on an on. I'm sorry, am rambling. I'll shut up.

From *A Personal Guide to West Wales*, anonymous authorship, privately printed, p. 47

The diversity of sediment deposition here makes for a most peculiar lithology, such variegation engendering, as it always does, uncertainty and its consequent contingency, ignorance. The district's mineral lodes can be seen to encapsulate such a process; the ores in these lodes are mainly made up of lead and zinc, together with associated ores of silver and copper. Precious arteries running through igneous rocks which here have travelled far, so far; pick up a palmful of pebbles at random and you will find amongst them chalk, coloured and speckled surfaces, coarse sandstone, fantastic eggs smoothed by the sea then chipped and scarred by contact with others during and after their long lonely journeys so is it any wonder then that they when endowed with our own necessary sentimentality cling to your clothes and intrude in your boots like burrs? Like smoke? Like moisture? Rub them together and some will crumble in your hands and block your pores with spoor. The rocks are highly folded and broken by many faults. The rocks are highly folded, and they are broken by many faults.

THEY ARE DANCING

THEY ARE DANCING sweaty and frantic with a deep and enormous sense of enjoyment, faces frozen in slippery grins below eyes wide and dilated and bright. The Selecter are on stage and the bounce of the music works like a drug as unfightable propulsion, as do the resurfacing memories of this music heard in past teenage years as a soundtrack to eruption and confusion and shocked awakening, that combination of cowering concealment and strident exhibition of the conviction of one's own uniqueness to which they peculiarly yearn to return or in which they have been for whatever reason arrested, adrift and whelmed in a dark hormonal cacophony. Allen's feet pound a table top; Liam and Laura weave rhythmically through the jumping crowd; and Colm jerks over to Beti, the heavily pregnant girlfriend of Jerry, to roar into her ear:

—Fuckin ace this, Beti, ey! A was more inter punk the ferst time this kinder stuff was out like burrav alweys adder soft spot fer ska! Just a bit too embarrassed ter admit i'!

Beti's reply goes unheard; Colm's ears are filled with the sound of his own teeth grinding.

—A berrit's a right fuckin pain inny arse been preggers at summun like this! When yer wanner dance n stuff!

—Oh God, yeh! Beti yells over the music, and Colm cranes his head towards her. —Worse thing's only bein able ter do just a little bit uv whizz for the babby's sake like! Gives yer the taste then, see! But see if a wasn like this – she points to her bulging belly —ad av two fuckin wraps inside me an ad be settin-a fuckin floor on fire!

She leans against Colm as she speaks and her stomach presses into his ribcage. The hardness of it disconcerts him somewhat, so he leans away to retrieve his pint from a nearby table top and gulps what's left of it.

—Ow much avyer ad then?

Beti shrugs. —Not much like. Bout a third of a gram. Ardly anythin rirly.

—Ah yer doan get much uvver hit off tha.

—No, yer carn get much uv a hit off a third. Got t'av somethin, tho, an yer? Fuckin borin without like.

—Yeh. Colm looks around. —Whir's Jerry?

Beti strains to look over her shoulder. —Dunno! Ee *was* ere behind me like but . . . ah thir ee is look, at-a bar!

Colm nods and jerks over to the bar, moving in that enthusiastically twitchy, anxiously jittery way of the speedfreak, smiling and shouting at people who he recognises. Some who call to him he fails to recognise, but he returns their greetings anyway, although his eyes never cease scanning the heads of the crowd jostling at the bar, seeking out Jerry's conspicuous dreadlocks.

—Oi, Colm, how y'doin?

—Sound, sound, lissen avyer seen Jerry?

A finger points and Colm follows it, finds Jerry about to bundle a bushel of bottles into his arms.

—Jerry me man!

—Colm. Ow was that base?

—Ah fuckin spot-on, man, avyer gor enny more?

Jerry takes in Colm's tennis-ball eyes and grinding jaws. —Jesus, duh yer *need* any more?

—Yeh, well, I adter give some awey yer see. Can yer lay us on another rock like? Al sort yer next week.

Jerry replaces the bottles on the bar, checks that the bar staff are preoccupied and with remarkable dexterity transfers a small bag from his left breast pocket to Colm's. Such rare legerdemain learned through long years of trafficking in illicit substances. The magical restoration of energy through two twists of the wrist.

—Ain't base tho, that stuff, sjust powder like. Resta me base is claimed.

Colm grins. —Fuck, this'll do, this'll do, sfuckin good enough fer me like. Already fuckin flyin. Al get the money to yer next week, yeh?

—Orright.

—Cheers, mate. Ar yer avin a good time by the wey?

—Fuckin buzzin. First band a ever saw, the Selecter. Brings back the memories like.

Jerry wrestles his bottles through the crowd, Colm buys a bottle of cold Budweiser and then goes and locks himself in a toilet cubicle. The music muffled, soft booms of pounding drums and feet through the walls. The opening chords of 'Pressure Drop', which Colm curses himself for missing.

Sniffing, grating his teeth, he squats and taps out a small heap of pinkish sulphate on to the toilet lid. The powder is coarse, so he crushes and chops it into a dust with the edge of his library card and then divides it into two ragged lines. He reflects that it could possibly, no probably, have been chopped a lot finer, but his appetite is strong and a stinging sinus is but a small price to pay for a more immediate hit. Through a rolled-up fiver he snorts one line up his right nostril and the other up his left, washing them down with gulps of beer. He licks the residual dust off the plastic lid and then feels embarrassed and nauseous. He sniffs hard, closes his eyes, murmurs in satisfaction and drifts momentarily away as the chemicals slide pleasurably down his throat, and then quickly covers his mouth with his hand as bile surges up in his chest. Grimacing, swallowing hard to suppress the gag reflex, he stands and stares and waits for his ravaged, boiling stomach to settle.

Outside, in the auditorium fervid with bodies, Liam and Laura rest at the side of the dance floor, knees pulled up to chests out of the way of stamping feet. Liam, his breast heaving, attempts to roll a cigarette on the twin humps of his knees, but each Rizla splits with dampness and is flicked away with a 'fuck'.

—Ah bollix. Ah'll gerrah straight from Colm when ee comes back. Whur is he annyway?

Laura, who has been watching Allen cossack-dance on the table top, shrugs. —A don't know. Last a saw of him he was up at the bar. Looking to score again probably.

—Ah he'll be back soon right enough.

—Look at Allen goin for it. What's he on tonight?

—Colm gave um some speed. A think ut was base. Certunly fuckin feels like base so ut does.

The music surges.

—Pardon?

263

—Ah sed ah think ut was base! Ut feels like base!

Laura, unsure whether Liam has just informed her that he thinks the music is ace or that he's right off his face, feels a hand ruffle her hair and turns to see Colm looming out of the lights and steam, his skin glistening, his eyes so enlarged that they look in danger of popping out of their sockets. His smoking hair appears to wave and sway as if under water, or mild electrocution. His lips tremble, close, open again, and he shouts:

—Am havin so much fuckin fun!

His whole face quivers:

—*Am havin so much fuckin fun!*

A giant grin splits his twitching face and he roars:

—*THIS IS SO MUCH FUCKIN FUN!*

And then an invisible tether yanks him back into the crowd, a marionette in the hands of a puppeteer with Parkinson's disease and for a moment his boots can be seen, kicking high, the cuffs of his jeans flicking moisture, then they too are swallowed up.

—Ah bollix, Liam says. —Ah fuckin fegot ter ask im ferra fag. Am gaspin fe wahn as wehl. Fuck ut.

He frowns.

—Ar yis dahncin some more?

—OK, says Laura, and then they are.

COLM

FUCKIN PACKIE BONNER fumbles, nah, fuckin *chucks* the ball into is own net an that's two–nil ter Holland an that's it, it's over, Ireland're out uv the World Cup. Bastard.

—Aw fe fuck's sake!

Liam springs up an storms out uv the room in disgust. A heer im stampin an mutterin down the hall:

—Ye useless fuckin *bah*stud . . . ball control uv a rapist so ye huv, Bonner . . . sick as a fuckin parrot ah am . . .

Me heart berns in me stomach ferra while an a open another can uv stout. Shite. The Republic uv Ireland out uv the 1994 Werld Cup. Quarter-finals, after beatin fuckin Italy as well. Did a rerly expect em ter get enny ferther, did a ever think thed fuckin win? Well, no, uv course not, but Jesus, it was good ter av thee oppertunity ter hope an pray an imagine that, yer know, just fuckin meybe . . .

Fuck it. Ts over now.

The last few minutes uv the gamer a formality only, Staunton an the lads just goin through the motions rerly. Fuckin Bonner . . . yer might uv been a hero agenst Romania four yeers ago, but now yerra yuceless twat. Well below international standard goalkeepin.

A gulp at me stout. Wharriz this, can number nine, ten? Fuck knows. Lost count. The Guinness logo, the harp like, comes on the telly an reminds me uv me uncle Tom cos ee useter av one tattooed on is forearm, a big one in faded perple an green. Ee's dead now. Burra remember bein a little kid an ee'd come round ter thee ouse an sey ter me mam: Ar, al just take wee Colm thur down te the Cast Iron Shore, an then ad spend the next two deys or so sittin underneath a pub table down the Dock Road bein fed bags uv crisps an arves uv stout evry few owers. Why Tom wanted me company on is marathon drinkin bouts a dunno, but ther a was, friend uv dusty floorboards an mucky pub dogs with waggy tails an great big boots caked in mud an cement. Ee only ad one tooth, Tom, a long, snaggled brown pointy thing liker stalagmite in is lower gum, an a remember this one time inner seventies when ee was mugged by some Teds outside the pub an ee pounced on one an bit is face an gorriz tooth stuck up the lad's nose. They adter go ter the ozzy like tha, stuck face ter face tegether, both uv um screamin at each other:

—Yer fuckin mad ahl cunt gerroff me! Gerroff! Help!

—Agl ucki gite ger uckin ace a er uckin gund!

Funny as fuck it was. A fuckin crazy man, Tom. Dead now, tho; the cirrhosis, among other things. But al always remember im like tha, face ter face with the Teddy boy, arms round each other an staggerin all over the road as if lost in the throes uv some tremendous passion, bernin an intense.

Liam comes back in with some more cold cans. Ee's been inner cocky mood all dey, struttin an loud; a like im when ee's like this. Makes me laugh.

—Ah Jaysis, Bonner, ee sez. —Fuckin shite so. Ye can kiss me whoit, black, Oirish ahrse.

A laugh. —White and black? Why's it white and black then, Liam?

—Wehl, the skin's white, an the hurs ur black. White, black n Oirish.

—Is yer arse *dead* hairy like?

—Oh Christ, yeh. Hairy as yer pet rat thur.

—Do, erm, do the hairs all cerl in terwards yer hole like, as if yer arse is imploding?

A only ask im this cos mine do. A sawrit inner mirror thee other dey when a was checkin fer zits.

—Nothin implodin about *my* arse, son. Srictly one-wey traffick up thur so ut is.

—Bollox, a sey. —Accordin ter Paulie yer can taker whole fuckin marrow up ther without flinchin an *still* ask fer more. Loster whole week's groceries up ther last week ee told me.

—Yer fuck. Paul wastin is shoppun ohn somwahn else's ahrse? Ee'd save ut fer is own so ee would. Ee gulps is beer. —Annywey, drink up. Wuv got te goan meet Paulie when the match finishes, doan feget.

—Ah it's fuckin finished, man. It's over, like, all fuckin over.

Wuv arranged ter meet Paul n Sioned inner pub onner prom, unless it's after nine, in which case ee'l be inner Crystal Palace, so a propose tha we wait until then cos the prom pub's owned by tha fat fucker Browntree an ee's alweys fuckin angin round in ther bein fat an lecherous an triner make out thareez some kinder fuckin gangster. A gangster in Aberystwyth: the prick. A herd another story about im thee other dey which just about sums im up rerly: some lad – a think it might uv been Rhun – was werkin as a commis chef in oner is restaurants, ee was a good one like, burree wanted ter leave ter go ter college so Browntree witheld is week-in-and-pey an told im thareed never find werk in the whole uv Dyfed ever agen. Fuckin typical uv im tharriz. A complete wanker; needser fuckin belt, ee does. Total fuckin gobshite.

So, ennywey, we ang around the flat until nineish, just drinkin an talkin like, then we hit the Crystal Palace. Instantly in ther an a regret it; not only is the big TV screen showin the lowlights from the footy but Browntree's holdin court at the bar wither load uv other fat fucks an the corner by the pool table's takin up byer load uv fuckin arse'ole students singin some tossy song, the twats. So fuckin self-consciously loud, those fuckers, so fuckin evryone-look-at-how-wacky-I-am . . . norall uv em ar like tha, of course; somer them ar sound, yer know, ther just triner gerron an improve ther chances, but the sad thing is is tha thel all soon discover ow truly werthless a degree rerly is; a mean, as if it ul help them ter lead the lives they want to, as if a fuckin knowledge uv post-structuralist terminology or the semiotics uv fuckin theatre or wharever ul assist them in obtaining ther top life-choice. As if thev gorrer fuckin choice; life's norra question uv wha yer want most, it's a question uv wha yer don't want least. Or most lives ar ennywey; mine's not, like, mine's different. Av made my choice an am fuckin stickin to it; al go ter pauperdom, the sanatorium, the grave an ter Hell in my own fuckin wey.

While am up at the bar, oner the students comes up ter me an tries ter engage me in conversation. A vaguely remember talkin to im one night some weeks ago when a was E'd up an feelin friendly, yer know, talk to enny bastard when am E-in. But now ee seems ter think thareez me best fuckin mate:

—Oh God, Colm, av bin on such a bloody binge, ee sez flickin is floppy hair back like Hugh fuckin Grant. —Haven't bin sober since Tuesday. Can't remember a thing.

A just raise me eyebrows, thinkin; an it's nor even the fuckin weekend yet. Am supposed ter be impressed, am I?

—I think am turning into an alcoholic, ee sez through a grin. —I mean I *must* be. Opened a bottle of whiskey on Tuesday and –

—Fuck off, a sey. —When yer crawlin along in the gutter with yer kex around yer ankles spewin up blood with shit runnin down yer legs an yer *still* gaspin fer another drink, *then* yer can talk ter me about fuckin alcoholism. Orright? Now fuckin do one an let me get wrecked in peace.

A tern me back on im an order a pint an wave to Antonella at the other end uv the bar, an she smiles an waves back. God, shiz got sucher beautiful face, tha gerl; me heart jumps in me chest when she smiles at me. Shiz with Sioned, who, a see, as gorra black eye. Fuckin Paul when ee's pissed up no doubt. Ee's arguin wither now like, leanin down ter sey summun inner ear. Er face flushes pink an she yells:

—At least a dunt leave *yew* on yer own out in bloody Pontrhydygroes!, an then she snarls an terns awey ter drink frommer can uv Hooch. Fuckin Paul; a sound lad like, burrer twat when ee's drunk. Ow ee can raiser fuckin finger ter Sioned, a don't know; a mean, shiz wee, God, shiz arf is fuckin size – one punch from im could fuckin killer. Ad never itter gerl, man, only fuckin arse'oles do tha. An ennywey, apart from ennythin else, Paul's a fuckin hypocrite; ow can ee avver go at Sioned about ennythin she does when a sawrim with me own eyes on me couch tha time shaggin Sarah when she came down from Liverpool ter stey? His hairy, spotty arse jigglin up n down. Orrible.

Liam taps me on the shoulder.

—Ah'm fuckin starvin, Colm. Ah could eat a fuckin horse so ah could.

Soon as ee sez this a realise with some dismay tha a havunt eaten for severul deys. Me belly rumbles, as if ter draw attention to itself, an a picture the poor bastard in me mind fuller dark curdled beer frothed wither green scum uv stomach acids, ashes an fag ends floatin in it, steam risin from it liker swamp.

—Yeh me n all, a sey. —A could eater scabby 'ed ter tell yer the truth. Wherjer wanner go?

—Dunno. Curry?

Tha sounds good, so a down me pint an we leave the pub, past Paul n Sioned screamin at each other outside on the pavement, tha mad bastard Richard just standin ther watchin them. Sioned's rerly goin for it, rerly fuckin screamin:

—Av *yew* ever had a psycho ex-boyfriend, ey, jealous enough to send yew dead fuckin animals in the post? NO! But now all uv a sudden yur the God's gift bastard expurt on it!

—Oh an what about Annie then? She's perfectly sane, is she?

—Annie carn beat yew up! Annie carn attack *yew*! Yew can defend yurself against her, but I can't with bloody Marc!

We leave em to it an ed off ter the curry ouse. Am not sure if Liam's gunner make it cos ee's staggerin all over the shop, wallopin inter cars, trippin over the kerb, eight owers on the stout biginnin ter tell on im like, burree does an we order poppadoms, egg vindaloo fer me, balti fer Liam, naans an loads n loads uv lager. Ace, but arfwey through me food an am thinkin; ooooooooooooorrrrggghhh, so a sey that a need a slash an sneak off to the bog an puke up in the sink. It's just as hot comin back up as it was goin down, an am already pityin me poor arse termorrer; irrul be like shittin Hades.

A feel grand after av yakked an am lookin forwards ter more beer an the rester me vindaloo, so a head back down to the table. Weavin through the restaurant tho a become awer uv all thee other eaters, all strangely quiet fer some reason an moster them glarin at me. A can feel ther eyes. Why? Probly cos am a drunken shambling fucker wearin the kind uv clothes tharra fuckin scarecrow ud dress down in, that's why. But I don't fuckin care.

Fuck me, Liam's gone n bought another balti.

—Jesus, Liam, another one! Christ yer *muster* been ungry!

Ee looks up at me through is hangin ropes uv hair an suddenly realise tharrit's not a second balti in is bowl but the ferst one come back up; thiz a saggin bridge uv grey spew joinin is lower lip to the rim uv the silver bowl. All eyes inner restaurant ar on us, an a mean the place's fuckin chocka, an as a sit down with me face in me ands laughin the waiter comes over wither bin-bag an puts evrythin in ther, boak, bowl, evrythin. Straight in.

—Little bit too much to drink perhaps?

Liam's babbling something, a think ee's triner apologise:

—Ahh Jayshish ahm shurry, am fuckin shurry, rilly rilly rilly rilly rilly, budder Republickah knock dow, mahn, er owva fuckin . . . djer know wha mean? Jer unnershtahn me now?

Am laughin me fuckin ed off. Liam hics an a think another puke's on its wey but ee swallows it back. The waiter shakes his head:

—I think you'd better leave. People are trying to eat here please.

Which is fair enough. An ennywey, ee can't be feelin too dandy imself; a mean, India or Pakistan or wherever the fuck ee's from never even got through the qualifying rounds, did they? Poor bastard.

Look at these zombie bastards. Just look arrum; the fixed ster at the telly, the drool . . . thee only signs of life out uv em ar thee occasional fit uv giggles at summun tha just isunt fuckin funny. Onner couch, inner chers, onner floor, ther just fuckin lyin ther. Stuffed. Like mummies. The livin bleedin dead.

A try agen:

—Come 'ed, oo's up fer goin out then? Cheap vodka night inner wine bar, fifty pee a shot. An Gareth's party after. We can get rat-arsed. Come 'ed, gerroff yer fuckin arses.

Mairead snores, Paul n Sioned grunt ambiguously in unison, Allen carries on lickin vapidly at is ice cream, Liam cackles at the telly screen. Malcolm, sprawled out in the cher liker mad woman's shite, goes:

—Ng. Later, maybe, an takes another toke on is pipe.

Jesus Christ. Ad av more fuckin fun, more adventure, wither wet log. *This* is why a hardly ever smoke draw; this is wharrit does ter yer, these six fuckin sacks of torpor n stupor mongin out at me feet. Ferget smack, crack, E; the real drug scourge uv this generation is draw. Weed sucks outer yer all fuckin life n motivation, it terns wharrever ambition or self-determination yer might possess into mere daydreams, things yer think yul do one day an of course yer never fuckin will. Other drugs goad yer n prod yer inter motion, even if tha motion involves, say, theft for another hit or a mile-long walk ter score; at least then yer fuckin movin, yer know, bein active an alive. Draw's just . . . uuuuuuuurrrrggghh. Crap. Nothun. And that's exactly what the fuckin system wants; it wants yer ter sit on yer saggin couch in yer mouldy bedsit gigglin at afternoon cartoons, empty an hollow an stupid . . . A mean, even, like, with skag; when yer off yer box on heroin yer might gerroff on pickin bogeys out yer nose fer owers on end burrat least yill do it wither sharp an focused intensity, wither real sense uv, a dunno, intrepid questing or summun . . . See, it's not the drugs that fuck people up, rerly; that would appen ennywey. If not drugs, then irrud be summun else – crime, violence, rape . . . It's not heroin that has decimated places such as Ton-yr-Efail an the New Gurnos – it's the void, the banality, the unbearable emptiness of evrydey life tha heroin is used ter fill. Trite observation, per'aps, but tha dozen make it enny less accurate.

Liam's eyes ar lost in circles uv inflamed redness. Ee's been on a marathon smokin session recently, all dey evry dey fer weeks, ever since ee came back from Newbury. And come ter think uv it, draw must be good fer somethin, cos ee asunt ad thee energy ter berate us fer not goin ter Newbury with im fer at least therty minutes. Altho then again, pot does serve ter fuel is self-deluded sense uv thee importance uv is trip; like Roger's mate Gareth, tha lad oo's alweys goin on about is time in Swansea nick (fer poaching fuckin trout; wooo, the therd Kray), Liam has a hugely inflated sense uv the werth and significance uv is actions. A mean, ee was in Newbury fer two deys, ee went n waved a banner, got stoned an stood inner line an chanted an ad a bit uvver dance ter the Tragic Roundabout. Did ee *fuck* live inner bash upper fuckin tree fer six months or fight the bailiffs, or even sabotage a fuckin bulldozer, let alone tie imself ter the highest branch. But now it's fuckin on with the solemn an martyred expression an: —Oh yeh, ah wis in Newbury orright, those fuckin cunts have gorra be stopped so they have, that fuckin land bilohngs ter us all mahn so ut does . . . Me fuckin arse. If yer pull im up about this ee'l retort with: —Ah shur, an ah nevurr fuckin wehl saw *you* thur!, which is true, like, but . . .

well, yer know wharrah mean; if yer not gunner let go uv the side, don't gerrin the fuckin pool.

A stand up.

—Wher's tha off? Mairead sez all slow.

—Oh so yer *can* fuckin speak? Thought yer were dead. Am gunner get some beer from the fridge.

An then uv course it's:

—Bring us one.

—Can yis purr us a wee whiskey?

—A fink there's some cider in the fridge. If not then al av a beer.

—Fuck off, fuck off, a sey. —If enny uv yis wanner bevvy yer can gerrit yer fuckin selves, an a goan fetch meself a canner lager. Fuckin pot'eds. Carn even ster themselves ter walk the ten feet to the kitchen ferra drink. Jesus.

When a go back into the front room Mags is in ther as well, rockin the cher tha Allen's sprawled out in an goin:

—Ahoy, me hearties! It's a right stormy night, cap'n!

Allen just groans an mutters: —Ah sod off . . . don't will yer . . . stop it . . .

Mags stands ther wither hands onner hips. —Jesus. Look at this picture uv vibrant youth, she sez. —Av seen more life in a . . . somethin that's dead. Stoned, are we?

—Nah, a sey. —Just fuckin dull.

Mairead pulls a face.

—Can anyone spair us a blim? Mags sez. —A fancy a spliff in the bath.

Wordlessly, Paul bites off a small chunk of resin an gives it ter Margaret and she buggers off. A hear the sound uv water runnin up the sters. One last effort:

—So this's it then, is it? Wer gunner just sit n watch crap on telly all night, ar we? Fuck sakes, yer wastin yer fuckin lives, do yer not wanner be out ther avin a laugh an gettin wrecked? This is so fuckin dull. So fuckin borin.

Sioned sighs an tuts in exasperation an Malcolm, in an indignant whiny voice, goes:

—Jast fuckin chill, Colm, fa fuck's sakes jast fuckin relax. Av ed no fuckin kip since larst fuckin Sunday an a jast wanna kick back, get stoned an watch telly. Fuckin ell. If ya rairly that fuckin desperate then go aht on ya own an give us awl a bit av peace.

—Cheeky southern blert, a sey an am about ter give im a real gobful but then a don't bother. It woulden be werth it like. Ee woulden fuckin lissen ennywey, an evryone else'd get pissed off an shout me down an ad get rerly wound up an the whole thing ud become a right fuckin pain inny arse. So wharrah do instead is, a eat tha temazepam jelly tharrah was plannin on neckin later before a went ter bed; a mean, these twats ar all fuckin arf asleep ennywey, I might as well go the whole fuckin hog. Apathy is infectious.

A get some more beer and drowsiness seeps in about arfwey through me therd can. It's nice, dead nice . . . but ther's a hideous fuckin programme on the telly, a think it's just called *The Eighties*, some kind uv retrospective on tha vile fuckin decade an presented by some odious, oily little gobshite wither tasteless demeanour uv unconfronted privilege. Ther's been a glut uv such programmes recently; objectionable attempts at the assuagement uv guilt is all they fuckin ar, invariably hosted by some plummy-voiced prick with an unforgivable bouff or ponytail. What ther sayin these programmes is, don't worry; don't entertain doubts about what you did under Thatcher, it was rerly OK to wer your hair liker total dick'ed, it was rerly OK ter step over tramps on yer wey ter thee opera or the restaurant, it was rerly OK ter make more money than yer possibly needed at the expense uv others; don't worry, it was rerly OK, evryone was doin it. It was rerly OK ter want more, and more, and more. More cars. More suits. More braces. More money. More holideys. More fuckin Phil tosser Collins an Whitney dog Houston CDs. It was rerly OK ter be a greedy grabbing braying wanker.

God, these fuckin people . . . not only do they want ter make unpardonable amounts uv money by enny vile means necessary but they wanner feel morally vindicated in doin so. Fuckers. Jesus . . . wha hope is ther? Ey? What the fuck can yer do?

—Look! It's Spandau bastard Ballet!

—Look at is kilt!

—The make-up! The poof!

—That ponytail! What a wankah . . . oo sorry, Liam.

At least this programme's prompted evryone inter avin a conversation agen, inter communicating. Well, of a sort; all ther rerly doin is goin inter fits uv hysterics at the old videos uv Adam Ant an Howard Jones an Spandau bastard Ballet an numerous other disappearin acts. Me, a coulden giver fuck; am driftin pleasantly awey inter chemical fuzzy fluffiness an composin an essay in me ed:

THINGS I DID IN THE EIGHTIES, by Colm Downey:

I left school inny eighties. A left Liverpool, went back ter Liverpool, left agen very quickly . . .

Lived in Cambridge, York, Doncaster, London, Nottingham, Birmingham, all over the fuckin place . . . France as well . . .

Fell in love inny eighties. A think.

On the orders uv a magistrate a checked meself into a drug an alcohol dependency clinic. Checked meself out agen four deys later on the orders uv meself. In the 1980s this was.

A nerly died in the eighties. More than once. Convulsin under pub tables in a pool uv me own spew.

A broke me heart in the 1980s.

Ferst had anal sex in the 1980s. Wither gerl like, a mean.

Started using hard drugs. Intravenously.

Dragged meself, or was dragged, up off menny floors.

A saw me own face reflected in

tiled floors
smashed mirrors
buckled chrome

in the 1980s.

A lost months, whole fuckin months, long long stretches uv deys in my life gone for ever gone for ever in which I remember NOTHING. Absolutely fuck all.

This is a disappointing, carelessly written piece of work, bereft of narrative thrust and with little in the way of descriptive drive or interest. The main protagonist is unattractive, indeed repellent; the reader must be able to empathise, or at least sympathise, if a writer is to make an impression. 2/10. Could, must, do better.

A drift off inter unconsciousness as the Human League start

singing 'Don't You Want Me Baby?', missing almost thee entire song. Which is one tiny mercy, a suppose.

So menny bodily fluids, so much goo an gunk; that's all wer made up of, us jellylike, dripping beings — blood, brine, piss, spunk, tears, smeg, spew, snot . . . It seems, sometimes, tharram afloat onner sea uv such stuff, an tha a wave uv it washed me up ere on Aberystwyth beach ow menny yeers ago now? Three? Four? Carn recall . . . ther's just loads n loads uv boak. An blood as well, ther's loadser fuckin blood; av been bleedin out me arse now ferra good few yeers evry time I av a dump. A don't know why like, but Geraint, the lad oo went ter Florida, ee told me once about internal haemorrhoids, yer know, piles on yer inner sphincter, actually *inside* yer body like; these sometimes bleed, ee said, thee, like, *berst* when yer strainin or pushin on the bog. Harmless, ee sed, burram not so sure; thiz certainly no pain down ther but, a mean, oo knows what's goin on inside, under the skin, wher yer can't see? Fuckin mystery ter me, man . . . tumours slowly blooming like coral. All a know is tha bingein leaves yer with only two things: one, an unshakeable sense of loss, an two, flecks uv blood on the toilet paper. Oh yeh, an empty pockits. A wonder if ther universal, a mean a wonder if such things happen to an bother people like, sey, Oily, tha bloke with aller tattoos on is face an the stitches permanently criss-crossin is chest. Or someone like Griff, or Ikey, tha psycho, tha killer . . . or, God, even someone like Roger ther, chuckin up noisily inter the sink:

—Hooooooark yew twat . . . groo . . . hurrrrreeeeeeerrgghh . . . fuck . . .

. . . whose sink? Wher am I? Whose fuckin room is this?

Roger groans an wipes is gob on is sleeve an sits back down onner floor biside me. Ee's been out uv it fer deys now, all mad n depressed cos is mate Bill is dead. Ee found the body imself, inner shack out in the mountains wher ee lived. Well . . . sort of lived; can't rerly call it life, just existence. Infection or summun it was, which a can't sey am *that* serprised ter hear; a mean, the last time a saw Bill, bout two months ago now, arf is lower lip ad been chewed off by rats when ee was out uv it on the skag. Fuckin orrible it was; liker skull bineath is beard. But that was Bill, yer see, a mean yud go out ther ter see im like up inter the hills, higher n higher, the mountains n sky ud get bigger n bigger, barren, wind howling, freezin cold, yud be expectin ter see Mr Kurtz — burall yud see instead was a one-armed fucked-up ole junkie inner shed. An ee lost the arm on the Falkland Islands *after* the war through fuckin about wither hand grenade when ee was pissed. Playin catch or summun. So no fuckin heroics ther like. Personally, I never knew what ter make uv Bill, a medic wither sadistic streak; ee was court-martialled on the Falklands fer machine-gunnin about eight hundred penguins. A know tha was partly due to is trainin like, a mean, ee was on the ship goin over ther when Argentina surrendered like so all is training, yer know, all tha conditioning ter kill an maim an hert had nowher ter go, an it needed *some*wher ter go a suppose . . . but penguins? Little smart waddlin fellers? Eight hundred uv them? Somethin fuckin deeply wrong ther, if yer ask me. The loss uv is arm was karma. Served im fuckin right, I reckon. But Roger, tho, Roger in Ulster; ee might not uv lost a limb over ther burree lost somethin. That's fer fuckin certain. Yer can see it in is eyes, man.

Ee groans agen an dry-washes is face with is hands. More fuckin inky-dink tats, a see, still inflamed an sore lookin; wha a think's serposed ter be a Welsh dragon but looks more liker fuckin teapot.

—Uuuurrrgh.

A pat is ot n sweaty ed. —Feelin berrer now?

—Uf. Might do arfter some more bloody ale like.

Ee sniggers like Beavis. Or Butt'ed. An a give im me last can, unopened; not cos am feelin generous but cos a doan wanner sher a can with im an avtoo drink out uv somethin tharee's drunk from, all bile on the rim an spewy spit dribblin down the side uv the can gor Christ. Djer see wharrah mean? Fuckin *drownin* in bodily fluids we are. All uv us fuckin are.

Roger opens the can an necks arf uv it in one go. Ee's oner those rare people oo can mix smack with bevvy; most smack'eds a know never touch booze, it makes em sick. But with Roger, tho, a serpose the spirit an the need is far stronger than the biochemistry.

—Ey, Roger.

—Wha.

Ee's lyin on is back, sterin up at the mildewy ceiling. Is crappy grey anorak's almost black with muck; same colour nerly, in fact, as the ceilin plaster.

—Wher the fuck ar we? Djer know?

—Wha, yer mean *yew* don't? Fuck me, boy, ow out-a it ar yew?

A look around the room. And a reckernise it then: Malcolm's in Llys Wen, the books piled up on the floor, slightly swollen with damp, the brown duvet cover, the blue puffa jackit over the backer the cher in the window bay. But what the fuck am a doin ere? An wer's Malcolm? Christ, a must uv hadder good time the last few days, a can't remember a thing . . . A notice a pair uv Paisley boxer shorts dryin over a radiator an a get a small pang in me chest; seein someone's underwear drying is liker glimpse into ther secret vulnerabilities. A don't know why, it just is.

Ah fuck. Ere comes sobriety. Feelin like shit. Fuck.

A ask Roger: —Wher's Malcolm gone?

—Do yer not remember? Christ, yewer fuckin memmury, mun . . . ed like a bloody siv yew av.

—Yeh, so? Wher's Malcolm gone?

—Ee's gone back t'London fer-a few deys like. Can yer not remember Iestyn's party on Saturdey? Malcolm was thir with is bags like.

Little bits start tricklin back now . . . Malcolm with a rucksack over is shoulder . . . all tha speed a did . . . someone bleeding, ferly badly, a remember that . . . the E . . . someone screamin tha Mairead was dyin . . . the bottle uv tequila, more speed, tha wee toot uv H . . . Mairead walkin round laughin, sound as a pound, nowt wrong with er . . . more E . . . hertin me knee . . . the bottle uv rum . . . somethin bizarre happenin with the house plant. Christ, was that Saturdey? Ow long ago was that? Seems like fuckin ages. An wher's Mairead at the moment? An all ee others? An why arn I back in me own fuckin flat?

An it starts comin down on me then, as a knew it would sooner or fuckin later, fallin on me liker big bagger wet sand berstin an fillin me chest cavity with heavy wet grit: depression. Comedown depression. Which am totally fuckin sick of ter tell yer the truth, sick uv this blur uvver life, this fuckin werld seen througher certain uv fluid, haze . . . av fuckin ad enough. A look down at me kex stained with fuck knows wha burrit's of many fuckin colours an the derty denim stretched tight over me swollen damaged knee, me boots encrusted with mud, me hands stained with wha looks like dried blood. Fuck it. Fuck irrall.

A look over at Roger an a sey somethin to im which am not sure tharra mean burrah sey it ennywey, It's:

—Fuck all this, Roger. Let's go back over the border an track down Malcolm. Av gorriz address. Ee knows people in France, a remember im seyin once, let's us three fuckin go over ther, man, come 'ed, new start, evrythin. Leave all this bollox be'ind. Whatjer reckon?

Quick flickering memories uv France uv Brittany wher a met tha gerl who a liked so much tha me whole fuckin biology was altered . . . a was younger, purer, a had more hope over ther. So much fuckin life ahead an a could do wharrever the fuck a wannid to.

Roger just sters at me an a ask meself if things rerly ar desperate enough ter run awey from. A mean, God, in tha wha brought me ere inner ferst place? Runnin awey from Liverpool an the Maguires an ther anger? Av been runnin all me fuckin life; from debts, beatings, pregnancies, deaths, embarrassments too fuckin acute ter bear . . . An even if a did go back ter Brittany, would it be enny different ther? Probly not, no, apart from the weather; ad still exist in a self-induced haze, but in the sun rather than the rain.

Christ, gerrer fuckin grip, Colm, this is your fuckin *life*. You're twenty-seven years old. Hold on to yerself. Keep it terfuckingether now yer on the verge uv losin it stey with it stey strong. Put down roots. Get some fuckin stability in yer life.

—Orright, Roger sez, an lurches over to the sink. —But yer's summin av got t'do, first like, an a doan mean be sick agen.

An then is face's back in the sink, pukin is fuckin ring up. A start thinkin about sleep, an about makin me wey ome. See if Mairead's ther. Gerra bottle so we can drink through the comedown tergether. Tharrud be nice, yeh, burrav got ter wait until am able ter fuckin move, ferst, uv course. That's the ferst thing; won't be able ter do ennythin until a can fuckin move.

An am suddenly awake cos uv the big bang in the kitchen, rerly fuckin loud: BANG! like tha, follered by the sound uv plates an glasses smashin on the walls an floor: CRASH! BLUNK! SMASH! Oh fuck. Must be Mairead fuckin freakin out agen. What for this time?

CRASH! SMASH!

Me eyes open wither faint rippin noise an a look over at the clock: 4:32. The throbbin red numbers like the inside uv me ed. Afternoon is it? Morning? Thiz light through the certains but tha means fuck all.

Footsteps come stampin down the hallwey an a sit up groggily, wipin me eyes an thinkin shitshitshit an then a look up agen an ther's gin in me face bernin an stingin an Mairead's on topper me punchin me inner fuckin face agen an agen an agen. Some fuckin alarm call this, eh? But the stupid cow, cos all that gin's done is ter shock me inter full alertness so a sit up and grabber arms an bundle er off the bed, both uv us slammin on ter the floor, ow me fuckin knee! A suddenly realise tharram in the nud, fuckin bollocko like so a protect me balls an tadger with one hand an grab Mairead's screechin face withy other. A squeeze hard, distortin er cheeks an lips. This is self-defuckinfence.

—What the fuck's wrong with you? EY! What the fucker you freakin out *now* for, yer soft fuckin get!

An the fuckin bitch, she jerks er head so that thee end uv me thumb slips into er gob an she bites down hard an a heer a crunch an feel er fuckin teeth grindin tergether through me skin. A yell an yank me hand awey; the ender me thumb's fuckin hangin off liker hat an the blood's already reached me elbow. Oh Christ, you mad fuckin psychotic bint. A scramble back up on to the bed an pull the duvet around meself fer protection feelin fuckin sick wither pain an Mairead's towerin over me lookin completely fuckin mental, blood runnin down er chin, er lips all twisted inner snarl, eyes on fuckin fire. She's lovin this, am fuckin sure she is; am positive she gets off on this kinder thing. Wooden fuckin do it so often, otherwise, would she? She can be a fuckin evil bitch sometimes, she can.

—Who wuh it, Colm? She slaps me in the face an me head jerks back. Me hand's in fuckin agony an me head is reelin burrah carn elp thinkin ow fuckin gorgeous she looks.

—Oo wuh it? Er voice is strained, horrible. —Oo wuh it tha fucked when a wuh in Aberdyfi? Eh?

Another slap. Oh shit. —What the fucker yer talkin about? A havvun gorrer bleedin *clue* –

Slap. An slap agen, this time not wither hand but with a little red notebook, a wee notebook tharrah sometimes write things in, just stuff, yer know, not rerly poems like, just, yer know, thoughts n things. Slap. An now a remember. Oh fuck.

—'My splendid secret'? She quotes, sneering. —'Those two days that we spent together'? 'The taste of your anus'? Tha fuckin *cunt*, Colm, tha bastard, tha twat, cunt, *wanker* . . .

She slaps me face with each swer werd which rerly fuckin winds me up so a clench me fist ignorin the pain an am about ter probly fuckin leather er one but bifore a can stand up even shiz grabbed a plank off the cher, the cher a put me foot through once inner rage an sort uv mended with the short thick plank uv wood shiz oldin now in both ands abover ed an she shrieks liker cat an brings it down on me skull with all er strength an a feel me teeth explode an then me vision goes grey an that's it, that's me, fucked, red card, out uv it, gone.

Sometimes, yer know, the erge just isunt ther. Sometimes it just goes awey. Last night, fer one; rain on the windows, freezin cold outside, me on the couch all wrapped up inner blanket with a big pot uv tea anner packit uv Jaffa Cakes readin some Cormac McCarthy. Amazin fuckin werds, in Cormac McCarthy. A wanted ter read is new one, rerly, a ferget wharrit's called like, burrit's still in ardback an is erlier stuff's in the cheaper, smaller, easier-ter-slip-down-yer-kex paperback editions. So ther a was, readin *Suttree*, all warm an sheltered from the rain. Oner the best nights av ad in fuckin ages. No craving, no hunger, no need, just safe an warm an comfortable. Which, in a wey, is a birruv a pisser too bicause no doubt when the hunger comes back al av ter scrat an scurry around for the munny ter assuage it an last night I ad therty quid on the bedroom sideboard. These things seem ter werk that wey. Birruver downer rerly. But, anyway, it was a fuckin ace night.

Even if people don't wanner heer about it, it was a fuckin ace night. No lie, man.

Hospital.

No confusion or bewilderment, a know exactly wher a am as soon as a wake up: ozzy.

Fuck. Me poor fuckin head. Christ.

Ther was a bonfire party out at Eglwys Fach, a remember tha much, on top uvver mountain somewher. The candles in the trees lightin the wey up, the glow uv the flames in the night sky, a remember Liam tellin us all ter follow im an walkin straight into the river ('try the othurr pahth, this wan's a bit wet so ut is'). Flyin on the E an whizz a was, up ther with the rockits like, feelin just fuckin dandy, a remember not wantin ter cause a barney with tha fuckin geek oo wouldn't stop strokin Mairead's legs when we wer out inner garden . . . a remember as well feelin a bit odd, panicky, not bein able ter breathe properly an stuff, sweatin far too much, me hands wooden stop shakin . . . what did a do then . . . oh yeh, a hadder toot uv skag ter calm meself down . . . went with Roger inter the house ter look fer more booze, inter thee upsters bedroom with the floor wobblin cos uv the techno downsters . . . another E, a Pink Cally a think . . . another wee toot uv skag . . . Roger angry cos a diddun sher me E . . . thinkin ow nice irrud be just ter lie down on the floor ferra bit . . . an then . . . an then . . . what the fuck then?

An then Malcolm sticks is ed round the ward door an goes:

—Well, look a tha fuckin state o' that.

A try ter laugh but me throat herts, kind uv berning; the stomach pump, a serpose. A become awer uv the daft green gown am wearin as Malcolm comes in, sniffin like mad, follered byer grinnin Paul anner scowlin Mairead, oo's arf pissed as well by the looks uv things – the unfocused look inner eyes like. Swayin on the spot. Am not entirely sure whether am pleased ter see em. A don't rerly know.

—They diddun av any flowers in thuh Spar, Paul sez. —So a brought yuh a leek instead.

Ee puts a mucky leek on top uv the bedside table, next ter me jug uv orange juice. The fuckin loon. A laugh.

283

—Oo's a silly sausage then?, ee sez, rufflin me ed. —Ow'd yuh get in here then, ey?

A shrug. —*I* doan fuckin know, do I? A was hopin tha you could tell me.

—Duh yuh not remembuh anythin?

A shake me ed. —Hardly. A remember avin a few toots with Roger like, an then another E cos a was feelin a bit odd, but –

Mairead butts in: —Ah, well, it's tha orn fuckin stupid fault then. Wha did tha expect, Colm? The bevvih, the speed, the E an the heroin as well? Nor fuckin wonder tha collapsed. Daft pillock. Tha's never fuckin satisfied, ar yuh? Tha can never av enough. Sort yersen out, Colm, fer fuck's serk.

—Oh, well, that's fuckin lovely, tharriz, a sey, startin ter feel a bit pissed off. —Nor even a fuckin ow ar yer, Colm? A good ter see yer still afuckinlive, Colm? Jesus.

She snarls. —Ad be a damn saht better off if tha wirnt. We all would.

—Ah yer fuckin –

—Ey, now, OI! Doan fuckin exert yaself, Colm. Yer an ill boy. An stop windin im ap, Malcolm sez.

—Like fuck, a sey, burra do make meself calm down. An anywey me fuckin throat's killin me.

—Well, wha happund was –

—No one ad seen ya fa abaht three owas –

—Someone goes: Whir's Colm? An –

—Will ya shat ap an fuckin let me tell it?

Paul pulls a face an starts sulkin liker kid. Malcolm carries on:

—We coulden find ya fa ages. Roger sed ee'd left ya somewhair but ee coulden rememba whair, an anyway by that time a could ardly undastand a fuckin waird ee sed, ee was so fuckin off it. Coulden even stand. An then these nippas oo wair thair – dja rememba the saucepans?

A nod, burra don't. Ther's always loads uv wee kids at parties tho.

—They came runnin aht inta the yard gowin: Thair's a dead fella apstairs! A dead fella!

—An then wuh knew exactly wuh tha fuckin wuh, Mairead sez.

—So we legged it apstairs, coulden rouse ya, you wair cowld, tairnin fuckin blue, we shat arselves, fawt you'd snuffed it, phowned a ambulance an that's it. They brought ya here.

A try, but no more memories retern. It's a blank. All tha a feel is stupid an useless and pathetic.

—Owja feel now?

—Whadder you think? Like apserlute fuckin shite.

—Well, doan worry yaself, cos av got jast the remedy fa that, my son, me ole spunka! Fret an fear not cos Dr Malcolm Baker is on tha case.

Ee tosses a wrap uv what I assume is whizz on the bed. A full wrap n all; still with the cling film on. —Aw nice one. Yerra fuckin star, mate.

—You stupid . . . fucking . . .

Mairead's werds ar bein forced out through gritted teeth an er hands uv cerled up inter claws an a think shiz about ter rip Mal's fuckin face off but then she storms stampin an flailing out uv the ward, spittin an hissin liker lynx. Paulie pulls a worried face an follows er an Malcolm shrugs an goes:

—What'd a do?

—Yer made me fuckin night is what yer did. Yerra fuckin saviour, man. Yud berrer follow er tho, see shiz alright like. She OK last night?

Ee shakes is ed. —Near fuckin hysterical, man. Fawt a was gonna hafta cawl a fuckin ambulance fa her as well. Fawt ya'd kicked it, ya see.

Ah. That's nice. Wee warm glow inside me.

—Anyway, look, sign yaself aht an wull meet ap in the wine bar later. Vodka promotion or sammink; two shots a quid. Yeh?

—Yeh. Give us about an ower.

—Orright. Be lucky.

Ee leaves an I unwrap the speed an pour it into a glass uv orange juice that tha babe uvver nerse brought me erlier, bless er. Right sweetie she is . . . mind you, a doan trust nerses any more, not since tha crazy one a was seein back in Birken'ed. Fuckin mad she was. Psycho. She found out that a was shaggin someone else be'ind er back, a don't know ow like, but she diddun lerron she knew until a was spread-eagled naked an tied toer bed (birrer bondage, yer know, av never been averse ter that), whence she proceeded ter push hatpins – long, thin, shiny cold steel hatpins – through me bollox. Not thee actual ball, like, just the skin, but Christ, tha was bad enough. A thought a was gunner die, or at least suffer irreparable damage. Fuckin terrified a was. A escaped when she sed that the last two pins were for me bell-end an went into the kitchen ter sterilise them; a wriggled out uv me bonds, skinnin me fuckin wrists an ankles, an ran fer me fuckin life. Left me clothes an stuff on the floor, just fuckin legged it. Runnin through Prenton in the nuddy with hatpins through me nadgers. Fuckin nightmer. A reverse-charged a phone call ter me mate an hid in the bushes until ee terned up ter take me ome. Ee sed it served me right, when ee'd stopped laughin like.

When the speed's dissolved a knock it back in one; me weakened stomach tries ter throw it back out agen but I cover me mouth with me hand an swallow it back. The ole biddy in the bed opposite scowls at me so a shower me teeth inner grin.

—Yer orright luv?

She just sters. Nor even blinking. Probly dead. A look awey an when a look back agen er eyes're closed. Which could mean that –

The speed kicks in quickly an pretty soon am fuckin *zoomin* up ther an am thinkin right that's me am offski but the fit nerse comes in as am fightin ter gerrout of the bed. Fuckin crappy hospital blanket's liker hairy bleedin python . . .

—What are you doing? What's going on?

—Wha does it look like am bleedin doin? A wanner goan sign meself out. Ere, gizzer and up, will yer?

She just sters n all, the corners uvver gob terned disapprovingly down. An wharrah gob; full, pouty, red . . . phwoar, Christ.

—That's not really advisable, Mr Downey, observation is –

—Aw fucks ter that, God, a can look after meself now, am orright, av never felt berrer ter tell yer the truth. But thanks fer yer elp in rebuildin the fine figger yer see before yer now.

A swing me legs out uv the bed on to the cold floor an me gown rides up, givin er a glimpse uv me plums all perple an swollen. That seems to appen when I. The whizz is fuckin rushin through me now an am a locomotive, unstoppable, a need ter be out uv ere an surrounded by faces, talk, music, life, a wanner be awey from this place with its smells and cleanliness. All neg and anti, hospitals ar. Death.

—I really do think that you should –

—Nah, nah, lissen, am off, am awey, am out uv ere. Carn stey a moment longer. Am rerly OK now. Jeez, ther wasn fuckin enny'in wrong with me in the ferst place. Av got people ter meet.

The coldness an clamminess uv the floor numbs me feet. Nersey stands ther, not knowin what ter do.

—Ey, yer could come with me if yer like. What time does yer shift finish? As anyone ever told you ow gorgeous yer ar?

This fails ter raise a smile.

A look around.

—Erm . . . can yer tell me wher me kex ar please?

Av gorrer be out uv ere. Av just got to.

Thiz a story tha me mam an dad ar fond uv tellin on the rare occasions tharra see em about a dey out to the Welsh Mountain Zoo when me n me brothers n sisters wer all little. We useter go ther quite a lot; me mam was born around ther somewher an we'd goan visit er family an then go ter see thee animals. A used ter love it, I did. Fuckin ace it was. Anywey, a was about four, a think, or five, an a doan remember it now but apparently a was fascinated by the wolves; ad drag evrybody awey from the elephants or giraffes or wharrever so a could goan see the wolves agen. This one wolf, soer story goes, was fascinated by me as well; irrud ster at me an lick its lips an whine an when a went awey irrud howl fer ages n ages. Just this one particular wolf, like; thee others wern arsed. Oh yeh, we wer good mates, me n this wolf. Anywey, this one time, me family wer all standin watchin the seals bein fed or somethin when someone noticed a was gone so they went n looked all over the zoo fer me, even back out to the car like, but they couldn't find me anywher so eventually thee told oner the guards or porters or wharrever ther called anner big serch was ordered. An a was found, ages later, outside the wolves' cage, but not, like, be'ind the hedges, wher yer serposed ter stey fer safety reasons, no, ad some'ow climbed over or crawled under the hedge an a was lyin on me side pressed up agenst the bars with me hand through inter the cage rufflin this special wolf's mane, an the wolf was simultaneously whimpering and growling as if, accordin to me da, ee was hating himself fer lovin thee attention a was givin im. Wid been lyin ther, pressed tergether like that, fer owers. Both uv us. Me n the wolf. Then the guard came an took me awey an the wolf started howling agen. I cried too, apparently.

And that's the whole story. Fuck knows wharrit means, like, or why a tell it all the time; a mean, it's just about a little scally kid anner caged wolf. An a doan even remember it happenin an neither am I triner make some hackneyed old clichéd analogy between me as a kid an the imprisoned wild animal burrah do remember dreams, certain dreams a yuced ter av, leapin through a snowbound forest an howlin blood-muzzled at the moon. But, anywey, it's juster good story an a like it an am dead glad tharram in it an that's all.

That feller Reich . . . Wilhelm, is it? Anywey, wharrever is fuckin name was, ee ad the right idea . . . sexual energy, like, it's . . . it's vital, yer know, a vital force, yer need to express it in order ter stay sane, more, the recognition, an appreciation, uv yer own sexuality allows you ter achieve satisfyin orgasms which then help ter free yer from yer preoccupations, an concerns, an neuroses . . . an thus allow yer ter become a whole person, true ter yerself like, stable n balanced an healthy . . . it's thee orgone, the blue force, this sexual energy . . . a can feel meself glowin fuckin blue like the phosphorescence yer see in the sea sometimes . . . oh it's the force tha unites an links all things, livin or inanimate, all things inner universe possess this force, possess or ar possessed by, it's like, all uv um ar linked an bonded tergether through this force, this cement . . . liker spunky Araldite it is . . .

. . . an moren that; thee exploration of the more, erm, adventurous (some would sey seedy but I fuckin wouldunt) side uv yer sexuality, tha, too, helps ter free yer frommer shackles an hang-ups uv which ther ar menny in sucher intolerant, repressive society as this one . . . leavin yer free to explore yerself . . . the achievement uv freedom, maybe thee only true possible freedom, in this werld uv fear an oppression, uv mistrust an ignorance . . . uv ·hegemonic control over class n race n gender an behaviour, those controlling forces which seek to an which will not rest until they have succeeded in pummelling evrythin tha lives outside them an which ar made uy diffrunt substances down into a paste as colourless an as bland an insipid as themselves . . . polymorphic perversity . . . my sexuality, thee only parter me which cannot be controlled . . . it frees energies inside me, mad energies, which threaten your cosy an proscribed view uv how the werld should be, they reinvest that werld wither rich colours an tastes tharrit was made in originally, before you crept out of the closet with yer fuckin bleach and sandpaper an sought ter destroy all which ley outside yer narrow weakly-beating breast cos it fuckin *scerd* you an you hated it cos it spoke ter parts inside you which you wanted to, *needed* to suppress an deny that you had . . . aw fuck . . . am alive here, man, a feel so fuckin alive . . .

A feel meself startin ter come, those familiar sensations beginnin wey down in me feet, ternin me thighs ter jelly an a thrust a bit harder and deeper an she groans bineath me, er face pressed inter the pillow, er fingers disappearin inter the sides uv the mattress. A put me lips down into er dreadlocks an pant:

—Ar yis alright? It dozent hert?

She murmurs: —No, God no, it feels fuckin great . . . gorgeous . . . don't stop fuckin me a love it yes a fuckin love it . . .

A push meself up on me hands an look downer smooth an muscular back ter wher ar bodies ar joined, my pelvis to her arse, er sphincter clingin tight ter the root uv me dick, me hips pushin er buttocks up into a creamy heart-shaped mound with evry push. Oh God . . . energy surges through me an a grit me teeth an start ter thrust agen, me heart pounding, she groans an a reach underneath er body ter tickler clit with thee end uv me finger an a feeler fanny gorgeously, sexily empty . . . phwoar . . . she grunts an thrusts back an a feel summun insider, some protruberance, not soft, feels like bone or summun press inter me bell-end which is a birruver shock, a doan know rerly if a like it or not, burra just carry on fuckin er upper arse'ole an caressin er clitoris an kissin an softly biting er neck and whisp'rin things inner ear, me lips agenst the metal uv the rings which run through er ear from lobe ter top in one unbroken silver line . . .

—Dyer feel me inside . . . right up inside yer anus . . . tell me it feels good . . . stretchin your tight little arse wide fuckin open . . . tell me how it feels . . .

She gergles inner throat an then thrashes and yells as she comes an then a let meself go, I explode into er arse, a massive jolt uv pure pleasure n ecstasy blastin through every cell uv me body . . . better than anythin, better than evrythin, better than any fuckin drug ever invented . . . God God God am in heaven am in fuckin heaven this is so fuckin *nice* . . .

A collapse on to er slippery back an me dick slides out wither soft, wet gergle. Panting I am, me chest heaving . . . soon's av got me breath back a roll off an lie on me side agenst er with me arms wrapped rounder, tryin ter remember er name . . . summun Welsh, a remember tha much . . . nah, sno good, it's gone. Never did av much uvver memory fer names like. A holder tight agenst me, feelin er heart boom behind er prominent ribcage. Ah, shiz nice, this one, sexy as fuck an was ace ter go speedin with last night . . . a hope Mairead didunt notice me slopin off like that. Probly not, cos when a left the pub she was almost bloody comatose in the back bar, an anywey she probly found someone ter fuck as well, like she alweys fuckin does. Still, God, this is fuckin great an is nowher fuckin *neer* as perverse as some uv the things av done, like shaggin Sharon. Biggest fuckin mistake uv me life, tha was, am tellin yer man, a regret it evry fuckin dey, specially when Malcolm woan stop goin on about it . . . but this, tho, this . . .

—Mmmmmmmmmm.

She mermurs inter me neck. A press the duvet tight ter me chest with me arm so the shite smell dozen waft up from me knob. Occupational hazard.

—Yew didn't mind doin it that way, didjer? She asks. —Only a carn feel much the other way like, not since a had me third.

—Oh Christ no, a sey, an kiss the matted top uvver ed. —A prefer it like tha, ter tell yer the truth. Terns me on.

—Good.

We just lie ther ferra bit. Glowing n happy. Then she sits up:

—A fancy a beer. Wouldjer like a can uv beer, Colin? Plenty in the fridge like.

Colin. She called me fuckin Colin. A fuckin *hate* it when tha happens.

—Nice n cold. Yew want one then?

—Yeh, orright.

She gets off the bed an walks across the room. A watcher shoulders move, er back, arse, legs, mane uv tangled hair reachin down to er bum . . . Fuckin Colin. Still, al fergive yer that, wharrever the fuck yer name is. Jesus, ow could a not? An three babbies, ey? Well, yuv still got yer figure, a must sey. Oh yeh, yer orright. You'll do.

Wher I stand on thee injection/ingestion debate:

Yer can never, in all onnesty, rerly sey tha yuv done drugs properly like until yuv used the needle. The needle's hard-core, thiz a vast gulf bitween snortin an jaggin. It's a rush uv such intense exhilaration tha yer can never get from any'in else, an am not just referrin purely ter thee effects uv the drug here (usually, in my case, amphetamines; oh, a know it's not fashionable ter inject speed any more, but fuck that – what's fashion got ter do with drug abuse?); no, am talkin also about thee act itself, the ritual – somer yer faverit tunes on, a few bottles uv yer faverit brew, the pulverised dexies bubblin in the spoon, the vein bulgin in yer tied arm liker blue umbilical cord . . . the needle breakin through yer skin, that lovely little flash uv pain (an once the needle goes in, once yuv broken tha barrier bitween blood and air, bitween inside and outside, then yuv entered a werld wher all bets ur off, a place wher few people go – uncharted waters like) . . . blood flowering in the barrel, rippling red ribbons . . . plunge, and slam the fuckin drug straight up an into yer sizzlin brain. Ace, man, too fuckin massive fer werds; yer feel liken angel evicted from Heaven. Fuckin indescribable. Try n explain sex to a vergin an yul see wharra mean. Fuck snortin, fuck bombs, fuck dabbin; ther orright, like, if circumstances preclude the needle, but amphets whapped straight into yer bloodstream is wha drug use is all about, that state tha can never be approximated by anythin else. An thee irony is tharrit's only when yer do this, this dangerous drama which flerts with dying, it's only then tha yer realise ow truly fuckin beautiful life can be. A mean, mostly, this life is beautiful, an I enjoy it too much fer werds – dancing, drinking, drugging, shaggin, talkin, laughin, playin with me rat, reading, swimmin inner sea, all this stuff, a doan giver fuck wha anyone else sez al tell yer heer n now tharra can love this life, this werld . . . yeh, the lives we lead ar magical, all uv us, but ther dulled and stupefied by what wer forced ter do, by what we *avter* do in order ter cling on to ar last scrap uv freedom which is a nominal freedom only uv course unless, and here's me point, unless yer can serch ferra diffrunt *kind* uv freedom through such things as drugs and sex, thee only arenas left to us wher we can be if not truly free then at least more free than anywher else. Djer know wharra mean? Drugs allow you ter realise an appreciate tha original magic tha lies under yer life an which, despite all thee ugly quotidian realities an petty obscenities uv diurnal existence, stubbernly refuses ter be banished. Why fight ter keep a job yer hate? Why struggle ter support a lifestyle that, evry minute uv every dey, yer deeply resent leading?

A streak uv rusty blood on the barrel uv the syringe. Cotton wool liker puffball inner scorched spoon.

There's no danger here, not fer me anywey, not rerly; me, am fuckin charmed. Born wither caul on me ed a was; a chosen one, oner God's faverits, oh yes, am fuckin invincible I am, a can dancer jig on the edge uv the grave an I will never ever ever fall in.

And wher the fuck am I? Am I insider fuckin mountain? A can feel wet on me back through me soppin clothes an seer stars above, spiky as if through tears. A can hear sheep bleating an me heart slowly booming, and the wind is callin me name: Ccccoooooollluuuuuuuummm . . . Is that the wind or voices? The wind has a Welsh accent . . . Me hands n feeter shakin like bastards an me teeth ar machine-gunnin tergether, but whether that's through cold or drugs or illness am not sure. Probly all three. Just genrully bein fucked up.

Huge spaces around me. Giant shapes in the night, vast humps uv a deeper blackness . . . must be mountains. Tha glittering, lapping, flat thing somewher on me right's a lake a serpose. Voices in the soil . . . callin me down to them . . .

This morning – or yesterdee morning or whenever the fuck it was – wazzer seventh, eighth, ninth dey without sleep or food, an yer know what that's like, when evrythin seems evil, infected wither force of pure malevolence . . . yer feel stalked, hunted . . .

fuckin awful like . . . yer hear people whisprin, plottin about yer, incessant hissing conspiracies, yer become painfully awer uv yer soft an intricate fragile flesh and how vulnerable, even prone, irriz to horrific damage . . . blood spertin from the gleaming muscle . . . a werld uv noise and hert, out here in the mountains, these places uv past massacres an ghosts an fields uv ber bones . . . pain and horrer's in every blade uv grass . . . a think those temazzies wer a mistake, especially with the Mad Dog . . . a hadder real go at Sharon, a seem ter remember . . . another one . . . flipped out a bit by the fire a did, a think, a seem ter recall . . . made a right arse uv meself . . . aw fuck . . .

Now the wind's soundin like Malcolm: Cccooorrrlllaaaaahhhmm!

Wakin up in the hills not knowin wher the fuck I yam; alone, freezin, exposed, fightin back hysteria and terrer with evry fuckin breath . . . lyin heer tremblin, lissenin ter wailin voices in the darkness callin me name. Fuck. Help.

—Sammy yew twat! What in-a name-a *fuck* av yew fuckin gorron?

A look up, and Sam is weavin across the crowded pub terwards me n Roger, a big daft grin on is face, an ee's wearin . . . well, what the fuck *is* ee wearin? Army boots, camouflage kex, a black vest wither bullet bandolier across it, a headband . . . an ee's carryin a placky machine-gun. What the fuck? Yer should see the looks ee's gettin.

—Jesus Christ. What's all this? Yer look liker right dick.

—Y'don't like it then?

—Wharrer yer serposed ter be?

—Am a Basque terrorist.

Roger splutters. —No yer not, mun, yewer a bloody tosser.

—Why? A ask Sam. —What for?

—The party. Fancy dress, innit.

—Oh yer soft arse! Who told yer tha?

Roger bersts out laughin. —Is it *fuck* fancy dress, mun! Yer gunner look a right twat swannin inter Twmi's in that fuckin get up! Twmi avin a fancy fuckin dress party, fuck, av fuckin ird it all now, I yav!

Ee shakes is ed an takes a gulp uv is pint, smiling around the glass.

Christ: Sam; a dick'ed. —What gave yer that idea?

Ee looks around wither redner, obviously feelin daft now, people laughin an pointin at im. Fuckin Basque terrerist, Jesus.

—Well, Malcolm said –

—Malcolm! Oh well, ther yer go. Tha explains it fuckin all now.

—Ee wuz windin yew fuckin up, boy! Takin yew fer the twat tha yer so obviously are! Twmi avin a fancy dress do. Ird it fuckin all now, I yav, Roger repeats.

—Shite, a sey. —So now wuv gorrer go ter this party with you lookin liker total knob?

—Maybe a could pretend am the bouncer.

Ow Sam keeps is life tergether al never fuckin know. If a was asked fer one adjective that best describes im, a think ad avter sey 'baffled'. Cos ee is; inner complete fuckin permanunt daze like . . . Fair pley to im tho, ee calms down after thee initial embarrassment as been seen off wither few whiskies an starts ter make a joke of irrall, callin the barman 'el capitan' and stuff, an the locals ar messin around with im, yer know, throwin ther ands up an goin 'don't shoot!' n stuff, an ee's evidently feelin a birruv an arse cos ee's neckin the whiskey like water, triner douse the flames in is cheeks, an when wer all pissed enough not ter cur we leave the pub and head down the dark wet lanes to the party. No street lights at all, a can ardly seer fuckin thing. Yer heer all that stuff about how country darkness is truly *dark* and, God, it's true; it's like walkin through soot or somethin. So fuckin black, like. Am not even entirely sure wher we ar; Goginan? Cwmbrwyno? Ponterwyd? Dozen rerly matter tho cos ter find the party all we avter do's follow the flashin glow an the techno thumpin across the fields, the thumpin bass. Sounds fuckin great. But ther's another noise as well, closer; Roger's the ferst to hear it.

—Can ennybody ir that? Tha scream, like?

We stop n lissun.

—Dunno, Sam whispers. —What does it sound like?

—Like a fuckin scream, yew soft twat. Whatjer fuckin think a scream fuckin sounds like then?

A strain me eers an stand very still. An then a can hear it, faintly, bineath the music, a high, tortured screech. Fuckin horrible – it sounds like real pain, real terrer. Me belly does a little flip.

—Fuck. It sounds liker gerl or a kid. Wharrer we gunner do?

Roger leads us off in the direction uv the sound, through a gap in the hedge and across a muddy field. Am gerrin me boots and kex all covered in shite, an ther me best ones n all, burram not rerly tha bothered cos me 'best' clothes ar all fallin ter bits anywey. An am scerd, like, a bit, burra carn elp laughin at Sam creepin silently through the grass, toy machine-gun held aloft as if ee's in fuckin Vietnam or summun. The idyit.

The scream gets louder. It's rerly fuckin horrible now, like EEEEEEEEEEEEE! EEEEEEEEEE! Am fuckin shitein meself. Somethin's in real distress, real agony; the sound's slicin inter me skull an sawin on the bone. It's awful. A look at Roger fer some kind uv reassurance but that just makes it werse; is dark eyes ar glitterin in the moonlight, is sharp n bony face focused and determined. Ee looks like a stalking predator, ee looks quietly berserk; terrible energy tightly coiled, about ter berst into a frenzy uv uncontrollable ferocity.

—Ah shit, Sam sez, standin still. —A can see what it is.

Roger's instantly at is shoulder: —Whir like? Wha? Wha-a fuck is it then?

Sam creeps over to a hedge, me n Roger close be'ind im, an then as well as the screech which is fuckin ear-splittin by now a can hear other sounds – branches breakin, somethin thrashin madly. Then it suddenly stops silent as Sam parts the hedge slowly an a can see it then, a can just about make it out inner dark; a fox, standing rigid and trembling, its lips drawn back over its teeth and its eyes bulgin like ping-pong balls. Me breath catches in me chest. It's thee image uv utter agony and fear; the fer around its neck is standin up all wet n spiky with blood an its whole body is quaking with horrer and pain. The sight uv it goes through me guts liken ice-cold sword.

—Aw fuck . . . yew poor little fucker . . . what's wrong then, bach? Roger's voice is serprisingly gentle.

—Am not sure yet . . . Sam creeps closer. The fox's trembling gets more frantic. —Shit. It's caught in a neck-wire.

Wer all just standin ther, wonderin what the fuck ter do, starin down at the trapped fox who trembles and bleeds. The distant techno drum matches me heartbeat and the thud of blood in me ed.

—Fuckin cunt's trick, tha, Roger whispers. —Fuckin neck-wire. Choke ter death on yewer own blood see. Fuckin evil like.

An then ee springs an lunges an with startlin agility ee grabs and raises the fox's arse so the pressure's taken off the wire, and it's thrashin around like fuck goin mad an it's snarlin an spittin liker fuckin demon.

—The fuckin wire, mun! Gerrit off! Don't just stand thir like-a twat, use yer fuckin gun!

Sam loops the wire off over the fox's ed with the barrel uv is placky gun an blood sperts up an Roger lets go an the fox leaps an snaps at Sam's and. Sam screams an falls on is arse inner mud an the fox takes off over the field, runnin all lopsided an floppy-edded terwards the booming music and the flashing lights.

Sam's lookin down at is and in is lap. Is voice sounds weak: —Fucker caught me finger. It's fuckin hangin off.

A strike me Zippo and we examine is finger. Yer can't seer lot because uv all the blood, burrit looks bad.

—Does it hert?

—Well, what d'fuckin you think? Me finger's just been nearly bitten off. It feels quite nice actually, all tickly and soft. Jesus Christ.

—Fuckin hospital fer yew, mun, Roger sez. —Rabies like.

So we ed back up to the pub and call fer an ambulance. What do we fuckin look like, ey, all three uv us pissed an covered in mud n shite, Sam in is terrerist geer an is toy gun, one uv is arms soaked in blood up ter thee elbow . . . fuckin mad. Diddun avter queue fer the phone, al tell yer that. We sink a few more whiskies waitin fer the ambulance and check out Sam's hand in the bogs, rinsin it under the cold tap ter reveal a wound all torn an jagged, exposed perple muscle throbbing, yellow sinew stretched tight . . . a was nerly bleedin sick. Flash uv white bone as well a think. Roger just shrugged an sed ee'd seen werse. Thee ambulance came an took us ter Bronglais an yer should've seen the face on the fuckin doctor when ee clocked us; terrified an tremblin. Just like the fox, in fact. Made me laugh. Ee takes Sam awey fer treatment an me n Roger goan sit in the waitin room. A fuckin hate hospitals. Hideous places, full uv sickness. Bring me right down.

Roger's manic, bouncin about on the lino, spinnin on the balls uv is feet. Ee catches sight uvver bunch uv rugby sherts round the coffee machine lookin agog at Sam as ee's led awey an legs it over to em, shoutin:

—Ah yeh, boys, yer it is, a War uv Independence! Front-line fuckin troops yer see! Kickin out-a fuckin English we ar, oh aye, a time as fuckin come! Free Wales Now, ey!

Oner them goes: —Aye, with every three gallons, eh?, an then can do nothing but ster at Roger as ee starts ter bellow 'A Nation Once Again' about four inches from is face:

> When boyhood's fire was in my blood
> I dreamt of ancient freemen!
> Of Greece an Rome where bravely stood
> Three hundred men and three men!
> And yet I pray ter see the day
> Da-dum-da-dee in twain!
> And Way-ells! Long a province!
> Be a fuckin NATION! Once! Ag – *eeeeeeeeennn*!

A nerse comes in an tells im ter shut up an ee starts dancin wither, spinnin er round, cacklin madly. The rugby boys're just starin at im, gobsmacked. Ee looks fuckin crazy. I just finder quiet corner and dab at me wrap uv whizz, rememberin the time not so long ago when a came ter visit Mairead in this hospital after she'd hadder miscarriage. A remember her in the bed, swallowed up in the gown, her hand with the nails all long an painted comin shakily out uv the huge sleeve ter wipe tears from er face. How pitiful she looked . . . how sad . . . I cried as well; it was the red nail varnish and the bracelets that did it, those futile attempts at a small amelioration uv a life whose savagery will brook no compromise nor knows no mercy.

Sometimes I hate this fuckin werld.

Sam comes back out, cleaned, injected and stitched up, an we jump a taxi back out ter the party. Roger's still onner high, singin an shoutin as we walk down the lanes, but Sam's subdued probly cos uv thee injection thee gave im at thee ozzy (lucky fucker) an I am n all cos . . . well, a dunno, rerly, a just am. The whizz asunt kicked in yet an am thinkin uv the fox, and Mairead, an how innocent things suffer and ar punished, of how meekness will be slaughtered. A remember when a was a kid an a useter paint me initials, 'CD' like, on big snails as a wey uv markin them, like, as mine, as my mates, burra never saw any snails crawlin round with 'CD' on ther backs cos the paint poisoned em an killed em. Thinkin ther all safe an sound inside ther shells an all the time ther absorbin slow lethal toxins. A diddun mean ter kill em, like, a just didn't know.

The night's completely black. Like walkin at the bottom uv an ocean uv Guinness.

—Colm, yer too quiet, mun, sey summin fer fuck seyk.

A shrug. —Well, yer know . . . tha fox n stuff. Poor little fucker. Could've ad pups or anythin. Probly dead by now. Slow fuckin torture. Put me onner right bleedin downer, tharraz.

—An the thing is, Sam sez, —those traps're fuckin illegal. Well within our rights t'spring em all y'know. We should; we should come back t'morrow an spring them all.

Is bandaged finger glows huge and white in the dark liker cartoon thumb.

—It's all shite, a sey, feelin the speed start ter tingle. —If tha fuckin fox wanted ter kill chickens n things it's cos irrad a family ter feed. That's all it wanted ter do, servive an feed its family, like us all, but *wer* too fuckin used ter avin too fuckin much. Slike tha herd uv deer out Pumlumon wey, yer know, been ther thousands uv yeers an ther now a fuckin venison farm, a mean wha kind uv –

—Oi, Colm, fer fuck's seyks cheer fuckin up, mun, yill av us in fuckin teers! Roger shouts, loud n sudden enough ter make me jump. —Yer'll av us fuckin cryin, yew will, boy! Get tha fuckin frown off yer feyce like, wir off to-a fuckin party arn we, Jesus! An can yew imagine-a fuckin faces on em when ey see iss twat yer!

Ee jerks is thumb at Sam an a have ter laugh at the state uv im. An a laugh even more when we go inter the party an a see Antonella sittin scowlin n red on the couch, dressed inner traditional Welsh costume uv shawl n stovepipe hat an buckled shoes, Malcolm standin be'ind er pointin atter an pissin imself with laughter. The speed kicks in properly now an me jaws start ter grind an am covered in mud an a see Mairead already pissed strugglin to open a bottle uv wine so a make me wey over to er. An at least av gorrer good story ter tell, ey? Yeh, at least ther's that. A feel orright now.

Bleedin Sharon. Er company's about as welcome as genital warts; all she ever fuckin talks about is oo might or might not fancy er, an whether Mairead can lender any more money. A mean, look atter now, spread out inner armcher liker mad woman's shite wither two-inch long ash onner fag an goin nasally on in tha gratin Wigan whine:

—Well, a knor forra *fact* that Rhodri fancies meeeerrr, cos ee's sed us much when ee wuh pissed up lahk, but thir's this slag Helena tha keeps sniffin round im and . . .

Jesus. Asn she got ennythin more fuckin importunt ter think about? An Mairead, she'll just sit ther lissnin ter this crap; shill purrup with enny amount uv shite from Sharon, fuck knows why like; a mean, Sharon contributes nothin uv enny werth ter *my* life, all she ever does is take. Shiz a fuckin leech. Mairead should teller ter fuck off. Although Mairead'll purrup with enny amount uv shite from ennyone, ter tell the truth. Except me.

Am triner block out Sharon's voice and concentrate on me buke, burrit's dead difficult; it's like tryin ter ignore a fuckin gnat buzzin incessantly round yer ears. Pain inny arse. An then the phone rings. Am not gunner answer it at ferst, cos am thinkin tharrit might be Sarah agen, phonin ter moan about Paul chuckin er. Shiz phoned five times in the past two deys an it's gerrin on me wick. An even if it's not Sarah, a know it's not gunner be good; it's quarter ter twelve, and as evryone knows, good news sleeps til noon (ter quote the Cowboy Junkies). It rings an rings.

—Tha just gornter sit thuh an let tha ring, Colm, or ar tha gornter answer it? Mairead sez, an a small sneer flickers across Sharon's face. Hag. A pick the receiver up.

—Hello?

—Ah, hello, it's Arfon Morris here . . .

Aw fuck. Whenever a heer me landlord's voice on the phone me heart plummets in me chest. With good fuckin reason n all;

299

ee's tellin me tha wer four hundred pounds in arrears, an tha if it isn cleered up by the end uv the month ee's gunner evict us. Four hundred quid. A shouldn av drunk the last two rent cheques. A tell im tha will do the best we can and hang up.

—Oo wuh that?

—Landlord, a sey, talkin ter Mairead but lookin right at Sharon. —Sez we owe four undred quid an if it's not paid up before thee end uv the month then wer ter gerrout.

Am hopin tha Sharon ul now offer ter repey somer the nine hundred pound she owes Mairead, but Christ shiz got the skin uv a rhinoceros. All she does is smirk an look awey from me an carry on wither selfish monotonous monologue:

—So enniwher, Jenny reckons tha Rhodri *does* fancih Helena, but ah wuh tokkin ter Rhidian last Frahder an he reckons tha Rhodri said that he –

Er ash finally falls off, over me *Illuminatus* trilogy stacked at the sider the cher. A carn stand any fuckin morer this. Onest, one more minute uv this an al drive me fuckin fore'ed right into Sharon's smug, self-satisfied expression. It's doin me fuckin ed in. An how can Mairead just sit ther an not sey anythin? Any moment now, a can tell, Sharon's gunner tap Mairead fer money an Mairead ul meekly and it over and I'll get fuckin mad and . . .

A move be'ind the cher Sharon's in. —Move.

She leans forward an a retrieve me coat hung over the backer the seat.

—Whir yer goin?

—Out, a sey, an Mairead looks hard at me. A know shill give me some stick later fer leavin er onner own with Sharon, but God, if she dozen wanner company then she should fuckin sey summun, shoulden she? Shoulden just sit ther an take it, Christ. Lerrin erself get walked over like this . . .

As am goin out the door a heer Sharon sey:

—Sor am askin Rhodri out t'naht lahk, ornleh a dorn't have enny munneh, an a knor he's skint cos ee sahns on sor am wundrin if . . .

A slam the door.

It's hot outside, rerly fuckin boilin; the sun's crackin the flags. A havn gorrer fuckin clue wharram goin ter do; a mean, av got no money, no wey uv gettin any . . . yes a have. A was gunner raid Mairead's perse burrah diddun av the chance, so al avter resort ter Plan B. Which is:

A goan nicker loader bukes from Smith's an the university bukeshop an take em round to the second-and shop, crackin the spines on the wey so it looks like thev been read. The woman tells me ter come back in an ower or so, after she's priced em like, so a wander round to the castle and just sit ther onner bench, smokin an lookin out at the sea. Thoughts uv Sharon ar a clenched fist in me chest, an poverty is weighin on me like chainmail, so a force meself ter think uv somethin nice like goin ferra pint after av been paid fer the bukes; a know a woan get much, just enough ferra few scoops like, which might make me even more frustrated cos then al have the taste . . . a don't know. But ther's fuck all else ter do an goin home's outer the question; at least out here, in the town, thiz alweys the chance tha somethin nice might happen, somethin unexpected.

A seer familiar figger walkin purposefully across the castle grounds, stridin through the ruins. A squint an make out Margaret. A call out toer an she comes over.

—What yer up to?

—Trying t'make some money.

—Soam I, a teller. —Am waitin fer some bukes ter be priced in the second-and shop. Bit bored ter tell yer the truth.

—Av got these, she sez, and olds upper big bagger coins. —Am gunner see ow much thel give me for them in the bank.

Thiz all kinds in ther, francs, pesetas, fuckin zlotys, lire, drachmas, some funny ones with oles inner middles which look like big, brass Polos . . . Mags tells me tha when she was little she yuce ter collect foreign coins an tha this is er collection. Sez shiz run out uv bukes an electrical appliances ter sell; she solder last one, a portable black n white telly, last week for a fiver.

—Ow much jer think yill get fer them? All them coins?

She shrugs. —Dunno. Dunno what the exchange rate is on most uv em. Wait and see. Fancy a pint?

Shiz gorrer few quid onner so we go to the Ship an Castle ferrer bevvy anner gamer pool. Murphy the dog sits onner bar stool an watches us pley, and it's nice in ther an a wanner stey but wir outer money after a pint n a arf each so a go round to the second-and bukeshop an pick up eight pound fifty. A thought irrud be more, like, but . . . berrer than fuckin nothin a serpose.

On the wey to the bank we meet Dai Datblygu, staggerin up Great Darkgate Street wither beard down to is belt-buckle. Ee's wearin carpet slippers and is pissed off is face, swiggin frommer bottle uv expensive-lookin wine.

—Yis orright, Dai?

—Knackered. Been wurkin see.

—Oh yeh? Djer win?

—Fifteen to one with a five-pound stake! Am fuckin rich, boy!

Ee roars an crushes both me n Mags tergether inner giant, smelly hug. Pwoar, Christ . . . as nicer bloke as ee is, ee could certainly do wither good wash.

—Fifteen times five, Mags sez. —That's . . .

—Enough fer two deys oblivion, darlin.

Ee gives er a big sloppy kiss on the cheek anner face gets lost in is beard.

—Thur's a few debts pressin on me, ee sez. —After that tho al be knockin em back in the Llew. My round.

—Nice one. See yer ther.

Ee shambles off. Lucky fucker. Maybe a should take up gambling. We go down ter Barclays an I stand around waitin outside while Mags is in ther stressin the cashier out. Shill be in ther fuckin ages probly, all those exchange rates ter sort out n stuff, so a sit down on the cold granite step and wait. A shrug apologetically at a *Big Issue* seller oo looks at me hopefully.

—Skint, mate.

Ee smiles an disappears in the crowd. Town's fuckin heavin, troops uv tourists wandrin aimlessly about an talkin in Brummie accents, a few stragglin students triner put off goin ome fer the holideys, aller locals out inner hot weather. The pubs'll be fuckin chocker. Av got eight fifty in me pocket an it's nowher neer enough. An am sure tha wha Mags'll get won't be anywher neer enough either; a mean, ferra good binge, yer lookin at seventy, eighty quid just fer yerself – twenny quid's werth a whizz (at least), tenner or so fer fags, loads n loads a beer uv course, take-outs ter get yer through the night an then more money ter drink through the comedown the next dey. Costs fuckin loads. Still, somethin might appen tho . . . Mags might gerrer lot more than she expects. Maybe ther'll be a dead rer coin in ther which is werth hundreds . . . an meybe the cashier is an avid coin collector ool buy them all out uv er own pocket fer much more than ther actually werth. Meybe Mags'll find some money in the bank. Meybe while am sittin ere a bundle uv notes'll fall out uv someone's pocket an land at me feet. Christ, it dozen even after be a bundle, juster twenny'll do . . . or a ten . . . even a fiver'd be a big help . . .

Maybe somethin nice will appen. Yer never can tell.

A pushcher nudges me inner shins an a look up. It's Sieffri Lewis, with is missus an an army uv little kids in tow.

—Ow's yurself then, Colm? Taken up beggin now eh?

—Norrer bad fuckin idea.

—Skint, is it?

A hold me palms out ter show im ow empty they ar. —The fuckin usual, yeh.

Sieff's left hand is done up inner mucky bandage an is missus, Amanda, as gorrer huge split lip. All eh kids' faces ar caked in chocolate and ice cream.

—Well, yer's a job goin, if yer intrested. That new site by er station? Eyr lookin for groundwurkers now they ar, with tha mater yours, Paul is it?

Is werds an movements ar all slow-motion underwater. Amanda's n all. Wooden minder a birrer skag meself rerly . . . take me mind off this grindin fuckin poverty . . .

—Werk? Oh fuck no, Sieff. Nor intrested ther, mate. Not one tiny bit.

—No, it's not bard, like, but a can make more dosh dealin. Tole the fuckin foreman that n all a did; ee goes why yer leavin? A said make more fuckin money dealin in a dey than a can wurkin on this fuckin place in a month. Should-a seen-a fuckin face on im.

A laugh. A like Sieffri.

—It's easy goin, like, not too ard, four quid un ower, early finish Saturdeys –

—No, no, Sieff, it rerly dozen move me, mate. Things arn

303

tha desperate yet. Save yer breath, mate, I am the Hercules uv disinterest.

Ee gets a bit more animated then as ee puts onner Harry Enfield Scouser accent:

—Ey! Ey! Caaaaarrm down, caaaarm down la, ey! Come ed la, come ed . . .

Oner the kids starts gerrin restless and Mandy picks er up.

—Hush, darlin, nirly thir . . . can yer see the sea?

She points to the end uv the road an the baby gergles.

—Can a intrest yer in a nice bit uv brown? Sieff's voice is low, confidential. —Good fuckin gear iss is like . . . picked it up off Fishguard docks meself, three o'clock iss mornin like . . .

A shake me ead. —Can't, mate. Skint. Gor eight fuckin quid in me pocket an that's it like, am fuckin brassic after tha.

—Well . . .

Ee crumples a fiver inter me shert pocket. —Yer. Ad give yer more if a could, like, but . . .

—No, Jesus, God, this ul fuckin do. Yerra fuckin star, man.

—Aye, a know. Spend it wisely now.

Ee gives us a big grin, revealin some choice dental pandemonium. Then ee winks an walks off, Mandy an the kids trailin after im, slowly like, weavin languidly through the people. Good one tha man. Maybe a *should* take up beggin. Been ere five minutes an got five quid an a wasn even tryin. Still, not evrybody's as generous wither cash as Sieffri, ar thee?

Maggie comes back out.

—Seven quid, she sez. —Expected more. Seven fuckin quid . . .

Which isn very much ferra childhood hobby, is it? It's always a shock when yer hobbies and intrests, even if they ar obsolete, ar translated into monetary units, cos then yer forced ter realise how, in the practical schemer things, they have utterly no value to anyone other than yourself. Outside uv yerself, ther not werth shite; and, since we measure the werth uv things in terms uv monetary exchange, then yuv wasted yer fuckin time. Done fuck all. Lernt fuck all. Might as well uv stacked fuckin shelves in Somerfield.

So; that's Mags's seven, my eight fifty, Sieffri's five . . . Twenty pounds fifty pence. After a packet uv ciggies wer down to just under eighteen quid which we sit an spend inner Black, Yr Hen

Llew Du, cool an gloomy pub awey from the heat an the shoppers' feet. But eighteen quid isn much more than nine pints, and after four each the end's in sight an av got the beginnings uv an alcohol buzz which is crying out ter be stoked ferther.

Roy comes in and Mags asks im if ee's seen Dai.

—Yeh, just now, ee sez. —Flat on is back on the beach singin is lungs out, completely fuckin rat-arsed. Carn even move ardly. A spoke to im an ee couldn't even recognise me. Why?

Mags shakes er ead an we sit ther nersin a final ahf each, waitin fer somethin ter happen. A mean, things *do* happen; that unexpected fiver off Sieffri, fer one . . . things *do* happen. But nothing does. We just sit ther slowly sippin an waitin an wharrever small buzz av got is robbed of its pleasure because nothing, fuckin, happens.

Am leanin on the bar up at Oxygen feelin the E in me system in me extremities an me teeth an a new rush is comin on from the new tab av just necked an a know tha inner few minutes al be inner place wher no fucker can disterb or dilute me joy but they won't want to anywey cos they'll all be feelin like this too. Paul's bellowin somethin in me ear, a carn ear it proply over the music burrah think it sounds like 'Tiger Feet' by Mud or some such shite, but am not rerly lissenin anywey cos am watchin Mairead an Margaret dance, rapture on ther faces, an am thinkin uv tha bruise a noticed on Mags's breast last night an wonderin how it got ther. I asked er like but she gor all embarrassed an sed she slipped over in the bath. Burrit dozen seem ter be botherin er now, er n Mairead dancin tergether, thee expressions on ther faces like angels', ther limbs lovely, skin shinin, both uv em lookin cool and beautiful . . . so happy . . .

Am standin ere watchin em both an am comin up fast on good MDMA. Things doan get much berrer than this. No fuckin wey.

My gorgeous women. My two beautiful gerls.

—Aaaaargh! Yer feeter like two blockser fuckin ice!

Mairead laughs and presses er feet harder agenst me legs.

—No, a fuckin mean it, Mairead; it *herts* theh so bleedin cold.

She takes em awey an squirrels in agenst me back, er face inner nape uv me neck, er knees like spoons in the backs uv mine. She asks me wharram thinkin about an a just shrug.

—Nothin rerly.

And sometimes ther rerly isn't anythin in me head . . . just floating white blocks uv nothingness . . . but right now am thinkin about the marvellous elasticity uv muscle and how amazing irriz that Mags's tight an tiny arsehole can stretch to accommodate me stiff dick.

Jesus. The cruelty uv human dynamics. Mairead here beside me, Mags up~at Llys Wen onner own. Doan we know anythin about mercy? What the fuck's wrong with me?

Mairead murmurs an pretty soon shiz asleep, a can tell cos er breathin gets slower n deeper, and I'm just lyin here, starin into the dark, lissenin to the rain onner window. Am hopin tha Mairead dozen start talkin inner sleep; she does sometimes, an it's dead unnerving – amongst the werds a can pick out, it seems that she talks to er grandmother, the one oo died an lefter all the money . . . It's unsettling. It becomes like another voice in me head, those sinister whisperings uv unknown provenance which sometimes come at night . . . an I imagine Mairead's granny here in the room with us, standin at thee end uv the bed in the dark, starin at me and breathin. Thiz no voices here at the mo, like, but the waiting for them can be werse than actually hearing them. Sometimes.

Am sober, completely fuckin sober. Ther might be a last trickle uv sulphate in me bloodstream from tha mound I ate three deys ago, but that's all. An am tired – fuckin exhausted ter tell yer the truth – burrah carn seem ter be able ter drop off. Avn slept properly fer deys, so rerly a should be out liker fuckin light, burram not; thiz loadser stuff runnin through me ed, me mind's inner mad fuckin wherl – will we be evicted (the past three housing benefit cheques av been cashed and spent), wha will Mairead do when she discovers ow little uv her inheritance shiz got left, will we go ter court fer non-payment uv council tax, will the bailiffs come round, will Mairead find out about me n Margaret? . . . all kindser shite bubblin awey in me tired, frazzled brain.

The speed paras. Amphetamine paranoia is a substitute fer dreams; yer carn sleep on speed an yer mind, yer psyche, needs ter dream so consequently yer start dreamin when yer awake. It's just yer mind triner sort itself out an makin evrythin werse . . . horrible images uv war and mutilation come at me outer the darkness, a sense uv a hooded army amassing at the end uv the road, me chest filled with guilt and shame for all the nasty, selfish things tharrav ever done . . . fuck. Sorrow sorrow sorrow. Regret. And silence except fer me heartbeat, the rain, an Mairead's deep breathing. A rhythm: Thud, patter, sss. Thud, patter, sss . . .

Out ther inner darkness, behind the window, ther ar owls, foxes, weasels, snakes, death, stalking, sharp teeth an shredding an shrieks uv pain an terror. Even in here, inside, inner bedroom, lice in the mattress, mites in the carpet, up ther inner corners wher wall meets ceiling ther ar those spindly spiders, snickering, ther stupid sucking sacks uv bodies just hanging ther, perfectly still an silent, just hangin ther in mid-air, waiting . . . evil little bastards . . . a hate those spiders wither long legs; not the chunky, hairy ones, a actually quite like them, it's those ones wither tiny bodies an ther nightmarishly, hysterically disproportionate legs; if yer could see a scream uv pain, that's wharrit would look like. Last week, a thought a was havin somethin uv a road-ter-Damascus experience with them; a was watchin one spin its web in the bathroom, its fuckin legs evrywher, an then all uv a sudden a sawrit as a creature uv the most fragile beauty and exquisite delicacy, a miracle uv evolution with its spinnerets an its silken trap twice the strength uv steel . . . but tha feelin only lasted a few seconds before a gished the creepy little fucker wither rolled up copy uv *Viz*.

Once, years ago now, me da was werkin onner site in Liverpool. Is labourer wen awey ter break open a new baler bricks an then came runnin back over, white as a sheet, oldin is and. Said a big yellow spider with long, long legs an huge black eyes ad come runnin out uv the bricks an bit im on is and, in tha webby bit bitween thumb an forefinger. In a minute or two ee was green, puking, gibbering . . . an ambulance was called out burree died before they could gerrim to hospital. Is last werds wer about the size uv this spider's eyes. Ee coulden believe tharree could've seen a spider's eyes.

Such fuckin things in this werld. Things we'll never know. Things that, if we *did* know them, would send us screaming running across the mountains across the clouds like scarecrows like dead berds hot shit runnin down your –

No. Hopeless. All fuckin hopeless.

This driftin round this fuckin island. Wher will a go after Aberystwyth, wher will a end up? Out ther into the darkness, behind glass: England, Scotland, Isler Man, other partser Wales . . . France, ah, fuckin France; hate the bleedin place like (it's full uv French, fer one), but it does hold fond memories . . . avter get Malcolm ter gerriz fuckin arse in geer an gerruz a place ter stey. Us three over ther, me, im, an Roger, a trail uv empty bars an pregnant women and, knowin Roger, broken noses right across the fuckin country . . . oh yeh.

But as if. As fuckin if. France me arse; yill stey poor an rained on an pissed off an yill continue ter do things which yill later wanner top yerself ter rid yer head uv the memory of. Yer know yer fuckin will. Yer carn fuckin help it, Colm. Yer fated ter be a fuck-up, and don't pretend otherwise.

No, nice things appen, man, they do sometimes fuckin appen; just believe. And wait. That's all yuv got ter do.

Christ. My life, man. Thud, patter, sss. My. Fuckin. Life.

Big mistake this, big big BIG mistake – speedin on yer own. End up climbin the fuckin walls, bitin yer nails till yer draw blood, chain-smokin until yer can ardly breathe an all yer can taste an smell is ash. Am sittin ere bein bombarded by sensory input; the telly's on wither sound terned down (fuckin Brucie showin off is new wig), tha Hallucinogen record *Twisted* rattlin the speakers, am flippin through the new issue uv *The Kop* tha Sarah sent me last week, chewin gum, smokin, an drinkin chilled cider with arf a gram uv top whizz rampagin through me system . . . fuckin sensual overload. Fuckin ace. Me whole body's twitchin, jitterin, me brain's spinnin liker washin machine under this onslaught. Am on fuckin fire. But what's missin is someone ter talk to, or at, anyone, desperately, am grindin me fuckin teeth down ter chalky stumps an a carn stop mutterin stuff ter meself, a need faces, crowds, moving bodies, other human presence . . . Mairead's gone down to the Glengower with Sam an Ella an Paul an Sioned an a think Laura's with em too, burrah doan wanner goan join em cos down ther it's alweys full uv fuckin students an rugby tossers an a doan want anythin ter compromise the wey am feelin . . . still, it might be berrer n steyin ere on me tod . . . a told em all ad meetem down ther in un ower or so an soon's they wer out the door it was out with the werks: needle, spoon, powder, et cetera . . . Buzzin ter fuck now, an am not that restless yet tharrah need ter leave the house, am avin a great time, burrah could use some company. Oh I doan fuckin know. Ow can a know anythin fer certain when ther's arf a grammer Pink Champagne an nerly four pints uv scrumpy hertlin through me veins? Me rat is scamperin about behind the wardrobe; a hadder conversation with im a few minutes ago burrit was a bit one-sided – I jabbered at him an ee just sat on me knee an cleaned is ears an twitched is nose. Borin little get.

A gerrup an start dancin on me own, wherlin about, hackin at the air with me arms . . . a love the Hallucinogen . . . the doorbell goes an me heart leaps an a go to answer it then leg it back an hide me werks under a cushion. Yer never know oo it could be. Burraz it terns out it's orright, no it's fuckin great cos it's Mags.

—Aw Jeez am a fuckin made up ter see you am eatin the fuckin carpets in eer Christ come in come in.

—You speedin?

—Off me fuckin box, yeh.

—Yuh look it. Aven't got any left, av you?

We go into the front room an a passer the bag from under the cushion an as she chops up a line on the coffee table wither sharp edge uv a Narcotics Anonymous card a babble atter, jabbering complete fuckin shite, overfuckinjoyed ter av someone ter talk to. She knows the score, like, shiz cool, Mags is, she just laughs an nods at regular intervals an concentrates on cuttin up the whizz an just lets me gerron with it. Evry time she leans forwuds ter chop or snort a gerrah glimpse down the baggy jumper shiz gorron, the deep, dark, creamy cleavage. Phwoar.

She snorts a last an sits back, sniffin.

—Ace, she sehs. —A was fuckin dying for a line . . . ar yuh plannin on goin out later an stuff?

—Yeh, yeh, if yer wannoo, like . . . Suddenly a remember summun: —Ah shit, av just remembered; am almost fuckin skint. A was gunner drink the scrumpy in the fridge or tap Mairead fer some money, if a can finder like. The whizz an tha cleared me out.

—Oh, so it's get Margaret tuh buy yuh drinks all night then, is it?

—No, yeh, ey ang on, *you* fuckin called fer *me*! AND thiz a fuckin fiver werther billy up yer nose!

She grins. —Ts OK, a got a giro t'day. Thair's about forty quid in me pocket. Whair jer wanner go then?

A shrug. —Well, am serposed ter be meetin evrybody on the prom, burrah fuckin hate it down ther. Tacky fuckin meat markets. We could go ferra couple, a serpose, an move on after. Whatjer reckon?

—Whair's Malcolm?

—Ee's werkin ternight, in tha chippy in Eastgate. Poor bastard. Sooner be fuckin skint. Jer wanner drink?

A pour us both some cider an we talk n mess about n get ready ter go out n do more speed n drink more cider an do more speed agen an when all thee others come back after midnight with placky bags bulgin with carry-outs an a crew in tow, me n Mags're inner centre uv the room goin fuckin mad ter thee Essential Selection, John Kelly a think irriz, ar boots thumpin on the floor. Am speedin me fuckin face off. An impromptu party: the best fuckin kind. Thiz a stringer drunken, drugged people five minutes long comin through the door.

Liam's ere, shit-faced, a bottle uv Rush jammed up is nostril, an Malcolm n all, smellin uv chip fat an vinegar an babblin awey appily about somethin involvin Paul and a boat, a doan catch much uv it. An thiz loadser people ere oo a don't know at all, or doan know very well; wher the fuck ud ee all come from?

A find Mairead in the kitchen, leanin crookedly agenst the cooker, pissed as a fart. She's bein chatted up by some tall gimp inner hooped rugby shert. A give im me best hard ster.

—Mairead, who the fucker all these people? Fuckin rent-a-party, is it?

She falls agenst me an puts er arms around me waist an rugby shert fucks off. A heer other blokes jeerin at im in the hallwey.

—We met em all in the Glen. Liam knors some a thum ah think. Tha dorn't mind?

—Nah, a sey. —Course a don't, an a rerly don't, like, burrit's fuckin unexpected, yer know? A mean, ther we wer, me n Mags, dancin about like, goin mad, an now look ... house is fuckin chocker.

Fuckin heavin. Iestyn's inner fridge, pullin out cans uv beer; ee ands a four-pack uv Stella ter me n Mairead.

—Nice one.

Mairead necks arf uv ers in one go then slides bonelessly on to the floor, curls up in the corner all greasy from the cooker. Shiz safe ther, outer the wey like, so a leaver ther an go serchin fer someone a know. By now, the kitchen's filled with weed smoke an people with glazed eyes and long lank hair ar driftin about aimlessly like remedial ghosts.

—This your place, man? some fuckin drippy hippy asks me.

—Yeh. Why?

—Nice fuckin gaff, man, can we use yer oven for hotties?

Nice uv im to ask. —Yeh, yeh, no problem. Just watch out fer me gerlfriend, she's passed out agenst the oven door.

Ee pats me shoulder with is bony and an a shrug im off an lerrim gerron with it. Fuckin hippies. If tha fuckin kitchen gets damaged in any fuckin wey ... or Mairead is at all disrespected ... anythin fuckin stolen ...

Nah. Ther orright. Polite uv im to ask, God, ther not doin any arm. The speed rushes through me, as exhilarating as diving into the sea; am fuckin flyin again. Airborne.

In the packed hallwey, Liam calls over huddled heads to Laura:

—Laura! Laura! Uh yis wantin another voddy?

—Filler up, babe!

A like it when Laura calls Liam 'babe'; it reminds me uv the Holling and Shelley couple off *Northern Exposure*. A flatten meself agenst the wall so Liam can squeeze past.

—Yis a happy mahn, Colm?

—As a pig in shite.

—Good mahn. Ye wantin a bevvy?

—Nah, av got one. Tell yer wha, tho, if thiz any fuckin about goin on in me kitchen lerruz know, will yer? Just keep yer eyes open like.

—Will do.

—An check on Mairead; she's flat out by thee oven.

A struggle down the hallwey, walkin side-on liker crab. A grin atter blonde gerl oo a once shagged on the beach an she smiles an sehs summun burrer werds ar drowned out byer voice singin the refrain from Blur's 'Parklife'. A Scouse voice; a wherl around quick burrit's alright, am safe, it's the barman in the Fountain. Could still be connected to the Maguires, tho, a serpose . . . but nah, probably not; a doubt very much tha they'd have a ragin queen in ther employ. The Maguires ur a family uv thick gets from Birkenhead, plastic gangsters like, oo, yeers ago, entrusted me with two grand uv ther money ter spend on Dutch heroin. Phuh. Fuckin idyits. A kept the fuckin money an went ter France an had the timer me fuckin life, but, obviously, a couldn't go back ter the 'Pool after tha, nor unless a wanted, at best, severe fuckin brain damage. Aberystwyth itself is still too close, a serpose, but . . . well, if it appens, it appens. Fuck all I can do about it. Gorrer accept. Some people call this kinder thing a death wish, but I call it servival. Lookin after Number One. Ter save face, the youngest Maguire, mad Tommy, fat sweaty back-permed psycho rapist Tommy, blew thee ed off a guy called Noel in is Toxteth bedsit, an purrit around that ee was the absconder. A think that's wha appened anywey.

A squeeze through inter the bedroom, wher Malcolm's talkin at a couple uv terrified specky types. Ee's gesticulatin wildly an is eyes're the size uv fuckin dinner plates:

—Am fuckin tellin ya, fa fuck's sikes, it's all fuckin owva! The game is up! Ya wanda through ya lives like thair's gonna be any kinda world receptive or othawise ta ya crappy little sociology degrees or whateva tha fuck they are an am fuckin tellin ya ere an now that thirl be fuck awl but ash! Ash an bones! How tha fuck can ya gow blithely on thinkin, actin as if there's any fuckin time left at awl let alown enough ta finish ya fuckin dissertations which anyway arn even worth tha fuckin paper tha written on? Ey? Ya taught fuckin nothin, pal, fuck awl, if ya ad any fuckin intelligence at awl dja know wha ya'd be, ya'd be off, the North fuckin Pole, Tierra del Fuego, Christ, anyfuckinwhere! Jesus! Anywher but here! Ya gonna fuckin die, man, I can awlready see ya skin breakin aht in immense grren pustules, ya –

Ad love ter stey n watch this, it's fuckin crackin me up, burram in strong need uv another toot so a tap Mal onner shoulder an ee terns a blotchy, twitchin, jaw-grindin face terwards me.

—Mal, wharrever the fuck irriz yer on, giz a bit. Am out.

Ee hands me a wrap.

—Strong fuckin stuff this, gow easy.

Then ee terns back to is audience who have been tryin to edge awey but they snap back to attention when Malcolm starts talkin at em agen:

—Gwan, gow an flog ya shitty little rag mags n delude yaselves inta believin that ya doin somethin uv tha utmowst impawtance when ya discussin tha role uv theatre in taday's society! Gawd, man, ya fuckin blind, ow can ya be so fuckin blind!

A go inter the front room fer me werks, people all over the bleedin place. Maggie is dancin, rerly goin for it by the stereo, lookin ecstatic an sexy. A see Plague standin on is back legs on the coffee table an a move over ter pick im up an purrim safely back in is cage but then a see tha some cunt's pointin a lit cigarette at is little pink nose an ee's just about ter sniff it.

—OI!

The cigarette is jabbed at is face an ee jumps an a scoop im up an purrim on me shoulder an tern ter the fat prick with the fag, anger swellin inside me and rushin with the whizz, big an black an welcome:

—That's me pet rat, yer fuckin prick! Oo the fuck ar yer anywey?

Ee looks up at me. Fuckin overweight dick'ed ginger'edded bastard.

—Um, me name's Dafydd, and I wasn't –

—Well, yer can fuck off. Gwan, gerrouter me fuckin ouse before a split yer fuckin face open, yer ugly fuckin cunt.

—But what for, I –

A see red an a grab im by is collar an fling im off the couch, Ratty's claws diggin inter me neck as ee tries ter stey on. The lad, this Dafydd cunt, slams on ter the floor an evryone terns ter look.

—Try un bern me fuckin rat, would yer? Ey!

A welly im twice in is fat arse, dead fuckin ard, as ard as a can anny yelps an scrambles awey, whimperin some pathetic defence which just makes me madder:

313

—Gerrout the fuckin house! If I find you anywher else in me fuckin flat ternight al fuckin kill yer!

Am bendin down an am screamin in is face. Ee stumbles to is feet an scurries out uv the room. Evryone's lookin at me burrah rerly doan fuckin cur like. Thee watch me as a put Plague gently back in is cage then retrieve me werks from underneath the cushion. Fuckin buncher pricks. Comin in me fuckin flat . . .

A put me werks in me top pockit, snarl at all the gawpin faces, kiss Margaret hard on the lips an then walk out. Wharrer fuckin exit; a feel like, a dunno, a cowboy, a gangster. A feel cool as fuck. An why the fuck shouldun I? My fuckin house, innit?

Back through the hall (the Scouse singer's now a comatose lump arf in, arf out uv the broom cupboard) and kitchen (Mairead's a slumberin lump bineath Liam's overcoat) and into the bathroom, wher some arse'oles ar buildin a spliff. They all look up.

—Orright, gerrout.

—What –

—Fuck off, we –

—Gerrout!, a scream. —Goan do it inner fuckin yard or somewher!

They leave grumblin an a lock the door. Fuck's sakes. Fuckin tossers come inter me flat . . . if I find one more sadistic twat tormentin me rat, al fuckin . . .

A sit down an set things up. Thiz a mouldy per uv reeking leggins in the corner by the bog, still smellin uv Mairead's piss from last week. Fuckin alkies; ther the werst fuckin addicts uv them all . . . A remember the clinic a was in once, in Cambridge. Thee alkies wer the werst. Even the smack'eds would get through it like, the withdrawal, but thee alkies ud do stuff like drink fuckin Domestos n aftershave and eat boot-polish butties ter trine gerra hit. Fuckin orrible it was. Me, a was in ther onner court order like, tryin ter overcome me serposed dependence on alcohol and amphetamines. A went through a couple uv deys uv cold chicken, which is like cold terkey, only cheaper. And as soon as a was lerrout a raided a chemist fer all its dexies an went straight ter the pub by wey uv celebration. Fuckin waster time n taxpayers' money that was.

Lighter, water inner spoon, powder, cotton wool . . . no cotton wool so a use the inside uv oner Mairead's tampons. It'll do. The little cauldron uv the spoon, the bubblin elixir; aqua vitae, uisce beatha, too fuckin right, la. A know av said this many times bifore, burrit bears repeatin: This is hard-core. This is beyond werds, beyond life an its simple biology, this is fuckin about in tha realm tha only angels and demons are familiar with. It is fearless. It is what livin is all about, yer never get yuced to it, it's alweys a fuckin thrill, there're alweys fuckin eagles flappin about in yer belly, alweys yer heart thuddin like fuck agenst yer ribcage . . .

The needle goes in the cotton wool. The needle goes in me vein, that gorgeous familiar prick uv pain . . . this is Malcolm's stuff . . . plunger in a wee bit an then back out agen, drawin out a thread uv blood which expands and frills like lace or the wing-feathers of a bright berd is wharrit alweys reminds me of . . . doan know how strong irriz . . . Malcolm was off is face an ee'd only been snortin it . . . fuck, a doan even know wharrit *is* . . . an then quickly and completely the plunger's pressed in.

Instantly am on me fuckin feet an pacin the floor the syringe still in me arm, the fuckin bathroom wherlin about me head an the floor like jelly or water and the drug surges through me an a dribble uv piss escapes into me jeans an am whimperin under thee onslaught an thinkin FUCK FUCK TOO MUCH TOO MUCH an a cling toer walls an press me face agenst the cool paint an me fuckin heart's berstin through me ribcage . . . too much breath am breathin too much my blood is goin much too fuckin fast . . . I don't think I can handle this . . . fuck . . . wharrav a done . . .

Then thee initial madness subsides an so does the fear with it an then guess wha? Yeh, a feel just fuckin dandy, ecstatic, am inner grip uvver joy which yull never fuckin know or experience, yull never come close ter this feelin man, yull never fuckin know . . .

A taker syringe out me arm with quakin fingers an stash me werks in the Ali Baba laundry basket an go back out toer party. All these people ere, they think ther appy, they think ther appy wither draw an ther booze, ther powders dabbed or snorted, an they avn gorra clue wha real appiness, real fuckin joy, is. A walk tall through em all, all the sad fuckers, grinnin so widely tharram expectin me face ter fall in two any minute now. I am the chosen one. I can strut through em all ten feet fuckin tall, I can crush em all with me thumb . . . Born wither caul. Romany blood. I *am* the fuckin chosen one. The whole fuckin planet will tremble when I pass.

Mairead's still snorin bineath Liam's overcoat inner forest uv legs n boots. Malcolm's over thee other sider the room, leanin agenst the table which is covered in bottles and cans an proddin some short-arsed geek inner chest an shoutin in is ear. A yell:

—G'wahn, Malcolm, give it some, lad!, an maker beeline over to im.

And so it goes on. On an on an on, an a never fuckin wannit to end.

Thir is one I remember, most clear an close, lyin onner back naked wither feet crossed at thee ankles, arms be'ind er ed, light shinin onner tight tanned stomach an er long long legs an perfect breasts. Just lyin ther smilin, waitin fer me ter touch and stroker when I was younger some years ago now.

The muscles outlined, the shadowed V uv the pubes . . . ther's been lots; lotser women, a serpose, lotser gerls like, but this one a remember most cleerly, even if this did occur all those years ago and all those miles awey . . . a still remember. An al never ferget tha one lyin ther naked wither whole uv fuckin France outside the window an me bleedin heart goin like mad.

Nah, fucks to it. Junkies, alkies, addicts uv all kinds, we don't have lovers; all we do is take hostages, human shields, ter barter with an hide be'ind on the long n lonely escape. That's all.

Hoip!

Bladoosh! Sssssssss . . .

Oo. Big one ther. Birruver ring-stinger, that . . . a red-wine dump, poo, mud-out, crap, shite . . . wonder wharrit is in red wine tha hardens yer shit ter thee consistency uv cast iron?

Layin some transatlantic cable.

A lean forwuds on the bog seat ter read the graffiti on the walls and door. Me belly feels queasy because uv the smell; a don't mean the shit-whiff, a can stand me own like, a mean tha cloying, detergenty, gagging speed-smell tha most pub toilets seem ter pong of. Sfuckin orrible. Must be somethin, some similar ingredient, in the cleaning detergent as ther is in the sulphate. Very unfriendly ter me sore, wasted stomach . . . makes me heave, dry-heave like, ther's fuck all in me belly sept beer n bile. Imagine shittin an spewin at the same time, like me mate Richey from Liverpool did tha time outside the tent in Tal-y-Bont when we'd gone on olidey as teenagers; the grand slam, an a can still picture im, on all fours in the grass an moonlight, yakkin up big gouts uv vom while rumblin, quackin sounds came from is arse end. A couldunt stop laughin. Ferst night a drank a full bottle uv spirits, tha. Gin a think it was. Puked fer deys.

Wuh! Just a trickle ther . . . oxtail soup . . . think am comin to the end . . . fuckin ope so, been in ere fuckin owers it seems like . . .

The end uv me knob, hangin down ther like bitween me legs, presses cold on the pissy porcelain an a think uv all the different dicks tharrav touched exactly tha spot an me belly rolls over agen. Jesus. The things yer avter do . . . all the little daily abominations . . .

A squint ter read the writing on the door. Agen; must av read it a hundred times, a almost know it off by heart. Couldn't tell yer wharrit means tho:

Tydi Alan
Ddim y'n hoffi
Myg y cwîn
Tydi Tudwal
Ddim yn dreifio
Limosîn
Tydi Bleddyn
Ddim yn caru
Blirdd bach blîn
Tydi Ieuan
Ddim am werthu'i
Drampolîn

Somethin about muggin the Queen, a think, that ferst bit . . . a get the general gist burrah couldn't translate it. Av picked up a birrer Welsh livin ere like an a also lernt a few werds from me nan as a kid; she was ferst-language Welsh speaker, like, but she adter ferget most uv it when she moved ter Liverpool when she was about sixteen, seventeen. Carn blamer; a mean, Christ, when yer twenty yeers old with three screamin kids an another one on the wey livin inner two-bedroom terrace inner fuckin Dingle the last thing on yer mind is keepin yr hen iaith alive. Yuv got more immediate things ter think about, such as keepin yer fuckin kids alive. Same with me da's dad an the Gaelic, like; triner find werk onner buildin site, wharrer yer gunner tell the foreman? Tha yerra bríceadóir? No, uv course not – a fuckin brickie is what yull sey. Yuv gorrer ferget such things, like, yer culture, yer heritage, yuv gorrer fuckin ferget all that stuff when survival's yer top priority, fer yerself an yer family. Me mamo as well like, full-blood Romany, born in Mayo, spent four fuckin yeers in the curragh durin the war like, she only ever uses the Bog Latin now when she's talkin to erself or er dead usbands. Or the fairies or the aliens or the people in the walls or ooever irriz she as conversations with now. Wee bit senile like.

Jesus. Some fuckin babel I grew up in, eh? Liverpool's like tha; even its version uv English ardly sounds fuckin English. It's an Anglo-Celtic city, as much as Edinburgh is, or Cardiff, or Dublin. It should av its own government. Self-autonomy fer Liverpool, too fuckin right. No lie, man.

A strain an squeeze out a small 'freep' of a fart, nowt else. It still feels like ther's more up ther tho so a sit tight. Well, loose-ish. Yer know.

It annoys me tho, the wey people alweys need ter categorise; am thinkin mainly about those two blinkered pricks in the wine bar that time, those two dick'eds oo sed they wer Welsh princes or summun an oo tried ter lay some uv the culpability fer the floodin uv Tryweryn on me. Fuckin gobshites. Me n Roger adter sort em fuckin out, give em a birruver dig like (altho Roger did moren fuckin *that*, diddun ee?). They, an ther's many people like em, wouldun fuckin understand like tha ther ar all fuckin sorts uv people oo suffer at the hands uv faceless inhuman bureaucracy, ooer trampled by quangos, oo av ther lives destroyed by self-servin organisations oo doan giver fuck ow many dreams they shatter or how many already struggling existences they toss catastrophes into. I've personally suffered much more at the hands uv Liverpool City Council than those two fuckers ever will, although ther desire fer martyrdom, righteous indignation, an the display uv false suffering as a badge uv belonging won't ever let them believe or understand that . . . In fact, come ter think uv it, oner those lads wouldunt understand wharrever yer sed to im now, not since Roger threw im off Trefechan Bridge, and the tide was out; ee hit the rocks an apparently ee's cabbaged now, a vegetable. Irreversible brain damage like. Or so it sed in the *Cambrian News*, which does haver propensity to embellish, so it could be bollox. Still, tho, I asked Roger if ee felt bad about this anny sed:

—Well, I *aimed* for-a fuckin water, mun, but-a cunt twisted around in mid-air like. Snot *my* fuckin fault if-a boy carn fuckin fall straight, is it like?

God knows ow ee gorrawey with tha one. Ee was never even questioned about it, an loadser people sawrim scrappin wither lad inside the wine bar. Fear, a serpose. They wer all too scerd ter identify im. Or at least, if they wernt at ferst then they certainly fuckin wer after Roger n Ikey ad adder wee werd with them.

Me stomach flips and bile trickles up inter me gob, tastin uv ashes. A spit irrout on to the tiled floor an some uv it splashes back on to me jeans. Fuck. A wee green egg uv it, liker temazepam capsule, glistens on the label of me kex, rumpled up ther bitween me ankles:

LEVI STRA	Quality clot
San Fran	TRADE
Original riv	Patented in U.S.

A wipe irroff with me thumb. Slimy, like oil agenst me skin.

Jesus Christ. Look at me sittin ere on the bog an mumblin awey ter meself when ther's drinkin ter be done with me mates, waitin fer me outside ther in the beer garden. Liverpool ar kickin off soon an all, agenst Arsenal on Sky. Wharram a doin? Fuck's sakes. Liverpool *always* beat the Arsenal, apart from in '89, of course.

A stand up an pull a shed snakeskin of bog paper off the roll on the wall. Snakes in the pan as well, thin dark ones, writhin in the water . . . umber vipers . . . a knot of . . . hot, dropped fodder . . .

That sounds good: 'hot, dropped fodder'. A like werds, a always have; av hadder wey with em ever since a was a kid. Me ferst werd was 'bird'. A like the sounds, the rhythms, the ability uv werds ter make the familiar unusual, an sometimes I can even taste them ('plinth' is banana-flavoured), burrit rerly means fuck all; my use uv language merely masks the fact tharrah doan have a fuckin clue, no fuckin idea uv wha any uv this is about. Am completely fuckin baffled.

Urgh, me poor guts . . . maybe al avver cheese roll or summun before a start drinkin again. Avn eaten fer over a week. No wonder tha crap was so horrific.

A wipe me arse clean an go back out into the bar. A feel much berrer fer that.

. . . is this it, then, is this all ther is? White n bloated, floppin about in the waves? Bein eaten by fish an crabs, floppin uselessly about, naked, rotting, bloated . . . aw fuck.

She's as white as, wha, a dunno, boiled fish flesh, white an purulent an pasty an yer imagine tha if yer touched er a piece uv flesh ud just, like, squelch off in yer hand . . . yud be able ter break er inter little bits with yer ber ands, like fuckin plasticine or summun . . . the harbour's ferly shallow but the tide must be comin back in cos the waves, the waves ar slappin er body about, each one billowin er bleached hair out liker fan an makin er limbs rock an slap lazily in the water . . . the waves make a hissing sound, like escaping gas. Oner those gooey sibilant farts yer do after a night onner stout, the ones that invariably stink ter high heaven. Sssssss. Maybe that *is* gas escapin; methane or somethin leakin out uv er orifices. A doan know.

Poor fuckin woman. To end up like tha, ey, completely impassive, nowt left juster wet an sagging wrapper, stripped utterly uv all dignity, lyin face-down nude inner derty sea, watched byer waster. Christ – wharrer fuckin life. Some fuckin werld this.

A should never uv done this, a should never uv acted on tha stupid fuckin idea uv comin down ter the harbour ter look out for the dolphins. A was crashin horribly after a speed-binge, yer know, feelin depressed as fuck. Ad done all the usual comedown activities – the bath, the chain-smoking, the wank, the bottle ur two uv red wine, the breakfast telly – tryin desperately ter stave off tha awful comedown depression when yer want to, need to, be on yer own but yer know tha when yer ar yull be consumed by a massive fuckin sadness tha promises ter stey around fer ever. Tha sadness liker physical fuckin pain, a howling black hole wher yer heart should be an a voice in yer ear explaining in a perfectly reasonable and logical wey why yer should commit suicide. A real fuckin hell. A mean it, a genuine hell. So a walked on me own down from Llys Wen wher we'd been partyin ferra few deys, leavin all ee others comatose onner ferniture an floor (but not before ad arf-inched Mairead's cash card frommer perse), went ome, did me stuff, an then came down ere, to the harbour. An ther she was, ther she *is*, my dead woman, my corpse, fallin ter pieces inner waves. Am sittin ere on the end uv the concrete pier lookin down atter, an the sun's only just up over the horizon an evrythin's glowin orange an lovely and Pen Dinas is juster big green blob in the thin mist an the fuckin wind's flayin the skin off me face an me arse's soakin fuckin wet an freezin bastard cold but fuck it all, fuck it all, nothin matters, evrythin's fucked, like I alweys knew it was. Or would be.

A jet, fuckin warplane like, Tornado or wharrever the fuck ther called, screams low over me head an tears thee air apart an I imagine blastin it down wither bazooka. Fuckin bastard.

Her limbs are tossed by a biggish wave an it's liker legs're kicking, as if shiz triner swim awey from what's appened toer. Too late fer tha now, love, yer shoulder tried doin tha bifore, shouldun yer? Unless uv course yer diddun want to, like, unless uv course it was suicide . . . doin a Reggie Perrin, just walkin into the sea. Only Reggie came back. Unlike this lady ere an tha mad lad, fergotten is name now, the one oo wrote tha funny Guide thing tha Liam's gorrer copy of; ee drowned imself as well, diddun ee? Carn fer the lifer me remember is name now . . . a remember *im*, tho, an the wey ee ad uv makin yer feel nervous an scrutinised, as if ee was alweys checkin yer out like . . . gazin inter yer soul . . . ee never yuced ter sey very much, an ther was alweys summun slightly creepy, eerie about im; like, when ee looked at yer, you wer bein assessed on some deep, unknowable level. As if ee could see evry bad thing yid ever done, or evrythin tha was hateful about yerself. As if ee could tell yer thee exact date an manner uv your death. Ee was a right fuckin odd one, im. Even Roger seemed ter be scerd uv im. A quite liked im, tho, if the truth be told; ee was, yer know . . . different.

Not any more tho. Just another corpse now, like all the billions uv others, just more fertiliser. Or fishfood like this woman ere. Makin me feel peculiar – the proximity uv death. Rot an decay. All spongy an putrid an pallid. Not tha I aven't seen a dead body bifore, fuck no; a probly would've seen loads at Hillsborough, had I made the train that dey an not been lyin in me own sick inner squat in Tuebrook when the ferst crushed corpses wer dragged out on to the pitch, but once when a was livin in Cambridge we founder dead tramp down an alley be'ind a pub; ee mussun uv been dead fer very long like cos is skin ad gone all plasticiny, all pliable like, an while we wer waitin fer thee ambulance we passed the time mouldin is face into funny shapes, givin im a witchy chin an ski-slope nose anner big dopey grin like Stan Laurel. Shoulder seen the faces on the ambulance crew when thee came ter fetch im. Hilarious. Funny as fuck at the time, like, but now . . . a dunno. A justified it ter meself by makin meself believe tha these physical fleshy bodies we inhabit ar just shells, just packages, an wha we truly ar, yer know, essence or soul or spirit or wharrever, goes elsewhere when we cark it an leaves an empty frame be'ind but maybe that's all juster loader shite rerly, isn't it? At the time, like, in Cambridge a mean, a was usin a lot uv acid, and a was much younger. A know better now. A think.

But this poor fuckin woman . . . floatin face-down with no clothes on, er legs lollin wide open, er hair all swishin about in long blonde fronds . . . a carn see any wounds onner body, but then me eyesight's pretty bad an am about twenny feet abover an anywey she could be wounded onner front or somethin or maybe nor even wounded at all, she mighter drowned by accident, yer know, pissed up, a midnight swim, she might've even fell overboard. Or been pushed. Oo knows? Ther ar so many fuckin things tha can appen to yer, thiz threat n harm fuckin evrywher, man, ar lives ar as fragile as insects' wings; a mean, yer walk across the fuckin room an things're snappin at yer, tearin at yer, when yer reach thee other side yer not the person yer started off as, yer less, yer diminished. An this happens a hundred times evry fuckin dey. Shadows hang over yer shoulder constantly, wherever yer fuckin go, ther ar guns, axes, cars, OD, derty needles, chokin on curry like Fat Charlie, hypothermia, cancer, AIDS, stumblin out uvver window on to iron spikes, steppin out in front uvver car, drownin in the bath, electrocution, blood clot, heart attack . . . it's all a big, sick joke, innit rerly, this fuckin life. A giant, twisted, warped practical joke. Even when you're feelin happy an content; a mean, well, wuv got, or if yerra Believer wuv been given, the capacity to experience an appreciate joy and rapture of and in this life, whether it's through drugs or sex or wharrever tickles yer fancy, an yet at the same time wuv also got the capacity to comprehend the complete extinction of such happiness, such joy! Wharrer sick fuckin joke! Wha was this dead woman doin last night? She could've been doin the exact same thing tha I was doin, speedin, drinkin, talkin, laughin, avin the fuckin timer me life. An now ere she is – just another piece uv pollution. Dead. Nothing.

Jesus fuckin Christ.

A start thinkin uv all thee animals which must've feasted onner; crabs, eels, all kinds uv fish, gulls peckin savagely atter face, lampreys, ick, *lampreys* . . . that's all she is now, a huge floatin smorgasbord fer all the sea creatures. Altho shid just be a morsel, bite-size like (or fun-size, wharrever the fuck that is) ferra larger animal, a shark sey, or a killer whale. Not tha yer likely ter find many uv *them* in Cardigan Bay. Funny thing about killer whales; apparently ther generally quite peaceful creatures, or so it sed in the wildlife magazine a was readin thee other dey, swimmin about in groups made up of family an friends, but occasionally in the pod ther's one mad bastard, one ferocious psychotic fucker oo attacks evrythin, so all thee others gang up on im (or her) an chuck em out, leavin them ter fend fer themselves. And somehow, no one knows how like, these crazy ones manage ter seek each other out an find each other over thousands uv miles uv deep ocean an they meet up an get tergether and form a gang, a separate gang uv insane, savage bastards, a prowlin pack uv fucked-up whales which will tolerate each other but have been known to attack anythin else tha moves, even blue whales, they'll rip anythin ter shreds. Funny ow the outcasts find each other. Some kind uv magnetics.

Another jet roars over an a neer shit meself an give it the V; a childish, pathetic, futile gesture. As a raise me arm me sleeve rolls down an a catch sighter me weepin, scabby track marks an am suddenly and completely filled with immense pity and sorrow for me own body, me delicate internal organs which av ravaged through long years uv abuse, me black lungs, me swollen liver . . . me exhausted brain. A mean, me poor liver; tryin its best to assimilate an purify all the shite a pump into me bloodstream, tryin its best ter keep me alive an functioning an how do a repay it? By givin it more fuckin werk, that's how, by chuckin more fuckin poison arrit evry fuckin dey . . . it's done nothin to deserve such punishment. No fuckin wey.

A look up from the floatin woman an down the coast ahead uv me. The last straggling street lights in Aberaeron and Newquay ar just about discernible through the swirls uv mist, miles awey like, shinin weakly out from an ungraspably huge line uv towerin mountains an cliffs. It looks beautiful, an if a had any fuckin breath left in me after last night's debaucheries then it would be taken awey by the view. This werld can be so fuckin gorgeous sometimes . . . a have this theory – probably read in a quickly-fergotten book once an then made me own – that, somewhere along the wey, things got mixed up and God gorall confused an put the beings oo wer designed fer *this* planet on the planet across thee other sider the galaxy tha was originally designed for us, an *that* planet, the one we humans should be on, is full uv hurricanes an volcanoes an perpetual storms an lightning and torrential rain an buzzin, bitin insects and *this* planet, the one we shouldn't be on, is . . . well, yer must know wha this planet can be like sometimes. An a offen trine imagine wha tha other race uv beings look like, those ones who wer made for ere, an a alweys seem ter picture them as bein willowy, rangy and graceful but also awkward an gawky an bewildered on the wrong werld, the one ther on now. An have ter stey on fer ever. Lost an longing and unsatisfied like us fer ever an ever an ever.

Nah. Too simplistic. Fer fuck's sakes, Colm, gerrer fuckin grip.

A light another ciggie an inhale painfully past the resistance in me throat an ster back down agen at the dead woman. A wave catches er leg an she drifts slowly sideweys ter bounce off the mossy harbour wall with each successive wave. Shiz spread out liker starfish, flopping, slowly bouncing, completely fuckin dead, totally dead, dead as fuck. Dead as yer can possibly be. Yer carn get any deader than this woman. An a haven't even seener face but a know al never ferget er; nor as a memento mori or anythin like tha ram's skull uv Malcolm's, no, fuck tha, me track marks fulfil that function very fuckin well, more as a pointer terwards what could possibly be: specifically, am thinkin uv Mairead – if any uv us ar a candidate fer suicide, or accidental death, it's Mairead. A mean, al never drown, the caul on me ed n stuff, burrah alweys imagine tha one dey Mairead'll be found like this, washed up onner beach or inner harbour with polluted cockles inner gob an seaweed inner hair. An this is painful ter sey burrav got ter fuckin admit it rerly: am no fuckin good fer Mairead. A maker werse. A doan know why she even steys with me ter tell yer the truth; shiz sed some fuckin ace things, a remember once she told me tha a was the real thing, tha shid been out with loadser blokes oo all tried an failed ter be the person that I genuinely am, which is oner the best things tha anyone's ever sed ter me, an al never fergerrit, burrah do think tha shid be berrer off without me an with someone else, someone oo can giver what she wants an wharrever tharriz I carn give, a haven't gorrit in me like. Doan even know what the fuck irriz even. Burrah do know tha shill probably end up drinkin erself into an erly grave, er good looks strafed by alcohol well before the usual time, an a do know also tha she deserves someone fuckin berrer than me. Berrer for her, a mean, shiz fuckin ace is Mairead, a know it mightn't seem tharrah feel tha wey about er burrah do, a rerly fuckin do. A wish she'd leave me. For her sake. Burrah know she never will.

Mind you, ace gerl or not, shiz been with some right fuckin tossers, Mairead has. A seer inner pub or summun talkin toer brain-dead slobber-lipped rugby-sherted beer monster no-mark an a find out tha she yuced ter shag im. Dozen do much fer yer fuckin ego, does it, know wharrah mean? Like tha fuckin Twmi cunt, tha arse'ole wither shaved ed . . . burrit was Roger oo told me tha Twmi fucked Mairead and she denies it so maybe it's crap. Arf the time a doan believer fuckin werd Roger sez. Burree's alweys bleedin smerkin, tha Twmi one, an lookin smugly at Mairead . . . am gunner smack the fucker oner these deys. Wait n fuckin see.

Ah fuck it. Noner tha shite matters rerly. This poor dead woman in the waves.

Me hands start up an uncontrollable trembling, a sign uv the drugs startin ter leave me system. A feel sick an me head throbs sore. The mist begins ter rise off Pen Dinas which seems ter suggest tharrit must be around eightish or somethin . . . pubs open in three owers. A could go ome, avver can or two frommer fridge, then hit the Glen or somewhere ter drink through the comedown, which a know is gunner be a bad one – a real deep despair job, wasted-body head-fuck type, sittin ther wither fuckin blade at me wrists. Ah fuck. No it won't. Yill be alright. Phone the police ferst tho, tell em ther's a corpse in the harbour. They might think I did it. They might think I'm a merderer. Arrest me an drag me into a nightmarish Kafkaesque werld uv red tape an questioning in which the inevitable outcome will be my slow death.

Bugger.

Tha kinder stuff's offen appened ter me, am offen gerrin accused uv things tharrah haven't done. Like when a was a kid, all the fuckin other kids ud be like: Gyppo, gyppo, derty fuckin gyppo, pooh gerrah bath yer smelly tinker bastard. All tha shit. An if anythin was ever knocked off in thee area the fuckin jacks'd be straight round me bleedin ouse: Where was your Colm last night, Mr Downey? Out sacrificin vergins yer fuckin prick. Altho avin sed that, a did gerra taste fer theft frommer very erly age; fuckin police puttin ideas in me young, impressionable ed. A still remember me very ferst heist; an El Cid scene Action Transfer lifted out the newsagent's. The buzz was incredible. A was about six.

Memories . . . like a shelterin thicket ter hide within. A defence mechanism an al tell yer fuckin why; cos nothin ever prepares yer fer this horror, nothin can ever help yer ter build up thee emotional defences yer need ter deal with the shite an terror inherent in this life, this werld, cos the shite an the terror ar too fuckin big, too huge and horrendous too shitey and too terrible ter ever be fuckin coped with, they'll eat you in one gulp and shit yer out bifore yuv ad time ter shed yer ferst fuckin tear. Ther's nothin yer can do. NOTHING. An if ther's nowt after death then why be afraid uv it? That makes sense, dunnit? But the thought uv tha nothingness, tha void, tha vacuum, adds horror and trembling an meaninglessness to the something tha precedes it, the life . . . An tha fear generates paralysis, an that's even more terrifying than death. Bein unable ter resist, defy, struggle, fight fuckin back . . . like tha sheep in Abergynolwyn tha time, the one with foot-rot an its eyes pecked out by ravens; wha was horrific an disgusting about it was not wharrad appened to it but the fact tharrit diddun seem arsed, yer know, it just continued ter go about its normal business. It shoulder been fuckin *raging*, screamin an kickin at wharrad befallen it, foul chance, furious at conspiring fortune and ill luck, the sickness uv this cellular fuckin existence . . . ah fuck it. Christ, it was only a fuckin sheep.

All these thoughts uv death n horror fill me with an overwhelming desire ter get abserlutely fuckin shit-faced, completely fuckin wrecked, so drunk tharrah carn even walk or talk . . . Roger's off the skag at the mo so ee's bound to av a large supply uv spirits, ee alweys does when ee's triner kick . . . maybe a should give im a knock . . .

Roger. A wonder wha Roger'd do in this situation, with the dead lady, a mean? A think about tha ferra minute an then shake me ed vigorously ter rid it uv the vile image uv Roger brutally fucking a waterlogged corpse, derty water spertin from its mouth with each thrust agh fuck no. A don't know why tha image arrived; Roger's norra necrophile, at least norraz far as a know. It's the comedown; does strange fuckin things to yer mind.

Yer just grit yer teeth. That's all yer can fuckin do, grit yer fuckin teeth an gerron with yer life cos yer liker fuckin gnat agenst an elephant, yuv got no fuckin chance bicause this is wher yer meant ter be, here at this exact time, doin precisely this, comin down from speed and watchin the body flap an slap in the water, some malign power as engineered evrythin so tha circumstances cannot help but lead you here, now, ter this.

Don't be daft. Christ, Colm, a classic symptom uv thee onset uv schizofuckinphrenia is the creepin certainty tha yer actions an thoughts ar bein planned an controlled by a force greater than yourself, unknown or maybe known . . . A mean, just think; diddun Jedburgh sell you the whizz last night, knowin full fuckin well that yer like ter go fer walks by the sea when yer comin down? An diddun ee then goan finder lone woman an taker down to the harbour and –

Oh fuck off. Yer goin fuckin crazy, man. Jed is norra merderer. Yuv flipped, gerra grip. Rid yerself of thee image uv a mountain-sized, demonically-grinning Jedburgh controlling a tiny puppet which looks like yerself. Get fuckin rid uv it.

The mist parts anner sunbeam slants whitely down into the water. The sun's light. Which takes eight anner half minutes ter reach thee earth. Imagine when it finally goes out, all the people werldwide just standin ther lookin up an blinking with eight anner half minutes ter contemplate not just ther own impending deaths but the utter irreversible extinction uv all life on this planet fer ever.

Al tell yer what, tho; ad love ter see this dead woman's face. A doan know why, a just would; maybe ad be able ter read summun ther like, some hint, some clue . . . maybe ad even recognise er! Not tha she looks like anybody a know from be'ind like, but then a doan know anybody oo looks liker decaying lump uv sodden and fish-nibbled lard. Except maybe Griff.

Poor fuckin woman. Someone's mam, lover, sister, daughter . . . all those hopes n fears n dreams n traits peculiar to her an nobody else in the werld ar now all gone, finished, more additives in the shitty sea. You poor, unfortunate woman. However you died, it was bifore your time. You should still be alive.

Ther's an empty crisp bag tangled round one uvver feet an ther's a Coke can wedged inner armpit. Which seems liker perfect summation, definition uv death: being unable ter push the garbage awey.

A goad me knackered body into action an walk awey from ther, from her. A use the phone box oppersite the horribly-closed Fountain Inn.

—Hello, emergency, which service do you require?

—Police please.

—Hold on a moment, I'll put you through.

Bring bring.

—Hello, police, how can I help you?

—Erm, ther's a body in the harbour. In Aberystwyth. A drowned woman. A was walkin anna sawrer.

—Can I have your –

A hang up an walk quickly awey, biginnin ter shiver. Fuck me, it's cold . . . Blind Huw, the tramp, is crashed out onner bench by thee old brewery wall. Ee's not rerly blind, like, or not completely; ee's just gorra cataract in one eye, looks liker blobber spunk in the socket, kind uv streaky blue. Carn see it now tho cos is eyes're closed. Is face's bright red and deeply fissured after arfer lifetime uv alcohol abuse an exposure to the whipping winds off thee Irish Sea. Even in sleep he looks mad and angry. Unless uv course ee's not sleeping; oh Jesus, no, surely norrim as well . . .

A lean down ter check if ee's still breathin an is eyes snap open, makin me jump. One bloodshot blue, thee other curdled milk. Ee yells somethin at me, somethin about needin to beware the dogs as a walk awey.

Two, three owers til the pubs open. A could go ome an bevvy, a could goan knock Roger up, see if ee's got any hard stuff . . . ah, life is so full uv choices. Either wey a just need simple oblivion.

If it takes me an even number uv steps ter cross the river, I'll go home. Odd, an I'll go ter Roger's.

A walk over Trefechan Bridge into the waking town, curled inter meself agenst the cold an wind.

Quick as a bullet an yellow as pee, a see it rocketin through thee air.

Irrad beener good mornin, so far; woke up refreshed an feelin kind uv dynamic an alive after the ferst night's proper sleep in ages wither big food-hunger inside me cos a hadn't eaten fer fuckin ages either. Nose still a bit runny tho. Mairead was lyin up agenst me, all warm n sleepy, lookin white and gorgeous. A stroked er face until er eyelids began ter twitch and whispered er name:

—Mair . . . Mair . . .

—Ng.

Er eyelids flickered an then opened wither faint rippin sound when a kissed er cheek. Er eyes look fuckin amazin when she's just woken up – all huge an dark with things, dreamy things, floating through them.

—Mairead.

—Ah dorn't, what?

—Ar yis hungry? Shall a go out an gerruz some scran?

She shifted in the bed.

—Oh ah ser . . . this meks a change.

—A know. Well, shall I then?

—Ah need t'sleep some more fust.

—Well, that's alright, yer can, al goan gerrit meself. What would yer like fer brekkie?

She just looks at me.

—A mean it, Mairead; no pub, no drugs, al be back ere with food in less than an ower. A rerly do mean it. Promise.

So we made a list; nice bread, butter, jam, eggs, bacon, a jar uv coffee anner few bottles uv red wine, and as Mairead nodded off agen a grabbed a quick shower and hacked upper loader snot into the sink. Had a birruver cold recently, nothin too bad like, just a loader mucus in me face and achin kidneys, tha kinder thing, exacerbated by whizzin me tits off all last week no doubt, burrit's beginnin ter go now an in me recovery a feel ace, strong and healthy. Avunt jagged any'in fer ages either and, a must say, am feelin miles berrer for abstainin. Plenty uv booze, like, God, booze is alweys fuckin ther, but that's ferly easy ter bounce back from if yer not usin anythin else with it an yuv been drinkin as long as I av. Yer body just gets yuced to it.

A stroked me body in the shower, soapin it like, an checked meself out; me arms still big an hard-muscled, track marks now just yellow memories, an the roll uv flab tharrav alweys had around me middle was almost completely gone, at least when a breathed in. Me knob felt big and chunky, fuller blood an power, an me face in the mirrer was free from blotches and berst veins and zits and even me recedin herline seemed ter be shrinking. Growin back maybe; av herd it can happen. And me eyes looked very blue an a could see in em tha twinkle tha people ar alweys remarkin on but which a can only ever see meself when ripped to the tits. A thought: Yep, me insides must look liker mixed grill by now like but thee external's in need uv minimal repair.

A felt just fuckin dandy.

A dressed in the bedroom, quietly like so as not ter wake Mairead. The floor n dresser n side table wer covered with little crusty balls uv snotty tissues, the legacy uv me cold. Bogeys, bogeys evrywher. Wherever yer look ther's a bogey. One uv Mairead's legs was hangin out uv the covers, long and finely-tuned. Phwoar. A wanted ter lick it. Maybe when we'd ad brekkie we could go back ter bed; a addun't ad sex with Mairead fer ages, irrad been mainly Mags an other women like, so it was about time we reopened tha chamber uv ar relationship. Been missin it as well, ter tell yer the truth.

A took Mairead's perse an went out into the bright and lovely dey. Still quite cold like, but the sun was shinin an thee air was clean and clear an it felt fuckin great ter breathe irrin; invigorating, liker mild drug. Lovely. Me body, me skin and brain, me whole body was tinglin an nice an a felt alright about fuckin evrythin – rent arrears, impendin court appearances fer non-paymenter fines, council tax an TV licence summonses, a diddun fuckin cur about any uv em. Not fuckin arsed. All a could cur about was Mairead asleep ther in the bed and some good food an drink for er when she wakes up. That's all. Evrythin else could fuck right off.

A walked inter town along the prom. Gulls an pigeons wer perched on the railings but thee all flew squawkin off when a coughed up another loader phlegm. Ug. Me cold's goin like, but the catarrh was still doggedly hangin on. A spatter big bundle uv green slimy stuff over the railings, into the sea. The sea looked fuckin incredible.

Up Pier Street an into the bukeshop, wher a browsed across the New Titles shelves. Not much, as usual; so much modern writing is so fuckin cold, so removed from wharrah know an hav experienced, a mean ad get more out uv readin a British Rail timetable, it's crap, snobby, elitist. Either that, or some brief foray into narco-tourism by some whinnying, middle-class wanker who thinks ee can pontificate about the contemporary drug scene cos ee smoked spliffs an had once took E atter rave. Ther was, however, a new collection uv Irish poetry in Gaelic with facing English translations, an al fuckin have that a thought so a whipped it down me kex an transferred it ter me coat pocket once outside. Changer plan then; after ad bought the shopping a would stop off inner Central on me wey ome ferra couple, juster couple, an reader few poems. Nice one. Mairead could do wither bit more sleep anywey. This could tern out ter be one ace fuckin dey. Ad avter pamper Mairead terdey; ad been neglectin er recently, an shiz too sounder person ter deserve such shitey treatment. In fact, al buy er a buncher flowers as well; waker up wither nice tray uv food an fresh flowers, wine an sex after. Al teller tharrah cur abouter an maker feel good. Ah. Mairead. Sucher lovely name.

After a stopped off at the Midlands cashpoint a terned down on ter Terrace Road, intendin ter visit the florists, the Spar, the bakery, an thee offy. As a was approachin the Spar a noticed tha ther was a beggar outside wither floppy blond mohican, sittin cross-legged on the pavement; at ferst a thought it was tha tosser oo Margaret knows, the one oo, after cadgin a quid off us a couple uv weeks back, then insisted on showin us is new navel an foreskin rings inner middle of the fuckin street. Burrit wasn im; as a got closer a could see tharrit was only a young lad, maybe twelve or thirteen, sittin ther with is and out, the ubiquitous mangy little dog asleep on is lap. A could see that is face was all bruised an battered an tha one uv is arms was all withered an fleshless, spindly liker twig. Polio or summun. Poor little bastard. Wha kinder life as ee got ter look forward to? Ey? A shite one, that's wha; never will ee wake up next to a beautiful gerl feelin great an go out shoppin fer nice food an drink with money ee asn't werked ard ter get. Probly won't even live ter my age. Poor little bastard. What cercumstances av conspired ter reduce im ter this sad state? Beaten up, diseased, beggin inner small Welsh seaside town with only a scabby wee dog fer company . . . Ad slip im a fiver, a thought; a fiver, an sod goin to the pub. Ee needed money more than I needed a couple uv pints.

A was walkin terwards im an gropin fer money in me back pockit. Ee looked up at me wither worried expression an I could imagine wharry saw; a mean, a was lookin ferly smart like in comparison ter me usual shamblin, scruffy self, an all ee could see was a stocky bloke in is late twenties wearin a clean denim shert an black jeans an big boots, descendin perposefully upon im. Probly ad abuse an kickins from people oo look like me all is young n unlucky life. So a smiled an cleared me throat ter speak ter im, a hadter cough ferly hard cos ther was an obstruction in ther, an then it flew out unexpectedly, just shot up from me blocked chest an out through me gob, quick as a bullet an yellow as pee, a great big fuckin oyster uvver snotter rocketin through thee air an landin splat in the centre uv this little kid's face.

Fuck.

Am standin ere an ee's lookin up at me an is expression now is, like, sheer terrer. The snot's across is cheeks inner slimy meniscus an ther's a big dewdrop hangin off the end uv is nose. Am feelin fuckin ashamed, mortified, an it's a few seconds before a can find me voice:

—God . . . am so sorry . . . a diddunt mean that, av gorrer

birruver cold, a sey but the kid's not lissenin; ee's gorriz ead in is derty ands an is shakin with sobs. Is dog sleeps on, oblivious to it all.

Fuck. Aw Jeez.

A heer voices:

—Did yew see that? Spat in that young feller's face. Disgusting animal.

—I don't approve of beggin but that's out uv bloody order. Should be bloody reported.

—Needs a good hiding. That's terrible that is. Twice is bloody size.

Ah Christ. A wanner lie down inner foetal position in the gutter and howl, a wanner be invisible, a wanner tern the clock back two minutes. Fuck.

fuck

fuck

fuckfuckfuckfuckfuckfuckfuckfuckfuckfuckfuckfuckfuckfuck

FUCK

A drop a crumpled fiver on to is dog an fuck off awey very fast. Straight into the Central, pinter cider wither Bloody Mary chaser, shoppin now completely fergotten. Al get shite from Mairead fer gettin rat-arsed onner money like but fuck it. Am not leavin this pub until they drag me out bodily. The whole thing's fucked now anyway. Shit.

Oh no . . . oh God no . . .

This's all a fuckin need; a come back from the bog after cleanin meself up avin just follered through, last night's whizz cut with fuckin baby laxative like, fuckin ignominiously perched on the edge uv the sink ter wash me shitey arse, fuckin sleazy sordid humiliation squalor, an oo do a see sittin ther with Maggie and Paul but that Nazi cunt Oxford bleedin John. That's all a fuckin need. Ee's a tosser at the bester times like, but now, with rivulets uv watery cack runnin down me inner legs an im off on one uv is mad rants . . . oh Jesus. Something come an carry this sad sack awey from all this vileness.

Mags just shrugs at me an pulls a snarly face. She yuce ter go out with Oxford John an she's a bit embarrassed about that now, not tharram serprised. A mean, ee's a twat; twisted; ther's somethin wrong inside. Ee preys on young, vulnerable, bewildered gerls, tries ter convert them to is warped werld-view. Lissen to im now, rantin awey ter Paul:

—I mean, what *is* a war crime, yer know? Who has the authority to say what is a crime and what isn't? War is war.

Jesus Christ. Systematically slaughtering ten million men, women, an children on account of ther spiritual, racial, an sexual characteristics is a war crime, dick'ed. Sick an twisted fuckin arse'ole ... A launch into a story about followin through, describin ow av just cleaned meself up in the bogs, gettin quite graphic like, which makes Paul n Margaret laugh but doesunt seem ter make any impression at all on Oxford John. His beliefs – awry as thee ar – ar is armour, an a difficult one ter dent. Ee's so sure uv imself, so certain tharreez right, tharry will not lissen to any contrary opinion. Ee talks about war as if it was a constant throughout is childhood, which is me arse. Ee woulden last two fuckin minutes inny army. Roger hates im, sez tha one dey ee's gunner cut im up. It terns me stomach sometimes when a see Roger go berserk with glass or knife or wharrever; but that's one 'punishment' (ter use Roger's werd) ad like ter see, may God fuckin fergive me.

Mags looks sadly at me an a just shrug. Drink off me pint. Am comin down rerly fuckin fast and hard an it's beginnin ter get very very very unpleasant an all a wanner do is get pissed with me friends, talk about all kindser crap, yer know, drugs, football, seagulls, moterweys, fuckin any'in. A doan wanner lissen ter some Nazi prick blather on about inferior races an life unwerthy uv life, as if some ugly white trash from some scummy council estate in the heart uv some sinking, stinking island is some'ow superior. Ther's alweys some cunt like John around ter spoil things, ter taint things with is diseased ideas. As if things arn bad enough. As if the werld needs another gobshite like im.

A raise me eyebrows ter Maggie an nod me ed backwards at the door. She shakes er ed; I understand, so a tern ter Paul instead.

—Paulie, let's go. Let's move on to another pub. Am fuckin sick uv it in ere.

Ee nods an starts puttin is coat on. John goes:

—Anyway, Paul, read *Mein Kampf*. It's all in ther.

Nah, a think, read Primo Levi, Robert Jay Lifton, Hannah Arendt, Martin Gilbert – that's wher it all is. A wanner avver real go arrim, wanner scream in is smug fuckin face like, burrah don't cos me body, me reflexes, me whole fuckin metabolism, is fucked an drug-ravaged an a know tha a woulden be able ter andle a confrontation. Ad go mad, ad end up breakin bottles, meybe even jammin glass in flesh, an ad hate meself afterwards. An besides, nothin a could ever do or sey would make the slightest difference ter John's extensive, iron-clad web uv self-delusion, so irrud just be a total waster time an energy. Not werth it. Best just ter ignore the prick.

A leave the pub with Paul as John goes off on one ter Mags about the law courts outside the window uv is bedsit. Paranoid, inflated shite. As if ee's that fuckin importunt ter them! As if they'd ever deem im werth watching! Christ, ee's a nothing, a speck, an insignificant blemish. Like us fuckin all, a serpose.

Christ, the people this bleedin town attracts, twats like the Cackler, or John, or Gladys Trevithick, or any uvver hundred fuckin others . . . Thee come ere ter be by the sea an take advantage uv relatively merciful DSS policies an hope that thee air here will cure them uv wharrever obscure, nasty little germ irriz that's buggin them an they sit an get stoned in ther poxy little bedsits an do fuck all all dey but watch portable black an white TVs an thee convince themselves that ther rebels, rejecting the system, trine to analyse the apparatus uv the State in ther little damp an mouldy rooms with intellectual tools borrowed from *The X Files* and interviews with the Shamen. It's all truly pathetic. An somewhere along the wey thee instil within themselves a false illusion uv power which then serves ter hide from them ther true impotence, a tiny amount uv disinfermation around which thee construct whole belief systems, unable ter acknowledge the massive processes uv self-delusion at werk. And not one uv em, not fuckin one, is ever able ter see the picture in its true hopelessness, thee ar inherently unable to appreciate how strong an insidious the system rerly fuckin is. The State knows ther lives; it knows ther thoughts, the places they live, it is fully awer uv the weys in which they will utilise the tiny trickles uv knowledge and autonomy that it grants to them. A mean, how threatening is a person oo sits in a mildewy box uvver room all dey, smokin weed an drinkin strong Spar cider, gigglin at *Kilroy* and *Teletubbies*, convincin themselves like Oxford John that they'd be berrer off if the Nazis had uv won the fuckin war? Ey? Exackly.

—Colm. Paul ruffles me hair. —Doan let it bother yuh. It's not worth gettin all worked up about, now, is it?

—No, a suppose not . . . it just rerly fuckin pisses me off tho. Fuckin arse'ole. Djer think Mags'll be orright?

—Oh yeh. She can look aftuh herself.

—A hope so. Am tellin yer, if ee leys one fuckin finger onner, al kill im. Al batter im up an down the fuckin prom til ee pisses blood.

We go on to another pub an drink an pley pool until neither of us can old our cues properly, then we get some bottles from the Spar an goan sit on the beach. Wrecked as I am, I'm enjoyin Paul's company; that's one yuce fer people like John, thee unwittingly make yer rerly appreciate the people yer like, the people ooer nice.

Thee Aberaeron and Newquay lights twinkle down the coast like sprinkles uv glitter. A cold wind whips across me face an the pebbles ar hard an cold on me arsecheeks burrah doan cur, a like it ere. Cold, yeh, but quiet an calm an peaceful as well. An av achieved me objective uv drinkin awey me comedown; av gorrer lovely low buzz goin in me skull an a think a might even be able ter sleep ternight, properly, without nightmers.

—There's uh Chinese king, Paul sehs, gulpin is wine. —In thuh olden days, yuh know, medieval times. An he wants a new castle cos is old one's buggered. Ee wants thuh most majestic an awesome castle in thuh whole wide wirld, one that will put evry othuh castle in thuh kingdom tuh shame. So ee calls for is best architect an tells im what he wants, sehs ee wants it built within three months. Architect sehs OK an gets down tuh wirk. Three months later, no castle. Whir's me bastard castle? sehs the king. Anothuh month, master, anothuh month. One month passes. Still no castle. The king's pissed off, but ee gives thuh architect one final month tuh finish it. So anothuh month goes by – this is five months in all now – and thuh architect calls thuh king to his house and sehs here's yuh castle. Whir? sehs the king, this is *your* house, I carn see any fuckin castle. So the architect unrolls a great big drawing uvver castle, amazin fuckin thing, hundreds uv turrets and ramparts an windows an rooves and balconies an cannons an evrything. Fuckin amazin it is. An the king sehs yeh velly good, now whir's the real thing? An thuh architect sehs here it is; this drawing, here, is yuh castle. In me arse it is, sehs thuh king, how can I fight off me enemies wither bruddy drawing? I'll just be raffed at. If yuh doan show me thuh real castle within five seconds, al chop yuh head off and feed it tuh thuh dogs. Ee draws is sword an starts counting: one . . . two . . . three . . . an when ee sehs five, thuh architect reaches out an opens one uv the doors on the drawing, steps through, closes it after im, an the king never sees im agen.

Am waitin fer more burrit doesunt come. Seagulls scream in the darkness an waves crash on the shore an wind howls through me earrings like an incoming shell.

—Is tharrit?

—That's it.

—Wharrappens to the king?

—A dunno. That's thuh end of thuh story.

A finish me wine. Pretty fuckin drunk now.

—A like that story.

—So do I, sez Paul, an then sez summun else which a doan hear cos just then a flare goes off wither shockin BANG an a very nearly shit me kex agen. Liker fuckin gunshot next ter me ear, jumped a fuckin mile. Some poor bastard drownin in the sea. In ten minutes or so we'll hear the helicopter roaring an rattlin over the waves an see its searchlight slidin over the water, unless uv course it's preoccupied somewher else with some other poor sod strugglin ter keep themselves alive. Which it probably is.

Oh well. Time ter go ome, a reckon. Knackered now. Not bifore a see the helicopter, tho.

Capel Seilo's bein demolished, the big comedown after the binge uv Calvinism. A know ow it feels. It's almost all gone; yer carn see any uv it at all over the tops uv the six-foot hoardings around it which av been decorated with painted symbols, largely Christian – dove, fish, ladder, et cetera – but thiz also a Celtic knot which is an intrestin addition but one which a carn be arsed fuckin thinkin about at the mo cos am comin down as well, crashin down agen

337

an a feel like shit, wasted an gutted, in bits, an it's sixish in the mornin an am roamin this small sleepin seaside town triner walk this orrible comedown off an a feel like shit, deeply sad, this fuckin life a string uv comedowns. That's all it fuckin is. Evrythin's comin down. The party's over. For us all.

Jesus, tho, wharrer fuckin party it's been, these last few deys; started off at tha rave, moved on to Ynyslas sands, the lights an the sound systems thumpin out from bitween the dunes, fuckin ace. Two Swans an arfer wrap uv Iain's hysterically strong speed, off me fuckin noggin a was, danced me arse off ten owers non-stop on the sand. It was fuckin great. Tha wind-down after a dey or so, then the party carried itself along through many pubs in several towns an villages, various houses, a barn out in the mountains above Penrhyncoch somewher . . . ad enough drugs ter flatten an elephant . . . an now after all that ere I am on me fuckin own, comin down agen, feelin as if all me guts av been yanked out through me ears an me brain as terned ter porridge. A feel old, an desolate, an completely fuckin empty. Hollow. Useless an stupid an senseless, liker toenail continuing ter grow onner corpse.

Ther's a newsagent's open over the road an in me indiscriminate speed-comedown horniness a start thinkin uv porn mags, voyeur-ism, glossy photos uv brown-skinned women with ther long legs open an aloft, smiling, cunts an arse'oles fer me ter see, the crinkled soles uv ther ber feet or ther insteps arched in high-heeled shoes . . . Burrah don't, a don't buy one cos a know al just feel liker sad bastard later if a do. Al feel liker lonely, derty ole fucker, av got several women on the go an a need ter gerroff on porn. Pitiful. A have bought porn bifore, course a have, am a fuckin bloke arn I, burrit's not thee act uv buyin so much as the reasons fer buyin, djer know wharrah mean? A doan serpose tha any reasons ar better than any others rerly, but some do seem tha wey, or at least easier ter live with. Ter me anywey. An a know tha, wer a not comin down so fuckin heavily, a woulden be intrested in pictures; a mean, a fit woman oo dozen move, laugh, talk? A prefer the real thing like, at least when am not crashin like this. An anywey, apart from any'in else . . . the town's too small; the people in the shop ud recognise me an ad alweys think uv them with an image in ther eds uv me bashin me bish over a copy uv *Razzle*.

. . . lyin ther pantin . . . trousers round me ankles . . . greasy spewin slug clutched in me grubby mitt . . .

Aw fuck. I dunno; a serpose a just wanner feel somehow alive.

A wander down on ter Queen's Road, littered with cans an bottles an empty foil cartons from the nearby take-aweys. Typical early-week detritus. A pool uv spew with pigeons peckin arrit. The crotch uv me jeans is angin down ter me knees, me boots ar shufflin along the pavement, ther's a foul niff risin up from me derty shert. A both feel and look a right fuckin state. Ahead uv me's Pen Dinas, be'ind me's Constitution Hill, two giant green doorposts or bars, imprisoning an restricting. A remember Malcolm once when ee was drunk goin on about how inner mountain country yer tend ter look either up at the sky or down at the ground or the towns cowering in the hollows, the valley floors. Ther's no in-between, ee sed; horizontal vision is rer — inner mountain country, yer can only be a dreamer or someone resigned to yer fate.

Which is shite. But the fact does remain tha recently av been thinkin moren more uv leavin. Gypsy blood. Itchy feet. A rerly must remember ter ask Malcolm about France. A never seem ter be able ter get round to it. A always ferget. Or am just about to ask im an either he, or me, passes out or spews up or wharrever. It's ridiculous. Burrah need somethin, some goal . . . am comin apart . . .

Down on ter the prom. The sea's nothin, juster loader grey, dull water, a lone goose flyin across it, lookin for is gaggle. Or is it skein when ther in flight? A look down at the water an a carn imagine any form uv life in it, but outer the corners uv me eyes a seem ter see large, triangular fins cutting through the waves. A look straight on but ther's nowt. Fuck all. The sea . . . if a walked into it terdey, irrud spit me right back out agen. Floppin an gaspin on the pebbles.

A see that fucker Peter on the beach, exercisin is two pit bulls. Ee's up erly. Ee goes badger-baiting with them dogs, the cunt. A remember avin a right go arrim once about it in the pub, burraz always when talkin ter bigots, it was like bangin me ed agenst concrete. Peter's defence was tharrit was natural, that dogs an badgers ar natural enemies; I countered that by seyin tharrin the wild tha mey be the case, burrin the wild (an in Britain ther ar no wild dogs anywey) badgers woulden av ther teeth an claws pulled or be whacked onny ed wither spade ter give the dogs a fighting chance, an in any case Peter's dogs arnt wild, ther domesticated. Well, yer can imagine is answer to that:

—Not fuckin wild, boy? Ey – if yew think them dogs arn fuckin wild you jes watch it, mun, inner pit wither badger or a fox. Soon see wha fuckin wild is then, aye.

Ignorant prick. A rerly fuckin hate tha, people exorcisin ther own confusions an anger through the torture an violent death uv somethin smaller an weaker than themselves. Makes me fuckin sick. Roger can be like tha sometimes, but mainly is drives terwards destruction ar terned back on imself. Most uv the time. But, uv course, ee could av secrets, coulden ee? Like us all.

Up on ter Terrace Road now. It's Tuesday; bread delivery dey at the Spar.

Mairead's money as all gone. Which was bound to appen sometime like; eleven grand dozen rerly last tha long when it's bein used ter support two big drink an drug habits. A putter card in the machine thee other night like, big fuckin therst on me, asked it fer sixty quid an it sed in green letters FUCK AHF, SON, YIS CAN FUCKIN WHISTLE, the fuckin bastard. Horrible, impersonal machines; a mean, wharrif a had uv been stranded somewhere an needed the money to gerrome? Wharrif ad been mugged or summun? No respect, nor even any acknowledgement, fer personal exigencies in sucher faceless, detached society. It's shite. So I asked it fer fifty an got NO; forty, still NO; therty an got OH ALRIGHT THEN, an went straight ter Ynyslas in Paul's car an necked two Pink Callies an found a nice secluded cove in which ter fill me bloodstream full uv amphetamines. An a sold some cut with tha fine white sand to a couple uv schoolkids, it was dark so thee diddun notice an a told em they'd gerrer better buzz if thee swallowed it, made some money back which a gave ter Mairead an shiz been pissed since. Within an ower she was comatose in the marram grass. Sfunny tho; a coulder sworn she adder couple uv undred left in er account. Oh well. Bit fucked now rerly. Don't wanner think about it.

But eleven fuckin grand. What now? Well, av still got me dole, an the extra bit uv disability benefit fer bein a registered alkie like, but oo the fuck can live on that? Even if yer didn't use drugs yud still find it a struggle to servive. Al avter start dealin onner larger scale or summun – sort somethin out with Roger. Need another fuckin mug like Maguire ter trust me wither coupler thou . . . fuckin take off awey somewher, just do one awey from evrythin. Fuck knows wharram gunner do. Al tell yer fuckin one thing tho; if tha fuckin bint Sharon doesent repey Mairead er nine hundred quid by the end uv the fuckin week am gonner smash up er fuckin car. A right fuckin twat, that one; nasty. A fuckin hater. She yuce ter run some crappy little theatre company or summun (which as since gone bust, due to Sharon's mismanagement skills an general social ineptitude), an she told Mairead tha she needed the money ter pey er actors or some such crap. Sed she was gerrin a grant, or a loan offer bank or summun, an tha shid pey the money back within a week. This was six bleedin months ago. An she waited til Mairead was drunk bifore she asked er (an was waitin fer all of, ooo, ten minutes), knowin shid sey yes, an even gaver an IOU, knowin shid never use it. Too nice for er own good, Mairead is, an Sharon's too fuckin sneaky. Mairead should uv listened ter me; A fuckin *told* er not ter trust Sharon. See, if she asunt paid by Saterdey . . .

Rent arrears; no wey uv peyin them now. We'll get evicted soon. And council tax arrears an all. An ther's no means uv movin anywher else now either, to escape like, the gap bitween dole cheques and the pricer train tickets bein an unbridgeable one, an engineered situation so tha the poor an disaffected sections uv the populace avter stey in one place and accrue no possessions. Fuckin shit. No wey ter buy drugs now. No wey ter do fuckin anythin apart from scream through the bars. What the fuck am a gunner do?

Nah . . . if a rerly need to, al get money. Al servive. A always have done, somehow. A mean, the council tax bill: just fuck it. A owe poll tax an council tax from Liverpool, York, Cambridge, Nottingham, London . . . loadser fuckin places. It's nothin ter worry about. This Government, it wants people ter stey wher thee ar, it wants ter restrict ther movements, burall it does is encourage them ter run. Evry person a know as run awey from some form uv debt, amongst other things like. In many cases, self-servin party politics av unwittingly generated remarkable new instances uv human ingenuity an innovation. It's either that, or die. The fuckin cunts.

So this is it, then, this is wharram' reduced to – foraging. Liker fuckin caveman. A watch the bakery truck unload utside the Spar, the white-coated driver lookin tired an unhappy, an when it pulls awey a move out uv the shadows uv the shop doorwey an goan fill me boots with stuff from the stack – bread, crumpets, teacakes, scones, Scotch pancakes, loadser stuff. A gerrer lorruv sweet stuff for Mairead cos, wither alcohol intake reduced so drastically now, er body will be cravin sugar an av seener bifore reduced to eatin spoonfuls uv jam or handfuls of Plague's special rat chocolates, not that ther's any fuckin sugar in them anyway. So a gerrer two packets uv iced buns an some Mr Kipling's apple pies an some odd little pancakey things which ar advertised on the packet as 'A Taste of Spain', an a wee smiling sultana or somethin wither sombrero on. Birruver coincidence ther, cos Mairead once lived in Spain. So she should like these then, burrah know what shill sey – shill shaker er ed wither cheeks all bulgy with food an sey: —Nowt lahk t'ones tha gets in Spern. Nowhere neer as good. Crap compared t'ones tha can get in Spern.

The quick movements uv me arms as a stuff cakes down me clothes breaks the scabs on me track marks an a feel warm, thick goo runnin down me skin. Wharrer fuckin mess. Still, av got no fuckin choice but ter get clean now. Withdrawal ere I fuckin come.

A must looker peculiar shape stumblin ome, stolen bread n stuff crammed into evry pocket, stuffed up me top, even packets uv flapjacks in me hood. A successful forage, but tha doesn't rerly make me any happier, the reason being yer see tharrit's norra choice any more. When it's a choice it's alright, it's fuckin great, but when it's a necessity it becomes a bore, no, moren that, it becomes fuckin meaningless. It's a nothing. A void. A hope tha never appens ter me drug use; a hope tha will alweys remain a choice. A never want that ter lose its value. Not tha ther'll be mucher tha shortly anyway, not unless a can find some wayer makin some money.

A open a packet uv muffins and eat em raw an dry as a walk ome.

Nor even arfer fuckin ower since a snorted tha cocaine an already it's wearin off. Fuckin shite. Al tell yer one thing about cocaine; it's fuckin shite. It's a wimpy, soft-core drug, a good initial buzz like burrit only lasts fer therty fuckin minutes followed by sixty fuckin minutes uv comedown, an the price! Christ! The same amount spent on good whizz an yer awey ferra coupler fuckin weeks, man. Fuck coke. A drug fer people who like ter think ther bigger wasters than thee actually ar, a drug fer wankers with too much fuckin money, fer pricks with jet-set, Groucho Club aspirations, Oasis fans. Drugs are all about the hit, not the mystique, not the stigma, nor any fuckin daft idea uv romantic rebellion; only the hit matters. Cocaine, puh; yer can stick irrup yer arse.

Still, got me faverit lunch on the table ere in fronter me; twenty Camel filters an a grammer speed slowly dissolvin in the bottom uvver cold pinter lager, drops uv moisture on the glass, lookit the bubbles rising. Gorgeous. Speed's me drug, a fuckin love speed; even the dick shrinkage is, perversely, parter the fun, the whole fuckin amphetamine experience is unbeatable. A love it. The coke might uv worn off by now burrah can feel the sulphate creepin slowly inter me system; the tinglin scalp, the twitchin extremities, the electricity flashin in me brain, the erge ter talk, touch, laugh, grind me teeth, expansive warm feelins beginnin ter fill me chest . . . yeh. Coke promises an fails ter deliver; speed just gives it to yer straight. Another forty minutes or so an al be a rantin twitchin fool, happy as a pig in shit.

What's tha fuckin barman lookin at? Ope ee diddun spot me droppin me powder inter me beer . . . nah; ad be out on me arse if ee did. Maybe ee's gay anny fancies me. A think ee clocked me in ere one gay night, when a wandered in with Malcolm by mistake, not knowin it was gays only. Well, sorry, pal, yer outer luck; one-way system, my arse is, unless uv course a gerlie has a probin finger. Al maken exception fer that, oh yes.

Mags is up at the pool table, bein talked at by tha crusty, Methadone Mickey, off is fuckin box, showin er is extensive selection uv downers. Must be script dey, the sad bastard. Fuckin lissen to im:

—Now if a laid oner these on yew, yurd be flat out in twenty minutes. An if a laid oner *these* onner yew, yurd be out before that fuckin glass touched yer lips. Spark out.

Danny outer *Withnail & I*; the fuckin spit.

—Ah yeh, straight out like a light. Bumph, there's yew, onner floor.

Oh yeh, fuckin great fun; a rerly wanner drug which sends me straight ter fuckin sleep. Toast, tea an telly ul do that for me very fuckin well. Wharriz it with some people that thee wannoo sleep ther whole fuckin lives awey?

Come on, speed, come on, speed . . . werk, man, werk . . . A coulduv mainlined inner bogs burrav lost me fuckin spike an am fucked if am gunner use anyone else's. Apart from Dodgy Derek, AIDS asunt rerly hit ere yet, at least norraz far as a know, burram not takin any more risks on tha score, not like a did in the Liverpool galleries, no fuckin wey, man. Al get some more needles frommer clinic up Plas Crug, or see if anyone's nicked any more frommy ozzy or the vets. Easy. An in the meantime, speed in me beer'll do just fine. Fine as fuckery.

. . . a think am goin insane. It might be drug abuse, or lack uv sleep, or no food, or some combination uv all three, burrah think am goin mad . . . a keep seein things . . . hearin voices, feeling infested by insects. Thoughts, mad, horrible thoughts, unwanted and of unknown provenance. A mean, tha fuckin stag's ed up ther on the wall as just winked at me. Am fuckin sure uv it, man. Now a look arrit straight on, tho, it's nothin, it's juster baldy ole stag's ed which should av been left on the shoulders uv the fuckin stag. Ah, I know wharrit is; it's a robot, remote-controlled, the barman's controllin it frommer secret panel under the bar which is why ee was starin at me bifore like, ter see my reaction to the winkin stag, if it freaked me out like. Well, hard fuckin lines, pal, cos am wise ter your fuckin game, you pretendin ter innocently mop the bar top with yer rag. Sneaky twat.

Unsure whether this rush goin through me is amphetamine or cocaine or thee onset of some type uv hysteria . . . am goin insane am goin insane; handy that, rerly, cos it's a well-known fact tharrif yer think yer goin mad then yer obviously not, astute if somewhat misguided self-analysis not bein one uv the reckernised characteristics of the journey into madness. Not like, sey, sucking dragonflies an coverin yerself in yer own faeces. So sey it loud an yull feel much, much berrer; am goin insane am goin insane. Help me someone cos a feel like am losing my mind.

A rhyme a made up when a was a kid:

> Last night I was warned by my dad
> If I stared at the moon I'd go mad
> But I stared at it last night
> And I'm perfectly alright
> So groodle mendle flad.

Margaret pockits the black an holdser cue up abover ed in triumph. Er jumper rides up and exposes er taut, flat belly. The bloke shiz just beaten is just standin ther starin atter, probly now feelin somewhat inadequate, and Mickey is flat on is back on the floor inner pool uv beer. The barman's triner wake im up, slappin is face wither wet beer towel, burry's avin none uv it, ee's fuckin dead to the werld. Try yer fuckin winkin stag's ed trick on im, yer sly fuckin twat.

Never ter wake up excited and think: Christ, a wonder what's gunner happen to me terdey. Never agen ter feel the blood thud in my ears. Never ter feel this freedom, never ter feel thee air hum and crackle with such possibility. Ter be slowly killed in a wey other than my own, to alweys look exhausted and unhappy. To hate life and its monotony. To accept ther proffered hell.

Never. Fucking never.

Mags walks across the pub terwards me, grinnin an shakin er head. She looks astonishing as she moves. And here's Uncle Sulphate come ter pey another visit, come with an armful uv fabulous prezzies, the same as alweys but no less ace and exciting and wonderful. Welcome back, man, avver seat, park yer arse; doan ever go away agen.

BILL

ROGER BROUGHT UP tha Malcolm one a month or two ago an he assed me what it's like to av nothin an a told im to fuck off. Nothin be buggered; I yav it all up ere, mun, I yav fuckin evrythin, anythin I need, or want, is available to me yer, shelter, clothes, food an stuff which Roger, God bless im, brings me, an more un those immediate evrydey necessities I yav things so fuckin valuable tha people will kill other people for em, fresh air, freedom, a chance t'live accordin completely ter my own methods an no bastard else's, a chance t'be truly me an juss watch-a pure sky an-a friendly mountains, be-a part uv-a changin seasons, see the sky change from-a angry black of oily smoke to total blue, so blue that it stains my skin, patterns my face an arms like woad . . . No money worries yer, no bills, no arse'oles in suits knockin on me door, no brown envelopes through-a letter box cos I yaven't bleedin *got* a letter box, no rent, no taxes, no phone, no government offices . . . I left all-a that shit back down in-a town like, way down at-a far end of-a valley, whir it can fuckin well stay. To them, like, those fuckers in suits be'ind eyr desks, I do not exist; I yav vanished off-a face uv the planet. I am on no known track or census up ere – they will never track me down. The only people oo come up yer ar those I want t'come up yer, those I invite, Roger an is mates like, no impositions, an ey bring me food an baccy an-a brown which stops-a orrible fuckin itchin in-a place whir me arm yuced t'be, the phantom limb like. Best antihistamine in-a world, the brown is like, oh yeh. An the only intruders on my personal space ar the birds an the insects an-a mountain rats, big, bold buggers them like, cat-size some-a em, an iss is their space as well so a can't complain. We share it, we do, me an-a animals, we share iss mountain, iss sky. I welcome them in my space. Like em, I do; good company, ey ar. So nothin be fucked; I yav it fuckin all up yer, I do. Don't fer one bastard moment think I aven't.

Patronisin bastard, tha Malcolm. Southern England, see; Sassenach. Saesneg shit'ed. Kept is ands deep in is pockets a whole bloody time ee was up yer, as if ee was ashamed uv em or somethin. Ardly said two words t'me either; juss stared down is nose at me like, wrinklin is top lip. Fuck off back to Essex, mun.

Am lyin on me back on-a hillside, sun startin t'go down, a last small hit uv brown keepin me relaxed an mellow. Although I'm *always* relaxed an mellow, me, mun. Roger's due up yer sometime today with more supplies like, so am keepin me eyes peeled fer Paul's car on-a valley road which a can see about thirty miles of from iss vantage point, a grey ribbon threadin its way between-a lakes an-a spurs all-a way to-a horizon whir-a town huddles up agenst the sea. Iss is the first thing I see of a mornin when I step out me shack to fetch tea water from-a stream, these mountains, the valley, the sea sparklin away over ther between two peaks, this vast expanse uv sky an space, all fuckin mine. The soarin birds, the buzzards, the merlins, the kites. Oh yeh, nothin fuckin bothers me up yer, mun. I don't need no one else.

Still, tho, a wonder oo Roger'll bring up with im . . . ee always brings someone up with im, at least Paul, cos Roger carn drive see, an no fuckin bus comes iss far into-a mountains, oh no. Good boy Paul is, built me a little lavatory last time ee was up yer, an outhouse like, deep hole in-a ground with wooden walls an-a roof around it an some big bags-a lime t'keep a pong down an elp with-a decayin process. Ardly *Homes an Gardens* like, but it does-a bleedin job, saves me squattin bare-arsed over-a river or a hole in-a woods dunnit, cartin me spade an all that fannyin around. Good hands, Paul as like, quick an efficient. Ee was with is girly, Sioned a think er name was; seemed a bit wary of me, she did, like, kept touchin Paul all-a time as if for protection or to keep im close to er or somethin. Can't blame er tho, really; fuckin Catweazle me, aye. Aven't touched a razor or cut me hair in nigh on three years. Al av birdies nestin in it soon, I will. Which would be nice; ther chirpin, a dawn chorus like, me own personal natural alarm clock. Watchin-a babbies grow an make eyr first flight, launchin emselves out over me chest an belly. I'd like that, I would. It'd be like, a suppose, payment or somethin, compensation or redress to-a bird world like for me killin all em penguins. Evry night I see em fallin, juss collapsin like skittles on the snowy beach, ther little wings eld away from ther bodies. I'm sorry for doing that, like, but it weren't my fault, tho, really; the real penguin-murderers are all tucked up nice n warm n safe in some fuckin MOD office away in bastard London. Fuckers. Wouldn't last two fuckin owers out ere, they wouldn't; oh yeh, they'd go out into-a Beacons an stuff like for several days but that's with full fuckin pack – *any* cunt can survive a few days with full bleedin pack, like. Without that, ey wouldn't last two fuckin owers out ere. No way.

Maybe tha Paddy'll come up, make me another superskunk spliff. Strong fuckin blow tha was like, whoof, blew me bleedin ead off, mun. Nimble fingers that lad aye, dextrous like, rolled me a five-skinner in seconds flat ee did, twistin, turnin, skilful fingers it was. Put it in me gob an sparked me up. Didn't smoke any isself tho, an then when a was good n wrecked ee tried t'sell me a bag, wavin it in front-a me nose like, goin through is patter. As if; ow-a fuck's ee think I can pey im like? No need for money up yer, mun, God no, it's all free, evrything. Occasionally, tho, to help Roger out, a have been known t'do a few days work on Thomas's farm down the valley, a bit-a milkin, spud-pickin, egg-gatherin, butcherin, yard-sweepin like, which int bleedin easy when yer missin yer full complement uv limbs like, and once, but only the once, when Roger was short like, a mugged a hiker with-a rock on-a foothills of Cader an gave is Bergen an boots an stuff to Roger in exchange for a small bag. Am not proud of it, oh no, but I had ter do it; juss crept up on im in-a fog like an boof, one belt, down ee went. One-armed bandit, that's me, mun. Not proud of it like, but a tell yer, people should watch out; the weather int the only danger in these mountains, Christ, no. The mountains'll punish yer, you don't give em enough respect like. He wouldn't leave it alone, tho, this Irish feller, kept goin on n on: 'Ah shur ah'll putchy down ferra quarturr so. Ah'm shur ye can get the money from somewhurr.' A mean, fuck. Got no need for that bleedin money stuff up yer, mun, evrythin a need is free; mushies (both edible and recreational) from-a field an woods, trout from-a river, vegetables from-a farms, eggs, chickens, it's all free. Wouldn't say no to-a spliff, tho; brown'll be wearin off soon like.

Hope tha Scouse lad dunt come up – pain inny arse im aye, ee'd be too fuckin much for me at-a moment, when am all chilled out, with is mad energy and is rantin an ravin. Last time ee come up ee was wearin a Liverpool Carlsberg shirt with 'DOWNEY' and '9' on-a back an flailin is ands around evrywhir, tryin to get me to go over-a mountain into Llangurig with im ter get lashed. 'Come 'ed,' ee was sayin, 'Come 'ed, irrill be a laugh, al get yer rat-arsed an bagged off with some buxom dairymaid called Rhiannon, irrull be fuckin top, man.' A wasn't avin any of it like. All bitten, is fingers were, an a remember noticin a wound onny end uv is thumb an while ee was goin on like shoutin an ramblin a was thinkin about infection an gangrene an amputation. A juss went off into me own head an let im get on with it like. Ee asn't been up for ages; Roger said that ee found out about-a penguins an said a was an evil bastard. Some fuckin understandin, some shred uv compassion, wouldn't go bleedin amiss yer like; it was-a fuckin trainin see, it was drilled fuckin into me, KILL KILL KILL, what-a fuck else could I do? A would've gone fuckin crazy like up ther on that bluff doin nothin but look out to sea for days, weeks on end. Mad with-a fuckin boredom, mun. An anyway, tha Scouse bastard can stay away for all I care, a won't fuckin miss im; too bleedin loud. Overbearin. Wouldn't mind a visit from is missus, tho, God no, fuckin great girl she was like; reminded me of me ex (oo fucked off to some poofy schoolteacher when a hit er once too often; trainin again, see). Brought a cassette player up with her, put on some-a that modern repetitive crap like an started dancin all round me shack, me n Roger juss gawpin at her like, shakin er hips, pattin an choppin-a air with er hands an I couldn't take my eyes off er fingers – long an slim, nails all filed an sharp, elegant's-a word like, loads-a bracelets an rings, sexy hands, women's hands . . . God, a started ter think about things a hadn't thought about in months, maybe even years. Awoke some old stirrings she did, an some good old memories n all, an a lovely girl she was as well – dead touchy like, friendly, er gorgeous hand on me half-arm, nattered away for owers we did me n er while Roger fell asleep in-a car an Paul went off explorin in-a hills. She was askin me about my life an stuff an a could tell that she was really lissenin, y'know really interested like, she wasn't juss bein like, emptily polite or anythin, she genuinely wanted to know, she truly was interested. So a told her, evrythin like, juss opened me gob an it all came out. Maybe it was er oo told er boyfriend about-a penguins like, a dunno, but a juss couldn't stop meself, out it came like a dam burstin, but she probly doesn't remember much uv it like cos she was a bit pissed. Fell over, if a remember rightly, tripped over me wellies an juss lay thir on er back roarin with laughter. As a rule, a don't miss people up yer like, a mean a moved up yer partly t'get away from people an their petty competitions an stuff, but God, it was nice to really av someone t'talk to, someone oo'd listen, an ask questions, an really fuckin hear what yer sayin to em, an not pass judgement. A nice change, it was. An maybe it's a feature uv the young women these days because tha other girlie was the same, er with-a short hair like, quiet girl, seemed a bit shy n nervous, a noticed that er hands were tremblin a bit when she rolled me a ciggie. God knows why like, she ad nothin to fear from me. But she was good t'be with n all – talkin, lissenin, interested in me an my stories like . . . made me feel, a dunno, sort uv important a suppose, not tha a *need* t'feel that, God, no – I am completely fulfilled out ere, there is nothin I lack, I want nothin more than I've got. I am not a part of tha greedy, money-grabbin, petty-minded an materialistic world tha exists on the valley floor an I could want for nothin else ever. This'll fuckin do me, mun. On a clear day a can see the town at the end of-a valley like an it looks brown an squat an dirty. Like a terminal moraine or somethin; all-a shit left behind after the glacier has melted.

I see a white car crawlin miles away up-a road an I'm hopin that it's Paul's but then it turns off down-a dirt track to Thomas's farm. Bugger. I hope ey come up soon, cos am needin all kinds-a stuff – tea, bread, baccy, especially fuckin baccy. Ikey it is oo sends me up-a tobacco, or oo brings it up isself like. Big two-ounce packets ee brings, look like boxes-a bleedin matches in is ands like, massive ands Ikey's got, farmer's ands like, all scarred an knuckly with a cross tattooed on each finger. Look more like tree roots than human hands. An am a bleedin dab hand with the Rizlas, I am, oh yes; a can roll quicker with one hand than most people can with two. Practice, see. Can even build spliffs one-handed, I can, altho nowhir near as fast as tha Paddy. Paul brought me up a rolling machine once like but I don't use it – don't need to. (A rolling machine! Ee means well, Paul does, an is heart's in-a right place like, but yer's many things a could use an a fuckin rolling machine int one uv em. Nice feller, Paul, but a bit thick; sarnie short uv a picnic like. Last time ee was up yer an ee was juss lookin round like an I said to im: 'Ah Paul, I can see yer rendered speechless by the sparkle an salubriousness uv your surroundings,' an ee was like 'Duh . . . wha?' Daft as arse'oles, mun.) Yeh, a can do anythin with one and, me, anythin I want to; gather an chop wood, make a fire, cook, dig a hole, fish, anyfuckinthing, mun, even cook up a fix like if am careful: hold the spoon in yer teeth, lighter under-a bowl, when it boils lean over an gently, gently, place spoon on flat surface, pick up needle an yer away. Easy. Patience an care, that's all yew need, mun. Patience an care.

But I'm no fuckin junkie, mun, Christ no. A use-a brown like cos it knocks me out, stops me from remembrin an sometimes, mun, it bleedin hurts t'remember. It was juss one-a those things, like, yeh, an sometimes a recall it all so clearly an a wish to fuck tha the grenade had uv knocked me out or even bleedin killed me. A remember laughin, like, takin me finger off the pin an lobbin it; I remember the noise, the BANG, I remember flyin through the air, I remember landin, I remember draggin meself t'me knees an Hughesy lookin at me with is eyes all big an-a wind rufflin is hair an then turnin away to throw up an a remember, in perfect detail, holdin my arm up in front uv my face an laughin again cos I just couldn't fuckin believe it, I couldn't believe it cos my arm had become two, it was split lengthways like down-a middle between-a third an fourth finger right between the two bones, the ulna an the radius like, right up to my elbow an a remember the two halves floppin away from each other an then t'wards each other, away from each other an then t'wards each other, makin a splat sound as they met an then fell away again as if they were fuckin applaudin somethin like. Ah yeh, a can tell you the sound of one hand clappin, I can. An all the colours an-a warm stuff squirtin in me face an Hughesy spewin an it was all juss like a dream, a bad dream that a don't ever want to remember. It was like ad stumbled upon somethin a was never meant t'see; it was like, ow can a explain it, seein the insides uv me arm, the bones an-a veins an-a exposed muscle an stuff, it's like seein all that equates itself in me mind with the time when a was a little boy an a came ome from school early an me uncle Maldwyn was givin me mother one over-a kitchen table. Me mam all bent over, tits swingin big an evvy cos she'd just ad me brother Gary, skirt up around er waist; me uncle Maldwyn slappin er arse, callin er names; me arm split in two, the bone gleamin blue-white, veins twistin like worms. They all seem part uv-a same event, the same dark secret a was never meant to see.

Ah fuck it. What's done is done like. Juss one-a those things. Juss got t'fuckin live with it, mun, aye. Nothin else yer can do.

The others, tho, Roger an is mates like, they can't bleedin live with it, they can't do what eyv got t'do; yer can see it in ther eyes, mun, often they look scared, they don't want-a live in-a town with all its pressures uv money an debt an men in suits, but they ant got the balls t'do what I've done an fuck it all off an find a space whir ey can be truly emselves. They're too scared to escape from-a world, even tho ey really want to, cos eyr even more bleedin scared uv a unknown. It attracts them, but it terrifies em at-a same time, so ey just go through cyr lives doin whatever ey can to ignore or blot out this duality. That's what I reckon, anyway. That's my theory.

The sun's sinkin behind Cader Idris in-a distance towards a sea an-a sky is filled with giant fires an this is all I fuckin need mun, I don't need nothin else. Evrythin I need, evrythin I want, lies up yer within reach. I yav it all up here, I do.

Where the fuck ar yew, Roger. Why won't yew come.

From *A Personal Guide to West Wales*, anonymous authorship, privately printed, p. 70

They can be heard, sometimes, the mountains, they can be heard as they shift closer; a deep, low rumble from within the earth followed by a slow and persistent grinding, the hunger pangs of an immeasurable beast in subterranean slumber embossing its vast shape on the landscape, spurnose, mountainnipple, cliffrib, immense, recumbent and green. Why do they do this, the mountains, why do they rush at the sea, why do they seem to seek that one element which always has and always will execrate and oppose them? Perhaps the possibility of union propels such gargantuan drift, the after-midnight keening of the Wicklow range at a pitch too high for human ear, the reuniting of a partnership once perfect, once powerful, now lost. So earth and water wrestle in deadlock, unstoppability against immovability, an eternal clash which will admit no stint or respite, and the breach between the two screams, knowing that like cilia in a digestive tract the mountains create a huge surface area in a narrowly-boundaried nation and that, when kind and whimsical, the ocean can on occasion permit escape. Concealment, then, or flight; the motives, aims and wherewithal will decide. You don't have to do anything. Just wait.

THEY ARE CELEBRATING

THEY ARE CELEBRATING with a ferocity which Geraint will half-remember with a shudder on his impending flight to Florida. He has been matching them drink for endless drink and now sits swaying in the corner of the pub listening with his right ear to Liam and Colm arguing and with his left to Malcolm's bizarre tales of an improbable visit to New Mexico a couple of years ago. It has been a long session, this, day melting into night and back into day again, and much fluid has been both consumed and ejected. As yet, this process is showing no signs of winding down; the desperate energies which fuel it are as resilient and demanding as stone.

—Well, a mean am just sain good fuckin luck ta ya, cawse a fuckin am. But am awlso sain that a down't fink ya'll like it thair. In fact, a know for a fact that ya'll fuckin hate it. Am tellin ya. A mean, the attractions, right, of the States, are, mainly, shite beer, a mean am talkin fuckin shandy here now, ya get sick of drinkin it befaw ya pissed; weed so fuckin strong that ya monged afta arfa spliff; unbridled greed an materialism, evry cunt drives so thair's no fuckin pavements ya can't fuckin wawk anywhair. Am tellin ya. The desert's fuckin pukka tho. As are the birds; plastic, like, oh yeh, sillycone tits an awl that but they cream fa the fuckin Brits, man, am tellin ya, English, Welsh, Jock, it's awl the fuckin same ta them. Ya'll be fightin em off with a shitty stick.

—Am warnin yer, Liam, Colm says, his voice rising. —Keep yer fuckin trap shut.

—Ah, a doan cur, slurs Geraint, raising his glass to his face and dumping a slop of Guinness on his left shoulder. —Z fuckin nothing for me yer, mun, is er? Ah yeh, new fuckin oppertunities, yer know, all that shit. New place, new faces like. Ah yeh. Ass all a need, mun, juss some new chances . . . like . . . ah yeh . . .

—Oh yeh, God, down't get me wrong, am not fuckin blamin

ya fa gowin. Christ, if a could ad be on the fuckin plane with ya. All am sain is that –

—AH YIS FUCKIN WANKER YER FUCKIN PRICK! A FUCKIN TOLD YER DIDDUN I, A FUCKIN WARNED YER! NOW FUCK OFF JUST FUCK OFF! DICK'ED!

Colm's spittle dots the table and he strides away from an overturned chair and a beer-soaked, abashed Liam, a limp and sodden roll-up drooping from his lower lip. He spits it out and shakes his head like a wet dog, spraying lager spindrift over the cold stone walls of the pub.

—Jee-sus! What tha fuck was awl that about? Malcolm wipes moisture off his face.

Liam slicks his wet hair back over his skull. —Ah, just summin ah said te yer man thir. Summin that mebbe ah shouldn't huv.

—Well, yeh, it certainly fuckin looks that way, down it?

Geraint asks: —What exactly was it, then? That yer said, like?

Liam shrugs. —Nowt rurly, ee just lost the fuckin head. All a said was that ee grrupnsnall ark erm . . .

—What?

—Ey?

Liam rolls another cigarette and murmurs: —Ah tole im tha ee only lirns about life t'rew bukes whereas ah lirn about it t'rew livin it. That's all.

—Ah well, thair ya fuckin go then. Count yaself lucky ee didn't fuckin chin ya. A know *I* fuckin would av. Malcolm shakes his head, bemused, exasperated, and drunk. —Ya shoulda known betta, Liam. Mighta known Colm was gowin ta react ta that. An anyway, it's not fuckin true, which am sure you fuckin know . . . whyja afta caws awl these arguments eh? Why can't ya just, ya know, chill out? Geraint's last night fa fuck's sakes . . .

—Whair's ee stormed off to then? asks Geraint.

Liam shrugs again. —Dunno. Doan curr.

Malcolm shakes his head. —Fuckin grow up, man. Childish fucker.

—Al, al goan seef a can find im.

Geraint finishes his pint and rises unsteadily, one hand on Liam's soaked shoulder, the other on the drenched table top. He stands swaying on the spot for a second until he is certain that he can walk without falling over and then he unmoors himself and staggers across the crowded pub, taking the slow and exaggerated cartoon steps of the hopelessly hammered. Were he not so numbingly inebriated he would probably be dwelling on the sadness of leaving a place in which he has largely enjoyed living for the past few years, and considering the apprehension and excitement of his imminent departure to a distant, wholly new location (and indeed, he has spent much of the previous two or three days doing precisely that, loudly and wetly and in any ear close to his mouth), but now, with his senses awash with alcohol, he only has a vague sense of needing to find Colm, who has become lost, a purpose which is jettisoned the instant he spots two pretty girls with whom he is acquainted slightly talking and drinking intently over a table in the corner. Standing, swaying, he struggles to focus on them and remember their names; the dark one with all the rings in her face and the legendary drink habit is from Yorkshire somewhere and has some kind of Gaelic name . . . Mary? Nah . . . Mairead; and the blonde one in the tight black dress, who moved away to Cornwall some months ago now, is called Rebecca. Clumsily he joins them, almost capsizing the table as he collapses into a sitting position, but they are amiable and receptive, as he knew they would be.

—So it's tomorrow yur off then, is it?

—Uh.

—A wee bit tipsy is tha, Geraint? Just a tad squiffy lahk?

Geraint grins sloppily and they laugh, loud, drunken, slatternly laughter which to Geraint at the moment is the most haunting and gorgeous of all.

—God, ah doesn't blame tha, Mairead says, swaying somewhat herself. —If ah wuh off t'Florida t'morrow lahk ah woulduv bin hospitalised three week ago.

Geraint narrows his eyes as he tries to make sense of this but then he gives up and yells: —DRINK! Oo's for a drink then?

—Al av one.

—Me n all.

He takes their orders and stumbles to the bar. Rebecca goes off to the toilet and Mairead, looking at the burning end of her cigarette, hears a slurred Liverpudlian accent say:

—Ello. Can a sit ere? Ooer you?

Up at the bar, Geraint is soon surrounded by a crowd of well-wishers who ply him with drink and shake his hand and slap his back. He accepts their offerings gladly and orders wrongly for Mairead and Rebecca, barely registering who these happy people around him are. Drinks spill and Iestyn slips a small paper envelope into the breast pocket of Geraint's damp white shirt.

—Sumthin for the plane journey, yeh? Make it go quicker like.

—Ta.

He fights his way back to the seat, drinks clutched in his large hands. His eyes open as he sees Colm sitting opposite and talking to Mairead.

—Ah thir yer ar! Who found yer? Been lookin all over, I yav!

Geraint gives Mairead her vodka and Coke and Rebecca her pint of Guinness. They had asked for a Jack Daniel's and a bottle of Newcastle Brown respectively, but they drink them anyway. Colm points at their glasses:

—Z oner them fer me?

Geraint shakes his head. —Didn't know what yew wir wantin, Col. Didn't even know you wir here.

—Aw yer bastard. Make way, them, lemme out . . .

—Nah, ts orright, al goan gerrit in for yer. Ah yeh. No bother.

—Nice one.

—What yavin?

—Erm . . . pinter . . . lager, a think.

Geraint hauls himself up and weaves back to the bar, hoping he'll meet more well-wishers; the reason, in fact, why he offered to buy Colm a drink. He slobbers his order and flops against the wall and Sharon squeezes her way through the crowd to stand by him.

—Hiya.

—N.

—Ah diddin knor Colm knows Mairead.

—Oh . . . Geraint smiles. —Ee doesn't. But ee's gettin to, ah yeh, he's gettin to.

—Mmm . . . anywer how ar yer?

—Fuckin sound . . . pissed off me face. Fuckin lashed, I am. Off ter Florida t'morror, see.

—Florida? T'morror?

—Aye.

—Oh . . . Do us a favour, will yer, gorn tell Colm ter come ere.

Geraint accepts the pint of lager off the barman and screws his face up at Sharon.

—Tell im yer fuckin self, he snarls, and retraces his steps once again, ricocheting off walls and people, eventually handing Colm half a pint of lager in a pint glass.

—Adder swig, did yer?

—Spilt it. An anyway, be fuckin grateful yer fuckin –

—Aw am only messin, Geraint, ta very much. Cheers.

They clink glasses and down their drinks in one. Geraint's ravaged stomach rebels and he heaves, slapping his hand over his mouth. Rebecca, sitting across the table from him, looks terrified.

—Not over me dress you don't! Only bought the bastard thing today!

Geraint makes an expression, half grimace, half grin. —It's alright, it's gone now . . . a juss thought for a minute tho . . . Ah yeh, how ter drink the same pint twice eh!

He laughs and feels himself falling, or something falling on him. Through descending greyness he hears Colm and Mairead singing together and he wonders how it will turn out between them, how everything will turn out, and as his eyelids slide heavily shut and his brain drowns in alcohol and he slides smoothly off his seat with a certain boneless grace on to the sodden and sawdusty stone slabs which make up the floor his last coherent and conscious thought for some hours is: only the losers stay.

GERAINT

TRAIN

So fuckin boring train journeys are aye but Christ how nice ter see green, so much green, the mountains green and the fields green rushin past-a window. An all a little whitewashed cottages an all; ah yeh, it's all like a great big fudge-box lid. Fudge-box Wales yer, aye. Ah yeh, Florida's just all brown, kind uv brown an yellow, gets dull after a while it does. Even the swamps're brown. This is a main thing a remember about Wales when am over thir – the green. The green evrywhir. Ah yeh.

Yer I am back ome in Wales, on-a train with-a suntan an money in me pocket, feelin healthy an hopeful. A was tempted t'bring some weed an maybe even some charlie back with me like but am weary uv customs, the sniffer dogs an the rubber gloves an that, an, ah yeh, they all carry fuckin machine-guns in Miami airport like so a didn't bother. An anyway, a can use me time back in Wales t'get cleaned up, ter flush out me system like; ah yeh, av bin doin a bit too much in-a States like, could do with a rest. Get rid of all-a toxins, jes soak up this good back ome feelin. Could do with somethin t'while away iss journey, tho; bored, I yam. Altho a could gaze all day at the sexy binty across-a aisle from me oo keeps tossin er hair back an crossin er legs. Short skirt shiz wearin, thick tights which show-a smooth skin of er legs between-a stitchin. Christ. Makes me think uv em pole-dancers like, all over-a bleedin States ey ar, ah yeh, yer tryin to order a drink an yer's some woman slappin er tasselled knockers in yer face. Mad. Fuckin gorgeous, iss girl is tho, auburn hair, an what's that shiz readin? Flann O'Brien? Oo's ee? Sounds like somethin yid av for yer dinner in an Irish theme pub. With crusty bread an salad.

Fuckin dead stewpid this train journey is tho; from Abergavenny down t'Cardiff, up from thir t'Birmingham, thir t'Shrewsbury an then down t'Aberystwyth. Fuckin daft, round the houses like.

Why ey refuse t'link mid Wales with-a south's fuckin beyond me like. Lucky a was able to crash for a few owers at me uncle's in Crickhowell or ad be jet-lagged t'fuck by now like. Ah yeh; never last-a fuckin train journey en, would I? Bit-a sleep an a bath an ah yeh, am alright, now, I am.

Chucka chucka chucka. Thomas-a fuckin Tank Engine, mun, aye. Back from Florida ome in Wales, back from Florida ome in Wales . . .

A train goes over a river. Fuckin huge mountains all around; so much *space*, boy, Christ . . . ah yeh, Florida's full-a space like, specially in a desert, but it's a different kind, innit? That's juss flat space like. This yer is . . . a dunno; fuckin *huge*.

The girlie puts-a book down an curls up t'get some sleep, er head leanin agenst a window. Pity rirly; a was about t'start up a conversation. Break a boredom like. Ah well, never mind, yew go for it, darlin, get some kip.

. . . wonder how evryone's doin. Wonder if Laura got me e-mail; a sent it up to-a uni like whir she wirks but didn't av time t'check me own number for a reply, a was that mad rushed. Fuckin ope so, or that's me with nowhir t'get me head down when a land in fuckin Aber. God, a wonder even if ther all still around like, it's been neer two fuckin years . . . maybe ev all fucked off like. Ah yeh, be juss my fuckin luck that would. Two yeers, tho, eh; a landscape still looks familiar tho, the old country, not alien or anythin like tha, but a suppose at's only t'be expected; a mean, Jesus, a fuckin mountains arn ever gunner go away, ar they? What's funny tho is tha if anythin a hills an a valleys an a rivers an stuff look an feel even more familiar than ey did before a left like, cos am comin back yer feelin even more Welsh, a can even speak more uv the language now cos when a was over in a States a did somethin av always wanted t'do an tha was visit Y Wladfa, in Argentina like, y'know a Welsh settlement in Patagonia? Ah yeh, a saved up an went down thir like, somethin ad wanted t'do ever since a read tha story about em durin a Falklands War when ey wir all gunner be deported by-a Argentine government but ey succeeded in convincin the fascist bastards tha ey ad fuck all t'do with a war, eyr Welsh, not English. An fuckin fair play to em I say. An ah yeh, a fuckin great place it was; a went an stayed with em, juss tirnd up like, an ey cooked me a South

American version uv cawl, probly ad fuckin llama innit instead-a lamb like (ad t'relax me vegetarian principles for that one like), an ey gave me ome-brew beer an taught me more Cymraeg than a ever fuckin lirnd at school an told me about St Madoc an all that stuff like. Fuckin great it was. But, a mean, y'know, ter rediscover me fuckin culture like I ad t'travel thousands-a fuckin miles away from Wales like; fuckin daft innit, ey? Makes me fuckin angry like. Grittin me teeth I am yer, tho that might just be cos am bored. An a tell yer, that's somethin al never eat agen as long as a fuckin live, them grits; all kind-a white an jellyish ey ar, like fuckin frogspawn or somethin. Kind uv porridgy. Oats. Porridge on-a same plate as yer eggs an bacon. Fuckin orrible like.

Fuckin train journeys . . . am drummin me fingers on-a table top like, all fuckin excited like a kiddie. Ah yeh, dead excitin iss is, am all excited t'be back like . . . lookin at-a mountains. A carn get enough-a seein em. An that's another thing a discovered recently; a was born in Crickhowell, see, an so was Sir George Everest, im with the mountain like. Ah yeh, ee was a colonist in India like. One uv the Patagonians, Bryddon is name was, told me all about im, an also about some fuckin giant massacre an betrayal tha happened in Abergavenny, years ago like, but a doan remember the details now. Ah yeh, knew is history, Bryddon did. Knew all about Wales like. And djer know wha? Ee'd never even been t'Wales once like. In is life.

Looks like this part-a Wales, Patagonia does. Same landscape like. Amazin. Apart from the fuckin huge council estates yer like, like giant cowpats lyin in a valleys, like-a New Gurnos, tha fuckin pit whir Roger's from; an no wonder ee's the way ee is, comin from a place like-a Gurnos – ah yeh, drive fuckin Mother Teresa crazy, that would. A fuckin Indian reservation's what it is, tha place, a fuckin piece-a the Third World in the middle of wha is supposed t'be the First. Ah yeh; the Celts are the Brit equivalent of the American Indians we ar, ah yeh, beaten, oppressed, fucked right up, mun, exactly-a same, only-a reservations yer ar immense warrens uv concrete an glass, an not, like, y'know, wigwams or wooden huts. Ah yeh, fuckin crazy boy. Tho maybe Roger's changed by now like, maybe ee's calmed down; but a fuckin doubt it. Set for fuckin life tha boy. An anyway, it doesn't always wirk like tha, y'know, yer doan av ter uv bin brought up on-a New Gurnos t'be a fuckin nutter like, ah no, a mean, look at fuckin Ikey Pritchard – from a lovely little village in-a mountains an ee's totally off is box like. Ah yeh, doesn't matter whir yer from like, yew can still get damaged in transit. A still remember Ikey freakin out the time in Jester's courtyard when ee found out tha Oily ad buggered off with a ton-a Phil's money, money tha Phil owed t'Ikey; yeers ago iss was, but al never ferget the fuckin rage an hatred an need t'harm in Ikey's face . . . fuckin frothin at-a mouth ee was like, an a can still remember what ee said:

—Yer's wha we fuckin do, right? We gerrer fuckin axe. We get fuckin Oily. We old the cunt's ands down on this table yer an we av is fuckin fingers off one by fuckin one, both fuckin ands, mun, yer fuckin ear me, boy? Maybe leave im is fuckin thumbs if ee begs enough so's ee can still av a fuckin wank like, but ee'l never nick fuck all again.

Course, Roger, Gareth, Phil an all ee other sickos wir well up fer this like but I fucked off t'Florida so a never found out what happened like. A wonder wha did . . . ah yeh, an a wonder if Colm ever got off with tha girl, wha was er name now . . . Mererid was it? No, Mairead, thass right, not a bad lookin bint either. Drank like a fuckin navvy, tho, a seem t'remember.

A tell yer, mun, since av been in-a States, me head's all over-a fuckin place. Ass wha livin in America does for yer, fucks up yer attention span. Fuckin evrythin's movin all-a time over thir, on-a go non-stop, ad breaks evry five fuckin minutes like, fuckin ad breaks within bastard ad breaks. Thir ar parts uv life over thir that a rirly fuckin hate; most uv the people I know ar spoilt tossers fer one, ey never fuckin walk anywhir ey always drive an en ey go on about a rainforests an ee ozone layer, honest, it's fuckin 'Afro-American' in one breath an 'niggers' in-a next. One twat defended imself by sayin that it was OK t'sey 'niggers' cos they use the wird themselves; ee couldn't see-a difference like which is tha they're black an ee's as white as a fuckin sheet. It's fuckin bollacks it is, all uv it, mun, fuckin political correctness of tha kind's juss fuckin cheap virtue if yew ask me, lip service like, it's a fuckin cop-out, a way uv deludin emselves tha they cur about the planet an ethnic minorities when rirly, deep down, ey don't cur about anythin sept emfuckinselves. Thick bastards n all, most-a em. 'Wales? Oh, ain't that abroad somewhere?' One daft fucker thought it was in Germany.

God, me fuckin head . . . bouncin all over-a fuckin shop it is. A need a pee.

A get up an go to-a bog. Yer's a couple uv fellers in red an green UMBRO footy tops quietly makin eyr way through a two-litre bottle-a blue label Smirnoff. Ey look pissed, an pissed off n all; Wales must-a fuckin lost agen. No surprises thir, mun. One a em gives me a wink as a pass:

—Alright, boy?

—Ah yeh, a say, an lock meself in a bog.

The stainless-steel pan's all overflowin with brown-smeared bog roll an lumpy turds so a piss in-a sink. British fuckin rail mun, cheeky bastards aye; charge extortionate amounts for eyr fares like an don't even clean ther toilets. Disgustin. Ah yeh, am already beginnin t'miss-a disinfected cleanliness uv-a States, evrythin so spotless an germ-free. A wish for a moment that a had some coke t'chop up on-a side like t'make iss journey go faster but a haven't so a think no more about it. Bollax. Could do with a drink tho.

A swill me face in the sink an go smilin to-a buffy car whir a buy four cans-a warm bitter an tip one-a em into a plastic glass. A much prefer me beer out-a glasses like, it's easier, yer can take big gulps, yer can bite at it like yer eating it . . . but iss is a mistake cos the train's rockin all over a place like as it tirns into-a Dyfi estuary an a beer's sloshin over a rim uv-a glass an on me way back a spill some on the fit, sleepin girl oo wakes up an gasps like an a say sorry an go back t'me seat with a beamer. Fuck. No chance-a talkin to er now like, av soaked er *and* er fuckin book, cheese an bacon Flann or whatever it's fuckin called . . . should-a used that, tho, that spillage, as an ice-breaker . . . maybe a will . . .

A look over at her dryin herself with a paper hanky. —Dead sorry about that, a say. —It's these bloody trains, all over-a place ey ar, aren't they? Ar yew OK thir, djer need a hand?

A start ter get up out uv me seat but she waves me back an shakes er head vigorously.

—No, God, no, I can manage. Just stay right where you are please.

371

A sit back down. Please yer bleedin self. Only offered ter help, yew snooty bleedin cow.

A lissen ter an old punk compilation on me Walkman an stir out-a window. Not far from Aber now, ah no. . . . Dyfi Junction, Machynlleth, Borth, Aber. Nirly thir like. A good thing about train journeys like is a constant movement; ah yeh, a fuckin hate bein still, me, it's not fuckin natural I don't reckon. If it moves, it lives like, at's all er is to it, mun. Simple as tha. Stasis results in brain-rot, stagnation, and death. Easy equation. Not tha a lirnd *that* in fuckin school; school taught me fuck all rirly, now a think back on it. All a important stuff av ever lirnd a lirnd after a left school, in-a pubs, factories, through me friends . . . an it's true, innit, ey, yew need t'move t'servive an thir's more than one type-a servival, people leave eyr omes like them in Y Wladfa like an ey do so not only t'escape danger an stuff like but also parts uv emselves, ah yeh, ey escape from betrayal an murder n stuff like cos if they stay in the one place too long then that's wha happens to them, at's wha they end up like. Ah yeh, movement's the thing, a only thing, but al be at Mach soon whir a hafter change an thir may be a long fuckin wait thir, like thir was at both Birmingham an Shrewsbury earlier t'day. Standin about doin fuck all, freezin cold on-a platform. Oh well. Christ, a wish a could slow things down . . . or speed things up . . . I don't know . . .

Ah yeh; back from America, home in Wales.

LIAM AND LAURA

God, Liam's up, way way up like, ee always is like but ee carn be on any uv a ard stuff t'night like cos ee's eatin like a fuckin moch an knockin back-a red wine like ee'l die if ee doesn't. Nice t'think that ee's so up cos-a me comin back, like, but . . . that's probly not the case; ee's just up cos ee's Liam, like, that's all thir is to it, mun. An on ee other and like, Laura's way way down, dead quiet like with red panda rings round er eyes as if she's bin crying. Shiz never been much uv a talker, like, Laura asn't, but even Stevie fuckin Wonder could see tha er's somethin up bad with er yer like. Ah yeh, she looks about t'fuckin top erself. An Liam's babblin on, fillin me bowl with pasta like an garlic bread an stuff an fillin me glass

372

with vino; Laura's snifflin an starin at-a table, one arm supportin er head like, ee other pushin food around er plate with a fork. Not a good omen for me visit, this, is it then? Ah no.

—So what's the quality uv gearr like Stateside? Liam asks. —Strohng, is ut?

A shake me head an blow air out through me lips. —Ah yeh. Far stronger'n anythin av ever ad over yer like, no fuckin messin. Honest; just a one-skinner like-a sensi an yer out the fuckin game, boy. It's like, say, three or four hotties uv resin yer. Never ad anythin like it in me life like. Unbelievable.

—Sounds mighty te me.

—Well . . . not rirly like. A mean, snot rirly much fuckin fun; snot like avin a sociable smoke like, or gettin a buzz on before yew go out like or anythin, it's just like, yer know, total headfuck. Paralysis like. Yew carn move out-a yer fuckin chair, mun. Ah yeh. This one time, like, we got these videos t'watch and –

An a tell em a borin story about stayin up with some friends (well, acquaintances like, yer's no real mates over thir, mun) t'watch films like an smoke an gettin so fuckin stoned that a woke up in-a bath, naked, like, in cold water, an only saw-a first five minutes uv a first film which, a still remember, was a strongest fuckin porn that av ever bloody seen like. Ah yeh, in-a first five minutes like it featured shit, an a set uv crockery (ah yeh, a fuckin Yanks'll av ter go over-a top in fuckin evrythin like, altho most uv-a people in this film wir Mexican). In-a first five minutes like. No story or anythin like, just a woman bakin a cake wearin shorts an-a gardener comes in like an next thing yew know it's down with-a trousers an out with-a novel type uv chocolate sauce. Fuckin disgustin it was like. A doan go inter details now tho cos Laura's yer, an yuv got t'censor such stories like when she's around unless yew want daggers stird at yew all fuckin night like. Which a don't. And, besides, she's already upset like.

So anyway, a say. —Am givin it a rest for a bit, like, while am home. Ah yeh, knockin it on-a head for a bit, sortin meself out, y'know.

—Yeh. A was just ahskin tho like cos ye rememburr Mickah? Out in Abergynolwyn?

A nod. —Im with Trapper-a dog like?

—That's the wahn. Well ee's been cultivatun some superrskunk in is shed an av nevurr smoked gearr like ut in all me life. Fair fuckin freaked me ou', din ut, babe?

Laura juss nods.

—Thought a was losin the fuckin head. Voices, panic, the fuckin wurrks, put the fuckin heart crossways in me. Like an acid trip so ut was. Rememburr ut?

He turns t'Laura agen who juss nods agen an Liam snarls. Yer's a bad atmos buildin like so t'change-a subject a ask Liam about tha strange feller ee used t'know, a one oo wrote tha mad guide thing. An ee answers, all deadpan:

—Brown bread. Walked inte the sea. Glug glug. Finito.

Laura yawns an stretches an goes: —Well, am tired. Lovely to see you an everything, Geraint, but av got work in the morning and . . .

—Ah that's orright, a say. —Doan yew bloody worry like. Get yerself off t'bed if yer tired like. An thanks for-a food an-a place t'kip an evrythin.

She kisses me on-a cheek like an goes off t'bed. A watch er walkin out an a notice a big, blue bruise on-a back uv er left leg, on-a fleshy bit, y'know, the calf. A wonder how she got that.

Ah yeh, lovely legs as Laura. Lovely body n all. In fact, shiz lovely all round rirly. Can be a bit snooty at times like but at's juss er way. Av always fancied er, t'tell a truth like. Ah yeh.

A start feelin a bit orny. A didn't get much-a that over in-a States like; yer was one, like, seemed orright, y'know, quite fit like, a started seein er an two weeks later she starts talkin about fuckin marriage like an babies. But not juss talkin about it, like, a mean goin on n on n on in a funny way with an odd look in er eyes like. So that was me, right fuckin out-a thir like, fast as me little legs could carry me. Ah yeh; too fuckin right, mun.

But tha bruise, tho . . . a look over at Liam but ee juss grins an hands me a bag of grass an goes:

—Skin um up then, me mahn, an al bring us both a scoop. Lagurr do yis?

—Yeh, a say, an build a big spliff on-a table. A doan put too much in it like but it still blows both ar fuckin heads off, mun. In a short time Liam's laughin uncontrollably like, but in a slow, drawly way, like a record played too slow or somethin like. I carn fuckin move. Here we go.

So that's it, then, me first night back in Aber; gettin completely fuckin wrecked with Liam. Ah yeh. Ploo sah shange or whatever-a fuck it is, tha French toss. Am sure yew know what-a mean like.

MALCOLM AND MAIREAD

Malcolm's torn between exuberance an worry; ee's juss bin sacked from is chippy job for stickin is fingers in-a till, so ee's free now, which makes for the exuberance, but is ex-boss as threatened t'report im to-a police, which makes for the worry. Is face doesn't know whether t'smile or t'frown like. An ee's speedin off is head an knockin a drinks back like nobody's fuckin business, an ee whiffs somethin terrible uv chip fat an vinegar.

—Ee's a useless fat fucka anyway, ee says, talkin about is ex-boss. —Guess ow much ee pays ya? Two fuckin ninety an owa. Oo can fuckin blame ya fa supplementin ya income out tha bleedin till? An besides, a ownly took manny from tha fuckin till on two, no, three occasions, cos what a did an it was a piecer fuckin piss, ad wait fa tha pissed up beer boys ta come in an eitha owva-charge em an pocket tha diff or unda-change tha cunts, an theid be too fuckin aht uv it ta nowtice. Whair's tha fuckin harm in that, ey? A could make an extrah thirty, forty quid a week sometimes doin that. I fuckin *ad* ta, din I?

—Ah yeh, get-a bloody beers in en yew tight-arsed twat.

—What ya avin?

Ee orders us up a pint an a vodka each like an after wiv finished em we walk across-a town t'Colm's house. Malcolm tells me on-a way like tha Colm n Mairead av bin livin t'gether for some time now, which serprises me; a mean, Colm's a total fuckin speedfreak oo'l shag anythin tha moves, an Mairead's a complete pisshead who will, at times, also shag anythin tha moves. Ah yeh, what a fuckin couple ey must make, eh? Recipe for disaster thir if ever av bloody seen one. Ah yeh.

A reflect, not for the first time, on-a circumstances which brought us all t'gether here. A mean, in a way, we wir sort uv allowed t'choose each other like, we wirnt thrown t'gether by school like or anythin like tha. We juss kind uv sought each other out like, found each other, juss like a group uv drifters driftin t'gether like. Which could mean, a serpose, tha we saw in each other some attractive things, some things tha we liked, some similarities . . . so, maybe, a serpose, in tha respect, choice never came into it like. Maybe wir t'gether cos we ad t'be, like me movin t'Florida; I didn't rirly av any choice in-a matter, it was juss somethin I felt I ad t'do like. Either way, tho, this is not a very comfortable thought, mun.

It tirns out that Colm's not in an asn't bin for a few deys like, an Mairead's lashed out uv er skull, watchin some crappy fuckin game show with tha twat Barrymore on it. She's down to-a last couple uv inches in a bottle uv tequila. She welcomes me with a hug an won't let go like; Malcolm juss stands yer gawpin, big cheesy grin on is face like.

—Jesus, Mairead! Yer chokin me! A carn breathe, mun!

She laughs an falls back on-a couch. Malcolm gets beer from-a kitchen.

—As tha seen Colm on tha travels at all?

—Um, no, we aven't like, no. Yew doan know whir ee is then?

She shakes er head vigorously. —Fuck im anywer, comen tell mih about Hawaii.

—Florida.

—Florida, aye, comen tell us about Florida.

So a tell er basically-a same stories av bin tellin evrybody else like; the drugs, the food, the climate, the beer, the cars, all tha stuff like, an when a tell er tha most Yanks ar fat bastards like she leaps up an pulls er shirt up t'juss below er tits like t'show off er tummy. Should see-a fuckin light in Malcolm's eyes, boy, Christ. Ah yeh, looks like yer's a fuckin searchlight birnin in is skull like.

—Look at mih! Mairead shouts. —Do yuh not think av lost lords uv weight since yuv bin awer? Do yuh not think ah look good?

—Ah yeh, a say but rirly am thinkin that she looks fuckin awful – er ribs're like a bloody xylophone like. She looks like a famine victim. Am shocked. A hadn't noticed it on-a face like but now, Christ, am findin it ard t'believe like that all uv er internal organs ar able t'fit into such a wasted, shrunken space. Fuck's sakes.

—Yew bin dietin, then? a say, juss for somethin t'say like.

—Yep. She sits back down an yew can almost hear Malcolm deflate with disappointment. —Well, bah necessiter, lahk, seen as av got nor fuckin munneh left. Carn afford tuh fuckin eat.

—What, yer whole fuckin inheritance like? Gone?

She nods.

—Christ. Whir?

She shrugs an points to-a tequila bottle. —Ask Colm. If tha can fuckin find im.

Jesus. What was it, eleven, twelve thousand? Fuck me.

Me an Malcolm drink beer an Mairead finishes off-a tequila an then opens a bottle uv wine. Whir-a fuck does she put it all like? Ah yeh, a imagine at any minute it's gunner start leakin out er ears an nose like cos she carn fit any more in er body. Which is sort uv right like, cos arfway through-a wine she collapses on-a floor an stays thir, but drags erself up evry fifteen minutes or so t'gulp more wine an spout gibberish. It's fuckin horrible t'watch like.

And this is sad. This is makin me rirly fuckin sad yer, boy. Ah yeh, am beginnin t'wish ad never even fuckin come back. What's fuckin happenin to evrybody?

—A think, Malcolm says, —tha wid best putta ta bed. Down't ya reckon? We cahn leava ere.

—Yer right.

We pick er up like, me on-a armpits an Malcolm on-a legs, take er through to-a bedroom an lay er down gently on-a bed. The bedroom's a fuckin bombsite like; books, clothes, magazines, dirty plates, empty bottles, crumpled crusty tissues, glasses uv yellow water filled with drowned fag ends. It's a fuckin pit, mun.

Mairead groans and mumbles somethin that a doan quite catch, so a lean closer.

—What yew say, Mair? What is it then, bach?

But shiz juss fuckin rambling, like, a haven't got a fuckin clue what she's goin on about. It's juss fuckin nonsense:

—Super, she says. —Nor, not super wuh *splendid*, thaz it, mah splendid secret wuh . . . never bin any fucker's *that* . . . fuckin never lahk, nor, sall fuckin shite . . . as tha, Geraint, as tha ever bin that? As tha?

377

—No, a say, juss t'calm er down like. She's juss rambling, just fuckin out uv-a game like, talkin shit.

—Florida, Geraint, tell mih aaaalll about . . . tha can get in t'bed wi me if tha wants lahk . . . tell mih stories . . .

—Best leava, Malcolm says quietly. —She's fuckin offa box, man. Fuckin lost it like.

She leans over the side uv-a bed an spews up. Hot sick splashes all over mine an Malcolm's legs an we leap back.

—Ow fa fuck's sakes! New fuckin pairah jeans n awl! Fuck!

Mairead's on er back, gurgling. A turn er over on er side so she won't choke on-a vomit like.

—Dorn fuckin care anywer any more, she's sayin, or at least that's what a think she's sayin. —Got mih fuckin tickets ah hav . . . Spern lahk . . . fuckin times ah hadder younger an not sor fuckin much . . .

She goes on for a bit about Spain for some fuckin reason an then she falls asleep. Ah yeh, snores rumblin in-a chest like.

—Yew think wid best clean iss up like?

Malcolm shakes is head. —Fuck that. Let fuckin Colm do it.

—What about Mairead then? A mean, she might choke like.

—Nah. Ain't appened so far, as it? An shiz like this evry fuckin night.

—A serpose yer right, aye.

—Cam on, let's go find Colm. She's is fuckin responsibility anyway.

—Ah yeh.

We leave the flat. An a carn say am sorry t'do so like.

MARGARET AND COLM

Thir's somethin up, a mean wrong like, with Colm. A mean it; a carn ever remember seein im like iss before like. Snot juss-a drugs like either, ah no, a mean ee's sittin yer in-a pub an ee keeps on puttin is ead in is ands like an mumblin to isself an is clothes-a fuckin filthy an all is teeth-a yellow an is skin, God, is skin's like meat, grisly an undercooked like-a lumps-a fatty lamb yer get in-a cawl in-a pubs round yer. A look at im like an a can almost ear things comin apart inside-a im. Ah yeh, iss fuckin sad

378

mun. An ee only adder pint-a Guinness for is dinner like, ah yeh, an I adder veggie burger an chips with some salad an garlic bread. Fuckin starvin a was like. An Margaret ad six vodkas an a bag-a crisps. She looks fucked as well like.

—Owjer know wid be in ere anyway? Colm asks me. A juss smile at im like. Ee nods an goes: —Yeh, a serpose. Avunt been out uv ere fer the past fuckin month it seems. All dey an all night. Am fuckin wrecked.

An en is eyes go back to-a door uv-a pub agen, waitin no doubt fer is dealer. Al tell yer oo ee's remindin me of; yer know tha feller oo drowned imself in-a sea, Liam's mate like oo wrote tha twatty little local guide thing? Im. Colm's remindin me now uv im; ee was like iss juss before ee walked into-a sea an never came back out agen like. Ah yeh.

A tell agen the same stories tha av told ter Malcolm n Mairead n Liam n Laura an evry other twat like oo av met since av bin back. It's gettin bloody borin it is like, an am sure it's borin ese two wasters n all like cos Maggie keeps rollin ciggies, a mean constantly like, shiz got one in-a gob like an she's rollin another an Colm keeps pickin at scabs on is arms an lookin round-a pub. Ee picks at a particularly chunky one an it starts-a bleed like, watery pussy blood tricklin down is forearm. Ee looks at it n goes: —Fuck, an wipes it up with-a paper anky a got with me dinner.

Ah yeh, iss is gettin more orrible by-a minute, mun.

Mags goes up to-a bar.

—Ey tell us, Geraint, Colm says. —In so far as yer trip ter Florida's beener voyage uv discovery, wha exackly av yer discovered?

A pretend ter think for a minute an then a say: —Tha Americans ar largely tossers, an fat, tha ther beer's sheep's piss, an tha grits taste like shit. Ah yeh; ey look like spunk an ey taste like shit.

Ee laughs an en is face lights up with hope as Margaret comes back from-a bar with a big black geezer in tow, a bloke with dreads oo a don't recognise. Thir's a marked improvement in Mags now, she's smilin an tellin-a black feller some story about a rave or somethin like:

—. . . an a didn't wanner stay outside or go in the barn cos it was all that gabba stuff in thair like, y'know, fuckin duvduvduvduv. So a went in the house instead cos it was all garage in thair n stuff,

379

started dancin n stuff on me own in the kitchen, rairly fuckin goin for it n stuff, an when a looked up thair was these three chickens on the windowsill, just like standin thair n watchin me n stuff. It was fuckin ace.

A black bloke smiles n grunts an Colm goes:

—Jerry, me main man. Wharrav yer got?

The guy looks at me sideways like an Colm says: —No, it's alright, Geraint's OK, an Jerry sits down by im like an ey exchange a great big bag-a pink powder for what looks like a fuck uv a lot uv money like. Am surprised tha Colm's been able t'get is ands on so much like, wha with Mairead's inheritance avin run out now. Wonder whir ee got it from? Margaret's twitchin, rippin up beer mats, scratchin, takin undreds uv little drags on er fag. Jerry – if that's is real name like – steys for a pint an en leaves an Colm n Margaret make a trip each to-a bogs. An en soon Colm's the old Colm a remember like, talkin ten to-a dozen, laughin, singin, drinkin like a fuckin fish, tellin stories which leave me both entertained an slightly soiled, whirlin Mags around-a pub, an a rest uv-a dey's spent runnin from pub t'pub an a carry on drinkin until a crash out back at Colm's around nineish a next mornin like. Iss time it's Mairead's tirn t'av vanished. A collapse on-a couch like an leave Colm n Margaret in-a kitchen, still talkin, still drinkin, sittin on-a greasy floor an lissnin t'music. Couple uv owers later am nudged awake an told t'go down-a pub. I do.

On one level, like, a fuckin great time; funny an mad an full-a energy like. Ah yeh. But on another . . . well, am sure y'know what am tryin t'sey like. Ah yeh.

PAUL AND SIONED

—No, Paul, am not bloody standing for *thattt*, Sioned says, er cheeks beginnin t'glow red with anger. Er eyes ar goin all fiery an er voice is risin. She looks at me. —Am sorry, Geraint, a know yur only back for a short time an yew don't want to hear this but this yer *twattt* . . . She gestures with er and at Paul like, oo's leanin back in is chair, face totally impassive.

—Well, yuh not standin for it, ee says. —Yuh sittin down.

—Oh har har, very fucking funneeee. About as . . . *comedic* as a boil on me arse.

What-a ey arguin about like? Fucked if I know; a switched off about twenty minutes ago like if-a truth be known an juss concentrated on enjoyin me food. Ah yeh, it's such-a bleedin relief t'be able t'get a proper veggie food; in-a States like, yer ask for refried fuckin beans which is about ee only non-meat stuff yer can get in-a take-aways like an ev bin cooked in fuckin lard with big chunks-a gristle floatin about in em. Ah yeh; ee only vegetarians over thir ar the fuckin cows.

Sioned goes on, er voice gettin louder, an ee other people in-a pub ar tryin-a best t'ignore us like.

—Yew said to me the other day thatt yew wur goin to gett my necklace back off Banon, righttt? Yew agree that's what yew said?

Paul juss shrugs.

—And now yur tellin me that yew've lost it.

Paul does nothin.

—No don't just fucking *sturr*, Paul, thatt fucking necklace was my mam-cu's. I want to know whur it is.

God. Ese two av bin at each other's throats since a called up for em iss mornin at Llys Wen. Ee idea like was t'come out for a bite an meet all the others like an make a dey uv it in-a town, y'know, beer, spliff, whatever. Av phoned around an Mal, Colm n Mairead ar on-a wey like, an all a want-a do's settle in for an all-dey sesh. Ah yeh. Paul n Sioned, tho . . . ev got other fuckin ideas like, it seems.

A feel a splash uv wet on me arm an look up t'see whir it's comin from an Paul's completely fuckin soaked, Sioned standin yer above im oldin an empty pint glass. Paul splutters an laughs, all mocking like.

—Well, that told fuckin me, dinnit? A can unduhstand yuh point now. Yes, it's all so clear tuh me now. How could I have been so blind?

—I'm sorry, Geraint, Sioned says. —Al make sure I see yew again before yew go. Preferably without this twatt yur makin a total arse uv imself aye.

She storms out-a pub an Paul goes after er, is teeth gritted an is fists clenched like. Ah yeh, an am juss left fuckin sittin yer like, drippin with beer an twiddlin me fuckin thumbs. An it was my fuckin pint n all, that Sioned threw over Paul. Fuck. Ah well; ee others'll be along soon.

ROGER

Ah, a juss knew-a twat'd be ere, in-a castle like. A juss fuckin knew ut, mun. Ah yeh, a was so sure in fact that a didn't even call up at is house, a juss came straight yer. It alweys as bin is faverit place like, a castle as, an ere ee is on-a war memorial steps like some fucked-up version uv-a knight, is armour iss orrible old overcoat covered in all kinds-a muck n stuff. Ah yeh. Yer's a bottle-a wine in is and an ee looks arf cut like.

—Yer twat! Ee yells when ee sees me. —A hird yew wir back like!

Ee jumps up an gives me a hug which a reciprocate for only a second-a two like cos a), av never rirly liked touchin other blokes, it fuckin embarrasses me like, an b), ee stinks. Judgin by-a whiff ee asn't fuckin washed isself or is clothes since a fuckin left for America. Ah yeh, a mean it; ee fuckin mings.

—So yer back then ar yer, from a land uv-a free to-a land uv-a fucked?

A laugh. —Looks like it, aye. Only for a bit, tho, only for a bit like.

—Yeh, so wiv got a fuckload-a drinkin t'cram in then, ant we ey? Load-a ground ter cover, mun. Wid bess get fuckin started.

It's good t'see im. Ah yeh, it's bin good t'see em all a s'pose like. Like all ee others, Roger looks wasted t'fuck, but en ee always as like, so yer's no difference thir. It used t'surprise me with Roger, like, ow anyone could look as bad as im an still be fuckin alive. A take im for a pint-a two in-a Angel (whir ee taps me for twenty quid; ah yeh, does anythin ever change?) an we arrange t'meet in-a Castle pub at night, an ee fucks off t'do whatever ee does with is days like an I juss spend ee arvo walkin around-a town like, seein-a old sights, callin on people, y'know, stuff like tha. A day passes, an in a Castle later an Roger's on time for once and, wonders ul never fuckin cease, ee's ad a bleedin bath an is wearin clean clothes; black jeans an a yellow T-shirt with black letters on it that say FFYCD. Nice t'see ee's finally ditched tha orrible fuckin snorkel parka tha ee always used t'wir, with-a generations uv muck on it like. Ee's movin all slow like an isn't entirely thir so ee's obviously usin somethin, some kind a downer my guess would be, but fuck ee looks appy so what's-a fuckin problem like? If it makes yer appy, if it makes things easier, en go on an fuckin do it, boy. Too fuckin right. An at least, when Roger's off is ead on-a brown or-a downers, y'know yer safe like; ah yeh, Roger with-a brown is like a reverse Jekyll an Hyde – ee's a fuckin monster til ee shoots up like, when ee becomes quiet as a lamb. Ah yeh, Roger's addiction should be sponsored by-a state for-a safety uv others. Too fuckin true.

A get shit-faced but Rog doesn't drink much an when-a boozer shuts we start eadin back across-a town t'call on Colm n Mairead, opin tha Colm'll av some uppers cos wir flaggin a bit like. On-a way we stop t'buy fags from-a all-night garage and, down Great Darkgate Street, Roger pulls us up outside Victoria Wine. Ee looks at me like all yellow in-a street light an a can see tha fuckin glint in is eyes, tha mad flicker a know only too fuckin well.

—Cunts tha we ar, wuv only gone an forgotten ter get enny teyk-outs, an we, ee says, grinning. —An yew know wha fuckin Colm's like, don't yew; think ee's gunner slip us enny fuckin billy without gettin ennythin in retirn, mun? Fuck no. Tight as arses tha one, innit?

Ee slips is and inside is jacket.

—An ennywey, a doan know about yew, like, but a know I don't wanner sit up all night on-a whizz without ennythin ter fuckin drink like. Carn av whizz without a drink, like, can we? Fuckin awful, that is. Need somethin t'take-a edge off, boy.

A nod, thinkin; oh fuck, as ee pulls a big, chunky glass ashtray out-a is jacket. A noticed im liftin it out-a pub before like but didn't think anythin uv it; amongst Roger's other vices like, yer's also a smidgeon uv kleptomania thrown yer in-a mix. Ah yeh. Ee looks up n down-a road t'check-a coast's clear an en looks back at me an goes:

—Remember yer isstry lessons, mun? A oes undod? Remember tha?

—Yeh.

—Well? Is thir?

'A oes undod'; Roger an is daft fuckin little games like. A know wha ee's up to yer; when Owain Glyndŵr eld is parliament in Machynlleth like, ee stood up in front-a all-a other delegates from-a different kingdoms in Wales (an Scotland, an France, an Spain, if yer b'lieve all-a stories like) an asked 'A oes undod', an evryone is supposed t'av stood up like an yelled 'Undod!' So that's wha Roger's gettin at; ee wants t'know if am still with im, like, ee's askin if yer's unity. It's some kind uv daft little stupid test uv me Welshness or somethin, checkin tha a know me history. Fuckin Roger. Daft little games ee plays sometimes like. Ah yeh, ee does nothin but slag Wales off most uv-a time an en ee comes out with somethin like this. Fuckin screw loose, mun, aye.

—A oes undod? ee asks agen an a look at im an go:

—*Course* a fuckin is mun, an ee chucks-a ashtray through a big window uv-a offy like an yer's such a fuckin CRASH an glass flies evrywhir an a alarm goes BBRRREEEEEEEEEEEE! an-a quiet night becomes fuckin chaos.

We kick the big spikes-a glass out-a frame like an climb in through-a hole (a realise later, back at Colm's, that a cut me arm), glass crunchin beneath ar feet like, ead straight to-a spirits section an fill ar fuckin pockets; whisky, gin, vodka, rum, all kinds-a fuckin stuff like an we jump back outside an Roger fuckin nutter that ee is clicks is fingers an goes back in. Am standin yer like fuckin shittin meself, ee alarm rippin me head apart, an Roger goes back fuckin in.

—Roger! Fuck sakes, mun! Less fuckin go!

—Old on! ee yells from somewhir inside-a shop. —Fergot me fags! An yew carn av-a whizz without-a drink an yew carn av-a whisky without-a chaser, can yer!

Ee reappears with-a big grin on is face an is pockets bulgin with fag packets, carryin two four-packs-a Wrexham lager an we leg it down Baker Street, on to a prom an then down on to-a beach, walkin close to-a wall like so we carn be seen from a-prom above. A get me fuckin shoes filled with wet sand an grit like but we make it safely back t'Cliff Terrace an Colm comes to-a door, staggerin, clearly out uv is tree.

—Jesus! All tha bevvy fer me, is i'? An Roger – what the fuck av yer done ter yerself, la, yer look fuckin clean! Fall inner fuckin sea didjer anyway come in come in a man with a bevvy's always fuckin welcome ere. Mairead! Get some glasses washed!

An a fuckin great night follows like. Ah yeh, sometimes tha can happen. So much for cleanin up tho.

A stey pissed an stoned til a retirn t'Florida five days later. A doan clean me shoes out, even tho eyr uncomfortable like, til am on American soil, in ee airport like; ah yeh, yer's now a tiny part-a Wales blowin across a fuckin runway mun. Aberystwyth grits in-a Florida sun. Ah yeh, a left sand n shit in me shoes for a whole fuckin flight like; sentifuckinmental, fuckin *sore* thing t'do. Still. A might never go back again like. Oo knows what's goin ter happen?

From *A Personal Guide to West Wales*, anonymous authorship, privately printed, p. 89

The unifying principle, the common squalid property of all forms of life-in-growth is competition, competition for light, air, nourishment, space to grow and feel and, primarily, move. Like vegetation, rocks too necessarily suffer the encroachment of aliens in weed-form and, like vegetation, need to banish or perish: thus wars, heroically sustained. Such clashes are fought out against a background of extinction, the loser's boon, a place grey as granite which crackles with static and endures for ever and for ever and for ever. So the unusual height of the coastline here is due only to the saw and slice of the sea; one element, one condition of matter performs a guerrilla raid on the other's magic arsenal and turns it to its own advantage. Such things do occur. The submerged forest at Borth, for instance, treetops at low-tide like carious teeth, evinces the sea's encroachment but not necessarily the surrender of the land, a demonstration of monumental resistance. Such things do occur. Cantre'r Gwaelod perhaps truly is a city sunk in the Cardigan Bay; conger eels may sit upright in the chapel pews at vespers, dolphins draw coaches down the main street over moss-fronded cobbles, Jones the Fish now *is* a fish selling slivers of suicides to worms rag and lug. Such things do occur.

THEY ARE FLOATING

THEY ARE FLOATING out of the swirls of mist like chimeras a-shimmer or phantoms, gradually regaining shape and dimension and locomotive idiosyncracies and at last declaring themselves as entities other than the volcanic stones, black and blasted, which sentinel here, Tan-y-bwlch, or the south beach. Swathes of dawn sunlight scythe softly through the layered mist, striping their mottled faces, pale and drifting, skin ash-blackened, hair reeking of salt and woodsmoke. Quiet they are, very quiet, except for their boots which crunch and crunch again on ground stone. Hidden seagulls shriek as if on fire.

Colm breaks the silence: —Wha was tha noise? He asks, looking around him, but receives no answer. —Did anyone else ear it? Tha screech? Sounded like some pathetic lost soul gropin frantically in the ether, pleadin desprutly fer the retern uv some kinder corporeality but knowin tharrit's doomed to eternal iserlation an agony. Maybe it was Sharon.

Malcolm splutters with laughter.

—Fucker yis ohn abou'? Liam's voice, lost in the mist.

—Ee's talkin is shite agern, says Mairead. —Asn't tha wukd it out yet? That Colm's the king uv the bullshitters?

—Fuck off, you. Least a can sey summun a bit more fuckin intrestin than 'Wher's me booze' or 'As anyone gorrah sper can?' At's all yer ever fuckin sey.

Colm's voice is venomous, spat into the mist which seems to curdle like clotted cream before his sallow face, his red and sleepless eyes boring like drills at the stumbling shadow which he takes to be Mairead. Which means that his next barb is launched at Antonella:

—In fact, I aven't erd you sey any'in either funny or intrestin or even inner slightest bit fuckin unusual or serprisin in any wey for fuckin, well, ever. A doan fuckin see *wha* fuckin right *you've* got ter –

—OH FOR CHRRRIST'S SAKE! WILL YOU STOP THIS FUCKIN SQUABBLING!

Sioned seems to be just a loud voice, disembodied on the foggy beach. Unseen waves hiss on the shore and the seagulls continue to cry.

—All av hurd all bloody *nighttt* is people at each other's throats. Gettin at each other for no bloody rrreason that I can see an am just about fucking *sick* uv it I am.

Colm is puzzled. —Is tha Sioned? Wher ar yer? I thought yer wen ome ages ago. All a can ear's yer voice.

—You an thuh rest uh bleedin Wales, Paul's voice mutters.

—That's not Sioned, Colm, Mairead says. —That's tha conscience speakin lahk. Unpleasant, int it?

Malcolm laughs again, somewhere.

—Stop bloody winding people up, Colm, for Christ's sake, Sioned continues. —Give us all a bit uv bloody peace, man, aye.

—Am fuckin well not! All am doin is defendin meself, quite fuckin rightly as well in my opinion, agenst Mairead's gratuitous scurrilities.

—Oh Christ.

Sioned asks: —Colm, whurr arr you?

—Over ere. On yer left, a think. Why?

—No, a dunt mean that, a mean, arr you on a beach in Wales afterr a night's drinking by a log fire or arr you prretending to be some kind uv poncey lawyer in a London courtroom? Cos thatt's what yur sounding like, boy.

—Neither. Am in the seventh cercle uv fuckin hell.

Nothing is said then for some time as they ghostlike drift and crunch across the pebbles and shells until Sioned's voice, rootless and beautiful, cuts through the mist, an auditory beacon. The sad tune and the sounds of the words calm each wasted walker and create around them each one a receptacle into which they can pour whatever longings and fears have been both eroding and driving them since yesterday's dusk when the first bottles were opened. The song leads them like a lifeline through the sharp unyielding rocks and dense fog, and they hold on to it gratefully:

O Iesu mawr, rho'th anian bur
I eiddil gwan mewn anial dir,
I'w nerthu drwy'r holl rwystrau sy
Ar ddyrys daith i'r ganaan fry.

Pob grâs sydd yn yr eglwys fawr,
Fry yn y nêf, neu ar y llawr,
Câf feddu'r oll-eu meddu'n un,
Wrth feddu d'anian Di dy hun.

Mi lyna'n dawel wrth dy draed,
Mi ganaf am rinweddau'th waed,
Mi garia'r groes, mi nofia'r don,
Ond cael Dy anian an fy mron.

The song ends as they stumble out of the fog bank and stand startled and blinking at each other in the weak and watery sunlight on the potholed harbour road. The Pen Dinas monument punctures the rising mist in the sky above them, some thousands of yards away. Liam, Laura, Sam and Antonella drive away home; Malcolm, Sioned, Paul, Colm and Mairead stand unsteadily squarely, on the brink of exhaustion and desperate for sleep but each fearful in equal measure of the prospect of aloneness and the approaching horror of sobriety. Paul, in particular, is feeling shipwrecked; he stands swaying with mist swirling around his feet making little whimpering noises in his throat as he ignores the ensuing conversation:

—Ey, wharrabout Roger?

—Ah, er'l bih fine . . . ah checked on him bifore wuh left an ee wuh still breathing.

They stand in silence, wind lifting their lank hair.

—Well. What now?

—What's a time?

Mairead wriggles her wrist so that the sleeve of her loose blue shirt goes up her arm and squints at her watch: —Ner quarter past seven lahk. Twelve minutes past.

Malcolm sighs. —Fuck. What do we do now then?

Colm spits. —No fuckin booze, no more drugs . . . what the fuck *can* we do? Wer fucked, la.

—Or we can shur the bottle uv vodka which *I* had the foresighttt

391

to stash under Mairead's couch before we came outtt, says Sioned, smiling.

—What?

—Yer messin.

She shakes her head. —Strrraight up, boy. Unopened, blue label, an even orange juice in the frridge.

Malcolm beams. —Fuckin blindin!

—Tha's a star, Sioned, Mairead grins, and crushes her in a hug. The tortuous, long and painful hours until the pubs open again can now be filled and, unexpected bonus, enjoyed, and the promise of such quickens and lightens their long journey home. Hangovers can be postponed once again. They move along the harbour road with steady step now except Paul who stumbles after them blindly, utterly unaware of where they are going or why they are going there.

And the mist leaves the planet in drifting airborne rags. Somewhere on the beach, between two boulders by a comatose Roger with a dirty syringe for a bedmate, embers continue to smoulder – perhaps the red-hot eggs of a bird plumed in flame.

SIONED

IT'S HORRIBLE – VILE. It's full of maggots – squirming in its eye sockets, in its ears – wriggling through its caked and rotten fleece. I don't want to look at it like but something is compelling me to – making me turn my head to stare. It's like something from a nightmare – making me feel sick. It's horrible.

This far up the mountain, the wind howls and whips – I'm sure if it wasn't so blowy, I'd be able to smell this dead ram here, smell its death and blackness. The mountainsides around me are dotted with white blobs of sheep – which ones are dead and which are alive I can't tell like – and several people – a different kind of sheep I suppose – are on all fours, picking the magic mushrooms and putting them into plastic bags – eating some as well straight out the ground. And I wish they'd hurry up cos I'm bored and fuckin freezing and can't wait to stop off at the pub in Derwenlas for a pint or ten on the way home like – that's if I can persuade Paul to do so – he's driving, see. Forget your fucking mushies, boy – can't beat a good skinful – oh no.

Liam, on the hillside below me, starts singing – the wind carries his voice up to my ears:

> Ooooooooooooooohhhh . . .
> There *was* an old woman an she lived in the woods
> A wéile wéile wáile
> There was an old woman an she lived in the woods
> Down by the river Sáile

On the green slope below Liam – hundreds of yards away like – I see Paul look up and squint at me. He grins and flicks the V and I do it back with both hands. He shouts something I don't hear.

—WHAT?

He shakes his head and carries on picking – the wind blowing his top tight against his back – I can see the knuckles of his spine – a little crescent shadow under each one.

> She had a baby it was three months old
> A wéile wéile wáile
> She had her baby it was three months old
> Down by the river Sáile

The cold wind blasts my exposed skin and stings the cuts on my hands and face that I got when we got lost in the woods earlier and Malcolm led us off the track – into a tangle of bushes and brambles and thorns – sharp sticks, spiky leaves in the skin. I imagine we'll sit and compare wounds in the pub later, but mine'll be the best – or the worst – whichever way you look at it. I caught a right bastard belt on the chin when I slipped off that mossy rock – these bloody boots – no fucking grip on them aye. They're called hiking boots like but they're not, really, that's just marketing like – fibs, crap – they look good like but, well, for hiking in these bastard mountains you'd be better off wearing a pair of fucking carpet slippers. And seventy quid nearly – rip-off – waste.

> She stuck a pen-knife in the baby's head
> A wéile wéile wáile
> She stuck a pen-knife in the baby's head
> Down by the river Sáile

One of those bastard fucking jets screams over and scares me shitless – fucking cowering in my hood I am. I can't tell you how much I hate them bleeding things – they give me the darks they do – loud, threatening – you can be out walking by a lake or something feeling perfectly happy with everything and then one of those twats roars over and ruins it all and that's it then – you're on a downer. Oh, the pilots need their training they say – aye – but no one can tell me that it's not also a show of strength – a threat – like, see what we've got to destroy you with – we can blow you to fuckin bits if we want. Saunders Lewis had the right idea aye – burn the fucking things up – or down – too fucking right, boy. Personally, I don't see how the pilots can be properly trained for warfare unless they're being shot at with massive cannons – no prizes for guessing who'd be the first to volunteer for *that* job.

—Oh Jesus. Looker tha.

Colm's looking down at the rotten sheep – his face all screwed up.

—Malcolm seen this, as ee? Ee'l be after its ed ter add to is collection when ee does. He gestures at it with his hand. —Yer see what ther is ter look forwuds to, Sion? Werms, maggots, decay, stink . . . ar bones'll be bared ter the wind an the gaze uv wasters. Wharrer fuckin mess. This is all we fuckin ar, innit?

Oh shit – he's off on one again. —Speak for your fuckinself, boy, I say. —No fuckin wool on me like. Or horns. Or flies.

—No, that's true, that's true. Still, tho, ar realities ar very thin; it only takes one wee step sideways out uv ar lives an wer in the swarmin horrors which lie under evrythin. That's all it fuckin takes.

—Oh Christ. And anyway, why arcn't you down there with all the others, pickin?

He shrugs and shakes his head: —A doan use hallucinogens. Or hardly ever. Aven't done any in ages like. A fuckin hatem, ter tell yer the truth. Doan agree with me, never av.

> They pulled the rope an she got hung
> A wéile wéile wáile
> They pulled the rope an she got hung
> Down by the river Sáile

We sit down – away from shite an dead sheep like – and smoke, watching the others crawl round below us after fungus. Paul is now rolling down the hill – going at a fair old speed – making siren noises while Malcolm flicks pellets of sheep shit at him. The others watch and laugh. I ask Colm something – just for like – y'know – something to say:

—Colm, the stuff you say, all that beyond stuff that you say like, about death and all that . . . know what I mean?

—Yeh?

—Well, where does it all come from like? Where do you get the thoughts from?

He shrugs – again – and curls his top lip: —Dunno. Me arse sometimes a suppose.

—Yeh, and that's another thing; why are you so obsessed with arses an shit an stuff? You're always goin on about em. Why're you so fascinated like?

He smiles: —I feel the need to mask my divine essence in scatological camouflage. In order to protect it like.

—Oh fuck off.

Malcolm shouts up from the mountainside: —Oi, Colm! Whatja cawl a Scouser in a white shell suit? . . . The bride!

I laugh and Colm shouts back: —I carn ear yer, mate! Yull avter shout louder!

—WHAT DO YA CAWL . . . OH FUCK OFF!

We sit and smoke and stare down into the valley. The wind whistles through my earrings like an incoming bomb, in an old film about the First World War or something.

> And that was the end of the woman in the woods
> A wéile wéile wáile
> And that was the end of the baby too
> Down by the river Sáileeeeeeeeeeeeeeee!

I'll talk Saesnag so you can understand – no bugger'll listen to me if I use my own language like – even though it feels strange – alien in my gob. Even after all these years it still feels bloody alien. I started to learn English when I was – what – thirteen? and even though hardly anyone speaks 'proper' English now like – if they ever fucking did – you'll still find that people don't really listen to you if you don't. They'll hear, like, but they won't bloody *listen*. Don't worry, my English is good – it's bound to be, I've been surrounded by it all my fucking life aye – but, of course, there'll always be bastards who won't listen to you no matter how you speak. To them, everything that doesn't come out of *their* mouths is just noise – not worth paying any attention to – especially the fucking Sais.

Margaret's talking here and is visibly upset – telling me things –

and I must admit it's come as a big bloody shock to me like, the revelation that she's been shagging Colm. I mean – I suspected it, kind of – vaguely like – but now that it's confirmed I don't really know how to react. I love Mairead, but I also care for Margaret and Colm as well – what can you do? These friends, here – these particular ones like – really they're like luggage which I took on board when I started seeing Paul cos he knew them first – before me like – but that doesn't stop me from liking them and classing them as friends, does it? Roger's, well, Roger's not exactly likeable – he's cold and he's hard, like a rock – a burden to know to be honest with you – and when friends burden you with their problems they can be kind of imprisoning – they can sometimes become part of that awful set of things which press down on you and make life difficult – give you the darks like – but, Duw, you're not much more than a twat if you can't lend an ear when your friend's in trouble like. And Margaret – Margaret's so fucking far in the darks that I can hardly fucking see her. Gets like this sometimes, she does – terrible depression like.

Over her shaking shoulder I see Trish and Rhun – in the corner of the pub – buy a wrap of something off Jed. Speed, probably, knowing Trish like. I watch her struggle to get into it like a kiddie with a bag of sweets and I hope Margaret doesn't start to cry because the pub's fairly full and I'll feel dead embarrassed like. And everyone knows me in here – they should do, I've been coming in since I was sixteen – and my sister before me – and my dad – and his dad before him – I know the barman by his first name – it's Rhobert.

—Why's it always happenin t'me, Sion? The blokes a like, the fuckin always with other women an stuff, other women always fuckin get thair fairst like, or a think at fairst the sound an stuff an then they reveal themselves t'be wankers. It's rairly not fuckin fair and I hate it . . . like John, yeh, a know he's a tosser n stuff, but ee's rairly deeply, deeply depressed. Is dad fucked off when John was about fifteen and it rairly fucked him up . . . he's not happy . . .

I'm waiting for another 'and stuff'; she always says that, Margaret does – she uses it like punctuation.

—All the men I meet are either obsessives, or arseholes, violent, or the fuckin married an stuff . . . a mean Reuben! Ee's gone an fuckin killed imself an stuff . . . a never meet anybody decent, or who's fuckin available an stuff. A mean, Mairead's ace, she's sound, what can a do? What can a fuckin do?

—Well . . . you could stop sleeping with her boyfriend for a start.

—It's not that fucking easy, is it? A mean a like him, a rairly rairly like him . . .

—Oh bach . . . Tears run down her cheeks and she puts her head in her hands. Behind her I see Colm and Paul leave the pub – their cheeks bulging like hamsters' with the sandwiches they stole from the darts club buffet earlier. Colm glances at Margaret's back – he looks concerned but he doesn't do anything like – just looks away again and leaves the pub with Paul.

Poor Margaret. There's something in her that seems to attract fucked-up men – I don't know what like – maybe it's got something to do with her reticence – the fact that she's weak on drink and drugs herself – her shyness – large breasts – I don't know. Whatever it is, fucked-up blokes are drawn to it like and some of them prey on it – on her. I remember – a couple of years ago now – I remember her going out one day with her hair all long and lovely and thick and curly – down to her bum it was aye – and she came back a couple of hours later with it all cut off – skinhead like – Sinead O'Connor style. She said that one of the reasons for her getting it done was that she was sick of attracting a certain type of bloke and she wanted to see if having short hair would make any difference. But it was more than that, though – I reckon – I could tell like – it was also a big FUCK OFF to all the things that were bothering her – and there was – and is – plenty of those like – there is for everybody, I know like, but . . . well, Margaret's not a happy girl.

—Everybody's just so fucked up n stuff, she sniffles. —No one a know is happy. A mean, y'know Dewi? The bloke with the wife Cerys who is a, erm, whatjer call it when you're addicted t'stealing things?

—Malcolm.

She laughs – a small, frightened noise.

—No, y'know, when it's like a disease . . . well, she's got it, anyway, an the other day like she was arrested after a ninety miles an hour car chase from here to fuckin Rhayader. A seven-year-old kid in the back of her car n stuff, an a massive mound of nicked stuff as well, including the fuckin car. Three police cars chasin er like . . . only caught her after she ran off the road into a tree; broke her pelvis and some ribs, the kid smashed all his little face up against the back uv the seat like . . . why's evrythin so fucked up, Sioned? Evrythin's fucked up. Whyer people so fuckin mad n stuff? You n Paul seem t'be the only sane couple around rairly . . . evrybody's unhappy, or addicted, or on the run . . . or a kleptomaniac, yeh, that's the waird, Cerys is a kleptomaniac . . .

Over her shoulder, Trish – drunk – is still struggling with the speed wrap. The people around her look on hungrily – twitching like. She twists it and wrenches it and suddenly it *bursts* open and sprays fine, white powder all over her velvet skirt. She throws back her head and laughs.

Paul, now . . . now there's a question. Sane, yes, I mean compared to some others we are sane – although some of the things that Paul says sometimes do baffle me – like we were watching telly the other night – a programme about stoats it was – they were eating a rabbit – and he suddenly sat up and shouted: —Captain Campion! Wouldn't tell me what he meant – although I don't think I asked – just one of his daftnesses like. He's forever doing things like that he is – probably just to wind me up like. Like the time he just disappeared – up at Llys Wen this was – for ages – I looked all over the fucking house for him – couldn't find him anywhere like – went into the big trunk freezer (which Paul nicked from one of the places where he used to live) – for something to cook for our tea and guess who was in there like – with frost in his hair and stubble and fern patterns of ice on his glasses – big stupid grin on his face. Bloody shat myself I did. When he got out I asked him what it was like in there and he said: —Freezing. That's all. He'd been in there half a bloody hour nearly.

So – OK like – not sane, then, and certainly not straight like – I like a drink, and Paul likes that as well and also a bit of E and acid – whatever he can get really – but compared to the others . . . No, there is one thing that he's addicted to – and I'm sick of it like – it hurts, it scares me, it shows no respect – I'm fucking sick of it aye – his temper. He likes to hit me. He's a twat for doing that

. . . yes, there are things which I like a lot about him — there's a kind of innocence there — I mean, take robbery — Malcolm and Colm go out on huge sprees like — every week they steal mounds of books, drink, food — I know, I've seen them do it like — I live in the same house as Malcolm and his cupboard is always much better stocked than mine — and Roger, God, he must've broken into every public building and private residence this side of the Dyfi estuary — but Paul . . . last week in Leo's — up there on the Waun like — we were at the checkout and I could see him going all red and sweaty like and trembling, twitching to get outside — I knew he'd nicked something, it was fucking obvious — and he gets outside and he was grinning, chuffed to bits, and what had he stolen? Batteries. And a packet of hairslides. And they weren't even big batteries — little diddy ones they were — useless like. Crap. Yet he acted like he'd knocked *The Black Book of Camarthen* out of the National Library or something. And the freezer — he'll get all panicky over some hairslides and some batteries — but he'll take a huge freezer out of someone's house and not bat an eyelid. I don't understand him — I don't.

The violence, though . . . Colm's got his rages, as has Mairead — Roger's got his psychosis — and Paul's got his kicking-the-bin fits on the promenade — and, of course, his slapping — punching — shoving — throwing — me. Which is typical really of that side of him that is cowardly and insipid — he wouldn't pick a fight with a bloke if he can use me as an outlet for his anger like — fuck no. And I can always tell when he's about to hit me — he gets a faraway, kind of absent look in his eyes — he starts to pant — I fucking hate it . . . Other things, too; he only lasted two lessons on his Welsh language course (an attempt to build better communication between us: HA), and he flatly refuses to tell that mad bastard Richard where to go. And he's always hanging round us, Richard is, he's bloody insane — only asked to get into bed with us the other night, didn't he — standing there in the moonlight at the side of the bed — his scrawny hard-on inches from my face. I know — he's mad — he needs help like — but enough's fucking enough. Paul should tell him to fuck off like — he's the only person Richard'll listen to. He's good with engines, Paul is — he can fix them sure enough — find out what's wrong like – but when it comes to human relationships – he's useless – complete crap.

—A hate it Sion, a rairly fuckin do, a don't think a can stand it any more . . .

Trish is now the centre of a feeding frenzy – people are on all fours around her – licking her skirt – taking rolled-up fivers to her woolly tights. She's laughing her head off – very amused.

—It just gets wairse n wairse . . .

The pub door opens and Colm and Paul come back in on a blast of cold air – with Liam as well – all three of them off their faces on something – it's obvious. Liam's got his amyl bottle stuck to his nose – as always – his face all red and sweaty – roaring. Paul grins at me and takes his glasses off – I see Colm look up at his face and say:

—But, Mr O'Riordain, without your glasses you're . . . you're . . . beautiful!

—A just can't see any fuckin hope anywhair . . . the whole thing's like a nightmair . . . what am a goin t'do?

There's tears in her eyes again so a give her a cwtch – a great big one and bollox to embarrassment. Liam walks past with a pint.

—Ah cheer up now, the pair o'yis. Smile anna wurld smiles wuth ye. Cry an ye –

—Cry alone, yeh, Margaret snaps. —Which only goes t'confairm me suspicions that most people are unfeeling, selfish, mercenary fuckin bastards.

—Christ. What's twisted *yur* fuckin knickers? Fuckin hell. Try an cheer sumwahn up an look what ye get. Jesus.

Liam goes off an Margaret cries against my shoulder. I look to see if Colm's watching but he's not – he's got his back to us playing on the quiz machine with Paul. I tell her not to worry and that things will work out OK but they're just words, aren't they? That's all they are – just fucking words like.

There's a bunch of twats up at the bar – you know the type – loud, beer bellies, rugby shirts – trying to wind Malcolm up cos he's English. I liked them before – when they were singing 'Gafr Goch' like – but now they're just being arseholes. They start singing

'Men of Harlech' and Malcolm joins in with his own words – a West Ham song like:

> Ian Wright fucks his mother
> Tony Adams fucks his brother
> All the Arsenal fuck each other
> Fuck off, Arsen-aaaawl!

He then shakes his head sadly and says: —Should neva ev picked that cunt Adams ta captain the England squad, fuckin *neva* . . . that's where it awl started ta gow wrong, I reckon . . .

One of the twats shouts over: —That the best yew can do, boy? Footy players? Try an name one famous Englishman who int a footy player. Go on then, less see if yer can. Jes one.

Malcolm puts his head in his hands.

—See! See! Yer can't, can yer!

—Oh fa fuck's sikes! What abaht tha Prince av fuckin Wales, then, ey? What fuckin nationality's ee?

I'm sure he's exaggerating his accent like – trying to wind them up in turn. Right bloody arseholes they are like aye. Met hundreds like them, I have. I mean, I'm not overly keen on the English myself, like, in general – you know – as a race – but some individuals are perfectly alright. Fucking beer boys like these, though – they were talking before – too loudly – about hiraeth like – and to people like them, hiraeth is just another form of and justification for blatant bloody racism. Twats they are like. It's not only the English who are racist – oh no – that's a fucking myth, boy, that racism's an English thing like – sometimes what starts off as anti-racism can become mutated into racism itself – and something as precious as hiraeth becomes like Aryanism was to the Nazis. Hiraeth is – it's – well, it's unexplainable really – or at least untranslatable like. It's like – the sense of a place – landscape – language – history – culture – all the big stuff which makes you what you are. Nothing can grasp the meaning of it like. I knew a bloke once – not very well like – I think he was in Liam's class at university (not that Liam lasted long in there like) – he wrote a book about hiraeth once – well, something quite close to hiraeth like – in the form of a guide book to the local area. It was never published like, but he photocopied it a few times and gave a copy to Liam – I read parts of it the other month when I was up at his flat and everyone else crashed out. It was nonsense – crap – I couldn't understand a bloody word hardly aye. But the bloke – the author of it, like – he went mad and ended up in North Road – soon as they let him out he flipped and went straight back in again like. When they let him out for the second time he walked straight from the doors of the hospital to the beach and just didn't stop walking like – straight into the sea – drowned himself like – poor bastard. Sometimes I think that trying to explain hiraeth will send you that way – daft – suicidal. But he was touched by the Teg, that one, the Tylwyth Teg – as my old mam-cu might say.

Malcolm hands me a drink – triple dry Martini. I feel like getting rat-arsed tonight – properly fucking lashed like aye – I love alcohol – I've had one drink at the very least – and usually much much more – every day now for about three years. Can't fucking leave the stuff alone – or maybe that should be the other way round.

—Some right cunts up at tha bar. Malcolm shakes his head.

—I know, I heard. Won't fucking shut up will they like.

—Right buncha fuckin wankas. Where's Colm got ta?

—Last I saw of him he was in the other room talking to a load of Scousers.

—Mighta fuckin guessed. Tha owld safety in numbas routine. Funny ow alla Scousers stick tagetha innit?

—Yeh. Apart from that one who drinks in the Ship and Castle – y'know the one? – the permed hair and moustache?

—Yeh! Im oo looks like Terry off *Brookside*? Colm hates him, danny. Memba he tried ta chat Mairead up once an Colm wanted ta kill im? Went fuckin banzai ee did. Paul an Liam had ta howld im back.

The twats at the bar start singing again:

> Mi sydd fachgern ieuanc ffôl
> Yn byw yn ôl fy ffansi

Malcolm pulls a face and jerks his head at the lower room – we go down into it. Colm's now talking to a girl with dreadlocks and about thirty earrings in one ear – it's just like one ear

is metal. Liam's drunk and is hugging a bloke in glasses, saying:

—Ah doan fuckin curr if ye are a fuckin Proddy. Suren wurr ahl
fuckin brothers now eh? Ceasefire, mahn, the fuckin war's ovurr
so ut is, the fuckin warr's ovurr.

We perch down on the end of a bench and too late I realise that
I'm sitting next to that animal Ikey – Ikey fucking Pritchard. He's
pissed off his face – aggressive, belligerent – and he leans over and
starts talking to me. I know him vaguely like – I mean, everybody
knows who he is anyway – but not well enough so that he can
grab my leg while he's breathing spewy-smelling words in my face.
Huge hand on my leg, a cross tattooed on each knuckle – his little
finger touches my knee and his thumb touches my hip. I take his
hand off my leg and he instantly puts it back on again. Malcolm's
pretending not to notice like – sipping his pint, looking around the
pub – he's fucking useless in situations like this he is aye. Ikey's
breath in my face is making me gag.

—An al tell yew one thing, now, Sion . . . one thing – we know
oo the rapist is, the campus rapist like? That dirty fuckin bastard.
Dirty fuckin . . . an doan breathe a fuckin werd-a iss to any fucker
like, but wer gunner do-a cunt in. We know oo it is, ah yeh, an
mean Griff like, wer gunner fuckin av im. Wer gunner slice is
balls off with a broken bottle an fuckin feed em to-a cunt, give
im some fuckin pain like, an en wer gunner fuckin top im. Doan
yew fuckin worry, bach; we'll make-a fuckin streets safe fer yer,
jes wait n fuckin see like, we'll follow-a fucker until we catch im
like an make sure ee never fuckin lazer finger on another fuckin
woman again. Am fuckin serious like. Yew believe me, don't yew?
Yer know tha am serious like?

He looks at me all sincere like – I nod and say: —Good on you,
boy. It's what he fucking deserves aye.

—Too fuckin right it is, mun. Fuckin pervert.

Fucking gorilla. Thinks I need his protection? Duw, I've got
karate, any bloke touches me without permission like an I'll rip his
bloody bollox off – I will. There's been about five students now
who've been attacked like – nothing too bad, I mean, no murder
or stabbings or anything like that – although of course rape's bad
enough. Duw, what kind of a fucking world is it where you don't

count yourself unlucky for being raped – you count yourself lucky for not being murdered? Christ.

And you can't trust anybody – no fucking body. Evil hides in the most unlikely places like aye – like Gladys Trevithick – or like that vicar in Tywyn with his collection of pickled pricks – in jars. Had a larder full of them apparently – used to cut them off the corpses lying in state – pickle them so he could play with them for years to come.

I'm getting sick of Ikey slobbering all over me like so I pretend to see someone I know and me and Malcolm move away – Malcolm probably with more relief than me – he's terrified of Ikey – but then who isn't? Ikey shouts after me:

—Any fuckin trouble an yew come t'me, girl, right! Al fuckin sort it fer yer! Yew hear me then?

I just smile and wave at him. We walk past Liam and his, erm, 'brother' did he call him?

—No yurr fuckin not, mahn, yer a fuckin Irishmahn. Will yis lissen te wha ahm sayin? British in me fuckin hole, yeer –

—See if ah fuckin wanter call meself British en ahl fuckin call meself British! Ooer fucker *you* ter tell me wha fucken nationality ah am?

—I'm a fuckin *Irish*mahn, is what! An am fuckin tellin yis that yurr wahn too!

Oh God. Not for the first time I find myself thinking of Liam's sister – how well he copes with her disability like – the bomb and all that – but I also realise now that – whatever capacity for forgiveness we – all of us – have – it's not enough. There is hatred – real, true hatred – everywhere.

The Proddy's mates are pointing at Liam and singing:

> Ee aye ee aye ee aye oh!
> Ee aye ee aye ee aye oh!
> Ee aye ee aye ee aye oh!
> Paddy was a bastard – ee aye oh!

Mairead's up at her grandparents' cottage in Aberdyfi – on her own – Paul's doing some late-night work on a house in Tal-y-bont (and probably shagging the owner) – Roger's disappeared, no one knows where – Margaret's staying in with an eighth and a video of *The Big Blue*. What have I got? Well, you've just seen it like – Malcolm's company and a raging thirst. Enough to get drunk with, anyway – at least.

—Yer Fenian fuckin bastard! Yer fuckin Taig!
—Typical fuckin Loyalist orange-ersed prick that yer ar!

It's Graduation Day – the top of Penglais Hill – up by the university like – is blocked with cars and proud mums and dads all dressed up – their sons and daughters all wearing flapping black cloaks and those stupid flat hats with the little dangling tassle – mortarboards like. All celebrating getting their degrees – which will qualify them for absolutely fuck all at great public expense. Not that they'll really need them anyway – I mean, they'll just go straight into daddy's company or something – or one of daddy's friends – rich bastards – the people who really need degrees can't fucking afford to do them any more.

I squeeze through the crowd – feeling scruffy and out of place in old jeans and a jumper – but fuck it, I don't care. I want to spit at their feet and really offend them – and I would, too, only I'm saving my spit for later on. I'm going to need it – plenty of better targets lined up aye.

At the bottom of the 'Glais I turn left, past Y Cŵps. There's a right wanker lives down this road – some rich English immigrant like – who flies the Union Jack from the crest of his roof. Imperialist prick like – smug bastard. He's had his house paint-bombed and stuff before like but that's just made him more determined not to give in – more determined to flaunt what he sees as some kind of conquest – some twisted superiority. I'm hoping that one day someone will pour petrol through the twat's letter box and drop a match in there – sort the stuck-up arsehole out. If he doesn't want to fly the dragon, fair enough – but why fly any flag at all then? Bloody asking for trouble, that is – so anyway – he gets my first salvo – I stop outside his big, wrought-iron gate – hawk up a load of frothy snot – blast it between the bars and all over the bonnet of his tan and pampered Volvo. Some of it sprays on the windscreen, speckles the tinted glass – what a shot, boy, aye.

Down the backstreets and on to Alexandra Road, making

deposits as I go on the window of a woman who shagged Paul once when I was away – fucking slag – and on the newly-painted door of a landlord who only ever rents his rooms – damp, crumbling, unhealthy rooms – to junkies, knowing that they'll let him shag them – men or women, young or old – in exchange for rent. Sick bastard. Duw, people get a sniff of money-power and they lose all fuckin morals – and when that happens, evil ensues. All inhibitions and moral restraints are thrown away with the power that money brings – and meanwhile, those who are suffering because they're poor are made to suffer more in newer, different ways. It's a sick, horrible, dirty situation.

I almost spit at the chapel on Gray's Inn Road, but at the last minute I change my mind – I can't – it still exerts a power like. My feelings towards the chapel are mixed – I mean, it's been there for me in times of trouble like but it's also turned potentially good times into their opposite – like, I rented my first room up this road when I was sixteen years old – lonely, looking for company like – and from my window all I could see was the front of this chapel – always there, like a strict auntie – telling me off. I would have lost my virginity in that room to a lovely lad called Iorwerth – but every time we'd go to bed I'd think of the chapel outside – stern and rigid – and get all tensed up like. First thing in the morning and last thing at night I'd see that bloody chapel – it was always – always – there – Reverend Thomas outside it on Sundays – scowling up at my room if I wasn't in the congregation. Iorwerth lost patience after a couple of months like so he left me and then I met that twat Marc – who didn't care whether I was too tense or not – just spat on his prick like and rammed it in. Hurt me badly. So I suppose that it was really Marc to blame – for being a twat like – but – I don't know – it seems somehow that – in Wales – chapels and houses are arranged in such a way that no bedroom is ever free from the sight of a chapel – every bedroom looks out on a steeple – or part of one. It's always bloody there like. You can never get away from it.

Not that that bothers some people like – oh no – like Gladys fucking Trevithick, whose house I stand outside now while I cough up a load of phlegm and snot and swirl it around in my mouth. I do this loudly, too, hoping that she'll be in and hear me and peer through her net curtains at what I do – oh yes – always has clean nets, does Gladys – it just wouldn't do to have dirty nets, now, would it? Handy for me, though, as well – it's easy for her to see how much I hate her.

My mouth fills with foamy, snotty, tobacco-tasting spit. I feel uncomfortable standing so close to her house – trying to stop myself from imagining what went on in there – when I've got so much spit up that it's beginning to overflow I fire it at close range at her window – it makes a kind of ringing sound – the nets twitch, which I'm pleased about, and I pause for a moment to admire my work – thick, yellowish, bubbly saliva running down the glass, seeping underneath the gap in the warped frame. Good one. Come out and clean *that* up, you evil old bitch.

I notice that there's a big, shiny turd on her doorstep – if it's dog, it's from a fucking big dog – thick as my arm like. Oh well. No more than she deserves.

I feel kind of light-headed as I walk away – all that hawking and spitting, an overdose of oxygen to my brain. What I could do with now is a drink – so I make my way to the cashpoint. At the top of Great Darkgate Street, though, I get waylaid – there's a load of gowned students and their parents milling around the square – probably just been in the Treehouse for lunch like – all trying to ignore the loud, mad figure of Dai Datblygu on the bench. By the looks – and the sounds – of him, he's well into a binge – matted beard and hair down to his chest like – filthy overcoat – carpet slippers. He looks absolutely crazy – a madman. People are either trying to ignore him or eyeing him surreptitiously – scared. There's a huge cigar sticking out of his beard and he's swigging from a bottle of champagne – a bulging plastic bag at his side. When he sees me he springs to his feet and roars:

—What is this *diamond* in my *eye*!

He hugs me too hard – it's painful like – and a bit wiffy.

—Dave, Dave, you're hurting me, boy. Let go.

He does.

—Oh am sorry, darlin . . . I know, darlin, I know . . . wanter see somethin nice?

He opens up the pastic bag and – Jesus Christ – it's full of money

– I've never seen so much in my life. If I had that amount of money all my financial worries would be over – I'd be able to pay off every last debt.

Dai's eyes are shining out of his face – looking at my reaction. —Amazin, darlin, aye . . .

—Christ. What did you do? Mug someone?

—Nah, course not – fuckin royalties, darlin, innit. Roy-al-teeees. God bless John fuckin Peel aye. An now what me n you are goin t'do is sit in the Llew an get ab-so-fuckin-lute-ly steamin. We can drink whatever we want, you name it – best whiskey, champagne . . . or go on the classy stuff if yer want. Like Blue Bols.

He picks out a fistful of fivers and waves them at the students and their parents – they look away – wary, uncomfortable – pretending not to notice him – or hear him as he yells:

—Yer see this? Yer see it, ey? Well taker good fuckin look like cos yew won't be fuckin seein it again!

Then he puts it back, slings his arm around me and we head off to the pub, where he buys a round for everybody in there (£73.28, it comes to) – stuffs a handful of pound coins in the jukebox – programmes it to play every Datblygu song on it twice over. He buys me a glass of champagne, a triple Jameson's and a pint of lager – and God it all goes down very well – reacts with the buzz that's already in my head like and pretty soon I know that I won't be arsed about anything – none of the shit – the darks will go away like – that fucking Union Jack – all of it – the knowledge that Gladys Trevithick – who always had a smile for everybody and who everybody liked – until she attempted heroin and liked it too much – used to fund her habit by renting her three children – five, seven, and eleven years old – out at a tenner per hour to known paedophiles – kiddiefiddlers – explaining away their inability to walk properly for a day or so after each session on some bone disease inherited from their father – who used to beat her and who buggered off with another woman years ago – sick – evil – they were taken away from her ages ago now like but when she was let out of prison she moved back here – don't know why like – stupid – her life must be a misery.

And I do my best to keep it that way. She'll be there now – wiping her windows with a damp rag – her neighbours laughing at her – throwing things. She deserves worse. And one day she'll get it.

Dai puts another pint and a whiskey in front of me.

—Plenty more where that came from, darlin. Don't hold yer horses like, gerrum down yer neck.

I'll tell you one thing, though – all that bloody spitting like – I'm sure it does me good – gets rid of all the toxins and poisons in me body – I'm bloody sure it does. I feel kind of new – ready to start again – rinsed out, sort of – shiny. I feel clean.

It started at Spank in Porky's on – when was it? – Thursday? Friday? – I can't fucking remember now like – a few days ago, anyway. All of us – that is, me, Paul, Colm, Margaret, Mairead, Malcolm, Laura – Roger was in hospital, I don't know what for – Liam was away in Cornwall – we all met in the pub a couple of hours before – then went to Spank – back to a party, I forget whose – drinking all day next day – and the next – and then –

Well. How these things always end.

With horrible hangovers – spew – people going mad. I remember a crap songs session – Colm standing in the middle of the room, belting along to 'Hot in the City' – Paul insisting on playing 'Sylvia's Mother' by Dr Hook – even though he knows I hate it cos it used to be one of Marc's favourites – people collapsing gradually – Mags disappearing into the bathroom for ages and then being sick in the hall and running out the door – fuck knows where she's gone like – food, sleep becoming just a memory – Mairead crashing out in the spare room – me and Paul eventually dragging each other off to bed and passing Colm in the kitchen – just sitting there he was – staring at the wall – still drinking like –

And finally sleep like the symptom of some kind of illness – it was so uncomfortable, I was so fucking wired aye – and then the vomit and the runs in the morning and the awful – crippling – hangover –

Jesus Christ – never again – no –

Well. How these things always end like.

I love it here, I do. I often come out here on my own, to Cwm Einion – only rich English tossers say 'Artist's Valley' – it's a beautiful place – the mountains and the trees and the lakes – despite the fact that that old fool Robert Plant's got a house here and has spray-painted his initials on all his sheep – arsehole – obsessive fucking ownership like aye. I'm due back in Camarthen tomorrow – boring work like – so I'm making the most of what time I've got left here. Daft really – it feels sad to be going away again – but I'll be back next weekend probably – maybe even sooner – if not to see Paul then to see the others. No, definitely to see the others – bollox to Paul.

That wanker. I'll never forgive him after last night – but what he did means that I can now forgive myself.

I've got lots and lots to think about out here.

I follow the track at the side of the Leri – through the woods where I can see the lake water shining through the trees – so peaceful here – not a bloody sound like – so calm.

Last night I shagged Malcolm.

We were out in the prom pubs – somehow we lost Colm – I don't know how, he was absolutely off his face on some combination – Mairead wanted to stay out though so she gave me the keys to her flat. Back there, Paul only wanted to tie me to the bed, didn't he – pissed as farts, the both of us – I wasn't having any of it like – I mean, the door to Mairead's flat opens directly on to the bedroom, what if she or Colm had've come in and there was me spread-eagled starkers – Paul began to insist – demand – I told him to fuck off – he belted me, I ran out the door straight past Mairead who was coming in – taxi back up to Llys Wen – knocked all upset on Malcolm's door – he had a bottle of brandy and an eighth – got stoned, cried – ended up in bed with him – screwed.

And that was it; it was that fucking easy. Never two-timed anyone in my life – not even Marc. Malcolm was very gentle – considerate like – a bit crap to tell you the truth – but I came, so . . .

And what do I do now, like? What the fuck do I do?

I walk out of the trees and follow the lake round. There are some swans on the lake and some smaller, darker bird making a high-pitched call. Thin mist floats across the water towards the burned ruins and the road at the far end of the lake. I head over there.

Paul's always said that he'd go fucking mad if I ever slept with someone behind his back like – well, now I have, and it was his fucking fault – he was so heartless – he becomes a right fucking ogre when he's pissed. And I'm not proud – oh no – I'd always seen fidelity as a virtue like – but this is the way of things – other people and their needs for power and control drive you into rejecting your principles because if you don't then you'll end up losing all self-respect – you'll become a fucking slave. There's many people I know who're like that – they'll harp on about sticking to their principles and refusing to compromise themselves – and what are they? – mere slaves to some bullying bloke – or some ignorant and insensitive boss – or some faceless and heartless bureaucrat who honestly couldn't care whether they live or die – no, actually they'd prefer them to go on living so they can exploit them some more – yeh, get as much money out of them as possible before they die – already a zombie – most people have been dead a long, long time before they're buried or burned. This is the way things are, boy – you have to join the great cycle of the giving and taking of pain if you want to save yourself. If there's anything left to save, that is. That is the situation. It's a fucking horrible one – and I don't know how it got that way like – but there it is. Just look around you.

I smile as I suddenly remember Malcolm's shyness. He went: —Erm . . . and gave a little cough every time I told him to do something to me – it was sweet. Feel me there, Malcolm: —Ummm, cough cough; Suck my tits, Malcolm: —Erm, ahem, cough cough; Go down on me now: —Harrumph, hack hack hack splutter. It was funny.

A fisherman waves to me and I wave back.

—Caught anything then?

—A bloody cold, that's it.

—Ah well.

I step carefully over the marshy bit at the end of the lake and go into the blackened shell of the burned-out house. Cars whoosh along the road behind the sooty wall – I can hear them. I've been here before – several times like – with all the others – we once sheltered in here from the rain when we were out picking mushies – I remember Roger squatting down over there in the corner – chasing the dragon – blowing smoke out of his nostrils – the thick mud which he had fallen in crusted into scales on his coat. And I remember us all stumbling out of the trees on to the road – a coachload of tourists had to swerve sharply to avoid us like – the faces at the window gawping at us. They come to Wales to see quaint little villages and mountains and lakes and maybe to check out the prices for a holiday cottage and what do they see? Wrecked scarecrows crashing through the woods – falling over – spewing . . .

Well – no – not really – they see whatever they want to see – they see only the little whitewashed houses in the valleys and not what goes on in them – the vile poverty – the violence – Satanism – incest – the substance abuse – the drug and bomb factories. I mean it like – you haven't got a fucking clue what goes on here aye. You see what you want to see.

There's a nest of syringes and matches and crumpled silver foil and yellow gas canisters in the corner – below the sprayed graffiti:

MEIBION GLYNDŴR
TAI CYMRAEG I'R CYMRY CYMRAEG
NID YW CYMRU AR WERTH
SAEFON MOCH ALLAN

My sentiments ex-bastard-actly. It's this fucking simple, right – if Wales ruled itself, the Welsh people would be different – more confident – more laid back – less disposed to self-destruction and infighting – it's as simple – and as complex – as that. Too fucking right it is, boy. That's why this place – Aberystwyth like, this west Wales area – attracts all the fuck-ups – on the surface, like, people come here to escape – or that's what they say – but underneath it all like what they're really doing is answering the call – the external realisation of their inner chaos – it calls to them across the countries – this little place on the western windy rim of Europe – this place between mountain and sea – this small colony of sadness and insanity.

Rain starts coming in through the charred rafters so I huddle back against the wall – light a fag. I can smell piss – it stinks – and through the ragged hole where the window used to be I see the fisherman begin to pack up.

I remember the surprised little noise Malcolm made when he came – kind of like 'oop!' I'm not going to compare him to Paul, or vice versa – it's unfair to do that – they are different – that's all.

Maybe I'll wait til I come back from Camarthen before I tell Paul – that'll probably be best. I don't know what he'll do – but I hope he doesn't hit me again. Bastard.

Big Charlie got burned today – in an extra-large coffin – in the crematorium on the Llangorwen/Clarach road – with a lovely view of the green mountains over the chimney, through the greasy smoke – Big Charlie got burned.

None of us knew him really well – apart from Roger, who wasn't at the burning – but his sister had asked us to come – so we stood there among the gravestones like – sniffing the air and smoking – in an odd assortment of dresses and suits. Colm's was so big it could've belonged to Big Charlie himself.

—Dig ya whistle, Col, Malcolm said, chewing gum and wearing the kind of outfit that wouldn't've looked out of place on a Nazi general in an old film. —Amazin what ya can pick up in Cancer Research, sometimes, innit?

—Yeh. An look – Colm turned round and flipped up the tail of his jacket. —If yer look closely yer can see wher av stitched over the stab marks. Not bad ferra coupler quid.

This brought stares and grumbles from a group of people standing close by us – Charlie's family and close friends like – clustered round a sobbing old lady in a red suit and a veil who I assumed was Charlie's mam. The graveyard was dotted with groups of people – us in one corner like – crusties in another – dealers in another – Charlie's mam and her entourage of plastic gangsters in the middle. I'd never heard such a variety of accents in such a small place before – it was like the whole of the British Isles compressed into one graveyard. And funny how people form cliques even at funerals like – death the great leveller – my arse.

Maggie and Mairead were pissed off their faces – holding each other up. Paul was in the first throes of an acid trip – the fucking idiot – and was trying to suppress giggles. It was just – awful. It was just fucking shit.

—Tha cunt thurr's got some fuckin neck so ee has, Liam said, nodding over at some weaselly little bloke in a grey suit and trainers. —Showin up hurr.

—Oo? Colm said. —The feller in the bags-more-buzz-at-Burton outfit? Why, what's ee done?

—Ee's the mahn tha sold Charlie is final fix. He's the fuckerr responsible fer is death.

—Nah, yuv gorrit wrong. Charlie choked on curry.

Liam shook his head. —No fuckin respect that. Tornin up hurr with blood on is fuckin hands. And Charlie's ma thurr fahlin afuckinpart.

Mags started crying – nuzzling into Mairead's neck: —I hate funerals . . . I fuckin hate death . . . why do we all have to die? Why is evrybody dying so fuckin young?

That's all she seems to do these days – cry – specially when she's pissed.

—Shhhh now . . . shhhh . . . Mairead stroked her back. Malcolm looked on, puzzled.

—I down't see wha all tha bleedin fuss is abaht, ta be onest wiv ya. It's ownly death, innit.

Paul suddenly spluttered and then disguised it with a cough.

Gradually people began to drift away – shoes crunching on gravel. The sky was blue and huge and hung over the valley like a – like a – oh I don't fucking know – it just hung there. And that was Fat Charlie's funeral – he choked on his own sick and was laid to rest – no, was burned – was cremated – was scorched into ash – among groups of fucked-up, grumbling, useless and rejected people who all seemed to be trying their best to follow him into the flames. The whole thing baffled me – bewildered like – none of it made the slightest bit of sense.

I looked up at the clouds of smoke. —Nos da'r, Charlie.

Malcolm sighed. —Av ad enough av awl this death lark. Let's gown get pissed.

—Yeh, Paul said. —An let's *not* go for a vindaloo afterwards.

I gave him a look and we left the graveyard for the long, long walk to the nearest pub. As I went through the big iron gates I heard someone crying – I looked round like – but I couldn't see anybody. I think it must've been Charlie's mammy – hunched up somewhere among the stones.

Christ – what a mess that was aye – what a total fucking mess. Sometimes it's really brought home to you how much of a fuck up it all is.

—. . . so, anyway, this feller comes leggin it over ter me dad yellin thareed been bitten byer spider, right? In fuckin Liverpool this was, a big spider came outer the bricks an bit im on is thumb. An –

—The vodka. Whir's thuh fuckin vodka?

—. . . oh a right tosser ee was, Toby is name was, is father owned Bass breweries or had shairs in it an stuff, so fuckin rich, God, an Christ he was a prick –

—Ack, Jesus, tha tastes like shite so ut does.

—So this lad said that ee lived in Colchesta, ya see, so a arsked im what rowd, an ee said Troon Close, an a couldan fuckin believe this, a used ta gow out wiv a girl from Troon Close, so a arsked im what numba an ee said –

—Oh me purr fuckin heart.

—Still hurts. Yeh, after four fuckin days it –

—Carn fuckin get over it like . . . just . . .

—Watch wha appens now; see? T'whole planet gets flooded lahk an t'car just carries on, t'message of the advert bein o'course that glorbal warmin is alright, tha knors, nowt t'worry about, cos t'car'll protect yer, which means –

—. . . lived next door to Phil, y'know, in that horrible place on the prom ee used t'live in n stuff –

—. . . yeh, Roger, as anyone seen im recently? Once again thuh fucker's disappeared off thuh map, he –

—. . . terrible fuckin pong –

—. . . oh my poor arse. An me knees n all. Nose dozen feel too fuckin dandy either.

—The Gibberer.

—Ip.

—Nah, nevurr saw ut mahn. Nevurr fucken wahnted te. Bicause –

—No, no, tha feller, whatsisface, Peter Lorre, I –

—. . . as long as tha's got this particular type uv car tha'll be Or-K. T'ultimate fuckin selfishness lahk, int it. Lahk some modern ark –

—. . . about this big, ee sed, size of yer and like, an ee kept goin on about ow it was bright yeller an ee could see its eyes, big black eyes like, so thee ran im toer ozzy an about an ower or so later—

—. . . evry so often ee does this, dozen ee. Just ups an disappears. Fwoo – an thir ee is, gone.

—Ah, ye missed a fuckin treat so ye did.

—An that's just fuckin typical uv you tharriz. Fuckin typical.

—What's that, thir, on thuh floor? By Liam's stupid pointy boot. Looks like seaweed.

—Wharrah cunt.

—Oo!

—Dunno. Size eleven a suppose.

—Christ!

—Fifty-three, an am like, *wha*? An rememba now this is in a tiny fuckin poxy little tavern outside Tijuana, so then a arsked im what bedroom an ee said tha back one by tha boila which ovalooks the alley, an –

—Ty'd ar whiskey yma.

—Speak English, bawh!

—Fuck off. Ga i'r blwchllwch?

—Aye, ut wuz in the *Cambrian News*. Evry last wahn. Cahn be a fucken venison fahrm now withou' anny fucken deer, can ut? Wild deer back in mid Wales now, cahn be fucken bad can ut, be nice te –

—Ah still remember t'fust pair ah bought. Fifteen quid thee wuh.

—Oo did tha?

—Ick, look, blood –

—Harrumph –

—Oof! Christ thill be some skiddies in yer shreddies after *tha* one bigad. Christ that's fuckin disgustin. It smells like bleedin sulpher.

—Goan wash yer arse out, boy –

—. . . poor bastard died. Brown fuckin bread. Fuckin fatal spider bite in Liverpool. The pathology, like, ther was an entymologist involved anny tested this feller's blood like iserlated the venom an got the spider's details, yer know, bright yellow with big black eyes an –

—Well thank you, Mr Chomsky, whups a mean Mairead –

—was shit. Might as well av necked a coupler aspirin for all the –

—. . . his little daughter'd come round like, fiver six years old n stuff, shid come round on her own and leave notes on Phil's door, they –

—It *is* seaweed.

—PAUL! NORRAFUCKINGEN!

—tha exact, same, bedroom. A mean, this fuckin blew me away. A just coulden fuckin believe it. Tawk abaht a fuckin coincidence –

—so now thurr's a possibility uv seein wild deer in the valleys again. Ace, I think.

—ah might gor horm around then lahk. Ant seen mih forks fer erges, lahk, must be, what, three year nirleh –

—an no known species uv spider fit tha description or tha typer venom. No known specie. On a fuckin buildin site this was, in Liverpool. Tellin yer man. Can yer fuckin –

—glue –

—in fact theser them! God!

—am not gunner tell yer –

—rirly fuckin hurt, it did, an –

—giz a bit. Gwahn.

—ther all twats, boy –

—ud say Ffion called; has anybody seen my daddy?

—gobshite. Fuckin –

—a wish a knew, a rerly fuckin wish a knew, man –

—carn do anythin more –

—would'n bleedin bother me like, as long as it wasn oner them long-leggedy fuckers, carn fuckin *stand* them, ug, Christ, freak me right out –

—Oo! OO!

Jesus Christ; this crystal meth off Jed, boy, fwoof.

Everybody wants a drink but no one can be bothered going to the off-licence – Roger and Colm won't go because they're both wasted, although Colm keeps complaining about being bored so you'd think he'd be glad of something to do – he keeps goading Mairead to go but she won't because she reckons – and bloody rightly in my opinion – that since it's going to be her who pays for the booze then someone else should go and get it. Which is fair enough – but I can't go because I've got an ingrown toenail and it hurts me to walk – it does – fucking agony, boy. And I've got a cold. I'm ill. Roger's been off heroin for a few weeks and he's looking better – if he wasn't coming down off a speed-binge he'd look healthy and well – and I've never touched the brown in my life and I look and feel like shit – bloody typical – not fucking fair aye. And Malcolm won't go the shop simply because he doesn't see why he should.

The phone rings, and Colm flaps his arms madly:

—Doan answer it! Doan fuckin answer it! Yer know oo irrill be, don't yer, fuckin Sharon, an a just carn be doin with er right now. No fuckin wey, man. She's a pain inny arse at the bester times like but when yer crashin down off whizz she's yer werst fuckin nightmer. Lerrit ring.

—It maht be someone else thor, Mairead says.

Colm shakes his head. —No, irrill be er. Doan answer it, Mairead. She can fuck off.

Roger agrees: —Aye, too fuckin right, boy. She comes round yer when am feelin like iss, mun, an starts er whinin an a tell yew al ring er fuckin neck for er. Throttle er like a turkey, I will. Ey, snot such a bard idea, mun – be well rid uv-a silly moo en, wun we, eh? Yeh! Bringer fuckin round! Lynch party, mun!

Malcolm laughs nervously, probably less out of amusement and more out of an urge to ingratiate himself to Roger. Creep. The insistent ringing gets annoying – it must be Sharon, no one else goes on this much – but eventually it stops. I'm glad Mairead didn't answer it – Sharon would've come round and asked Mairead for money, she would've said yes like she always does and Colm would've got annoyed and then there would've been a row and it all would've been too, too much. The way Sharon uses Mairead is shameless – but what puzzles me is the way Mairead allows herself to be used. I mean – last week I think it was – I was round here – Sharon phoned – asked if Mairead wanted to go out – could she borrow some money to go out with her – Mairead said yes, Sharon said she'd be round in a few minutes – ten minutes later – Sharon phones again – she's now changed her mind and is going out with

421

Rhidian and Jenny and Rhodri – but she'll be round for the money anyway. Ten minutes later – ring ring – Sharon – she's in a rush, can Mairead take the money round to her? Right on the other side of town – Mairead said she'd drunk too much to drive – Sharon's like, oh no bother, take a taxi but hurry up because she's meeting Rhodri in a few minutes. Mairead agreed to all this and went out in the rain to hail a taxi and give money to Sharon. I would've told the daft bint to fuck off – I mean, if you're borrowing money, you *don't* fucking ask the person who's lending it to you – or, in this case, giving, Mairead'll never get it back, no way, boy – to bring it to you – they're already doing you a favour by lending you money – *you* go round to *them*. It's all to do with respect, respect and gratitude – that's all – qualities which Sharon evidently lacks. She's an abuser – a parasite – I've never liked her. It baffles me the way Mairead offers herself as a doormat to her – I mean, if you do that, you're sure to be trampled on – do that to someone like Sharon and she'll bleed you fucking dry like.

Malcolm, Roger and Colm all cheer as the phone stops ringing – Mairead just stares at it silently. She reminds me of my auntie Menna, Mairead does – they even look alike – the dark hair and eyes, the full lips – although Menna hasn't got any facial piercings, of course – but if you want to see what Mairead'll look like in thirty years' time, look at Menna – she's an alkie as well – lost her two children in the Aberfan disaster in 1966 – thirty fucking years ago – imagine it – your own two children drowned in sludge – and she hasn't stopped drinking since like. I'm waiting for her to die – we all are – she can't have much time left, she looks like a corpse – in and out of hospital all the bloody time – she's hardly got any internal organs left – soon as they let her out she's back on the bottle, straight into the pub on the way home. Thirty years. She still lives in Aberfan – says she wants to be close to her children. She lives in the darks perpetually – imagine it – has done for thirty years. Thirty fucking years, boy.

Ah well.

Colm's bored – trying to wind Malcolm up – Malcolm's just ignoring him:

—Malcolm Baker, wharra squirt. He wers lipstick and a skirt.

Malcolm just watches the telly – arms folded, face impassive.

Blind Date is on – the-lucky-girl-who-gets-to-choose-one-of-these-three-lovely-fellas comes on – slim and pretty and dark – looks like the girl who lives in the flat above. Colm – being his usual letchy and insensitive self – so easily bored that boy – grins and goes:

—Phwoar. Body on *er*.

Mairead – and I don't blame her – gives him daggers.

—Ey, what's tha fuckin look for? A was only *sayin*, Christ.

—Yeh, well, keep tha twisted observertions in tha sewer tha calls a mind. Wuh dorn't wantuh hear thum.

—No, *you* don't wanter hear them. Thee others arn arsed.

—Fuck off an shut tha gob.

—Eeeeewwww! Who's at home ter Mister Tetchy ternight then? What's wrong with you?

Mairead scowls and turns the telly over.

—Oi! A was fuckin watchin tha!

—Well, tha's not now.

—Pain inner fuckin arse. Colm sits frowning for a minute and then turns back to Malcolm: —Malcolm Baker, wharra nance. Wearin knix an stockings under is pants.

Malcolm just sighs.

The news is on this side – midway through an item about the discovery of a child's body in the Rhondda – mutilation – evidence of sexual interference. I don't have time to feel depressed about it because Roger's reaction – even by his standards – is extreme – sudden and shocking. He strains towards the screen, veins bulging on his neck – frothing at the mouth – scary, horrible – eyes so big they look like they're about to pop.

—Yer see! Yer FUCKIN SEE! Iss ul appen agen an agen, mun, until yer bring in a decent fuckin punishment fer ese cunts! Fuckin KILL em! Kill-a fuckin cunts, mun! TORTURE-a fuckers! Cut-a fuckin BOLLACKS off an makem wear em UN A FUCKIN NECKLACE MUN! EYR SCUM!

This knocks me back – the fury in his face – his voice – I feel like running away from him. Colm's staring at him as if he's just breathed fire or something – Malcolm's chin is on his chest – and Mairead puts her hand on his shoulder and says softly:

—God, Roger, calm y'sen down sausage. Just calm down.

—But eyr EVIL fuckers! CUNTS! Eyr FUCKIN –

—Ah knor, ah knor . . . shhh . . . shhh . . .

She strokes his shoulder and pretty soon he's calm again – or calmish anyway. As calm as Roger could ever be like aye. What is it inside him? What is it that makes him so – well – you know.

Colm goes: —See wha yev done now, Mairead? A told yer we shoulda watched *Blind Date*.

He turns back over to see Cilla waving goodbye bucktoothily. He stands there and watches it for a minute then turns back to Mairead: —Al need yer cash card then.

—Oh yuh goin! Nice one!

She stands up and kisses his head.

—Not too much, tho. A doan wanner after carry fuckin loads back like.

Mairead gives him her cash card – we give him our orders.

—Erm . . . what's yer number agen?

As if he doesn't know like.

Mairead smirks: —1270.

—Oof, says Roger. —Bard fuckin number that like.

We look at him. Malcolm goes: —An why's that?

—Cos thass-a yeer tha Prince Llewellyn wrecked Caerphilly castle innit? Easy ter remember see?

—Oh, Malcolm says and Colm shakes his head and leaves for the off-licence. A moment later though he pops his grinning head back round the door and goes:

—Malcolm Baker, wharra poof. Ee wears a dress with –

Malcolm bites this time: —Oh fa fuck's saikes! Will ya just give it a rest fa one fuckin minute? Gow tha off-licence an stop making a twat av yaself, Colm, Christ.

Colm cheers and raises his arms up over his head and goes: —Victureee! Victureee!, an then closes the door. Right wind-up merchant when he's bored. Like a big bloody kid aye.

Malcolm sits there moodily and Roger sniggers, his rage seemingly completely gone now. He's mad, Roger, I'm sure he is – the way he switches so suddenly and so drastically like – the stuff he keeps in his head – useless history stuff like aye. He scares me, he does – I don't particularly like him either – but he really does surprise me on occasion and I don't suppose there's many people you can say that about aye.

I'm a bit wary of being alone with him like – just me, him, and Mairead – oh, forget Malcolm, like, at the first sign of trouble you wouldn't see him for dust – he's stronger – madder – than us, but all he does is chain-smoke and stare at the telly. Doesn't say one word to us except 'ta' when Malcolm passes him the spliff we make and smoke to pass the time waiting for Colm. The promise of booze is making all of us a bit twitchy – Malcolm writhes in his seat as if he's got worms – Mairead frantically files her fingernails – some of which are long like talons – others short and split. I'm dying for a drink – I didn't realise how badly I want one until Colm actually went like – now I've got a big fucking thirst on me, boy, aye – too right – And not just in my throat – in my lungs – my head – my legs –

And then there's a voice singing in the road outside – a Scouse voice – Colm's:

> There is no pain that can't be eased
> With the devil's holy water an yer rosary beads!

He shouts: —Oi! Someone come down an let me in quick!, and Malcolm and Mairead rush to the door to let him in. I turn the telly off and put some good music on – a Welsh compilation tape that I made last week – Catatonia – 60 Ft Dolls – Super Furry Animals – Datblygu – Dom – Manics – loads of fucking great stuff aye. The first song to come on is 'Australia' – a song I fucking love – I turn it up and Roger expresses his approval by roaring.

And that's it – we get pissed – simple as that, boy.

Nos da'r, spwriel Saeson. Nos da'r, twpsyn.

From *A Personal Guide to West Wales*, anonymous authorship, privately printed, p. 102

Elongated slabs of rock, narrow, fat, then narrow again, here litter the littoral. No Ishmael would survive on these shapes, but he may take a pointed hint from them and flee, fast and far . . . Ah, but this is the end of the line; to run with this clutch of descending debris would be, simply, to drown, so one must turn to other tracks and retrace one's steps – inland. Back inland. The railway line is still here, and here you'll find its end; this is Europe's terminus. So: either to sea, or back inland; the choice is restricted, limited. There really is no choice at all. Swim.

THEY ARE STANDING

THEY ARE STANDING in these desolate hills, sniffling and dripping in drizzle. They seek out whatever shelter offers itself in the lees of hills or rocky outcrops or beneath their own hoisted hoods, and they stand greyed by the rain like a sect or army, faces hidden, limbs still. Their trembling skin has very little to do with what some would like to call earth-power or natural electricity, stemming instead from chemical intake, alcohol-shiver, drug-thrum. Nevertheless, their passage through these gargantuan green spurs wind-flayed and hostile has about it an undeniable air of determination and purpose, as if the only stasis ever possible will be decided by them and only them. They crouch and huddle like an army in ambush.

Malcolm, hands in pockets, collar raised, woolly hat pulled down to his eyebrows, watches, for a moment, Roger and Colm attempting to chase the dragon, hunched in the lee of a hillock. Leaning shoulder to shoulder, touching, bowed, they appear like initiates engaged in some dark and secret ritual, rolled-up money snorkels in their mouths as they cajole and create fire and smoke. Watching them through the opaque grey curtain of rain Malcolm feels a pang of he knows not what and then shuffles over to Paul, who has been standing by a cairn and staring at a fixed spot on the lake edge for quite some time.

—What ya lookin at?

—Ssshh. That bird thir, on thuh rock. See it? A think it's a heron or somethin like that.

—Whair?

Paul points. —Maybe a buzzard or somethin. Sittin down like. Av bin waitin for it tuh move for ages. Am thinkin it might be dead.

Malcolm squints but can see no bird.

—What fuckin bird?

—Sshh! Yull scir it away!

429

—Paul, thiz fuck awl thair. Yuv been stairin at a branch. Jesus, tha acid must be fuckin blindin.

Paul deflates and sighs and Malcolm squats down on his haunches, quivering in the cold. The acid he swallowed earlier is now beginning its tingling tread into his system and he feels, not for the first time today, apprehensive. He is well acquainted with the hallucinogenic experience but there remains fresh and feverish in his mind a memory of madness in New Mexico when, among the twisted dreamscapes of the badlands lava beds, he witnessed his first genuine case of LSD psychosis; the sudden nakedness of his friend Davey from Plymouth, the intense and nonsensical babbling, and a panicked disappearance into the tortured rocks. Malcolm himself found Davey after a nightmare six-hour search through moaning ghosts and screaming magma, trembling in a small cave and covered with countless cuts and bruises with no real recollection of the incident, only an unshakeable sense of utter horror. Davey was never the same again. And since then, Malcolm has always been aware of the possibility of a similar calamity befalling and befouling him, although as yet he has not been so unfortunate. However, it is beneficial, he thinks, to always be aware that such a thing could happen; it produces respect for the drug and, maybe as a consequence, for oneself.

He stares at the dark, sombre waters of the lake unmoved by wave or ripple and imagines a past massacre happening here, tiers of bone white and seething in the soil beneath his boots. He pictures a man squatting in the shallows, a man dressed in rags and blood with spirals of flesh in his matted hair and beard, holding his head in his cracked hands and sobbing uncontrollably down the centuries. A man with an axe and murder. A man adorned with a necklace of entrails.

A picture to be, at this moment, resisted, although the sight of Colm and Roger offers no viable alternative – they are both, now, flat on their backs in the sheepshit and the mud. Still, Malcolm reflects, they are an image of some small sort of success; isn't that what they wanted? Pale, strange urchins in the sheepshit and the mud.

Surrounded by mountains, Malcolm stares at the lake. His leg muscles have frozen and cramped in this hunkered position but he knows full well that, when the acid accelerates and begins its unstoppable rampage through his cellular structure, then, even though it will hurt him to do so, he will move. Oh yes.

MALCOLM

FUCK ME, A down balieve this. A down know whetha ta sing or scream; av neva seen anyfin like it in me life an a down know how ta react.

—Jesus. Here's another one, Harvey says in the long grass.

So that makes eighteen. Can ya balieve it? Eighteen of tha fuckas, eighteen dead sheep in tha one field, each in diffarent stages av decomposition. Terrible fuckin smell. Eighteen av the cunts. Al tell ya what it's like, ere, it's like tha Welsh equivalent av tha elephants' graveyard in Africa; this is whair awl tha sheep come ta die. An it is no fuckin plaice for an Essex boy.

Allen an Harvey are wawkin ahead av me, bowth av um as gobsmacked as I am. Ain't just tha dead animals, like, it's this whole fuckin plaice, it's strainge, thiz summink not quite right about it. No birds're singin, fa one; an ya'd imagine tha, with so many rottin carcasses lyin around, thir'd be crows an buzzards an things, but no – there's fuck awl. Funny fuckin crackle in tha air an awl; a càn awlmowst hear it, tho that could just be my imagination. It's bizarre. A feel dead fuckin strange.

An strainger agen when a nowtice it stairin at me from undaneath a clumpa nettles, starin out at me wiv its big black eyes. A pull it out, free from tha bindweed an stuff wrapped rahnd it an owld it up ta tha sunlight so's a can get a good gander at it; tha mowst perfect fuckin thing av eva seen – a ram's skull, wiv orns, curved orns like, an teeth an eyebrows an ridges and suture marks across the top ov it. It's fuckin amazin, pukka. Perfect. Some people get freaked out by skulls; even Roger fa fuck's sikes, even ee went doofuckinlally when ee saw tha stag's skull on tha wawl ov tha pub that time. Not fuckin me tho, mate, I fuckin love em, I do; thiz summin just so fuckin perfect abaht em, so well fawmed, white wiv tha life tha once throbbed inside em, tha mystery like. Cawse, a down like ta fink av me own grinnin away thair baneath me face; fuck no.

—What've yer got there?

A owld it up ta show Harvey. —Skully.

Ee grins. —Alas poor Flossie, I knew her well.

—Yeh, 'knew' in the Biblical sense, Allen goes. —That's wha wiv stumbled on ere, y'know; the site of a Welsh gang-bang. All these sheep av bin shagged to death. A bet yer.

An then we find tha oddest thing av awl; a pile av dead sheep, abaht six av em in a little tower, one on top av tha otha. A stack of tha bleedas. A mean, how tha fuck? Why? What's fuckin gowin on? Summink not quite on tha fuckin level ere. We get *rairly* fuckin freaked out by this like so we leg it back ta the car an head howm, back ta Llys Wen. Gotta get owm soonish anyway; Paulie, tha darft bastard, is cookin evrywan a big lasagne in tha sadly misguided balief that it'll elp us awl ta kick ard drugs. Tha fool. What's ee on? I, personally, fully intend, arfter av digested me nosh like, ta snawt a line av showbiz sherbert as big n thick as one av tha lines in tha middle av the rowd an make a fuckin night av it. Still, if it makes im happy, then ee can do whaeva tha fuck ee likes. A still fink ee needs is ead read tho.

As we drive up tha hill ta tha Waun a begin ta get a bad, bad feelin. A mean, tha field, awl them dead sheep, an am gonna be takin tha skull av one inta me owce; what if it's cursed? What if a bring doom n disasta down on us awl? Well, fuck awl a can do about it now. Al arsk Colm wha ee finks abaht it, im an is gyppo shit like. It's lookin up at me thir, from tha seat; one ugly fucka. Awl it is is bone, lifeless, dead, harmless bone. Calcium. But a still carn shake tha feelin that av made a great big fuckin mistake.

Christ, thir are fings in this world . . . bizarre fuckin things . . . things that'd make ya run screamin if ya looked at em too closely.

So down't fuckin look at em then. Easy.

An if I am cursed then it carn be too bard cos a down't get cawt in tha Spar when a wawk aht wiv a bottle av brandy up me sleeve. An tha bird oo wairks bahind tha counter's a fuckin babe.

Speed. Am baginnin ta wonda whetha the hit is wirth tha fuckin comedown. When am speedin, then yeh, obviously, it is; the firthest thing from me mind then is tha comedown. But when am comin down, tho, it's just tha fuckin opposite; the firthest thing from me mind now is feelin good.

Fuckin speed comedowns are tha wirst in tha world. A feel raw,

> vulnerable
> wasted
> exposed
> terrified
> depressed
> suicidal
> disgusting
> guilty
> vile
> like av bin eaten an shat
> out.

It's just fuckin awful. Lyin in me bed, me own smell risin up aht of the dirty sheets, an am curled up baneath em like a fuckin foetus. Me brain humming, me ears ringing, awl me nerve ends, every single fuckin one, frayed an shredded arfta tha larst few days partying. Fuckin payin for it now, tho, arn I, too fuckin right. Maybe this is, like, buried memory or sammink, maybe this is ow it felt ta be bawn, ta be fawced out dahn me mother's birth canal – from wawm, maroon safety ta screams an blood an blindin lights an a man in a mask oo eld me upside down an smacked me arse. Jesus. Some fuckin life, this, innit?

. . . If ownly I could fuckin sleep. A sleep well, am a heavy sleeper neva plagued by nightmirs, a down care wha any otha bastard says. When a *do* sleep, that is; and, at tha mowment, av got abaht as much chance av doin that as a have of gettin a hard-on the next time a see Roger vom down is shirt.

I am one useless cunt. Truly I am. I am a blemish, a pimple, I can do no good here eva. I have neva done anythink of any use or wirth or value whatsofuckineva. I am one useless cunt.

Yeh, some fuckin life this. A sick fuckin joke. Next time someone arsks ya why ya take drugs, just fuckin outline tha fuckin lives fa them; trawma of birth an cruel childhood (an awl fuckin childhoods are cruel, neva balieve othawise), adolescence filled wiv pus an wankin an soul-shreddin insacurities, baffled by tha immense changes appenin in ya body an mind, the tawture of school, sadistic teachers, terrible pressure ta succeed so's ya can get a good job an be a nice safe responsible upstandin citizen an memba of a society which as neva offered ya anythin of any interest or excitement an which doesn't give a shit whetha ya happy or unhappy, safe or in danger, dead or fuckin alive . . . a nice wife an a coal-look gas fire in tha suburbs, new car unda tha corrugated plastic carport, fifty fuckin years of ya one shawt life in a job which ya hate but ya fuckin terrified ta lose an which ya'd kill ta keep, ya whole fuckin life controlled by somebody else, somebody uglier, eviller, an ultimately wirth far less than yaself howldin ya in ther thrall. An fa what? Fa what? Fa sprinting senility, piss an shit in ya kex, dribblin dahn ya shirt-front an tryin desperately ta get some semblance of life out of ya useless cock which ain't even good fa pissin out of any fuckin maw. An then the big blackness: Death. Buried in a nice plot with a nice view of the park, paid faw by ya own hard-earned cash which ya had ta wirk months ta make in tha same shitty job which helped ta put ya in tha fuckin ground anyway. A mean, sick! That ya hafta wirk awl ya fuckin life in awda ta buy a place where ya can be respectably, socially-acceptably dead.

Fuck.

Actually, senility might be sammink ta look forward to; a can't eat that, docta, it's maggots an toenail clippings. Didn't you die twenty years agow? Elsie? Is tha you, Elsie? Whoops, diableedinrrhoea in me bed again. Owld out ya hands, nurse, av got a lovely saprise fa ya . . .

Fuck.

There is no hope. There is *no* hope. All of us, we are doomed, an fucked, an useless. We lie ta each avver, stab each avver in tha back, pray to a God oo neva fuckin listens if at awl ee's even fuckin thir. Filled with secrets an hatred we are, we are, awl of us fuckin are.

Av neva known such depression as when am comin down from billy. That's why a try not ta comedown, that's why a try ta keep it gowin as long as a can, fa three days, faw, five, six, ow eva long it takes ta burn away every larst scrap of energy an adrenalin . . . Funny fing is tho, is tha this comedown depression invariably comes with a rampagin, irrepressible hawniness. A twisted combination. Like, the avver mawnin (was it Saturday? Fuck knows), a was hitchin back from tha party in Ynyslas, Robbie's leavin do like (awltho Robbie imself ad well fucked off), buzzin me tits off, legs fucked from darncin awl night, drums still bangin in me ears, an a got picked up by a Bedford van, in tha back of which was a group of young kids, well, about sixteenish, awl of em sufferin ther first E an amphet comedowns. Shoulda seen em; white as sheets, shiverin, teeth chatterin, a fuckin mess. An one of em − a right fuckin darlin an awl − looked up at me awl tearful like an said:

—How do you cope? What's the best way of dealin with this?

A lit a fag, pontificated faw a bit, an went: —Well, personally speakin, unless av got a shitload of downers ta knock me aht, a drink a couple of bottles av red wine, go ta bed wiv some slow music on, wank me cock til it's red raw an try an usually a must say fail ta persuade meself tha life rirly is worth livin.

She neva said one maw wird ta me awl tha way howm.

A curl up inta a tight bawl unda the duvet which if a don't wash soon al be able ta snap ova me knee. Involuntary groans escape me cracked an scummy lips. Creepy sheep cawl ta each avver outside the winda, an a start thinkin of tha skull downstirs, in tha kitchen; maybe they can sense it in ere. Maybe they want it back. Al tell ya, the sheep oo live in tha field between ere an tha university av started ta attack people, an that's no fuckin joke − not just the ram, a mean, the sheep, tha little fluffy baa-y fings. Harvey towld me about it first, said ee'd bin bitten, so a tried it out fa meself, an it's fuckin true − the sheep see ya an peg it tawards ya full fuckin pelt, teeth bared, evil fuckin look in ther eyes. A managed ta get ta tha gate in time, but Harvey said tha they butted an bit im, an true enough is lower legs wir awl covered in bruises. Fuckin man-eatin sheep now. Whole world's fucked up, man.

. . . someone ta tawk to. That would be nice.

. . . oh well. Might as well get it ova with; ya know ya gonna do it soona aw later, so thir's no sense in puttin it off any longa.

A lie on me back on coax me knob inta some approximation of stiffness. The amphet dick-shriv; a burden indeed. Ya awl confident when ya buzzin, sparklin wit, a bird gets intrested an she comes back with ya aw you gow back ta hers an wha does she see when ya get ya kit off? An albino sultana. A one-eyed white acorn. Just one maw twisted cruelty, innit. A know, lyin ere, that in a while am gonna be twitchin in a pool of sour sweat wiv a slimy spewin slug clutched in me grubby mitt, feelin filthy an pathetic, but a carn elp meself, this speed-hawn's irrepressible. It is. What awlsow scares me is tha thawt of what's gonna rise unbidden inta me head when a come; it's odd, but sometimes, when a come, images flash through me mind which a don't fuckin want an which a don't find hawny in tha least, in fact just the fuckin opposite, a find em a complete turn-off; stuff like me mum, Paul's bare toes when ee wirs is sandals, tha crack of Roger's spotty, scrawny arse when ee bent ova yestaday ta chuck up in tha sink. What's gowin on here? Why does this happen?

A start ta stroke, long smooth strokes, an once again, Mairead's lesbian experience is reconstructed in me head. She towld me abaht it once; didn't give me many details like but just tha idea is enough, a solid foundation ta build on. Am sure that she didn't get up ta tha fings I imagine er doin, but God, tha magical power of tha human imagination eh? Yeh.

In a surprisingly shawt time, a come: Mairead's slim, long-nailed middle finga entas er mate's (Rebeccah, tha bird oo went ta Cornwall) tight n puckered hairless arsehole fa the third time, er delicate wrist twists an turns as she probes an that's it, a groan an blurt painfully on me belly. Av wiped meself off an am out of the bed an scannin me tapes befaw the self-loathin an depression can grab tha opportunity ta set in: Tom Waits is too slow an growly; the Cowboy Junkies' first album makes me wanna weep an top meself; any ambient sounds are too fuckin floaty an insubstantial wiv nowt ta hang on to; an anythin else's too loud and grating. So a think fucks ta it an get dressed an gow downstirs inta tha cold an mouldy front room which smells uv fag smoke an stale whiskey. An the mould's fuckin horrible; wawkin inta this room's like wawkin inta a constipated bowel. It's so fuckin damp tha the Rizlas split as a spliff up.

A lie on tha couch an watch *The Chart Show* an get stoned as a bastard. Am tryin ta knock meself out with the weed but a spend a fascinated hour watchin an incredible fuckin sight: a daddy-long-legs cawt in a lanky spider's web in tha cawna, the fly strugglin ta escape an the spider strugglin ta wrap it up in a little silken coffin. Legs fuckin evrywhir, it's a pandemonium of insect limbs. This'd drive Colm fuckin insane; ee hates things wiv long legs, aw, ta quote tha mota-mouthed cunt, legs which are 'hysterically disproportionate'. This'd drive im gibberin an droolin straight inta North Road. Me, tho, a find it fuckin incredible; am completely fuckin agog, watchin it. Some fuckin amazin, unbalievable fings goin on around us. Ya just afta look faw em.

The spider fucks off wiv is prize an faw hours later am still ere. Ain't moved a fuckin muscle, apaht from me fingas ta change tha channels with the remote controwl an roll up a succession of spliffs. Mawnin telly shit, some awful fuckin Oprah-style public confession/exhibition on now, offensive an sickly, but a carn be arsed ta move. Av even got tha vid, *The 100 Best Goals*, perfect headfuck viewing, but the act of gettin off tha couch an crawlin across tha flaw to the telly ta put it on just seems sow fuckin strenuous . . . an anyway, fuck football; it's awl just about money now, it's become a middle-class thing; the players now down't av tha drive anymaw, tha drive ta escape tha slums, or mowst of em don't anyway. That's why teams like Brazil are so good, because it's not so money-oriented ova thir yet an the players are awl driven, full of fanatical energy. Universities are tha same; students now don't get ther places due ta talent aw passion faw their subject, they get them simply cos they can fuckin affawd to. Mummy an daddy'll pay fa them. That's why mowst students nowadays are wankas; the uncontested privilege. An they've awl got tha same drawly, laid-back public-school accent an a perpetual smirk playin abaht their smackable gobs. Not a decent one among em. It's fuckin shit, an it's gonna get worse.

Aw Christ. Bawd an fed up. A wait faw the sahnd av music in tha house – people gettin up – company. But naffin fuckin appens. Sweet fuck awl. Av smoked enough weed ta knock aht a fuckin horse but ere I am still, wide abastardwake, filled wiv loathin an disgust. Faw evrythin. Awl av it.

Maybe I'll knock on Mags's daw, see if shiz got any downas. See if shiz cheered up enny n awl; I adta step in sharpish tha avver day, at tha rave out in tha mountains, Robbie's party like. A could see er startin ta crash, sittin there starin aht owva tha mountains, a could see blackness descendin on er, like it awlways bleedin does. Not a happy girl, Margaret. Which is why shill probly av some downas, an a can knock meself aht, wake up feelin betta, awl tha comedown leaked aht av me in my sleep. A wish a could sleep, a really fuckin do. Why can't a sleep? Why am a still awake?

Fuck it. Fuck it awl. A just can't be bleedin bothered.

An am *still* fuckin buzzin from that E. Twenty-faw hours nearly since a ate tha larst Dove, out at tha rave in tha hills, Tal-y-Bont like, an am still fuckin buzzin. Flew awl tha way through the party out at Borth sands n awl, fuckin great it was, blindin, an it's pukka still, just sittin ere in Colm's gaff, Mags dowzin on tha bed, wir drinkin red wine an lissenin ta good music, the telly on with tha sahnd tirned down. Happy, awl of us, buzzin still, just enjoyin tha shared experience av larst night an tha night befaw . . . A love these times, me; just gently comin down, drinkin, tawkin, just bein tagevva an gettin off on each avver's company. It's fuckin great. An Colm n Mairead ar feelin it as well; ther flopped aht on the sowfa, wrapped up in each avver's arms. Sweet. Nice ta see. It's awl gentle an lovely an easy. One thing, tho; a wish they'd hoova tha fuckin carpet.

—Jesus, ow long is it since eitha of ya pushed the fuckin vacuum abaht? Evry time a take a drink av got ta look at awl this crap stuck ta tha bottom of me glass. Look at it – fuckin pubes, toenail clippins fa fuck's sakes, owld food . . . does me fuckin ead in.

Colm larfs. —Thiz probly a few winnits n all, if yer look. A was pickin me arse bifore like, avin a right good dig a was. Oi, Mairead! Pull yer fuckin skert down, gerl!

Mairead's leanin ova tha coffee table ta change tha channel an er tiny skirt's awl ridden up at tha back. I carn see anyfin tho.

—We don't wanner see yer arse angin out! Purrit awey, Christ.

She sits back dahn agin. —Well that's nice. Ther wuh a time when a glimpse uv me arse would've ad tha cartin mih orver t'bed. Nice t'see t'magic asunt gone out uv t'relationship.

—No, it's still ther, albeit in a Paul Daniels fashion. Colm's voice then gows awl high n squeaky: —Now yer see me . . . an now yer don't! An that's magic!

Dead on. A laugh. Colm then crushes Mairead in a big hug an

a feel a pang. A like Mairead, even if she does drink like a fuckin fish — she's ahfway through a bottle av brandy now — but she's still got a lovely smile an a lovely way abaht er . . . A reckon, right, that if I ad av got in thir first, shid be livin with me now. Fuckin defo. No two ways abaht it, man. If I ad av got in thir befaw Colm, me n Mairead'd be an item now, livin tagevva, the lot. Just anovver missed charnce, innit?

A owpen anovver bottle uv wine an paw some fa me n Colm. A shout ta Mags if she wants some but thir's no ahnsa; probly nodded off.

—It was a fuckin pukka party, tho, wannit? A say, energy bubblin up inside me. —Fuckin top E as well . . . did *you* av a good time on it?

Mairead shrugs. —Yeh, ah had a fuckin grert time lahk. Just the comedowns ah cannot stand. Er voice is awl slow an slurred. She looks fuckin wrecked.

Colm hugs er agin. —Nah, this is nice, this is nice . . . am still buzzin a little bit. This is fuckin ace.

Ee shakes is messy head at the aceness av it awl an then gows off on anavver one of is little stawries:

—Guess wher a had me ferst E. Go on, guess.

—Now how are we suppowsed ta know that? Just fuckin tell us.

Ee grins: —The Mersey ferry. Ages ago now like, late eighties, a serpose. We wer goin to a rave over on the Wirral, inner place called Thurstaston. We all necked the gear on the Pier Ed an came up on the ferry an it was so fuckin ace tha we stayed on ther fer ages, just goin back n forth bitween Liverpool an Birken'ed . . . it was fuckin brilliant. The ferst one alweys is, innit?

Mairead shakes her head. —Not fuckin mine. Merd mih spew it did.

—An mine was fuckin ketamine so it was fuckin orrible, a say, which ain't quite true; I have had ketamine, unknowingly like, several times, and it has been horrible, but me first E was fuckin perfect, blindin, nowt wrong wiv it at awl. Fuck knows why a said tha ta Colm. A just did.

Ee ignores us an carries on: —A went ter fuckin loadser raves round that time, late eighties, erly nineties like. Evry fuckin weekend. An a mean proper raves, yer know, in fields or hangars or wer'ouses, not poxy little clubs. Big, huge events these wer. Yuced ter fuckin love em, until a got pissed off with em; a started ter realise ow fuckin shallow thee wer, yer know, ow, like, empty an conformist thee wer, all those people all on the same drugs, in the same place, doin the same thing, wearin the same clothes . . . people oo coulden get enthusiastic about any'in apart from drugs. Wid go back ter someone's house like for a chill out or summun an ad be fuckin flyin, out me fuckin tree, wantin ter talk about anythin, yer know, fuckin bukes, parsnips, kestrels, icebergs, fuckin any'in like, burrall ad fuckin ear would be these fuckin drug stories all night fuckin long. What's the most Es yuv done in one night? Ever mixed E with skag? Borin as fuck it was . . . Back inter raves now tho, specially thee outdoor ones like; all the tossers go clubbin it now. The people oo just like the dancin an the drugs, an not the poncey fuckin posin, go ter thee outdoor ones. Maybe it's just cos am older now, a dunno, but ther seems ter be more uv a connection. Beats sittin at ome anyway, dunnit, wond'rin which fuckin tacky trinket or tawdry bauble ter save up for next.

Ee leans back on tha couch, as if sayin so much as exhausted him. Maybe it has. David Bowie comes on tha telly an ee murmas: —Oh look oo it is. The Thin White Puke.

A larf. 'The Thin White Puke' . . . a do like tha way Colm uses words; a like lissanin ta im sometimes. It can be entatainin. Tha avver day, in tha pub, ee came aht av the bog wiv a great big grin on is face an said sammink like:

—Ther's somethin absurdly satisfyin about sittin on the bog ridin the ripe, risin reek of yer own hot, dropped fodder an then standin ter peer down at a statically seethin knot of beige vipers.

Cracked me up. An the way ee says fings like that, wiv a strut, as if ee's paradin abaht on a stage . . . makes me larf. Altho, a suppowse, in is mind like, Colm's always bin famous; ya can tell. In is mind, ee moves abaht in a spotlight. An the reality of it is is that ee'll spend tha little slice of lucid adulthood ee experiences befaw ee dies in a scummy little bedsit somewhere, fundin whateva drug habit he'll av by then by petty crime, rantin abaht imself an ow great he is an becomin an embarrassment, a burden, an a bore ta evryone oo knows im. He will die unloved, lonely, loathed. Sad, like, but that's what's gonna happen. It's fuckin written. Colm, undaneaf it awl, is just as confused an bewildered as tha rest of us, maybe maw so; that's why ee's sow addicted ta tellin stawries, cos they seem somehow ta give im some focus, aw meaning, aw goal. A mean ee's good, like, is stawries are good, an a like it sometimes when ee rants on; but tha drugs are baginnin ta tell on im now (not saprisin, arfta fifteen fuckin years of heavy abuse) an is shawt-term memory's awl shot ta fuck. Ee drifts off mid-sentence, ee repeats imself loads a times. Which is dull.

—An of course ther's thee attraction of the E itself, ee continues. —When yer gerra good un, E's the best fuckin drug ther is. Apart from tha fuckin Pink Cally tha put me in the ozzy tha time.

—What merks yuh think the E did that? Mairead says. —Could it not hav bin the speed lahk? Or the downers?

—Aw the smack? I say.

—Or the bottle uv vodka?

—Aw tha mawphine?

—Or the rum?

—Aw tha coke?

—Or the twentih-odd pints o'beer?

—Orright, orright, Colm shakes is head. —Shut the fuck up now ey. An al tell yer, Christ, when a woke up in the ozzy tha time like, a had bollox the sizer fuckin tennis balls. Doan know why like. An they wer perple as well.

The phone rings.

—Doan answer it! He hisses. —Irrull be the landlord or Sharon, an a doan wanner speak ter either of em. Lerrit ring.

—But it maht bih Sioned. She said shid ring us if er n Paul wanted t'come round or go out, Mairead says. —Shill think wuh not in if wih dorn't answer it.

Colm curls is lip an puts tha receiva ta is ear. Immediately ee scowls an ands it ta Mairead.

—Sharon, ee spits. —Fuckin knew it. Teller ter fuck off, Mairead. Shill come round ere, bring us all fuckin down, go on n on n on about why we didn't invite er ter the rave with us. 'Why didn yer invaht meeeerr? Why didn yer invaht meeeerr?' Cos yer a sour-faced, competitive, nasty little cow is why, Sharon. Fuck.

Ee lights a fag an scowls at tha TV screen. Mairead tawks politely on tha phown ta Sharon, as she awlways does, an fuck knows why. Sharon ownly seems appy when she's abusing, using or ridiculin someone . . . a down't like er, but a can feel sorry for her; her burden was ta be bawn ugly, a mean physically like, an it can't be easy bein ugly in this wirld . . . it turns ya ugly inside, awl that abuse. Howeva, I have no fuckin sympathy fa the way she exploits Mairead; thir's a niceness in Mairead which people like Sharon will always fuckin prey on. Sharon just takes – she gives nothin back. A mean, when Colm or Mags're on the scrounge a down mind payin fa them cos their, like, entatainin, intrestin people ta be wiv. Mowst of the time. Sharon, tho, is just a pain in tha arse.

—Shit, a say. —That's awl we fuckin need.

Colm just grinds is teeth.

A watch Mairead tawkin, bein polite an nice ta someone oo ownly seems ta see er as a potential sawce of ready money. Tha MDMA that's still tinglin in me brain is sparkin off thawt prowcesses, fings which could be insights but am not sure. Am thinkin, am lookin at Mairead an am thinkin, that what would solve her problems, what would stop her drinkin, what would give her a new reason fa livin is a baby. A fink a baby would sawt her out . . . but then a rememba what Colm towld me once, in confidence like when ee was pissed, that she's ad sow many miscarriages an abawtions that she's now incapable of carryin a child ta term. She's barren. Whevva that's true aw not a dunno, but maybe that's why she stays wiv Colm, because he's like a baby; he also needs lookin arfta, he's also a monsta of appetites . . . ee even shits is kex at times n awl.

Am down now. Now am down. Aw Christ.

—Let's go aht, a say ta Colm. —A down wanna be ere if Sharon's comin round. Let's go tha pub.

Colm nods an gestures wiv is head at tha phown. —Let's see wha shiz said ferst. She might not be comin round.

—OK then, Mairead says. —Orright . . . yeh . . . see yer then, darlin . . . bye.

She replaces the receiva.

—Wharrud she say?

—Said shiz goin back up Wigan way for a few ders. Assed if you had any speed left an a said nor.

—So that's it? Shiz not comin round?

—Just for a bit, yeh, bifore she gors lahk.

—Fuck. Why?

—She wants t'borror thutty quid.

Colm looks at er. —An you said yeh?

She nods.

—Oh Jesus fuckin Christ.

He stabs is fag out savagely an stands up.

—Come ed, Mal. Let's go the fuckin pub.

—Sor am t'be left here on mah orn wither, am ah?

Colm shrugs. —*You* fuckin invited the silly twat round. *You* can fuckin entertain er. Al fuckin belter one if am ere when she calls.

He stamps out inta tha kitchen as ee gows ta fetch is jacket. Fuck. A was avin such a good time n awl.

—Am sorreh, Mairead says, shruggin. —Ah coulden ser nor, could ah? Shiz off t'see her parents lahk. A dorn't think shill ster very long, shiz ornleh comin round ferrer bit shih said.

Yeh, a think, that'll be right; shill just take tha money an fuck off. Typical.

—Down worry abaht it, a say. —A feel fuckin sorry fa ya, that's awl, avin ta put up with tha fuckin bint. Comen meet us in tha pub when she gows, yeh? But ownly when she goes. Don't, whateva ya do, bring er wiv ya.

Mairead nods an a go inta tha bedroom ta wake up Margaret. Fuck. A can hear Colm mutterin to imself in tha kitchen, an a can feel tha remnants of tha E leavin me system awlmowst like fluid pawrin aht of me pores as if a tap's bin turned on. Reality rearin its ugly fuckin head. Shit.

It's fuckin freezin aht here, really really cowld, an tha rowd aht ta Devil's Bridge is awl iced up. The car's fuckin slewin evrywhere, an Paul's fuckin mad n erratic drivin ain't makin anyfin any fuckin easya.

—Fa fuck's sake, Paul, slow fuckin dahn, will ya? Wir gonna end up in tha fuckin valley!

Ee cackles like a madman. Thir's ownly a flimsy wire fence at the

445

side av tha rowd – some crappy wooden powsts an a few strands av chicken wire are awl that lie between me an excruciating, mutilated death. Paul down't seem arsed tho, ee's larfin away like a mad fucka an swervin awl ova tha fuckin place, avin tha time of is fuckin life. Ee's not got a death wish aw anyfin, ee's just a dipstick. I cling on ta me seat an ope fa tha fuckin best, shittin meself like, teeth chatterin both in fear an in tha icy wind that's blowin through tha car's browken vents. When awl's said n done, tho, am probably safe wiv Paul drivin; far as a know, ee's neva ad an accident in is life. Car accident, a mean. Ee might be actin tha cunt but ee knows wha ee's doin.

An no soona do a fink that than ee loses controwl; the car swerves on tha ice, skids, a piss meself as it starts driftin ova to tha fence an tha massive drop tawards death but at tha larst mowment Paul yanks tha wheel an it straightens up again. Arm fuckin angry now.

—Ya see! Ya fuckin stupid arse! Coulda fuckin ad us bowth fuckin killed! Slow fuckin down, you twat!

Ee larfs, but a can tell ee's a bit freaked n awl; there's a tremor in is larfta an in is voice as ee speaks:

—Ah stop yuh moanin. Old fuckin biddy. Yuh want to live for ever?

—Well no, a say, —but nor do a wanna die at twenty-fuckin-seven.

Ee slows down, an as we gow through Pisgah a council grit lorry pulls aht in front av us, shittin out a lowd uv salt an grit from its back end awl ova tha icy rowd. Bits av grit ping off tha windscreen. Paul gows: —Cunt, an a larf as ee's fawced ta slow to a crawl.

—Don't even fink abaht ovatakin im, Paul. Wir nearly there anyway.

—Fuckin ope so. Av got tuh be back soonish tuh pick Sioned up from thuh station.

Just outside Pisgah an thir's a couplea vans parked in a lay-by at tha side of tha rowd. Thev bin converted inta mobile houses; chimneys in tha rooves wiv smowk comin aht av em n stuff, stacks of logs an bags of rubbish outside. Thed look cosy if it wasn't for awl tha detritus, awl tha shite; rusty supamarket trolleys, burst bin-bags, twisted prams. Awl kinds of stuff like. It's a fuckin pit.

—This them? Paul arsks.

—A guess so.

—Al wait ere.

Ee pulls ova an a get aht. Fuckin freezin it is. A can feel me face turnin blue. A helicopta flies ova, low, an disappears ova tha hill inta tha mountains; probably lookin fa those hikers who've disappeared recently. Faw uv em, a think it is now. Hikers. Just vanished in tha mountains.

Tha sahnd of its rotors dies aht an then thir's silence agin, towtal silence apart from tha wind. A little skinny brown dog looks up at me from whir it's lyin in tha scrappy grass. —Good boy, a say, an knock at the daw uv one of the vans. Some crusty geeza arnsas it, lookin just as a expected; cammy jacket, dreads down to is arse, rings in is nowse an lips. Runes on a string rahnd is neck. The usual crap.

—Yeh?

—Erm, am lookin fa Suzannah. Mickey sent me.

—Mickey? Oo's Mickey?

—Er, Methadone Mickey. From Aber.

Ee looks me up n down an then gows back inta tha van. A hear is voice, maw Southern than mine:

—Zannah! Sam can et the daw faw yah!

Charmin. Twat.

A girl's voice, fainta:

—Oh can you sawt it aht, am on the bog!

The crusty cunt reappears again.

—Wha is it ya arftah?

—Just a quart.

—Yeh, of wha? Smoke?

—Yeh.

—Cam in then, cam in. Down't let awl the fuckin cowld air in.

A follow im inta tha van. It's so fuckin dark in there that a carn see a fuckin fing ahtside of a three-foot radius, an in tha three feet there's a lowd uv dried plants, a set of weighing scales an dirty plates on an upturned crate an a baby asleep in a bundle of clothes and blankets. At the baby's feet is a big tabby cat, lookin contentedly at me wiv bright green eyes. The place smells of fried onions an patchouli oil an tha funny, milky whiff tha ya awlways get arahnd babies.

447

—Drought still on in tahn, is it yeh?

—Yeh, a say. —Lowds of avver stuff like but no blow. Place's fuckin flooded wiv brown.

—Oh a know that. Money.

A give im me dosh an ee ands ova a chunk of resin. Fair size awlright but it looks crumbly in texture an light in colour; probably crap, weak as fuck no doubt. Beggas carn be choosas tho, can they?

—Ya arftah anyfin else, man?

—What like?

Ee gets awl pally now, actin awl matey, puttin is and arahnd me shoulda an leanin clowse. So clowse tha a can see bits of food cawt in is beard.

—Well nah . . . ah've got on me person a very special, very new kind av MDMA. I personally av nevah, ah say nevah, ad anyfin remowtly like it in my fuckin life. An that's a fahkin troof, man, a say that's a fahkin *troof.*

A just raise me eyebrows. This twat sounds like Foghorn fuckin Leghorn.

—Evah ad a Dennis the Menace then?

—Fuck yeh, a say. —Loadser times.

Ee grins an nods. —Well –

—They're crap.

Ee looks awl insulted. —Rhubarbs an Custards then? Them mental fuckahs?

A nod.

—Well, this gear makes em look like fahkin aspirin, man. Am tellin ya; ah was buzzin fa seventy-two fahkin hours, man, an that's no fahkin jowk. Free days, free nights. Am tellin ya, man; this gear is *special.* Ya won't want naffin else evah arftah this.

A probably carn trust this geeza but a have heard that thir's some mad pills goin round; Iestyn's bin ravin abaht em fa the past two weeks. An a fuckin love E like and, well, when it's good, it's awlways worth tha risk.

—OK, a say. —Ow much?

—Well nah . . . ow match would ya be prepared ta pay fa such a hit? Once-in-a-lifetime buzz, man.

A pretend ta think. Startin ta feel cocky now. Colm's right when ee says that it don't behove a physical coward ta be as cocky as a am sometimes (an I *am* a fuckin coward, ah yeh, av got no qualms abaht admittin that; first sign av lumba an am away like tha fuckin clappers), but a carn fuckin help meself. It'll probably get me fuckin hospitalised one day like, but . . . an anyway, this cunt deserves it; ee's a prick. So a pull meself up ta me full height an say:

—Well, given that what am *prepared* ta pay is inevitably commensurate with what am *able* ta pay, let's say, ooo . . . seventy-three pence?

Ee just stares, expressionless.

—Twelve pahnd.

—Orright.

Av still got some money left ova from tha wanky chippy job a did; me mowst recent haul from tha till netted me an extra fawty quid so even if this E's a dud a still won't really lose aht. Be a bit uvver pissa if it is tho; it's not sow much tha money spent as tha fuckin disappointment. Awl tha excitement an anticipation wasted. A should av arsked Reggie, tha mate of Robbie's like, if thir was any news abaht tha latest tabs on tha Internet when a saw im in tha park yestaday. Ee's clued in abaht E, Reggie is.

A give im tha cash an ee gives me tha pill. Small n white, as they usually are; just looks like a common-or-garden dove ta me. Al save it for a special occasion an hope it does tha job.

There's a figure movin abaht in tha shadows at tha back of the van; pale n thin n ghostly. It's probably Suzannah like, but aht tha cawna av me eye it's awl spindly an pallid. Movin slow. Like a huge albino spider doin t'ai chi. Freaks me aht a bit so a fank im an fuck off.

A go back ta the car an Paul drives us back inta town. Ee drops me off at Llys Wen an then gows ta fetch Sioned from the station. A hide in me room, lissen ta some good music an sample tha pot: not too bad. Av ad betta, but av alsow ad a lot worse.

> Some say the devil is dead
> The devil is dead, the devil is dead
> Some say the devil is dead
> And buried in Killarney!

I know he rose again!
I know he rose again!
I know he rose again,
Ter lead the Tory Party!

Liam an Colm singin their stupid fuckin rebel songs. Thev bin doin it awl fuckin night. They sing it again, ownly this time they change tha larst line ta 'join the British Army'. They sing it wiv gusto, some real venom, as if theh bein really fuckin subversive, as if gettin pissed by a lake in the Welsh mountains at two a'clock in tha mawnin will in any way alta that cunt Major's policies in Ulster. As if. Pair av bleedin dipsticks.

Colm moves jerkily in an aht tha light of tha fire where Liam's fryin sausages. They smell fuckin gorgeous. Laura's behind im, runnin a brush through is long hair, which looks poncey when not in a powny-tail. Fuck, what am a sayin? It looks poncey when it's in a powny-tail as well. Colm is completely boozed, pissed off is face, a mean utterly, a doan fink av eva seen im this aht av it wivaht bein in a coma. Ee keeps on fawlin ova in tha mud by thá side av the lake an just lyin there on is back cavvered in crap, larfin an babblin gibberish ta imself. Is jeans cawt fire befaw an ee ran inta tha lake ta put tha flames aht an then made us awl lissen ta im while ee towld us again tha fuckin stawry abaht findin a dead body in tha harba, a stawry which wiv awl hird abaht twenty fuckin times now an which am not so sure is even true. Ya can neva tall wiv Colm; a mean, ee embellishes, ee exaggerates, sometimes ee tells downright lies . . . it's like tha stawry about when ee was a sawcepan an ee met tha wolf in the Welsh Mountain Zoo; evry time ee recites tha fuckin stawry it's different. Sometimes it ends wiv im actually *in* tha wolf's cage, which am sure must be bullshit. Ow could ee av climbed ova tha bars, if ee was ownly a nippa? A down't fink ee knows imself any maw what's true or not, what really happened. A down't fink tha distinction between fantasy an reality exists fa Colm any maw.

The lake shines silva in tha moonlight an tha mountains loom up arahnd us, immense lumps av a deepa blackness against tha night sky. People's faces, sittin in a circle rahnd tha fire, are like orange moons, complete wiv craters an plains an hills. There's no music (apaht from the God-awful singin); there was, like, befaw; someone brawt a ghetto blarsta an was playin Leftfield on it, but Colm fell ova on ta tha machine when ee was drippin wet an it won't work now. Colm didn't apologise, of cawse; just larfed. Ee's bin in a foul, aggressive mood awl night, verbally attackin evrybody; ee sent Sioned off in a huff befaw by callin er a racist cow (prompted by a stawry Sioned towld abaht er sista playin a joke on er by arskin er tha Welsh word fa 'dog' – which is 'cŵn' – as they were wawkin parst a black fella). Ee went on abaht ow racism ain't purely an English disease, it's endemic throughaht tha British Isles, which Sioned, in er dangerous idealisation of awl things Welsh an blinkered demonisation of awl fings English, disagreed with, which was tha trigga Colm needed ta gow on tha offensive. Personally, I agreed wiv Colm like, but . . . best just ta keep ya gob shut.

. . . he's in . . . great danger, Colm is. Ee's fawlin apaht. Av awlways liked Colm; ee useta be completely imself, individual, wild wiv a really deep an incisive mind. Ya know like a dog is just so much a dog? Well, Colm was like that; awl Colm. One av the best blowks av met during me time in Wales. Now, tho, ee's rapidly becomin . . . well, sammink completely different, sammink which ee useta hate, a pitiful burden, a sad, wasted fuck-up. Ee's showin maw signs of ravage than any of us; burst veins on is nowse, even is teeth an hair are fawlin aht, ee's got no shawt-term memory ta speak of, which means that ee tells tha same stawries ova n ova agin which is deadly fuckin borin an annoyin, ee finks ee's lent ya money when ya know for a fact ee hasn't, insists ee's paid ya back money ee owes ya when ee hasn't. An is tempa now, Christ, ee's awlways ad a bad tempa, but now ee flies off tha handle at tha mowst negligible fings. Like befaw, when ee was staggerin abaht evrywhir around tha fire an Roy towld im ta watch imself; Roy was ownly tryin ta make sure tha Colm didn't hurt imself, but Colm was like:

—Oh, an why's tha? Cos a carn fuckin look after meself, is tha wha yer sayin? Yer think al fall an hert meself, do yer, yer think am a fuckin invalid?

With real aggression, like, ya know, as if ee was genuinely insulted. It was pointless. It's fuckin sad. Ee useta carry imself as if ee was impawtant, as if ee was special, but now, well, just fuckin look at im; ee's standin ere in full view of evrybody (an there's lowds of people ere, abaht thirty-odd, a lot of em we down't even know), swayin, dribblin, is knob angin aht of is flies an sprayin piss awl ova is boots. One girl is shakin er head an mumblin 'disgusting . . . disgusting' to erself. An it fuckin is n awl; is dignity's gone. A neva fawt ad say that abaht Colm, an as soon as a do a feel a horrible, heavy weight settle inside me. Is dignity's gone an left im, an that was awlways tha fing ee eld mowst dear.

Mairead isn't lookin at im, althow she's so drunk she probably down't even know ee's there. An am wonderin ow Margaret would react ta seein im like this; a know she likes im, in that special way like, an a wonda what shid do. Maybe, in tha long run, it'd do er good ta see im like this; shid realise then that ee's got a wide narsty streak as well, like tha rest av us. She ain't here, tho, she's off drinkin wiv that fat fucka Martin; a hope shiz awlright wiv im − av neva really trusted that bastard. Too creepy. Too shiny of face.

A take anavver swig of brandy. Mairead, somewhir on me left, says in a low, sad voice:

—What's it called when tha kills tha boyfriend? Is thuh a special nerm fer it, y'knor, like summat cide? Partnericide?

Sharon gows: —Twatticide!, an then cackles loudly. Mairead larfs n awl.

Colm stares at them bowth an then puts is knob away (a see, in tha firelight, a new wet stain spread ova tha top part of is knackered jeans).

—Fuck off, Sharon. An you too, Mairead. Just do one, the bother yer.

—Well, that's nice, Sharon says. —Tellin yer orn girlfriend who yer s'porsed t'love t'fuck off.

—Least a don't owe er nine undred fuckin quid. Leech.

—No, you owe er about fawer grand.

Colm strides ova ta Sharon, is teeth grindin sow loud a can fuckin hear em echoin off tha trees. A fink ee's gonna belt er wiv tha bottle of orange Mad Dog ee's owldin but ee doesn't; ee just stands thir ova her, lowds av people watchin, an says:

—Sharon, fuck off right now right outer me fuckin life an never come back inter it, yer ugly fuckin fatuous piecer shite. Am fuckin sicker yer angin round us liker bad fuckin fart, no one fuckin wants yer ere, when yer phone de owce we doan answer it, when yer knock on the door we pretend ter be out cos yer company's so fuckin unwanted. All yerrah is a pain inny arse, yer stupid, yer annoy evryone, yer totally fuckin useless, complete waster space. Al tell yer, the biggest mistake of me ole fuckin life so far was goin ter fuckin bed with you. Wharrever the fuck was a thinkin of? Wooden a done it if a wasn't so fuckin drunk, an a regret it every single fuckin day. A was rat-arsed, yeh, a fuckin *needed* ter be, burrit was sucher vile fuckin experience tharrah can still remember it. Liker nightmer. Yerran ugly fuckin pig. Avter stop meself from bein fuckin sick whenever a fuckin think of it. You truly ar the werst fuckin *dog* av ever ad the horrer of shaggin. I've been with some fuckin hounds like, but you wer by far the werst.

—Ah now, yeer out uv fuckin ordurr!, Liam yells. Mairead puts er face in er hands an Sharon runs off, back up ta tha cars.

—Pay de fuckin money back!, Colm yells arfta her. —Al smash up yer fuckin car if yer don't! Twat!

Ee turns on Liam.

—An what the fucker *you* buttin in for? Any o'your fuckin business is it? Ey? Wanker.

Ee stands unsteadily in tha firelight an fumbles in is pockets for a lowd av pills which ee washes down wiv a gulp of Mad Dog. Fuck knows what they are. Downas, ad imagine; an not befaw fuckin time.

—In fact, yer *all* a buncher fuckin wankers. Arse'oles, the lotter yer. Youse can all fuck off.

An then ee stumbles away inta tha blackness, inta tha mountains, parst tha plaque which commemorates tha battle of Hyddgen or whateva it is. Some owld fuckin bloodshed anyway. A tell meself tha Colm's behaviour is largely due ta tha drink an tha drugs an tha several sleepless nights, but a know, really, tha sammink's gone wrong with im. Sammink deep inside im as gone wonky, an it's gonna be very fuckin difficult, maybe even impossible, for im ta put it straight agin. What's appenin ta im? What's appenin ta awl of us? Where did tha fuckin rottenness begin, where are its roots?

A turn ta Mairead an offa er me brandy. She seems ta have sowbered up somewhat.

—Ya awlright?

She nods, but a can see wetness on er face an er mouth is shut tight in a thin line. Tha light av tha flames flickas off er cheeks an tha rings in er face an then off tha bottle as she tilts it to er lips an takes a massive swallow.

—Christ, Mairead, gow easy.

—Why?

A take tha brandy back off er an gulp at it meself. A feel a bit tingly, sittin ere close ta Mairead, just me an her. A tell ya, she should be wiv me. Ad be fuckin good ta her, I would. Am sittin sow close that a can smell the sowp she uses an a wanna lick er neck, er back, er arms. Malcolm an Mairead sahnds good. Proppa.

An maybe am drunk enough ta tell her this as a turn ta face her but she's awlready aht, lyin there on her back beneath the stars, comatose again through booze. A watch her lyin there, wrecked on the shores of the lake. A gorgeous heap of despair, if there can be such a fing.

There's a thawt gowin through my head. An idea like, slowly becomin an urge. A down't do fuck awl ta prevent it from germinating.

—Ah Jaysis fuck!

Liam as shook tha fryin pan an one av is sausages as leapt out inta tha flames. Ee reaches out fa it awtomatically but Laura, still brushin is girly hair, yanks im back an ee snaps at her:

—Will yis stop brushin me fuckin hurr as if it's a fuckin *sheep* that ah am! Jesus!

—Oh well. Sorry.

She lets go av is hair an sits back in a huff. Scowling, arms fowlded.

An a can see tha rest of tha night ahead, a can just see what's gonna happen: will awl get drunk, then thowse oo need ta will make friends again, then when dawn comes will awl gown search fa Colm in the mountains, tha wildaness, whereva tha fuck ee's got ta. Great fuckin fun. That's how it will happen. A can hear Sharon sobbing in tha car behind me, up on tha ridge. She didn't deserve that abuse from Colm. Ee was well out av fuckin awda.

A drink me brandy next ta tha snorin Mairead an watch tha sausage in tha fire become just anavver glowin emba. A can't believe tha life could offa me such a cawny fuckin symbol. A can't believe tha life would insult me fuckin intelligence so; a mean, aht av tha fryin pan an inta tha fuckin fire? Give me a break. Well cawny. A decide that this can't be a prophecy, because real life is neva so clichéd an shallow, althow a know that, of cawse, sometimes it certainly fuckin is.

Right: busy fuckin day taday as it appens so am gonna need a bit av a kick-start, so arfta av ad a showa a snawt a coupla lines – coke mixed wiv bill. Well rough on me fuckin shnozz like, burnin away in me face, an a fink am gonna chuck n awl on tha foul taste av it as it trickles dahn tha back ov me throat but a just gag a few times an drink some water an smowk a fag an then am away.

It's a fuckin beautiful mawnin as a walk dahn inta tha town, across tha fields an through tha uni. Thir's a group of students loungin around in tha cawtyard, arahnd tha bell tower like; a stride through em awl with tha drugs kickin in me chest an head, chewin gum, me eyes behind me shades scannin fa babes, of which thir's fuckin plenty, wearin ahdly anyfin in the hot wevva. It's fuckin great. One av em wawks parst me an brushes me arm; she wants it. Carn be maw than eighteen, tight tiny shawts an a cut-off top wiv 'NAUGHTY – BUT NICE' on it. Jesus Christ. If it wasn't faw tha whizz an that ad av a fuckin riot goin on in me trahsers. Fuck me.

Thir's a spring in me step an am fuckin whistlin as a wawk dahn Penglais Hill. Me brain's transmittin thawts at an incredible fuckin rate an me heart's hammerin farst. Jesus, Colm fuckin injects this stuff – mad barstard. That's why ee's flippin out; ya can't use drugs intravenously fa ten fuckin years an expect ta stay sane. A mean, look at Lou Reed; ee's now doin a collaboration wiv Dave bleedin Stewart. I rest my case.

From this vantage point I can see tha whole town below me, sandwiched between tha two huge green humps of Pen Dinas on tha left an Constitution Hill on tha right, awl hazy in tha bright sunshine, the sea awl grey an calm between them, behind tha town. They look like two immense guards, jailers like, standin watch an makin sure tha no fucka leaves. At tha mowment like a couldn't give a fuck, arm just buzzin, but sometimes a do feel that livin among mountains is difficult. Kind av oppressive. They hang ova ya, colossal an immovable, ya feel constantly watched. Not everyone can live in a place like this; frinstance tha mad geeza oo wrote that 'Guide' fing – he couldn't live here, literally – poor fucka topped imself, din he. Poor barstard. Still, thow . . . a can't rememba eva meetin im, like, but from wha people av towld me abaht im, it sounds like ee was a bit avver twat.

Well. Me legs're sweatin in tha heat – it's fuckin swelterin. A rememba Colm sayin once tha ee was so hot tha bein inside is kex would be like livin in a hairy deep-fat frya. A larf. A like that; hairy deep-fat frya. Ha.

First stop: dole office. A didn't receive a rent cheque larst week an am worried that they might av found out abaht me workin in tha chippy, but Paul, oo knows abaht these fings, said that if they ad uv they would've cawld me in fa intaview straightaway. That's what happened to im when that crazy bint Annie grassed im up. Arm still a bit fuckin worried, thow; fa one fing, am dahn ta me larst fuckin thirty quid an am near aht uv drugs n awl, so a need that fuckin cheque. A hate bein skint, I do. Bein on tha dole's fuckin awful, man, yav gotta work on tha side; a mean, it's governmentally acknowledged that tha dole is the barest minimum ya need ta savive, but I down't wanta merely savive an I down't see what tha fuck's wrong wiv that; a wanta drink, buy clowthes, books, drugs, rent videos, av fuckin fun while arm still young. A want that sensation of bein in controwl av your life that ya get wiv money in ya pocket; bein paw is so fuckin repressive, ya feel imprisoned, when yav got fuck awl money ya rirly become aware that there are fawces – people – aht there who controwl ya. I mean, they pull ya strings an press ya buttons as they would a machine. It's fuckin orrible. An yet, if ya get a job – pawly paid, like, which mowst jobs fuckin are, particularly thowse available to an Essex lad wiv fuck-awl qualifications – an ya sign off, then they hit ya fa council tax, full whack on tha rent, on public transpawt, prescription costs, fuckin evryfin. Terrible state av affairs. Ya can't let it get ya down tho, cos that's just what tha fuckas want. Awl ya can do is get by tha best ya can, an cultivate certain shopliftin an defrawdin skills. That's awl ya can do. An fuck it – it's enough, ain't it?

Grindin me teeth in tha dole office an the sound's echoin off tha wawls. Place's empty sept fa Dirty Derek an is snot-nosed sawcepans up at tha counta; he's gettin rirly fuckin exasperated, huffin an puffin an slappin is ands on tha glass barrier. Tha girl's tryin ta stay calm, tryin ta explain somefin to im, but ee won't av any of it. Ee's like a fuckin anorexic scarecrow, Derek is; ee's HIV-positive like, but arm sure ee's got tha full-blown AIDS by now cos ya can awlmowst see im wastin away befaw ya very eyes. Ee moved up ere from London when ee was diagnosed like, brawt is kids an is missus wiv im (oo quickly fucked off back dahn south on er own), probably finkin that it'd be healthier faw im ta live by tha sea an the mountains, sammink like that. Tha healing waters an awl that toss; apparently tha Victorians useta bring TB patients ere ta bathe in tha sea. Wevva it did em any good aw not a down't know, but it wouldn't now, not wiv tha turds an chemicals. An no amount av sea water, polluted aw not, will cure the Virus. It's certainly done fuck awl faw Derek.

—Ah yeh, yer can say that with this sheeta fuckin glass between us but yer wouldn't say it round this side, would yer? No! Cos ad fuckin throttle yer, that's why! Ya smug fuckin bitch! Ow can I be fit fa work when am HIV-positive? An ow tha fuck can I feed these, ey, can you fuckin feed them? Here – *you* fuckin feed them!

Ee picks is kids up an plonks em down on the counta, whereupon they start ta bawl. Screams rubbin on me fuckin nerve ends. Well annoyin. Tha girl behind tha glass is tryin ta calm tha Dirty Clan dahn but they're not avin any of it; the kids carry on screamin an the back av Derek's neck turns purple.

Fuck it, al come back later. Ow tha fuck can a sit an wait fa anyfin when av got a fuckin V8 engine roarin in me body? This gear's fuckin brilliant. Well good. Tha coke gives it a push like but this speed, God, arm tellin ya, when it kicks in ya fuckin know abaht it. Am buzzin me fuckin face off. Pukka. A feel like a god.

A leave an bump inta Roger ahtside tha Western Vaults. Ee's lookin a lot healthier than nawmal, puttin a bit uv weight on, an is hair's grown aht av its customary crop an am saprised ta see that it's actually curly. Fa some reason, a would neva of thawt of Roger as avin curly hair. Curly an blond; awlmowst cherubic in fact, it disturbs me somewhat ta say. Ee's wiv that bloke Ianto oo av met once aw twice, im from tha mountains wiv tha buck-teeth an tha inbred drool an tha manic giggle. No one knows oo is farver is, but ee's got is uncle's lolling tongue. Fuckin *Deliverance* ain't in it, man.

—Malcolm, yew twat!, Roger shouts. —What's-a fuckin news en, boy?

A shrug. —Ya see it awl, mate; skint, speedin . . .

Ee leans in clowse. —Yev not got enny left av yer? Only a could do with a toot like.

A shake me head. —Ad it faw breakfast, mate. Awl gone. Up me shnozz.

—Oh well. I believe yer. Thousands fuckin wouldn't like. Ey, yew doan know whir we can get old of enny E, do yer? Ianto's fuckin dyin ta get loved-up, in yer, boy?

Ianto giggles and dribbles an is ead bobs on is neck like one av thowse noddin dogs ya see in the back windows av family cars. Ee freaks me aht when am straight, but when am whizzin a can larf wiv im. No danger.

—Ya could try Jed, a say. —Or Jerry's. Scottish Iain did av some, some stars a fink, but ee's fucked off somewhir, fuck knows where like. No one's seen im fa ages.

Roger nods. —Al av a call up at Jed's en. Got somethin ter get tho first, an we, Ianto? Arfter a big fuckin dildo we ar.

Anavver giggle from Ianto.

—Mad Cyril still sellin em, is ee?

—Couldn't tell ya mate, a say. —Got no cawl fa them meself like.

—Ah no, yew still usin them cucumbers then ey? An a fuckin carrots an-a parsnips an Paulie's fuckin lad when ee feels like it aye!

Ianto finds this hysterically funny an am wonderin what these two want wiv a big dildo. Don't like ta fuckin fink.

Roger says ee'll be in touch an we go are separate ways, me up Great Darkgate Street an im to . . . well, whireva tha fuck ee's gowin. Down't rirly wanta know. Roger, he's, well, a mean sometimes ee's a good larf like but ya neva know whir ya are with tha fucka, ya can neva tell what ee's gonna do. He's sow unpredictable, ya can neva feel safe wiv im. Like the time at Iestyn's party when Roger nodded aht an that bloke from Wrexham, Tansey is name was, drew a moustache an beard on is face. Roger larfed about it when ee wowk up like, ee even left it on an ad a few drinks wiv Tansey, just tawkin like, bein pally an avin a natta, an then abaht five owas later in tha kitchen Roger crept up behind im an wiv awl is fawce it im on tha top uv is head wiv a full bottle uv Newcastle Brown. Well sick it was. A rememba it clearly; the sahnd like a gunshot, tha bottle birstin an sprayin tha room wiv beer, Tansey gowin down instantly like awl is bowns ad tirned ta jelly, tha blood streamin, gushin from is ears, is nose . . . it was orrible, it was; twisted an terrifying. A rememba finkin a was gonna throw. An Roger just stood thir lookin dahn at im, the beard an moustache (a big curly Three Musketeers-ish one) still on is face, spat on Tansey an booted im in tha bawls a coupla times an then went off ta jack up. A down't know what appened ta Tansey arfta that; I adta gown sit in tha garden for a bit. I presume someone took im ta hospital, cos thir was no sign av im when a went back in; just a dark n bloody stain.

This memory leads me on ta annaver, just as unpleasant one as a weave in n aht av the shoppas; abaht two months agow a was doin this very same fing – wawkin up tha main rowd, speedin – an a spotted Peter, tha badger-baitin cunt, lurchin across tha rowd an in n aht av shops, howling, leavin a trail av blood behind im. A dived inta Superdrug cos ee was scarin me like but not befaw a nowticed that ee ad a machete buried in is shoulder, just above tha collarbown like, sunk right in. Staggerin awl ova tha busy rowd ee was, bleedin evrywhir, people runnin away from im like, draggin imself inta shops an screamin. One av tha wirst fings av eva seen. Apparently, as a fahnd out later, Fat Charlie ad done it ta him arfta burnin im aht av is caravan in Bow Street. A down't know what faw like, but Fat Charlie was foreva doin fings like that – blood money, ya see. Ee'd break people's legs fa twenty quid; what ee charged fa machete-ing some paw cunt, a down't know. Ee was anavver fuckin psycho ee was, Fat Charles. An what a farce is fuckin funeral was; none av us liked im anyway, an Paulie was thir trippin away on acid, Mags n Mairead pissed off their faces an fawlin ova tha gravestowns . . . a neva wanted ta gow in tha first fuckin place. No loss ta tha world, one less violent barstard. But is sista invited us so I had ta gow a suppowse.

Anyway.

A see Dai Datblygu in tha square but ee's incoherently rat-arsed an ain't makin any sense at awl so a nip for a pint an a toot in tha Ship an Castle an then head off dahn tha supamarket. Somerfield; it's tha easiest one ta nick from, a piece a piss, cos a know some people oo wirk thir an they've towld me tha codes; 'Manager ta checkout three' means they've spotted someone, 'Staff announcement fa Bill Rhodes' means there's a team on tha rob, et cetera. So when ya hear that ova tha tannoy ya know yuv bin rumbled like so ya can put ya nicked stuff back on tha shelves an righteously demand an apology when ya leave tha shop an the staw detective searches ya pockets an finds fuck awl on ya. Ace. A need lowds av stuff taday like, food-wise av got faw slices of bread an a tin of tuna up at tha owce but cos arm speedin food is tha larst fing on me mind; it's not a good idea ta gow shopliftin when ya speedin – ya fink that ya'll neva eat again, so ya end up swipin useless stuff like mugs an magazines an toys. Ya get tha confidence wiv tha speed like but ya powers av reasonin ain't exactly up ta scratch, but anyway tha practicalities down't really fuckin matta – it's tha buzz, tha thrill . . . not tha a get much av that any maw. Shopliftin's really just anavver job now; anavver chore that needs ta be done.

It's nice an cool inside Somerfield wiv tha air-conditionin but a can't stand that hideous fuckin muzak. Av neva undastood why they play that; it's suppowsed ta create a relaxin atmosphere ta shop in, but awl it does is grate on ya nerves an make ya wanta get aht av thir fast's ya fuckin can. Tha fruit an tha vegetables are awl garishly coloured; they look fake, too vivid, plasticky. Am grindin me jaws an sniffin like av got fuckin pleurisy an arm wandarin through tha shoppin people unda tha bright lights an am feelin fuckin great.

Thir's Roy by tha fish counta.

—Ya awlright, Roy?

—Sound, Malcolm. Stand there, will yer.

A guard im while ee pockets some smowked salmon an shoves a packet av Irish oystas dahn is trahsers. That must be cold.

—Nice one. Ta.

—Maw than welcome, Royston.

A go dahn tha next aisle. This is ace, this, just wandarin through these commodities an not wantin any av em. Tha drugs av shrunk me stomach ta tha size av a fuckin peanut an the thawt of food is bleedin awful; a could no soona eat right now than a could mainline spew (which may be one av Colm's comparisons, am not sure; sahnds like it). Wiv ya natural appetites taken away from ya an relatively freed from need ya can see these products fa what they really are – false wants, manufactured requirements, useless, empty, vapid, merely a piss-poor representation uv choice designed ta provide ya wiv a sham sense of shallow fulfilment. Hollow offerings, that's awl. A mean, do we rirly need fawty types of deodorant? Baked beans wiv HP sawce added? Do we bollox. Let them decay.

A take an extra strong sniff an the chemicals burn nicely dahn me throat. Standin by these silent objects an waitin fa the consequent rush an a feel fuckin wondaful. Pukka.

Rhodri, by tha dairy counta, winks at me as ee pockets a block of cheese. It's a big one n awl, angin down thir on is hip like some kind av fuckin hernia. Griff wawks past wiv a big grin on is face an is jumpa bulgin as if ee's preggas. A see Cerys – an for a kleptomaniac she's a bit too fuckin casual abaht tha way she steals – slip a frozen chicken in er bag an then take off, followed by a middle-aged fella in a tie who is quite conspicuously tha staw detective. Am safe, then; while ee's off followin Cerys a can pay a visit ta tha booze section.

A pass Laura on tha way, lookin through tha damaged goods shelf fa Liam's tea. Dented peas an smashed pie. See? Obey tha law an ya eat like a fuckin tramp.

At tha booze section an a slip a half-bottle av vodders dahn the front av me trahsers an annaver one dahn tha back. Quarta-bottle av Scotch in each front pocket an a bottle uv red wine up me baggy sleeve an a take a faw-pack av Heineken up ta tha checkout. Yav gotta buy sammink in awda ta allay suspicion; attracts attention if ya down't. A buy a magazine as well an ownly muzak comes aht of tha tannoy as a do so, a smile at tha doris operatin tha till an awlmowst burst out larfin at tha pained expression on Roy's face as ee pays fa is tea bags; those oystas must av fuckin frozen is bawls by now. They'll be like two Brussels sprouts in tha freeza section.

As arm leavin tha shop a hear a voice cawlin tha manager ta checkout three; wonda who's bin spotted. Ad like ta stay an watch tha action but am carryin too much contraband like so a wawk aht inta tha sunlight an weigh up me choices: find somewhir ta sit on tha beach, read me magazine an get wrecked; gown do tha same at howm; call on Colm an Mairead . . . So many choices. *Real* fuckin choices n awl; things a wanta do.

Then a rememba that av still gotta gown see what's appened ta me cheque in tha dole office. Shit. Ad fagotten abaht that, in me fun. Still, that shouldn't take too long like, an av got pockets filled wiv booze an a good few lines left in me wrap. Carrots befaw tha donkey, blindin. A squeeze one nostril shut an sniff up hard with tha avver one ta get any residue from me larst toot an head off ta tha dole office as annaver rush starts a-tinglin in me thighs. Great fuckin day. So far.

Twelve fuckin quid fa a dud E. Barstard fuckin crusty rip-off merchant wankas. Takin a fuckin liberty. Ad get someone ta Molotov tha cunt's caravan if there wasn't a bleedin baby in it. Let's howp ee ain't sowld any ta Roger aw Griff aw Ikey, someone like that; they'll fuckin disembowel tha tossa, which is no maw than ee fuckin deserves. Cunt. A fuckin hate it, a rirly fuckin do; av not got much money as it is, an not ownly av a wasted twelve quid on that fuckin paracetamol or whatevva tha fuck it was but av ad ta buy two wraps uv bill as well sow's a can at least get a hit off fuckin sammink. Fuck. Selfish mercenary sly barstards. World's fuckin full av em.

Av bin pissed off since yestaday arftanoon, when a discovered that the E was dud. Tha whizz helped for a while like, but now arm comin down agin arm fuckin twice as fed up as a was. A know arm bein a grumpy fucka but a carn fuckin help it; anyone would be. Such a bleedin disappointment. Yestaday teatime, when a finally adta admit that the pill wasn't gonna work a went ta buy a pizza an while we waitin faw it ta cook Colm grabbed tha awda pad an wrote on it awdas faw stuff like 'one toejam an winnit deep-pan . . . side order of fanny batter . . . pube an egg salad', an a towld im ee was childish an puerile an stupid an was makin a fool av imself, but rirly it was me – it was me oo was actin tha twat. Nawmally a would've fahnd it funny, what Colm did like, but yestaday . . . a just couldn't help it. Gettin ripped off is such a bleedin downa.

An it's just my fuckin luck ta be sittin by a bunch av E kids. Naive fuckas. Listen to em:

—Ah yeh, man, it's the only way ter sort out the world's problems, innit? Make every politician, every banker, every fuckin straight-peg drop a Dove an go to a rave an I'll guaranfuckintee yer there'll be no more wars, or starvation, or greed . . . nothin like that, ever again.

—Yeh. Everywahn will lav each avvah . . .

—An end to fighting all over the world. Can yer imagine it, man? An end to violence. All over the fuckin world.

Rolf, whose garden we're awl sittin in, butts in then an tells em that they down't avver fuckin clue an starts gowin on abaht how ee was thir when it awl kicked off, the whowl scene, he was at Horizon, he was at Shoom. The E kids just look at im as if ee's tawkin Greek aw sammink. They ain't nevva heard av Shoom befaw; probly fink it's some kind av new n trendy hi-energy drink faw when ya startin ta crash.

Sad, misguided fuckwits. Oh yeh, E is tremendous, an incredible fuckin buzz like, maybe tha very best, but it's worlds away from bein any sawt av panacea. It's just anavver drug which takes ya away from evryfink an allows ya ta have a great time. That's awl. It can't solve naffin outside tha personal, an whevva it can help even in that way aw not is debatable. A mean, look at acid in tha sixties; evryone thawt it was tha saviour, a step on tha way to a new, higha consciousness, an what's become av such people now? Three wirds: Richard fuckin Branson. Genesis. Roger bleedin Waters.

—Yer still up on that whizz, Mal?

A tirn ta Colm an shake me head.

—Nah, not rirly. Wearin off now like. Could do wiv some maw ta tall ya tha truth.

Ee passes me a wrap an a take a few dabs. The waster's Sherbet Fountain. Thir's a wodge uv gum in Colm's gob tha size avver bleedin tennis bawl an is eyes're twitchin awl ova is face. Sheep're munchin tha grass a few feet behind im in tha field.

The girls're tawkin abaht . . . what are they tawkin about? Words faw 'fanny', it sounds like:

—In America it means bum, apparentlih, Mairead says. —Geraint torld mih.

Maggie gows: —It's the waird 'vadge' I hate. 'Vadge' . . . it just sounds all kind of fat an splayed an stuff. It's horrible.

—Hairy clam.

—Oh yeh!

—Or 'frontbum', that's t'wust. As if it has nor function other than tuh excrete lahk. 'Cunt' is actually t'nicest one, cos it comes from t'serm linguistic root as 'queen'. Sow when tha thinks about it lahk . . .

—Ah, that's nice, Mags says, awl wistful. —My own little queen . . .

—That's bullshit, Mairead, Colm says. —Yer carn praise a werd simply cos of its etymology. A mean, it's become so fuckin detached from its roots now, 'cunt' is a harsh, brutal werd. Wharrif someone referred ter you as a cunt, like av seen some fellers doin ter women, in the streets like? As if that's all yerrah, nothun else, juster fanny like, would yer think yud been complimented? No, would yer fuck. Would yer feel regal an majestic?

An so on. Colm continuin is prowcess av bludgeonin Mairead inta submission. Not physically, av cawse, but thir are avver ways, aren't thir? Ee's bin doin this faw a long time now, Colm has; an tha distressin fing is that ee down't even know ee's doin it. Am tellin ya, Mairead would be far better off wiv me. Too fuckin right.

Mags is now bein towld off by some hippy earth-mavver type faw smowking. Ya know the sawt; late thirties or early fawties, flowery dress, patchouli oil, ratty hair, dim an dazed expression. She's gowin on abaht ow Maggie's body is a temple which shouldn't be polluted. Maggie's just starin at er. A rememba this woman; it was her at Iestyn's party oo was awl ova Liam an Colm, followin em arahnd, fetchin em drinks, actin as if they wir some sawt uv divine twins when awl they were wir drug-addled Scouse Mick gits wiv recedin fuckin hairlines. A rememba Colm windin this bird up; she said that ee looked like a 'dissipated angel' an Colm went off on one, sammink like:

—Djer fuckin blame me fer bein dissipated? Fuck all romantic about it, like, Christ, life is short, dull, an ultimately humiliating. All yer dreams'll sooner or later tern ter dung. Without drugs an drink life isn even werth fuckin livin; it's not werth the fuckin effert. Angelic me arse.

This upset tha doris like an she started tawkin about ow shiz got a son of Colm's age an that if ee eva began ta fink like im it would be tha wirst fing she could eva imagine. It was quite sad, actually; a mean, she seemed genuinely upset. An Colm, tha cunt, when she went off ta get anavver drink, spewed up in er handbag. Hand-stitched by Guatemalan peasants it was n awl. Colm didn't do it maliciously like, a mean it just shot aht, but yav still got ta feel sorry faw er, ain't ya? Her heart's in tha right place, like, an ya can tell that she was once very pretty an that losin er looks as probly bin a fuckin catastrophe in er life, specially losin em sow young (altho ad still give er one, as it appens). A fink thir's some fawm av addiction in er parst; ya can see it in er eyes. But now she's cleaned up an she exhibits the self-righteous smugness of the bawn-agin an refawmed, which does tend ta wind people up, a mean even Mags is avin a gow at er now:

—Crap! That's just crap! Am twenty-two years old, djer think a cair whether smoking'll give me wrinkles? Smokin is fuckin ace! A love it when av been speeding for days an smoking like a chimney an me lungs're red raw and I inhale an a can feel the nicotine fuckin rippin through me n stuff! It's ace! Smoking is enjoyable, satisfying, and what's more a think it's cool!

An ta prove er point she takes an extra long drag on er Camel. The E heads are lookin worried. The earth-mavver's lookin sad again, an I imagine that, to her, it must seem like awl tha people arahnd her who possess that which she held mowst dear an which she deeply mourns tha passin of – youth, a mean – are tryin ta throw it away in tha mowst rapid, undignified, dirty way possible. Poor ole doris. She probly down't wanta accept ow much fings have changed since she was in er twenties.

Colm's still rantin away at Mairead. The earth-mavver watches im an when ee stops fa breath she taps im on tha shoulder an says:

—I can help you, you know. Your two chakra is blocked. That's why you're so uptight. Let me remove it, let me free your energy. You poor soul.

Colm just stares. —Yer wha?

Anavver woman joins in, hard-faced sawt wiv dyed black hair an bangles. Ovagrown Goth: —It's not that, Di, she says. —It's cos he hates women. Like all men. He hates women.

Colm throws back is head an larfs: —I don't hate women! I've fucked hundreds of em!

They ignaw him an start tawkin to each avver abaht their shawls, one av which is Peruvian, the avver's from Afghanistan. But Colm wown't leave em alone:

—Djer know wha? Ee says, leanin towards em. —Aller this is so much shite. Political correctness is just lip-service fer you, inni? Just werds like. An what yer do – this fuckin combin of shops fer foreign artefacts which yer buy simply for the political kudos an which yer then wear as an ostentatious badge of phoney compassion – is tantamount ter plunder. It's fuckin bollox. I see more fuckin colonialism ere than I do liberality. Loader fuckin shite.

Thir's a smile playin across is face an a know what ee's doin, a can recawl is words from abaht a month agow when ee ad a row wiv a lecturer from tha university at a party: 'They think I'm a Scouse gyppo tea-leaf, well, that's wha they'll get. An they'd berrer fuckin watch it cos am a great fuckin thief n all. But then, yer see, when they think they've got me nicely pigeon-oled, I'll hit em with some intelligence, some articulacy – watch the gawps on ther fuckin dials. Offend them with ther own stupid prejudices.'

He cawls it, arfta some sixties Black Power fing, 'Mau Mau-ing'; I cawl it acting tha cunt. An not fuckin knowin when ta stop:

—An anyway, why's Afghanistan so fuckin great? If yer went over ther wearin tha shawl now, as yer are, with yer face an hands uncovered like, yud be stoned ter fuckin death. When Russia was at war with Afghanistan, a young pilot crashed in the desert. Injured, lost, fuckin terrified, not knowin what the fuck ter do, ee called at the nearest tent fer help. The tent was fuller women peasants, probly makin fuckin shawls ter sell ter Westerners like, an yer know what thee did? Thee stripped im naked, tied im to a tree, an *pulled* is balls off. Not cut, or sliced – pulled. Tied a rope around em an heaved til thee came away from is body. Nice, eh?

Jesus Christ. Ee's losin it, Colm is, arm tellin ya. Ee's comin afuckinpart.

A tirn ta Mags but she's off in a world avver own. Tha bawda av Rolf's garden is marked by a row of pretty stones an shells n stuff, probly put thir by is sawcepans like, an one av tha objects is a big chunk of perspex wiv a sea hawse embedded in it. Mags has this right up to her face an is smilin an mutterin ta erself:

—Ah . . . small sea horse . . . God, you're so gorgeous . . .

She's tawkin to it, rapt. Probly tha shroom tea she drank faw mugs av earlier.

A nowtice a big, black, scabbed-ova wound on tha end av Colm's thumb an am just abaht ta arsk im ow ee got it when Liz runs inta tha garden yelling:

—Rolf! The police are outside! Ther coming in!

—Oh fuck.

Instant action: Rolf leaps up from tha swing ee was perching on an legs it inta tha house, thir's a mad scramble as evryone stashes their gear in bushes, socks, shoes, some people gobble em down, one fella grabs Rolf's cat an tries ta shove is bag av pills up it's arse, thir's hashchunks, E, whizz, skag, downas, acid, evryfin. Black Jerry, oo a know faw a fact was carryin coke an smack as well as whizz, owpens awl is wraps up inta is drink an necks tha fuckin lot. A whole fuckin pharmacy straight dahn is gregory. Wir awlright, tho, me, Mairead, Mags, et cetera, cos we did awl owa drugs in owers agow, when it was still dark. Apart from tha wrap Colm passed me earlier, which ee now swallows the rest of.

Mairead ain't bovvered anyway, she's pissed as a fart. Arsehowled. She starts arskin Colm, as two filth wawk purposefully up tha garden tawards us, abaht some syringe she fahnd in tha laundry basket tha avver day:

—Oo's wuh it, Colm? A want t'knor, now. Av got a right t'fuckin knor.

—Fuck knows, not mine, now shut the fuck up, ere's the busies. Shut yer gob.

—Well, ah pricked mih fuckin finger on it. Could av AIDS now or owt for all ah knor.

—Shurrup.

One av the Bill speaks ta us in Welsh, an one av tha E kids in a trembly voice gows:

—Dunno watcha sayin, mistah. Can only speak English.

Plod looks indignant, but awlsow smug:

—Well, yew would know what I was saying if yew spoke God's language, now, wouldn't yew?

Fuck's sakes. Fuckin Welshies. Bill sirches us but fails ta find anyfin. One av the E kids starts cryin, Black Jerry starts tryin ta waltz rahnd tha swings wiv an owld coppa oo's avin none av it.

—Ey, yer carn fuckin search er, Colm says as a coppa starts friskin Mairead. —Is ther norra WPC with yer?

—Afraid not.

—Well, ther fuckin should be. Yer carn search er. It's illegal.

Plod sighs. —Yes. Of course, there are plenty of female officers back at the station. Ee looks Colm an down as if ee's sammink just bin wiped off is size ten.

—Aw Colm, Mairead says. —Ah'm not fussed.

—And we don't need profanity, plod gows on. —Sign of laziness. Surely there are other words you can use? You *do* know some other words, don't you?

—Yeh. Me arse.

Plod sneers at Colm an Mairead howlds er arms out.

—Go on then. Do tha wust. Ah'm clean.

Colm watches the pig like a hawk as ee pats Mairead dahn. Rolf yells ta us from tha bottom of the garden, a coppa on each arm:

—Well, am off to the station, peeps! Bastards found me stash! Elp yuhselves tuh home-brew!

Ee's led away arahnd the house.

—I'm afraid none of you will be drinking any more, says the Bill oo frisked Colm. Fuckin hook-nose an ginger beard. An down't ya hate fuckwits oo say 'I'm afraid' as they deny ya sammink?—At least, not here anyway. Party's over, I'm afraid.

—Oi yer carn bleedin –

—Oh yes we can. Been watching the news recently? Heard of the Criminal Justice Bill? A perfectly lovely piece of legislation. I'll outline it for you, shall I?

Colm mumbles.

—What was that?

—A said wer on private property. Criminal Justice Bill dozen apply.

—Ah, well, now . . . Ee toes a brightly-painted rock wiv one uv is polished shoes. The symbol of tossas worldwide; polished black shoes. —This, here, is the limit of Mr Maddox's garden. You are standing beyond it. Where you're standing, that ground belongs to Mr Reece, the farmer, and I'm quite sure he didn't invite you on to his land.

Ee smirks an Colm steps back ova tha boundary, is eyes fuckin blazing. Ee mumbles again.

—I'm sorry, what did you say?

Colm just glares at him.

—Yes. Keep your no doubt offensive opinions to yourself and go home. I'm sure that urine tests, blood tests on you all would yield some very interesting results, wouldn't they? Yes. Now *move*.

That gets evryone's arses in gear awlright. The E kids are practically fuckin sprintin away, Linford fuckin Christie aw wha. Fuckin Pontrhydygroes ta Aberystwyth; one fuck uv a wawk. Just when arm comin up on tha dab of whizz n awl.

—Dorn't wurrih, says Mairead. —T'pubs orpen at eleven lahk. Am sure thull be one ont wer horm.

Maggie says nothin; she just stares at tha sea hawse.

We start wawkin. It down't really matta, does it? Nah. Naffin does. Weren't that good a party anyway, ta be honest wiv ya.

A wake up in a horrible pool av cowld sweat in the middle of the night awlmowst fuckin certain that thir's a figure at tha end av me bed wiv sammink risin up behind it black an billowy wings aw a cloak. A lie thir faw a bit, pantin, until tha sensation gows, an then a just lie thir. Creepy barstard feelin inside now . . . a turn me light on ta check but av cawse thir's naffin thir so a turn tha light back off again an smowk a fag in tha darkness, tha end av it glowin orange, fiercer whenevva a take a drag. The whowl house is silent; the ownly noise is tha rain on the windah an tha occasional sheep complainin ahtside, in tha field. The whowl bleedin world is lyin ahtside tha windah. A can sense it kind av, awl immense an open an available . . . it makes me itch, inside in me lungs. It's just thir, like it awlways has bin; just lyin there waitin faw me.

A stub me oily rag out an curl up in tha darkness. As arm driftin off back ta sleep again memories, images come crowdin inta me brain, unspoolin in front av me like a film aw sammink. A watch them, an a see:

A blarsted tree on a windswept hillside.

Mairead dahncin on er own in the middle av tha wine bar; evry blowk's eyes in tha place on her.

Playin pool wiv Colm n Margaret on the sixth day wivaht sleep aw food. The bawls flyin fuckin evrywhir, except the pockets. Utterly, totally, fucked. Colm gowin: —Ey, yer know them things which jig about in the corners uv yer eyes on the therd day? Well, terday a can catch them. They got little claws. Haver try, go on.

Paul angin upside down from tha rafters in tha garage, a grinning gibbon.

Mist on tha mountains.

Margaret surfacin aht av tha sea, er T-shirt awl tight to er tits. Er large, soft, welcomin breasts. Nipples stickin aht like bullets. A mermaid.

Flyin on E in tha blizzard; seein tha lights av Mairead's grand-parents' cottage through tha fawlin snow.

Sheep, sheep, sheep.

Colossal green space; wantin ta leap off the cliff into it awl.

Comin dahn by tha side avver lake; tha dawn sunlight on tha water an tha birds cawlin.

Watchin a seal swimmin in tha harbour as a wait faw tha pubs ta owpen.

Sioned's bare back.

Dahncin in a field in darkness, me, Colm, Mairead, Liam, no lights, no music, just us an the drugs an tha stars.

Trippin on top av Cader Idris an lookin down on tha soarin buzzards. So fuckin amazin, that, ta be able ta look down on tha birds. Ya can ownly do it on mountains aw in tower blocks. Sammink about large, soaring birds . . .

Singin rahnd tha beach-fire, pissed as fuck, spuds tirnin inta coal.

Tingling, throbbing.

Shelterin from tha rain in a ruined farm'ouse wiv whiskey an weed.

So much bleedin rain.

Jets screamin ova me head, scarin tha shite aht av me.

Dark, quiet pubs wiv tha sahnd av the sea ahtside.

Watchin faw dolphins; neva seein any.

Pub hovels in tha mountains; blackness an cowld ahtside, fire an beer inside.

Snawtin whizz off greasy toilet seats.

Spewin up inta tha waters av an ancient lake.

On a wave av mushrooms in a medieval castle.

Bare an blarsted trees.

And maw, many maw mowments av me time ere in Wales, lost now in that succession av unremembered an unrecawded instants which drugs generate as a defence against tha vast blankness ahead, not just av death but awlsow of tha unknowable, unmapped future. Lost now.

A fawl back inta sleep again as tha rain lashes on tha glass.

Paul's on automatic pilot, whippin through the gears, rippin through tha town's narrah streets as if is fucked old station wagon's tha size avver Mini aw sammink. There ar buildin sites evrywhir; fings goin up, fings comin dahn. Aberystwyth looks fuck awl like it used ta when a came ere on holiday as a kid wiv me folks. Arm just sittin back in tha seat like an lissenin ta Paul's stream-of-consciousness ramblins:

—Look at thuh little old man with thuh little old dog . . . ah . . . bofe of um white an doddery . . . oi! . . . oh nice hat, love . . . gerraht thuh fakkin way, you cant! . . . oo, sorry! . . . nice car . . . arse on that! Giz a grab, darlin! . . . look out, pigeon! Nnnnyyeeow, almost winged im . . . look arrim; looks like Alexei Sayle . . . I wish I ad time tuh sit on uh fuckin bench!

An ee gows on like this awl rahnd tha one-way system ta tha estate agent's, which is owa destination, but then ee drives straight parst.

—What ya doin? A fawt we wir gowin ta pay tha rent?

—We are.

—Well yav just driven straight fuckin parst. Whatja gown do that faw?

—Phone box. Got tuh call Sioned first.

Me heart begins ta beat a bit farsta an when Paul gows inta tha phown box a stay in tha car repeatin ova n ova ta meself downfuckinsaynaffindownfuckinsaynaffindownfuckinsaynaffin. A can't blame meself faw gowin ta bed wiv Sioned; Christ, I hadn't ad me leg ova faw awlmowst two years, an thir it was, on a plate, just offad ta me like, Jesus, whatja fuckin expect me ta do? Arm not exactly gonna tirn it dahn, now, am I? Sioned's fit as a butcher's dog. An she needed comfatin arfta bein smacked arahnd by Paul, which ee does awl too fuckin often if ya arsk me. An if ee adna done it, then Sioned wouldn't av come ta me, an then we wouldn't av ended up in kip tagevva, so fuck it it's Paul's fault. Not mine, not Sioned's, Paul's. An a down't fink she'll say anyfin like, but ya neva can tell . . . she might be regrettin it now, ya know, feelin guilty an awl that shit. She towld me that she liked me an awlways had done an she even suggested that tha bowth av us gow back ova tha bawda, but that's crap, a reckon, just tha emotion tawkin; a mean, she complains abaht how no one can undastand ow much avver strain it is avin ta speak tha foreign language av English awl tha time yet she wants ta gown live in tha bleedin place! That's wha made me think she wasn't entirely serious. An avver fings she's said, like fibs − like tha time when we wir awl pissed off arfta the beach party cos we wir awl aht av booze an drugs, terrified av the hangowva that was comin on, an Sioned said that she'd stashed a bottle av vodka back at Mairead's place. Well, av cawse, there was no fuckin vodka; she said that she'd ownly said thir was ta cheer us awl up so we'd not suffa too much on tha long wawk howm. It did, partly, have tha effect, but . . . what a fuckin disappointment.

Anyway, that's Sioned. Full av shit. Pukka shag, tho, as it appens . . . came fuckin buckets, I did.

Paul gets back in tha car wiv a face like a bleedin storm. Arm finkin oh fuck, an av got me and on tha daw andle ready ta bleedin scarpa. A arsk im what's wrong.

—Sioned's just told me somethin, ee says, shakin is head. —An am shocked . . . a can't fuckin believe it. No way.

—What?

—Am fuckin gutted.

—*What?*

—It's Roger. He's dead.

—. . . What?

—It's true. Fuckin Roger's dead. Sioned just told me, now. Can yuh believe it?

First, like, thir's relief, relief that Sioned's kept er gob shut abaht owa, erm, dalliance, an then it hits me like a welly in tha guts. Roger's dead.

—Roger's dead?

—Yeh. Am fuckin gutted.

—Jesus Christ. How?

—Well, that's thuh thing. It appened up there, in Camarthen or Caernarfon or whirever thuh fuck it is. Apparently ee was beaten tuh death. Stabbed as well. It's in all thuh papers, Sioned said, probly be in thuh *Cambrian News* on Wednesday. Stabbed ovuh twenty times, smashed skull, stuff like that. Can yuh believe it?

A shake me head but really, yeh, a can believe it awl too fuckin well. If any av us was destined faw a violent death it was Roger. It was written in fuckin stone, man. Live a violent life an ya die a violent death. Roger went up ta Camarthen, aw Caernarfon, aw whirevva, a few days agow ta sell a lowd av old war medals an stuff like that; there's a deala in such things up thir apparently. Ee said that ee didn't wanta sell em, but ee was brassic. They wir his grandad's aw sammink, from tha war . . . maybe even is own, but I doubt it. By awl accounts, is army experience affawded im no fuckin medals; all ee took from those years was a liking faw physical violence, a few survival skills an that twisted, crippled camaraderie which went some way towards destroyin im. Oh yeh, fuck, if it wasn't tha violence then it would av bin tha skag, aw misadventure, aw sammink. Ee was doomed. Ya could see it in is face. Paw fucka, a sappowse a should say, aw sammink like that.

—Am just fuckin gutted, Paul says again. —A doan know what tuh do now . . . what duh we do now?

A put on me sensible hat: —Well, we do what we came ere ta do. We gown pay tha rent. Then we gown get shit-faced. Ow's that sahnd?

—Yeh.

—Ere, give us tha money, an al gown pay the man.

Ee wordlessly gives us a big wad av nowts an a run ova ta tha estate agents. It's in me mind, God, it's clamouring in me mind . . . shitlowd av money in me hand . . . train station's just rahnd tha cawna . . . Roger's dead . . . Sioned's shagged . . . load av money on me pirson . . .

The geek behind tha desk looks up at me.

—Ah! Rent, is it?

A give im tha dosh.

—Is this everbody's?

—Yeh. It's awl there. Fa Llys Wen like.

—Yes I know. If you could just sit tight a moment while I count it.

—A can't, mate, I say, an then befaw a can stop it it jumps out: —Am leaving. A havta gown pack.

Ee looks up from tha bundle av money which is now his.

—Pardon.

—Arm leaving.

—When? Today?

—Yeh. A dunno; soon.

—I'm afraid you can't. The contract requires two weeks' notice.

—Av got ta. Death in tha family.

—Well I'm very sorry to hear that but you signed a contract stating –

—Look, what is this, a fuckin guvnor's office? Are ya deaf? Am leavin. Am goin. Am fuckin off. There's ownly me gowin, tha rest are stayin like, so ya'll still get some money. Get some avver paw mug ta live in tha bleedin bug hutch yav got tha fuckin cheek ta cawl a house.

An a leave tha office feelin, like, a turmoil av fings; angry, sad, relieved, anxious, awl sawts av stuff. Where tha fuck arm a gonna gow? Still, tho, movements should be spontaneous, a know that; if ya carefully plan fings then ya create opportunities fa fings ta gow wrong. Yav got ta act on impulse, awlways, an I just have. So a down't rirly know what ta feel yet.

A down't tell Paulie what av just done, a just get im ta drive us up ta tha Ship an Castle, whir ee gets tha drinks in while I leg it rahnd ta the bank. It's a bright sunny day an Great Darkgate Street is heavin; shoppas, tourists, people on their lunchbreaks . . . arm seein an hearin an feelin fings an arm finkin that Roger'll neva do this stuff again. From now on, thir'll be a Roger-shaped hole in tha world. . . . what do a feel abaht that? Roger was a nutta, a psycho, damaged fuckin goods, ee used ta glass people, give em Stanley facials, break ther legs wiv iron bars, a wouldn't be fuckin saprised if thir's even a topping aw two in is parst. Do a feel sad that ee's gone? *Should* a feel sad that ee's gone? An what abaht tha manna av is death – poetic justice, is it? The fing is, a sappowse, is that finally, in tha act av dying, av bein killed, Roger's done sammink useful; a mean, is stawry's ended, it's finished, an this is just a chapta in mine like,

474

but Roger's death, is murder, will give meaning ta this slice av me existence. It's time ta go. Is life wasn't entirely in vain.

Arm rememberin him, at the Cnapan festival larst year, muggin two buskers faw their instruments wiv a syringe av is own blood. Owldin it like a little sword. Ee towld them ee ad tha AIDS virus an that if they didn't and ova their guitars ee'd stick them. Cawse, they did, an Roger got fawty quid faw em back in Aber. Arm pretty sure tha Roger wasn't infected, like, but God, a mean, would *you* take tha risk? I fuckin wouldn't. And that's how al rememba Roger; scruffy, skinny fucka, weasel-faced, arms mottled wiv track marks an crap howm-made tats, wieldin like a weapon a syringe av is own blood. That image will remain in me mind long arfta every avver memory av Roger has disappeared; when a can't even rememba tha sahnd av is voice aw tha way ee smelled, al awlways av a picture av him grinning an ferocious usin is own polluted plasma as a weapon.

Roger. Ee's free from awl this now.

Inside tha foyer av tha bank, whir tha cash machines are, there's some sagging bag av sweaty, piss-stained rags givin people grief, arskin them fa money. There's an awful fuckin stench comin off im in waves. Some fuckin tramps, a tell ya; no bleedin shame. A ignaw im an put me card in tha machine as ee angs ova tha shoulda av one ole geeza who's makin a withdrawal.

—G'wahn, a fiver, juster measly fuckin fiver, won't fuckin hert yer, yuv got fuckin loads there. Go on, la, don't be stingy, when a write a bestseller –

—Leave me alone or I shall call the police!

—Ah yer mingy arl fuckin cunt. Wha d'you need money for anyway, God, yer gonna be fuckin dead soon, Christ. Stater yer. Fuckin ole gobshite.

Oh Jesus. A recognise tha accent, tha voice. Is it? This is worse, a fink, this is even bleedin worse . . .

—Colm. What tha fuck are ya doin, man?

Ee just stares an gurgles: —Ey, lad, lend us a fuckin fiver ey?

—Colm, it's me, Malcolm.

Is eyes are glazed ova, lifeless. Ee reeks av piss an shit n sick; there's a horrible yellow crust at the crotch av is jeans an is T-shirt is caked wiv blood an spew. One av is eyes is awl black an swollen an is foul breath comes aht at me ova blackened rotting teeth.

—A know oo yer fuckin ar. Juster fuckin fiver, al pay yer it back, onest.

This ain't Colm. This ain't him. This is a vile facsimile av im, a robot, a warped an twisted image. In tha week aw so since I saw him larst, the real Colm was abducted an replaced by this pathetic creature. This ain't Colm.

There's a slurry voice in me ear as am takin money aht tha machine, breathin in me face an makin me heave. An a ain't got tha first fuckin clue what ee's ramblin on abaht:

—France, ey, when's fuckin France? Us two n Roger, ey, ey yeh an where the fuck's fuckin Roger? As ee fucked off as well as ee, like that fuckin bitch? Left me on me fuckin own? Ey, av thee fucked off ter France tergether av thee, ey! EY!

What the fuck's awl this abaht France? A mean, me stepdad lives ova thir, but ee's a wanka. A hate im. Aven't seen im fa abaht three years. Am about ta arsk Colm what ee's on abaht when ee belts me on tha arm an shouts:

—Av those cunts gone already without tellin me? Av thee? Answer me, twat!

Ee grabs me arm an shakes it roughly.

—Fucked off an left me as she? With *im*? An you n all, yer fuckin joinin em ar yer is tha wha yer needin money for?

Ee's off it, just ramblin. Frightenin me. Tawkin fuckin gibberish. Is eyes are awl bloodshot an wide an it's like lookin inta hell. A carn bleedin stand this. A howld is arm an say:

—Colm, take it easy, man, calm dahn . . . ere, av this . . .

A give im a tenner.

—Take this. Calm dahn. It's awlright, man, it's awl awlright . . .

Ee looks at tha note in is hand.

—Ah just twenny quid ey . . . just twenny fuckin quid . . .

A leave im as a police car pulls up an ee sees it an collapses in tha cawna an starts screaming an shouting, really fuckin hysterical like:

—NO! NO! GERRAWAY! GERRAWAY FROM ME! HELP ME! HELP ME! AH NO! PLEASE NO! FUCK OFF! FUCK OFF! FUCK OFF!

A can still hear him from tha top av tha rowd. People are lookin round, apprehensive, worried, as if they've just heard a wolf howl aw sammink. A week; little maw than a week is awl it took. It's just one step away, innit, tha void, tha obscenity, just one tiny fuckin step.

Back in tha pub an Paul's sittin at a table wiv Iestyn an Phil, the Gibberer. A knock back me wawm, flat pint an immediately awda up anavver wiv a vodka chaser. There's a black vortex, a yawnin howl, in tha core av me being that ownly chemicals can fill an am abaht ta arsk Iestyn if ee's carryin anyfin cos ee's definitely buzzin on sammink but then as a listen ta what ee's tellin Paul, a realise it's sammink like fear:

—Never fuckin happened to me before like. Av only ever had a great time on E, I have. Ad *hurd* of it happenin, like, but . . . y'know, yew never think it'll happen to yew. It was the second one that did it, a think, at, uh, five in the mornin, was it? Didn't even need it, really, an a wish ter fuckin God now ad never taken it.

Ee drinks from is pint an a see that is hands're tremblin like fuck. Ee's terrified. Av neva seen Iestyn like this. Never thawt a would, neeva.

—A smashed up the whole club. A was convinced all the blokes in thir wir plannin ter get me in the bogs an rape me up the dirtbox. Convinced of it, I was. Absolutely fuckin para. A jumped out through the window, walkin round fuckin Cardiff crying not knowin whir tha fuck a was, a bought forty-six quid's wirth-a fruit from a market, melons, fuckin guavas, took a bite out of each an then lobbed it away. Goin fuckin mad a was aye. Insane, truly fuckin insane. The bloke a was stayin with, this gay lad, a bought a baseball bat an smashed fuck out-a his car with it in the middle of the street. A just didn't av a clew what a was doin, absolutely fuckin off me head mad a was.

Ee shakes is head an a can see tha fear on is face. It looks like ee'll neva smile again.

Phil, oo dives inta tha silence, is a frightenin fuckin contrast; Iestyn's expression says toxic withdrawal, Phil's says toxic psychosis. Ee's fuckin frothin at tha mouth, is eyes like cauldrons av boilin blood. Is T-shirt says: 'YOU WILL NEVER UNDERSTAND', an ee down't fuckin know how right that is:

—Fuh fuh fuh fuh fuh fuckin ma ma magistrates doan gih give a fuh fuh fuh fuck, ey duh doan fuh fuh fuh fuckin care that a ppppppppppput a bih bih bih bih blan blan blanket on a fuh fuh fuckin deh deh dead mmmmman. Guh Guh Guh Gareth? At th th th th th th th th th the ruhruhruhruhave th th th th thuh thuh night G Gareth wuh was rrrrrrreleased from puh puh prison, ee wuh wuh was on mmmmm, mmmmm*meth*adone an c c c c c c c rashed out in sssssssomeone's van an it was cccccccccold s, suh, suh so a puh puh puh puh put a buh buh buhlanket oh over him, an eeeeee wuh wuh was duh duh duh duh dead in the mmmmmmmmornin. Oh oh D. A tuh tuh tuh tuh tucked up a d, d, d, dead mmman. An the cuh cuh cuh cunts in th th the c c c c c c court lookin duh down theh fuckin noses, puh puh puh possession of a fuh fuh fuh fuckin blim – th th th th th th thirty quid. A ttttttt*took* th th th thirty quid out me fuckin ppppppocket an goes: Ere, an a fuh fuh fuckin cccccunt sssssssays: Cuh cuh cuh cuh contempt. Ad like tuh tuh tuh tuh tuh *tooooo* chuck a fuh fuh fuh fuh fuh fuckin guh guh guh-ren-*ade* at the bbbbbbench, huh huh hide an la la la la la fuckin *laugh* as all the bbbbbbbb*its* fuh fuh fuh fly over. Oh yeh; ad fuh fuh fuh fuh fuh fuh fuh fuh fuh fuckin lllllove that, I wuh would. Ey – djer nuh nuh know Guh Guh Guh Guh Guh Guh Griff got sssssssssssix yih years fuh fuh fuh for sssssupplyin E?

By now av fagotten what Phil started tawkin abaht an tha table's awl cavvered in spit. Phil's oozing a chemical smell an Iestyn's lookin at im like ee'd look at tha Devil. Am surrounded by drug casualties an madness an Roger's dead an arm knockin back vodkas tryin ta douse this fuckin turmoil inside me. Arm tryin ta distance meself from awl this shit, awl this horror. Phil Collins comes on tha jukebox an a rememba one av Geraint's rants against im, ow ee'd gladly murder im an do tha time cos ee'd know that when ee came aht ee'd be comin aht to a Collinsless world. But even that can't make me larf now, an as a nowtice Sharon come inta tha pub a take me cue ta leave. A tell Paul al see im back up at tha house an fuck off. Mairead, arm finkin, arm finkin abaht Mairead; if Colm's in that state, what will Mairead be like? A toy wiv tha idea of cawlin rahnd ta see her but then a decide that a rirly down't wanta know. A rirly down't wanta know. Come ta fink av it, a ain't seen Mairead arahnd faw a coupla weeks. Wonda whir she's got ta . . . Cawse, whireva she is, a know she'd be in a far betta state if she was wiv me. A truly fuckin believe that; she would've bin far betta off if she ad av met me instead av Colm. No bleedin messin.

A fink awlsow av cawlin up ta see Liam an Laura but a dismiss that as well. Liam's now on ta a lucrative little earna sellin cultivated supa-skunk aht av Mickah's barn, swannin arahnd in Tommy Hilfiger gear, even tawkin abaht puttin a deposit dahn on a house in Eglwys Fach wiv tha prowceeds. Well, good fuckin luck ta him. An Laura too, who was recently made redundant, so she deserves a bit av luck. She'll av maw fuckin money now, anyway. High-profit merchandise, ya supa-skunk.

Mags, tho. Yeh, Mags. A could gown see her. Apart from anyfin else, a wanta arsk her if it's true what that sleazy tossa Twmi said, that she let im fuck her faw a tenna larst week, in the bogs dahn Plas Crug. A howp it ain't.

Yeh, Mags. But it neva ends, tho, does it? It just gows on, extremity on extremity on extremity. Human misery knows no absolutes.

Back up at Llys Wen a knock on Margaret's daw – there's a temazepam jelly sellotaped ta it wiv the wirds 'SWEET DREAMS' written nearby – an then gow in. She's lyin on er bed, smilin at me, her eyes arf-clowsed. A can smell sick.

—Mags, a say. —Arm leavin.

—Mmmm, she murmurs, an then a see it awl; tha hideous scabs an bruises on tha inside av er arm; the syringe an spoon an stuff on tha duvet; the bedroom towtally devoid av any electrical appliance aw even fuckin furniture apart from tha bed. Pools av sick on tha carpet. Blood-streaked bawls av cotton wool awl ova tha place.

It just gows on. On an on an on. Screaming wivaht end. Loss an horror.

A clowse tha daw slowly. Al neva see Margaret again in me life. Needles, smack . . . al tell ya, it's awlways bleedin shit me up. Av awlways bin too scared ta try it. When a saw Colm an Roger that time up by tha Bearded Lake, bowth av em hunched ova an chasin, the ownly thawt that entered me head was: Pair av pricks. An a was right n awl; look what's happened ta them bowth. But Mags, tho, lovely little Margaret; heroin will kill her. Naffin maw certain – smack will kill her. What's wirse is the thawt that, fa some reason, that seems ta be what she wants.

A feel ill as a run upstirs ta pack. So much fuckin stuff . . . av got ta be quick now, no time ta dwell, no time ta waste; a wanta be aht of here befaw Paul comes back wiv Sioned. Quick. Fuckin *move*.

Listen ta me:

There are fawces in this world that controwl ya. Hostile, malignant fawces which try ta bend an break you to their will, their twisted ideas of what you should be. Immensely powerful, they will stop at naffin ta achieve their aim which is ta drag evryfin dahn to a unity; one nation, one personality, one voice. Fuck them awl.

Life is hard enough faw some people. Margaret, faw instance, wouldn't be happy even if she ad unlimited money an tha freedom ta live oweva she wanted to. She's just inherently unhappy, fuck knows why; chemical imbalance, hereditary depression, whateva . . . Life is hard, heavy, and horrible faw her, yet thir are cunts who wanta make it worse. Torture is not confined ta tha Middle Ages, aw tha Third World; an insistence on unifawmity is tha modern rack on which we ar awl broken, or would be if those cunts ad their way. Evil is not an amorphous, anonymous fing; it has a house an a family, it eats breakfast, it wears certain clowthes an squirms tentacles inta every àspect av your life. It will neva give in.

Make no mistake, it is there. It will bring death upon you in worse ways than the physical. Right now, someone is lacing up their polished black shoes an double-checking your address. Run like fuck.

A nice day, wawm through the windows av the carriage, bright n sharp and clear. The Welsh weather tho; could well be pissin dahn in tha next few minutes.

A put me feet up on tha seat opposite, me legs stretched undaneath tha table. Wonderin what they'll do, what they'll think, when they discover that av gone. A wown't really care by then anyway. Failure is part av tha prowcess, innit?

The hills roll by outside tha windah an the outskirts av tha town begin ta disappear in a cluster av estates an cooling towers. Big green hills take ova. A used ta fink tha countryside was a clenched fist, befaw a went ta live in it like, now a down't know what it is. But arm a city boy, a like cars, noise, carbon monoxide, neon, clubs, tawl man-made structures, awl that stuff. It's easier ta escape in a city, ta become anonymous if ya want to. Better fuckin drugs n awl; no twelve quid faw a pill that does fuck awl but cure ya headache. New Age fuckin travellers. Al shit em.

It's this fuckin Government's fault. If drugs were legal, there'd be none av this bleedin hassle; the chemicals could be screened, an then ya'd know what you were gettin. That's neva gonna happen tho. Still, a total blanket ban on drugs is betta than no drugs at awl, a suppowse.

Rollin away on tha train. Llanbadarn, Borth, Dovey Junction, Machynlleth . . . no, wait, thir ain't a stop at Llanbadarn; useta be, a fink, but not anymaw, unless ya on tha Cwm Rheidol steam train ta Devil's Bridge, an ya'd be a fuckin mug if ya were – ten bleedin quid that costs, an it ownly takes ahf an owa. Towtal fuckin rip-off if ya arsk me. Still, nostalgia leaves itself wide owpen ta exploitation, dunnit?

A look aht av the windah an up at tha passin hill. A can just abaht see tha side wawl av Llys Wen, a slice of white between tha trees. Wonda what's gowin on in there right now . . . There's one av them bleedin jets flyin through tha blue ova tha house, probly rattlin the fuckin windahs in their frames, scarin evryone shitless. An arm glad that a can't hear it at this distance an through the glass – fuckin horrible noise they make, when they useta fly ova dead low like that it'd be like a fuckin hacksaw on me bones. A wown't miss those fuckas, al tell ya that.

We pass anavver train travellin in the opposite direction, tawards Aberystwyth an tha extreme edge av the land. No doubt bringin maw; maw expectant faces wawkin through tha station, blinking, hoping, lookin faw a certain somefing which they've neva bin able ta find anywhir else. A hope they find it there. Good fuckin luck to em. By tanight they'll be screamin-stoned on Liam's skunk, covered in Mags's vomit, they'll av ad awl their money stolen by Colm an they'll av bin beaten up by Roger. Oh no, not that larst bit.

A crack owpen one av me cans av lager. Twelve uv em should larst tha journey, this journey, ahead av me away from Wales . . . Thir's a voice in me head gowin 'selffulfillinprophecy' ova n ova again so a drown it wiv a bangin John Kelly mix on me Walkman. It's a lowd av shit anyway; such fings down't really happen. An anyway, the sheep's skull is now at tha bottom of the River Ystwyth, little fishes swimmin in an aht av its eye sockets an weed growin ova it. Fuckin stupid. A fink av that an then once again a can hear Roger's voice, his whiny, insulted lilt, tellin me abaht the time ee was in tha army avin target practice wiv heavy machine-guns in the Brecon Beacons; in a lull in the shooting, ee said, while they were awl reloading, a sheep wandered across tha firing range, 'an en-a twat wuz fuckin vapourised, mun, fuckin red cloud's what it wuz see, evry fucker thir aimin is gun at iss fuckin sheep like, blew-a cunt apart', ee said an then ee did is fuckin Beavis laugh with is top teeth out ova is bottom lip an drool runnin down is bleedin chin. Fuckin Roger. Fuckin Roger wiv is little blood gun. Fuckin Roger dying in tha gutter.

The doris pushes er refreshment trolley parst an a wave er away. Pay British Rail prices? Fuck that. Al bring me own beer. Far cheapa. A adta pay tha ticket price av cawse, which was fuckin astronomical, but this journey, this movement, feels good. London is tha destination on tha ticket, but, well, arm finkin; av got ta change at Birmingham New Street, an av got a mate in Dudley – aw, as ee cawls it, Dudlaaaaayy – an a know someone in Wolverhampton n awl, an fuck, from New Street ya can get connections fa anywhir in these islands, Aberdeen, Penzance, fuckin anywhir, man. An av got money as well – the blowk in tha estate agent's'll get a shock when ee counts tha rent like, an av awlsow got tha deposit a paid faw Llys Wen (in a cheque, but I'll find somewhire aw someone ta cash it), so tha fuckin country's me cockle. A can go anywhere. Trains, buses, money'll take me fuckin anywhere. Pukka. Where shall a go, where shall a go? . . . Love this fucking freedom.

A down't know, yet, what a fink abaht me time in Wales. It's too early ta make any judgement. Al avta wait an see.

The mountains are still crowdin up around me and the train rattles through em but av done this journey befaw an I know that they'll soon start ta fawl away. As I get closer ta England, these mountains arahnd me will fall away.

So what av a got now? Well, av got lager, music, movement, an tha new edition of *Viz*. Should be a good journey. An see, look, a towld ya; there's rain clouds in the sky now. An as we pull inta Borth the speed that a snawted in the bog befaw tha train pulled aht of Aberystwyth begins ta kick in wiv the usual lovely tingling in me scalp an pleasant pressure in me teeth an a know that it'll carry on kicking in and kicking in until evrything's awlright. There's happiness ahead. It's fucking great.

A SELECTED LIST OF CONTEMPORARY FICTION
AVAILABLE IN VINTAGE

☐	LONDON FIELDS	Martin Amis	£6.99
☐	STRANGER THAN FULHAM	Matthew Baylis	£6.99
☐	BURNING ELVIS	John Burnside	£6.99
☐	DISGRACE	J M Coetzee	£6.99
☐	MR IN BETWEEN	Neil Cross	£6.99
☐	WHAT ARE YOU LIKE?	Anne Enright	£6.99
☐	DEAD LONG ENOUGH	James Hawes	£6.99
☐	MARK OF THE ANGEL	Nancy Huston	£6.99
☐	COLUMBUS DAY	Janette Jenkins	£6.99
☐	THE FOOTBALL FACTORY	John King	£6.99
☐	THE NUDIST COLONY	Sarah May	£6.99
☐	ENDURING LOVE	Ian McEwan	£6.99
☐	FIGHT CLUB	Chuck Palahniuk	£6.99
☐	THE HUMAN STAIN	Philip Roth	£6.99
☐	POWDER	Kevin Sampson	£6.99
☐	ECSTASY	Irvine Welsh	£6.99
☐	FILTH	Irvine Welsh	£6.99

* All Vintage books are available through mail order or from your local bookshop.

* Payment may be made using Access, Visa, Mastercard, Diners Club, Switch and Amex, or cheque, eurocheque and postal order (sterling only).

☐ ☐ ☐ ☐ ☐ ☐ ☐ ☐ ☐ ☐ ☐ ☐ ☐ ☐ ☐ ☐

Expiry Date:_____ Signature:_____

Please allow £2.50 for post and packing for the first book and £1.00 per book thereafter.

ALL ORDERS TO:

Vintage Books, Books by Post, TBS Limited, The Book Service,
Colchester Road, Frating Green, Colchester, Essex, CO7 7DW, UK.
Telephone: (01206) 256 000
Fax: (01206) 255 914

NAME:_____

ADDRESS:_____

_____

_____

Please allow 28 days for delivery. Please tick box if you do not
wish to receive any additional information   ☐
Prices and availability subject to change without notice.